THE
PUSHCART PRIZE, XXVI:
BEST OF THE
SMALL PRESSES

BEST OF
THE SMALL
PRESSES

The
PUSHCART
PRIZE

2002

XXVI

Edited by
Bill Henderson
with the Pushcart
Prize editors

Note: nominations for this series are invited from any small, independent, literary book press or magazine in the world. Up to six nominations—tear sheets or copies, selected from work published, or about to be published, in the calendar year—are accepted by our December 1 deadline each year. Write to Pushcart Press, P.O. Box 380, Wainscott, N.Y. 11975 for more information.

Acknowledgments

Selections for *The Pushcart Prize* are reprinted
with the permission of authors and presses cited. Copy-
right reverts to authors and presses immediately after
publication.

Distributed by W. W. Norton & Co.
500 Fifth Ave., New York, N.Y. 10110

Library of Congress Card Number: 76–58675
ISBN: 1–888889–30–6
      1–888889–31–4
ISSN: 0149–7863

*In Memoriam: Theodore Wilentz
(1915–2001), a Founding Editor of this series.
With thanks to Drake McFeely
and W.W. Norton & Co.*

INTRODUCTION
by BILL HENDERSON

L AST YEAR IN THIS SPACE I celebrated the remarkable survival of this series, from a hopeful first edition issued by an unknown press in 1976—published without grants or financial backing of any sort and not expected by most to endure more than a year or two—to a thriving annual that has somehow confounded the naysayers and lasted a quarter century. All credit for this endurance belongs to our Founding Editors, to the hundreds of Contributing Editors, and to the thousands of writers who have kept the faith with thoughtful, passionate and compassionate words through the years. In an age of glitz, celebrity and the obscene worship of whatever's happening now, primed by an electronic instant info juggernaut, our small press writers have continued to insist on what matters.

As of this edition, five empires now dominate general publishing: Rupert Murdoch's News Corporation, Viacom, England's Pearson, and Germany's Bertelsmann and Holzbrinck. Just about every major trade book publisher is owned by these five firms, which also often control other media sources such as Paramount Pictures, MTV and hundreds of magazines and journals. Meanwhile Borders and Barnes and Noble dominate distribution.

This situation would be a cultural nightmare—placing the United States on a par with Russian publishing which is controlled by a handful of oligarchs in collusion directly or indirectly with the government—if it were not for a few surviving independent publishers like W. W. Norton & Co. (Pushcart's distributor) and the hundreds of small presses that we honor each year.

What about the next twenty-five years? If the past is any guide to what comes next, I predict there will always be a Pushcart Prize for the simple reason that our writers and presses have never lost our faith. The louder the media noise, the stronger we become. This Prize now receives more than 8,000 nominations of poetry, essays and stories each year, and the quality has risen with the numbers. Nobody pretends that all of these nominations are spectacular—most aren't—but in heart and soul they are light years beyond what is coughed up by the "content providers" of mass cult.

I predict thoughtful books and journals will remain for the most part paper and binding objects like the one you hold in your hand. Beeps, bongs and whistles conveyed at light speed into E-books and computers are not appreciated by most small press readers. And the temptation of instant publication via the Internet will soon weed out impatient writers who usually have nothing to say but want to be noticed in a hurry. We small press critters tend to take our time. What's zippy is of little note to us. We know you can't just dash out a terrific short story, essay or poem and feed it into a gizmo for fast fame. Small press readers and writers appreciate taking time, savoring ideas, daring to think long thoughts. The rest of this so-called culture may dash hither and yon whenever dollars and celebrity beckon, but we will hunker down with paper and binding and low electric bills. Speed corrupts and high speed corrupts absolutely. As to power corrupting—well look around you as the big five try to outdo one another and become the big One.

That's the view from Pushcart's 8 × 8 shack in the backyard. It will take luck and determination for all of us to endure in the next 25 years. This ongoing rebellion has never been easy. Thomas Paine, Walt Whitman, William Blake, Bobby Burns, Mark Twain, Herman Melville, James Joyce, Virginia Woolf, Stephen Crane, Carl Sandburg, Ezra Pound, D.H. Lawrence, Anais Nin, Alan Swallow, Lawrence Ferlinghetti, Barney Rosset, James Laughlin, Allan Ginsberg and other small press legends knew very well the value of true grit. We won't forget.

❀   ❀   ❀

Pushcart's 26th edition is unique, as is every edition before it. To comment on each of the 71 selections from 49 presses (ten of them new to the series) would be futile.

I helped read the fiction this year with David Means, Jack Driscoll and Monica Hellman. David Means's *Assorted Fire Events* (Context), was nominated this year for a National Book Critics Circle fiction award, and won the *Los Angeles Times* book prize. Jack Driscoll's *Lucky Man, Lucky Woman* (Pushcart) named a best novel of the year by *The Independent Publisher*, is out in paperback from Norton. Monica Hellman for many years helped her dad, Oscar DeLiso, run Phaedra Press, a tiny Manhattan outfit with a terrific list in the 60's and 70's.

The fiction this year is notable, as usual, for an array of subjects and styles, but what's special is the hoot out loud humor of tales by Stacey Richter, Ian Frazier, Nicola Mason, Stephen Dobyns, Melissa Pritchard and others. Laughs are back in style.

As in every edition we feature the work of newcomers, but we also welcome the best work of some not so new: Ann Beattie (her first ever *Pushcart Prize* appearance), Rick Bass, and Russell Banks for instance. Beattie's "The Big-Breasted Pilgrim" (*Conjunctions*) also introduces Bill Clinton and George Stephanopoulos to our pages in a Florida feeding frenzy.

A few years ago (PPXIX) I asked our fiction editors at the time, Rick Moody and Lee Smith, to compose statements on their visions of the state of the storyteller's art (if they had any eyesight left) after they had read boxes of nominated stories. This year I requested that Tony Brandt, our essays editor, and Judith Kitchen and Sherod Santos, our PPXXVI poetry co-editors, describe their reading experiences.

✧ ✧ ✧

Tony Brandt has been our essays editor for fifteen years. He is that rarest of birds—a free-lance writer and a real good one. He makes his living unattached to any institution, without a financial safety net. He refuses to grind out the usual schlock that most commercial magazines require. He has lived this way his entire life, with a brief stint as a columnist for *Esquire* and as author of a book about the mental health industry, *Reality Police*. Right now he is selecting what may prove to be one of the defining collections of the past century—*The Pushcart Book of Essays*. For his Pushcart Prize efforts each year he receives a small honorarium or, in lean years, dinner at Pushcart's house.

TONY BRANDT

"If this year's essays are any indication the current renaissance of the essay form has reached its golden age. There were not more es-

11

says this year than in previous years, but they were better overall, and a good many were brilliant. The inescapably self-righteous ideological essay, whether feminist or neo-Marxist or conservative or multi-cultural, was not much in evidence, while more and more writers seemed to come at their subjects in a nuanced way and with a sophistication about their own and other's experience that the editor can only welcome. The essay at its best is written out of some sort of pressing inner need, or from a unique insight, and not from mere professional ambition or to scratch an ideological itch. What makes an essay great is intensity, emotional or intellectual, however calmly expressed. There were more of them this year, and fewer essays written with an eye on a collection, or because somebody is teaching creative non-fiction in a writing program and needs to get in print to maintain his or her credentials. Three cheers.

"Reading so many essays at once it's impossible not to notice trends, and this year had its share. Nature essays were surprisingly scarce; the best, the one by Kim Barnes about fighting forest fires in Idaho, was also one of the few. Death was a major preoccupation, much more than usual—death by murder, as in Gary Amdahl's amazing piece, death in warfare, death by drowning. We all know the old saw, that all art is essentially about death, but this year it was quite explicitly so. At the same time there were fewer essays written by people who have suffered some sort of personal illness or accident and must live with the damage. Let's put it this way, that all art is about loss; if so, that kind of loss was less, if this is the word, inspiring to this year's nominees. There were also fewer essays remembering or memorializing dead writers. But the great trend, again, was a growing excellence. What a thrill to come upon so much of it. Make that four cheers, and shout them out."

✿   ✿   ✿

Sherod Santos is the author of four books of poetry, most recently *The Pilot Star Elegies* (W. W. Norton 1999), which was both a National Book Award Finalist and a nominee for *The New Yorker* Book Award. He is also the author of a recent book of literary essays, *A Poetry of Two Minds* (University of Georgia Press, 2000), a finalist for the National Book Critics Circle Award in Criticism. Santos' poems appear regularly in such journals as *The New Yorker, The Paris Review, The Nation, Poetry*, and *The Yale Review*. His awards include the Delmore Schwartz Memorial Award, the Discovery / *The Nation*

Award, the Oscar Blumenthal Prize from *Poetry* magazine, a Pushcart Prize in both poetry and the essay, and appointment as Robert Frost Poet at the Frost house in Franconia, New Hampshire. He has received fellowships from the Ingram Merrill and Guggenheim foundations, and the National Endowment for the Arts. In 1999 he received an Award for Literary Excellence from the American Academy of Arts and Letters. He is currently professor of English at the University of Missouri.

SHEROD SANTOS

"On the basis of the large (and I mean *large*) body of poems we reviewed this year, I am happy to report that—despite how often contemporary critics have hastened to administer its last rites—American poetry is not only alive and well at the beginning of this century, but as unfazed, robust, and wide ranging as at any other period in our history. And if one of poetry's first responsibilities is to *unbecome* the mirror image our institutions hold up to it, then this year's gathering has taken to heart the gravity of that charge. For all the range of their styles and formal affiliations, for all their experiments and mindful reclamations, together these poems form a heartening glimpse into the future of this art."

✿ ✿ ✿

Judith Kitchen is the author of *Only the Dance: Essays on Time and Memory* (University of South Carolina Press) and *Distance and Direction* (Coffee House Press, 2001). Her critical study of William Stafford, *Writing the World*, was reprinted by Oregon State University Press in 1999. Kitchen's awards include a Fellowship from the National Endowment for the Arts, a Pushcart Prize for an essay, the Anhinga Prize for poetry, and nomination for a National Magazine Award. Kitchen is an Advisory and Contributing Editor for *The Georgia Review*, where she regularly reviews poetry, and she was recently selected to serve on the Artists' Advisory Committee of the New York Foundation for the Arts. In addition, for the past twenty years she has been editor of the State Street Press Chapbook Series which has published over eighty authors chosen in a national competition. She is Writer-in-Residence at SUNY Brockport.

JUDITH KITCHEN

"The boxes arrived—thousands of poems—a variety of poems such as I knew existed, but had never seen all in one place before. As a reviewer, I usually read a book cover-to-cover, noting the way the poems speak to each other, how they add up to what we might call themes. So judging individual poems, selecting from among so many, restored for me the sense that a poem is—first and foremost—a singular event. What made a poem stand out, all on its own? I'm not sure that I can answer my own question, but I've been mulling it over. It's made me think hard about how a poet's voice distinguishes itself as unique. The poems I chose have a spark of individuality—an oddball angle of vision, a precision of craft, a cadence of thought—something that takes me into the world of the poet as well as the world of the poem.

"Perhaps the best thing about judging poetry for *The Pushcart Prize* was meeting and conferring with my co-judge, Sherod Santos. Together, we discovered that each of us had selected just as many poets we did not know as those we know. It is always interesting to see fine work by poets you admire, but it is doubly exciting to be able to discover and single out distinctive new voices. And we discovered new presses as well, proving that poetry is still a vital art with editors willing to devote time and energy to its publication. In short, Bill Henderson has seen what is really happening—and he is making it possible for others to share in his vision."

THE PEOPLE WHO HELPED

FOUNDING EDITORS—*Anaïs Nin (1903–1977) Buckminster Fuller (1895–1983), Charles Newman, Daniel Halpern, Gordon Lish, Harry Smith, Hugh Fox, Ishmael Reed, Joyce Carol Oates, Len Fulton, Leonard Randolph, Leslie Fiedler, Nona Balakian (1918–1991), Paul Bowles (1910–1999), Paul Engle (1908–1991), Ralph Ellison (1914–1994), Reynolds Price, Rhoda Schwartz, Richard Morris, Ted Wilentz (1915-2001), Tom Montag, William Phillips, Poetry editor; H. L. Van Brunt.*

CONTRIBUTING EDITORS FOR THIS EDITION—*Katrina Roberts, Mary Yukari Waters, Sharon Solwitz, H.E. Francis, Richard Siken, Marianna Cherry, Karl Elder, Ted Deppe, Caroline Langston, Daniel Stern, R. C. Hildebrandt, P. H. Liotta, Thomas E. Kennedy, Michael Bowden, Daniel Henry, Ken Kalfus, Morton Elevitch, Ron Tanner, Richard Garcia, Katherine Min, Steve Yarbrough, Donald Revell, Tom Paine, Maxine Kumin, Jeffrey Hammond, Elizabeth Gaffney, George Keithley, Nancy Richard, Kristin King, Jane McCafferty, Robert Wrigley, Jim Simmerman, Mike Newirth, Rosellen Brown, Jewel Mogan, John Kistner, Jessica Roeder, Karen Bender, Sharman Russell, Mark Irwin, Lucia Perillo, Wally Lamb, Joe Ashby Porter, Tom Disch, Kenneth Gangemi, Philip Dacey, Stuart Dybek, Eugene Stein, Richard Tayson, Marie Sheppard Williams, Robert Phillips, Elizabeth McKenzie, Diann Blakely, Jody Stewart, Robert McBrearty, Martha Collins, Joyce Carol Oates, Paul Maliszewski, Reginald Shepherd, Kay Ryan, Daniel Orozco, Alice Mattison, C. S. Giscombe, Laurie Sheck, Jim Daniels, Ed Ochester, Gerald Shapiro, John Drury, Maura Stanton, Kim Addonizio, Alicia Ostriker, Ed-*

MANAGING EDITOR—*Hannah Turner*

FICTION EDITORS—*Jack Driscoll, David Means, Monica Hellman, Bill Henderson*

POETRY EDITORS—*Judith Kitchen, Sherod Santos*

ESSAYS EDITOR—*Anthony Brandt*

EDITOR AND PUBLISHER—*Bill Henderson*

CONTENTS

THE
PUSHCART PRIZE, XXVI:
BEST OF THE
SMALL PRESSES

THE CAVEMEN IN
THE HEDGES

fiction by STACEY RICHTER

from ZOETROPE: ALL STORY

THERE ARE CAVEMEN in the hedges again. I take the pellet gun
from the rack beside the door and go out back and try to run them
off. These cavemen are tough sons of bitches who are impervious to
pain, but they love anything shiny, so I load the gun up with golden
Mardi Gras beads my girlfriend, Kim, keeps in a bowl on the dresser
and aim toward their ankles. There are two of them, hairy and squat,
grunting around inside a privet hedge I have harassed with great la-
bor into a series of rectilinear shapes. It takes the cavemen a while to
register the beads. It's said that they have poor eyesight, and of all
the bullshit printed in the papers about the cavemen in the past
few months, this at least seems to be true. They crash through
the branches, doing something distasteful. Maybe they're eating
garbage. After a while they notice the beads and crawl out, covered
in leaves, and start loping after them. They chase them down the al-
ley, occasionally scooping up a few and whining to each other in that
high-pitched way they have when they get excited, like little kids
complaining.

I take a few steps off the edge of the patio and aim toward the An-
derson's lot. The cavemen scramble after the beads, their matted
backs receding into the distance.

"What is it?" Kim stands behind me and touches my arm. She's
been staying indoors a lot lately, working on the house, keeping to

25

herself. She hasn't said so, but it's pretty obvious the cavemen scare her.

"A couple of furry motherfuckers."

"I think they are," she says.

"What?"

"Mother fuckers. Without taboos. It's disgusting." She shivers and heads back inside.

After scanning the treetops, I follow. There haven't been any climbers reported so far, but they are nothing if not unpredictable. Inside, I find Kim sitting on the kitchen floor, arranging our spices alphabetically. She's transferring them out of their grocery-store bottles and into nicer ones, plain glass, neatly labeled. Kim has been tirelessly arranging things for the last four years—first the contents of our apartment on Pine Avenue, then, as her interior decorating business took off, other people's places, and lately our own house, since we took the plunge and bought it together last September. She finishes with fenugreek and picks up the galanga.

I go to the living room and put on some music. It's a nice, warm Saturday and if it weren't for the cavemen, we'd probably be spending it outdoors.

"Did you lock it?"

I tell her yes. I get a beer from the fridge and watch her. She's up to Greek seasonings. Her slim back is tense under her stretchy black top. The music kicks in and we don't say much for a few minutes. The band is D.I., and they're singing: "Johnny's got a problem and it's out of control!" We used to be punk rockers, Kim and I, back in the day. Now we are homeowners. When the kids down the street throw loud parties, we immediately dial 911.

"The thing that gets me," I say, "is how puny they are."

"What do they want?" asks Kim. Her hair is springing out of its plastic clamp, and she looks like she's going to cry. "What the fuck do they want with us?"

When the cavemen first appeared, they were assumed to be homeless examples of modern man. But it soon became obvious that even the most broken-down and mentally ill homeless guy wasn't *this* hairy. Or naked, hammer-browed, and short. And they didn't rummage through garbage cans and trash piles with an insatiable desire for spherical, shiny objects, empty shampoo bottles, and foam packing peanuts.

26

A reporter from KUTA had a hunch and sent a paleontologist from the university out to do a little fieldwork. For some reason I was watching the local news that night, and I remember this guy—typical academic, bad haircut, bad teeth—holding something in a take-out box. He said it was *scat*. Just when you think the news can't get any more absurd, there's a guy on TV, holding a turd in his hands, telling you the hairy people scurrying around the bike paths and Dumpsters of our fair burg are probably Neanderthal, from the Middle Pale-olithic period, and that they have been surviving on a diet of pizza crusts, unchewed insects, and pigeon eggs.

People started calling them cavemen, though they were both male and female and tended to live in culverts, heavy brush, and freeway underpasses, rather than caves. Or they lived wherever—they turned up in weird places. The security guard at the Ice-O-Plex heard an eerie yipping one night. He flipped on the lights and found a half dozen of them sliding around the rink like otters. At least we knew another thing about them. They loved ice.

Facts about the cavemen have been difficult to establish. It is un-clear if they're protected by the law. It is unclear if they are responsi-ble for their actions. It *has* been determined that they're a nuisance to property and a threat to themselves. They will break into cars and climb fences to gain access to swimming pools, where they drop to all fours to drink. They will snatch food out of trucks or bins and eat out of trash cans. They avoid modern man as a general rule but are becoming bolder by the hour. The university students attempting to study them have had difficulties, though they've managed to discover that the cavemen cannot be taught or tamed and are extremely diffi-cult to contain. They're strong for their size. It's hard to hurt them but they're simple to distract. They love pink plastic figurines and all things little-girl pretty. They love products perfumed with synthetic woodsy or herbal scents. You can shoot at them with rubber bullets all day and they'll just stand there, scratching their asses, but if you wave a little bottle of Barbie bubble bath in front of them they'll fol-low you around like a dog. They do not understand deterrence. They understand desire.

Fathers, lock up your daughters.

Kim sits across from me at the table, fingering the stem of her wine-glass and giving me The Look. She gets The Look whenever I con-fess that I'm not ready to get married yet. The Look is a peculiar expression, pained and brave, like Kim has swallowed a bee but she isn't going to let on.

"It's fine," she says. "It's not like I'm all goddamn *ready* either." I drain my glass and sigh. Tonight she's made a fennel-basil lasagna, lit candles, and scratched the price tag off the wine. Kim and I have been together for ten years, since we were twenty-three, and she's still a real firecracker, brainy, blonde, and bitchy. What I have in Kim is one of those cute little women with a swishy ponytail who cuts people off in traffic while swearing like a Marine. She's a fierce one, grinding her teeth all night long, grimly determined, though the object of her determination is usually vague or unclear. I've never wanted anyone else. And I've followed her instructions. I've nested. I mean, we bought a house together. We're co-borrowers on a thirty-year mortgage. Isn't that commitment enough?

Oh no, I can see it is not. She shoots me The Look a couple more times and begins grabbing dishes off the table and piling them in the sink. Kim wants the whole ordeal: a white dress, bridesmaids stuffed into taffeta, a soft rain of cherry blossoms. I want none of it. The whole idea of marriage makes me want to pull a dry cleaning bag over my head. I miss our punk rock days, Kim and me and our loser friends playing in bands, hawking spit at guys in BMWs, shooting drugs and living in basements with anarchy tattoos poking through the rips in our clothing. Those times are gone and we've since established real credit ratings, I had the circled-A tattoo lasered off my neck, but . . . But. I feel like marriage would exterminate the last shred of the rebel in me. For some reason, I think of marriage as a living death.

Or, I don't know, maybe I'm just a typical guy, don't want to pay for the cow if I can get the milk for free.

Kim is leaning in the open doorway, gazing out at the street, sucking on a cigarette. She doesn't smoke much anymore, but every time I tell her I'm not ready she rips through a pack in a day and a half. "They'd probably ruin it anyway," she says, watching a trio of cavemen out on the street, loping along, sniffing the sidewalk. They fan out and then move back together to briefly touch one another's ragged, dirty brown fur with their noses. The one on the end, lighter-boned with small, pale breasts poking out of her chest hair, stops dead in her tracks and begins making a cooing sound at the sky. It must be a full moon. Then she squats and pees a silver puddle onto the road.

Kim stares at her. She forgets to take a drag and ash builds on the end of her cigarette. I know her; I know what she's thinking. She's picturing hordes of cavemen crashing the reception, grabbing canapés with their fists, rubbing their crotches against the floral arrangements. That would never do. She's too much of a perfectionist to ever allow that.

When I first saw the cavemen scurrying around town, I have to admit I was horrified. It was like when kids started to wear those huge pants—I couldn't get used to it, I couldn't get over the shock. But now I have hopes Kim will let the marriage idea slide for a while. For this reason I am somewhat grateful to the cavemen.

It rains for three days and the railroad underpasses flood. The washes are all running and on the news there are shots of SUVs bobbing in the current because some idiot ignored the DO NOT ENTER WHEN FLOODED sign and tried to gun it through four feet of rushing water. A lot of cavemen have been driven out of their nests and the incident level is way up. They roam around the city hungry and disoriented. We keep the doors locked at all times. Kim has a few stashes of sample-sized shampoo bottles around the house. She says she'll toss them out like trick-or-treat candy if any cavemen come around hassling her. So far, we haven't had any trouble.

Our neighbors, the Schaefers, haven't been so lucky. Kim invites them over for dinner one night, even though she knows I can't stand them. The Schaefers are these lonely, New Age hippies who are always staggering toward us with eager, too-friendly looks on their faces, arms outstretched, like they're going to grab our necks and start sucking. I beg Kim not to invite them, but at this stage in the game she seems to relish annoying me. They arrive dressed in gauzy robes. It turns out Winsome has made us a hammock out of hemp in a grasping attempt to secure our friendship. I tell her it's terrific and take it into the spare room where I stuff it in a closet, fully aware that by morning all of our coats are going to smell like bongwater.

When I return, everyone is sipping wine in the living room while the storm wets down the windows. Winsome is describing how she found a dead cavebaby in their backyard.

"It must not have been there for long," she says, her huge, oil-on-velvet eyes welling up with tears, "because it just looked like it was sleeping, and it wasn't very stiff. Its mother had wrapped it in tinsel, like for Christmas."

"Ick," says Kim. "How can you cry for those things?"

"It looked so vulnerable." Winsome leans forward and touches Kim's knee. "I sensed it had a spirit. I mean, they're human or proto-human or whatever."

"I don't care," says Kim, "I think they're disgusting."

"Isn't that kind of judgmental?"

"I think we should try to understand them," chimes in Evan, smoothing down his smock—every inch the soulful, sandal-wearing, sensitive man. "In a sense, they're *us*. If we understood why that female caveman wrapped her baby in tinsel, perhaps we'd know a little more about ourselves."

"I don't see why people can't just say 'cavewoman,' " snaps Kim. " 'Female caveman' is weird, like 'male nurse.' Besides, they are *not* us. We're supposed to have won. You know, survival of the fittest."

"It might be that it's time we expanded our definition of 'humanity,' " intones Evan. "It might be that it's time we welcome all creatures on planet Earth."

I'm so incredibly annoyed by Evan that I have to go into the bathroom and splash cold water on my face. When I get back, Kim has herded the Schaefers into the dining room, where she proceeds to serve us a deluxe vegetarian feast: little kabobs of tofu skewered along with baby turnips, green beans, rice, and steamed leaf of something or other. Everything is lovely, symmetrical, and delicious, as always. The house looks great. Kim has cleaned and polished and organized the contents of each room until it's like living in a furniture store. The Schaefers praise everything and Kim grumbles her thanks. The thing about Kim is she's a wonderful cook, a great creator of ambiance, but she has a habit of getting annoyed with her guests, as if no one could ever be grateful enough for her efforts. We drain a couple more bottles of wine and after a while I notice that Kim has become fed up with the Schaefers too. She starts giving them The Look.

"Seriously," she begins, "do you two even like being married?"

They exchange a glance.

"No, c'mon, really. It's overrated, right?" Kim pulls the hair off her face and I can see how flushed she is, how infuriated. "I think all that crap about biological clocks and baby lust, it's all sexist propaganda meant to keep women in line."

"Well, I haven't noticed any conspiracy," offers Winsome, checking everyone's face to make sure she's not somehow being disagreeable. "I think marriage is just part of the journey."

"Ha," says Kim. "Ha ha ha." She leans across the table, swaying slightly. "I know," she pronounces, "that you don't believe that hippie shit. I can tell," she whispers, "how fucking lost you really are."

Then she stands, picks up her glass, and weaves toward the back door. "I have to go check the basement."

We stare at the space where Kim was for a while. Winsome is blinking rapidly and Evan keeps clearing his throat. I explain we have an unfinished basement that's been known to fill with water when it rains, and that the only entrance to it is outside in the yard, and that Kim probably wants to make sure that everything's okay down there. They nod vigorously. I can tell they're itching to purify our home with sticks of burning sage.

While Kim is gone I take them into the living room and show them my collection of LPs. I pull out my rare purple vinyl X-Ray Spex record, and after considering this for a while, Winsome informs me that purple is a healing color. We hear a couple of bangs under the house. I toy with the idea of checking on Kim, but then I recall the early days of our courtship, before all this house-beautiful crap, when Kim used to hang out the window of my 1956 hearse, which was also purple, and scream "Anarchy now!" and "Destroy!" while lobbing rocks through smoked glass windows into corporate lobbies. It's difficult to worry about a girl like that.

It doesn't take long for the Schaefers and me to run out of small talk. I have no idea how to get them to go home; social transitions are Kim's jurisdiction. We sit there nodding at each other like idiots until Kim finally straggles back inside. She's muddy, soaked to the bone, and strangely jolly. She says there's about a foot of water in the basement and that she was walking around in there and it's like a big honking wading pool. She giggles. The Schaefers stare with horror at the puddle spreading around her feet onto our nice oak floors. I put my arm around her and kiss her hair. She smells like wet dog.

I come home from work a few days later and find Kim unloading a Toys R Us bag. I notice a diamond tiara/necklace set with huge, divorcée-sized fake jewels stuck to a panel of pink cardboard. Again, she seems happy, which is odd for Kim. In fact, she's taken to singing around the house in this new style where she doesn't sing actual words, she goes "nar nar nar" like some demented little kid. It drives me crazy, in particular when the game is on, so I tell her to fucking please cut it out. She glares at me and storms off into the backyard. I let her pout for a while, but I'm in the mood to make an effort, so I eventually go out and find her standing on a chair, hanging over the hedge, gazing at the alley. I lean in beside her and see a caveman shambling off with a red bandana tied around his neck, like a puppy.

"That's weird."

"Look at his butt."

I look. There's a big blob of pink bubble gum stuck in his fur.

"God," says Kim, "isn't that pitiful?"

I ask her what we're having for dinner. She looks at me blankly and says I don't know, what are we having for dinner. I tell her I'll cook, and when I get back from picking up the pizza she's nowhere to be found. I walk from one empty room to another while the hairs on my arms start to tingle. I have to say, there's a peculiar feeling building in the household. Things are in a state of slight disarray. There's a candy bar wrapper on the coffee table, and the bag from the toy store is on the kitchen floor. I yell Kim's name. When she doesn't appear I turn on the TV and eat a few slices straight from the box. For some reason that starts to bother me, so I get up and get a plate, silverware, and a paper napkin. Kim walks in a little while later. She's wet from the waist down and all flushed, as if she's been doing calisthenics.

"I was bailing out the basement!" she says, with great verve, like basement bailing is a terrific new sport. Her hair is tangled around her head and she's sucking on a strand of it. She is smiling away. She says: "I'm worried about letting all that water just stand down there!"

But she doesn't look worried.

On the news one night, a psychic with a flashlight shining up under his chin explains there's a time portal in the condemned Pizza Hut by the freeway. Though the mayor whines he wasn't elected to buckle to the whim of every nutbar with an opinion, there are televised protests featuring people shaking placards proclaiming the Pizza Hut ground zero of unnatural evil, and finally they just bulldoze it to shut everyone up. A while after that, the incident levels start to drop. It seems that the cavemen are thinning out. They are not brainy enough for our world, and they can't stop extinguishing themselves. They tumble into swimming pools and drown. They walk through plate glass windows and sever their arteries. They fall asleep under eighteen-wheelers and wander onto runways and get mauled by pit bulls.

It looks like we're the dominant species after all; rock smashes scissors, *Homo sapiens sapiens* kicks *Homo sapiens neanderthalensis*'s ass.

As the caveman population drops, the ominous feeling around town begins to lift. You can feel it in the air: women jog by themselves instead of in pairs. People barbecue large cuts of meat at dusk. The cavemen, it seems, are thinning out everywhere except around our house. I come home from work and walk through the living room and peek out the back window just in time to see a tough, furry leg disappear through a hole in the hedge. The hole is new. When I go outside and kick around in the landscaping, I find neat little stashes of rhinestones and fake pearls, Barbie shoes, and folded squares of foil wrapping paper. They can't see that well, but have the ears of a dog and flee as soon as I rustle the window shaders. One time, though, I peel back the shade silently and catch a pair skipping in circles around the clothesline. One of them is gripping something purple and hairy, and when I go out there later I find a soiled My Little Pony doll on the ground. They are not living up to their reputation as club-swinging brutes. More than anything, they resemble feral little girls.

Also, our house has become an unbelievable mess. Kim walks through the door and drops the mail on the coffee table, where it remains for days until I remove it. There are panties on the bathroom floor and water glasses on top of the television and scraps of food on the kitchen counter. I ask Kim what's going on and she just says she's sick of that anal constant-housekeeping-bullshit, and if I want it clean, I can clean it myself. She looks straight at me and says this, without flinching, without any signs of deference or anger or subtle backing away that had always let me know, in nonverbal but gratifying ways, that I had the upper hand in the relationship. She tosses an orange peel on the table before marching outside and descending into the basement.

I stand there in the kitchen, which smells like sour milk, shaking my head and trying to face up to the increasingly obvious fact that my girlfriend of ten years is having an affair, and that her lover is a Neanderthal man from the Pleistocene epoch. They rendezvous in our moldy, water-stained basement where he takes her on the cement floor beneath a canopy of spiderwebs, grunting over her with his animal-like body, or perhaps behind her, so that when she comes back inside there are thick, dark hairs stuck all over her shirt and she smells like a cross between some musky, woodland animal gland and Herbal Essences shampoo. Furthermore, she's stopped shaving her legs.

The next day, I duck out of the office claiming I have a doctor's appointment and zip back home around noon. I open the door with my key and creep inside. I don't know what I'm looking for. I think I half expect to find Kim in bed with one of those things, and that he'll pop up and start "trying to reason" with me in a British accent. What I find instead is an empty house. Kim's car is gone. I poke around, stepping over mounds of dirty clothes, then head out back and take the stairs to the basement. When I pull the door open, the first thing to hit me is the smell of mold and earth. I pace from one side to the other and shine my flashlight around, but I don't see anything suspicious, just an old metal weight-lifting bench with a plastic bucket sitting on top. Maybe, I think, I'm making this whole thing up in my head. Maybe Kim just goes down there because she needs some time to herself.

But then on my way out, I spot something. On the concrete wall beside the door, several feet up, my flashlight picks out a pattern of crude lines. They appear to have been made with charcoal or maybe some type of crayon. When I take a few steps back, I can see it's a drawing, a cave painting of some sort. It's red and black with the occasional pom-pom of dripping orange that looks like it was made by someone who doesn't understand spray paint.

I stand there for two or three minutes trying to figure out what the painting is about, then spend another fifteen trying to convince myself my interpretation is wrong. The picture shows half a dozen cars in a V-shaped formation bearing down on a group of cavemen. The cavemen's flailing limbs suggest flight or panic; obviously, they're in danger of being flattened by the cars. Above them, sketched in a swift, forceful manner, floats a huge, God-like figure with very long arms. One arm cradles the fleeing cavemen while the other blocks the cars. This figure is flowing and graceful and has a big ponytail sprouting from the top of her head. Of course, it's meant to be Kim. Who else?

I go upstairs and sit at the kitchen table, elbowing away half a moldy cantaloupe, and hold my head in my hands. I was hoping it was nothing—a casual flirtation at most—but a guy who makes a cave painting for a girl is probably in love with the girl. And girls love to be loved, even high-strung ones like Kim. I admit I'm hurt, but my hurt switches to anger and my anger to resolve. I can fight this thing. I can win her back. I know her; I know what to do.

I put on rubber gloves and start cleaning everything, thoroughly and with strong-smelling products, the way Kim likes things cleaned. I do the laundry and iron our shirts and line everything up neatly in the closet. I get down on my knees and wipe the baseboards, then up on a chair to dust the lightbulbs. I pull a long clot of hair out of the drain. There's a picture of us in Mexico in a silver frame on top of the medicine cabinet. I pick it up and think: that is my woman! It's civilization versus base instinct, and I vow to deploy the strongest weapon at my disposal: my evolutionarily superior traits. I will use my patience, my facility with machinery and tools, my complex problem-solving skills. I will bathe often and floss my teeth. I will cook with gas.

A little after five Kim walks in and drops the mail on the coffee table. She looks around the house, at the gleaming neatness, smiling slightly and going "nar nar nar" to the tune of "Nobody Does It Better." I stand there in my cleanest suit with my arms hanging at my sides and gaze at her, in her little professional outfit, pretty and sexy in an I-don't-know-it-but-I-do way, clutching her black purse, her hair pulled back with one of those fabric hair things.

"God, I can't believe you cleaned," she says, and walks through the kitchen and out of the house into the yard and slams the basement door behind her.

Kim is so happy. The worst part is she's so disgustingly happy and I could never make her happy all by myself and I don't particularly like her this way. For a couple of weeks she walks around in a delirious haze. She spins around on the porch with her head thrown back and comments on the shape of the clouds. She asks why haven't I bothered to take in the pretty, pretty sunset, all blue and gold. Like I fucking care, I say, forgetting my pledge to be civil. It's as though someone has dumped a bottle of pancake syrup over her head—she has no nastiness left, no edge, no resentment. Her hair is hanging loose and she has dirty feet and bad breath. She smiles all the time. This is not the girl I originally took up with.

Of course, I'm heartstick; I'm torn up inside. Even so, I do my

35

best to act all patient and evolutionarily superior. I keep the house clean enough to lick. I start to cook elaborate meals the minute I get home from work. I groom myself until I'm sleek as a goddamn seal. I aim for a Fred Astaire/James Bond hybrid: smooth, sophisticated, oozing suaveness around the collar and cuffs—the kind of guy who would never fart in front of a woman, at least not audibly. She has a big, inarticulate lug already. I want to provide her with an option.

Kim takes it all for granted, coming and going as she pleases, wandering away from the house without explanation, hanging out in the basement with the door locked and brushing off my questions about what the hell she's doing down there, and with whom. She doesn't listen when I talk to her and eats standing in front of the refrigerator with the door open, yelling between bites that it's time for me to go to the store and get more milk. One evening I watch her polish off a plate of appetizers I have made for her, melon balls wrapped in prosciutto, downing them one after another like airline peanuts. When she's finished, she unbuttons the top button of her pants and ambles out the door and lets it slam without so much as a glance back at me. Without so much as a thank you.

I trot out after her, figuring it's about time I give her a suave, patient lecture, but I'm not fast enough and she slams the basement door in my face. I pound and scream for a while before giving up and going up into the yard to wait. The night is very still. There's a full moon and the hedges glow silver on the top and then fade to blue at the bottom. I get a glass of iced tea and pull a chair off the patio, thinking to myself that she can't stay down there forever. I think about how maybe I'll catch the caveguy when he comes out too. Maybe I can tie on an apron and offer them both baby wieners on a toothpick.

After a while I hear a rustling in the hedges. At that moment I'm too miserable to be aware of the specifics of what's going on around me, so I'm startled as hell when a cavegirl pops out of the hedge, backlit in the moonlight, and begins walking toward me with a slow, hesitant gait. I sit there, taking shallow breaths, not sure whether or not I should be afraid. She has a low brow and a tucked, abbreviated chin, like Don Knotts', but her limbs are long and sinewy. When she gets closer I see that she looks a lot stronger than a human woman does, and of course she's naked. Her breasts are like perfect human pinup breasts with bunny fur growing all over them. I can't unstick my eyes from them as they bob toward me, moving closer, until they come to a stop less than an arm's length from my chin. They are simultaneously furry and plump and I really want to bite them. But not hard.

She leans in closer. I hold very still as she reaches out with a leathery hand and begins to stroke my lapel. She lowers her head to my neck and sniffs. On the exhale I discover that cavegirl breath smells just like moss. She prods me a few times with her fingertips; after she's had enough of that she just rubs the fabric of my suit and sniffs my neck while sort of kneading me rhythmically, like a purring cat. It's pretty obvious she likes my suit—a shiny sharkskin number I've hauled out of the back of the closet in the interest of wooing Kim— and I guess she likes my cologne too. For a minute I feel special and chosen, but then it occurs to me that there's something sleazy and impersonal about her attention. I'm probably just a giant, shiny, sandalwood-scented object to her. The moon is behind her so I can't see her that clearly, but then she shifts and I get a better view of her face and I realize she's young. Really young. I feel like a creep for wanting to feel her up, more because she's about fourteen than because she's a Neanderthal.

She swings a leg over and settles her rump onto my thigh, lap-dance-style.

I say: "Whoa there, Jailbait."

The cavegirl leaps up like she's spring-loaded. She stops a few feet away and stares at me. I stare back. She tilts her head from side to side in puzzlement. The moon shines down. I reach into my glass and draw out a crescent-shaped piece of ice, moving with aching slowness, and offer it to her on a flat palm. She considers this ice cube for a good long time. I hold my arm as still as possible while freezing water trickles off my elbow and my muscles start to seize. Then, after a few false lunges, she snatches it from my hand.

"Nar," she says. Just that. Then she darts back into the hedge with her prize.

I remain in the moonlight for a while, shaking with excitement. I feel almost high. It's like I've touched a wild animal; I've communicated with it—an animal that's somehow human, somehow like me. I'm totally giddy.

This is probably how it was with Kim and her guy when they first met.

I guess I'm a complete failure with every category of female because the cavegirl does not come back. Even worse, Kim continues to treat me like I'm invisible. It's painfully clear that my strategy of suaveness isn't working. So I say screw evolution. What's it ever done for me? I go out drinking with the guys and allow the house to return to a state of nature. The plates in the sink turn brown. I shower every other day, every third. Kim and I go days without speaking to each other. By this time there are hardly any cavemen left around town; the count is running at one or two dozen. I go to the bars and everyone is lounging with their drinks, all relaxed and relieved that the cavemen aren't really an issue anymore, while I continue to stew in my own miserable interspecies soap opera. I don't even want to talk to anyone about it. What could I say? Hey buddy, did I mention my girlfriend has thrown me over for the Missing Link? It's humiliating.

One hungover afternoon I decide to skip the bars and come straight home from the office. Kim, naturally, is not around, though this barely registers. I've lost interest in tracking her whereabouts. But when I go into the kitchen, I catch sight of her through the window, standing outside, leaning against the chinaberry tree. It looks like she's sick or something. She's trying to hold herself up but keeps doubling over anyway. I go outside and find her braced against the tree, sobbing from deep in her belly while a string of snot swings from her nose. She's pale and spongy and smudged with dirt and I get the feeling she's been standing there crying all afternoon. She's clutching something. A red bandana. So it was him. The one with gum on his butt.

"Where is he?"

"He's gone," she whispers, and gives me a sad, dramatic, miniseries smile. "They're all gone."

Her sobs begin anew. I pat her on the back.

So she's curled over crying and I'm patting her thinking well, well; now that the other boyfriend is gone she's all mine again. Immediately I'm looking forward to putting the whole caveman ordeal behind us and having a regular life like we had before. I see all sorts of normal activities looming in the distance like a mirage, including things we always made fun of, like procreating and playing golf. She blows her nose in the bandana. I put my arm around her. She doesn't shake it off.

I should wait I know, I should go slow; but I can see the opening, the niche all vacant and waiting for me. I feel absolutely compelled to exploit it right away, before some other guy does. I turn to Kim and say: "Babe, let's just forget about this whole caveman thing and go back to the way it was before. I'm willing to forgive you. Let's have a normal life without any weird creatures in it, okay?"

She's still hiccuping and wiping her nose but I observe a knot of tension building in her shoulders, the little wrinkles of a glare starting around the edge of her eyes. I realize I'm in grave danger of eliciting The Look. It dawns on me that my strategy is a failure and I'd better think fast. So I bow to the inevitable. I've always known I couldn't put it off forever.

I take a deep breath and drop to one knee and tell her I love her and I can't live without her and beg her to marry me while kissing her hand. She's hiccuping and trying to pull her hand away, but in the back of my mind I'm convinced that this is going to work and of course she'll say yes. I've never made an effort like this before; I've only told her I love her two or three times total, in my life. It's inconceivable that this effort won't be rewarded. Plus, I know her. She lives for this. This is exactly what she wants.

I look up at her from my kneeling position. Her hair is greasy and her face is smeared with dirt and snot, but she's stopped crying. I see that she has created a new Look. It involves a shaking of the head while simultaneously pushing the lips outward, like she's crushed a wasp between her teeth and is about to spit it out. It's a look of pity, pity mixed with superiority; pity mixed with superiority and blended with dislike.

"I don't want a normal life without any creatures in it," Kim says, her voice ragged from crying, but contemptuous nonetheless. "I want an extraordinary life, with everything in it."

The Look fades. She brings her dirty, snotty face to mine and kisses me on the forehead and turns and walks away, leaving me on my knees. I stumble into the house after her. I can smell a trail of scent where she's passed by, cinnamon and sweat and fabric softener, but though I run through the house after her, and out into the street, I don't see her anywhere, not all night. Not the night after that. Never again.

Some psychic with a towel on his head says the cavemen passed through his drive-through palm-reading joint on their way back to the Pleistocene epoch, and I finally go over and ask him if he saw Kim with them. He has me write him a check and then says, Oh *yeah*, I did see her! She was at the front of this line of female cavemen and she was all festooned with beads and tinsel, like she was some sort of goddess! He says it in this bullshit way, but after some reflection I decide even charlatans may see strange and wondrous things, as we all had during the time the cavemen were with us, and then report them so that they sound like a totally improbable lie.

It's bizarre, the way time changes things. Now that the cavemen are gone, it seems obvious that their arrival was the kind of astonishing event people measure their entire lives by; and now that Kim is gone it seems clear that she was astonishing too, regal and proud, like she's represented in the cave painting. I once thought of her as sort of a burden, a pain-in-the-ass responsibility, but now I think of her as the one good thing I had in my life, an intense woman with great reserves of strength, forever vanished.

Or, I don't know; maybe I'm just a typical guy, don't know what I have until it walks out on me.

I've been trying to get over her, but I can't stop wallowing in it. One night we hold a drum circle on the site of the old Pizza Hut, and I swear that after this night, I'll force myself to stop thinking about her. This drum circle is the largest yet, maybe a couple of hundred people milling around, having the kind of conversations people have these days—you know, they were annoyed and frightened by the cavemen when they were here, but now that they're gone they just want them back, they want the weird, vivid feeling, the newness of the primitive world, et cetera. My job is to tend the fire. There's a six-foot pyramid of split pine in the middle of the circle, ready to go. At the signal I throw on a match. The wood is soaked in lighter fluid and goes up with a whoosh. Everyone starts to bang on their drums, or garbage can lids, or whatever percussive dingus they've dragged along, while I stand there poking the flames, periodically squirting in plumes of lighter fluid, as the participants wail and drum and cry and dance.

We are supposedly honoring the cavemen with this activity, but in truth no one ever saw the cavemen making fires or dancing or playing any sort of musical instrument. Apparently the original Neanderthal did these things; they also ate one another's brains and worshipped the skulls of bears, though no one seems anxious to resurrect these particular hobbies. Still, I admit I get kind of into it. Standing there in the middle, sweating, with the sound of the drumming surrounding me while the fire crackles and pops, it's easy to zone out. For a moment I imagine what it might be like to live in an uncivilized haze of sweat and hunger and fear and desire, to never plan, to never speak or think in words—but then the smell of lighter fluid snaps me back to how artificial this whole drum circle is, how prearranged and ignited with gas.

Later, when the fire has burned out, some New Age hardcores roll around in the ashes and pray for the cavemen to come back, our savage brothers, our hairy predecessors, et cetera, but of course they don't come back. Those guys look stupid, covered in ash. When the sun comes up, everyone straggles away. I get into my hatchback and listen to bad news on the radio as I drive home.

Nominated by Zoetrope: All Story

NARROW ROAD TO THE DEEP NORTH

essay by GARY AMDAHL

from THE GETTYSBURG REVIEW

I AM WALKING DOWN A NARROW HALLWAY. *A phone rings. I come to an open door at the end of the hallway. The phone rings again. I stand at the threshold, convinced, as I often am, that the room I am poised to enter is, for a reason or reasons unknown or unclear to me, a room I should not enter. My mother appears. She glances at me in a distracted, ready to answer the phone way, then answers the phone. The house shifts slightly in the hot August wind.*

My mother's face changes. She is recovering from surgery, so my first thought is that the wound is hurting, but then she says the name of my aunt, her sister, her only sister, Nada, gone now, too—a strange name perhaps for hispanophones, but she was christened so by Ted and Clara Nestegard, who spoke only English and Norwegian, and however strange her name might be, it is appropriate to this ominous and attenuated moment. My mother says "Nada" once, twice, three times. My aunt and uncle are due in town, coming up for a visit from Jackson, in southwestern Minnesota, where they farm a great many acres of corn and soybeans. When they return from this visit, the purpose of which is to cheer my mother, preparations for the harvest will begin.

But here is the news: my uncle will not participate in this harvest. He has been shot. He is dead.

I have told this story a number of times. The reaction is almost always one of disbelief. Because I appear to be telling the truth, listeners want to believe me, but for reasons I do not fully understand—perhaps they do not either—they want not to believe me, too. Murder in Lake Wobegon? There can be no murder in Lake Wobegon; it is not possible. Anything that disturbing must be absorbed by sly humor and transformed into pleasant melancholy, the deeper pools of which are fenced off by simple common sense. One cannot even tell the story of a murder there: the words fly up from the teller's mouth as if caught in a tornado.

Which is not the worst way to live, but it is a narrow discipline and tends to make a certain sort of person feel unwelcome: me, for instance, at least in the way I saw myself then, a tiny male figure, neither man nor boy, on his back in a vast and neglected meadow of foxtail barley and timothy, under a boiling, luminous silver-and-green sky, telling a story that can be heard only as a roaring, seen only as a black cloud funneling from his mouth.

I told the story to a psychiatrist once. I was being bad in ways I do not want to recall, was depressed, had been identified as a candidate for a course in grief management and spiritual renewal—and, more importantly, had begun to see the blackness of the whirlwind as composed of equal parts self-indulgence (fear of my own sudden death, fear of my own sudden murderousness) and shame over the uses to which I was putting or knew I would soon put the story. I told the story sensationally, for its shock value; I told it so that people might feel as sorry for me as I did for myself, told it so that I might be seen as having heroically withstood horror, told it knowing I would write about it and, while the rest of my family simply grieved, profit from it. As Barry Hannah's narrator says in the story "Carriba": "Murder is not interesting, friends. Murder is vomit. You may attach a story to it but you are already dishonest to the faces of the dead. . . . I knew I had no place arranging this misery into entertainment, a little *Hamlet* for busybodies and ghouls. . . . My whole professional life reared up in my mind. I was a hag and a parasite. I was to be grave and eloquent over their story. . . . They were to get nothing. I was to get fame and good bucks, provided I was interesting. A great sick came on me."

Such was the tenor of my conversation with the psychiatrist. His response was remarkable. I realized only after I had fled his office that he had simply chosen not to believe me. I gave him the murder in précis, with a suggestion of the emotional discord I claimed to be experiencing, and he said, "That's interesting." I waited a good long while for him to continue. He was a kind of Kilroy behind his desk, getting smaller and smaller by the second. Just when he was about to vanish entirely, he said, "I make a special study of stories like the one you've just told me, but I don't recall reading or hearing about this one. Where did you say it happened? And when? I'd like to check the papers. Your uncle's name is . . . ?"

I said that his name had been, when he was alive, Art Storm. It struck us both, I think, as sounding made up, the name of a character in a bad novel (if you punch up *art storm* on the Lexis Nexis newspaper searching service, you get thirty stories on Robert Mapplethorpe and one on my uncle), so I said, "Arthur William Storm, Jr." I then described *where* pretty convincingly but was shaky on *when*, which bolstered, I guess, my inquisitor's sense that I was making it up, in a play, I guess, for sympathy. He wrote a prescription for Prozac and sent me on my way.

That was the last time we chatted. Now that I have gotten my facts straight, I want to share them. But I find I cannot recall the name of this psychiatrist, nor when I saw him, nor, precisely, where. The building was located in a downtown St. Paul backwater; the program was part of that city's social service safety net; and the decor of the waiting room was dominated by fiery orange shag carpeting and dark imitation-wood paneling. My fellow clients either spoke in harsh whispers to themselves ("Not now, you fool, not here!"), turned in very small circles before the magazine rack—which had dizzied and deflected me, too—or stared, stonily or stonedly, into midair. They were both a fright and a comfort to me. Then there was the doctor—elusive, peeping. I took the Prozac for a month; it, too, was both a fright and a comfort. I imagined I felt clear-minded, but predatory. I felt as if the number of rods in my retinas—those receptors responsive to faint light—had multiplied rather demonically. I could see in the dark and had lots of energy for the hunt but missed both the peace of deepening twilight and the nervous dread of a sleepless dawn. I failed to make my next appointment, failed to have the prescription refilled, failed to balance my chemicals.

A violent act in a violent culture: what of it? Violence can be both fun and rewarding, if you watch the right movies. And I do not mean only those on television or in theaters; I mean the ones we film day after weary day, loops of resentment and frustration and greed and fear and ignorance in which we get the last word, beat senseless

44

those who have annoyed us, and sometimes even kill them, if the annoyance is grievously deep and can be shown to be the cause of a chronic social ill.

Arnold and Sly and Clint simply make entertainingly explicit the features and character of the man many of us daydream about being: a good man—i.e., one who knows how to fight but appears to be reluctant to do so, one who is cool under psychological and moral pressure but can explode like a volcano when he needs to, a man not prone to doubt or confusion, a man of deeds not words, a man of action who can gather and manage the collective rage of the savagely annoyed and perfectly righteous people who have defined and approved his goodness, a man who can marshal the virtues and skills his employers say are pertinent and conducive to good public relations. I am talking about a man who can dodge bullets. What better man could we possibly hope for! A man who can see it coming, who can turn aside just in time, engage bad violence with good violence, use the flabby weight of the enemy's badness judo-like against him and hurl him into the never-never land of soulless, heartless, mindless evildoers, a man who can perform the Alchemy of the Good Man: make the lead of superior violence into the moral gold of justice. Above all, I am dreaming about a man who can *remain alive and in control, no matter what, forever.*

My uncle's murderer, a Green Beret from what is always termed the "tough" Eighty-second Airborne, honorably discharged after the invasion of Grenada—in which he saw action of an undisclosed sort—and sophomore English major at Iowa State in Ames, knew all about this massive fraud. "Thank you," his suicide letter read, "for keeping me alive so long." The hero, hoodwinked and helpless. "Thank you for keeping me alive so long." He was twenty-four.

I turned eighteen in 1974 and thus was spared the Vietnam that had troubled me so. Neither sincerely "born again" in Jesus Christ (I did walk down the aisle in answer to that call but really only to get the autograph of a Minnesota Twins pitcher—either Jim Kaat or Al Worthington, cannot remember which now) nor apostate, I sometimes felt a Lutheran call to be obedient to the prince, to serve my country, and sometimes felt a Christian pacifism welling up in me. But I was also a fan of Heroic Violence. I even had a specialty: I was something, I fancied, of an after-dinner speaker, a guy who could mouth off while trading blows with pinheads.

45

For instance, the episode that precipitated me into the lair of the shrinking Kilroy: I fought a man on a highway. He had rammed my car from behind, enraged by the way I had gotten in line ahead of him, or "merged," if you will. My first thought was to get his license plate number, and I tried to read it in the rearview mirror—difficult even if he had not been hanging on my bumper. Then I decided I would get behind him. He took the next exit, but I was in a rather taut-handling little German thing and whipped in after him. Still, my only conscious desire was to get his number. Which I got, and began to calm down. But then we came to a red light. I pulled up behind him and then thought, *I cannot pretend this has not happened. I will seek an explanation.* So we tumbled out of our jars of formaldehyde, this sales rep and I, and before I knew what hit me, he hit me. "Is that the best you can do, Chumley?" I demanded to know, but before he could answer, I saw the famous red haze. I began to choke him with one hand, forcing him back to his car and wedging him between the open door and the frame. His arms snugly pinned, his face darkening, I drew back my free fist, in hopes of pounding his insolent face all bloody and askew. But I came to my senses and saw only the natural colors of a cloudy spring day in Minnesota. I released the man's throat and stepped back. I was about to lecture him, but he came flying out at me and landed a good one right in my mouth. The light had changed, and traffic was approaching. I grabbed hold of him and threw him directly in the path of a big orange utilities maintenance truck.

The driver of the truck managed to avoid running over and killing my fallen foe, but the feeling that he had almost, that the sales rep was dead and that I was responsible—that has stayed with me. It is a perplexing feeling, not so much because it is not true, or because I am filled with shame, but because it is a *good* feeling.

It was one of the first times I had acted on an angry feeling, rather than stewing in my own bitter juices. While getting out of the car, approaching the other—right up to that moment when I started smashing my fists against his window—I was calm. I felt I was "in the right" and was merely going to "redress the wrong" that had been done to me; I was going to be forthright and reasonable. I had already noted the license plate number and was planning only an assertion of righteousness, acceptance of which on the part of the sales rep would have short-circuited my decision to tell on him, as talking to the cops has always been the last thing I want to do. But the next thing I knew, he was sprawled upon the road, and a huge truck was describing a screeching salient around him.

I acknowledged, privately, the shamefulness of my actions, noted the "mistakes in judgment," and worked out the causes and effects, but I could not help but interpret it positively. I had appealed to no authority, handed off no responsibility, called out to no one for help or confirmation of what I believed was right and what I believed was wrong. This all seemed perfectly proper to me, even heroic. I had had a bone to pick with an asshole and had nearly killed him. I had understood, in a flash of violently heroic insight, that he was a bad guy, and I was a good guy, and neither of us was going to brook recourse to armed bureaucrats. And I nearly killed him.

What if he had had a gun?

What if I had had a gun?

I had wanted one for a long time. I knew some fellows who owned guns, and I liked them. I went to sporting goods stores and priced them, listened to salesmen describe them, picked them up and hefted them. I began saving money toward the purchase of one.

Television, computer, automobile, handgun: they were all the same to me, tools of American cultural welfare. When they were managed properly, nobody died. My adversaries would be only persuaded—just as they would be by the rigors of any other religion— and corrected.

My uncle's killer did have a gun, a Ruger Security Six (a .357 Magnum revolver, serial number 156-52069) loaded with Peters .38 Special copper-jacketed hollow-points. It was his father's gun, but having been a commando, he was no stranger to sidearms. I do not know if he killed anybody in Grenada, but I do know that he was said to have "come back changed" and that he had tried to kill himself once before. "The last time he attempted suicide he went to Missouri," his father was quoted as saying in an Iowa newspaper. "There is no doubt in my mind he went to Minnesota to commit suicide." The implication is that he could not, for some reason, bring himself to do the deed in Iowa, his home state—an inability I found curious. Were I planning to do myself in, I would most certainly get the hell out of California, which I have designated as the last place I want to die, and go home. But home, of course, is precisely where they keep you alive so long.

The next question is, why Minnesota? "It's strange," said Eric Ha-

47

gen's mother, "but if you follow Highway 169 from here" ("here" being the towns of Ogden and Perry in central Iowa), "Jackson is almost straight north." Put a ruler on the map, and fill the tank with gas. When you run out, you kill yourself.

Jackson is about fifteen miles north of the Iowa border and seventy east of South Dakota: *coteau des prairies*, the first step up of the great high plains from the Mississippi valley toward the Rockies—the "true prairie" as it was sometimes called, the tallgrass prairie, grass as high as a horse's back and occasionally even higher, up to twelve feet. It is often described as oceanic, a vast swelling sea into which despairing pioneer women cast themselves and drowned. But of that ocean nothing remains, as if ten million years have elapsed from the time my great-grandparents appeared on its shore—geologic time, time enough for an ocean to vanish, exposing a bed infamously flat, across which, in pesticide dispersal grids, immense machines move.

For several years after his father's death, my cousin, who farmed in partnership with him (and who found him on the porch), would sit high atop one of those machines in a little air-conditioned cube and listen to self-help tapes while he plowed or sowed or cultivated or harvested. Once in a while he would suffer what they call a "false heart attack" (which seems as "true" as the other kind to me). He would become suddenly overwhelmed by panic, feeling that his loss, his terror, was not in the past but was steady and continual and happening *right now*, and he would be rushed off to the hospital, where, after a while, the present would expand enough to give his heart, again, the space to beat.

The Des Moines River runs roughly north and south through the country, originating about forty miles to the northwest and emptying into the Mississippi at Keokuk, Iowa. The land for no more than a mile on either bank of the river is folded into hills, giving some parts of town a little elevation and a view, and altering the character of some of the farms along the river: basically, more livestock, less corn.

It was on one of these river farms that my aunt and my mother grew up and that I was born. When I think of farms, this one, and the one on which my father was born and raised (in northeastern Iowa), are the ones I think of: hill farms, polyculture, cattle, hogs, chickens, corn and wheat and alfalfa and sorghum, norghum and flax and beans, wagons and tractors tipping over on steep hillsides—"Just roll with it," my grandfather instructed my mother. There was no running water on the farm, no indoor plumbing. There were bedpans and buckets and pitchers and basins, an outhouse and a well. My mother carried water from this well every day of her life until she left for college. My life on the farm lasted only a month, but what a month! From there it was on to the unspeakable luxuries of Minneapolis: running water, central heating (the farmhouse had a single big woodstove, with a grate in the ceiling to heat the upstairs bedrooms), refrigerators, toasters—luxury upon luxury, to the point where I now do not think twice about jetting to Europe or filling a large plastic bag every week with trash.

Rural America was pretty well electrified by the time my mother was born, which meant, for her, two or three lightbulbs and a radio. There was also a telephone. My mother speaks of her childhood as a kind of idyll of clean and happy poverty—and the orange and the pencil that she got as Christmas gifts, the wood she chopped and the water she carried, do indeed seem integral to paradise. I grew up in the suburbs but can hardly bear to drive through them now. I do not even like reading novels set in the suburbs. My father, who left farm life eagerly at eighteen, saw, with his BBA and CPA diplomas, his income rise sharply the first eighteen years of my life, allowing him to present me with a profoundly different world upon graduation from high school than the one he and my mother had known. My brother and I had already been to California, to Florida (and if I now know a more desperate and corrupt Miami, I will never forget the way the palm trees rattled that first night in the hot, muggy wind), to Jamaica and the Bahamas! I had fished for, and caught, a barracuda. I had already known the impatience Liz Taylor was said to have known in the Joan Rivers joke about slow microwave ovens. I had already experienced the wave of hatred a motorist whose skills I judged to be subpar could excite. There was more money. Our standard of living was very high. You may have heard about this; sociologists and investment fund managers alike have been advertising the phenomenon for years: *rising expectations*.

I think rising expectations are what killed my uncle, actually. How, I cannot say, but I began to think of the .38 Special hollow-points emerging in the bright smoke of the muzzle flash as merely the exploding fragments of the grotesquely ignorant and self-righteous sense of expectation and entitlement that—I began to think—characterized American culture.

49

I knew nothing of the killer. I knew he felt strongly enough about what he had done to kill himself ("Justice will be done by me," wrote the hero), but what I wanted desperately to understand, was how, step by step, he had come to my uncle's farmhouse porch and shot him in the head. This is perhaps the way in which the story became a black whirlwind: uneven breathing in which inquiry became panic slowly rotating clockwise around a void, the void slowly sinking from brain to heart. The killer disappeared. I looked to his country and lo, it was murderous. Each inhalation took in more and more of the cultural atmosphere, each exhalation grew blacker and blacker. Everything about the United States seemed designed to encourage or induce murder: capitalism, technology, the law itself—all nothing more than oppressive religions. I repudiated them, just as I had Christianity and the Lutheran Church that has aided—not frightened—and comforted so many of the people closest to me, my mother and my father particularly, whose devotion is genuine and whose freethinking returns them again and again to the bosom of the Savior. And as I went about perfecting the terrible beauty of the black tale—the writer of fiction assuming the pompous posture of truth-teller and coming more completely undone by the duplicity of it than he would have, had he simply told lies—the little farmhouse on the prairie came to seem a psychic refuge. By the time I began to think seriously about the place, it had been abandoned for decades. I dreamed of inhabiting it like a character in a Beckett story, or like a Timon of the Great Plains, spitting and howling malediction.

It was not just that my uncle had been murdered, but that my uncle had been murdered *and* I could not make a living. My gifts were being rejected or ignored. My wife had left me once already and was drifting toward a second departure, and I felt sorry for myself: *nasty country, run by knaves for fools, or vice versa, I do not know which.* I closed my ears to the drip and hiss of agrochemicals, to the firm, quiet phrasings of agribusiness executives, and told myself that if I were not the lazy man of letters that—at best—I am, I would be working in a field somewhere, walking neat rows of beans like my grandfathers did. I walked around the farmhouse in my mind, saw the fireflies in the twilight, heard the grossly articulate speech of cattle and hogs—the grunt, the bellow, the squeal, the moan—and the black tale became a murmur and a plume of cigar smoke. Then, in that fairyland of peace and sociologically verifiable contentment, the phone would ring. The farmhouse disappears as suddenly and vio-

50

lently as if a nuclear wind had blasted it. I can see it up there in the tornado swirling down upon me, just like Dorothy's house in Kansas.

The violent act in a violent culture: every one of us is familiar with the ethos of murder. As Freud pointed out, where there is a grave taboo there must also be a powerful desire. The most popular question in the story of my uncle's killing quickly centered on the randomness of it: why would a Green Beret turned English major quit his job as a hired hand on a farm, drive one hundred and sixty-eight miles north, choose a farm out of the blue (the green, rather, a million acres of it), and shoot to death the first man he saw there?

It sounds like a joke: to get to the other side?

"We felt, I guess, all along that this looked like a random deal," Jackson County Sheriff Pete Eggiman said at the time. The random deal of the rising expectation: the quintessence of our time and place. Randomness is all the rage, because cause and effect degenerate so quickly into name-calling and scapegoating. But insofar as randomness is a special effect or a magazine cover or a business fad, it is a useless idea, a fraudulent one, a dead end—because, after all the cool graphics and inspirational speeches, it is about precisely what it says it is not: control and manipulation. I used to write videoscripts for business seminars and was amazed to see so many people, day after day, equate *excellence* and *chaos* and *huge profits*. Mid- and upper-level managers taking a day or three off at a convention have a very different understanding of chaos than the guy who appears one fine morning on the loading dock, armed to the teeth and "disgruntled": *I want my job back, I want to feel needed, I know I'm weird, I know I lack people skills, but I am a human being anyway, after all, oh it's too late, it's too fucking late, I've killed someone.* Chaos cannot be measured along a spectrum: there are six billion varieties of chaos alone, and the only taxonomy of importance concerns the ways in which these forms disguise and display their essence, the celestial matter at the bottom of the deep well (this is a line from Neruda to which I came via an epigraph in a book by Gina Berriault) into which artists are forever falling.

I am a novelist (proud to say so, and equally proud to admit that only one-tenth of one novel has seen the light of a bookstore) and operate under the belief that novels and people are ideally suited to each other. Reading a novel is all about the immersion of oneself in the comfortingly familiar incomprehensibility of life and living, in

51

observant incomprehension, in the disorder and beauty of the houses that languages and minds build, in the disordered architecture of language itself. And of all the thoughts I have had of the murdering soldier and his short life, the most compelling is that he was a frustrated writer, that if he had so much as been able to begin to think about a novel of the invasion of Grenada, about a Green Beret who had "never wanted to be strong" (I am quoting his suicide letter again), all would have been well. He would have returned to Ames and Iowa State, continued to read, study literature, write. My uncle would still be farming. His friends would never have had to say things to reporters like, "He was gentle and affable, the nicest guy you could hope to meet." My aunt too, I believe, would still be alive (only in my mind did she die of causes related to my uncle's death; everyone else chalks it up to the tumor on her colon that was to be removed—prognosis for recovery, excellent—and the sudden heart attack—"sudden" in that she was not in any of the risk categories and was only sixty-four), and my mother would not feel quite so lonely, would not wake up every morning to memories of her sister, would not feel the need to wear my aunt's sweater, trying to reconstruct the warmth of her hug. I would be hard at work on an unpublishable novel, not cashing in on private grief and the public taste for mayhem. Or maybe reviewing Eric Charles Hagen's novel, listening to him on a panel with Tim O'Brien and David Rabe, though he was not that good a writer; although, on the other hand, the only work of his I have read was written at a time of profound emotional distress, and he had really only just begun.

Why? For what? *Everyone has tried to help. I love mom and dad and Sandy and Mike and Jer and Julie and Tami—all those that tried their best. But I saw this coming in a walking dream, seems like years ago. I hate to be so much alone, though I love the animals. I realize now I won't leave this town. I'm not going anywhere.*

Thank you for keeping me alive so long. There were beautiful times. I only wish I could come back.

I'm no criminal, just scared and falling.

Directed inward or outward—pain is still pain.

Sandy—I wish I could meet you again. Stay strong, your strength held me together for so long, I love you forever.

Not only couldn't I change the world, I couldn't even keep it still.

There is a surcharge of violence in me that is not safely directed at anything in this spectacular mystery of a world, though the violence may die, I will not, I will survive as a piece of dust, a fallen leaf, tranquil, unawake, forever a part of this world, forever more at peace. No one should blame themselves for what I have done save me, and justice will be done by me.

I never wanted to be strong.

It is strange that the future can be foreseen, but not averted.

I am allergic to love, a fatal allergy, and in the end I have discovered courage, it is a calm (my first) and it is facing the world face to face, and only seeing the mirror.

> *Finis*
> *end of game*
> *no more*
> *will I quench this thirst*
> *the drink is too ugly*
> *the love lost*
> *is too great*
> *these are terrible times*
> *sometimes*
> *we danced*
> *we laughed*
> *those memories*
> *I bring to the wind*
> *the lightning storms*
> *were beautiful*
> *on the front porch*
> *and the purrs and*
> *wagging tail*
> *knowing that then*
> *I was home*
> *I miss you*
> *I miss the simple sanity*

But those frames cannot die.

I'm not sure what I have done but I have a horrible feeling, win the battle to lose the war.

I wish I could explain

I wish there were words to express the love I never showed
I'm hearing voices, like, the whispers of last fall but stronger, all
too clear
I am barely here.

The letter was written sometime in the late afternoon or evening of Friday, August 21, 1987, after the death of my uncle, in a room at the Danish Inn Motel in Tyler, Minnesota, a town a little less than a hundred miles northwest of Jackson. The motel was not open for business, but the owner sometimes rented rooms anyway. Hagen paid for his room with a fifty-dollar bill, which turned out to be quite important in knowing who killed my uncle. Once he had rented the room, he went for a walk. Passing Mrs. Bruce Meyer, he noted her pregnant condition and greeted her. "You're pregnant," he said, smiling and friendly. "You could probably use some money." He tried to give her two fifty-dollar bills, which she declined to accept. Hagen carefully placed the bills on the sidewalk, weighting them with a chip of concrete. This was about 9:30 P.M., right around the time I had gone to my friend's house with the idea of borrowing one of his hunting rifles, thinking, *sooner or later I'll be close enough to "this guy" (Hagen), and I'll kill him.* By eleven o'clock my "murderous rage" had passed, and Hagen had written his letter, crawled into bed, drawn up the covers, and killed himself.

"We knew Jackson was missing four fifty-dollar bills," the Lincoln County sheriff said, illuminating the foundation of what we mean when we talk about closure. There was also "blood-stained clothing in the room not related to the suicide." The state Bureau of Criminal Apprehension ran ballistics and blood tests, checked Hagen's fingertips, and found they matched prints on a red disposable lighter found between the porch (the porch!) of my uncle's house and the driveway—it was spotted first by my cousin, who, according to deputy Leonard Rowe, shouted *"Watch out for that lighter!"* as if it were an unexploded bomb.

And that was that. Special Agent Dennis Sigafoos put it this way in Item Seven of his "Report of Investigation": "The homicide of Arthur William Storm, Jr., has been cleared. The perpetrator of the crime Eric Charles Hagen committed suicide ending this investigation."

Once upon a time, a young man who had been working on a farm in Iowa took his father's car—a white Volkswagen with a black tail fin—

54

and his father's gun and drove north for three hours. A few miles west of the town of Jackson, Minnesota, he saw a remote and prosperous looking farm. He went to the door of the farmhouse. The farmer who lived there was in the kitchen making lunch. He heard a noise on his front porch and went to see who or what it could be. No one knows if words passed between the two men when they met. Some people believe that a struggle ensued, for life or death, for life and death, but a man who professed to know said that the few minor bruises he found on the two bodies did not indicate any such thing. Silently or not, struggling or not, the younger man shot the farmer four times, twice in the head and twice in the upper torso. There was a large and bloody hole in the farmer's back, and smaller bloody holes in the back of his head, the hair of which was well known for its tendency to rooster-tail. When the sheriff's deputy arrived, he noted that "it was real obvious the party had expired." An investigation revealed the absence of four fifty-dollar bills from the farmer's billfold, money he had just taken that morning at a coffee shop in town as a down payment for a truck he was selling. A cry went up that a vagrant, a drifter, a madman had appeared, had robbed and murdered, had fled, and was at large. But the truth was that by the time most people heard the story, the killer was dead.

Fifteen hundred people filed past the open casket at the wake. The farmer's nephew, at the end of the line, was seen to thump his uncle's hollow chest and cry out. At the funeral the next day, the church was filled with the sound of people sobbing loudly, people who made a point of being cheerful and strong in the face of disaster or misery or sorrow—or at least strong, or at least stone-faced and dry-eyed.

After the service, in the basement of the church where mourners ate plate after plate of cold cuts and hot dishes, roll after buttered roll, slice of ham after slice of ham, news that a young man who had killed himself in a town to the north had been "positively linked" to the murder of the farmer made its way through the crowd. Each person looked into the eyes of the person nearest, then quickly at another and another, saw tears filling those eyes and spilling from them in stern, exhausted relief, felt the force of a hundred spines burning like fuses, shook hands all around to keep those hands from trembling, and smiled, then looked away.

The subject of the death penalty sometimes arises when I tell this story. I am opposed to it, and I present myself as a "crime victim." I say, murderous rage flashing whitely, blackly, in my mind, that if the murderer were alive today, I would want to forgive him. To which the obvious reply is that the murderer is not alive. My feeling, however, continues to be that once you get to know someone, it is hard to want to see them dead.

Plus, what is two plus two? It does not add up to a novelist weakening under a load of ominous dread, every day more and more frightened by—simply and frankly—other people. Clearly, the only way out is to find the well of other souls and drink from it.

Nominated by Pamela Stewart, The Gettysburg Review

GRATITUDE

by ROBERT CORDING

from THE PARIS REVIEW

In his prison letters, Bonhoeffer is thankful
for a hairbrush, for a pipe and tobacco,
for cigarettes and Schelling's *Morals* Vol. II.
Thankful for stain remover, laxatives,
collar studs, bottled fruit and cooling salts.
For his Bible and hymns praising what is
fearful, which he sings, pacing in circles
for exercise, to his cell walls where he's hung
a reproduction of Dürer's *Apocalypse*.
He's thankful for letters from his parents
and friends that lead him back home,
and for the pain of memory's arrival,
his orderly room of books and prints too far
from the nightly sobs of a prisoner
in the next cell whom Bonhoeffer does not know
how to comfort, though he believes religion
begins with a neighbor who is within reach.
He's thankful for the few hours outside
in the prison yard, and for the half-strangled
laughter between inmates as they sit together
under a chestnut tree. He's thankful even
for a small ant hill, and for the ants that are
all purpose and clear decision. For the two
lime trees that mumble audibly with the workings
of bees in June and, especially, for the warm
laying on of sun that tells him he's a man

created of earth and not of air and thoughts.
He's thankful for minutes when his reading
and writing fill up the emptiness of time,
and for those moments when he sees himself
as a small figure in a vast, unrolling scroll,
though mostly he looks out over the plains
of ignorance inside himself. And for that,
too, he's thankful: for the self who asks
who am I?—the man who steps
cheerfully from this cell and speaks easily,
without hatred to his jailers, or the man
who is restless and weary and trembling
with anger and despair as cities burn and Jews
are herded into railroad cars—can,
without an answer, say finally, *I am thine*,
to a God who lives each day,
as Bonhoeffer must, in the knowledge
of what has been done, is still being done,
his gift a refusal to leave his suffering, for which,
even as the rope is placed around his neck
and pulled tight, Bonhoeffer is utterly grateful.

Nominated by William Wenthe, Theodore Deppe, Jeffrey Harrison

ABOUT TERE WHO WAS IN PALOMAS

fiction by DAGOBERTO GILB

from THE THREEPENNY REVIEW

GUILLERMO SANTILLAN didn't like the nickname Memo so he was Willie. He pronounced it "weee-lee," you know, like popping "wheelies" on a bike. He liked to say he was from Mexico, or sometimes Nuevo Méjico, and sometimes Pinche Tejas. He was just from Canutillo, living out of an old adobe. It was square, four sides, and three windows, and a door. The plaster on it was falling off and it wasn't so it would look real hip but just that it'd been there a long time. The man who owned it, who Willie was renting it from real cheap, he poured the cement floor himself, so the inside wasn't plain dirt no more, and it had high and low spots and cracks. He stood up two stud walls and drywalled them—he never got around to the taping and bedding part, just nails and seams, hammer marks—to make the bathroom a room and then the bedroom a room. No door to the bedroom. The whole house was so dinky that when you opened the front door—which was hollow, a fist could go right through, but it was a lot cheaper than a solid door—and stepped in, pues, you were on the other side of the house.

Willie got to living there with Teresa Gámez. He was in that kind of love with her that he also hated her. He didn't trust her, didn't like how he was about any of it. He didn't want this love. She was married to a person who was so ugly. Willie wouldn't even call him a man. He stunk like an alley winos piss in. He plain stunk. When this person walked, he slumped like a tecato, but he didn't do no chiva or roca or

59

meth, he wasn't a sniffer, nothing, he just drank beer and smoked grifa and didn't do nothing for work except sell some to other stupids. No, it wasn't just Willie who thought this way. Everybody asked how could Tere be with such a person. Something about her past, something wrong about her. And so something he didn't trust about her. It wasn't like everyone didn't talk the same thing. Like about that body of hers. That figure. This person, her man, he didn't fight Willie to keep her. Willie offered her a place to stay, y ya, she was there. But how come it took her so long, and then how come she came over so fast? He hated how he wanted her and how he had her. Even after she moved in and lived with him in the adobe, which he got nada más because he was passing through and it was cheap and the dude who rented it to him gave him some work. That was Willie. Passing through. So he was scared of Tere. Then after a while she told him she was leaving him, going back home to Palomas. Fucking good, he said. Why? he asked her. She was crying. So leave, he told her! Just leave. She left.

So he left too, and now he was talking with this woman and they were at a Mexican restaurant and he wasn't going to tell her one thing about Tere. He didn't tell his cousin, he wouldn't tell this gringita. Nothing about how he loved Tere so much his muscles clenched the air out of his body and his heart and like he couldn't breathe, and it made him sick like a flu.

He and this Irene—Irene Something, he couldn't get her last name—were done talking about the three weeks he would babysit her house. She liked to talk, this woman. She was going to France and Spain, which yeah of course he knew about. But no, not about Hemingway or Cervantes, or Matisse or Miró, Prado or Louvre. He'd been to L.A. and Phoenix and Vegas and took planes to get there. No, he didn't really like to drink wine. Yeah, he loved New Mexico, he agreed with her, nodded his head at the same time he said yes. Then they were done talking about these jobs he planned to look into, which was what he told her he was doing, and when there was no more gossip about his cousin Julie, who worked for this Irene, they didn't have too much left to say to each other.

"Yeah, it's all right here," he said. The restaurant chairs weren't easy to sit on, and he wasn't hungry.

"So many people get here and can't ever leave," she said.

"If you want to stay and you can, I guess no reason to go."

"Are you next?"

60

He phony laughed and shrugged. "I don't seem to stay in any-wheres that long."

"Maybe we can change your ways," she said. She played with her voice like her fingers did her airy, shoulder-length hair on her forehead and neck.

They finished margaritas as their waiter turned the corner. He wore high-top hiking boots and old jeans and a restaurant logo T-shirt, sleeves rolled up to show off matching, bracelet-like tattoos on either side, a gold stud-earring, and moussed messy hair. He was cool in how he moved and talked too. They each said yes, they would have another, frozen, salt. Irene made winks at Willie while the waiter first listed the sauces she could choose for her enchiladas and then the kinds of beans she could select to go with them.

"You're probably not used to that," she said.

"It's that we always order like enchiladas and they come with frijoles."

"Mexican food is totally big here," she said.

"Hey, I'm not complaining."

"You're probably used to the best Mexican food."

"I dunno. It's like food, if you know what I mean."

"Probably people would want to go out to an American restaurant."

"Yeah," he said. "Like a Luby's cafeteria. You know, hot rolls, meat loaf, mashed potatoes and green beans, and coconut cream pie."

She laughed real. "I live close. Just around the corner."

"These drinks are pretty cheap, so I'm sure I'll like the food a lot."

Hers was a pretty two-bedroom bungalow in a rich, green neighborhood, oak trees tangled up in it, squirrels scratching the tar-shingled roof. Her tour took him over the sanded, glossy wood floors, past bubbly lamps and padded chairs and little tables, a double bed, head- and footboard part of a set of matching tables and a bureau of a thousand drawers and vanity with a mirror that was like a wall. Another bedroom made into an office, all the manila-folder-colored machine tools—computer, fax, scanner, printer. Books. Bookcases all formica white. The kitchen was small, sink and faucets and tile the originals, but shining cappuccino maker and microwave and toaster. She was new mommy bright.

"No," he said, "not exactly my place in Canutillo." He told her that part of his story.

"I bet it was beautiful there. Authentic."

"Yeah, right."

"I think you miss it."

"You kidding? When I get to stay in here?"

"I am really glad you like it. It's my first home."

He wanted to go to sleep now. Willie was sleepy all the time. His body already had fallen into the soft sofa—his bed, sheets and pillows and blanket waiting neatly. She told him how there was too much light above it, under the picture window. She'd just had that put in, the rotted sliders taken out. The new blinds didn't fit though, and others were being made. He couldn't say nothing. It wasn't moonlight but light and it was bright like being awake and he hoped he could go to sleep, try, she'd let him, soon. She'd turned on the air-conditioning when they'd come in from the restaurant and already it wasn't so hot and he waited on her.

This Irene was just out of the shower. Like all the other rooms, the bathroom was not far from where Willie sat. She opened the door, a thick towel around her, stood in the tight space between rooms. "There's plenty of hot water," she told him.

"It is pretty hard to not get all sweaty," he said.

"I can't sleep if I am." She stood there. "This humidity here. Not like where you're from."

"Maybe I will, gracias."

"I left a towel out for you," she said. She was still standing there holding up her towel where she had it tucked in.

"Thanks," he said. He didn't want her to talk no more. Please. He wanted to sleep but knew he wouldn't right way. Knew he didn't want to talk to this Irene no more. He couldn't. What else was there? He hadn't imagined this part, the days to stay with her before she left and he'd be alone. Her talking all the time.

"Yeah," he told her, "I think I will take a shower if that's okay."

"Of course you can!" Her voice all cheerful and generous. "Well, good night then," she told him. She went into her bedroom, closing that door, the light from her bedroom, behind her. He could hear a radio go on.

When he got back from his shower, he wrapped himself into a sheet and shut his eyes. He couldn't stop it. It was so horrible to him, he hated this so much, but he couldn't stop. He could feel her body fill out like the light coming through the window, like heat. Then she'd be above him, squeezing her chiches. He'd feel them in his face. He'd move his hands to the curve of her waist, then to her butt.

His mouth would be between her legs, where he could taste and feel the slick labios, all her sexual muscle pushed into him. She'd want him inside her mouth. He'd see them both, every angle. He'd listen to her, her sounds, he could hear them in his ears. She'd be turned around, and he'd see her arching her neck and back, and she'd be tasting him with her own taste on him, and he'd be on top, and he'd watch her face, eyes closed and lips open and wet, and he'd see every part of her, nipple, belly button, thigh, panocha, and she'd tell him do it to her, a voice, do it to her, loud as hearts, and he'd both taste her there and be in her there and he wanted to break her, this? this?, her breasts under him, his hands gripped onto each nalga and he's telling her he's got her he's having her he's got her she can't stop him and she's moaning she doesn't want him to stop she wants him wants what he's doing.

It came out on the couch and he felt both relieved of the torment and embarrassed by its strength over his weakness, and because it was a mess and it was a pretty, new couch. He jumped up to get the towel he used for his shower and he tried so hard to be quiet both times there and back but the wooden floor creaked under his bare feet. He thought he heard Irene moving but no light or sound from under the door and so he'd been quiet enough and at least it didn't seem like she heard anything.

And all the day he thought of her. Glimpses, nothing like at night, but her when he opened a simple cabinet door in the kitchen. When he pulled out a drawer, digging around, her. Bored, he rummaged through the cabinets beneath the drawers, where Irene and every-one kept nothing but the pots and the pans, and he thought of her. He opened the drawer by a table next to the stuffed chair, one with papers and receipts and an address book, as though he could say he looked for Tere's name and number in there and then went through them all thinking of her, trying not to think of her, going through this Irene's stuff. He was awake and he was standing and he was dream-ing of her in Palomas without him. It ran from what she'd told him: They had a dripping wall unit air-conditioner, and so it was better in-side, and she had told him about touching herself while her dad was away working, when her mom was at her sister's, when they were asleep and she wasn't. It was summer in Palomas and her body would get wet, all her body, until it would become as wet as inside her, where she would rub herself. He had listened to her tell him about this and it made him so enraged with jealousy because he didn't be-

63

lieve her that she was alone and so he would fuck her right then, take
her so hard so that there would be nothing left in him to make him
imagine.

He wished he could sleep and not wonder if she were already go-
ing out. Would her cousins or brothers introduce her to someone
else? Every man wanted to get her. Would she have a date already
tonight? Would she like to kiss him? Would she let him touch her?
Would she like it? He tried to sleep and he tried to wake himself up.
How could she go to Palomas? Didn't she say she hated Palomas?
Dirt and scratchy weeds and rocks, and rocks, and boredom, norteña
radio a siren outdoors from the earliest morning until so late. The
only time she might like it there, she'd told him, would be if she was
with him, if they were together. He started holding her, touching her.
They were on the mattress, in darkness, staring. He was so sick of
her, of his want of her. The rhythm of he wanted her, he didn't want
her. The fever again, this time and that time and no time.

"Mattie's my best friend," she said. It was gray dusk, and she'd been
home for almost an hour. "We talk about everything." She saw his ex-
pression was not enthusiastic. "We won't get back that late."

He didn't want to go over there with her, but he didn't see how he
could stay back in her house without her, not do what she wanted.

"You must have some dirty clothes," she said. "It's your last chance
to wash for free."

He did have a few cositas.

"Let me have them." She reached out her hands.

Some socks and underwear were in his hand.

"It's all right, you can give them to me." She was smiling again.

He didn't know how not to.

"Maybe you're right, maybe it does kind of turn me on to hold
your underwear," she said.

"If all it takes is some stinky chones."

She cracked up. "We working girls learn to get it where we can."

He gave her a pair of dirty jeans.

"What about the ones you have on?"

"I don't got any others."

She was really laughing. "Be that way then."

Her friend's house, a Spanish villa, whitewashed and red-tile roof,
was a drive only a few blocks away.

"Didn't I tell you?" Irene said. She gave Willie one of the plastic clothes baskets, and she took the other. "Andrew's done well."

"Man, I wish I knew that secret."

She took a few beats before she spoke. "It helps if you come from it."

The heavy front door on the other side of a Mexican tiled entry patio opened with almost intentional elegance. "Hi!" Her friend Mattie looked like she was modeling the casual clothes she wore. Even the sandals looked sexy on her feet. "You better be hungry!" she said. Irene introduced her to Willie. "Hi!" she said. He pronounced his name and she tried to say it like he did. She had naturally what magazines tried to pose. "Well, Willie, I want to apologize beforehand that we're having a no meat night!"

"You don't gotta worry about it."

"You're so sweet!" She turned to Irene and winked. "You had to find yourself a dark Latin man."

"He's already got me washing his clothes," Irene said.

"Honey, I'd wash his clothes too."

"You guys are starting to make me feel funny," Willie said.

Under the ceiling of light in the kitchen, Mattie was even more beautiful than in the shadows outside. She had a shape, and long thick brown hair, and hazel eyes set off by an earth shade of skin. Next to her, Irene was bony and no soft bumps, her skin both too transparent and thin, too rough. Her blinking eyes seemed colorless. Around her friend, this Irene had even become jittery, jerky, both insecure and conceited. As she took charge of cottage cheese and salad, a big bowl of fruit, she was mad at them.

Andrew, Mattie's husband, was fat. Not blubber slob fat, but fat. Overweight in the soft, never was an athlete, never worked outdoors, never been in the military, in that never worked out way. Not so much that anybody'd stare, or even care. Nobody'd notice this guy. He wasn't so handsome either, and here he was married to the sexy woman, and so you saw the fat.

Willie drank bottled dark beer and Mattie and Andrew drank bottled spring water and Irene drank wine. Willie watched a basketball game with this Andrew in a TV room until the clothes were dry and they were all folded real neat. Andrew was into investments, he told Willie. Software and software companies. All obvious now, he explained, but he got there before it was.

"Come wash your clothes here anytime, Willie!" Mattie told him, leaning that body over to look at him in the passenger's seat. She put her arms through the car window and around Irene. "And you make sure you call me before you leave!"

"Isn't he kinda like big to her?" Willie said when they were back.

She did not chuckle or smile. "He's been trying to diet," Irene said.

Willie thought maybe he was messing up, being impolite about a friend of hers. "I'm sorry, I guess I shouldn't. . ."

She seemed distracted. "It's okay, I know what you mean." She headed for the bathroom.

Willie sat on the couch. He could see her leaning into the mirror in that putting on the makeup way.

"You like her, don't you?" she said loud enough, still staring at the mirror.

"Like her? Whaddaya mean?"

"That you like her. That you think she's so beautiful."

Willie couldn't figure out a reply. He stopped watching what she was doing in front of the mirror.

She turned toward him, away from the mirror. She'd washed off her make-up. "You think Mattie is gorgeous, like every other man." She walked into the bedroom. "It's all right, I know," she said from in there. "She is."

He had taken off his shoes and socks, and he relaxed his head into the pillow on the couch, and he shut his eyes. God, he was already in a dirty-minded dream, already visualizing Tere naked, and he was talking to her in language he never used to her or to anyone: He wanted to fuck her. He was going to fuck her. He'd say to her, You want me to fuck you? I'm going to fuck you. His language and attitude made her excited, but he didn't care, though he did like it too, and that he said it and that she liked that he did made him more aroused, but it wasn't just that. It was that he meant it.

Irene came out of the bedroom in a nightgown. White cotton wasn't satin or even polyester, and it didn't have lacy frills at the top or the bottom, wasn't low-cut or designed to emphasize, was not a see-through. But it was a night-gown, thin enough that her nipples were not much of a secret.

She left the kitchen with a glass in her hand, she stood near him for a little moment, and then she sat down in the stuffed chair near the couch and he sat up.

"I'm thinking I'll invite some friends over the night before I leave. Have a big meal for them."

He wasn't sure what she was saying, why she was telling him. She wasn't concentrating on the dinner. He tried to make himself more awake.

"I'm so sorry," she said. "It's orange juice." She stood up. "I'm so rude."

"No, it's okay," he said.

"Are you sure? There's plenty."

"Yeah I am. De veras, honest."

She sat down again but on the edge of the chair. "Everything in the refrigerator is yours when I'm gone. It'll go bad, and I don't want to throw it away."

"Thanks. I'll check it out after you leave."

"Squash and tomatoes, and a cucumber, and those carrots. I haven't even opened that bag. I think there are two apples and an orange in there."

"I'll see."

"Maybe I can use the vegetables for the dinner."

"Porqué no."

"You can help yourself now, too, you know. Anything you want."

"I'd feel better about it once I'm alone here."

"You don't have to, though."

He nodded.

She sipped her juice.

"You don't sleep in those clothes, do you?"

He smiled back. "No, course not."

"I don't think you should feel uncomfortable around me."

"I'm not," he said. He couldn't help but look. Too much of her skinny thighs were showing because her nightgown, which was short, had ridden up even higher. He didn't let his eyes follow their path, though. "You're so nice to let me stay. A lot of help to me, you don't know."

"It's nothing. You're doing me a favor." It was a breezy night, clear, and the moon, in the picture window, seemed to sway between the branches and leaves. "I want you to trust me. I know I do."

"Yeah." He had turned his head to see out the glass too, then back. "I like it here."

"I don't trust everyone. I really don't. I don't know why I know I can trust you."

"You can."

"You have pretty feet," she said.

He looked down. "I do?"

"Yes," she said. "They're just right."

"Oh yeah?"

"My first years of college I was in a studio art program."

"So that's why the stuff on the walls. It's all pretty."

She smiled, sipping her orange juice patiently.

"I'm not keeping you up, am I?" she suddenly asked.

"Me? You're the one who's gotta get up early for your job."

"I don't really need to go in the morning."

"Take the day off," he said. "You probably could use it to get ready for the trip, right?"

She nodded, but she wasn't really paying attention. "You wouldn't like salmon, would you?"

He bobbed his head a little, trying not to say no.

"I'm thinking I'll make poached salmon. It's so easy. Everybody loves it."

He nodded agreeably. "I'll try it if you make it. I know salmon's supposed to be the best."

She made a noise between a sigh and a yawn. "Well, it's probably getting late enough."

"I feel like I'm just starting to wake up."

"Too bad you don't like wine," she said. "I feel like another glass of wine."

"Pues, ándale."

"I'll save it for the dinner. I can't believe you don't like wine."

"It gives me a headache."

"Not good wine," she snapped. "You've probably only had cheap wine."

"No ways," he laughed. "Where I'm from you can get Mad Dog at any corner store."

"Mad Dog?"

"Yeah," he said. He stopped laughing at his own joke since she didn't get it. "Really, it's all right to drink without me, go on."

"I always have at least vodka around, but we finished it a few days ago. I wish I had some for this orange juice." She was shaking her head. "You like screwdrivers, don't you?"

"Sure. Hey, if you want, I can go out and get some vodka for you."

"I usually have some around. Some gin too for a while." She took a

68

little time. Adjusted the top of her cotton nightgown. "I should go to bed."

He didn't say nothing.

"I guess I've had too much wine tonight already," she said.

He yawned unintentionally.

She stood up, lingered. "So, see you in the morning."

"You're chickening out, huh?"

She waited.

"Not ditching school."

"Oh," she said. "No, I better go in."

"Do you mind if I take a shower?" he asked.

"I should," she said, "but I'm not going to."

It was his worst night. The hunger and need felt more like numbed wounds, his confused body and mind throbbing with their pain. His dream body became as fuzzy and fragmented as Tere's, shifting and floating. He wanted to talk, use his actual voice. He wanted to hear hers with his real ears and so he whispered, saying what she would say, and he would answer for her. No, he had never been through anything like this. He couldn't stop. He would see her bedroom as he imagined it—a single bed, that bed, a bedspread she told him was the same since she was a child, a diploma above it, a cross, a guardian angel, the Virgin, and then he was ravishing her, she was ravishing him, the lust and desire upside down and rolling around without gravity, floating like dust on a hot night, and they were moaning. He was moaning, almost there, doing her from behind.

Irene opened her bedroom door. He was naked under the sheet, and he was sweating. He could still feel himself, stopped.

"I heard something," she said as she approached.

He tried to shake it off but couldn't. "What?"

She didn't seem right. "I can't sleep," she said.

He was really embarrassed.

"I'm sorry," she said. She lowered her head and rubbed her palm over her eyes.

She'd gotten too close to him, she was standing too near. His mind was still a wanton fume, his heart was going, pushing blood down there.

He hadn't seen her walk off but he heard her weeping in her room. He put on his underwear and pants and stood at her door. "Are you okay?" He was still mostly hard.

She was on her bed, face down. Her nightgown had scooted up above her pearl panties. They shined like silk, and they were cut to reveal. She didn't answer.

"Irene?" he said. "Are you okay?"

She said something too softly so he went in the room and sat next to her on the bed. "Irene?" He didn't want to touch her. He did not want to. He touched her leg. He wanted to be polite because she was drunk. She wasn't sobbing. It was a light, gentle cry. "Irene? Are you okay?" He heard her say yes. He wanted to do what was right. "Are you sure you're okay?" he asked her. She didn't answer, and his hands moved higher onto her, he really was touching her skin now, and then she responded too fast, too hungry, and she cried the whole time, and she kept on crying. He left the door open when he went back to the couch. He could still hear her in there. He listened until it was inaudible, or no more, he couldn't be sure.

He went out in the morning—he really looked for a job—even before she left for her job, before she'd made coffee. It was getting hot. When he got back into her house, he turned her air-conditioning down. He still felt too hot no matter what. He felt bad, like he was getting really sick. He was going to call Tere. He opened her refrigerator and he downed her orange juice from the carton and he cut two slices of her cheese and he went into her bedroom. He got on her unmade bed and he picked up her phone next to the blinking message machine and punched in the list of numbers and Tere's brother answered and told him que no está, no, no sé donde, quién sabe, no sé donde cuando nada, hombre, nada, boss, nada, y no, their mom couldn't talk to him. He felt so tired and he put his head down and for a while he didn't notice that it was on her nightgown and her panties. Then it started. He imagined but the need and want were too real. It felt like a convulsion and a scent had become a musk that stained the air. He took a shower and he came back to her bed and he held the phone again and he thought about more phone calls but he stopped himself and opened the cabinet drawer on the end table and he heard something drop as he did. It rolled on the hardwood floor. It was a penny. He wasn't sure where it came from or what it was doing there. He hadn't knocked it down from above. Maybe it was so the door shut well. No, it wasn't that. It hadn't dropped and fallen on the top ledge either, couldn't have. There wasn't even a phone book inside. This was wrong, he knew this was wrong, this was

70

something else bad about him and his life. He still looked. It was personal stuff. In a box was some cash, twenties only, and coins from other countries, and credit cards. Another box of letters, personal letters, and birthday cards, another of photographs. Piles of paper, in folders and not. Finally he put it all back. He wasn't really thinking much about them. He was sick, that disoriented. He didn't take anything, he didn't even think of taking anything, but he knew he was doing wrong. Everything about him was wrong, was bad. He was bad. So bad he was already dreaming about Tere again, dreaming of being in Palomas. So awful. He was so miserable, so wrong, so in love with her. He was worried. Even more embarrassed. He knew it was there still, an animal odor, even though he couldn't smell it anymore. He tried to figure where to put that penny back. He couldn't know if he had opened it in such a way that it fell or if it would fall any time. He locked the penny in on the hinge side, so it would drop again when it was opened again. He decided he'd make her bed. To let her know that he'd been in there. He put her undies on top of the chest of drawers. So he'd tell her he used her phone and made a long distance call.

She seemed to be in a good mood when she came in, earlier than the other days, early afternoon. She had groceries, a few bags with her, and he went for the last one.

"I guarantee that you're even going to like this dinner," she told him when he got back from her car.

"I'm sure it'll be great."

"You don't seem to eat much."

"I just haven't been hungry. It's the heat."

"It's so cool in the apartment," she said. She went in and came out of the bedroom. "Thank you for making my bed."

She didn't say more. They weren't talking right. He felt he would be caught any minute. That she would tell him. It was like he'd done something even worse but couldn't remember some horrible detail.

He came around to her side of the kitchen counter. "I used your phone in there," he admitted. "Made a long distance call, and, I dunno, I thought I might as well, you know, make your bed."

"And it was nice of you, thanks," she said.

He didn't know what to feel worse about, what to feel the most guilty about, what it was with her.

"So last night," he told her.

You could see her listening to him, heard well, waited for him to finish until she knew he wouldn't. "I was in a mood." She wanted to say something else, almost leaning over with the words.

"Seemed like, I think, you were mostly in a good mood," he said.

"I think I was too drunk."

"You weren't so bad," he said.

Suddenly she said, "Was that all that you did in there?"

"Whaddaya mean?" he said. It was shame, complete shame that drained him.

"Did you talk to Mattie?"

"Mattie?"

"There was a message on the machine from Mattie."

"For me?"

"Yes and no."

He stood, no idea what she was talking about. "I don't understand, I really don't."

"She asked for you. Like you were screening calls."

"I didn't even hear that phone ring."

"It sounded like you picked it up once, and then she called again while you were here."

He had no idea.

"She was asking for you."

She'd taken all the food out of the plastic bags. She went back into the bedroom and into the shower and then back into the bedroom again, doors opening and closing too hard.

She was wearing a white blouse, white shorts, white sandals. She did not have make-up on.

"You look so pretty, just your, like, face," he told her.

"Thank you." She didn't even pretend to go along.

"What is it?" he asked, not sure to be close to her or farther away.

"Nothing."

He went in to the bathroom and then he went over to the couch and he looked out the window and he was remembering Tere and how angry she was when she left and then he came back to this kitchen where Irene was cooking the dinner.

"So, what's wrong?" he asked.

"Nothing," she said. "Everything's fine."

"No, it's not."

"Nothing's wrong."

"I'm sorry I was in your room," he said. "I'm, you know, sorry."

For a long time he didn't know what to do and he didn't say anything and she didn't say anything until finally she said, "Willie, I've changed my mind," and as he got his things together he wanted so much to confess about that penny but since she might not have noticed—not yet, or wouldn't ever—he just left.

Nominated by The Threepenny Review, Cyrus Cassells

TOMORROW'S BIRD

fiction by IAN FRAZIER

from DOUBLETAKE

SINCE MAY, I've been working for the crows, and so far it's the best job I ever had. I kind of fell into it by a combination of preparedness and luck. I'd been casting around a bit, looking for a new direction in my career, and one afternoon when I was out on my walk I happened to see some crows fly by. One of them landed on a telephone wire just above my head. I looked at him for a moment, and then on impulse I made a *skchhh* noise with my teeth and lips. He seemed to like that; I saw his tail make a quick upward bobbing motion at the sound. Encouraged, I made the noise again, and again his tail bobbed. He looked at me closely with one eye, then turned his beak and looked at me with the other, meanwhile readjusting his feet on the wire. After a few minutes, he cawed and flew off to join his companions. I had a good feeling I couldn't put into words. Basically, I thought the meeting had gone well, and as it turned out, I was right. When I got home there was a message from the crows saying I had the job.

That first interview proved indicative of the crows' business style. They are very informal and relaxed, unlike their public persona, and mostly they leave me alone. I'm given a general direction of what they want done, but the specifics of how to do it are up to me. For example, the crows have long been unhappy about public misperceptions of them: that they raid other birds' nests, drive songbirds away, eat garbage and dead things, can't sing, etc., all of which are completely untrue once you know them. My first task was to take these misperceptions and turn them into a more positive image. I decided the crows needed a slogan that emphasized their strengths as a species. The slogan I came up with was "Crows: We Want To Be Your Only Bird™." I told this to the crows, they loved it, and we've been using it ever since.

Crows speak a dialect of English rather like that of the remote hill people of the Alleghenies. If you're not accustomed to it, it can be hard to understand. In their formal speech they are as measured and clear as a radio announcer from the Midwest—though, as I say, they are seldom formal with me. (For everyday needs, of course, they caw.) Their unit of money is the empty soda bottle, which trades at a rate of about twenty to the dollar. In the recent years of economic boom, the crows have quietly amassed great power. With investment capital based on their nationwide control of everything that gets run over on the roads, they have bought a number of major companies. Pepsi-Cola is now owned by the crows, as well as Knight Ridder Newspapers and the company that makes Tombstone Frozen Pizzas. The New York Metropolitan Opera is now wholly crow-owned.

In order to stay competitive, as most people know, the crows recently merged with the ravens. This was done not only for reasons of growth but also to better serve those millions who live and work near crows. In the future, both crows and ravens will be known by the group name of Crows, so if you see a bird and wonder which it is, you don't have to waste any time: officially and legally, it's a crow. The net result of this, of course, is that now there are a lot more crows— which is exactly what the crows want. Studies they've sponsored show that there could be anywhere from ten to a thousand times more crows than there already are, with no strain on carrying capacity. A healthy increase in crow numbers would make basic services like cawing loudly outside your bedroom window at six in the morning available to all. In this area, as in many others, the crows are thinking very long-term.

If more people in the future get a chance to know crows as I have done, they are in for a real treat. Because I must say, the crows have been absolutely wonderful to me. I like them not just as highly profitable business associates but as friends. Their aggressive side, admittedly quite strong in disputes with scarlet tanagers, etc., has been nowhere in evidence around me. I could not wish for any companions more charming. The other day I was having lunch with an important crow in the park, me sipping from a drinking fountain while he ate peanuts taken from a squirrel. In between sharp downward raps of his bill on the peanut shell to poke it open, he drew me out with seemingly artless questions. Sometimes the wind would push the shell to one side and he would steady it with one large foot while continuing the raps with his beak. And all the while, he kept up his attentive questioning, making me feel that, business considerations aside, he was truly interested in what I had to say.

"Crows: we want To Be Your Only Bird™." I think this slogan is worth repeating, because there's a lot behind it. Of course, the crows don't literally want (or expect) to be the only species of bird left on the planet. They admire and enjoy other kinds of birds and even hope that there will still be some remaining in limited numbers out of doors as well as in zoos and museums. But in terms of daily usage, the crows hope that you will think of them first when you're looking for those quality-of-life intangibles usually associated with birds. Singing, for example: crows actually can sing, and beautifully, too; however, so far they have not been given any chance. In the future, with fewer other birds around, they feel that they will be.

Whether they're good-naturedly harassing an owl caught out in daylight, or carrying bits of sticks and used gauze bandage in their beaks to make their colorful, freeform nests, or simply landing on the sidewalk in front of you with their characteristic double hop, the crows have become a part of the fabric of our days. When you had your first kiss, the crows were there, flying around nearby. They were cawing overhead at your college graduation, and worrying a hamburger wrapper through the wire mesh of a trash container in front of the building when you went in for your first job interview, and flapping past the door of the hospital where you held your firstborn child. The crows have always been with us, and they promise that by growing the species at a predicted rate of 17 percent a year, in the future they'll be around even more.

The crows aren't the last Siberian tigers, and they don't pretend to be. They're not interested in being a part of anybody's dying tradition. But then how many of us deal with Siberian tigers on a regular basis? Usually, the nontech stuff we deal with, besides humans, is squirrels, pigeons, raccoons, rats, mice, and a few kinds of bugs. The crows are confident enough to claim that they will be able to compete effectively even with these familiar and well-entrenched providers. Indeed, they have already begun to displace pigeons in the category of walking around under park benches with chewing gum stuck to their feet. Scampering nervously in attics, sneaking through pet doors, and gnawing little holes in things are all in the crows' expansion plans.

I would not have taken this job if I did not believe, strongly and deeply, in the crows myself. And I do. I could go on and on about the crow's generosity, taste in music, sense of family values; the "buddy system" they invented to use against other birds, the work they do for the Shriners, and more. But they're paying me a lot of bottles to say this—I can't expect everybody to believe me. I do ask, if you're un-convinced, that you take this simple test: next time you're looking out a window or driving in a car, notice if there's a crow in sight. Then multiply that one crow by lots and lots of crows, and you'll get an idea of what the next years will bring. In the bird department, no matter what, the future is going to be almost all crows, almost all the time. That's just a fact.

So why not just accept it, and learn to appreciate it, as so many of us have already? The crows are going to influence our culture and our world in beneficial ways we can't even imagine today. Much of what they envision I am not yet at liberty to disclose, but I can tell you that it is magnificent. They are going to be birds like we've never seen. In their dark, jewel-like eyes burns an ambition to be more and better and to fly around all over the place constantly. They're smart, they're driven, and they're comin' at us. The crows: let's get ready to welcome tomorrow's only bird.

Nominated by DoubleTake

AT HORTICULTURE PARK

by MARIANNE BORUCH

from THE GEORGIA REVIEW

They make a great noise in the leaves,
trying to be quiet, these
ROTC boys, to be stealth
as the bomber eaten
by fog. Their faces
smudged black, their slow
passage under maples, under
the huge oaks. It's fall,
its wild ravishments. Everything's
past camouflage into almost
freeze and rest
and the last thought. They do not
look at us, my son and me, where
we might walk, or where
we've been in these woods.
And their emptiness, which is
a kind of focus, they practice it
like prayer, like the sad violinist, fierce
and without any hope
of song, climbing his C minor scale
for the twentieth time. The afternoon's nearly
lost to twilight. They look—where else?—
perfectly ahead. A line

is a line. And their rifles—even
the smallest holds his
not gently, hard against him.
Oh, to be
a threat, to swallow
anything. *Dear boy, go home.*
Go home, where you left your longing.

Nominated by The Georgia Review

RETURNING TO PROVIDENCE

essay by DAVID PLANTE

from IMAGE

Over half my life had been lived in Europe, but I felt that, however far from my parish in Providence, Rhode Island I got, I was still within hearing distance of its church bell. Sometimes, in a foreign city, it seemed to me I did hear that bell, especially as it sounded on a Saturday evening for vespers, and I would be filled with a sudden, deep grief. But grief for what, I had no idea.

On a visit to New York, where I stayed with a close friend, I thought, falling asleep one night, of a dream that I had had often when I lived in the house in my parish: that of being inside the house, terrified that the door was locked and I, pulling at the knob, couldn't get away from what was inside, and, simultaneously, that the door couldn't be locked and I, pressing my body against it, wasn't able to stop what was outside from coming in.

Now that I was in New York, my parish was just a few hours' ride along the southern New England coast.

I telephoned Mary Gordon, whom I wanted very much to see, and she told me to come to her right away, as if there were urgency in our seeing one another.

I no longer believed in God, but if I'd said to anyone, "I'm grieving because I do not believe in God," the expected retort would have been: "You are using that as an excuse for some deep, deep, deep, self-regarding, self-indulgent, even self-aggrandizing helplessness in yourself that you *must*, if you expect anyone to accept you as sincere,

80

get out of. Your grief at the impossibility of being with God in eternity is, really, nothing but the longing to be helpless, and therefore blameless. You know that God, who alone could justify you in your longing to be blameless, does not exist and *cannot* justify any longing, least of all the longing to be with Him blamelessly in eternity. You *must* look into yourself for the real reason for such an impossible longing. Your 'spiritual' crisis is, and can only be, a 'neurotic' crisis, because it has only to do with you." And my only consolation against such a retort would have been my own retort: "But all 'spiritual' crises are, for *everyone* who has had a spiritual crisis, nothing more than 'neurotic' crises." This would be a consolation because it would at least raise me out of myself enough to see myself among an accused number of people, and not alone.

Mary, however much I felt she above all had the right to because she knew me so well, would never reduce my "spiritual" crisis to a "neurotic" crisis. Mary believed in therapy, had had it herself and said it had helped her, and she even suggested it to me to help me, but Mary believed also that if a person *was* suffering "neurotically," which *was* to suffer, that person *could* be helped "spiritually" out of his or her suffering. Mary believed in impersonal, universal suffering beyond personal suffering which was, and had to be, spiritual suffering, and which *all* suffering could lead to, and which did not make you feel you were alone.

But when I went to see Mary in her apartment near Columbia University, I didn't want to talk about anything "spiritual." It seemed to be a banal subject, one we would give too much importance to by talking about it, an importance that embarrassed me. Sometimes Mary herself embarrassed me when she used, however matter-of-factly, words like "moral" and "immoral." She embarrassed me when she asked such questions as, "Do you think Henry James was a *good* man?" Also, I, who never felt I had the right to make judgements, was a little intimidated by Mary's, which she felt she had every right to make: some people were "good" and others were "evil."

We talked about writing.

I told Mary that all I had been writing was one image a page, all remembered from my parish, so I had over five hundred pages of one phrase images, such as:

A plastic statue of the Virgin Mother and a pot of plastic flowers on a refrigerator—

I tried to explain to Mary what I was hoping images would do if they were vivid enough—that is, create a world in themselves, beyond what *I* could intend them to create.

She said, "You believe in images."

After a moment of wondering, I said, "Yes, yes, I do."

I embraced and kissed Mary and left her.

On my way back to my friend's apartment, I asked myself, Did I believe in images? No, no, no, I answered myself.

But wasn't I at moments of writing images overwhelmed in such a way that I had no choice but to believe in them? Sometimes, yes, I felt overwhelmed, but I didn't know by what. And then it occurred to me, as though it were the strange realization of my deepest longing, that what the images, which seemed to come from some darkness all outside me, most overwhelmed me with was grief—grief in no way for myself, but for those images.

Why grief?

I wanted to see Mary again soon, and not only because I loved Mary. I did see her again soon. She asked me to her place for dinner with her family and close friends, those people who belonged to the moral city within the immoral. Among them was her close friend, the Jesuit priest Gary Seibert.

Gary, good-looking and spirited, was wearing an open-collared shirt and a pullover. His church was Holy Cross on West Forty-second Street, and his congregation consisted in large part of theater people and the homeless. He would, the next day, which was Ash Wednesday, hold morning, afternoon, and evening services for those who wanted to receive ashes.

Mary said to me, "Why don't you come with me?"

If it were for communion, I said, I couldn't, because I'd be presuming on my immortality and committing a sacrilege. But I wouldn't feel that by receiving ashes and being reminded of my mortality I'd be committing a sacrilege.

"So you'll come?"

"Tell me once more where the church is," I said.

Before I left, Mary said, "Look, I don't want to force you to come, though I think I *should* force you. I'll be in the church at three o'clock, and if you come, fine, and if not, fine."

The next morning, out in the streets of the city going from one appointment to another—because, as I was in New York, I thought I must *try* to be professional as a writer—I often saw on the foreheads of people I passed along the crowded sidewalks the crude cross of black ash. People who, from the point of view of their native identities, were so different their differences implied separate worlds, were for this one day visibly marked as all belonging to the same world. I passed a small, wrinkled Oriental woman with a great black cross from the bridge of her nose to her hairline, from one side of her forehead to the other, and as I looked at her she glanced at me then quickly away. I knew something essential about her that she didn't know about me.

I returned to my friend's apartment. When the time came for me to go to Holy Cross church to meet Mary, I thought I wouldn't go, and yet I thought I would go. The contradictory feelings I had were just like the feelings roused in me by that recurring dream of simultaneously being in a house unable to open the door to get away from what threatened me inside and unable to lock the door against what threatened me from outside. In the apartment where I was staying, I delayed leaving without directly intending to, delayed until I'd be too late, but, at the same time, whatever I did to delay I did so quickly— telephone calls, lunch on my own from the refrigerator, notes in my diary. I found I had plenty of time.

I had enough time to walk across town to the West Side along Forty-second Street, past the shops that had been, when I'd last been in New York, porn shops, now all with corrugated metal sheets painted pink, green, and blue pulled down over their fronts and locked with shining steel locks, to the Port Authority Building, where out-of-state buses were entering and leaving and where the homeless gathered. Holy Cross church was just across Forty-second Street from the side entrance of the Port Authority.

I was, in fact, early. A few people were in the pews—each one of them, again, of a different identity, or so it seemed to me—but Mary wasn't among them. Without genuflecting or making the sign of the cross or kneeling first to pray, I sat in a pew halfway down. I was among people who, kneeling or sitting, were deeply silent and still, so there was a great silence and stillness in the church, and I, in that silence and stillness, went into what I can only call a trance.

I was deep in that trance when Mary sat beside me. She didn't appear surprised to see me, though I was surprised to see her only because everything surprised me. And yet Mary's presence beside me was exactly as expected.

Gary and another priest, the actual pastor, came out from the vestry, both in green chasubles with yellow crosses, and while Gary sat, the pastor, a large man who looked as though he had at one time been a heavyweight boxer, talked to the congregation. He talked about why people should come to church: if for nothing else, to be near one another bodily, to be aware of one another, and, during Mass, to wish one another peace. I listened with an attention I had never before in my life given to a sermon. What the pastor said sounded so reasonable to me, but, then, my trance made everything seem both reasonable and at the same time surprising—made, maybe, reason itself surprising. It was entirely reasonable, enlightened even, that people should gather together and wish one another peace, and yet it was an extraordinary idea that I seemed never to have heard expressed before.

The two priests stood side by side before the altar and people formed lines in the main aisle to receive ash on their foreheads. I followed Mary out of the pew and with her joined the line leading to Gary. As we advanced toward him, I felt both very far from and very near to everything happening, and the closer I got to Gary the further away I felt I became and also the nearer, so I was seeing the whole interior of the church from a vast distance, seeing the stitching of the hem of the chasuble Gary wore, seeing his hands, seeing the little silver boat of ashes in his hands. Mary received ashes before me and turned away, and Gary, smiling, embraced me before marking my forehead with the cross of black ash. I followed Mary down a side aisle and directly out of the church into the street.

I couldn't speak. I told myself that of course I could speak, of course, but what stopped me was that I had nothing to say. Mary didn't speak, but took my arm and we walked toward Eighth Avenue.

She asked me, "Why don't you give in?"

I must have had an answer for not giving in, but I couldn't think of it.

"Why don't you?"

My mouth open, I wasn't able to get my breath. Mary held my arm more tightly in hers. As we crossed Eighth Avenue, a car sped close by her, and Mary shouted at the driver, "Fucker," then, turning back to me, said, "It's just that Canuck stubbornness that won't let you give in."

On the other side of the Avenue, trying to catch my breath, all I could say was, "This only happens when I'm with you."

"Then what I'm saying means something to you that you insist on denying, but that won't be denied."

I stopped her, and, suddenly a little angry because she was pressing me and I had had enough of being pressed, I said in as assertive a voice as I could manage, "Mary, I *do not* believe in God. All I believe is this: *There is no salvation for us, there is no life after death for us, there is no eternity for us. God does not exist.*"

Mary reacted to my anger with argumentative insistence. "This world exists," she said, "and we've got to have a reason for going on living in it all together without destroying it."

I didn't answer, but we resumed walking to Seventh Avenue, where we waited on the corner for the light to change.

I said, with my own argumentative insistence, "It's impossible to give in to something that doesn't exist."

But Mary insisted even more on her argument. "No," she said. "What you long for exists in the very longing for it. If you believe in images the way you do, you believe in God."

Mary could always stop me with her arguments.

I said, "I can't believe we're having this conversation here in New York City."

She said, "It's just because we are here in New York City that we're having this conversation."

We crossed and she left me to go down into the subway station, and I continued to walk across town, now marked with the cross of my religion, which, however, was not my religion, but which everyone passing would have assumed to be mine. When I passed someone marked as I was, our eyes very briefly met in recognition of one another, though what the passerby recognized on me had really nothing to do with me, because, though marked as a believer, I would have had to say, if approached by someone who spoke to me as one, that I wasn't.

I kept telling myself, the images I write have nothing to do with belief in God.

Maybe because so many people saw me as an introspective person, a person who was impelled to act much more in terms of feelings that made him look inwardly than that made him look outwardly, a person who was altogether more subjective than objective, I had assumed the same about myself. But, more than ever before, I realized that this wasn't at all true of me. I wasn't a person who would find faith, or even love, or even the inspiration to write, from a depth within my subjective self, which I wanted in fact to leave behind me by dying to myself, but was instead a person who needed confirma-

85

tion of faith and love and the inspiration to write from outside me, from a depth as objective as all the outer space that surrounds the world. No belief, ever, that came from within myself would convince me of the existence of God. To believe in God, I would have to be convinced by a force as positively outside me as a bright light flashing through the darkness of all that space. Mary didn't understand about me, and I only now really understood: I expected to be made to believe, not by giving in to my feelings, but by being taken out of my feelings into something entirely other than my feelings. That was my deepest longing. That was the longing that most made me the Catholic I was.

And I rejected, right away, any imputation that I was only committing the sin of pride in such an expectation, the sin of assuming I was worthy of such attention by an omnipotent force, that I would be taken out of myself and brought elsewhere by that force, the sin of assuming I counted.

It wasn't pride that made me think that if I were to be a believer, God, as I expected God to do, would have to come down and overwhelm me totally, so I would be knocked to the ground, unable to rise unless God helped me. It wasn't pride because I knew God would not do it. God had never, even in my youthful years of great devotion when I went to early Mass every morning before going to school, come down, and all I could honestly say I believed was that God would never come down.

Mary woke me the next morning by telephone to say she'd decided we were going to drive up to Providence to visit my parish. I may not have wanted to see it, but she did.

I said, "I'm sure my parish doesn't exist any more."

"Then you should see that," she answered.

I realized how much Mary tolerated in me, which I, when I was aware of it, found intolerant in myself: not that Canuck stubbornness, but, on the contrary, that Canuck will-lessness, that deepest Canuck longing to give in to what was beyond will. My mother had all her life tried, and failed, to save herself from that longing. What Mary was doing was to make me at least try to use my will, and she was right to do this, as right as my mother had been to try to use her will, even if she had failed.

I met Mary at her apartment early in the morning a few days later, and she drove us out of Manhattan along the West Side Highway, past great, craggy ledges of stone on the side of the highway from the cracks of which winter-bare trees grew. Those ledges gave me a disorienting sense of suddenly being far from the city. There was little traffic; the highway seemed abandoned, littered with broken branches.

Mary drove along the Connecticut coast, from where the Atlantic Ocean was dark grey, and into southern Rhode Island and through low scrub woods, where a war between a native tribe and colonists had been fought, and which the colonists won. We crossed over-passes into the city of Providence.

I got lost guiding her out of downtown Providence onto Atwells Avenue that led up Federal Hill, where there was so large an Italian parish the traffic line down the middle of the avenue was red, white, and green. We rose up the hill through the Irish parish, through the Polish parish, all with brick churches with rosette windows, which I told Mary I used to visit during Holy Week when, on a certain day I couldn't remember, you received a plenary indulgence—meaning you were completely cleared of sin and any punishment in purgatory due to sin—if you said a certain prayer in seven different churches. Mary knew the day—Good Friday—and was able to recite the prayer. We drove up past bare maple trees along either side of the highway, clapboard tenement houses with snow drifts still unmelted in the yards between them, bars on corners with wide but blackened windows in which little neon signs flashed: BUD. And we came to the French parish, Notre Dame de Lourdes, brick with a rosette window, as opaque as if covered by a huge cataract.

Mary wanted to see, first, the house where I was born and brought up. Again, I lost my way, now among the narrow streets that were so familiar and so strange, and, impatient to go on and also frightened and wanting to pull back, I told her to turn at corners without know-ing where they would lead. It was exactly as though I was dreaming, and in my dream I began to tremble. We rose over the crest of a hill and started down the other side, and I, still disoriented, saw the white clapboard bungalow on a corner. I shouted, "There it is." Mary parked the car in front of the house. I was trembling more with fear, and if it hadn't been for Mary I would not have gotten out of the car. If it hadn't been for Mary, I wouldn't have been there. I looked at the front porch, the glass storm door and the wooden door behind it, the porch lamp of a hanging lantern with yellow glass, the black numbers 128 over the door. I began to shake. Mary was the first to get out of the car. I got out.

The house looked dilapidated, as it had looked, I recalled, when it had been sold to a Franco couple after the deaths of my parents. The floorboards of the porch were rotting, the shingles of the roof were curling about the edges, and the maple trees that had spread their branches over it had been cut down to stumps.

Looking around at the other houses of the neighborhood, Mary said that she'd been brought up in a very similar place.

Suddenly, I felt that I no longer had anything to do with this house. I never had. I couldn't imagine living in it, couldn't imagine my parents living in it. It was not a haunted house.

As Mary and I left, I thought, I'll never come back here again.

We stopped at the church, which was locked. Mary suggested we come back in the morning for Mass, and I wanted to say, Never mind, it doesn't matter, but I said yes. And we went downtown again to book into a Holiday Inn—a hotel, Mary said, suitable to our class. We had dinner in an Italian restaurant on Federal Hill.

"For all my fantasies when I was growing up in Providence," I said, "never, never would I have fantasized about having dinner here with a fellow writer. My fantasies about being a writer were all based somewhere far, far outside Providence."

Before we went to our rooms for the night, Mary and I went to the pool, and there, alone, floating about each other in the illuminated lapping water, we talked quietly and intimately about our childhoods. And as we talked I became aware, in the closeness of Mary's full body, of a sadness I always felt with her. It was not, I thought, the sadness of our sexual incompatibility, but, instead, of our supra-sexual compatibility.

Mary woke me at six o'clock to go to my parish church for early Mass. She had found out about the hour. The parish seemed deserted, and we parked on a side street where there were no other cars. As we approached the church, I noticed a hole in a stained glass window at the side, made as if by a stone thrown through it. I expected the door to be still locked when Mary pulled at the handle, but it did open and we went into the foyer, where the linoleum tiles on the floor, brown and green, struck me with the force of years and years of fear. I was terrified of entering that church. There was the rounded marble holy water font and the glass in the double doors, each door with a translucent purple cross, and, beyond the doors, the main aisle of brown and green tiles into the nave.

Mass had started. A priest I didn't recognize was at the altar, facing the congregation of about five people. Mary went right up to the first pew and I followed her in.

I remembered the long kneeler along the pew on which I knelt with Mary. She went to receive communion while I remained kneeling, my face in my hands. I went on kneeling, my face in my hands, when Mary returned, and I went on in that position until the end of the Mass.

I wanted to leave, but Mary said, "We're going into the vestry." I had never been into the vestry. As devout as I'd been, I'd never been an altar boy, and had never viewed Monsieur le Curé as a man I could have visited in the vestry after Mass. I had never spoken to him outside of confession. I would have been as incapable of opening the door to the vestry, as Mary did matter-of-factly, as I would have the tabernacle on the altar. Mary went in first. The priest, already unvested, was putting on a yellow baseball jacket over his black shirt and clerical collar. He seemed to have expected us, and said, "Come on in." Father was grey-haired and almost immediately said he was going to retire soon.

I didn't remember him, but when I gave him my name he said he'd buried my father and mother, and that was all he had to say about them.

Mary, who talked to him familiarly, asked him more about his retirement.

Then he said he had to go, a baseball team of kids he coached was expecting him. "Stay and look around the church," he said. And when Mary asked him where she could get a couple of candles, he said, pointing to a brown cardboard box on a counter, "Help yourself." He left.

I watched Mary take two large votive candles from the box. She said, "Let's go light these." We went, she carrying the candles, into the nave of the church again. Dim grey light was showing through the windows on the left side, and the church was chilly. We went up this side and up a little flight of circular wooden stairs into the organ loft where the organ was very dusty, then down and into the foyer and into the little space to the side of the foyer where the baptismal font was, and beside the font lay a pile of cardboard boxes as in a storeroom. Back in the nave, we went down the side aisle on the right side, the side where there was a window with a hole in it, reading, below each window, the names of the French parishioners in black Gothic script who had donated money for them. The brown and green floor tiles were cracked and some unglued. Mary still carried the candles, looking for a place to light them.

Mary said, "This church looks like the butt end of something."

"Yes," I said.

In a niche was a life-sized statue of the Virgin Mother with large, sad eyes before which, I told Mary, I had as a boy coming into puberty fervently prayed for purity, and sometimes I'd been sure the Virgin Mother's eyes had filled with tears.

"We'll light our candles here," Mary said.

"No, no," I said, "not here."

"Why?" Mary asked.

"Because I'm not pure."

Mary held the candles out.

I looked round at both side altars and said, "In front of the crucified Christ."

Mary lit her candle from the only one burning in the stand, and I lit mine from hers. She knelt to pray and I stood behind her, looking at Christ's white body hanging on the black cross, blood running from his thorn-entangled head, from his nailed hands and feet, from the lance wound in his side, from his scourged flesh.

I looked away, and, staring into space as I had often seen my father stare into space, I thought that the God of my ancestors—ancestors who from generation to generation had lived through the stark facts that the doctor would not arrive in the snow storm in time to save the dying mother, that the crop would fail, the bank foreclose—this God was the God of the greatest grief, which was the greatest grief of His own helplessness toward us, the greatest grief of His not being able to help us. His greatest grief was His greatest desire to help us, but all He could do for us was to purify us in His grief. In His grief we were forgiven. In His grief was our tenderness, our gentleness. In His grief was our love for Him, and in our love for Him was our love for one another.

Nominated by Image

SUITCASE SONG

by ALBERT GOLDBARTH

from POETRY

John-O was given a key to the apartment. The deal
was this: if Phil died suddenly, and John-O heard,
he would rush on over, enter the apartment, leave
unseen with Phil's brown suitcase, and secretly pitch it
into the mounded deeps of the city dump.
Simply, there were things that Phil didn't want
to hurt his family with. Do you have *yours*?
I have *mine*. The brown suitcase. Sasha's sister,
on her death bed—dinky, frail, just a mild
skim milk trickle of a hospice patient—
tensed, sat up, and unloosed
such confessional invective that it seemed the walls
and the sheets would have to be splattered in shit,
her cancer having acted with the harsh, disbursing
force of a tornado on the brown and hardshelled
suitcase in her electrochemical memory webs.
Is yours secure? from love? from sodium pentathol?
Last year, when a tornado hit our fringe
of downtown businesses, the air was alive for counties around
with the downward dance of naked cancelled checks,
handwritten notes, hotel receipts, e-mail transcripts,
smeary Polaroids, a swirl of lacy underwisps
that jellyfished the skies, and from The G-Spot Shoppe
a rain of plastic pleasure aids, of which one prime example
pierced a cow between the eyes and struck her dead.

✿

Maybe AIDS—I wasn't sure. But he was dying,
that was sure: as dry as a stick of human chalk,
and making the terrible scritch-sound of a stick of chalk,
in his throat, in the community air, in the room
across from Sasha's sister. Something . . . *hidden*
in the trace of run-down aura still around him
as we chatted there one morning . . . a tv? a sissyboy tv?
I wasn't sure, but it was obvious
his life-chalk held a story not yet written,
not confessed yet
for this storynivorous planet.
And when I remembered my mother's own
last days . . . the way a person is a narrative,
the strength of which is either
revelation or withholding. It was summer, and the garden
at the nursing home was fat with summer's pleasures:
flowered mounds like reefs of coral,
bees as globular as whole yolks.
In her room, my mother disappeared a breath
at a time, and everything else was only a kind of scenery for that.
The wink of pollen in the light. The birds. Their feather-lice.
The bursting spores. Those opened-up
cicada husks abandoned on the patio
—the small, brown, unlocked luggage
that's completed its work in this world.

Nominated by Poetry, David Kirby

AN OFFICIAL REPLY

fiction by HA JIN

from SHENANDOAH

Professor Pan Chendong, Party Secretary
English Department
Beijing Humanities University

Dear Professor Pan:

Please allow me to express my deep admiration for your paper on Theodore Dreiser's novels, which you presented at the Shanghai conference three years ago. My name is Zhao Ningshen, and I have chaired the Foreign Language Department at Muji Teachers College for two years. You may still remember me: a man in his mid-thirties, bespectacled, of slender build and medium height, with slightly hirsute arms and a head of luxuriant hair. After your talk at Splendor Hotel, we conversed for a few minutes in its lobby, and you gave me your card. Later I wrote you a letter and mailed you under separate cover a paper of mine on Saul Bellow's *Adventures of Augie March*. I assume you received them.

In response to your inquiry about Professor Fang Baichen of my department, I shall refrain from dwelling too much on his character, because he was once my teacher and I can hardly be impartial. Although you may have heard anecdotes and depictions of him—he is a fool, a megalomaniac, an incorrigible lecher, a braggart, a charlatan, an opportunist, and so forth—none of those terms can adequately describe this unusual man. In the following pages, let me provide you with some facts, from which you may draw your own conclusion.

I came to Muji Teachers College as a freshman in the winter of 1977 and met Mr. Fang on the very day of my arrival. At that time he was a lecturer, in charge of the instruction of the freshmen. I had been disappointed by being made to major in English, for I was not interested in any foreign tongue. I had applied for philosophy and Chinese literature in hopes of becoming a scholar of classics. To this day I am still unclear how the hand of fate steered me into the field of English studies. Probably because I was among the few applicants bold enough to tackle the English examination—I mean the written part—some people on the Provincial College Admission Committee had decided to make me specialize in this language. In my heart I resented their decision, though there was no way to express my indignation. On our first evening on campus, all the freshmen were given a listening comprehension test in a lecture hall. Mr. Fang dictated the test.

He read slowly in a vibrant voice: "In the old days, my grandfather was a farmhand hired by a cruel landlord. Day and night he worked like a beast of burden, but still his family did not have enough food and clothes. . . ."

I was impressed by his clear pronunciation, never having met anyone who read English better than this dapper man. But I felt miserable because I couldn't write down a complete sentence and had to turn in my test sheet almost blank. More disappointing was that the result of this test determined our placements in the classes, which were immediately divided into four levels. The freshmen of our year were the first group to take the entrance examinations after the Cultural Revolution. During the previous ten years, colleges had partly or mostly shut down and young talents had accumulated in society, so the student pool now was replete with all kinds of creatures. In our English program, three or four freshmen could read *Jane Eyre*, *The Gadfly*, and *A Tale of Two Cities* in the original, and they even scored higher than the graduating seniors in a test. On the other hand, many freshmen, like myself, knew only a couple of English words and had been assigned to study the language mainly on the strength of our high scores in the other subjects. A few boys and girls from Inner Mongolia, who had excelled in mathematics and physics, didn't even know a single English word; nonetheless, they had been sent here too, to learn the language because their region needed English teachers.

Naturally I was placed in the lowest class. I was so upset that I began to play truant. Mr. Fang's class was from 7:30 to 9:30 in the morning, so I often skipped it. He was a good teacher, amiable and conscientious, and I bore him no grudge. In truth, I liked his way of running the class—he tried to make every one of us speak loudly, however shy or slow of comprehension we were. He loved the word "apple" because its vowel could force our mouths open. He would drop his roundish jaw and bare his even teeth, saying, "Open your mouth for a big apple." That was his way of building our confidence as English speakers. Later I came to learn that he had been labeled a rightist and banished to the countryside for three years in the late fifties. I also could tell that his English pronunciation was not as impeccable as I had thought. The tip of his tongue often missed the edge of his teeth when he pronounced the interdental *th*, which Chinese does not have. Once in a while he would say "dick" for "thick" or "tree" for "three." In addition, he spoke English with a stiff accent, perhaps because he had studied Russian originally. In the early sixties, when the relationship between China and Russia was deteriorating, Mr. Fang, like thousands of college teachers who responded to the Party's call, had changed his field from Russian to English. (I always wonder who among our national leaders at the time had the foresight to discern the drift of history. How could he, or they, foresee that within twenty years English would replace Russian as the most powerful linguistic instrument for our country?)

One evening I was lying in bed with a pair of earphones on my head, listening to an opera. Someone knocked at the door, but I did not bother to answer. To my surprise, the door opened and Mr. Fang's face emerged. He was panting slightly, with his sheepskin hat under his arm; his left hand held a pale-blue tape recorder that weighed at least thirty pounds (at that time a cassette player was as rare as a unicorn here). On his steaming forehead a large snowflake was still melting, right beside a giant mole. His neck was muffled with a gray woolen scarf, which made him appear shorter than he was. I got up from my bed.

He sat down on a decrepit chair and said to me, "Young Zhao, why didn't you come to class this morning?"

"I'm ill."

"What's wrong?"

"Stomachache."

"You can't walk?"

"Just barely."

"All right, since you still can speak and hear, I'm going to teach you here and now."

I was too shocked to respond. He moved the chair closer, took a mimeographed textbook out of his jacket pocket, and said, "Let's begin with Lesson Four."

Reluctantly I pulled out my textbook from the single-shelf bookcase above the head of my bed.

"Turn to page thirty-one," he said.

I found the lesson. He went on, "Repeat after me, please: This is a bee." The tip of his tongue moistened his heavy upper lip.

I read out the sentence beneath the drawing of the insect, which looked more like a horsefly.

"That is a cabbage," he intoned.

I read out the line under the vegetable. Together we practiced the variation of some simple syntactic patterns—changing statements into questions and vice versa. The whole time I was nervous and couldn't resist wondering why he was so determined to keep me abreast of the class.

After the reading practice, he plugged in the recorder and turned it on to let me hear how a British man pronounced those sentences. As we waited for the machine to produce the genuine English voice, he sighed and said to me, "All your classmates repeat the text after the recording for at least two hours a day, while you don't do a thing. If you continue to be like this, you'll have to drop out soon. You're wasting your talent."

"I've no talent for English," I said.

He raised his long eyebrows and told me calmly, "In fact you don't need talent for learning a foreign language. What you need is endurance and diligence. The more time and effort you put into it, the better your English will be. There's no shortcut."

When the British man's voice finally emerged, I was made to follow it, repeating every sentence in the long pause after it. Meanwhile Mr. Fang was chain-smoking, which soon turned the room foggy. I read out the lesson along with the recording several times. He stayed almost two hours, until one of my roommates came back for bed. How relieved I was after he left. We kept the transom open for a long while.

I did not expect he would come again the next evening. His second appearance disturbed me, because obviously he knew I was not ill. Why did my truancy bother him so much? Despite not showing any temper, he must be exasperated at heart. Was he going to flunk me if I missed more classes? Indeed it was not his fault that I got trapped in the Foreign Language Department. He must take me for a major troublemaker. Burdened with all these worrisome thoughts, I could hardly concentrate on the reading practice.

To my amazement, we ended an hour earlier this time. But before he left, with his hand on the doorknob, he said to me, "I know you don't like English, but think about this: What subject taught in our college can promise you a better career? Last year two of our best students passed the exams and went to Africa to serve as interpreters. They travel between Europe and Africa a lot and eat beef and cheese every day. Another graduate of our department is working as an English editor at *China Times* in Beijing. Every year we'll send some students to the Provincial Administration, where they manage international trade, cultural exchanges, and foreign affairs— all hold important positions. You're still young. All kinds of opportunities may turn up in your life. If you don't get yourself ready, you won't be able to seize any of them. Now, to master English is the only way to prepare yourself, don't you think?"

I didn't answer.

"Think about it. See you tomorrow," he said and went out with the bulky recorder, whose weight bent his legs a little.

His words heartened me to some degree. I had never heard that graduates from this department could enter diplomatic service. That was a wonderful profession and would enable one to travel abroad. I would love to visit some foreign countries in the future. By and by a ray of hope emerged in my mind. There was no way to change my major, so probably I had better not laze around too much. It was not too late to catch up with the class.

So on Mr. Fang's third visit to our dormitory, I told him that I was well enough to go to class the next day.

Gradually I became a diligent student. In the morning I would rise at 4:30, pacing back and forth in corridors and lobbies (it was too cold to stay outside), reading out lessons, and memorizing vocabulary, idioms, expressions, and sentence patterns. Some freshmen got up even earlier than I did. To save time, a few would stay in the classrooms at night and just sleep three or four hours, fully clothed, on the long platforms beneath the blackboards. They would return to the dormitory every other night. On the face of it, we studied feverishly because we cherished the opportunity for a college education, which the majority of our generation dared not dream about; and the department commended us for our dedication. But at bottom there was a stiff competition among us, since better grades might help one get a better job assignment on graduation. I overused my throat so much in practicing English pronunciation that I had to swallow painkillers every day.

Soon Mr. Fang was promoted to professorship. To our dismay, he stopped teaching us. The department at the time had only two associate professors in English, and Mr. Fang was one of them. He was highly respected by the students and the young faculty members, whom he often taught how to waltz or tango. Every Thursday afternoon some teachers would hold a dance party, which we students could only peep at through a keyhole or a door left ajar. By far Mr. Fang was the best male dancer. He didn't have a paunch, but when dancing, he would stick out his belly and make himself somewhat resemble a paunchy businessman, and in this way he also got physically closer to his female partner. We were impressed and thought he was something, truly a man of parts. At our annual conference on foreign literature, he presented a lengthy paper on *For Whom the Bell Tolls*, in *Modern Literature*. Before that, I had never heard of Hemingway.

I was unhappy during my undergraduate years because I remained in the lowest class all the time. This stung my pride. Twice the students of the lower classes staged a strike, demanding new class placements based on merit. After two years' study, many of us in the lower classes had caught up and knew English as well as some of those in the top class, which had always been taught by a British or Canadian expert. Whereas we had never had a native speaker to teach us. As a result, our spoken English was deplorable. The department refused to consider our demand seriously, but to forestall another strike, Professor Fang, who had been appointed its vice chairman lately, agreed to have a dialogue with us. So we all gathered in a classroom and listened to him explain why the hierarchical order of the classes should remain unchanged. His reason was that we could hire only one foreign expert at a time, and that this person should teach the best students. He mentioned the saying "Give the hardest steel to the blade." We did not disagree about that. What we contended against was the permanency of the top group.

We argued with him tenaciously. Neither side could persuade the other. Gradually Mr. Fang lost his temper, and his face turned the color of pork liver. His voice grew more nasal. He declared with his hand chopping the air, "No, the continuity of instruction must never be disrupted. If we changed the top group constantly, who could teach such a class? Impossible!"

Zhang Mingchen, a willowy fellow with curved eyes and caterpillar brows, who was the monitor of Class Three, stood up and said smilingly, "Professor Fang, this is ludicrous. You've made us feel as if we were all retarded. Why do we have to remain always the same? Why can't we develop? Even you—haven't you added some stature and weight to yourself?"

We exploded into laughter. Glowering at Mingchen, Mr. Fang thumped the lectern and bellowed, "Stop pretending you're Mark Twain! You should know who you're talking to." He turned his head slowly, glaring at us.

More laughter rose from the students. Abruptly Professor Fang wrapped up the meeting and stalked out of the room with a white cotton thread dangling from the hem of his black herringbone blazer. I had not expected he would take so much umbrage. He seemed to have become a different man, no longer the humble, conscientious teacher, as though he had been a high-ranking official all his life. In fact, besides his brand-new vice chairmanship, he had held only one official title—as president of the Regional Bridge Association, which consisted of about two dozen members, mostly old intellectuals.

The next spring Mr. Fang joined the Communist Party. I had some reservations about his induction, but I only represented the students' voice and was among the minority in the Party branch. I couldn't stop wondering whether he had been helpful and considerate to me because I was one of the few student Party members, and so could speak for or against him at Party meetings. In other words, by going to the dormitory to teach me, he might deliberately have curried favor with me so as to earn my support for his Party membership in the future. What a calculating man! But that was just a conjecture without any proof, so I couldn't communicate my doubts to the other Party members.

My suspicion of him was deepened by another occurrence, which unsettled me greatly. At our graduation the next year, Mingchen, an archtroublemaker in Mr. Fang's eyes, was assigned to a coal-mining company in Luomei County; that was the worst job assignment in our department that year. Mingchen got drunk at the graduation banquet and declared he would stab Mr. Fang to death. Lifting the bottom of his jacket, he showed us a bone-handled knife in his belt, which he had bought from an itinerant tinker for fifteen yuan. I turned to look at the table where the departmental leaders were dining. Lucky for Mr. Fang, he was not there, or he would definitely have seen his own blood that evening. When Mingchen collapsed in a stupor, I took the large knife from him. Surely he would have created a disturbance if he had kept the weapon handy. Two days ago his girlfriend, assigned to teach English at a military college in Shenyang City, had insinuated that they should split up. He believed her change of heart was another consequence of Mr. Fang's vengeance.

Fortunately I had done well in the examinations for graduate studies and enrolled in the English Department at Harbin University; it meant I did not have to seek employment upon graduation, so that Mr. Fang could not punish me with a bad job assignment. Otherwise I might have ended in a situation as grim as Mingchen's, for I was positive that Mr. Fang knew I had voted against his admission to the Party. Besides, he must have believed I had masterminded the strikes.

During my three years' graduate work in Harbin, I was well informed about the happenings in this department, because my fiancée, after her graduation, remained here as an instructor in Japanese.

Mr. Fang went on prospering in the meantime. He founded a journal entitled *Narrative Techniques*, which you may have seen, since for several years it maintained a circulation of 90,000 and was quite popular among young people, especially among would-be writers. He lectured at colleges throughout the Northeast, mainly about stream of consciousness as the most advanced narrative technique in the West. He even tried his hand at fiction writing. One of his short stories, "Beyond the Raining Mountain," about a tragic love triangle, won the first prize in a provincial contest. It has been anthologized several times. To be fair, he is a capable fiction writer. In his stories, you often can perceive a kind of primitive passion and peasant cunning that you rarely find in fiction written by academics. In truth, sometimes I cannot help thinking that he might have become an accomplished novelist had he concentrated solely on fiction writing. He spent a great deal of time editing the journal. His energy was dissipated, and he could not sustain the momentum generated by the initial success of his short fiction. Perhaps he has suffered from the absence of an artistic vision, or having misplaced his ambition, satisfied merely with getting ahead of his peers and with temporary fame. He has never planned to follow the masters' way—writing a hefty novel, a monumental chef d'oeuvre, something intended to revise and rejuvenate the genre. Apparently he no longer has the strength for such a book. He always worked on small, minor pieces. In brief, although he was a promising late bloomer, he has not blossomed fully.

My relationship with him began to improve as I contributed to his journal regularly. He treated me well and always published my papers and reviews, often giving me top-rate contribution fees. Besides translations and criticism on foreign literature, *Narrative Techniques* also carried a section of short stories and poems by Chinese authors. I was baffled by this format. Why would such an academic journal publish original poems? Never had Mr. Fang studied poetics. Why did he include a dozen pages of poetry in each issue? No doubt he was aware of the incongruity. He must have been up to something.

In the summer of 1984, I finished my graduate work and returned to my alma mater, where my bride was teaching as a lecturer. I heard that Professor Fang's journal had been suspended because a number of young women, both students and faculty, had accused him of sexual improprieties. A few said he had published their writings in exchange for their favors, while some claimed he had turned their works down because they had resisted his advances. To be frank, I suspect that some of the women might have entered into a relationship with him of their own accord. Of course this is not to deny that he must have taken the initiative. His wife had been ill for years, and sex was out of the question in their marriage. He must have been lonesome and quite concupiscent. Yet one of these affairs was absolutely beyond forgiveness, to wit: he had gotten a student pregnant, which was technically due to the substandard quality of a condom. An old nurse, who had been present at the abortion, spread the scandal, and within a week the student's pregnancy had become a household topic. I knew the girl, who was a fledgling poet and a gracious person, I must say. I had been her older brother's friend for years. She was two grades below me. One of her poems, which she had once recited in our auditorium, had moved me almost to tears and instantly made her the object of numerous young fellows' attentions. It was entitled "The Love I Have Is All You Can Have," such a wonderful poem that our school's radio station broadcast it twice a day for a whole week. In appearance she was demure and blushed easily, with dimmed eyes like a lamb's. I couldn't imagine that such a fine girl would allow an old man like Mr. Fang to explore her carnally, while there were many young men who would be happy to serve her in any way she desired. Later I learned from her brother that Professor Fang had published many of her poems under the pen name Sea Maiden and had promised her that he would help her get accepted, with a scholarship, by the Comparative Literature Department at Indiana University—Bloomington, with which Mr. Fang had claimed to have powerful connections. Oh, a young girl's heart so easily overflowed.

Although Mr. Fang was in disgrace—having received a disciplinary action from the Party Committee and lost his vice-chairmanship—I did not shun him. One day I invited him to a simple dinner in my apartment. My bride had left to teach summer school in an oil field south of Tsitsihar. I had just made some money from translating a play by Eugene O'Neill, so I bought a braised chicken, two pounds of beef sausages, tomatoes, a packet of white sugar, salted duck eggs, and ten liters of draft beer. I did not invite anyone else, because other faculty members were reluctant to mix with Mr. Fang at the time. As he and I were drinking and eating, he turned loquacious. He told me that his wife suffered from a cardiovascular disease and that his son had just graduated from Nanjing University, specializing in international trade, and was going to work for a German auto company in Shanghai. His wife was upset by their son's lucrative but far-away job, for she had expected him to come back to Muji City, to marry and settle down near home.

I noticed Mr. Fang had not aged much. His hair was still dark and bushy, and his facial muscles looked quite elastic. Behind the front of his white short-sleeved shirt, his belly seemed firm and flat. You could easily take him to be in his early forties. Half jokingly I asked him how come he was so well preserved. To my amazement, he replied in earnest, pressing his hand on his chest, "First, you must have a large heart and never be depressed by anything, eat well, and sleep well. Second, you must exercise every morning in any kind of weather, hot or cold." He smiled with a shrewd twinkle in his eye. He knew I was a night owl and always went to bed in the wee hours, never bothering about morning exercises. Again I expressed my admiration for his good health.

Soon he was inebriated, and his tongue went unbridled. He sighed and said, "I'm fifty-three already. My life has come to a dead end."

"Don't be so down," I said.

"I'm going to die soon. Ah, to die without achieving any-anything. How sad!"

"Come on, have a larger heart."

He looked tearful and pathetic. I tried to comfort him by pointing out that he was a reputable scholar, at the peak of his powers, and still had a long, bright journey ahead. But the more I said, the more heartbroken he was. "After I graduated from college," he declared as though to a roomful of listeners, "I dreamed about going to Russia to study esthetics. Then Russia became our enemy, and I was made— made to study damned English, which I didn't like until I could read D. H. Lawrence in the original. Now our country is finally o-open, but I'm too old to go abroad to do gra-graduate work. I'm no match for you young people, too old." He dissolved into tears, wiping his cheeks with the back of his short-fingered hand. "Oh I should've had a Ph.D., or at least an M.A., like you!" He patted my forearm.

That was inane. He was already an associate professor. To side-track him, I said, lightheartedly, "Stop crying, all right? You've been a lucky old man here, so many girls were around you. Who ever had such luck as you?" I was being slightly ironic, but he took my words as a compliment, or a cue. He grinned and poured another glass of beer.

Then he began talking about the young women he was involved with in recent years. I was surprised that one of my former class-mates, who used to be seeded number two in badminton in our province, was among them. She had married an officer, a dog han-dler, who was often away from home. How could Mr. Fang match that amazon in bed? It made me giddy just to think it. I felt embar-rassed by his disordered talk, yet I was fascinated and eager to hear more. What amazed me most was that one of the women had even been willing to marry him, provided he divorced his wife, which he would not do. He explained to me, "I'm not heartless, Young Zhao. I can't abandon my sick wife. When I was in the countryside, she came to see me every two months. Another woman would have divorced me under the circumstances. She alone suffered with me and never complained. Now our son's far away from home, and I'm the only family she has here." His eyes, misty with tears, gazed at me.

I couldn't help wondering what had contributed to his apotheosis in those young women's eyes. His knowledge? His power? His vital-ity? His pen? His tricks? His optimism? What was the magic wand with which he had held so many of them in thrall? I thought of my friend's younger sister, the lamb-eyed girl, who had been banished to a county town to teach middle school. Before departing for the coun-tryside, she was so distraught that she had almost defenestrated herself, pulled back just in time by her parents. Had Mr. Fang ever felt guilty about her ruin?

"Ah, how I adore those girl poets!" he confessed, rubbing his broad nose.

"Why poets?" I asked.

"You don't know how sweet and innocent girl poets can be. They all have a te-tender heart. Just give them a few words they want to hear, you-you can sweep them off their feet and set their hearts flying like ca-catkins." He giggled.

"So, no fiction writers, only girl poets, eh?"

He grinned. "Yeah. If I come back to this life again, I'll try to be a poet myself. Young Zhao, one of these days you should get to know a girl poet."

"No, I want a nymphet," I said. He reminded me of Nabokov's lecherous Humbert.

"Okay, a nymphet poet then." He burst into laughter.

You see, Professor Pan, that was the advice he gave to me, his former student. I would not try to know a girl poet. My wife is good enough for me, although she is not an extraordinary beauty. Besides, I am in poor health and ought to save my energy and time for completing my book on the Oriental myths in Eugene O'Neill's plays. After that dinner, whenever I ran into Mr. Fang, he seemed evasive and often hurried away as though I were carrying hepatitis, which had broken out in our city that summer. Apparently he regretted having divulged his secrets to me. But I never held that talk against him. Even three years later, when I became the chairman of this department, I wouldn't allude to that talk. No, I did not change my feelings about him because of the secrets he had let slip.

After the suspension of *Narrative Techniques*, our department was pestered by thousands of letters from its subscribers. They demanded a refund. Because the money had been shared out by the faculty as a holiday bonus long ago, all we could do was promise the subscribers that a new issue of the journal would reach them soon. Nobody here was able to edit the journal at the time except for Mr. Fang. So in the fall, *Narrative Techniques* was reinstated, with him as the editor-in-chief again, but now he was ordered to eliminate the section of creative writing. This time the journal turned out to be more focused and more impressive, each issue having a glossy cover and a photograph of a modern master novelist on its back. Gradually, Mr. Fang's fame rose once again. He worked hard and even pub-

104

lished a volume of short fiction, *At the Blossoming Bridge*, which he dedicated to Ernest Hemingway as if the American writer were still alive and in correspondence with him. Probably he meant that Hemingway had been a source of inspiration. The book garnered a good deal of critical acclaim and got him ranked among the better contemporary authors for a while. He was promoted to full professor the following year, the first one in our department. He seemed destined to become a minor man of letters, but few people can remain coolheaded on the merry-go-round of success.

His fall occurred on our trip to the United States, in the early summer of 1987. He and I were both chosen for the provincial cultural delegation that was to visit four American cities. I was selected because I could speak English fairly well and was somewhat knowledgeable about American literature. Mr. Fang joined the group as a fiction writer and literary scholar. The trip was partly sponsored by Wellington University in Connecticut, which was eager to become our sister school. That was why half the delegates were from our college.

On this trip, I discovered another aspect of Mr. Fang's character which I had not noticed before, namely parsimony. When we had lunch together, he would, if possible, avoid sharing the cost. Twice I paid for him. Despite having a bedridden wife, he was by no means destitute; his son sent him a handsome sum of money every month. Unlike us, he even had a foreign-currency account at the bank. It was less problematic if he took the gratis treatment for granted only among ourselves, the Chinese. What angered me most was that he played the same trick on some Americans, often waiting for them to pay for his coffee or tea or drink, as though everyone in the world owed him a favor or a debt. I could not understand why he acted like a mendicant. Our country had given each of us twenty-two dollars a day for pocket money, which was indeed not much, but a man ought to have his dignity. I could not imagine how a skinflint like Mr. Fang could be a lady-killer. Once, he even wanted an American woman novelist to pay for a cheese strudel he had ordered; he told her, in all insouciance, "I have no money on me." The tall redhead wore a sky-blue bolero and a pair of large Ching Dynasty coins as earrings, apparently for meeting with us. She had an irksome habit: after every sentence, she would add, "See my point?" She was so shocked by Mr. Fang's pointed words that she gave a smile which changed into a sour grimace; then she turned to me, as if questioning me with her green, deep-set eyes to determine whether he was in his right mind. Outraged, I pulled a ten-dollar note out of my pocket and said to him in Chinese, "Take this, but I want my money back tomorrow morning." That, for once, made him open his wallet.

Probably he acted that way because he had misunderstood the capitalist culture and the so-called American spirit, having confused selfhood with selfishness. A few months before the trip, we had invited an American professor, Alan Redstone, to our college to lecture on Faulkner. That florid-faced man from Kentucky was truly a turkey; he wore a ponytail and a flowered shirt and played the banjo. He said that in America the self was absolutely essential, that one had to make every effort to assert one's own selfhood, that a large ego was fundamental for any individual success, blah, blah, blah, all that kind of flatus. He even declared that self-interest was the dynamo of American culture and economy, and that if you were an American, the center of your life would have to be yourself. I swear, if he were a Chinese I would have had him hauled out of the lecture hall before he was done. But Mr. Fang told me afterwards that he was deeply impressed by Redstone's talk, which apparently had set his mind spinning. Now, in Hartford, Mr. Fang asserted himself so aggressively in front of the American woman that he would not mind smirching our country's face. It was as though he were altogether immune to shame. How could he, a well-learned man, be such a credulous ignoramus? This is still beyond me.

Our American host informed us that there would be a writers' conference at the university on Saturday. The organizers would love to arrange a special panel for the Chinese writers, meaning those in our delegation. We agreed to participate, quite moved by such a friendly invitation. I was asked to talk about American literature in contemporary China, while the six writers wouldn't have to speak, just be prepared to answer questions about their writings and experiences. We were all excited and put on our best suits or dresses for the occasion. To fortify my spoken English, I read out articles in *The New York Review of Books* for a solid hour before we set off.

The university was in a small town, which lay in a wooded valley. It was clean and eerily quiet, perhaps on account of the summer break. The roads on the campus were lined with enormous tamaracks and maples. A cream-colored minivan dropped us before a low brick building, wherein several talks were to take place at the same time. Because our panel had not been advertised like the others, most of the conference participants didn't know about it and were heading toward the other rooms. I was nervous, whispering to my comrades, "If we just have a dozen people, that will be good enough."

How we were worried! Ganlan, the woman playwright, kept wringing her fingers and said we should not have agreed to take part in such an ad hoc thing.

Suddenly Mr. Fang shouted in his broken English to the people in the lobby, "Attention, please, ladies and gentlemen, I am Professor Fang Baichen, a great contemporary Chinese fiction writer. Please come to my lecture!" He pointed his index finger at the entrance to our room while his other hand was beckoning every American around us.

People looked puzzled, then some started chortling. We were astounded and had no idea what he was up to. I thought perhaps this was just a last-ditch attempt to fetch an audience. Mr. Fang went on shouting, "Room Elefen. Please. A great writer is going to speak."

If possible, I would have fled through the roof. We stepped aside to make ourselves less conspicuous. But Mr. Fang's performance did attract a sizable audience—about thirty people came to our panel. I made an effort to keep calm so as to talk.

To our astonishment, after the woman moderator introduced us, Mr. Fang grabbed the microphone from me and began delivering a lecture. He was reading loudly from a paper he had written in advance. His voice sounded as domineering as if he were a government official delivering an admonitory speech. My head was tingling and my mouth went numb.

"What's he doing?" whispered Ganlan.

Another writer said, "This is a blitzkrieg."

"Academic hysteria," I added.

Why didn't the moderator stop him? I wondered. Then I saw the woman's oval brown face smiling at me understandingly; she must have assumed he and I had agreed to switch positions.

Mr. Fang was speaking about how he had successfully experimented with the most recent fiction techniques (which were, in fact, all outdated in the West) and how he had inspired the younger generation of Chinese writers to master the technique of stream of consciousness. At first, the audience seemed shocked by the immense volume of his booming voice. Then some of them began chuckling and snickering; many looked amused, as if they were watching a comedian performing a skit. How ashamed we were! He made a fool of

107

all the Chinese in the room! We couldn't help cursing him under our breath.

It took him more than half an hour to finish his lecture. The audience laughed and smirked when he finally stopped. A few young men, who must be students, whistled as Mr. Fang stood up to acknowledge the pitter-patter of applause, which was obviously meant to mock him.

I did not give the talk I had prepared. Completely flustered, I simply couldn't do it. But meanwhile, Mr. Fang kept smiling at us, his compatriots sitting along two folding tables. His broad face was glazed with perspiration, and his eyes glowed complacently. He was engulfed in a rectangle of sunlight falling in through a high window. Again and again he looked at us with a sort of disdain on his face, as if challenging us, "Who among you could deliver a lecture like that in English?" Were I able to reach him, I would have pinched his thigh to restore his senses.

The audience asked us some dull questions. We managed to answer them perfunctorily. Every one of us was somewhat shaken. My English became incoherent, marred by grammatical mistakes, as I struggled to interpret the questions and answers. In fact, I couldn't help stuttering, half throttled by scalding rage. My pulse went at 120 a minute at least.

Finally the whole thing was over, and every one of us felt relieved. Thank heaven, we survived it!

You can imagine how disgusted we were with Mr. Fang after that episode. Nobody would have anything to do with him. We wanted to let him wear the halo of "the great writer" alone. Ganlan even suggested we depart for San Francisco in secret, leaving him behind so that he would have trouble finding money for the return airfare. Of course we could not do that. Even if he had died, we would have had to bring his ashes back; because if he had remained in America, the authorities would have assumed he had defected, and would have criticized us for neglecting to anticipate his motives and, ergo, being the occasion of such an opportunity for him.

When we had returned to China, he was reprimanded by our college's Party Committee, which ordered him to turn in a thorough self-criticism. He did that. Then the Provincial Writers' Association revoked his membership. He became persona non grata again. *Narrative Techniques* was taken out of his hands, this time for good. He was returned to teaching as a regular faculty member and has been barred from attending conferences and giving talks.

Professor Pan, do not assume that this is his end. No, he is very much alive. There is one most remarkable quality in this man, namely that he is simply insuppressible, full of energy and resilience. Recently he has finished translating into English the autobiography of the late Marshal Fu; the book will be published by the International Friendship Press. He has made a tidy sum of money from the work. Rumor has it that he claims he is the best translator of Chinese into English in our country. Maybe that is true, especially after those master translators in Beijing and Shanghai either have passed away or are too old to embark on a large project. It seems Mr. Fang is rising again and will soon tip over. These days he brags that he has numerous connections in the capital, that he is going to teach translation and modern British fiction in your department next year, and that he will edit an English journal for your university.

Professor Pan, please forgive me for this long-winded reply. To be honest, I did not expect to write with such abandon. Actually this is the first time I am composing on a computer. It's quite an experience. The machine has undoubtedly enhanced my eloquence, and perhaps some grandiloquence; I feel as if it could form sentences by itself. Now, I must not digress anymore. Let me conclude by summarizing my opinion of Mr. Fang, though I will withhold my moral judgment: he is a man of vitality, learning, and stratagems; although already in his late fifties, he is still vigorous and may have many years left; as long as you have a way to contain him, he can be very useful and may contribute a great deal to your department. In other words, he can be used but should never be trusted, not unlike the majority of intellectuals, who are no more than petty scoundrels.

My respectful salute!

Zhao Ningshen, Chairman
Department of Foreign Languages
Muji Teachers College
March 29

Nominated by Shenandoah, Tony Ardizzone

GRIEF

fiction by PAMELA PAINTER

from PLOUGHSHARES

Harris was walking his usual route to work, up Beacon Street
and past the State House, when half a block ahead he saw their
stolen car stopped at a red light. It was their missing car, all right—a
white '94 Honda Accord, license plate 432 DOG, easy to remember—
and it was still pumping out pale blue exhaust, portent, Harris re-
membered thinking, of a large muffler bill and so much grief.

He quickened his pace to get a look at the driver leaning against
his door, the driver's fingers drumming impatiently on the wheel as if
he had better things to do with his time and Harris's car than wait for
the light to turn green. Or maybe the police cruiser idling two cars
behind was making him nervous.

Harris ran back to the cruiser and rapped sharply on the window,
passenger's side. It scrolled down at a snail's pace. Pointing, Harris
told the cop, "See that car two cars ahead? The white Honda. That's
my car. It was stolen two weeks ago. See it? That's my car." As the
light turned green, the Honda pulled away with the rest of the morn-
ing traffic. Bursts of adrenaline shot through Harris—the first thing
he'd felt in the year since his wife's death.

The cop looked after Harris's disappearing Honda and then back
at Harris, as if trying to decide if he was a nut. "Okay, mister, get in,"
the cop said. For once Harris was grateful for the respectable-
looking briefcase his wife had given him on their twenty-fifth an-
niversary.

Harris yanked on the door handle, but it was locked.

"No, in back," the cop said. "Get in the back."

Harris threw his briefcase onto the back seat and slid in behind what was surely a bulletproof window between him and the cop, taxi-style. Siren blaring, they crept down Beacon Street in a low-speed chase and swung right on Tremont. Cars parted for them reluc-tantly—giving up feet, not yards.

Thirty seconds later they were bumper to bumper with Harris's stolen car, and the cop was strongly suggesting on his loud-speaker that the driver pull over. Harris was sitting forward, his nose inches from the scratched plastic divider. "That's it, that's my car," he said.

"You wait here," the cop said, as if Harris had foolishly been plan-ning to accompany him on the dangerous stroll to the stolen car. Un-bidden images came to Harris's mind. He pictured a stash of cocaine or a weighty little handgun the new owner had tucked under the driver's seat or hidden among their maps of New England. If the thief had noticed all the hiking guides, he probably wondered why Harris needed a car.

Now the cop was standing outside Harris's car, legs spread in cop-stance, no doubt asking to see the driver's license and registration. Good luck. The registration was in the glove compartment where it belonged, but hidden—his wife's idea—inside a paperback mystery involving root vegetables. The cop car's siren and flashing lights had drawn a business-suited crowd, which gathered at a safe distance from any anticipated mayhem.

Knowing Boston, Harris had never hoped to get their car back—and still road-worthy. He'd merely expected to come home to some message from the police on his answering machine saying they'd found his car trashed and wired on the campus of Tufts or MIT or abandoned in a bad part of town. The day after his wife died, he'd driven an hour west on I-90 until he came to a rest stop with an out-side phone booth. He'd pulled the folding door shut against the out-side world, and he'd called home over and over to hear her voice say, "Hello, please leave a message. We don't want to miss anything." Then he'd saved the tape and left a message of his own.

"No license on him," the cop said as he dropped into the front seat. "Says he left the registration with his sister cause she's trying to sell the car for him." He punched 432 DOG into a black box on the dash. Seconds later, like a fax—maybe it was a fax—out scrolled a sheet of paper with not much written on it, but the cop studied it thoroughly. He verified Harris's name, address, and when he'd re-ported the car missing. Then once again he told Harris, "Wait here," and approached Harris's stolen car, where he motioned for the driver to get out. The crowd drew back.

The driver's Red Sox jacket had a ripped sleeve, and his jeans were faded to a pale blue. Short and stocky, he was this side of forty, a limp ponytail hanging off a bald rump of a dome.

The cop spun him around and told him to lean against the car, his legs spread apart, then he patted Ponytail down movie-style before clamping handcuffs on his wrists. Satisfied, the cop pointed to where Harris sat waiting and gave Ponytail a slight nudge toward him. Soon Ponytail was peering in at Harris on one of those fake freeze frames Harris would trust in any movie from that moment on. His gaze was cool, not giving anything away. Real static hissed on the cop's radio as the dispatcher asked if the cop wanted backup. "Nah," the cop said through the front window, "I'm bringing him in."

Somehow Harris couldn't picture himself and Ponytail locked in, side by side, in the back seat of this cruiser. He tried to roll down the window, but it wouldn't budge.

The cop nodded for Harris to get out—what else could his nod mean? Harris gathered up his briefcase and waited for the cop to open the door. Harris's peripheral vision assured him that Ponytail and he were not going to do anything rash like make eye contact a second time.

"The car's all yours," the cop said. "Keys are in it."

All three of them looked at Harris's car, helping the police cruiser hold up traffic. Their bottleneck was doing a bad job of channeling three lanes of angry drivers into two.

"Thanks," Harris said. Then, "You mean I just drive it away?"

"Anywhere you want," the cop said. "I can't take custody of him and your car at the same time. He's coming with me. I guess that leaves you with the car." His mustache twitched with humor, impatience, and pride.

"Sure thing," Harris said, something he knew he'd never uttered before in his life. "Well, see you around." Feeling a bit ridiculous, Harris took possession of his car. He moved the seat back and adjusted the rearview in time to see Ponytail disappear into cop-car-land, the cop's hand on the back of Ponytail's neck to make sure his head cleared the doorframe. The cop pulled out and around Harris, no siren, but his lights still flashing.

Slowly, Harris drove back to his apartment and parked in front, in the same spot from which his car had been stolen. For the first time, he assessed its state—then set to gathering up Dunkin' Donuts cups, McDonald's cartons, and candy wrappers, and stuffed them into a white Dunkin' Donuts sack. The paperback mystery—*Roots of All Evil*—was still in the glove compartment and, just as his wife had predicted, had disguised the registration well. The walking guides and maps were still under the seat; there was no handgun. And when Harris got home after work that night, there was no wife to tell the story to.

Three days later, he was matching socks and watching the six o'clock news when the phone rang. He hoped it wasn't the solicitous new tenant from the upstairs apartment, a woman whose roast lamb and braised chicken tempted Harris to emerge from his solitary gloom— a gloom he always returned to well-fed but even more despondent. She had probably noticed his car in the street and wanted to hear how he'd got it back, perhaps help him celebrate. He didn't know how to tell her that more than the car was still missing. When he said "Hello," he felt instant relief that it was not the woman upstairs, but a man's gravelly voice. "You got my TVs," the voice said.

Harris told him he had the wrong number.

"No I don't," he said. "I want my TVs."

Harris hung up and went back to sorting socks. Mostly black, they were draped over the back of the couch, side by side, toes pointing down, the way his wife used to line them up. Now, fewer and fewer of them matched. The phone rang again. It was probably the guy missing his TVs, and Harris thought, Let him.

Next night, about the same time, the phone rang. Harris was sitting on the couch beside the leftover socks, again dreading the cheerful voice of the woman upstairs. A man's gravelly voice said, "They're in the trunk of your car."

"The TVs?" Harris said.

"See, I knew you had them."

Harris matched the man's TVs with his own stolen car. Ponytail. Knowing Boston, what made Harris think that Ponytail would be arrested, indicted, convicted, put away? The cop never suggested to Harris that he should press charges, a failure pointed out by his cynical colleague in the accounting firm where Harris spent his days.

"The cop probably dropped your Ponytail-guy at the next corner," Rentz had said. Clearly, Ponytail wasn't calling Harris now from some jail. Lord, Harris didn't need this. "Look—"

The man cut him off. "You got your car back safe and sound. No harm done. I just want my TVs."

"How did you get my number?" Harris asked.

"Information," the man said. "AT&T."

"Someone's here," Harris said. "Can we talk about this another time?"

"You'll talk TVs tomorrow?"

"Tomorrow," Harris said and hung up, picturing Ponytail carless, standing in some phone booth near a bus stop or subway, figuring his chances. Harris put a Stouffer's lasagna in the oven and headed out to visit his car.

The car was where he'd parked it when he got it back four days ago. In the beam of his flashlight, he unlocked the trunk and found three TVs wedged in tight, just like the man had said. Harris had to admire the way he packed. With a sharp pang of regret he recalled his annoyance that his wife insisted on packing up the car for their camping trips. She'd assemble everything outside by the car, eye it thoughtfully, then begin with the large items first—the tent, the kerosene stove. At the end, there'd be no extra space, but nothing left behind.

The TVs weren't new, but newer than Harris's, with large blank screens. All of a sudden he felt very tired.

The next night he waited for the call, not sure what he'd say. He turned the news on with no sound. The back of the couch was free of socks, the socks put away. Who said they had to match? When the phone rang Harris was ready with a gruff hello, but this time it was the woman upstairs calling to say she'd just slipped a stuffed free-range roasting chicken into the oven and it was far too much for one person. It would be ready in about two hours. Cornbread and onion stuffing, she said, and quite a bit of tarragon. Harris's wife had always used sage and rosemary. For what must have been the fifth or sixth time, Harris thanked her and said he'd bring a bottle of wine. He imagined the new photographs his upstairs neighbor would show him, her son's gourmet peppers, or alarming images from her daughter's latest assignment with Doctors Without Borders—a daughter who had his neighbor's same pale hair and deep-set, discerning eyes. He could hear his neighbor's stories of Sip, her cat, who carefully

114

coated his trousers with hair, her hints about a new movie she'd like to see at the theater down the block. He wouldn't tell her, and she couldn't know, that his wife and he had held hands in every movie they ever saw—her hand in his, their fingers changing pressure in her lap of wool, or denim, or silk. Often now, his hands felt empty. His neighbor couldn't know he was afraid, no, terrified, that in a moment of high emotion or fright at the images on the screen, he might reach for her hand—her perfectly good, but achingly unfamiliar hand. He'd bring a bottle of red wine, he said, because he didn't know how to say no. Then he clicked off the silent news and hauled out his briefcase. Two hours was enough time to get through tonight's office work.

Ponytail called five minutes later.

To Harris's surprise, he found himself taking part in complicated, delicate arrangements to give back the TVs. Of course, this was after Ponytail explained that they had once been in dire need of repair, but now they were ready to be returned to their impatient owners. "I pick up and deliver," he said. "This won't take long. You got any TVs, toaster ovens, anything giving you trouble?"

"Just the TVs," Harris told him. They said goodbye.

Ten minutes later Harris was driving to the appointed place, wondering if he really would go through with this maneuver. He didn't feel prepared for anything since his wife died. He probably wouldn't be meeting Ponytail if his wife were at home waiting for him, worrying. They would have talked it over, together come up with a plan. It saddened him that he didn't know what she would have wanted him to do.

As arranged, Ponytail was standing on the corner of Government Center, near the subway stop, only a few blocks from the spot where Harris had been given back his car. Neither of them had suggested Ponytail come to Harris's house. Though the September night was warm, Ponytail's hands were tucked into the front pocket of his Red Sox jacket. This made Harris a little nervous. He pulled to the curb and beeped his horn twice. Ponytail glanced at Harris's car, and then, as if to shield himself from a brisk wind, he slowly turned full circle to light a cigarette behind cupped hands. Clearly, he was looking for a trap, and somehow his caution made Harris feel a little better. Finally, Ponytail sauntered over and leaned down as if to make sure it was Harris, then casually he flicked away his cigarette and tugged on the handle of the passenger door. It was locked; Harris had made

115

sure it was locked before setting off. Ponytail didn't seem to find the locked door strange and stepped back with a nod. Harris, embarrassed by his own unaccustomed display of caution, got out. His car idled in a light cloud of blue exhaust.

Across the roof, Ponytail squinted at him, straight in the eye. "Like I said on the phone, this won't take long. An hour maybe." He took his hands out of his pockets and placed them flat on the car's roof—as if to offer Harris, with this gesture, his assurance that he was not going to do anything rash. No doubt he was counting on the same from Harris.

"Okay," Harris said, thumping the car's roof with the flat of his palm. "Let's do it." Once again, adrenaline was pumping through him as it had when he first spotted his car. He slid behind the wheel, leaned over to unlock the passenger's door. Ponytail got in, the first passenger to ride in his car since his wife died. Although he'd never thought of his wife as a passenger. Ponytail's knuckles were white, and his fingers drummed on worn denim knees.

"Where to?" Harris said, belatedly thinking he should have told someone—maybe the woman upstairs—where he was going.

"Get onto Storrow and head up Route 1." Ponytail buckled his seatbelt and slouched against the door, eyeing his side mirror, his ponytail a wisp on his solid shoulder. Stealthily Harris rubbed the back of his neck, unable to imagine securing his hair with a rubber band, unable to feel a ponytail swishing against his collar, surprised even to consider it.

Once they were on the open road, Ponytail said, "Hear that rattle? Oil needs changing."

Harris glanced down at the dash, which was reassuringly dark. "A light usually comes on if—"

"Them lights don't know nothing."

"So, you think it's the oil?" Harris said.

"I was gonna do it."

"Yes, well, thanks," Harris said.

"You probably know about the muffler," Ponytail said.

Harris told him he did. Then, "You been repairing TVs long?"

Ponytail thought for a moment. "Nah. Not too long. What do you do?"

"Mostly tax returns," Harris said.

"Repairing tax returns long?" Ponytail said.

Harris had to wrap his mind around this one, but finally he said,

"Not too long." They settled into silence as the neon of roadside small businesses flashed by. After a while Ponytail told Harris to turn off Route 1 and take the overpass, then make a right at Cappy's Liquor. Three streets over they were in a neighborhood of two-story houses, lanky trees, and sloping cracked sidewalks. Aluminum siding glowed in the evening's dusk, and one house had a horizontal freezer on the front porch, another an old-fashioned gas oven. Harris had seen such things on porches before, but now they seemed strange and menacing. He tried for a little light-hearted humor. "Okay, first stop coming up," he said. But it turned out—and why was he again surprised—that all the TVs were going to one house. Ponytail's house.

"I said it wouldn't take long," Ponytail said, as if he was doing Harris a favor by consolidating the deliveries. They pulled into a narrow driveway bordered on one side by a chain-link fence. Lights were on in the downstairs of the house. A green pickup on cement blocks loomed off to the side. Now it was Harris's turn to think about a trap as Ponytail got out and slammed the car door. A jungle gym took up most of the small backyard.

Harris guardedly emerged from the car. Clothes flapped on a clothesline in the skinny side yard next to the driveway: blouses or shirts, workpants, kids' clothes, socks, and a long red dress or robe of some shiny material that caught the light from the street-lamp. Ponytail followed Harris's gaze. "Damn dryer's broken," he said. "Wife's been nagging me to fix it. I keep forgetting to order the part." At the fence, beneath a window, he gave a sharp whistle.

Harris backed up fast till he was flat against the car door with thoughts of taking off, TVs and all. Why on earth was he here? As if on cue, a woman came to the window and peered out through the screen. She was jiggling a kid about two on her hip. Absurdly, Harris found himself noticing that her blond ponytail was fatter than her husband's.

"Hey," Ponytail called out to her, his thumb jabbing the air in Harris's direction. "He's gonna help me put the stuff in the garage." Another kid, not much older, butted his head under her arm. "Bring in the clothes when you finish," she said without acknowledging Harris, then smartly wheeled the children away.

"Let's do it," Ponytail said. His voice startled Harris, who had been imagining what it would be like to park in this driveway, to live in this house. Reaching down, Ponytail heaved up the garage door and

117

turned on the light. "They're going in there," he said. With a jerk of his head, he indicated four sawhorses covered with boards at the rear of the garage. This makeshift table sat under a large, neat wall-board display of tools—most of which Harris didn't recognize—and three small blue cabinets of tiny drawers labeled screws and nails and nuts and bolts. To one side, Harris could make out the sturdy shapes of five microwaves still in their shipping boxes and four spiffy new leaf blowers. Ponytail swiped the table with a rag—it was a kind of "no comment" gesture, and Harris was grateful for it.

Together, they hoisted the first TV out of the trunk. Hobbling sideways, they carried it up the driveway, arms wrapped under and around it, foreheads almost touching across its top.

"Set her down—right—here," Ponytail panted, wiping his face on his jacket sleeve. The TVs were heavy. After the second one, Harris was sweating and huffing; his arms burned. He flexed his fingers and bent to wipe his face on his shirtsleeve, out of shape from no exercise, no long hikes for over a year. They trooped back to the car for the last delivery.

"Done." Ponytail patted the last TV. Carefully, he spread a brown tarp over the TVs and microwaves, then turned off the light. Harris stood off to the side while he pulled down the garage door.

"Well—" Harris said. Because he didn't know what else to say, he turned toward his car. It had probably been parked on and off in this same driveway for three whole weeks. The candy wrappers must have been from the kids. Beyond the fence, the shiny robe or dress was fluttering back and forth. It was actually a bathrobe, and Harris could see now that the hem was a little ragged and one of the elbows had a hole in it, but it was still of use. Without thinking, he walked past his car to the clothesline and reached up to undo the clothespins holding the robe in place. The robe was red; it was light and slippery as he folded it over his arm.

Ponytail touched his shoulder. "Hey, man, you don't need to do that."

On the way home, Harris forced himself to drive slowly even though the upstairs neighbor was waiting for him. She'd want to know all about his getting the car back, so over dinner he'd recount how he'd spotted his car in traffic, and his surprise that it was still road-worthy. He'd tell her about the telephone calls, the tense drive up Route 1, the wife and kids at the window, the garage full of companionable leaf blowers, microwaves, and TVs. He'd tell her how, as he was pulling out of the drive, Ponytail had slapped the side of his car, hard, and Harris had jumped like he'd been shot, but Ponytail only wanted to tell him to remember and check the oil. Then maybe somewhere along toward dessert, Harris would tell her more about his wife.

Nominated by Thomas Kennedy

MY NIGHT WITH PHILIP LARKIN

by RACHEL LODEN

from HOTEL IMPERIUM (University of Georgia Press)

Rendezvous with dweeby Philip in the shower:
"Aubade" taped up on pale blue tile;
I can hear him grumbling through the falling water.
Uncurling steam is scented with a trace of bile,
And I'm as grateful as a thankless child can be.
Someone has been here in this night with me,
Someone whose bitterness, I want to say,
Is even more impressive than my own.
Talking with Larkin on the great white telephone
I let the night be washed out into day

Until it's safe enough to go lie down
And dream of my librarian, my bride.
Perhaps he sits and watches in his dressing gown;
I know he won't be coming to my side
For fumblings and words he simply can't get out.
That stuff was never what it was about
When he would wake at four o'clock to piss
And part the curtains, let the moon go on
With all the things worth doing, and not done,
The things that others do instead of this.

Nominated by Paul Zimmer

120

THE ASHES OF AUGUST

essay by KIM BARNES

from THE GEORGIA REVIEW

LATE SUMMER LIGHT comes to Idaho's Clearwater Canyon in a wash of color so sweet it's palatable: butterscotch and toffee, caramel and honey. It is as though the high fields of wheat, the darker ravines tangled with blackberry, sumac, and poison ivy, the riverbanks bedded in basalt and shadowed by cottonwood and locust—all have drawn from the arid soil the last threaded rindles of moisture and spun them to gold. By four o'clock, the thermometer outside my kitchen window will read 105°. In another three hours, a hot whip of wind, and then those few moments when the wheat beards and brittle leaves, even the river, are gilded in alpenglow. Often my children call me to the window, and even as we watch, the soft brilliance darkens to sepia. But soon there will be the moon, illuminating the bridge that seems to levitate above the pearlescent river. Some nights my family and I spread our blankets on the deck and lie uncovered to trace the stars, to witness the Perseids of August—the shower of meteors so intense we exhaust ourselves pointing and counting, then fall asleep while the sky above us sparks and flares.

Other nights there is no moon or stars, only clouds gathering in the south and the air so close we labor to breathe. "Storm coming," my daughter announces, and we wait for the stillness to give way, for the wind we'll hear first as it pushes across the prairie and down the draws, bringing with it the grit of harvest. Bolts etch the sky, hit the ridges all around us; the thunder cracks above our heads. Perhaps the crop-saving rain will come, or the hail, leaving our garden shredded and bruised. Sometimes, there is nothing but the lightning and thunder, the gale bending the yellow pines to impossible angles, one

121

tree so old and seemingly wise to wind that we watch it as the miners once watched their caged canaries: should the pine ever break, we may do well to seek concrete shelter.

These are the times we huddle together on the couch, mesmerized and alarmed. We know that the storm will pass and that we will find ourselves to have again survived. We know, too, that somewhere around us, the lightning-struck forests have begun to burn; by morning, the canyon will be nearly unseeable, the sunset a smoky vermilion.

The West, Wallace Stegner so famously noted, is defined by its aridity, and this stretch of north Idaho canyon land where I live is no exception. The Clearwater River is the reason for the numerous settlements along its reach as well as those of its tributaries. Logging, mining, agriculture: all are dependent on the presence and ways of water. Fire, too, defines this land, and at no time more so than in the month of August, when the early rains of spring have given way to weeks of no measurable precipitation, when the sweet blossoms of syringa and chokecherry have shriveled and fallen, when wild plums hang blistered with ferment. We must go high into the mountains where the snowpack held longest to find huckleberries, our belt-strung buckets banging our legs, our mouths and fingers stained black, and we go prepared to defend ourselves against two things: the bears who share our fondness for fruit, and fire. Our bear defense is little more than loud conversation and an occasional glance toward the perimeters of our patch. For fire, we carry in our pickup a shovel and a water-worthy bucket. If called upon to do so, we could hope to dig a fire line, or drown a few flames if lucky enough to be near a creek or spring.

Born and raised within a fifty-mile radius of where I now live, I have memories of late summer that are infused with fire. As a child growing up in the logging camps of the Clearwater National Forest, I knew August meant that my father would rise at two A.M. to work the dew-damp hours before noon, when a machine-struck spark could set the wilderness ablaze. But no one could mandate the hours ruled by lightning, and with the lightning came the fires—as many as fifty or sixty from one storm—and with the fires came the pleas for volunteers to man the Pulaskis, buckets, and bulldozers. Often, the loggers were not asked so much as pressed into service, ordered from their sites and sent to the front lines still wearing their calked boots and pants cut short to avoid snags.

Like my father, my uncles had taken up the life of the lumberjack. Our communal camp was a circle of small wooden trailers, out of which each morning my cousins came, still in their pajamas, rubbing the sleep from their eyes. I remember my mother and aunts in those weeks of searing high-altitude heat, how they rose with their husbands and made their biscuits and pies so that the wood-fueled stove might cool before dawn, then loaded a pillowcase with sandwiches, fried pies, jugs of iced tea and Kool-Aid that would chill in the creek. Somewhere just over the ridge the men battled to keep the fires at bay, while my cousins and I explored the cool recesses of the stream bed, searching for mussels whose halves spread out like angel wings, prying the translucent periwinkles from their casings to be stabbed onto hooks that would catch the trout we'd have for supper. My sensory memories of those afternoons—the sun on my shoulders, the icy water at my knees, the incense of pine and camas, the image of my mother and aunts lounging with the straps of their swimsuits pulled down, the brush of skin against skin as my cousins sifted the water beside me in their quest for gold—are forever linked with my awareness of the smoke rising in columns only a few miles away and the drone of planes overhead, belly-heavy with retardant, the smell of something dangerous that caused us to lift our faces to the breeze as it shifted. When the men returned they were red-eyed and weary, smudged with pitch and ash, smelling like coals from the furnace. I watched them drink tumbler after tumbler of iced tea, wondered at the dangers they faced, and thought that I might want to be like them and come home a fighter and a hero.

As a child raised in the woods, I gained my awareness and wariness of fire by way of the stories told by my elders as they sat around the table after dinner, picking their teeth with broomstraw, pouring another cup of the stout coffee kept warm atop the cookstove. New fires brought stories of old ones, and so August was full of fire, both distant and near, burning the night horizon, burning the edges of my dreams.

There was the fire of 1910, the one most often remembered by those old enough to have witnessed its destruction, their stories retold by the generations who have sat and listened and seen with their own eyes the scars left across the land. That year, July had come and gone with only .05 inches of rain. Thunderstorms had started spot fires throughout the Clearwater National Forest; the Forest Service and its small force of men, working with little more than shovels and picks, could not hope to suppress so much flame. And then came August, "ominous, sinister, and threatening," according to Forest Service worker Clarence B. Swim's account of that summer. "Dire catastrophe seemed to permeate the very atmosphere. Through the first weeks of August, the sun rose a coppery red ball and passed overhead . . . as if announcing impending disaster. The air felt close, oppressive, and explosive."[1]

"Ten days of clear summer weather," the old-timers say, "and the forest will burn." No rains came, and the many small fires that crews had been battling for days grew stronger and joined and began a run that would last for weeks. It swept up and down and across the Clearwater drainages: the Lochsa, Warm Springs Creek, Kelly Creek, Hemlock Creek, Cayuse Creek—the Idaho sky was black with ash. One Forest Service veteran, Ralph S. Space, whose written history of the Clearwater Forest contains lively anecdotal recollections, remembers smoke so thick that, as a nine-year-old boy rising to another day of no rain, he could look directly into the sun without hurting his eyes. The chickens, he said, never left their roost.[2]

On 21 August 1910, the wind began to blow, picking up velocity as the sun crested, until the bull pine and white fir swayed and snapped, and the dust rose up from the dirt roads and fields to join the smoke in a dervish of soot and cinder. Men along the fires' perimeters were told to run, get out, it was no use. Some took to the creeks and rivers, pulling their hysterical horses along behind them. (One legend tells of a panicked horse breaking away and racing the fire some fifty miles east to Superior, Montana—and making it.) Others fled northward, subsisting on grouse whose feathers were too burnt for them to fly.

As in any war, many who fought the fires came away scarred, some bearing the marks like badges of courage while others, whose less-than-brave actions in the face of disaster had earned them the coward's stripes, hid themselves in the backrooms of saloons or simply

[1]Stan Cohen and Don Miller, *The Big Burn: The Northwest's Forest Fire of 1910* (Missoula, MT: Pictorial Histories Publishing Company, 1978), 3.
[2]Ralph S. Space. *The Clearwater Story: A History of the Clearwater National Forest* (Forest Service USDA, 1964), 96.

disappeared. One man, part of a group sent to fight the blaze near Avery, Idaho, was so undone by the blistering heat and hurricane roar of the approaching fire that he deserted, pulled his pistol, and shot himself—the only casualty to beset his crew.[3]

One of the heroes was a man named Edward Pulaski. When he found himself and the forty-three men he led cut off from escape, he ordered them into the nearby War Eagle mine, believing the large tunnel their only hope for survival. As the heat rose and the fire ate its way closer, several of the men panicked and threatened to run. Pulaski drew his pistol and forced the men to lie belly down, faces to the ground, where the coolest air would gather. He hung blankets across the tunnel's entrance, dampening them with what water he could, until he fainted. By the time the flames had passed around them, sucking the oxygen from the cavern, replacing it with a scorching, unbreathable wind, five were dead from suffocation. Another man who had chosen to run before Pulaski could stop him was found a short distance away: the rescue party had stepped over him on the way in, thinking the blackened mass a burned log; only on their return trip did they recognize the charred body for what it was. Pulaski had stood strong in the face of events "such as sear the souls of lesser men," declared the Washington, DC, *Star*.[4] He would go on to become even more famous for his invention bearing his name, the Pulaski—a combination shovel, ax, and mattock that since has become standard equipment for fighters of wildfire.

Pulaski's story is just one of many that came from that time of unimaginable conflagration. For three days and nights the wind howled up the canyons and down the draws, taking the fire with it. The ash, caught by updraft and high current, traveled for thousands of miles before falling in places that most Idahoans had only heard of: in Saskatchewan, Denver, and New York, the air was thick with the detritus of western larch and hemlock; in San Francisco, ships dropped anchor outside the bay and waited for days, unable to sight land through the blue-gray smoke that had drifted south and descended upon the city.[5] Norman Maclean wrote that in his home town of Missoula, "the street lights had to be turned on in the middle

[3]Stan B. Cohen and A. Richard Guth, *Northern Region: A Pictorial History of the U.S. Forest Service 1891–1945* (Missoula, MT: Pictorial Histories Publishing Company, 1991), 61; Stan Cohen and Don Miller, 18–19.
[4]Cohen and Miller, 18.
[5]Cohen and Guth, 58.

of the afternoon, and curled ashes brushed softly against the lamps as if snow were falling heavily in the heat of August."[6] The "Big Blowup," they call it now, or the "Big Burn"—not one large fire, but 1,736 smaller ones that had come together across the Clearwater Region. By the time it was over, three million acres and many small towns across Idaho and Montana lay in ruins; at least eighty-five people, most of them firefighters, were dead.[7]

The Big Blowup of 1910 was not the last August fire to rage across the Clearwater: 1914, 1919, 1929, 1934—major fires every five to ten years. The fire of 1919 is synonymous in my mind with the North Fork of the Clearwater, where I spent much of my childhood, for it is there, in the middle of the turquoise river, that a small rise of land bears the name Survivor Island. I remember how, aware of its legendary significance, I studied the island each time we passed along the dusty road, how the heart-flutter of danger and adventure filled my chest. What written history I can find records how two packers and their packstrings, two Nez Perce, and several wild animals had found safety from the fire by swimming to the island. But the story I remember has only three characters: an Indian grandfather, his grandson, and a black bear, all secure upon the island as the fire raged by, the winds it generated whipping the water into whitecaps. At some point, the story became embellished with a detail I still can't shake—how the child, emboldened by the success of their escape, wanted to kill the bear, and how the grandfather would not let him. Perhaps the elder understood the mythical ties he and his charge would forever have to that bear; perhaps he believed that nothing else should die in the face of the carnage that surrounded them.

With each year's August, I feel the familiar expectation that comes with the heat and powder-dry dust boiling up from behind the cars and logging trucks. Expectation, anticipation, sometimes fear of what lies just over the horizon—August is a month of waiting for storm, for fire, for rain, for the season to change and pull us away from our gardens, our open windows and doors, back to the contained warmth of the hearth and the bed that comforts us.

Yet some part of me loves the suspense of August, the hot breath

---

[6]Norman Maclean, "USFS 1919: The Ranger, the Cook, and a Hole in the Sky," in *A River Runs Through It and Other Stories* (Chicago: The University of Chicago Press, 1976), 140.
[7]Cohen and Miller, v.

of morning whispering the possibility of high drama, the calm and complacency of dog-day afternoons giving way to evening thunderheads brewing along the ridge. Something's afoot, something's about to happen, and I shiver with the sureness of it.

Years when I have lived in town, surrounded by asphalt, concrete, and brick, there was little to fear from the dance of electricity lighting the sky except the loss of electricity itself. Here in the country, on the south-facing slope of the Clearwater Canyon, what surrounds us is something as volatile and menacing as the tinder-dry forest: miles of waist-high grass and thistle the color and texture of straw. Just such desiccated vegetation fueled the flames that killed the men made famous by Norman Maclean's book *Young Men and Fire* (1992), the story of the tragic 1949 Mann Gulch blaze.

We have no rural fire district here; those of us who have chosen to call this small settlement home know that should a wildfire come our way, we have only our wits to protect us—that and every available gunnysack, shovel, hoe, and tractor the community can provide. All through the summer we watch from our windows as the sun leeches the green from the hills and the color from the sky, and the land takes on a pale translucence. Come August, we have counted the days since no rain, and we know that somewhere a storm is building, perhaps just to the south where the horizontal plane of the Camas Prairie intersects the vertical thrust of the Seven Devils—the mountains whose peaks rise jagged and white through the brown haze of harvest.

We check our flashlights, our candle supply; we fill our bathtubs with water. There will be wind, which will switch the sumac and send the sagebrush busting across the gravel roads; it will tear the limbs from the trees, drop them across the power lines in some part of the county so remote that the service crew will take hours, sometimes days, to locate and repair them. Then comes the lightning, blasting the tops from the tallest pines, striking the poles that carry our phone and electricity. The lights will flicker, then fail; the air conditioner will moan into silence. Pumps that pull the water from the springs will lapse into stillness; our toilets and faucets will gurgle and go dry. If we're lucky, what passes over us will be nothing more than the black raft of storm clouds, and the seconds we count between lightning and thunder will never fall below five. But there have been times when the bolt and jarring crack have come simultaneously, and we have known, then, that the lightning has touched somewhere near us, and that we must watch more carefully now and smell the air and be ready to fight or to run.

The summer of 1998, on just such an evening, we sat at the dinner table with my in-laws, who had arrived from Illinois for a weeklong visit. My husband Bob and I had each kept an eye on the clouds mushrooming behind Angel Ridge; to my Midwestern relatives, the oppressive humidity seemed nothing unusual, but to us, accustomed to zero percent air moisture, the too-still air signaled a weather change. When I stepped out onto the deck, I could hear the wind coming, huffing its way up the canyon like a steam engine. Within minutes, I was hit with a blast of hot air, then felt the cool come in behind it. The first reverberating boom made the hair stand up on the back of my neck, a response so atavistic I could barely resist the instinctual urge to take shelter. Instead, I raised my face to the wind, redolent with fennel and sage, locust and mullein, the arid incense of a summer's rich dust; along the edges of the breeze, I could smell the dampness of distant rain.

Back at the table, we drank our coffee and shared stories of the past year. I got up once to fill a few pitchers with water. The lightning moved closer—only a few seconds between the flash and thunder—and then a clap so loud and close we all jumped. Not really a clap, not even a boom, but a sharp, ripping roar. Bob and I looked at one another and headed for the porch, and then we could see it: to the west, a narrow column of smoke just beginning to rise. Even as we watched, the column grew thicker, and then we felt the wind gain momentum, pushing east toward us.

The country road, we knew, was our best hope, cutting between us and the fire, providing a fuel-free strip where the flames might falter. Earlier in the summer, Bob had cut, raked, and burned a fire-line around our house, decreasing the chances that fire could reach us, but what we couldn't shield ourselves against were the airborne cinders already beginning to descend.

"It's right behind the Bringman place," Bob said. "If we don't get it stopped, they'll be in trouble."

I had a vague acquaintance with Mr. and Mrs. Bringman, a retired couple who have worked the canyon land for decades. Their house and outbuildings sit a quarter-mile above and to the west of us, in the middle of what was then a good crop of ripe wheat. We had come to know them as we have come to know most of our neighbors: by our happenstance run-ins at the PO. Mr. Bringman is also known for his homemade wine. Local history holds that his land had once belonged to a man of some note who had imported grapevines from France and planted them in the sandy bluffs above the river. "Noble vines," Mr. Bringman pronounced, and we began saving our empty store-bought bottles so that, once a month, he could swing by on his four-wheeler to collect them and drop off a sample of the wine he had put up the past summer, which we dutifully shelved, though he insisted it was quite ready to drink now.

"You get on the phone," Bob said. "I'm going up there." Already the smoke and ash had darkened the sky to a deep shade of gray.

"Wear boots," I said. "Take a wet handkerchief and gloves."

While Bob gathered his gear, I picked up the phone and dialed. Mrs. Bringman's voice came on the line, high-pitched and quavering. "Tell your husband to get here as fast as he can," she said. "Call anyone you can. It's coming our way."

I hung up, then began a series of calls, knowing that for each call I made, two more would go out, word of the lightning strike spreading faster than the fire itself, fanning out across the ridges and high prairie for miles, until every family would be alerted. I knew that every wife and mother would dial the next number down the road, that each man and his oldest sons would don their hats and boots, grab their shovels and buckets and be out the door within minutes, all guided by the pillar of smoke that marked the point of danger as surely as a lighthouse beam.

I paused in my calling long enough to kiss Bob as he hurried out the door. I could see the change in his eyes, the urgency and excitement, and I felt the regret and longing and resignation I had as a child when the men had gone into the wilderness, to the front where the stories were being made and the dramas played out.

"Remember how fast the fire can move," I said. I had a momentary image of my husband scrabbling across the canyon's steep pitch and felt my heart jerk with fear. "Do you have a lighter?"

Bob nodded, remembering, as I remembered, the story of the ranger who survived the Mann Gulch fire.

"Be careful," I cautioned.

"I will," he said, and was gone.

In *Young Men and Fire*, Norman Maclean researches and describes the 5 August 1949 blaze that caught and killed all but three of the fifteen Forest Service smoke jumpers who had parachuted into the Helena National Forest of Montana. They had been on the ground for less than two hours and were working their way down a hillside toward the fire—an error that would cost them dearly, for a fire racing uphill can easily catch even the fastest man. But what they had found was a simple class C fire, no more than sixty acres. It was a "ground" fire, one the men expected to mean hard work but little danger.[8]

Yet there is always danger when a wildfire is present, and so the crew knew that this one might "crown," as its charred path suggested it had done already before moving back down into undergrowth. The fire that has crowned is what creates the great roar of sound so many survivors describe as the noise of a fast-moving train descending upon them, so loud that communication becomes impossible. A crown fire creates its own weather system: the warmer air rises and the cooler air rushes down to replace it, creating a "fire whirl," a moving convection that can fill the air with burning pine cones and limbs, as though the forest itself has exploded. This incendiary debris gives rise to spot fires that can flare behind or in front of the fighters; crews find themselves suddenly surrounded, ringed by fire that seems to have come from nowhere, sprung up from the ground and converging.[9]

With these conditions comes the possibility of the phenomenon fire-fighters most fear: the "blowup." Blowups occur when fresh air is drawn into the "fire triangle" of flammable material, high temperature, and oxygen. Few have witnessed a true blowup and lived to tell of it, but those who have speak with wonder of the fire's speed. Maclean recounts the experience of fire expert Harry T. Gisborne, perhaps the first to observe, survive, and describe a blowup. The 1929 fire Gisborne detailed occurred in Glacier National Park and burned ninety thousand acres with almost incomprehensible swiftness, demolishing "over two square miles in possibly two minutes, although probably in a minute flat."[10]

The Mann Gulch smoke jumpers were young and had dropped onto a terrain that may have seemed at the time less threatening than the densely wooded ridge in the distance. They were at a point where the tree-studded mountains broke open to grassy plains dried to amber. Perhaps they believed themselves safe amid the loose-rock

---

[8]Norman Maclean, *Young Men and Fire: A True Story of the Mann Gulch Fire* (Chicago: The University of Chicago Press, 1992), 33.
[9]Maclean, 34–37.
[10]Maclean, 35, 37.

slope and low-lying vegetation, but they were tragically mistaken. They had their tools—their shovels and Pulaskis—but what they did not have was knowledge of the ways of this fire and of how, within an hour, it would cross the gulch and push them screaming up the steep hill, crest at the top, and die there with them. Bunch grass, cheat grass, some immature pines mixed in with older growth—these were all that was needed to create the blowup that engulfed the men. Two of the three who survived did so by racing the fire to the ridge and winning; the third, the crew's foreman, saved himself by escape of another kind: instead of running, he stopped, struck a match, set fire to the grass at his feet, then stepped into the flames he had created. He lay face down on the still-smoking earth, covered his head with his hands, and waited for the main fire to catch and sweep over him. And it did.[11]

A steeply pitched basalt-strewn slope covered with dry grass and scattered patches of timber—the very terrain into which Bob was headed. I prayed that he would have the foreman's presence of mind should the fire overtake him. I could see the flames themselves now, flaring twenty feet into the sky. I let the screen door swing shut, went back to the phone, and began another call.

The men came in their pickups and stock trucks and cars, on their four-wheelers and tractors—a steady parade passing by our house. Having exhausted my list of numbers, I gave up my station to stand with my children and in-laws where our gravel driveway met the gravel road. We tried to determine what we could of the fire's direction. We waved our support as our neighbors flew by—driving too fast, we thought, though we understood their urgency. On the slope just above us, the Goodes and Grimms and Andersons had set their sprinklers atop their roofs, dampening the embers and sparking ash that floated and fell around us like fireflies in the darkening sky. I'd instructed my ten-year-old daughter and eight-year-old son to stand ready with the hose, knowing that should the power lines go down, our electric pump that drew water from the spring below would be useless; our only defense against the fire would be whatever water remained in the storage tank. But if we used that water for prevention, we would have none left should the fire reach us.

As twilight deepened, the fire's glow grew more distinct along the

---

[11]Maclean, 74–75, 102–106.

western horizon, until the last rays of sunlight were indistinguishable from the orange-red aura melding sky to land. My mother-in-law, city raised and only half understanding her son's desire to live in such a wild place, did her best to rein in her fear; my father-in-law, nearing eighty, paced in frustration: he should be out there, offering what help he could. Had it not been for the fire's location along the breaks of the canyon, our ability to keep him clear of the battle would have proven much more difficult.

We all knew the immediate danger Bob and the other men faced—the fire—but there were other concerns I kept to myself. Just down the road from our house is a jut of land named Rattlesnake Point: we kill an average of two diamondbacks per year in our yard; the annual score we spy along the roads and paths outside our property we leave be. In times of fire, every living thing flees from what threatens it—cougar, deer, elk, rabbit, pheasant, field mouse, bear, and rattlesnakes, too, slithering ahead of the heat faster than most could imagine, sometimes smoking from their close brush with death. My hope was that, should Bob encounter a snake, it would be too intent on escape to strike at the legs of a man.

And then there was the terrain itself: fragile shelves of talus, slanted fields of scree. The land could give way beneath your feet, begin moving like a tipped mass of marbles. I have had it happen before, while hunting chukar, and found myself grabbing at the smallest outcroppings of sage and buckbrush, feeling them pull loose in my hands, the only thing below me a chute toward an outcropping of columnar basalt that would launch me into the canyon. I've always been lucky, able to catch a knob of stable rock or wedge my foot into the roots of a stunted hawthorn, but that memory of falling, of gathering momentum, of hurtling toward endless open space, has never left me. I knew that Bob was sure-footed and careful; I knew, too, that in the lapse of light, the ground's definition would fade.

The smoke thickened. We covered our faces with our hands, coughing, our eyes watering, unwilling to abandon our vigil, knowing how much more those closer to the fire were having to endure. I ordered the children back to the house, but they would not go. They wanted to be of some help, perhaps believing, as I did, that our standing guard might somehow keep the fire at bay. The glow had moved higher up the ridge; the flames leapt, receded, then leapt again. With the wind and lack of equipment, we had little hope that simple manpower could contain the fire. I estimated that a half-mile of pasture land separated us from the conflagration—that and the road—and I told myself we could hold our ground for a little while longer before loading the cars with what we most treasured: photographs, books, laptop computer, the children's most precious belongings. The possibility of losing our home and everything in it seemed very real to me, but I considered it with little emotion. What was uppermost in my mind was the safety of my loved ones: the family that gathered closer as the smoke increased, and my husband, somewhere just over the ridge, risking his life to save the nearby houses and barns, the crops and timber, perhaps even an entire small town should the fire run the ridge and drop over into the next draw. At that moment, I wasn't sure the saving was worth the risk. How could I weigh the loss of my husband against nothing more than property and economy? There was little chance that anyone other than the firefighters was in danger—by now, everyone in the county had been warned. Why not stand back, allow the fire to meet the river on one side, the linkage of creeks on the other? In the end, it would burn itself out.

But then I remembered the stories—the fire of 1910, the young men who had died so suddenly by thinking the distance between them and the fire enough—and I realized that this wasn't about the wheat field a mile down the road or the home of the family at the bottom of the draw. It was about fire. It was about crowning and whirls, convection and blowups. It was about August and a summer's long drought. It was about three million acres burned in a matter of days—the width and breadth of many whole states.

What I wished for, then, was the help of all the technology and knowledge such fires of the past had brought into being. The fire of 1910 showed everyone that crews of men scattered about the burning edges would never be enough, and then the Forest Service began its study and transformation of firefighting. But we do not live in a forest; we live on private land, too distant to warrant the protection of the city, too sparsely populated to afford the luxury of a volunteer fire department. That August of 1998, our situation was little different from the one facing the farmers and loggers and townspeople of 1910: our primitive tools had not changed, and at that moment, I began to realize that our chances of saving our home had not, either.

I moved down the driveway, preparing myself to announce that it was time to pack up, to position ourselves by the river where Bob might find us. But then came the roar of something overhead—the thrum and air-beat of a helicopter. I looked up to see what I had believed would not come to us: help from the outside world.

From beneath the helicopter hung a length of cable attached to a large vinyl-and-canvas bucket. The pilot did not head for the fire but for the river, where he hovered and dropped and filled the bucket with nearly one hundred gallons of water—a half ton hoisted up and swinging from the Bell Jet Ranger. As we watched, the helicopter leaned itself toward the fire's furthest point, the bale opened, and a sheet of water rained down.

My daughter and son let loose with whoops of excitement. My in-laws and I clapped and hugged, jubilant at this unexpected turn of events. Again and again, the pilot followed his path from river to fire, until the ribbon of flame along the horizon had dimmed to a faint glow; within an hour, we could no longer point to even the smallest flare.

We stood watch as night came on, unable to see the helicopter now but tracing its direction by the deep hum that drifted to us on the smoky breeze. Although we were safe, rescued by the graces of the Clearwater-Potlatch Timber Protective Association, who had sent the helicopter because they were fighting no fires of their own, we all knew our wait was not over: somewhere in the darkness was our father, son, and husband. The line of vehicles that had sped by us earlier now came in reverse—a slower-moving column whose lights passed over us as we held up our hands in a gesture of greeting and gratitude.

"Bob will be coming soon," I said. "Let's go make him some fresh iced tea."

We walked the few yards back to the house, turned on the porch light. Our jubilation had been replaced by a quiet fear that grew with each passing minute—fear that receded and then leapt up each time another pickup approached but did not slow and turn into our driveway.

"He should be back by now," my father-in-law said, pacing from the window to the door and back again. "Maybe I should go see if I can find him."

I knew that Bob and the other men would have driven off-road and into the fields, gaining what time they could against the fire. Even if we could locate our four-wheel-drive, there was no guarantee Bob would be near it. Without light, the diminishing fire behind him and the total blackness of rural night before him, he could walk for hours before finding his way back to where he had parked.

"I think we should wait," I said. "He'll stay as long as he's needed. Someone will come and get us if there's trouble." I listened to my own words, only half believing. What if Bob had gotten turned around, fallen into a ravine, been isolated and trapped by the fire? What if he were lying somewhere in the dark, injured, unable to save himself?

I thought again of the rough terrain—familiar to me from the many walks Bob and I had taken, the many hours we had spent exploring and visually mapping the area. The fire likely would have eaten its way across Bedrock Canyon, down to the river and up to the top of the ridge, creating acres and acres of charcoal earth, charcoal sky—like a black blizzard. How could we hope to find him?

We made the tea. We gathered and washed the dinner dishes. We distracted the children with books and puzzles until none of us could be distracted any longer. We gathered outside in the cooling air, still heavy with smoke that would hang in the canyon for days.

"Come on, Bob," I whispered to myself. "Come on." I thought of my mother and aunts then, waiting as I waited, fighting the growing panic with the mundane details of daily life. How many hours had they spent watching from the window above the sink, their hands submerged in soapy water, their fingers blindly tracing the knife's edge? How many Augusts had passed in a haze of worry and despair as the lightning came down and the flames rose up and the men disappeared into that place where no one could reach them?

But then, the lights at the top of the driveway, the held breath, the release as the engine idled and died.

I let my daughter and son reach him first, escort him into the house. He was covered with soot, his white T-shirt scorched, burned through in some places; his face was red, nearly blistered beneath the ashy smudges. We hovered around him, offering tea, voicing our concern and sympathy. I stepped up close, breathed in the familiar smell of everything burned—the dead grass and live trees, the cloth on his back, the singed hair.

"I'm so glad you're okay." I wanted to cry—out of relief that he was home, out of anger at the fire, out of frustration that I had found myself caught up in the same cycle that my mother had known so well. I knew that the stories Bob would tell of the fire would become part of our family's shared history, that we would recite and embellish the narrative with each passing summer, that we would always remember the way he shook his head when he told us: "There was no way we were going to be able to stop it. But then I heard the helicopter, directly overhead. I looked up just as the bottom of the bucket opened. I've never felt anything so good in my life."

The next day, we drove downriver to view where the fire had burned—an oily pool spread across the golden hillside. After the fire subsided, Bob had found himself disoriented and had wandered in the dark for an hour before coming across several other men. Together they were able to find their way back. "I can look up there now," he said, "and have no idea where I was."

Later, when I asked my son what he remembered about the fire, he answered quickly: "I remember that I couldn't breathe." My daughter recalled the ash falling and my concern that we would lose our water supply. And she reminded me of something I had forgotten: "What I remember most," she said, "is how badly I wanted to go and help fight the fire, and how you wouldn't let me."

Perhaps she will be the one to leave the phone and go to the place where stories are being made, the one who will not be left behind. One of the most respected smoke jumping crews in the country is composed entirely of women; of the fourteen Oregon-based firefighters who died in the Colorado fire of 1994, four were female. I shudder with the thought of my son or daughter choosing to try himself, herself, against such an adversary. I wonder if I would come to dread and despise the month I love so well, for I am strangely wedded to the tyrannical heat, the thunderstorms, even the fire—the absolutism, the undeniable presence of August in my life.

Instead of wading the ashes of August, I spend many late summer days wading the river. This is Nez Perce land, and the water's flux covers and uncovers the remnants of their ancient industry: arrowheads, spear points, blades of obsidian. I come to the Clearwater armed only with a hook and line, meaning to fool the fish with a tuft of feather, a swirl of bright thread. I step in to my waist and feel the strange dissonance of temperature—my feet numbing with cold, the crown of my head hot with sun. I stand for a moment, brace myself. I am all that is still, an island anchored by nothing more than the felt soles of my boots. I load my line, cast toward the calm above the current. I imagine the fish rising, its world a kaleidoscope of shattered light.

Through the cooling nights of fall, during the long nights of winter when ice rimes the eddies, I dream of August, the water at my hips, my line lacing the sun. I wake to the odor of woodsmoke—my husband firing the stove—but for a sleepy moment it is the warm wind that I smell, the burning of yellow pine and prairie grass and wheat stubble. I smell summer sage and mullein, the licorice spice of dog fennel. I smell the cool drift of fish scent off the river. I open my eyes, expecting early light, the windows still open to the morning breeze, but what I see instead is the darkness before sunrise, the frost that glisters each pane of glass, and I am bereft.

Nominated by Claire Davis, Ron Tanner

INVENTORY

by EAMON GRENNAN

from HAYDEN'S FERRY REVIEW

To lay claim to something, even
this old half-barrel with its
rusty hoops and painted staves,
weather-bleached, as it starts
to look back, be a true thing
in the world, offering crumbs
to small birds, two streaks of
birdshit brightening its side.
Or bodies stretched to a limit
in that incessant present
they'd stumbled into, living
the truth of hand to mouth.
But there they go now, falling
forward with small cries of pain,
calling back the long vowels
and that short clamouring
from her mouth riding the
air, eager for it, swimming into
his open mouth. Evening,
he can hear the wind
off the Atlantic—oceanic uproar
among the high branches
and see the sycamores which
sky the garden, swaying shipwise,
and two gulls down the valley
backlit by brightness. A swallow

reams the garden's air and
ragged bushes show at once
their bones and bright flowers,
their leafy summer-swollen
plenitude taking the wind in
to sigh its big life among them,
waves and waves of it
gathering, greeting, going on,
where he sits singing the
praises of shelter, trying to
fathom what it is that glints
through hedge-windows or at the edge
of clouds, or what the wind
insists to high branches or among
the agitated leaves. Clouds now
changing shapes and changing
as they marshall and disperse: their
weight unimaginable, almost
on fire with themselves, coasting
towards change and change about
in such bodies, maybe, as angels
might borrow, spreading themselves
in light and through it, or turning
all to tears while the mountains
like immense gentle animals
lie down under the hand of light
itself and are settled by it.

Nominated by Hayden's Ferry Review, Theodore Deppe, Gibbons Ruark

SEMPER PARATUS

fiction by ALYSON HAGY

from GRAVEYARD OF THE ATLANTIC (Graywolf Press)

WE WERE A GOOD BOAT CREW. A lot better than anything I saw in boot camp, which you would hope was true. We drilled, ran constant checks on our equipment. We had to. There were only seven of us assigned to the station—a station with an Area of Responsibility of 1,350 miles—and we had hundreds of pleasure craft and beaucoup bad weather to deal with. That made it a choice billet for me. Much better than galley duty on the cutter *Harriet Lane*, which was where I started. At Station Ocracoke, I had what I wanted: plenty of contact with boats and water. I can't speak for the guys. We were all after different things in our careers and our lives, and maybe we still are.

I'd been with Group Cape Hatteras two months, working on promotion to petty officer, when I drew a three-week rotation on Ocracoke Island. James Leggett was our Boatswain's Mate. I believed I could deal with him. He'd been supervisor on crews with women before. He was career and steady and stuck to his business. The kind of guy you wanted to kid about officer school, tell him he needed to get his lieutenant's stripes so he could kick some Academy ass. He'd gnaw on a laugh if you said that, then shake his blondish head. He liked taking the Coast Guard at an enlisted man's pace.

Leggett knew how to run things. Burgoyne, our Machinery Tech, was slick with engines and every other piece of metal in the harbor. Like a lot of shop rat MTs, Burgoyne kept to himself when he could. So did I. The crew accused me of studying all the time, then they'd ask why I bothered, every apprentice seaman from here to Alaska knew I didn't have to bust it for promotion, promotions were handed to women like candy. I ignored the shots like I was supposed to. It was basic shit, part of our lazy downtime talk about R&R and money. The shit that meant something was stowed underneath our work blues. Where it was safest.

Those weeks at Ocracoke it was me, Leggett, Burgoyne, Paul Toshiko, Trey Buckner, Lyle Pozek, and Sammy Walker. There were five other women at Hatteras, but I was the only one who pulled the straw. Which didn't concern me, like I said. I can eat anything a guy cooks, and I know how to be good crew. I was sure we'd catch some hardcore Search-and-Rescue on Ocracoke, the stuff that makes my blood run best. There'd be no dry rot for us.

Buckner and Pozek asked me out to play pool at the Jolly Roger the afternoon we transferred down. They'd done their calculating and rank toting and knew we'd be hitting the waves together. I was senior to them both, though not by much. We needed to be able to look each other in the eye. I'm a lousy pool player. So is Pozek, who's not much good at anything he's not made to focus on. Buckner shoots a mean game and likes to hip-slide around the corners of the table like he's on a waxed dance floor even when there aren't any girls to impress. A shimmy, Pozek calls it . . . as in *Shimmy for me, Buck*. At least once a day Buckner tells me—and everybody else—that he can't wait to finish his hitch, he should've been a marine. He's got restlessness like it's a four-season allergy. Makes him a ball-slamming shooter though, all focus and heat, just like it can make him awesome on drills. His body knows how to burn unhappiness for fuel.

So we're playing Cut Throat and I'm doing all right and the Jolly Roger is empty except for a couple of kids eating french fries in a back corner that smells like trapped crab. The jukebox is looping through some old Trisha Yearwood songs, Pozek's choice. We've got time to bitch about our assignment, but we don't, maybe because I don't feel like clipping Buckner's claws when he gets snotty, which he will. I've got this feeling it's better if we stay quiet on the subject. Then Leggett walks in, all broad shoulders and regulation. I can tell by the stoked way he moves in from the black square of the door that he knew we'd be here. He orders a Coke, comes over to the table. Lyle, he says, Trey, Randall. Using my last name like they all do. Pozek invites him into the game but he says no, not this time. He'll just stand by. Leggett is a watcher, we all know that. Question is, what's the man, our superior, hope to see?

Some cold coast in Michigan—that's where Leggett is from. He told me once that seeing the big cutters on the Great Lakes did him in as a kid, worse than a junior high romance. The Coast Guard kissed him hard. Tonight, he seems so keyed his voice drags on a drawl I haven't heard before, and I hear him talk to Buckner about a mutual friend of theirs who's a Tech on the Hatteras buoy tender. The friend has racked up some negatives with the chief. Pozek then has to go goofing on me, doing the male-dog thing that guys do to get attention when they outnumber the girls in a room even if the girls aren't ones they're thinking about screwing, not with the front part of their brains. He tells Leggett I suck as a pool player, it's a good thing I toss line better than I slide a stick. He says it every way he can to make Leggett laugh. Which doesn't happen. Then it's my turn, and I can feel Leggett surveying my back, casting a shadow between my shoulders. I miss a semi-tough shot on the ⑪ ball. Pozek slaps the rail of the table. Buckner nails me with his brown eyes, which always go darker around the edge when there's a Boatswain or anyone else close by who might call his number. Buckner looks at me and shrugs, turning away to the bar to get a refill for his beer. Yeah, his eyes say, Randall sucks at pool and everything else outside the system. What else is new?

I spend a little time—like three seconds—trying to frame up why Buckner might have it in for me, then I drop it. We all have our moods.

Then something about the satisfied way Pozek is chewing his bottom lip takes me back to recruit training at Cape May. My Company Commander never made a face like that; CC was never satisfied. But there was a girl in my company—name was Yancy Treet from some pothole town near St. Louis—who practiced twisting her brown mouth that way. She was in the Guard to get a government job and keep it. Don't waste your blood heat on a paycheck. Don't pretend. Yancy liked to tell me how she was going to wait out all the bullshit boat procedure, how soon she'd be behind a desk forever. Snacking on her busy lip. Last I heard she was a seaman on the *Mohawk* down in the Florida Keys, collecting Haitians from Lincoln Log rafts and sailing them away from fenced-in America.

We finished up our game when Buckner sank two cracking bank shots on the ② and the ⑤. Leggett left before that. As he hit the door he told me he'd see me whenever. His mouth was as straight as a ruler, and his left hand cupped the knobby bone above his fresh-shaved neck, a thing it always did when he was thinking hard. He was making the effort, I could see that. But it was still true he was fighting to keep things even between us. I'd noticed it for a couple of weeks, ever since I spliced a moor line on a drill and turned to see him memorizing me. It was like an uncorked smell in the air, rank and sweet at the same time. Temptation. We both recognized it. And being old hands, we knew better than to do anything about it.

I was driving and Buckner asked me to stop at the store so he could get cigarettes, which I did. Pozek went with him just to wander the aisles and flirt with the high schooler pecking at the cash register. A few of our guys play up the sailors-in-a-port attitude, acting like their haircuts and wrapped-in-plastic dress uniforms mean something. But we aren't navy. That gets drilled into our heads in boot camp and beyond. For us, there isn't ever any shore leave, not like the swabbies have it. Maybe at the air stations, yeah, where we have pilots and jumpsuit officers, but not in these tiny harbor towns. *Semper paratus*. You don't shit in your own nest. If Buckner and Pozek wanted to screw around, they'd be smart to go way up the beach to Nags Head to do it.

Me, I liked to go even further. When I had the chance.

So we got to the station without much talking, though Buckner, at least, seemed to think he'd checked something off his list by including me in the game. The way he said good night dropped him just short of being a full-bird asshole. I went to the prefab I had all to myself, finished unpacking, sat on my bunk for a while trying to decide which manuals I was most likely to read. At 2200 the klaxon rang for the Motor Lifeboat crew to respond to a foundering cabin cruiser a mile southeast of the inlet. The call went well. We were able to bail the cruiser with the portable pump before we escorted her in. I was asleep fifteen minutes after I went off watch.

We'd served most of our stint before the bad thing happened. It was early spring, the days were clearing off in twos and threes, but we'd seen gale-force winds a couple of times, taken ten to twelve calls. This is why I can say our crew was good. We'd handled some tricky stuff, including a night tow of a ketch through Teach's Hole. We weren't cocky. That's not a feeling any of us believed we could afford. But we knew how to make certain kinds of decisions together. So it's hard, even now, to bring it all into focus. Parts are as clear as can be. I can run them like high-resolution video behind my eyes again and again, even though visibility was poor near the end because of the darkness and the storm. I've got stark mental snapshots

143

I have to live with. What I don't have is enough peace or logic. If there are such things.

Sammy Walker was standing watch when the call got relayed. An inshore charter scooting down the sound with the tide, out late like they sometimes are if they want to catch mullet for bait, spots what looks like an empty skiff banging off the lee side of a dredge island southeast of Howard Reef. The captain calls it in. He can't get close enough to see much. The sandbars there are crazy, especially at ebb tide. Plus, the wind is kicking pretty good, he's got it at twenty or twenty-five knots out of the north. He thinks we ought to take a look. Sammy gets a position, asks if the captain sees any other craft in the area, but the captain gives a negative on that. Sammy rings in Leggett, shows him the chart that puts the skiff's position close to the northern border of our AOR. Leggett orders up a crew for the Rigid Hull Inflatable, the position is way too shallow for the Motor Lifeboat. That's when we got our bell. Three minutes after the call. Three more minutes and we've suited up and cast off, leaving Burgoyne, Toshiko, and Walker to man the fort.

Some good news, some not so good. We had fifteen or twenty minutes of daylight left, mostly because the weather was clear to the west and we were catching a lot of reflected sun off a hanging cloud bank. But the barometer was dropping, and that northern wind was as fresh as the charter captain said. We took it full in the face as soon as we changed course out of Big Foot Slough Channel. Sammy radioed us with two bits of information. One was that Station Hatteras had been called out on a possible Gulf Stream collision and the air station at Elizabeth City was pitching in on that, so everybody was tied up. We might not be able to snag a 'copter if we decided to look for floaters. Second was the report of a squall headed right down the coast, hard rain, winds over forty knots. None of it bothered Leggett, who was at the wheel as our cox. What bothered him was how the tide was running with the wind, which meant a man overboard, if that's what we had, would be damn hard to find in the dark.

We rode in silence, catching plenty of stinging spray off the bow, each thinking our own thoughts. Buckner loved Search-and-Rescue as much as I did. Seated portside in his dry suit, helmet, and vest, he was dog alert, nose in the air. Both hands were fisted together between his knees. I was stationed as lookout just off the starboard bow, my fingers clove-hitched in anticipation. Pozek was in the stern, close enough to Leggett to hear him without shouting.

I thought about the possibilities, arranging my ideas in checklists and columns as I imagined Leggett, or any good Boatswain, would. I didn't think about how well Leggett wanted me to perform on calls, how that seemed to vent his steam some, seeing me do well. I dodged that thought as I had before. I figured a tourist wouldn't be out in a skiff this early in the year; I wanted to think the person or persons connected were natives smart enough to wear life jackets and have good habits. An old hand working his crab pots. Or laying nets for mullet. Though most of the locals got off the water for their suppers when they could. Engine trouble, maybe. There ought to be oars aboard, however, unless the operator was a fool. Truth be told, I didn't like my tally. Either the skiff had been abandoned and some lazy bastard had failed to notify us like he was supposed to, or the occupant was in the water, maybe hurt, maybe not.

We passed our first cluster of dredge isles as last light drained away. Because the Banks are so unstable, summer dredges have to suck sand from the channels and spit it into piles to keep things passable. And we weren't into summer yet. There were sandbars scattered like thrown rice on the backside of Ocracoke. Leggett knew the subsurface well, though. We'd run it enough in recent days. And he was counting on me to keep my eyes peeled in the bow. He throttled back the diesel when he had to, waiting for my read on the chop.

We sighted the charter boat who'd made the call at 2007. Without a dinghy aboard, she'd been able to do little but stand by with her lights ablaze. Leggett swung us to starboard, then idled the engine about a hundred feet off her stern. Instructions from Sammy put the skiff near a steep bank of dredged sand, maybe three hundred yards east. Pozek stood spread-legged beside our Boatswain and aimed a light. Sure enough, she was there. Low in the water and white as hot metal in our beam. Buckner, who had binoculars, shouted off her registration, what little he could see with her gunwales so low. Leggett called it in as he gave us enough throttle to counter the pulling tide. He also radioed the charter captain to ask if he'd seen or heard anything. He hadn't.

The idea was to slide in above the skiff and secure her first. The RHI is plenty maneuverable, especially in good hands, but there was still a chance one or two of us would have to go into the water. The charts showed depths of one to four feet, but we all knew how to be skeptical about the charts, especially after a hard winter. If the skiff wasn't anchored, we'd need to steady her for a search, then proceed from there.

Buckner saw the bow line when I did, a tight thread dropping straight off the prow, and we both agreed the skiff might be anchored fore and aft, which would account for her being swamped in the chop. Leggett ordered out the tow line and bridle anyway. I got them ready. He put the diesel in neutral, gave me the order to hail and go board as we came alongside. Pozek was still bleaching everything with his light. We caught some rogue swells coming in, however, and that caused our first bit of trouble.

Buckner was supposed to grab the craft midship and make fast a line while I boarded. And that's what he started to do. But he heard something, he said later, something animal and pained. We clipped the skiff pretty hard making our approach in the swells. Maybe that was Leggett's mistake. But he didn't know what we had out there, none of us did. And the rain had started to come at us in needles. What we'd done was knock the kid loose from the starboard side of the skiff.

I was in the swamped craft, about to run my regs. Check for onboard survivors. Check anchor lines. Check fuel leaks. But Buckner came aboard right behind me and was out again, overboard in at least five feet of rough water before I could turn and cuss him out. He claimed he shouted before he went in, but I don't remember that. What I remember is Pozek's huge white moon of a light and how it shielded me from the dark spar of Leggett as Buckner busted procedure and took matters into his own hands.

The asshole went in without orders or a line. He figured it was shallow enough and he said he could actually breathe that kid's fear, it rushed into his lungs and head before he even processed it. Like a grab for a falling baby, he told me later. He shouted to Leggett, *Man in, Man in.* He did do that when he surfaced, and we knew right away we had more than a floater. But I had to tie off the lines Buckner had neglected first. I had to. Meanwhile, Leggett ordered Pozek off the light and into the skiff with me, life buoy in hand. This was good crew. Buckner left a blank, Pozek filled it. I didn't have time to look at Pozek's face, what little was visible beneath his helmet, but I didn't have to see his full black eyes to know he was still calm, still greased and ready.

Unlike Buckner. He was so damn sure his strong body could fix this one. He pushed the prow of the skiff backward—I felt the

146

shove—then went under for the kid. No lights, the kid was struggling to grab the skiff, weighed down by the damn waders put on to check nets, unable to get out of the waders because an ankle was wedged—and broken—in the rusty, shitty mass of rebar that made up the guts of the dredge island. The same rebar that had fouled the kid's nets in the first place. Buckner got the kid up for air, shouting for assistance, saying the kid was trapped, cut the nets, cut the nets. He thought the kid was wrapped up that way. I went in on Leggett's order, clear of Buckner and his armful of thrashing. Pulled my light. Spit out a high, cold slap of surf. My eyes burned with the first rinse of salt, but I saw Buckner's wide mouth moving under the orange cup of his helmet, repeating something soft and calm I couldn't hear. The kid was still alert enough to cough some. I saw that, too. Then came another rank of swells, God damn Pozek and Leggett for not seeing they needed to clear off. The water surged in over us and brought the skiff right at Buckner's head.

He took the kid down. Heave to, I screamed, back off. Leggett saw my waving arms and hauled the diesel into reverse, gave me as much room as the skiff's anchor lines would allow. Now that I was in the water, I could feel how bad and strange it was to be caught in the yanking backwash. The surf was hammering. My feet searched for purchase on the chunked concrete. I could touch bottom every few seconds but it didn't last. It took Pozek too long to realize he had to cut the skiff's lines and get the damn thing out of there. Too long. Holding the useless life buoy in position, he seemed to want the order relayed through Leggett, who was fighting the wheel, as though he couldn't hear the words any other way. I had to tell him twice. I went under with my light until I could see the huddled shape that made up Buckner and the kid. He was waiting until he was sure it was safe. When the skiff was finally towed free, I signaled Buckner with my light. He powered up with the kid wrapped in his arms. God damn, Randall, he shouted between gulps of air. You gotta cut this kid free.

But it wasn't the nets. I went down and found the foot clamped between iron and rock. Cut away some mesh, I did that. Cut away the waders. Living all the time in the single-tone roar of the under-sea. No go, I told Buckner, no go. All gasping and spit. Let me re-lieve. We were doing it on our own now, together, caged by rain and waves, Buckner squeezing water out of the kid's lungs, or trying to, me diving less than five feet, not able to shift the rebar, taking the kid

147

from Buckner's rimrock arms, the transfer gentle even with the froth and breakers. That's a snapshot I have: spikes of black hair around a child's white face. We all look more like children when we're that soaked and cold. I worked that kid. Floated her, kept her head up, kissed her with mouth-to-mouth, wiped the vomit. I felt what Buckner hadn't felt, the berry breasts under my clamping forearm. Not that it mattered. Buckner tried like hell to rip her free. I'm gonna cut him, he said, shooting up for air. Tell me to cut his ankle, Randall, it's our only chance. His eyes were round and glazed like they get when we run through our adrenaline into the sledge of exhaustion. He was gagging salt water but didn't seem to know it. Another shot I have: savage, demanding Buckner. Leggett was thirty yards away, bucking the RHI in the surf. But Buckner wasn't looking for orders, he was looking for a way. No, I said. You get the tow line from Leggett and you pull that rebar free. We'll all pull. Now.

We were so different. That fact took hold like a death grip right then, and it nearly stopped us both. I was the best one on the crew for him to work with—he knew it, he damn well did—but it made Trey Buckner hate me. I was the one who reeled his crazy, muscled self in, and he never hated me more than then. The hate welded a new color into his full-flushed eyes. I hated him, too. He'd fucked procedure from the word go. But it was a good hate, hot and furious in that night water, and it gave us what we needed to try and save that kid.

Leggett was trying to keep the inflatable from being beaten ashore, trying to sort out what was happening in the water. Buckner stroked out and signed to Pozek for the gear. It was a long shot. The RHI might not have enough power, especially running against the current. But it was a chance. Burgoyne babied that engine. I was sure I could feel the kid shiver against me while I held her, I believed that. It wasn't too late. Buckner rigged the line right beneath us, then gave Pozek the thumb. I did what I had to do, cradled that girl against a pillow of concrete so I could shield her from the waves. Buckner dove to rip at the rebar with his hands. He was frantic now, though I only knew that from the sandpapering of his breath. He no longer yelled or wasted motion.

Tore the kid free, that's what he did. Somebody later told me the whole operation took a little over fifteen minutes. It's a slo-mo distortion I don't need to relive. The inside of the kid's foot was peeled out of its skin, half of Buckner's fingers, even with gloves, were no better.

It didn't matter. We couldn't revive her. Not with Pozek and Leggett working fresh. Not with the airlift thirty minutes later. We broke her ribs, her sternum, never got her back. Sixteen years old from a long-time island family, she'd gone to pull nets for an ailing grandfather. Not the first drowning they'd suffered, I was told. Probably not the last.

For me, either. Or any of us. I'd pulled floaters before, but I'd never lost a live one. I thought I knew enough not to let her haunt me. Part of this job demands coping with being too late. I think of frost-faced Yancy Treet when I think of that. Then there are the mistakes. Did you make them? Can you admit them? Do you blame a man—or a woman–for not acting the way you think you might? Do you *want* them to act the same? Buckner tortured himself over that girl's death, claimed he knew her from the ice-cream shop or some place like that even though we knew it wasn't true. He believed what he wanted to believe. That we could have done it. I'm not so sure. You don't get to pick your weather out here, and you don't get fair chances. *Always ready*. That's our responsibility, and it's the only responsibility I'll ever swear by, in the Coast Guard or out. You don't get to find your luck in this life. You have to be prepared for anything, including the worst.

Leggett kept us together for the next few days. That was his job, and he did it. He gave us no time to think or brood. The calls kept coming. We kept responding. *Semper, semper.* A small yacht ran aground because the skipper was drunk and stupid. A trawler out of Wanchese was reported overdue. A ferry had engine trouble. The Hyde County Sheriff passed on a tip about marijuana being smuggled through the harbor by some sailboat yuppies. I worked the girl's loss out of my system like soreness out of my muscles. I made it a physical matter. Things went blank between me and Leggett, though. He wide-eyed me, but it wasn't the same. It was like the failure with the girl—which we didn't talk about except officially—and the forgiveness—which we somehow owed each other—froze all channels between us. He didn't write Buckner up for jumping the gun, that may have been a scrap thrown my way. I don't know. It was a while before we could pass each other in the hallways or on the docks like normal people, no shuttered faces, no stops and starts, and then it was all right. The scent trail was gone.

Pozek was another matter. He went big-sister pissed at Buckner, rabbit-punching him with fake newspaper headlines to make him mad. *Selfless Rescue Swimmer Fails. USCG Witness to Teen Drowning*. But Pozek had nothing to say to me. He knew he should have reacted faster when he was on the skiff, but he couldn't be sure his screwup had made any difference. Instead of running the scenario over and over in his head, sanding it down to livable, he tried to scrape his way into Buckner's thick hide, which was the exact wrong place to be.

With me and Buckner it was more complicated. We developed a thundercloud survivor's bond, all gloom and hovering. He still called me Randall, and it wasn't a friendship in any way. Not one. It wasn't a sex thing either though we had to try that, with Buckner's stiff, scabbed hands, to know it. We didn't shoot pool anymore and had only one halfway regular conversation over warm coffee and that was mostly about his growing up in South Carolina with a son-of-a-bitch dad and how he was no longer in touch with any of his brothers. What we had between us was the dirty fact we fit together when things were dire and messed up. And only then. I could see how he wanted another dose of it, Buckner did. But not by talking about what happened or about that girl, Karla Wahab. I'll bet he didn't mouth the syllables of her name more than once, even when he was cutting himself up about her death. What he wanted was more rage and swimming. A merciless heart pounding harder than the merciless surf. Risk. Blind rescue. I'd been there with him, and he knew I wanted it, too.

I meant to tell Pozek that what we'd been through wasn't worth it. Even after he lay down hints about my body like he was some kind of jealous when all Buckner and I had gained was one fuck and coping. Who wants deafness and loss of speech, the inability to communicate with anything except a sea you can't change? Except telling Pozek that would have been a lie. I thought of those castaway moments when I polished brass in the stale, mosquitoed harbor. I'd riptide into daydreams about them, surrounded by men as I was. Buckner and I truly could not bear each other, not in orgasm or chore, but we had found the pitiless, unwinnable world we all imagine. All know. And it was, in ways I didn't yet understand, the world we'd clearly trained for.

Nominated by Graywolf Press, David Romtvedt

KINDS OF SLEEP

by KEVIN PRUFER

from THE SYCAMORE REVIEW

THERE IS THE SLEEP of the plastic soldier and it is olive green and terrible on the windowsill where the sun speckles the dust so, like mortar, it hangs in the air

and there is the sleep of the window, which is clear and cool to the touch.

I love the dream of the yard beyond the window, which is at peace, how the sun swags over the trees like a little gold watch suspended from a chain, the hypnotist saying, *sleep, sleep. I will count to three.*

My daughter lines plastic soldiers on the windowsill. This is a serious game, picking one soldier after another from a coffee can.

I have never been to war, though I often dream about a battle in Super8, where extras pose on a ridge while the night air trills and the mortar falls like a hot glass net.

Always, the mind goes back to a story about angels rising from the trees. First there was a fluttering in the leaves above the war, then they spread their golden wings

over the bodies of the retreating. This is the myth, dreamed in grainy black & white, the camera shaking while the soldiers slipped on the ice, slipped and fell but—gratefully, gratefully—made it over the hill and back to their tents where the director yelled *cut* and the extras smiled and collected their checks.

I fear most the sleep of the dead, strewn like spent cartridges where the guns eject them.

Nominated by Lucia Perillo

THE SECRETS OF BATS

fiction by JESS ROW

from PLOUGHSHARES

ALICE LEUNG has discovered the secrets of bats: how they see without seeing, how they own darkness, as we own light. She walks the halls with a black headband across her eyes, keening a high C—*cheat cheat cheat cheat cheat cheat*—never once veering off course, as if drawn by an invisible thread. Echolocation, she tells me, it's not as difficult as you might think. Now she sees a light around objects when she looks at them, like halos on her retinas from staring at the sun. In her journal she writes, *I had a dream that was all in blackness. Tell me how to describe.*

It is January: my fifth month in Hong Kong.

In the margin I write, *I wish I knew.*

After six, when the custodians leave, the school becomes a perfect acoustic chamber; she wanders from the basement laboratories to the basketball courts like a trapped bird looking for a window. She finds my door completely blind, she says, not counting flights or paces. Twisting her head from side to side like Stevie Wonder, she announces her progress: another room mapped, a door, a desk, a globe, detected and identified by its aura.

You'll hurt yourself, I tell her. I've had nightmares: her foot missing the edge of a step, the dry crack of a leg breaking. Try it without the blindfold, I say. That way you can check yourself.

Her mouth wrinkles. This not important, she says. This only practice.

Practice for what, I want to ask. All the more reason you have to be careful.

153

You keep saying, she says, grabbing a piece of chalk. E-x-p-e-r-i-m-e-n-t, she writes on the blackboard, digging it in until it squeals.

That's right. Sometimes experiments fail.

Sometimes, she repeats. She eyes me suspiciously, as if I invented the word.

Go home, I tell her. She turns her pager off and leaves it in her locker; sometimes police appear at the school gate, shouting her name. Somebody, it seems, wants her back.

In the doorway she whirls, flipping her hair out of her eyes. Ten days more, she says. You listen. Maybe then you see why.

The name of the school is Po Sing Uk: a five-story concrete block, cracked and eroded by dirty rain, shoulder-to-shoulder with the tenements and garment factories of Cheung Sha Wan. No air conditioning and no heat; in September I shouted to be heard over a giant fan, and now, in January, I teach in a winter jacket. When it rains, mildew spiderwebs across the ceiling of my classroom. Schoolgirls in white jumpers crowd into the room forty at a time, falling asleep over their textbooks, making furtive calls on mobile phones, scribbling notes to each other on pink Hello Kitty paper. If I call on one who hasn't raised her hand, she folds her arms across her chest and stares at the floor, and the room falls silent, as if by a secret signal. There is nothing more terrifying, I've found, than the echo of your own voice: *Who are you?* it answers. *What are you doing here?*

I've come to see my life as a radiating circle of improbabilities that grow from each other, like ripples in water around a dropped stone. That I became a high school English teacher, that I work in another country, that I live in Hong Kong. That a city can be a mirage, hovering above the ground: skycrapers built on mountainsides, islands swallowed in fog for days. That a language can have no tenses or articles, with seven different ways of saying the same syllable. That my best student stares at the blackboard only when I erase it.

She stayed behind on the first day of class: a tall girl with a narrow face, pinched around the mouth, her cheeks pitted with acne scars. Like most of my sixteen-year-olds she looked twelve, in a baggy uniform that hung to her knees like a sack. The others streamed past her

154

without looking up, as if she were a boulder in the current; she stared down at my desk with a fierce vacancy, as if looking itself was an act of will.

How do you think about bats?

Bats?

She joined her hands at the wrist and fluttered them at me.

People are afraid of them, I said. I think they're very interesting.

Why? she said. Why very interesting?

Because they live in the dark, I said. We think of them as being blind, but they aren't blind. They have a way of seeing, with sound waves—just like we see with light.

Yes, she said. I know this. Her body swayed slightly, in an imaginary breeze.

Are you interested in bats?

I am interest, she said. I want to know how—she made a face I'd already come to recognize: *I know how to say it in Chinese*—when one bat sees the other. The feeling.

You mean how one bat recognizes another?

Yes—recognize.

That's a good idea, I said. You can keep a journal about what you find. Write something in it every day.

She nodded vehemently, as if she'd already thought of that.

There are books on bat behavior that will tell you—

Not in books. She covered her eyes with one hand and walked forward until her hip brushed the side of my desk, then turned away, at a right angle. Like this, she said. There is a sound, she said. I want to find the sound.

18 September

First hit tuning fork. Sing one octave higher: A B C. This is best way.

Drink water or lips get dry.

I must have eyes totally closed. No light!!! So some kind of black—like cloth—is good.

Start singing. First to the closest wall—sing and listen. Practice ten times, 20 times. IMPORTANT: can not move until I HEAR the wall. Take step back, one time, two time.

155

Listen again. I have to hear DIFFERENCE first, then move.

Then take turn, ninety degrees left.

Then turn, one hundred eighty degrees left. Feel position with feet. Feet very important—they are wings!!!

I don't know what this is, I told her the next day, opening the journal and pushing it across the desk. Can you help me?

I tell you already, she said. She hunched her shoulders so that her head seemed to rest on them, spreading her elbows to either side. It is like a test.

A test?

In the courtyard rain crackled against the asphalt; a warm wind lifted scraps of paper from the desk, somersaulting them through the air.

The sound, she said, impatiently. I told you this.

I covered my mouth to hide a smile.

Alice, I said, humans can't do that. It isn't a learned behavior. It's something you study.

She pushed up the cover of the composition book and let it fall.

I think I can help you, I said. Can you tell me why you want to write this?

Why I want? She stared at me wide-eyed.

Why do you want to do this? What is the test for?

Her eyes lifted from my face to the blackboard behind me, moved to the right, then the left, as if measuring the dimensions of the room.

Why you want to come to Hong Kong?

Many reasons, I said. After college I wanted to go to another country, and there was a special fellowship available here. And maybe someday I will be a teacher.

You are teacher.

I'm just learning, I said. I am trying to be one.

Then why you have to leave America?

I don't, I said. The two things— I took off my glasses and rubbed my eyes. All at once I was exhausted; the effort seemed useless; a pointless evasion. When I looked up she was nodding, slowly, as if I'd just said something profound.

I think I will find the reason for being here only after some time, I said. Do you know what I mean? There could be a purpose I don't know about.

So you don't know for good. Not sure.

You could say that.

Hai yat yeung, she said. This same. Maybe if you read you can tell me why.

This is what's so strange about her, I thought, studying her red-rimmed eyes, the tiny veins standing out like wires on a circuit board. She doesn't look down. I am fascinated by her, I thought. Is that fair?

You're different than the others, I said. You're not afraid of me. Why is that?

Maybe I have other things be afraid of.

At first the fifth-floor bathroom was her echo chamber; she sat in one corner, on a stool taken from the physics room, and placed an object directly opposite her: a basketball, a glass, a feather. Sound waves triangulate, she told me, corners are best. Passing by, at the end of the day, I stopped, closing my eyes, and listened for the difference. She sang without stopping for five minutes, hardly taking a breath: almost a mechanical sound, as if someone had forgotten their mobile phone. Other teachers walked by in groups, talking loudly. If they noticed me, or the sound, I was never aware of it, but always, instinctively, I looked at my watch and followed them down the stairs. As if I, too, had to rush home to cook for hungry children, or boil medicine for my mother-in-law. I never stayed long enough to see if anything changed.

Document everything, I told her, and she did; now I have two binders of entries, forty-one in all. *Hallway. Chair. Notebook.* As if we were scientists writing a grant proposal, as if there was something actual to show at the end of it.

I don't keep a journal, or take photographs, and my letters home are factual and sparse. No one in Larchmont would believe me—not even my parents—if I told them the truth. *It sounds like quite an experience you're having! Don't get run over by a rickshaw.* And yet if I died tomorrow—why should I ever think this way?—these binders would be the record of my days. Those and Alice herself, who looks out of her window and with her eyes closed sees ships passing in the harbor, men walking silently in the streets.

157

26 January

Sound of lightbulb—low like bees hum. So hard to listen!

A week ago I dreamed of bodies breaking apart, arms and legs and torsos, fragments of bone, bits of tissue. I woke up flailing in the sheets, and remembered her, immediately; there was too long a moment before I believed I was awake. *It has to stop,* I thought, *you have to say something.* Though I know that I can't.

Perhaps there was a time when I might have told her, *This is ridiculous,* or, *You're sixteen, find some friends. What will people think?* But this is Hong Kong, of course, and I have no friends, no basis to judge. I leave the door open, always, and no one ever comes to check; we walk out of the gates together, late in the afternoon, past the watchman sleeping in his chair. For me she has a kind of professional courtesy, ignoring my whiteness politely, as if I had horns growing from my head. And she returns, at the end of each day, as a bat flies back to its cave at daybreak. All I have is time; who am I to pack my briefcase and turn away?

There was only once when I slipped up.

Pretend I've forgotten, I told her, one Monday in early October. The journal was open in front of us, the pages covered in red; she squinted down at it, as if instead of corrections I'd written hieroglyphics. I'm an English teacher, I thought, this is what I'm here for. We should start again at the beginning, I said. Tell me what it is that you want to do here. You don't have to tell me about the project— just about the writing. Who are you writing these for? Who do you want to read them?

She stretched, catlike, curling her fingers like claws.

Because I don't think I understand, I said. I think you might want to find another teacher to help you. There could be something you have in mind in Chinese that doesn't come across.

Not in Chinese, she said, as if I should have known that already. In Chinese cannot say like this.

But it isn't really English, either.

I know this. It is like both.

I can't teach that way, I said. You have to learn the rules before you can—

You are not teaching me.

Then what's the point?

She strode across the room to the window and leaned out, placing her hands on the sill and bending at the waist. Come here, she said, look. I stood up and walked over to her.

She ducked her head down, like a gymnast on a bar, and tilted forward, her feet lifting off the floor.

Alice!

I grabbed her shoulder and jerked her upright. She stumbled, falling back; I caught her wrist, and she pulled it away, steadying herself. We stood there a moment staring at each other, breathing in short huffs that echoed in the hallway.

Maybe I hear something and forget, she said. You catch me then. Okay?

28 January

It is like photo negative, all the colors are the opposite.
Black sky, white trees, this way. But they are still shapes—
I can see them.

I read standing at the window, in a last sliver of sunlight. Alice stands on my desk, already well in shadow, turning around slowly as if trying to dizzy herself for a party game. Her winter uniform cardigan is three sizes too large; unopened, it falls behind her like a cape.

This is beautiful.

Quiet, she hisses, eyebrows bunched together above her headband. One second. There—there.

What is it?

A man on the stairs.

I go out into the hallway and stand at the top of the stairwell, listening. Five floors below, very faintly, I hear sandals skidding on the concrete, keys jangling on the janitor's ring.

You heard him open the gate, I say. That's cheating.

She shakes her head. I hear heartbeat.

The next Monday, Principal Ho comes to see me during the lunch hour. He stands at the opposite end of the classroom, as always: a tall, slightly chubby man, in a tailored shirt, gold-rimmed glasses, and Italian shoes, who blinks as he reads the ESL posters I've tacked up on the wall. When he asks how my classes are, and I tell him that the girls are unmotivated, disengaged, he nods, quickly, as if to save me the embarrassment. How lucky he was, he tells me, to go to boarding school in Australia, and then pronounces it with a flattened *a*, *Aus-trahlia*, so I have to laugh.

Principal Ho, I ask, do you know Alice Leung?

He turns his head toward me and blinks more rapidly. Leung Ka Yee, he says. Of course. You have problem with her?

No sir. I need something to hold; my hands dart across the desk behind me and find my red marking pen.

How does she perform?

She's very gifted. One of the best students in the class. Very creative.

He nods, scratches his nose, and turns away.

She likes to work alone, I say. The other girls don't pay much attention to her. I don't think she has many friends.

It is very difficult for her, he says, slowly, measuring every word. Her mother is—her mother was a suicide.

In the courtyard, five stories down, someone drops a basketball and lets it bounce against the pavement; little *pings* that trill and fade into the infinite.

In Yau Ma Tei, Ho says. He makes a little gliding motion with his hand. Nowadays this is not so uncommon in Hong Kong. But still there are superstitions.

What kind of superstitions?

He frowns and shakes his head. Difficult to say in English. Maybe just that she is unlucky girl. Chinese people, you understand—some are still afraid of ghosts.

She isn't a ghost.

He gives a high-pitched, nervous laugh. No, no, he says. Not her. He puts his hands into his pockets, searching for something. Difficult to explain. I'm sorry.

Is there someone she can talk to?

He raises his eyebrows. *A counselor*, I am about to say, and explain what it means, when my hand relaxes, and I realize I have been crushing the pen in my palm. For a moment I am water-skiing again at Lake Patchogue: releasing the handle, settling against the surface, enfolded in water. When I look up, Ho glances at his watch.

If you have any problem you can talk to me.

It's nothing, I say. Just curious, that's all.

✿

160

She wears the headband all the time now, I've noticed: pulling it over her eyes whenever possible, in the halls between classes, in the courtyard at lunchtime, sitting by herself. No one shoves her or calls her names; she passes through the crowds unseen. If possible, I think, she's grown thinner, her skin translucent, blue veins showing at the wrists. Occasionally I notice the other teachers shadowing her, frowning, their arms crossed, but if our eyes meet they stare through me, disinterested, and look away.

I have to talk to you about something.

She is sitting in a desk at the far end of the room, reading her chemistry textbook, drinking from a can of soymilk with a straw. When the straw gurgles she bangs the can down, and we sit, silently, the sound reverberating in the hallway.

I give you another journal soon. Two more days.

Not about that.

She doesn't move: fixed, alert, waiting. I stand up and move down the aisle toward her, sitting two desks away, and as I move her eyes grow slightly rounder and her cheeks puff out slightly, as if she's holding her breath.

Alice, I say, can you tell me about your mother?

Her hands fall down on the desk, and the can clatters to the floor, white drops spinning in the air.

Mother? Who tell you I have mother?

It's all right—

I reach over to touch one hand, and she snatches it back.

Who tell you?

It doesn't matter. You don't have to be angry.

You big mistake, she says, wild-eyed, taking long swallows of air and spitting them out. Why you have to come here and mess everything?

I don't understand, I say. Alice, what did I do?

I trust you, she says, and pushes the heel of one palm against her cheek. I write and you read. I *trust* you.

What did you expect? I ask, my jaw trembling. Did you think I would never know?

Believe me. She looks at me pleadingly. Believe *me*.

Two days later she leaves her notebook on my desk, with a note stuck to the top. *You keep.*

1 February

Now I am finished
It is out there I hear it

I call out to her after class, and she hesitates in the doorway for a moment before turning, pushing her back against the wall.

Tell me what it was like, I say. Was it a voice? Did you hear someone speaking?

Of course no voice. Not so close to me. It was a feeling.

How did it feel?

She reaches up and slides the headband over her eyes.

It is all finish, she says. You not worry about me anymore.

Too late, I say. I stand up from my chair and take a tentative step toward her: weak-kneed, as if it were a staircase in the dark. You chose me, I say. Remember?

Go back to America. Then you forget all about this crazy girl.

This is my life, too. Did you forget about that?

She raises her head and listens, and I know what she hears: a stranger's voice, as surely as if someone else had entered the room. She nods. *Who do you see?* I wonder. *What will he do next?* I reach out, blindly, and my hand misses the door; on the second try I close it.

I choose this, I say. I'm waiting. Tell me.

Her body sinks into a crouch; she hugs her knees and tilts her head back.

Warm. It was warm. It was—it was a body.

But not close to you?

Not close. Only little feeling, then no more.

Did it know you were there?

No.

How can you be sure?

When I look up to repeat the question, shiny tracks of tears have run out from under the blindfold.

I am sorry, she says. She reaches into her backpack and splits open a packet of tissues without looking down, her fingers nimble, almost autonomous. You are my good friend, she says, and takes off the blindfold, turning her face to the side and dabbing her eyes. Thank you for help me.

It isn't over, I say. How can it be over?

162

Like you say. Sometimes experiment fails.

No, I say, too loudly, startling us both. It isn't that easy. You have to prove it to me.

Prove it you?

Show me how it works. I take a deep breath. I believe you. Will you catch me?

Her eyes widen, and she does not look away; the world swims around her irises. Tonight, she says, and writes something on a slip of paper, not looking down. I see you then.

In a week it will be the New Year: all along the streets the shop fronts are hung with firecrackers, red-and-gold character scrolls, pictures of grinning cats, and the twin cherubs of good luck. Mothers lead little boys dressed in red silk pajamas, girls with New Year's pigtails. The old woman sitting next to me on the bus is busily stuffing twenty-dollar bills into red *lai see* packets: lucky money for the year to come. When I turn my head from the window, she holds one out to me, and I take it with both hands, automatically, bowing my head. This will make you rich, she says to me in Cantonese. And lots of children.

Thank you, I say. The same to you.

She laughs. Already happened. Jade bangles clink together as she holds up her fingers. Thirteen grandchildren! she says. Six boys. All fat and good-looking. You should say live long life to me.

I'm sorry. My Chinese is terrible.

No, it's very good, she says. You were born in Hong Kong?

Outside night is just falling, and Nathan Road has become a canyon of light: blazing neon signs, brilliant shop windows, decorations blinking across the fronts of half-finished tower blocks. I stare at myself a moment in the reflection, three red characters passing across my forehead, and look away. No, I say. In America. I've lived here only since August.

Ah. Then what is America like?

Forgive me, aunt, I say. I forget.

Prosperous Garden no. 4. Tung Kun Street. Yau Ma Tei.
A scribble of Chinese characters.
Show this to doorman he let you in.
The building is on the far edge of Kowloon, next to the reclamation; a low concrete barrier separates it from an elevated highway that thunders continuously as cars pass. Four identical towers around

163

a courtyard, long poles draped with laundry jutting from every window, like spears hung with old rotted flags.

Gong hei fat choi, I say to the doorman through the gate, and he smiles with crooked teeth, but when I pass the note to him all expression leaves his face; he presses the buzzer and turns away quickly. Twenty-three A-ah, he calls out to the opposite wall. You understand?

Thank you.

When I step out into the hallway I breathe in boiled chicken, oyster sauce, frying oil, the acrid steam of medicine, dried fish, Dettol. Two young boys are crouched at the far end, sending a radio-controlled car zipping past me; someone is arguing loudly over the telephone; a stereo plays loud Canto-pop from a balcony somewhere below. All the apartment doors are open, I notice, walking by, and only the heavy sliding gates in front of them are closed. Like a honeycomb, I can't help thinking, or an ant farm. But when I reach 23A the door behind the gate is shut, and no sound comes from behind it. The bell rings several times before the locks begin to snap open.

You are early, Alice says, rubbing her eyes, as if she's been sleeping. Behind her the apartment is dark; there is only a faint blue glow, as if from a TV screen.

I'm sorry. You didn't say when to come. I look at my watch: eight-thirty. I can come back, I say, another time, maybe another night—

She shakes her head and opens the gate.

When she turns on the light I draw a deep breath, involuntarily, and hide it with a cough. The walls are covered with stacks of yellowed paper, file boxes, brown envelopes, and ragged books; on opposite sides of the room are two desks, each holding a computer with a flickering screen. I peer at the one closest to the door. At the top of the screen there is a rotating globe and, below it, a ribbon of letters and numbers, always changing. The other, I see, is just the same: a head staring at its twin.

Come, Alice says. She has disappeared for a moment and reemerged, dressed in a long dress, silver running shoes, a hooded sweatshirt.

Are these yours?

No. My father's.

Why does he need two? They're just the same.

Nysee, she says, impatiently, pointing. Footsie. New York Stock Exchange. London Stock Exchange.

Sau Yee, a hoarse voice calls from another room. Who is it?

164

It's my English teacher, she says loudly. Giving me a homework assignment.

Gwailo a?

Yes, she says. The white one.

Then call a taxi for him. He appears in the kitchen doorway: a stooped old man, perhaps five feet tall, in a dirty white T-shirt, shorts, and sandals. His face is covered with liver spots; his eyes shrunken into their sockets. I sorry-ah, he says to me. No speakee English.

It's all right, I say. There is a numbness growing behind my eyes: I want to speak to him, but the words are all jumbled, and Alice's eyes burning on my neck. Goodbye, I say, take care.

See later-ah.

Alice pulls the hood over her head and opens the door.

She leads me to the top of a dark stairwell, in front of a rusting door with light pouring through its cracks. *Tin paang*, she says, reading the characters stenciled on it in white. Roof. She hands me a black headband, identical to her own.

Hold on, I say, gripping the railing with both hands. The numbness behind my eyes is still there, and I feel my knees growing weak, as if there were no building below me, only a framework of girders and air. Can you answer me a question?

Maybe one.

Has he always been like that?

What like?

With the computers, I say. Does he do that all the time?

Always. Never turn them off.

In the darkness I can barely see her face: only the eyes, shining, daring me to speak. *If I were in your place,* I say to myself, and the phrase dissolves, weightless.

Listen, I say. I'm not sure I'm ready.

She laughs. When you be sure?

Her fingers fall across my face, and I feel the elastic brushing over my hair, and then the world is black: I open my eyes and close them, no difference.

We just go for a little walk, she says. You don't worry. Only listen.

I never realized, before, the weight of the air: at every step I feel the great mass of it pressing against my face, saddled on my shoul-

165

ders. I am breathing huge quantities, as if my lungs were a giant re-circulation machine, and sweat is running down from my forehead and soaking the edge of the headband. Alice takes normal-sized steps, and grips my hand fiercely, so I can't let go. Don't be afraid, she shouts. We still in the middle. Not near the edge.

What am I supposed to do?

Nothing, she says. Only wait. Maybe you see something.

I stare, fiercely, into blackness, into my own eyelids. There is the afterglow of the hallway light, and the computer screens, very faint; or am I imagining it? What is there on a roof? I wonder, and try to picture it: television antennas, heating ducts, clotheslines. Are there guardrails? I've never seen any on a Hong Kong building. She turns, and I brush something metal with my hand. Do you know where you're going? I shout.

Here, she says, and stops. I stumble into her, and she catches my shoulder. Careful, she says. We wait here.

Wait for what?

Just listen, she says. I tell to you. Look to left side: there's a big building there. Very tall white building, higher than us. Small windows.

All right. I can see that.

Right side is highway. Very bright. Many cars and trucks passing.

If I strain to listen I can hear a steady whooshing sound, and then the high whine of a motorcycle, like a mosquito passing my ear. Okay, I say. Got that.

In the middle is very dark. Small buildings. Only few lights on.

Not enough, I say.

One window close to us, she says. Two little children there. You see them?

No.

Lift your arm, she says, and I do. Put your hand up. See? They wave to you.

My God, I say. How do you do that?

She squeezes my hand.

You promise me something.

Of course. What is it?

You don't take it off, she says. No matter nothing. You promise me?

I do. I promise.

166

She lets go of my hand, and I hear running steps, soles skidding on concrete.

Alice! I shout, rooted to the spot; I crouch down, and balance myself with my hands. Alice! You don't—

Mama, she screams, ten feet away, and the sound carries, echoes; I can see it slanting with the wind, bright as daylight, as if a roman candle had exploded in my face. *Mama mama mama mama mama mama mama*, she sings, and I am crawling towards her on hands and knees, feeling in front of me for the edge.

She is there, Alice shouts. You see? She is in the air.

I see her. Stay where you are.

You watch, she says. I follow her.

She doesn't want you, I shout. She doesn't want you there. Let her go.

There is a long silence, and I stay where I am, the damp concrete soaking through to my knees. My ears are ringing, and the numbness has blossomed through my head; I feel faintly seasick.

Alice?

You can stand up, she says, in a small voice, and I do.

You are shaking, she says. She puts her arms around me from behind and clasps my chest, pressing her head against my back. I thank you, she says.

She unties the headband.

6 February

Man waves white hands at black sky
He says arent you happy be alive
arent you
He kneels and kisses floor

Nominated by Ploughshares

A SHORT HISTORY
OF THE SHADOW

by CHARLES WRIGHT

from YALE REVIEW

Thanksgiving, dark of the moon.
Nothing down here in the underworld but vague shapes and black
   holes,
Heaven resplendent but virtual
Above me,
         trees stripped and triple-wired like Irish harps.
Lights on Pantops and Free Bridge mirror the eastern sky.
Under the bridge is the river,
               the red Rivanna.
Under the river's redemption, it says in the book,
It says in the book,
Through water and fire the whole place becomes purified,
The visible by the visible, the hidden by what is hidden.

Each word, as someone once wrote, contains the universe.
The visible carries all the invisible on its back.
Tonight, in the unconditional, what moves in the long-limbed
   grasses, what touches me
As though I didn't exist?
What is it that keeps on moving,
              a tiny pillar of smoke
Erect on its hind legs,
      loose in the hollow grasses?

168

A word I don't know yet, a little word, containing infinity,
Noiseless and unrepentent, in sift through the dry grass.
Under the tongue is the utterance.
Under the utterance is the fire, and then the only end of fire.

Only Dante, in Purgatory, casts a shadow,
L'ombra della carne, the shadow of flesh—
                                        everyone else *is* one.
The darkness that flows from the world's body, gloomy spot,
Pre-dogs our footsteps, and follow us,
                                        diaphanous bodies
Watching the nouns circle, and watching the verbs circle,
Till one of them enters the left ear and becomes a shadow
Itself, sweet word in the unwaxed ear.
This is a short history of the shadow, one part of us that's real.
This is the way the world looks
In late November,
            no leaves on the trees, no ledge to foil the lightfall.

No ledge in early December either, and no ice,
La Niña unhosing the heat pump
                            up from the Gulf,
Orange Crush sunset over the Blue Ridge,
No shadow from anything as evening gathers its objects
And eases into earshot.
Under the influx the outtake,
                        Leonbattista Alberti says,
Some lights are from stars, some from the sun
And moon, and other lights are from fires.
The light from the stars makes the shadow equal to the body.
Light from fire makes it greater,
            there, under the tongue, there, under the utterance.

Nominated by Yale Review, Linda Bierds, Arthur Smith, Bruce Beasley, Jim Barnes

HIPPIES

essay by DENIS JOHNSON

from THE PARIS REVIEW

It FELT LIKE the International had one last trip left in it. Two shocks had blown and the frame was cracked and quite a bit of the electrical system had gone dark. This thing's from 1970 and it's been a while since it went on a ride. But you could feel that last trip coming. And Joey said these people he knew from Austin intended to pick him up in Long Beach on their way to the Rainbow Gathering in the national forest over in north-central Oregon. The Gathering of the Tribes, it used to be called, tens of thousands of hippies in the woods, seven days of Peace and Love. Four hundred miles to over there where it is—a distance the International could surely make and even possibly manage to retrace back home. You could feel that one last trip coming.

Peace and Love! This tall skinny mean guy in Iowa City in the seventies had a poster on his wall of a peace sign, the upside-down Y symbolizing peace, which he'd altered with a Magic Marker into a lopsided swastika, and he'd added words so that the Peace and Love slogan beneath it read PEACE OF THE ACTION / LOVE OF MONEY. I never forgot it . . . I who have had so much of peace and so much of love, I have never really believed in either one.

•

The Magical Mystery Message to see the Rainbow was coming from a couple of directions, wasn't just coming from Joey and the teenage past. All spring Mike O, a friend of mine from north Idaho, had been bothering me I should go. Mike O, a regular Mr. Natural: Barefoot Mike, Underground Mike, one of the originals, close to sixty years old now; his white hair hasn't been cut or combed since youth and his white beard looks inhabited. How did we all get so old? Sitting around laughing at old people probably caused it.

•

How long since I'd seen Joey? We'd taken our first acid trip together, Carter B and him and me and Bobby Z. Hadn't seen Carter in nearly thirty years. Joey since—wow, since 1974. That summer of 1974 I was with Miss X. Bobby Z and Joey came to see us on the second floor where we lived in this place like a box of heat. They owed me a disruption—Joey did anyway, because Carter and I had invaded him two years before, when he'd been living on the side of this mountain in Hollywood and studying to be, or actually working as, some kind of hairdresser. "What do you want?" I said when I answered the door. "You're not gonna stay here." The place had only one room to sleep in, and a kitchen the size of a bathroom, a bathroom the size of a closet. There weren't any closets.

Miss X and I were always fighting. Every time a knock came on the door we had to stop screaming and collect our wits.

"We're economizing on space," I said when I saw who it was this time.

"Obviously," Bobby said.

Joey had his guitar case leaning up against him and his arm draped around it like a little sibling. Miss X stood behind me breathing hard with the mascara streaking her cheeks, radiant with tears and anger and her wet eyelashes like starbursts.

In short, three weeks or two weeks or one week later I made loud vague accusations in a scene, basically the result of the August heat, that ended with Bobby Z and Joey heading north for Minnesota, taking Miss X. I was stabbing through the windowscreen with a pair of scissors as they headed down the back stairs, and I didn't see Bobby again until he was sick on his deathbed five years ago in Virginia.

It's funny, but Joey called me from Huntington Beach just last night—two years after this trip to the hippies I'm describing—just to say hello, partly, and partly because his band broke up and he's just started AA and begun a program of meds for his depression and needs a place to lay back, because he's homeless. He mentioned he'd heard from Carter B. Carter said he's got hepatitis C and thinks I probably have it, too, because he must have picked it up way back during the era we were sharing needles when we were kids. I feel all

171

right. I don't feel sick. But it's funny. Thirty years go by, and the moves we made just keep bringing this old stuff rolling over us.

•

The International throws a tire down in the tri-city area of Hanford, Washington. It's so hot on the tarmac I get confused in my head and forget to put the nuts back on when I change the flat, and the loose rim tears up the wheel a good bit before I figure out what's happening and pull over, and I have to roll the thing in front of me a half mile to a garage and get the whole business straightened out. But the truck still works when all is said and done. After I'm in the mountains I start getting glad I agreed to go. Our vehicles, our hamlets and commerce miniaturized in the shadow of these mountains . . . RU FREE—Minnesota places on a VW bus in the one-street town of Mitchell not far from the beginning of the Ochoco National Forest. Five youngsters all around twenty years old and a dog, gassing up.

The eastern end of the Ochoco Forest seems quiet enough, a showcase for the public administration of nature, having narrow roads of unblemished blacktop with level campsites scattered sparsely alongside them. The Rainbow Gathering's website has provided a map leading out toward the wilder part of the mountain and down a dirt road toward a cloud of dust where hundreds of pickups and vans and tiny beat-up cars have parked at the direction of a bunch of wild-looking toothless young pirates under a plastic awning with a handheld radio and a dirty illegible flag. Even down here where people wait for the shuttle vans that take them up the mountain to the gathering or where they shoulder their frame backpacks and start up the hill on foot, all dressed up in the ashes of their most beautiful clothes, in their long skirts and tie-dyed shirts, just like the hippies of thirty years ago, even down here there's a feeling of anarchy third-world style, the pole and tarp lean-to, the people with shiny eyes, the lying around, the walking around, the sudden flaring madness, only this is celebratory and happy madness rather than angry or violent. The shuttle van climbs up past further checkpoints where serious authoritative hippies make sure nobody's just driving up out of laziness to park all over the mountain and get in each other's way. Past the first camp—the A Camp, the only place where alcohol is permitted, although this segregation has been accomplished voluntarily and nobody would think of enforcing it. Past other camps of

172

teepees, dome tents, shacks of twigs and plastic tarp to where the WELCOME HOME sign stands at the head of the footpath. The path heads into the series of clearings and copses where a whole lot of hippies (nobody can accurately count how many) have come to celebrate themselves, mostly, right now, by walking around and around, up and down the trails, past the kitchens set up under homemade awnings and canvas roofs, food centers staffed by those who want to give to those who need to take. Mike O has instructed me to equip myself with a big enamelware cup, a spoon and a sleeping bag—to come as a taker, and be confident I won't need more. No money changes hands here, at least that's the idea, everything is done by bartering. But I've brought a couple hundred dollars in my pocket because Joey and I might look for mushrooms and seek some sort of spiritual union together through exotic chemicals like in the old days, and I don't care what they say, I've never seen anybody trade dope for anything except sex or cash.

You hear wildly varying figures, eleven different guesses for every-thing—4,000 feet elevation, 6,700 elevation, 8,000 elevation. Claims of anywhere from 10,000–50,000, as far as attendance. But let's say 10,000 or more hippies touring along the paths here in the American wilderness just as we did up and down Telegraph Avenue in Berzerkeley almost thirty years ago. Yes! They're still at it!—still moving and searching, still probing along the avenues for quick friends and high times, weather-burned and dusty and gaunt, the older ones now in their fifties and a whole new batch in their teens and twenties, still with their backpacks, bare feet, tangled hair, their sophomoric phi-losophizing, their glittery eyes, their dogs named Bummer and Bandit and Roach and Kilo and Dark Star. And as they pass each other they say, "Loving you!"—Loving you! It serves for anything, greeting and parting and passing, like aloha, and might burst from a person at any time as if driven by a case of Tourette's, apropos of absolutely jack. Everybody keeps saying it.

Scattered over about one square mile of Indian Prairie in the Ochoco National Forest we have the pole-and-awning kitchens and camps of various tribes and families and impromptu more-or-less hobo clans: Elvis Kitchen. 12-Step Kitchen, Funky Granola, Avalon, Greenwich Village. The billboard map near the welcome entrance lists and vaguely locates the groups who wish to be located and who have notified someone among the oozing anarchic strata from the el-ders down to the children as to where they'd be:

173

Aloha
Bear Fish
Bliss Rehydration Station
Brew Ha-ha
Cannabis Confusion Café
Carnivores Café
Cybercamp
Faerie Camp
Eternal Book Assembly
Madam Frog's Dinkytown Teahouse
Northwest Tribe
Ohana Tribe
Omklahoma
Shama Lama Ding Dong
Rainbow Solar Bubble
Deaf Tribe
Jesus Kitchen
Ida No & Eye Don Kare
Free Family
Sacred Head Church
BC Tribe
Twelve Tribes (w/ star of David)
Thank You Camp
Camp Discordia

. . . and the infamous A Camp, the only region whose temporary residents have agreed that among them alcohol shall be one of the chemicals of happiness.

> Alcohol: Near the parking area there is a place called "A-camp." Rainbow says, "We love the alcoholic, but not the alcohol." Personalities change on alcohol (and hard drugs). Sometimes people can't control themselves as well. Therefore you are respectfully asked to leave the alcohol in A-camp when you hike in to the main gathering space.

—so says the unofficial Rainbow website. The whole region commandeered by the Rainbow tribes, as always without benefit of permits from the U.S. Forest Service, parking and all, covers about four square miles. The givers, the ones who hand out food and take care of things to the extent they're taken care of, the putters-up of portable toilets and showers and medical stations and crude signs like the directory and map or the small billboard illustrating how germs get from dog shit to flies to foodstuff and then to human fingers and mouths, along with advisos to interrupt this process by keeping your hands clean, these who make it all possible arrived and started erecting their camps a week or so before the general celebrants showed up, the takers, the bunch of us who just arrive and stash our stuff under a bush and hold out our blue enamelware cups for hot cereal offered every noon by, for instance, the orange-garbed bald-headed Hare Krishnas, who ladle out three to four thousand such lunches every day of the party.

Joey and I have planned to meet up at the camp of the Ohana tribe, a nomad family of twenty or more who caravan around North America living only in government-owned forests like the Ochoco. I don't find Joey right off and have no real explanation for my presence among them, but the young teenagers who seem to make up the most of the Ohana don't care where I put up my tent and don't seem to hold it against me that I look like somebody from a TV news team, olive shorts, khaki shirt, baseball hat and jogging shoes. Hey. Even socks. On the other hand nobody seems inclined to talk with me, either. At a glance they see there's no sense asking me for reefer. *Ohana* means something in Hawaiian, they tell me. Peace, or Love, they're not sure.

●

I've located Joey. He looks the same, only older, just as sad or perhaps more so, having lived thirty years longer now and found more to be sad about.

Joey and I sit out in front of my tent in the dirt while he tunes up. He's played professionally for decades now and he doesn't do it just for fun very often anymore. But just to oblige me . . . We sing a few of the old ones while the teenage Ohanans get a fire going about six feet away and start good-naturedly hassling whoever wanders past for drugs.

It's the second of July and anybody who's coming is probably here. The woods aren't quiet. You can hear the general murmur of thousands, as in a large stadium, just a bit muted by the forest. The sky turns red and the day dies and Joey has to put away his guitar thanks

175

to competition: drums start up all around, they call from far and near and not quite anywhere in the forest, they give a sense of its deeps and distances and they sound like thoughts it's thinking.

We stumble through the dark woods amongst them: the drums, the drums, the drums. All over the forest pockets of a hundred, two hundred dancers gather around separate groups of ten or twenty maniac percussionists with congas and bongos and tambourines and every other kind of thing to whang on loudly, and the rhythm rises up from all directions into the blackness of space, until the galactic cluster at the center of Andromeda trembles. The yellow strobing light of bonfires and the shadows of the dancers on the smoke. Naked men with their penises bouncing and topless women shaking their beautiful breasts. Every so often when the mood gets them a cry goes up and a hundred voices lift in a collective howling that really just completely banishes gravity for a moment and dies away.

We hear it rained quite heavily two nights ago, but this night is all stars and stillness, the smoke of fires going straight up in the orange light, and the ground isn't particularly uncomfortable, but just the same camping out always feels wrong to me—to sleep outdoors feels desperate, broke and lonely—brings back those nights under a billboard on Wilshire where Joey and Carter and I found a bush to hide us, panhandler punks moving up and down the West Coast drunk on wine and dreaming of somewhere else, brings back those nights in a bag in the hills above Telegraph Avenue when I literally—literally, because I tried—could not get arrested, couldn't land a vagrancy charge and a bed and a roof and three meals of jail food. In my tent on the earth of the Ochoco Forest I don't sleep right. Neither does Joey. By next day noon we're already talking about finding a motel. The morning's too hot and the party's bumping off to a bad start, we keep running into many more people looking for dope than people who look stoned, and the Krishnas run out of gruel twenty minutes after they start serving. Joey and I join what they call the Circle, about a thousand people sitting in a pack on the ground—no standing allowed, please—getting fed with one ladleful each of spiceless veggie broth, courtesy, we believe, of the Rainbow elders.

Once upon a time in the cataclysmic future, according to Rainbow lore, which filters down to us from the ancient Hopi and the Navajo through the cloudy intuitions of people who get high a lot, once upon a time in the future "when the earth is ravaged and the animals are dying," says the unofficial Rainbow Internet website, claiming to quote an Old Native American Prophecy, "a new tribe of people shall come unto the earth from many colors, classes, creeds, and who by their actions and deeds shall make the earth green again. They will be known as the warriors of the Rainbow." I spot hardly any blacks, hardly any Indians from either continent, but it's astonishing to see so many youngsters on the cusp of twenty, as if perhaps some segment of the sixties population stopped growing up.

The Rainbow Family, consisting apparently of anybody who wants to be in it, not only has a myth but also has a creed, expressed succinctly, way back when, by Ralph Waldo Emerson in his essay "Self-Reliance": *Do Your Thing*; and with great reluctance they've allowed to evolve out of the cherished disorganization of these gatherings a sort of structure and an optional authority, that is, an unenforced authority, which defaults to the givers, the ones who actually make possible things like this gathering and many other smaller ones around the country every year since the first one in 1972; and the givers defer to the tribal elders, whoever they are.

An online exchange of letters headed "God can be found in LSD" winds up urging that those participating in these experiments in spontaneous community-building only

1) Be self-reliant
2) Be respectful
3) Keep the Peace
4) Clean up after yourself

and that anything else going on is nobody's business unless someone's getting hurt. "In that event, our system of PeaceKeeping (we call it 'Shanti Senta,' not 'Security') kicks in, and the unsafe situation is dealt with." Speaking as a congenital skeptic, I have to admit that no such situation occurs all weekend, as far as I can learn. And nobody can tell me what *Shanti Senta* means, either.

I go walking in the woods with Mike O, who's spent the last few days under a tiny awning dispensing information about the Course in Miracles, a heretic sort of gnostic brand of Christian thinking that doesn't recognize the existence of evil and whose sacred text is mostly in iambic pentameter. He's a grizzled old guy, wiry and hairy, lives in the Idaho mountains in an underground house he dug out with a shovel, never wears shoes between April and October. He stops a time or two to smoke some grass out of a pipe, a couple of times also to share a toke with passersby, because Mike is a genuinely unselfish and benevolent hippie, and after that he has to stop once in a while and rest his butt on a log because he's dizzy. We pass a gorgeous woman completely naked but covered with black mud. She's been rolling in a mud hole with her friends. I guess I'm staring because she says, "Like what you see?"

"In a day full of erotic visions, you're the most erotic vision of all," I tell her. To me it's a poem, but she just thinks I'm fucked.

Somehow these flower people sense I'm not quite there. They see me. And I think I see them back: in a four-square-mile swatch of the Ochoco Forest the misadventures of a whole generation continue. Here in this bunch of ten to fifty thousand people somehow unable to count themselves I see my generation epitomized: a Peter Pan generation nannied by matronly Wendies like Bill and Hillary Clinton, our politics a confusion of Red and Green beneath the black flag of anarchy; cross-eyed and well-meaning, self-righteous, self-satisfied; close-minded, hypocritical, intolerant—*Loving* you!—*Sieg Heil*!

Joey and I have discovered that if we identify ourselves as medical people ferrying supplies, the Unofficials at the checkpoints let us pass and we don't have to bother with distant parking and the wait for one of the shuttle brigade of VW vans and such, and in the comfort of Joey's pretty good Volvo we can come and go as we please. Coming back up from a burger run in town, we pick up this guy hitching. He says he's staying in the A Camp. "I'm not the big juicehead," he says, "but at least those folks understand I like cash American currency for what I'm selling."

"And what's for sale?"

"Shrooms. Twenty-five an eighth."

I don't ask an eighth of what, just—"How much to get the two of us high?"

"Oh, an eighth should do you real nice if you haven't been eating them as a steady thing and like built a tolerance. Twenty-five bucks will send you both around and back, guaranteed."

And this is why certain people shouldn't mess with these substances: "Better give me a hundred bucks' worth," I say.

It makes me sort of depressed to report that as we accomplish the exchange this man actually says, "Far out, dude."

We now possess this baggie full of gnarled dried vegetation that definitely looks to be some sort of fungi. Back at my tent I dig out my canteen and prepare to split the stuff, whatever it is, with Joey, while he finds his own canteen so we can wash it down quick. And here is why I can't permit myself even to try to coexist with these substances: I said I'd split it, but I only gave him about a quarter. Less than a quarter. Yeah. I never quite became a hippie. And I'll never stop being a junkie.

For a half hour or so we sat on the earth between our two tents and watched the folks go by. In a copse of trees just uphill from us the Ohana group had started a drum circle and were slowly hypnotizing themselves with mad rhythm. Joey revealed he did, in fact, eat these things once in a while and probably had a tolerance. He wasn't sensing much effect.

"Oh," I said.

In a few minutes he said, "Yeah, I'm definitely not getting off."

I could only reply by saying, "Off."

I was sitting on the ground with my back against a tree. My limbs and torso had filled up with a molten psychedelic lead and I couldn't move. Objects became pimpled like cactuses. Ornately and methodically and intricately pimpled. Everything looked crafted, an inarticulate intention worked at every surface.

People walked by along the trail. Each carried a deeply private shameful secret, no, a joke they couldn't tell anyone, yes, their heads raged almost unbearably with consciousness and their souls carried their bodies along.

"Those are some serious drums."

Anything you say sounds like the understatement of the century. But to get hyperbolic at all would be to hint dreadfully at the truth that no hyperbole whatsoever is possible—that is, it's hopelessly impossible to exaggerate the unprecedented impact of those drums. And the sinister, amused, helpless, defeated, worshipful, ecstatic, awed, snide, reeling, happy, criminal, resigned, insinuating tone of the message of those drums. Above all we don't wish to make the grave error of hinting at the truth of those drums and then, perhaps, give way to panic. Panic at the ultimateness—panic at the fact that in those drums, and with those drums, and before those drums, and above all *because* of those drums, the world is ending. *That* one is one we don't want to touch—the apocalypse all around us. These concepts are wound up inside the word *serious* like the rubber bands packed explosively inside a golf ball.

"Yeah, they sure are," Joey says.

Who? What? Oh, my God, he's talking about the drums: Very nearly acknowledging the unspeakable! He's a mischievous bastard and my best friend and the only other person in the universe.

Loving you!

According to the psychiatrists who have embarked together on a molecular exploration of what they like to call "the three-pound universe"—the human brain—what's happening right now is all about serotonin—5-hydroxytryptamine, or 5-HT for short, "the Mr. Big of neurotransmitters," the chemical that regulates the flow of information through the neural system.

I read this article in *Omni* called "The Neuroscience of Transcendence" that explains the whole thing. Having ingested the hallucinogen psilocybin, quite a bit more than my share, I've stimulated the serotonin receptors and disrupted the brain's delicate balancing act in cycling normal input messages from the exterior world—adding special effects.

At the same time, the messages outward to the motor cortex of the brain are disrupted by the same flood of sacred potent molecules, bombarding key serotonin receptors and sending signals *unprovoked by any external stimulus*. What's happening *in here* seems to come from *out there*. The subjective quality underlying all of experience at last reveals that it belongs to everything. The mind inside becomes the mind all around.

> Serotonin and the hallucinogens that act as serotonin agonists—like LSD, mescaline, DMT and psilocybin—also travel to the thalamus, a relay station for all sensory data heading for the cortex. There, conscious rationalizings, philosophizings and interpretations of imagery occur. The cortex of the brain now attaches meaning to the visions that bubble up from the limbic lobe—of burning bushes or feelings of floating union with nature. The flow of images is scripted and edited into a whole new kind of show.

EXACTLY!

YES! Bugs Bunny with a double-barreled twelve-gauge shoots you in the head with a miracle.

I watched helplessly as two beings encountered one another on the trail. Two figures really hard to credit with actuality. But they weren't hallucinatory, just very formally and exotically got up as if for some sort of ceremony, covered in black designs and ornamental silver. They greeted one another and transacted. It was brief and wordless with many secret gestures, the most sinister transaction I've ever witnessed, the most private, the most deeply none of my business. Initiates of the utterly inscrutable. My eyesight too geometrically patterned to allow them faces. They had myths instead of heads.

That is very definitely *it* for *me*. I crawl into my tent. It's four feet away but somehow a little bit farther off than the end of time. It's dark and closed and I'm safe from what's out there but not from what's in *here*—the impending cataclysm, the imploding immenseness, the jocular enormity.

It's been between twenty-five minutes and twenty-five thousand years since I ate the mushrooms, and already we have the results of this experiment. The question was, now that a quarter century has passed since my last such chemical experience, now that my soul is awake, and I've grown from a criminal hedonist into a citizen of life with a belief in eternity, will a psychedelic journey help me spiritually? And the answer is yes; I believe such is possible; thanks; now how do you turn this stuff off?

Because what if the world ends, and Jesus comes down in a cloud, and I'm wrapped in a low-grade fireball all messed up on chemicals? *Is* the world ending? God looms outside the playroom. The revelation and the end of toys. The horrible possibility that *I might have to deal with something*.

And: ludicrously proliferating mental-cartoon sausages fat with a sly and monstrous significance—OH so significant and EVER so coy about just what they mean to impart. And the drums, the drums, the drums. Fifty thousand journeys to the moon and back in every beat.

Four hours later I succeed in operating the zipper on my sleeping bag: tantamount to conquering Everest. I got in and held on.

Sure was raining hard. Sure was looking bad. Sure was dark and twisted in the soul. Sure was wild in the mind. And the drums like ruthless neon, like busted candy.

Me and this sleeping bag! People, we are going places now!

And that strange lifting away of the illusion of discontinuity—I am not a story of eras and epochs, of beginnings and endings, deaths and rebirths, not "a route of occasions" as Alfred North Whitehead claimed—no. I'm the same person I was the day I was born. The one

181

I was inside the womb. I am not my thoughts, not my mind, not my ideas of myself—I am the place and time through which parade those passing things.

After several hours I crawled out into the universe and took up my rightful position in outer space, lodged against the surface of this planet. It wasn't raining rain, it was only raining starlight.

This musician friend of Joey's from Austin, this guy named Jimmy G, sits down beside me with a magic-mushroom guitar and serenades me with his compositions until almost dawn. He's about fifty maybe, white-haired, very skinny, with a variety of faint colors washing over him ceaselessly. It's incomprehensible to me that a genius of this caliber, whose rhymes say everything there is to say and whose tunes sound sweeter and sadder and wilder and happier and more melodic than any others in history, should just live in Austin like a person, writing his songs. Songs about getting our hearts right, loving each other, getting along in peace, sharing the wealth, caring for our mother planet.

By then, all over the world, the drums have stopped. Teenage Ohanans in the tent across the trail make tea on a campfire without uttering a word amongst them. Nobody talks anywhere in the Ochoco Forest; it's a time of meditation. Today is the Fourth of July, the focal hour of the Rainbow Family's gathering. Despite all the partying, this is *the day of the party*. The idea is to enter a silence at dawn and meditate till noon. Then get real happy.

Joey and I walk around watching folks start the day without talking. The strange silence broken only by two dogs barking and one naked man raving as if drunk, really raving, feinting and charging at people like a bull, stumbling right through the fire-pit down by the Bartering Circle.

Noon sharp, the howling starts. The wild keening of human hippies emulating wolves. Minutes later, the drums. In the big meadow where the Circle gathers for meals everybody jumps up dancing, some naked, some dressed in clothes, others wearing mud. The sun burns on them as the crowd becomes a mob the size of a football field. A guy pours Gatorade from a jug into people's upturned open mouths, another sprinkles the throng with a hose from a backpack full of water, like an exterminator's outfit—he's a sweatbuster. Higher and higher! I crash under a bush.

Just before sunset I wake up and get back among the Circle and encounter a definite palpable downturn in the vibes. There's not enough food and not enough drugs. The party has scattered among the various camps, the drum circle that must have included a hundred or so wild percussionists mutters back and forth to itself from just a couple places hidden in the woods.

As the sunset reddens the west, black thunderheads form in the south: a lull, a dead spot, a return of the morning's silence as the Rainbow Family watches a squall gathering, bunching itself together in the southern half of an otherwise clear ceiling.

Then a rainbow drops down through the pale sky. The sight of it, a perfect multicolored quarter-circle, calls up a round of howling from everywhere at once that grows and doesn't stop, and the drumming starts from every direction. Then it's a double rainbow, and then a triple, and the drums and howls can't be compared to anything I've ever heard, it's a Rainbow Sign from Above—*Loving* you!—then a monster light show with the thunderheads gone crimson in the opposing sunset, the three rainbows, and now forked lightning and profound, invincible thunder, every crooked white veiny bolt and giant peal answered by a wild ten-thousand-voiced ululation—a conversation with the Spirit of All at the Divine Fourth of July Show! Far fuckin out! The Great Mother-Father Spirit Goddess Dude is a hippie!

And this is why a certain type mustn't mess with magic potions: I'm thinking, all through this spectacle, that I should have saved a couple buttons for today, I should be *high* to *dig* this. Forgetting how I dug the starlight last night by zooming around somebody's immense black mind in my sleeping bag and almost never witnessing the sky.

But after the rainbows and the storm the night comes down and we get just a little flashback: I close my eyes and remember that first ride on White Owlsley's acid, remember surfacing behind a steering wheel behind which I'd apparently been sitting for some hours, trying to figure out what to do with it; and there was Joey, and Carter B, and Bobby Z, the four of us coming back to the barest fringes of Earth, a place we'd never afterward be able to take quite so seriously because we'd seen it obliterated, finding each other in this place now—none of us having ever taken acid before or even really talked to anybody about it, four teenage beatnik aspirants returned from an absurd odyssey for which none of us had been the slightest bit prepared and which we felt we'd just barely survived—remember watching Joey and Carter disappear into an apartment building and

183

remember heading with Bobby, somehow *traveling* through streets like rivers behind this *steering wheel*—five hundred mikes of White Owsley's!—remember steering magnificently through Alexandria, Virginia, in a gigantic teacup that once had been a Chevrolet under streetlights with heads like glittering brittle dandelions, remember letting it park itself and remember floating into a building and down the halls of the Fort Ward Towers apartments, down the complicated curvature of the halls, and finding, at the end of the palatial mazes, finding—Mom! Mom in her robe and slippers! Her curlers from Mars! Mom from another species! Mom who said, It's five in the morning! I nearly called the police: WHERE have you BEEN, and remember turning to Bobby Z, who's dead of AIDS, at his funeral I threw dirt onto his coffin while his sister, my old high school sweetheart, keened and screamed, turned to Bobby Z and said, Where have we been?—and the question astonished and baffled and shocked him too, and we both said, Where have we been? WHERE HAVE WE BEEN?

Bobby, them drums are riding themselves up to the very limit and right on through like it was nothing. Where where where have we been?

Where did we go?

Nominated by Diann Blakely, The Paris Review, Wally Lamb, David Means

CREELEY CURSING IN CHURCH

by RICK CAMPBELL

from QUARTERLY WEST

Fuck, he said.
Why not? Where I come from *God damn it*
was a curse on every sooty thing
in our graveyard shift life.
God heard them mutter *Damn*
as they crowded the bus stop, winter
cracking off the river.
God heard men cry *shit*
when the hammer busts a thumb.
Heard them scream *oh christ*
when the saw blade
ripped through sweet skin.
Heard *oh jesus, mary*
mother of god,
when Louie fell
into the smelter and left
his strange mark on every beam
poured that week.

Nominated by Quarterly West

THE BIG-BREASTED PILGRIM

fiction by ANN BEATTIE

from CONJUNCTIONS

Our house in the Florida Keys is down a narrow road, half a mile from a convenience store with a green neon sign that advertises "Bait and Basics." Lowell's sister, Kathryn, called to get us to arrange for a car to drive her from Miami. She considers everywhere Lowell has ever lived to be Siberia, including Saratoga, New York, which she saw only once, during a blizzard. TriBeCa, circa 1977, was Siberia. Ditto Ashland, Oregon. In all those places, Lowell had what he now calls The Siberian Brides: his first and second wives, who gradually became as incomprehensible to him as foreigners: Tish, who lived with us in Saratoga and later in TriBeCa; Leigh Anne Leighton—a name so melodic he always speaks of her that way, even though it seems inordinately formal—who lived with us for a month in Ashland before flying to Los Angeles for her grandfather's funeral, from which she never returned. This was no case of riding forever 'neath the streets of Boston, however: she got a Mexican divorce and re-married a youth Lowell and I recently saw on *Late Night with Conan O'Brien*, playing soprano sax with a group called "Bobecito and the Brazen Beauties."

My own life is nothing like Lowell's. The joke is that I am his Boswell, and to the extent that I used to take dictation in Lowell's precomputer days, I suppose I have been a sort of Boswell—though I doubt the man, himself, ever scrubbed down a shower with Tilex, or would have, even if shower stalls—to say nothing of the excessively effective cleaning products we have now—existed. Nor, say, did we mistake Ashland for the Hebrides, though Lowell and I have inevitably arrived at pithy pronouncements as a prelude to packing up and leaving place after place.

I, Richard Howard Manson, was an Army brat, living in thirteen different locations by the time I started high school. The one good thing about that was that it made me pretty unflappable, though at the same time it's given me a wanderlust I've tired of as I've aged. Lowell makes fun of me for trying to decondition myself by accepting vicarious travel in place of the real thing: I subscribe to almost every travel magazine, and view cassettes of foreign cities, or even silly resort promo tapes, almost every night before bed. Lowell calls this "nicotine patch travel." Passing in front of the TV, he'll drag hard on an imaginary cigarette, then toss the phantom cig on the floor, grind it out, and slap his right arm to his left bicep, exhaling with instant relief. As it happens, I quit smoking—I mean real cigarettes—cold turkey. The travel addiction has not been so easy to break, but since I like my job, and since my employer is terminally itchy, he has often been pleased to take advantage of my weakness. The way wheedling wives have talked husbands into second and third babies, Lowell has persuaded me to give a month at the Chateau Marmont, or a few years in a rented Victorian in upstate New York, a try. He never claims we're staying, though he doesn't present the trips as vacations, either. When he had a larger network of friends—that period, about ten years ago, when everybody seemed to be between marriages—our ostensible reason for going somewhere would often be that we were on a mercy mission to cheer up so-and-so. Once there, so-and-so would be found, miraculously, to have cheered *us* up, and so we would stay for a longer infusion of friendliness, until so-and-so became affiliated with the next Mrs. so-and-so, who would inevitably dislike us, or until that moment when a blizzard hit and we thought of being in the sun, or when summer heat settled like an itchy, wooly mantle.

In most of the places we've lived, there have been constants, Kathryn's visits among them. Other constants are a few ceramics made by a friend, a couple of very nice geometrically patterned rugs, and our picture mugs, depicting each of us sitting on camels in front of pyramids. There's also the favorite this, or the favored that—small things, like jars of homegrown herbs, or the amazing sea nettle suntan lotion that can be ordered by calling an 800 number that relays a request for shipping to the apothecary in St. Paul de Vence. Our Barbour jackets are indispensable, as is a particular wine pull, no longer manufactured. When you travel as much as we do, you can seem to fixate on what looks to other people to be trivia. I make it a point to be casual about the wine pull, letting other people use it whenever they insist upon being helpful, though I often awaken in the night, convinced that it has been thrown away during the clean-up period, and then I go downstairs and open the drawer and see it, but return to bed convinced that I have nevertheless had an accurate premonition of its fate following the next dinner party.

Lowell is a chef, and a quite brilliant one. He has one of those metabolisms that allows him to eat anything and remain thin. I, too, can and do eat anything, my diabetes having been cured by a Japanese acupuncturist, but unlike Lowell, everything I eat increases my weight. At six feet, I am two hundred and seventy pounds—so imposing that the first time I hurried inside to pick up some items at our "Bait And" convenience store, the teenager behind the counter raised his hands above his head. This has become a standing joke with Lowell, who sometimes imitates the teenager when he and I cross paths in the house, or when I bring the evening cocktails to the back deck.

Lowell and I met more than twenty years ago, when I was driving for my cousin's private car company in New York City. Lowell was in town that evening to be a guest chef for the weekend at the short-lived but much-admired Le Monde Aujourd'hui. I picked him up at La Guardia in a downpour, and on the way in—he was coming from a birthday party for Craig Claiborne, in upstate New York—we talked about our preferences in junk food, rock and roll and—I should have been suspicious—whether any city that was a state capital had any zip to it. But this gives the impression that we chattered away. We spoke only intermittently, and I had little to say, except that I liked Montpelier, Vermont, very much, but that was probably because I'd only visited the state once, during a heat wave in New York, and it had seemed to me I'd gone to heaven. This brought up the subject of gardens, and I heard for the first time, though others no doubt knew it, the theory of planting certain flowers to repel insects from certain vegetables. On the streets of Brooklyn you didn't hear things like that—Brooklyn Heights being the place I had settled when I was discharged from the Marine Corps. I was living in my uncle's spare bedroom, driving for my cousin's car company, making extra money to help support the baby that would be born to Rita and me—that was going to happen, whether she left me or not, as she was always threatening to do—though less than four months from the day I picked Lowell up, my twenty-two-year-old, in-the-process-of-becoming-ex wife, as well as the child she was carrying, would be dead after a collision on the Merritt Parkway. In the years following the accident, this has never come up in conversation, so even if I'd been able to look into a crystal ball, I would still have chatted with Lowell about Sara Lee chocolate cupcakes and the extraordinarily addictive quality of Cheetos. I do not care to discuss matters of substance, as Kathryn has correctly stated many times. Both she and Lowell know the fact of my wife's death, of course. My uncle told them, the time they came to a barbecue at his apartment, six months or so after I met them. By that time, I was in Lowell's employ, and he was working on the second of his cookbooks, trying to decide whether he should take a very lucrative, full-time position at a New Orleans hotel. I had become his secretary because—as it turned out, to my own surprise—I seem to have a tenacity about succeeding in minor matters, which are all that frustrate the majority of people, anyway. That is, after some research, I would find the telephone number of the dive shop in Tortola that was across the street from a phoneless shack, where the non-English-speaking cook had used a certain herb mixture on the grilled chicken he had served to me and Lowell that Lowell felt he must find a way to reproduce. (Not that these things ever struck him in the moment. He often has a delayed reaction to certain preparations, but his insistence on deciphering the mystery is always in direct proportion to the time elapsed between eating and doing the double-take.) My next step would be to send Chef Lowell T-shirts to the helpful salesman in the dive shop, one for him, his wife and their two children and—FedEx's ideas about not sending cash in envelopes be damned—money to bribe both salesman and chef. It was a minor matter to get a friend of a friend, who was a stewardess, to use her free hours before her flight took off again from Beef Island to take a cab to the dive shop and pick up a small quantity of the ground herb concoction, which chemical analysis later revealed to be powdered rhino horn (one could well wonder how they got that in Tortola), mixed with something called dried Annie flower, to which was added a generous pinch—as Lowell suspected—of simple ginger. Of course I see these small successes of mine as minor victories, but to Lowell they seem a display of inventive brilliance. He describes himself, quite unfairly, I think, as a plodder. He will try a recipe a hundred times, if that's what it takes. But to me that isn't plodding; it's being a perfectionist, which, God knows, too few people are these days.

Tonight, before Kathryn arrives, Lowell's new love interest will be arriving for drinks. She has no idea that he is a famous chef, who has published numerous cookbooks, writes a monthly column for one of the most prestigious food magazines, and teaches seminars on the art of sautéing in St. Croix, where we are put up annually at the Chenay Bay Beach Resort. I have met this woman, who has a name like something out of a cheap, English romance, Daphne Crowell, exactly once, when I stumbled into them—literally—on the back deck. It was a moonless night, exceedingly dark, and the two of them had gone downstairs to observe our neighbor's speedy little boat coming around the point with another load of drugs. She had been wearing *my* bathrobe, which she simply helped herself to, after taking it from the hook on the back of *my* bathroom door. There she was, leaning against the rail at the edge of the deck like a car's hood ornament, when I awoke from slumbering under a blanket on a chaise longue just in time to see her untie the sash and pull off the robe, giggling as she held it forward to flap in the breeze—*my* robe—like some big flag at a parade. I'm sure the silly gesture was equally appreciated by our neighbor, whose own "secretary" wears night goggles for land-to-shore vision, in case the police are waiting in ambush with their panthers, or whatever intimidating beasts they currently favor. Anyway: Daphne is a fool, but nobody ever said Lowell didn't like to waste his time. A recipe he will fret over forever, but any woman will do—particularly on a night when Kathryn, whom he is still intimidated by, is arriving, all big-city bluster and Oh, how are you doing out here in the boonies? Since starting a graduate program in writing at The New School, she treats everyone as interesting material. She has been trying for years to see if she can make me mad by insisting that I read *The Remains of the Day*, which—I have not told her, and will not—I have, in fact, viewed on television. I understand completely that she wishes me to see myself as some pathetic, latter-day servant who has wasted his life by missing the forest for the trees. If she thinks I live to serve, she's wrong. I simply live to avoid my previous life.

"Everything ready out here?" Lowell calls. He has opened the

French doors and is propping them open with cement-filled conch shells. Everything ready, indeed: he's the one who set out the cheese torte, under the big, upside-down brass colander. All I had to do was bring out the gallon of Tanqueray, the tonic and some Key limes. My Swiss Army knife will do for slicing, and even mixing.

"Are you going deaf, Richard? Half the things I ask you, you don't respond to."

He's mad at me not because I haven't answered, really, but because I refused to drive to Miami to get his sister. The ride wouldn't have bothered me, but two and a half hours with Kathryn in a car would be more than I could take, by approximately two hours and twenty-five minutes.

"Richard . . . is there a possibility that not only do you not hear me, but that you have no curiosity about why I'm standing here, moving my lips?"

"I thought maybe you'd just had something tasty," I say.

A pause. "You did hear me, then? You just chose not to answer?"

"What's the point of these random women?" I say.

He walks toward me. "I don't know why it upset you so much that she borrowed your robe," he says. "Anything that smacks of exuberance, you insist upon seeing as drunken foolishness."

"Remember the Siberians," I say. "And the one you picked up in South Beach, who wanted to sue for palimony after one weekend."

He looks at my knife, open to the longest blade, next to the bottle of gin. "This was your idea of a stirrer?" he says.

"She's so spontaneous and uninhibited," I say. "Let's see if she doesn't just use her finger."

As if that were a cue, we hear the crunch of gravel under Daphne's tires. Since today is Friday, she will have spent the day making fruit smoothies for tourists. On Monday and Tuesday, the only other days she works, she has been substituting for a dentist's receptionist, who was mugged in Miami during her ninth month of pregnancy. Six weeks after the mugging, the woman has still not given birth. If nothing happens by Monday, they are going to induce labor—though apparently what the woman is most afraid of is leaving her house. I know all this because Daphne phones the house often, and when I answer she always feels obliged to strike up a conversation.

Much oohing and aahing at the front door: such a lovely house, so secluded, such beautiful plants everywhere. The unexpected delight of seeing roses growing in profusion in the Keys, blah blah blah.

191

She has brought me—the absurd cow has brought me—a plastic manatee. She has brought Lowell three birds-of-paradise, wrapped by the flower shop in lavender paper, which she pronounces "coals to Newcastle." But the manatee . . . we don't already have one of those, do we? No, we don't. We don't even have a rubber ducky to float in the bathwater. We're so . . . you know . . . old.

Behold: she has on gold Lycra pants, gold thong sandals and a football-sized shirt with enormous shoulder pads. The material is iridescent: blue, shimmering gold, flashing orange, everything sparkling as if Tinker Bell, in a mad mood, applied the finishing touches. The sparkly stuff is also in her hair, broken lines of it, as if to provide a passing lane. All this, because she put a heaping teaspoon of protein powder into Lowell's smoothie, gratis. I see Lowell slip his arm around her shoulder as the two of them walk to the edge of the deck. I go into the house to get glasses and ice.

When I return, with the three glasses on a tray, she is in mid-banality: the loveliness of the sky, etc. Well: Kathryn's pathetic butler would bow out at this point, but in our house the servant drinks and eats with the employer. The employer has no real friends except for the servant, in good part because he is given to sarcasm, periods of dark despair, temper tantrums and hypochondriacal illnesses, alternating with intense self-appreciation. Similarly, the servant has been co-opted by a life of leisure, a feeling of gratitude. Lowell is far easier to take care of than a wife, certainly easier to care for than a child, much easier to look after than the majority of dogs, by which I mean no disrespect to either party, as a dog was the one thing I ever had a strong attachment to and deep admiration for. The Marines, I found out, were sociopaths. Imagine the days of my youth when I thought I would prove my manhood and patriotism by outdoing my Army Lieutenant Colonel father by joining the Marines. *Sir, Yes Sir!* And Lowell thinks there might be a problem with tracking down a particular herb mixture? I could kiss his feet. Though I settle for shining his shoes—or did, in pre-Reebok days.

Lowell and Daphne have decided to take a ride in the kayak, tied to the end of the pier. This may leave me alone to greet Kathryn, who should arrive in twenty minutes or so, if everything goes according to schedule. Lately, I have begun to think that she is angry because she has had to pity me for so many years. The choked-up version my uncle gave her of the event that ostensibly ruined my young life registered so strongly with her that she has never been

192

able to put it aside. The sheer misery of what I went through gets superimposed, I suspect, on her desire to be competitive with me, makes her back off from trying, more tenaciously, to solve the puzzle that is me: a street kid who gradually became educated (nothing else to do those four long, cold years we lived in Saratoga), only to shun those with similar education—to shun everyone, in fact. What she doesn't know is that I knew almost immediately my marriage was a mistake, I never wanted to become a father—the accident was my way out, not only from that situation, but for all time. Daphne could have spooned so much protein powder into my fruit drink it would have had the consistency of sawdust, and I would only have paid her and walked away. I've faltered a bit, from time to time; Kathryn would love to know with whom, and when, but my uncle spoke so graphically to her, years ago, that he managed to instill even future shame—that's the way I think of the service he inadvertently did for me—so that she still can't bring herself to ask outright what the story is with some hulking street kid who has no girlfriend and no friends, who is aging companionably, in the lower Florida Keys, with her bizarre, neurotic brother.

They descend into the kayak. Daphne has found something, already, to giggle about. She has left one shoe on the dock, it seems. I am summoned to help. Once seated, Lowell doesn't want to risk toppling the boat, I suppose. I don't play deaf; I respond to his entreaty, and at the edge of the dock I bend and pick up her gold flip-flop, for which she thanks me profusely, and then Prince Charming and Cinderella set sail. Which leaves me with the four-cheese torte with rye saffron crust that I don't mind being the first to cut into, taking out a neat wedge with the knife and admiring its firm, yet creamy consistency. It is flecked with rosemary and ground pink peppercorns: the appetizer other chefs have been stealing and altering almost from the minute Lowell invented it. What none of them have guessed, to my knowledge, is the presence of the single, simmered vanilla bean. I bite off a tiny piece, chew slowly and consider the possibility that anything as ambrosial as this might be interchangeable with love.

The Triple J Cab pulls into the drive as the sun is setting. Kathryn alights from the front seat—wouldn't you know she'd be so ballsy she'd sit up front. She seems to have only a small bag with her, which means, thank God, she won't be visiting longer than she said. But then, from the backseat, a skinny woman emerges, holding her own small bag, wearing a beret and a long white scarf, which matches her white shorts and her white T-shirt, over which she wears a droopy vest. "Paradise!" she exclaims, throwing back her head and enthusing, as if the sky were awaiting her verdict. Yes, indeed—but who is she?

She is Nancy Cummins—Cummins without a "g"—who is en route to a bris to be held in a suite at the Casa Marina hotel, in Key West. She is an acquaintance of Kathryn's from New York—a highlighter, whom Kathryn arranged to meet at JFK, when it turned out the two women would be taking trips at the same time, almost to the same destination. ("Highlighter"—meaning that she paints streaks in rich people's hair.)

I carry their two small bags. Inside one, it will later turn out, is a narcotized kitten.

"Where's my brother?" Kathryn asks. Rushing to also ask: "Did he forget I was coming?"

"He's in a kayak with his girlfriend," I say.

"See?" Kathryn says to the highlighter. "No one meets anybody in New York; you come to Siberia, and *bingo*."

"Bingo," I say. "I haven't thought of bingo in a million years."

"They don't play games. They read books," Kathryn says to the highlighter, as if I'm not there.

"You know," I say, realizing I'm about to make a fool of myself, but not caring, "when she said you were a highlighter, I thought at first she must mean of books. Those yellow markers you underline with. You know: highlighters."

"No," the highlighter says. "I've always stayed as far from school as I could get."

I put their bags on the kitchen counter. It's only then that the highlighter unzips her bag and removes what I take, at first, to be a wad of material. It is a six-week-old black kitten, sleeping what looks to me like the sleep of death, though the thing does twitch when she puts it on the counter.

"Isn't it adorable?" Kathryn says.

Oh, absolutely. Now we have a cow, a manatee and a kitten.

"Did he chill my favorite wine, or did he forget?" Kathryn wants to know, pulling open the refrigerator door. In the shelf sit four bottles of Vichon Chardonnay, with two cans of Tecate at either end seeming to brace the bottles like bookends. Kathryn plucks a bottle from the shelf. I open the drawer and pantomime that I would be happy to extract the cork. But no: she's a liberated woman, none of that harmful stereotyping of the helpless female allowed. Flip forward until two A.M., when I'll have the anxiety dream.

The highlighter opens the door and seizes a Tecate.

"Key lime?" I offer, reaching behind the slightly quivering kitten and extracting one from a basket.

"What do you do with it?"

"You squirt some in your beer," Kathryn says.

"I hope . . . I hope it isn't too much trouble, my just, you know, *coming here*," the highlighter says, as if the idea of limes used to enhance the flavor of drinks has just defined some complexity for her.

"Look at this! Next Sunday's *Times Book Review*—by subscription!" Kathryn says.

"Yes. We alternate with our reading of *The Siberian Daily*."

"Didn't I tell you he has a clever comeback for everything?" Kathryn says.

As if this weren't a put-down, the highlighter extends her hand and says, "I can't believe my good fortune in being here. I mean, it's very generous of you to have me. Because what a coincidence, my flying to this part of Florida—I *guess* I'm in the right part of Florida!—just when . . ."

I shake her hand. It is what we might have done from the first, if she had said immediately how happy she was to be where she was, and if Kathryn hadn't plunked the two bags in my hand. Does this happen to other people? This finding oneself suddenly greeting someone, or introducing oneself, long after things have gotten rolling? Roger Vergé once introduced himself to me on the second day of his visit, following his dinner of the night before, and after preparing lunch, for which he'd had me shop earlier that morning. Does some strange, sudden formality overcome people, or is there something I do that makes them feel so immediately a part of the family that they forget social form? I've asked Lowell, and that is his explanation. Just as his sister would never miss an opportunity to express skepticism about me, Lowell lets no opportunity pass when he can reassure me of my worthiness, by putting a positive spin on things. Leaving aside those periods when he is too depressed to speak, that is.

"And so you . . . you stay out here and create recipes together?" the highlighter asks.

"That sounds so domestic," I say. "No, actually. I have nothing to do with composing the recipes, and now that Lowell has mastered the computer, I sometimes don't even—"

"Tell her about tracking down the powdered rhino horn," Kathryn says, stroking the collapsed kitten.

"She's talking about my tracking down an herbal mixture Lowell had interest in," I begin.

"Did you go to jail?"

"Pardon?"

"For importing the rhinocerous."

"I didn't . . . I didn't import a whole rhinocerous. . . ."

"The drug smuggler around the corner would probably be willing to do that for a price," Kathryn says.

The highlighter looks at me, wide-eyed. "She told me about the guy who runs drugs."

"And did she tell you that we disapprove, and that we're spying on him for the Federal Government?"

"No."

"Only kidding. We don't care what our neighbors do."

"For one thing, you'd have to be delusional to live here on the edge of nowhere and think in terms of having a neighbor," Kathryn says.

"I know everybody in my building," the highlighter says. "Of course, there are only four apartments."

"Apartments," Kathryn muses, strolling onto the back deck. "Can you stand here and imagine one going up across the way?"

"No," the highlighter says.

"We've left places because of equally ridiculous scenarios," I say.

"Kathryn told me that you two have lived just about everywhere."

"She did? Well, as an adult I've only—"

"Rhinoceros," the highlighter says. "Isn't that an aphrodisiac, or something?"

The wall phone rings, sending a short spasm through the kitten, who has dragged itself almost underneath it, before collapsing again.

That is what we were doing, what the three of us were talking about, when a chef whose name I faintly computed called from Coral Gables, in quite a dither, wanting me to inform Lowell that George Stephanopoulos would be calling momentarily.

The president, it seems, is a lover of mango. He has recently sampled Lowell's preparation of baked mango gratinée—usually served as an accompaniment to chicken or fish—at the home of a friend, who prepared it from Lowell's newest cookbook. The president loved it, as well as the main course, which was apparently prepared out of the same cookbook. Furthermore, Mrs. Clinton has become intent upon sampling some of Lowell's newer dishes (*but no chocolate chip cookies*, goes through my mind) and wonders if they might recruit Lowell to cook for them during an upcoming weekend at a friend's borrowed home in Boca Raton. Mrs. Clinton herself will call to confer about the menu, which would be for ten people—three of them teenage girls—whenever it is convenient.

I cover the receiver with my hand and whisper: "When can you talk to Hillary?"

Kathryn, from the back deck, maintains this is all a prank.

"Any time," Lowell whispers back.

"Would Mrs. Clinton be able to talk to Mr. Cartwright now?"

"Probably she would right after the Kennedy Center performance," George Stephanopoulos says. "Give me five minutes. Let me get back to you on that."

The phone doesn't ring for an hour. By the time it does ring, the kitten is upright and spunky, chasing after Key limes rolled across the kitchen floor.

"George Stephanopoulos," the voice says. "Are you . . . there's a landing field in Marathon, correct?"

"Yes," I say.

"Big planes don't come in, though?"

I see the dinner slipping away. "No," I say.

"Is there a roasted pig? Not at the airport, I mean. I mean, is there a recipe for roasted pig?"

"Prepared with a cumin marinade, and served with pistachio pureed potatoes."

"The Clintons have left for an evening performance, but if it wouldn't be inconvenient, I think Mrs. Clinton would like to call when they return. It might be eleven, ten-thirty or eleven—something like that."

"Mr. Cartwright stays up until well after midnight."

"I'll bet I'm interrupting your dinner right now. Tell me the truth."

"No. Actually, we've been watching what has turned out to be an incredible sunset and we've been waiting for your call."

"Sunset," Stephanopoulos says, with real longing in his voice. "Okay," he says. "Speak to you later."

197

"This is *amazing*," the highlighter says.

"Sting and Trude Styler rented a house in Key West last winter," Daphne says. "Also, David Hyde Pierce, who plays Frasier's brother, took a date for dinner on Little Palm Island, and he tipped really well."

Since the moment they were introduced, Daphne and the highlighter have gotten along famously. They're sitting on the kitchen floor, rolling limes around like some variation of playing marbles, and the kitten is going gonzo.

"When would the dinner be?" Lowell asks.

"They're going to call around eleven," I say. "You can ask."

"You ask," Lowell says. "I'd make a fool of myself if I had to talk to Hillary Clinton."

On the deck, Kathryn plucks a stalk of lemon grass growing from a clay pot, puts it between her two thumbs and blows loudly. The kitten slithers under the refrigerator.

"Reminds me of certain of the doctor's patients," Daphne says, watching the kitten disappear. "You know, what really drives me crazy is that when they call, they give every last detail about their problem, as if the dentist cares whether the tooth broke because they were eating pizza or gnawing on a brick."

The kitten emerges, followed by what looks like its own kitten: a quick moving Palmetto bug that disappears under the stove.

"Jesus Christ," Lowell says. "Don't we have bug spray?"

Antonio, the chef from Coral Gables, calls back. He wants Lowell to know that since the president will be having lunch at his restaurant, he is not at all offended that the president wishes to dine with us. Every effort must be made, however, not to duplicate dishes. He asks, bleakly, if we have had any success in finding fresh estragon in Southern Florida.

"If this were *Frasier*, Niles would run out and buy a speaker-phone before the president called back. He'd hook it up, but then in the middle of the call it would blow up, or something," Daphne says.

We all look at her.

"I always watch because I like my namesake," Daphne says.

"That's what he said?" Lowell says, pouring chardonnay into his glass. "He came right out and said the president liked my potato-mango gratinée?"

"What do you think he'd say to lead into the subject that Clinton wanted to come to dinner? That the president had been very depressed about the Whitewater investigation?"

"No mention of Whitewater!" Lowell says.

"It's like: don't think of a pink elephant," the highlighter says.

Kathryn comes in from the back deck. "The bugs are starting to bite," she says.

"Also, where are we going to seat them?" Lowell says.

I say: "At the dining room table."

"Twelve, with the leaf up, but fourteen? Where will we get the chairs?"

"You can probably leave that up to someone on his staff."

"This isn't going to happen," Kathryn says. "You really think the Clintons are going to come bumping down that dirt road like the Beverly Hillbillies?"

"Gravel," Lowell says. "Also, we could easily get it paved."

"Remember when Queen Elizabeth went to Washington, and they took her to the home of a typical black family, or whatever it was, and the woman went up to the Queen and gave her a big hug, and all the newspapers had the photograph of the Queen going into shock when she was touched?" the highlighter says.

"A good suggestion: a simple handshake with the president and first lady," Lowell says to the highlighter.

"If I had to talk to them, I'd probably piss my pants," the highlighter says.

"We could mention to Hillary that treatment for adult incontinence was not often covered under current health policies," I say.

"We could say that *yellow water* was better than *white water*," Daphne chimes in.

"I just realized: I didn't put the carpaccio out," I say, going to the refrigerator.

"Let's spray ourselves and knock back some more wine out on the deck before we eat," Kathryn says.

"Yes, but . . . *we won't swallow!*" the highlighter says.

Well before eleven, we've run out of jokes.

"This is *the* most strange and exciting day I have had since Madonna came in to get her roots retouched after closing. There she was, looking like a little wet dog, with her hair shampooed and the handkerchief-size towel behind her neck, and she wouldn't speak to me directly, she said everything to her bodyguard, who relayed it to me. All of a sudden, instead of touching up her roots, I was supposed to dry her hair, set the dryer on low and give it to him, actually, and let him dry it, and I was supposed to highlight her wig, instead. And then we had a blackout. The whole place went dark, and do you know, her bodyguard thought it was deliberate. It wasn't Con Ed fucking up again, it was a plot to kidnap Madonna! He kept lighting this butane lighter he had with him and looking incredibly fierce. She was smoking a cigarette and talking to herself. She was dabbing at her neck and saying that she wished she could be somewhere else, and then, in almost no light, the bodyguard kept telling me to hurry up with highlighting the wig."

"What did she name that baby?" Kathryn asks.

"Lulu," Daphne says.

I correct her: "Lourdes."

"He reads the tabloids in the food store," Kathryn says.

At eleven-thirty, George Stephanopoulos has not called back. After Letterman's monologue, we decide to skip Burt Bacharach and call it a night. The kitten has been sleeping on its back, like a dog, for quite a long time. The highlighter casually reaches for it, as if it were her evening bag.

"You're sure it was George Stephanopoulos?" Lowell says to me, as Kathryn volunteers to lead the ladies to their rooms.

"It had the ring of truth about it," I say.

"I bet the president would have liked the dinner we had tonight, and then he could have played 'Last Year at Marienbad' with the three of us!" Daphne giggles, as she follows Kathryn toward the stairs.

I am amazed that the twenty-something highlighter doesn't ask, "What's 'Last Year at Marienbad'?"

Then she does, pronouncing the last two words so that they resonate amusingly. The words are "Marine" and "bad."

The mere idea that I might have thought to take down George Stephanopoulos's phone number provokes merriment at breakfast (frittata and an orange-coconut salad; two-shot con leches all around).

Antonio, his wife informs me when I call, is spending the day fishing off a pontoon boat. She will have him return my call when he returns.

"Maybe he decided McDonald's was easier," Daphne says.

"Impossible. His wife was going to be along," Lowell reminds her.

Someone who is driving from Miami for the bris will pick up the highlighter at the discount sandal store ten minutes from our house, and give her a lift to the Casa Marina. I'll give her a ride out to the highway in another half hour.

"You'd think they'd call," the highlighter says.

We sit around, like a bunch of kids nobody's asked to dance. In a little while, when I go out to sweep the deck, the highlighter follows me.

"Are you guys gay?" she says.

"No," I say, "but you aren't the first to wonder."

"Because you're hanging out in the Keys. And you've been together so long, and all."

"Right," I say.

"What kind of tree is that?" she says, stepping around the pile of leaves.

"Kapok. It doesn't always drop its leaves, but when it does, it does."

"So listen," she says. "I didn't offend you by asking?"

"No," I say.

"Because if you're not a couple—I didn't think you were a couple—but I mean, since you're not, I'm going to be at that Casa Marina place for a couple of days after Izzy gets snipped, and I wondered if maybe I could take you out."

It's the first time a woman has ever invited me on a date. I haven't been on a date in years. I only vaguely remember how to go on a date.

"There's a private party in some place called Bahama Village. Gianni Versace's sister invited me. It's some house where they took out the kitchen and put in a swimming pool. He's given her a bunch of ties to give out. Not that you'd want a tie," she says.

"No particular use for them," I say.

"Doesn't seem," she says. Then: "So. Would you like to do that?"

"To swim in someone's kitchen?"

"If you'd rather we just—"

"No, no. Party sounds fine. I should come around to the Casa Marina, then? What time?"

"I think the party starts at ten."

"Little before ten, then."

"Great," she says.

201

"See you then," I say. "Of course, I'll also see you in about five minutes, when we should leave for the sandal store."

She nods.

"Like to sweep for a few minutes?" I ask.

That drives her away.

The next day, there is still no word. Could the potato-mango gratinée have been a moment's passing fancy? Antonio knows nothing, except that the Clintons will be arriving at his restaurant February 11, and that the restaurant will be closed after the first seating on February 10, when it will be secured by the Secret Service. The following day, they will watch Antonio and one assistant prepare all the food. He worries aloud about finding good quality estragon.

Just as I am about to step into the shower, the phone rings. It is George Stephanopoulos. He is apologetic. The president has been put on a new allergy medicine, which had unexpected side effects. Mrs. Clinton has been preoccupied with other details of the trip, and only realized that morning that further communication was needed from her. She is prepared to talk to me in just a few minutes, if I'm able to hold on.

I hold on. To my surprise, though, it is the president, himself, who comes to the line. "I'm very glad to talk to you, sir," the president says. "Hillary and I have greatly enjoyed your recipes."

"Actually, Mr. President, Mr. Cartwright is the person you want to talk to. I'm his assistant. I'm afraid he's out, right now, kayaking."

"Kayaking? Where are you all?"

"In the Florida Keys, Mr. President."

"Is that right? I thought you were in Louisiana."

"We're in the Florida Keys. A bit short of Key West."

"I see. Then where will we be having lunch before we come over to you?" the president asks.

"I believe you'll be lunching in Boca Raton, which is about three hours by car from where Lowell—Mr. Cartwright—lives."

"We're going to be coming to your restaurant that evening? How are we getting there, George?"

A muffled answer.

"I see. Well, that's fine. Wish I could take the time to do some fishing. But your restaurant—it's not a fish restaurant, is it?"

"Oh, no sir. It's . . . the thing is, it's not a restaurant. It's"—Is this going to screw the whole deal, somehow?—"It's where we live. Mr.

Cartwright prefers to have favored people dine with us in his home. The view of the water from the back deck is splendid."

"A house on the water?" the president says. "Has George registered that?"

More muted discussion.

"I'm sorry," the president says. "I get caught up in logistics, when it's better to leave it to the experts."

"*Water*," I hear George Stephanopoulos hissing in the background.

"You know, I'm a chef's nightmare," the president says. "If I had my way, I'd eat a medium hamburger with extra mustard and go fishing with you guys." He says: "Isn't that what I'd do, George?"

"*Papaya*," Stephanopoulos hisses. Is he hissing at the president?

"Hillary got all excited about that papaya dish," the president says. "I'm going to let you speak to the boss about this, but if there's one thing I might request, with the exception of shrimp, I'm not overly fond of seafood."

"No seafood," I say.

"Well yeah, that kind of cuts to the chase," the president says. He clears his throat. "Just out of curiosity, how far is the airport from where you are?"

"Less than an hour, sir."

"That's fine, then. George and Hillary will firm this up, and we're looking forward to an exceptional meal."

"Mr. Cartwright will be so sorry he missed your call."

"Fishing in the kayak?" the president asks.

"Just paddling around with a friend," I reply.

This seems to cause the president several seconds of mirth. "Quite different from my plans for the afternoon," the president says.

George Stephanopoulos cuts in: "Thank you very much," George Stephanopoulos says.

"We look forward to making plans," I say.

"Good-bye," George Stephanopoulos says. "Thanks again."

I am standing there in my barracuda briefs, preparing to shower and go on my date. I fully realize that when Kathryn finds out, she will raise an eyebrow and say something sarcastic about my having a date. She will no doubt see my going into Key West as analogous to the butler's going off to find the former housemaid: a sad moment of self-protective delusion. Like him, I also won't be bringing her back. I'll be swimming with her at some party. Then, if we have sex, it can very well be in her room at the hotel. Simple white boxers are almost always preferable to the barracudas, when one is disrobing for the first time. The tangerine sports shirt that is my favorite is probably a bit too tropical-jokey; slightly faded denim seems better, with a pair of new khaki trousers.

"I'm going into Key West," I say, coming upon Lowell, pouring glasses of iced tea at the kitchen counter. "See you tonight."

"Why are you going into Key West?" he says.

"Date," I say.

"You have a date? With whom?"

"The highlighter."

"She just left," he says.

"Yesterday."

"I see," he says.

"Mrs. Clinton, or her secretary, will be calling. I spoke to the president briefly, and he doesn't want seafood."

"You spoke to the president? When?"

"Just before I showered."

He looks at me. "You've cleaned up beautifully," he says.

"Thank you," I say.

"Nothing else you want to tell me about anything?" he says.

"She asked if we were gay and I told her we weren't, and that seemed to provoke her to ask me out to a party."

"I meant, was there anything else you wanted to report about your conversation with the president," he says.

"If you get to speak to the president himself, tell him about kayaking," I say. "When I mentioned it, the idea seemed to please him."

"Maybe we could borrow a couple of kayaks and take them all for a predinner ride."

"Right. They can bring in the Navy SEALs."

"You're saying that would be too complicated," Lowell says.

"I suspect."

"You should leave before Kathryn begins to cross-examine you."

"Good idea."

"Be sure to fill the gas tank to the level you found it at."

I turn to look at him. He does a double-take, and raises his hands above his head. "Joke," he says.

The party is at a house with crayon-blue shutters. Broken pieces of colored tile are embedded in the cement steps. A piece of sculpture that looks like a cross between Edward Munch's scream and a fancy can opener stands gap-mouthed on the side lawn, but the lawn isn't a lawn in the usual sense: it's pink gravel, with a huge cement birdbath that is spotlit with a bright pink light. Orchids bloom from square wooden boxes suspended from hooks on the porch columns. A man who makes me look like an ant to his Mighty Mouse opens the door and scrutinizes us. Nancy—I am thinking of her as Nancy, instead of as the highlighter—reaches in the pocket of her white jacket and removes an invitation with a golden sun shining on the front.

"That's the ticket to ride," the man says. "Party's out back."

We walk through the house. Some Dade County pine. Ceiling fans going. Nice. The backyard is another story: a big tent has been set up, and a carousel revolves in the center, though instead of carousel animals, oversized pit bulls and rottweilers circulate, bright-eyed, jaws protruding, teeth bared. One little girl in a party dress rides round and round on a rottweiler. In the far corner is the bar, where another enormous man is mixing drinks. Upon closer inspection, I see that he has a diamond stud in one ear. Wraparound sunglasses have been pushed to the top of his shaved head.

"I guess . . . gee, what do I want?" Nancy says. "A rum and Coke."

"The real thing, or diet?"

"Diet," Nancy says, demurely.

"A shot of Stoli," I say, as the man hands Nancy her drink.

He pours me half a glass of vodka.

"Thank you," I say.

"Nancy!" a woman in a leopard print jumpsuit says, clattering toward her in black mules.

"Inez!" Nancy says, embracing the woman. She turns to me. "This is, like, absolutely *the* best makeup person in New York."

"Did you make friends with Madonna?" Inez asks.

"No," Nancy says. "She didn't like me. It was clear that I was really a menial person to her."

"She didn't know you," Inez says.

"Well, you can't meet somebody if you won't speak to them," Nancy says.

The woman disappears into the growing crowd, and Nancy sighs. "I didn't do a very good job of introducing you," she says.

"Can I be honest? I'll never see these people again, so it really doesn't matter to me."

She squeezes my hand. "I'd like to think that maybe there's a

205

chance that I'll see you again, at least," she says. "Maybe sometime you'll want to come to New York and check out what's new in some restaurants there."

"Maybe so," I say. "That would be very nice."

"It would," she says. "There are hardly any straight men in New York."

Two ladies in hats are air kissing. One holds a small dog on a leash. It's so small, Nancy's kitten could devour it. On closer inspection, though, I see that it's a tiny wind-up toy. I overhear the woman saying that she's bringing a non-pooping pet as a gift for the hostess. People begin to play Where's-The-Hostess.

"I think it's so exciting you're going to meet the president," Nancy says. "Hillary, too."

"Are you talking about my friend Hillary?" the woman who'd been talking to a woman with the toy dog says.

"Nothing detrimental," I say quickly.

"Priscilla DeNova," the woman says. "Pleased to meet you both."

"I'm Nancy," Nancy says. "This is my friend Richard."

"Richard," the woman echoes. "And do you know George, if you know Hillary?"

"I've only spoken to him on the phone," I say.

"Oh. What were you discussing with my friend George?"

"The president's coming to dinner," I say.

"I see. Is he going to drop by to fish, first?"

"He did mention the possibility. But no. He's just stopping by to dine."

"Conch fritters?" the woman says. She seems very amused by something.

"I think we can do a little better than that."

"What he really likes is burgers," Priscilla says. "I guess anyone who reads the paper knows that." She tosses back her long hair and says, almost conspiratorially, "Tell me the truth. Have you been having me on about Clinton coming for dinner?"

"No. The whole family will be coming."

"You must either be a fascinating conversationalist or quite a cook," she says.

"Or quite delusional," I say.

"Yes, well, that possibility did cross my mind." She looks around for someone more interesting to talk to.

"Tell us how you know George Stephanopoulos," Nancy says.

"My sister cleans house for a friend of his," the woman says. "She was a brilliant teacher, but she ruined her mind with drugs, and now about all she can remember is *Get the vacuum*. George has always been very kind to her. He gave her a ride once when she got stuck in the snow. He has a four-wheel drive, or whatever those things are. One time he saw us out hailing a cab, and he dropped us at the Avalon and came in to see the movie." She looks down, considering. "You know, I've never gotten straight on whether George, himself, goes on some fishing expeditions—so to speak, I mean—or whether Clinton gets some idea in his head, and then it just disappears. What I mean is, I wouldn't get my hopes up about them coming to dinner." She looks around, again. "Though if Hillary's involved, I suppose it might happen."

She drifts off without saying good-bye.

"Would I scare you off if I said that part of the reason I came to a bris in Florida was because a psychic told me that on this trip, or the next trip, I'd find true love?" Nancy says suddenly.

"You don't mean *me*."

"Oh, of course not," she says, straight-faced. "The woman who just walked away."

"You did mean me," I say.

"Yes, I did. I don't mean that right this moment I'm in love with you, but you do seem like a real possibility." Her eyes meet mine. "Come on: you must have had some interest, or you wouldn't have come tonight."

I smile.

"And you have such a nice smile," she says.

"Excuse me for interrupting, but have you seen Gianni?" a small man asks. He has on a Gianni Versace shirt and black pants. He might be five feet tall, he might not.

"I'm afraid I don't know him," I say.

"But he's about to meet the president," Nancy says.

"The president of what?" the short man says.

"The United States," Nancy says.

"I'm Cuban," the man says. He walks away.

"So maybe it would be more fun at the Casa Marina," Nancy says. "Did you bring your bathing suit? There's a hot tub there."

"It's in my car," I say. "But didn't you say there was a pool here, in the kitchen?"

"Oh, right. I almost forgot," she says. "Let's find it."

We make our way back into the house. Two women are making out on a sofa in the hallway. The bouncer looms in the doorway, checking invitations. We take a left and find ourselves in a Victorian parlor. We turn around and go in the opposite direction. That room contains a stainless steel sink, where two women are washing and drying glasses. Nothing else that resembles a kitchen is there: no refrigerator; no cupboards. An indoor hot tub bubbles away, with several men and women inside, talking and laughing. There is a mat below the three steps leading to the hot tub. It depicts a moose, and says, in large black letters: WELCOME TO THE CAMP. The people in the hot tub are all speaking Italian. At the sink, the women are speaking Spanish. From a radio above the sink, Rod Stewart sings.

"Bathroom?" one of the women at the sink asks us.

"No, no. Just looking," Nancy says.

"Mr. Loring," the woman says, puckering her lips excessively to say, "Loring." She looks at Nancy. She says: "He went to the bathroom."

Nancy considers this. "Thank you," she says.

"*De nada*," the woman says.

"I think it would be more fun at the Casa Marina," Nancy says.

"Welllllll," Kathryn says. "Somebody got home *very* late."

"Refill the tank?" Lowell asks.

"Just imagine me blushing deeply," I say.

"But at least somebody thought to bring the *New York Times*. Good, good, good," Kathryn says.

"If you like all these things so much why do you leave New York?"

"To check the level of depradation," she says.

"Any update on the president?" I ask.

"You'd better not be responsible for my favorite hair highlighter of all time leaving New York City to live in the boonies," Kathryn says.

"Don't worry. I didn't ask her to marry me."

"You don't have to. Sex with a straight guy is enough to drive them over the edge."

"Quiet," Lowell says. "I don't want to hear the two of you sniping at each other before I've even had a cup of coffee."

On the counter, the coffee is slowly dripping into the pot.

"We went to a party," I say. "Gianni Versace was there, but he was peeing the whole time. We left and got into the hot tub at the Casa

Marina. We watched *Grand Hotel* on the tube and had room service deliver a steak."

"It's love," Kathryn sighs.

"Well, don't sound so despondent about it, Cruella," Lowell says. The phone rings. Lowell ignores it, resting his head on his hands. Kathryn is fanning herself with the travel section.

I answer the phone.

"George here," the voice says. "I just found out there was a screw-up, and that no one from Mrs. Clinton's staff got back to you. My apologies for that. I didn't awaken you, did I?"

"No, not at all. You'll want to be speaking to Mr. Cartwright," I say.

"Well, actually, if you could just relay the message that things are pretty much on hold at this end, I'd appreciate it."

"Of course," I say.

"I hope we can do it another time," George Stephanopoulos says.

I don't know what makes me do it, but I say, "You know, last night I was at a party—Gianni Versace and some other folks, down in Key West—and I met a woman who knows you. Apparently her sister cleans house for a friend of yours. Does this ring a bell?"

"What?" George Stephanopoulos says.

"Nice-looking woman. From Washington. With a sister, who—"

"Oh, sure. You're talking about Francine Worth's sister Priscilla."

"Yes," I say.

There is a pause. "What about her?" George Stephanopoulos says.

Lowell and Kathryn are staring at me. The dripping coffee is making deep, guttural, sexual sounds.

"The party wasn't that much fun. You weren't missing anything," I say.

"Is that right? Well, a lot of the time I feel like I am missing something, so maybe I'll feel better now that I know I'm not."

"It wasn't so bad, I guess. I haven't been to a party for years. Not on a date, either, to tell the truth. So last night was quite out of the ordinary for me."

"I guess so, then," George Stephanopoulos says, after a slight pause.

I can't think what to say. I realize that I'm being watched from one end, and listened to carefully at the other.

"Well, we'll see if this can be worked out sometime when things are less hectic," George Stephanopoulos says. "Just think of me stuck at the desk the next time you step out."

"Oh, there isn't going to be a next time. She's going back to New York tomorrow." I add: "Priscilla had only good things to say about you. Your kindness in giving people rides, I mean. Very generous."

"Yeah, I caught a movie with them one time. Seems like that was in another lifetime."

"I often have that same feeling of disorientation. I've lived so many places. Thailand. All over France, at various times. Le Moulin de Mougins, when the cooking was still brilliant. In the U.S., there's a place called Lava Hot Springs. Lowell and I went there when he took part in a steak barbecuing competition, I guess you'd call it. A very nice place. And the country is full of places like that."

"I know it," George Stephanopoulos says. "Man, you're making me chomp at the bit."

"You should come here and fish and have dinner, yourself, if you ever take a couple of days off. We're right on the water. Plenty of room."

"That's very nice of you. Very nice, indeed. Certainly be easier than trying to get everybody together to caravan down there in early February, Mrs. Clinton converging from one place, the president with no idea what time his meeting is going to conclude. And you toss into that three or four teenage girls, some of them who'll back out at the last minute because some boy might call, or something."

"Feel free to call us," I say. "Some of Lowell's uncollected recipes are his very best. The Thai-California fusion dishes he's been working on have really come together."

"My mouth is watering," George Stephanopoulos says. "Think of me when you're having some of that terrific food."

"Will do," I say.

"And thanks again," George Stephanopoulos says. It doesn't seem like he really wants to hang up.

"See you, then, maybe," I say.

"I'll keep that in mind," he says. "Good-bye."

Kathryn is the first to speak. She collects her cup, and her brother's, and pours coffee, giving me a wide berth to indicate her skepticism. She's jealous; that's what it's always been with Kathryn. She's very possessive, very set in her ways. In spite of passing judgment on anything new, she's still trying to come to terms with things that are old. How many years have I been around, now—years in which I've been pretty decent to her—and she still wishes that she

210

had her brother all to herself? Kathryn says: "The new effusiveness."

I say nothing.

"Well, for God's sake, would you mind letting me know the out-
come of your little chat? Am I correct in assuming that the president
is not coming, but that George Stephanopoulos might?" Lowell says.

I nod.

"What is this? Twenty Questions? The president is not coming . . .
why?"

"Some meeting is probably going to run late, and Mrs. Clinton
would be rendezvousing with him from wherever she was, and
Chelsea and her friends apparently drive him mad, because they're
so unpredictable."

"He didn't know this when he called?" Kathryn says.

"How would I know?"

"Don't you two start in on each other. Think about me, for once.
What about my feelings, when I was prepared to be cooking for the
president and suddenly he decides to blow the whole thing off be-
cause some meeting might run a little late."

Kathryn and I take this in. I get a mug and pour coffee. We all sit
at the table in silence.

"I'm not sure it quite computed with me," I say. "The president
visiting, I mean."

"I wonder if the bastard's still having lunch at Antonio's," Lowell
says.

"Read the *Times*," I say. "Would you like me to make you some
toast?"

"No thank you," Lowell says. "But it's nice of you to offer."

"I'll be on the deck," Kathryn says. She picks up her mug and half
the paper and walks outside.

"Still," Lowell says. "Not everyone gets a call from the president."
He looks at me. "Remember a few months after we met, when we
had that barbecue at your uncle's?"

"Of course I remember. He was a great guy. Never charged me a
nickel for room and board. A totally generous man. 'Never get too
big for your britches that you turn your back on your family,' my un-
cle used to say."

"You never did," Lowell says. "You sent him food every time we
went somewhere exotic."

"Pistachios from Saudi Arabia," I say.

"And I've taken his advice, too. Which means that Kathryn will tyrannize us forever," Lowell says.

Back in Key West that evening, on impulse, I'm almost giddy. I go to the Green Parrot and have a cold draft before going over to the Casa Marina to meet Nancy and her friends in the bar there. Some bikers are at the Parrot with their girlfriends. Somebody who looks like a tweedy professor, except that he's got on pink short shorts with the tweed jacket with elbow patches, so he might be just another unemployed oddball. He's playing a game of Nintendo while sipping some tropical drink through double-barrel straws.

I am thinking about what I might have said to the president if he came to dinner.

But then I think: he no doubt already knows the Marines are a bunch of dangerous psychos. He always had better sense than to truck with any of that stuff.

What would Nancy say if I suggested moving to New York with her?

Probably yes. She dropped enough hints about the lack of straight guys in Manhattan.

What do you get when you fall in love?

You get enough germs to catch pneumonia.

What happened to all the great singers of yesteryear?

Replaced by "The Butthole Surfers."

"You hear the one about this guy's girlfriend who's leaving him?" a skinny guy in cutoffs and a "Mommy and Daddy Visited Key West And All I Got Was This Crummy Shirt" T-shirt says, sitting next to me on a bar stool.

"Don't think so," I say.

"The girlfriend says, 'I'm leaving you. I'm out of here.' And the guy says, 'Whoa there, can a guy even know why?' and she goes, 'Yeah, I've heard something very, very disturbing about you.' He says, 'Oh yeah? What's that?' She says, 'I heard that you were a pedophile.' He says, 'Hey, that's a pretty big word for an eleven-year-old.'"

Today I have spoken to this unfunny jerk, and to the president's assistant, George Stephanopoulos. Also to my employer, who is depressed, because the president was going to come to dinner and then suddenly he didn't want to, and to Kathryn—the sarcastic Kathryn, who always brings both of us down—though soon I will be talking to the lovely, though fleeting-as-the-breeze Nancy. Somewhere in the middle of these thoughts, I manage a strained, "Ha ha." I ask for the check and pay the bill before the guy gets wound up again.

I drive on Duval, to check out the action. A bunch of middle-aged tourists, who wonder what they're doing in Key West, a lot of T-shirt shops, quite a few kids beneath the age of consent, not yet at the age of reason, who have never even heard of the Age of Aquarius. Duval looks like Forty-Second Street, although maybe by now Forty-Second Street looks like Disneyland.

I meet Nancy and her friends—both women—where she said they'd be: at the beach bar. The women give me the once-over, and the You-Might-Hurt-Her-Permanently squint. Nancy flashes bedroom eyes, but only gives me a discreet peck on the cheek. "There's another party, in a condo over by the beach. But first Jerri has to go back to the photo place where she works, because she needs to double-check that the alarm is activated," she says.

"Nobody has a car. Would you mind driving?" Jerri says.

"Not at all," I say.

"Some customer left a bottle of champagne for the owner, but he's a beer drinker, so he just gives me those things. If you want, we could take that out of the fridge and drink it."

"Mmmm," Bea, the other woman, says. Bea looks like she might eventually forgive me for being a man.

"This new alarm system has been screwing up in a major way," Jerri says. "It will take me ten secs to make sure it hasn't depro-grammed itself. And to round up the bubbly."

"So," Bea says. "I hear you're the assistant to a famous chef."

"Yes, I am."

"Do you cook, too?"

"Just help out," I say. "I'm not innovative, myself."

"So how does somebody get a job like that?" Bea says.

"Lowell and I became friends when I picked him up for a car service I used to drive for. It was back in the days when you'd meet somebody and check them out, and basically, if you liked the person, you never minded running some strange proposition past him."

"What was the strange proposition?" Nancy says.

"It wasn't so strange in and of itself. But there I was driving for a car service, and basically, he wanted to know if I had any interest in coming to work for him. Letting the other job go."

"Did he talk about money? I had two job interviews last year and it

213

turned out they didn't want to give me any money at all! They wanted me to take a full-time job as a volunteer!"

"He didn't mention money, now that you mention it. But people went more on intuition then, I think. I figured he'd pay me a decent wage."

"So where did he get a name like Lowell?"

"I'm not sure."

"Everybody who meets me wants to know absolutely everything about me," Jerri says. "Full disclosure, even if I'm, like, trying on a pair of shoes. I wouldn't get out of the store without saying how much I pay in rent. Though I suppose people in Key West are obsessed with that."

"They are? Why?" I ask, grateful that something has come up that I can ask about.

"Because it costs so much to live here," she says.

"Oh. Right," I say. I open the car door, and everyone gets in.

"Guess what I pay in rent," Jerri says.

"I wouldn't have any idea."

"It's a one bedroom, and the bedroom isn't mine. It's on the top floor of a house on Francis that has a separate entrance. I share it with the landlady's granddaughter, who's not all there, if you know what I mean. She's forty years old, and all she does all day is read gardening books and drown all the houseplants so they die."

"When she moved in, they gave her a mattress that used to be the dog's bed," Bea says.

"God," Nancy says. "Things were never that bad back in New York, were they?"

"Oh, I didn't *sleep* on it," Jerri says. "But it was really depressing, because all these little fleas were using it as a trampoline. You could see them jumping up and down."

"I suppose you're going to tell me that the rent costs a fortune," I say.

"One fifty-five a month," Jerri says. "Take a turn here. The next street's one way."

"Isn't that reasonable for Key West?" I ask.

"Yeah, it's reasonable, but I had to buy my own mattress and box spring, and the granddaughter insists on keeping lights on in every room, all night."

"You couldn't find another place to live?" I ask.

"For *one fifty-five?*"

214

Jerri indicates that I should take an empty parking space. I park, and we lock the car and start down the street. From a clip hanging off her belt, Jerri removes a key ring. She opens two locks with two different keys and flips on a light inside the back of the shop. We walk in behind her. She looks at a panel, flashing a number, on the same wall as the light switch. "Whew," she says. "Okay, this is cool." She pushes a couple of buttons and walks to the small refrigerator in the corner, from which she removes the bottle of champagne. She reaches up on a shelf and takes down a tower of upside-down plastic glasses. She counts out four and puts the rest back on the shelf.

But my attention is drifting. In the back of the shop there are life-size cardboard cutouts with cutout faces. One is Marilyn Monroe, with her skirt blowing up. Another is Tina Turner, all long legs and stiletto heels and micro-mini skirt with fringe. There is the American Gothic couple, and there are a couple of Pilgrims, complete with a turkey that retains its own face. There's Donald Duck, and Donald Trump with Marla Maples, who also has her face; Sylvester Stallone as Rocky; James Dean on his motorcycle. There is also Bill Clinton, arm extended to clasp the shoulder of whoever stands beside him. Jerri has walked over to the figures; first she becomes Marilyn, then Tina Turner. Her young, narrow face makes her unconvincing as either. Nancy is the next to wander over. Champagne glass in hand, she tries her luck as Rocky. She motions for me to join her. I do, and together we peer out from behind the Pilgrim couple. Behind the cutouts she passes me her glass, and I duck back to take a sip of champagne.

"I look at this stuff all day long. It doesn't seem so funny anymore," Jerri says. "And what's really not funny is when some guy who thinks he's a real stud comes in to be Stallone, or when some guy who smells like a brewery wants his girlfriend to be Marilyn. *Really* wants her to be Marilyn."

"I notice they don't have one of Ike with his gun," Jerri says, sticking her face through Tina Turner's highly teased hair.

"Too bad there's not one of your good friend, George Stephanopoulos, just his flunky," Jerri says. "Nancy was telling us about that before you came over."

Nancy smiles, mugging from behind the female Pilgrim again.

"Well, we all know Nancy. Nancy's only interested in the rich and famous. Or in people who hang with the rich and famous," Jerri says.

"That cowboy she lived with was hardly rich or famous," Bea says.

215

"You were always so jealous you couldn't see straight, because somebody followed me all the way from Montana to New York," Nancy says. "It really made you crazy, didn't it, Bea?"

"Oh, look who's talking! Like you didn't call my old boyfriend the day he moved out!" Bea says.

"I called him to get my canvas bag back."

"Listen to her! She called about eight hours after he moved into his new place because she needed a bag back!" Bea shrieks.

"You are so sadly misled," Jerri says. "I mean, fun is fun, but this is one time I've got to defend my friend Nancy. She always thought your boyfriend was a *jerk!*"

It's as if I'm not there, suddenly. While they continue to go at it, I wander over to the plastic glass of champagne that's been poured for me and take a long, bubbly sip. So she lived with some guy who followed her all the way to New York from Montana. When? How long were they together?

"And you look so much like him!" Bea suddenly says to me. "If you were, like, fifty pounds lighter, and if you wore cowboy boots some armadillo gave its life for instead of those goony shoes, you'd be a dead ringer for Les."

"*Jesus*! I can't believe you're so jealous I've got a date that you're insulting him about his weight!" Nancy says.

"Oh, sit on it," Jerri says. "Both of you."

"Bea has really got it in for me!" Nancy says to Jerri.

"*I've* got it in for *you*? Nancy, you need to ask yourself why, every time somebody says something that's true, but maybe you don't want to hear it . . . you should ask yourself why you find it necessary to say that that person is *crazy*. I mean, Fuck you!" Bea says. She pushes past Marilyn and storms out the back door, crushing her empty plastic glass.

"Je-*sus*," Nancy says. "What is *wrong* with her?"

"Well, don't get on your high horse," Jerri says. "You didn't have to tell her how mean and spiteful she was."

"I didn't say that. I only said she was jealous of me and Les."

"Who's Les?" I ask.

"I don't see why we should be talking about this now," Nancy says.

"You mean, you thought we were having a conventional date?" I ask.

"No, I didn't . . . I mean, we're going to a party, aren't we? We stopped by here because Jerri had to check the damned alarm."

216

"She wanted an excuse to say mean things and run off," Jerri says. "It pisses her off that Nancy and I can discuss things and be really honest with each other, because she introduced the two of us, and she's got some weird thing about how each of us has to have her as our best friend, so we're not supposed to care that much about each other."

"I can't follow all this. Maybe we should go to the party," I say.

"I feel bad," Jerri says. "I should have tried to cool her out."

"Why should you feel responsible for Bea's state of mind?" Nancy says.

"Let me get a picture of you two," Jerri says. "Souvenir of our wonderful evening, so far."

She goes to a safe and turns the combination lock. When the door swings open, she takes out a Polaroid and fiddles with the camera. I'm still wondering: Who's Les? How long has he been gone? And: what constitutes goony shoes?

Nancy seems quite shaken by Bea's exit. She is fighting back tears, I see, as Jerri gestures for us to make a choice: for a couples shot, it's either American Gothic or the Pilgrim couple. Nancy, sniffing, moves behind the Pilgrims. I stand beside her, crouching so my face peers out where it's supposed to.

The camera spews out the photograph. We both converge on Jerri, to watch it develop.

"Let me get you with the president. Go on," Jerri says, gesturing for me to stand next to Clinton.

"You know, she can really be a terrible bitch," Nancy says. "But now I feel like everything's all messed up."

The flash goes off. Jerri takes the first photograph out of her pocket and nods approvingly. The second photograph—the one she just took—begins to quickly develop. There I am, probably closer to the president than I'd ever have gotten if he'd come to the house, and obviously on much chummier terms. Probably just as good as meeting him, the photo op being interchangeable with real experiences in recent years.

"You're mad at me for dragging you into this," Nancy says. Tears are rolling down her cheeks.

"No, it's just one of those things that happened," I say.

"One of those things that happened?" she repeats. She seems confused. "You mean you think this was okay? It's okay if somebody insults you and if the person you slept with the night before turns out to be in love with some other guy?"

217

It takes me a minute to respond. "I didn't know until now that you were in love with him," I say.

"I am! And I think that if the mere mention of his name, by that bitch, can make me this upset, maybe I should swallow my pride and go out to Montana and get him. He didn't hate me, he just hated New York."

I raise both hands, palms up.

"That's fine with you?" she says.

"What can I do about it?" I say.

"You know, I think that once again, I've found an apathetic jerk," Nancy says. "I guess it's all for the best that this happened, because this way you and I won't waste any more time with each other."

"I cannot believe this," Jerri says. She puts both pictures in her shirt pocket. She walks over to the safe, shaking her head. She replaces the camera in the safe and shuts the door. "Lights out, kids," she says, tiredly.

"Yeah," Nancy says. "I think I'll be the first off to dreamy dreamland. I think I'll just spend the night alone with my fabulous new scenario."

We watch her go.

"I suppose I should have gone after her, but I couldn't see the point in it. I think she meant everything she said. So why would I go after her?" I say.

"Is that really a question?" Jerri says.

"Yes," I say.

"In my opinion, you did the right thing not to," she says.

"Thank you," I say.

"You don't have to thank me. I wasn't trying to flatter you. I was just saying that I think you made the right decision."

"What do you say, if you don't say thank you?"

"You don't have to say anything."

I consider this. "I think I'll drive home, but if you'd like a lift anywhere . . ."

"You know, you really didn't deserve that. You really seem like a very nice man."

"With dorky shoes," I say, extending my foot.

"Topsiders are dorky? Millions of people wear Topsiders."

"But I can see that they aren't exactly cool."

"We're not teenagers anymore," she says. "I don't think any of us will perish if we don't have the exact newest thing."

"No," I say.

"Thanks for the offer, but I think I'll just walk over to a friend's house."

"Fine," I say. "I'm sorry about all this, too. It's a lame thing to say, but I sort of appreciate the fact that at least one person is still talking to me."

She shrugs. "You take care," she says.

I'm out the door when she says, "Oh, wait. Take your pictures."

I turn around, and she puts the photographs in my hand. For the first time, I see that they're joke Pilgrims: the woman excessively big-breasted, the man with his fly unzipped. Stallone, of course, you wouldn't dare joke about. And Marilyn is almost a sacred cultural icon. People who don't like James Dean would nevertheless realize that he was the embodiment of cool. But the Pilgrims, I suppose, have become so anachronistic that there's no harm in joking about them. I hand that photograph back to her. "Two turkeys and one big-breasted babe," I say. "I think I might as well pass on that one."

Then I'm out on Duval, going around the corner to the street where I parked the car.

A guy in dreadlocks walks past, bouncing on the balls of his bare feet. On the steps by a guest house, a man lies sprawled on top of a coat, a small pile of clutter next to him. He's wearing a beret, is shirtless and almost trouserless. His pants are down around his hips. He's lying on his side, mouth lolled open. I walk past a store selling silk-screened bags with tropical birds on them. I stop to admire a traveller's palm in someone's front yard, spotlit. As they pass by, a middle-aged woman says to the man she is walking with, "So what part of town did they film *Key Largo* in?" In a shop window, I see a verdigris crane, flanked by gargoyles in graduated sizes. Just as I get near the car, someone's light sensor is activated by my presence; the light blinks on and floods the street with light, and I feel embarrassed, as if I've been caught doing something bad. Or as if I've unnecessarily caused some commotion. But the light blinks out after I pass, and the whole block—surprising, this close to Duval—is eerily quiet. It gives me more time than I want to hear the voice in my head telling me that I've done everything wrong, that years ago, I took the easy way out, that if I think I'm indispensable to Lowell, that's only a delusion—like the delusion that I'm a nice-looking man, or at least ordinary, wearing inconspicuous clothes and conventional shoes. What must it be like to be the president? Pictures in the paper of you jogging, sweating, your heavy legs caught at a bad angle, so they look like tree trunks? Cry at a funeral, and they zoom the lens in on you. "It's love," I hear Kathryn saying sarcastically. Well, no: it certainly isn't, and apparently wasn't going to be. But what version is Nancy going to give Kathryn, back in the great city of New York? On the other hand, what do I care? What do I have to be embarrassed about?

I get in the car, not much looking forward to joining the weekend traffic exiting Key West. It seems that half the world is intent upon getting to the Southernmost point, and half the world is intent upon fleeing it. Half an hour up the Keys, there's a police roadblock. A cop standing in the street is motioning cars over to the side, but thank heaven: I was feeling so sorry for myself, and so preoccupied, that I was creeping along, barely going the minimum. Once past, I turn on the radio. The tape deck has been broken for weeks. I fiddle with the dial and find Rod Stewart, singing, "Do you feel what I feel? Can we make it so that's part of the deal?" which reminds me of the party the night before, which reminds me of afterward, at the Casa Marina. Bad luck, I think. Bad timing, bad lady, bad luck.

"A Whiter Shade of Pale" comes on, which really takes me back. I'm probably among the few Americans who first heard that song in a bar in Tangiers. I think about returning to my room, my VCR, my travel tapes. It seems a pleasant notion. And if I'm lucky, there will be leftovers to eat while I take the nightly imaginative voyage.

Then I see it: the police cars in the driveway. Police on the front steps. Police standing by the rose garden, writing whatever they're writing. The grating noise of their radios seems to stab the quiet of the night. I catch Kathryn, like a stunned deer, in my headlights. Then, suddenly, she is on her way back to the house, accompanied by a policeman. Lowell. Something terrible has happened to Lowell.

"What?" I say to the first cop I see. I only say that word; I can't manage a full sentence.

"Who are you?" he says.

"Lowell's assistant," I say.

"His assistant? You live here?"

I nod yes.

"There was an accident," he says. "The gentleman fell out of a tree."

"Fell?"

"Fell," the cop says, his shoulders going a little limp and his knees slightly buckling as he slumps toward the ground. "From a tree," he says again.

"What happened to him?" I ask.

"He was airlifted to Miami," the cop says. "I wouldn't want to speculate about the extent of his injuries."

"He's alive," I say.

"He might have broken his neck," the cop says. He swivels his head and puts his ear as close to his shoulder as it can get without actually touching the shoulder.

I go in the house, where every light is on.

"They wouldn't let me on the plane," Kathryn says, turning toward me in the glare. Then she collapses in tears. "That stupid whore you've taken such a liking to, with her mangy kitten. She just turned it out and then . . ." Tears interrupt Kathryn's story. Then she pulls herself together, or tries to imitate someone who's pulled herself together. She looks into my eyes. "You knew she left the god-damned thing here, didn't you? It got away, and she just left it. She told me to find it, like I was her servant, or something." She stops. "I didn't mean that the way it sounded," she said. "I didn't mean anything personal. Oh, God, if he lives, I'll never be awful again. I really won't. All I'm saying is, why am I supposed to find some scrappy cat and get it back to her in New York? That's something perfectly normal to expect, like she left an earring here, or something? She didn't even tell you any of this, when the other morning it was such a crisis I thought she was going to jump out of her skin if the ratty thing didn't come back?"

I shake my head no. This can't be happening. Just a few hours ago, everything was fine.

"It's impossible," Kathryn says to a cop who passes by. "This morning we were talking about the president coming here for dinner."

I reach in my pocket and take out the photograph of myself with Clinton. I stare at it, as if it's evidence of something.

"Hey! You and President Clinton!" the cop says. He's young. Blond with blue eyes. He looks like he's barely more than a teenager. But can he really be so unobservant that he doesn't know it's a joke photograph? My head begins to pound.

"It's my fault for ever bringing her here," Kathryn says. "She let her cat go, like it was a dog that would come back from a walk." She turns to me. "He was fixing dinner, and I saw it. It ran up a tree, like a squirrel. Lowell was inside. He turned off the stove and went out

221

on the deck, and eventually we got the ladder and put it up. Lowell was trying to coax it down from the kapok tree. Then he started to climb, and the next thing I knew, he was in the water, but he wasn't moving. I thought he didn't move right away because the fall had stunned him. I waded out and got him. Otherwise, he would have drowned. You don't live where there's anyone who can help you in an emergency. I could have screamed my head off, and nobody would have come. He went after that stupid girl's stupid cat, and now they think something horrible happened to his spine."

The young cop has listened attentively to this avalanche of information. Finally he turns to me. "Was he also a friend of the president's? Should someone let the president know?" he says.

Is he possibly making some bizarre joke? I look at the photograph again, as if I might be the one who's missing something. Clinton, in a gray suit, stands smiling, his arm, with its inexactly cutout hand, too stiffly extended to really appear to be clasping anyone's shoulder.

Words tumble through my mind, as I imagine the letter I might send: *"Dear George, I enclose a photo that's as close as I'll ever come now to the real thing. This evening Lowell was airlifted to Miami, with serious injuries: quite probably a broken neck. Which leaves me wondering—if things go as badly as they seem to be going at the moment—what a person who has always been a maverick in this country is supposed to do when the comfortable life he more or less stumbled into unexpectedly disappears out from under him. The first woman I dated in years turns out to be in love with another man. . . ."*

I open the kitchen drawer. There is the wine pull, foolish contraption that it is. An item guaranteed to be puzzled over if found years hence in a time capsule.

"How you doing, big guy?" a cop I haven't spoken to before says to me.

"This is a joke," I say, removing the Polaroid from my pocket and holding it out. "You see that, don't you?"

"Sure," he says slowly, as if I'm playing some sort of parlor game. He studies my face. "I had a picture taken of myself one time in one of those fake stockades. Used it as a Christmas card. One of those 'From Our House To Yours' things. Turned out pretty funny."

"Thank you," I say, so quietly I can barely hear my own voice. I put the picture back in my pocket, clamping my right hand over it as if it might fly out and disappear. As if I were a boy again, in one of the many schools I attended, dutifully reciting the Pledge of Allegiance.

Those days when life consisted of ritual, wherever we lived; ritual was the one constant, as predictable as my father's patriotism, as inevitable as my mother's churchgoing. I would get away from all that, I vowed. And I did—researching hotels and restaurants around the world, booking flights, arranging for any necessary letters of introduction, Lowell and I greeted by interesting and important people wherever we journeyed—people with whom we drank wine and dined. And now, it seems, that travel has concluded in the Florida Keys.

The note—the note in response to the letter I do eventually write to George Stephanopoulos—is very brief. It is addressed to Lowell, naturally enough, not to me. It concludes, in a heartfelt, yet predictable way, yet in a totally sincere way, if you know George: "*You are in the president and first lady's prayers.*"

Nominated by Conjunctions

THREE CROWS

by CAROL POTTER

from A SHORT HISTORY OF PETS (Cleveland State University Poetry Center)

How the falling snow erases sound from the air.
It pleases me that the slur of cars on 47 is gone.
That I can hear no squirrels running in the dry leaves.
And the tree frogs, crickets that sang all summer
this is it, not much time, not much time they sang, are gone.
We subtract the color green, take away leaf from tree
and add the bare backs of hills that the leaves hid.
The ground has become stone and the small pond sheeted over.
What was alive in the water has buried itself in the mud.
Is dead. Does not bat itself against the bottom of the ice.
Does not stare at the sky through that shut door.
You can knock on the ground and nothing comes out.
Take away the voices summer plaits inside the green.
That profusion of leaf, each blade singing and the air
thick with sound. If grief comes walking now, you can see it.
Something dark, and glossy in the bare field. Three crows.
Voices clear and gratified by their own clarity. It is too late
to paint the house before winter comes, to finish raking leaves.
It is winter. Let the snow fall. Let it freeze and the roads get slick,
the wind drag itself house to house fingering what needs to be
    taken.
What needs to be blown before it. The dead branches off the trees,
and the leaves that didn't fall but hang like paper rattling.
Let the wind take them down. Scrub the trees and cover the ground
around this house. Let it be done. Let it be over with. Take away

what needs to be taken. Let it be taken. Even the beagle all day
on the neighbor's stoop crying *oh, oh, oh,* has gone inside.
Sleeps in front of the fire, the great pink tongue retracted.

Nominated by Kathy Fagan

THE BAD SEED: A GUIDE

fiction by NICOLA MASON

from THE OXFORD AMERICAN

MANY SEEDS DO NOT GERMINATE WHEN PLACED UNDER CONDITIONS
WHICH ARE NORMALLY REGARDED AS FAVORABLE.
—*The Germination of Seeds*

Recognition is all-important. None of us is safe. You could be at the corner grocery, on a lonely bus to Tucson, in the emergency room with a bleeding gash. You could be tossing Mini-Wheats to birds in the park (because most people feed them crap) or sprinting for Gate B *(Gate B, where the hell is Gate B?)*. You could be jazzercizing (if you are *wont* to jazzercize). You could be pumping fuel at a local Shell or finger-ing your tresses in a Paris café. Anywhere, at any time, *you could encounter a Bad Seed*. You could *miss the warning signs*. And if you do, you could sink like a stone into a life of untold misery. Of redoubtable doubt. Of lies that mask truths and truths that mask lies that mask truths. Of throbbing migraines. Of hope that blinks in and out, a distant galaxy. You could sink like a stone, like a waterlogged corpse, like a sack full of hammers—and you will. Because the Bad Seed is always someone you could love. And you always do.

SEED PRODUCTION NORMALLY RESULTS IN AN OPPORTUNITY FOR THE
SEGREGATION AND RECOMBINATION OF GENES SO THAT THE SEED
POPULATION CONTAINS SOME NEW GENETIC COMBINATIONS.
—*Seed Dormancy and Germination*

Bad Seeds come in all shapes and sizes, from all walks of life. They look just like you and me, and this makes them hard to spot. Do not be lulled by their appearance of viability. Bad Seeds like to imagine they are good seeds, and if they think you are fooled—if you laugh too long at their limericks or let your bra strap slip into view— you will become their target *may God help you*. Your only chances of repelling a Bad Seed are (1) to become frowzy (but not *too* frowzy or he will see you as a challenge); (2) to become invisible (yet not so much so that you can't grasp objects and dial phones); (3) to become a robot. TIP: *Do not act like a cast-iron, stone-cold bitch, as this only attracts the Bad Seed.* Usually none of these tactics work, and you are approached anyway.

The initial encounter is a time of extreme danger, because the Bad Seed excels at first impressions and has an endearing persona for every situation. If you are waiting in a block-long line, bored out of your skull, he is the Stand-Up Comic. If you are frantically late, he becomes Kind Soul Who Shares His Cab. At the Suds 'n' Spin, he is the deceptively helpless Guy Who Mixes Whites and Darks. In a crisis, he is Man Who Knows CPR, Man Who Can Land Plane, Man Who Can Cauterize Wound If Necessary, Man Who Can Shimmy Through Small Opening at Great Peril and Not Die. But perhaps his most insidious identity is the Bumbler. EXAMPLE: You are at a party, content with your third tequila and lime, enjoying the taste of your tooth enamel, and the Bad Seed bumbles into you and spills juice (yes, juice, that's the genius of it) on your dress. "Oh, jeeze," he may say, "I'm such a dork. Do you want to use my Stain Stick? I live across the hall." He may say, "God, I feel terrible. I'll never forgive myself if I've ruined your bodice." (Bad Seeds like to say "bodice.") He may say, "Figures I'd spill on the most beautiful woman here. Now you'll never go out with me." He may say, "I know this sounds nuts, but you look great with juice on you." If you show vulnerability, if you are flustered and flattered and sputter words of comfort—"Oh, honestly, this dress is as old as Yoda" (your MasterCard is blood-warm from the purchase); "I was conflicted about it anyway. I mean, who wears eyelet anymore?" (you adore the lace-exercising-restraint look); "Where did you say that Stain Stick was?" (his apartment, i.e., TRAP)—then he will employ the Bad Seed refrain: "Please say you don't hate me." If you allow these words to pass his lips, you are doomed to a date.

227

IT CAN BE INTUITIVELY UNDERSTOOD THAT SOME FACTORS WHICH
PREVAIL DURING SEED DEVELOPMENT COULD INFLUENCE THE
SUBSEQUENT . . . BEHAVIOR OF THE SEED.
—*The Germination of Seeds*

When going out with a seed of unknown viability, play it safe:
bury your heart in the backyard (deep, as dogs and Bad Seeds have
formed an unholy alliance). Remember that you are your own worst
enemy—because you believe that most convicts just got confused;
because you want Chicken Little to have a forum though he's wrong;
because "trust" has become a four-letter word even for people good
at math; because you are lonely and your cat's opinion matters to you
("Do you think I have a pear body? Be honest, Cumin").

The Bad Seed may take you to the ballet or the bowling alley. To
the gallery opening or the Tastee Freeze. But no matter where you
go or what you say (whether you use *chiaroscuro* improperly or insist
the lane gutter has a magnet in it), sometime during the date the Bad
Seed will reveal a Tortured Past That Has Damaged Him Irrevoca-
bly. Instead of alarming you, instead of causing your brain to fire off
the following internal memorandum: MAN MAY BE THE DEVIL,
this will intrigue and draw you to him. As he reveals the Shocking
Facts, you will listen raptly and feel your spleen go limp with com-
passion. You will nod, nod, nod and maybe cry some when he says,
"The musky smell of horses still haunts me," or, "Most people don't
consider that animals can rape. It's a largely unaddressed issue in our
society," or, "If only I'd used the spurs . . . but I was just a boy."

After his confession, you will feel shy and secretly honored that he
has entrusted you with his shame. You will offer him a sip of your
Sprite to show him that you don't think he's befouled, and when he
accepts and sucks on your straw you will think, *This is how the rav-
aged suck straws.* Later, at your door, his mouth will press yours
chastely, and when you try to deepen the kiss he will pull away, duck
his head, and whisper, "I'm sorry . . . the horse, the horse." You will
be understanding and give him a big hug (you always overestimate
the allure of the big hug). You will tell him he can call you if he
wants, and he fervently says he wants, so you imagine he will phone
the next day, or maybe even in the middle of the night to say, "I just
had this incredible dream, and you were in it," or to entrust you with
the name of the horse: "It was Pierce. *Pierce.* I don't know why I
called. I just wanted you to know."

Despite your expectation, he doesn't phone in the middle of the night, but you decide this means nothing, and though it is *far too soon* to dig up the heart, there you are at 3:00 a.m. in your Mighty Mouse nightshirt, carving a crater the size of a minivan out of your flower bed, the neighbor's schnauzer looking on all the while, grinning its soggy, doggy grin. When you finally unearth the heart and go inside to rinse it, the Bad Seed is experiencing REM sleep across town, dreaming he is a jockey riding a mare with straining neck muscles and foaming withers. The mare's face is your face.

SEEDS. . .OF PARASITIC OR SEMI-PARASITIC PLANTS HAVE BEEN
SAID TO DEPEND UPON SECRETIONS FROM THE ROOTS OF
THE HOST PLANTS FOR GERMINATION.
—*Physiology of Seeds*

On the second date you will go somewhere alone, just the two of you, maybe to the levee to watch the river grow luminous with contaminants, or the park so he can swing you too high and hear you shriek. You stroll arm in arm, like in old movies but with far more flying insects, and as you pretend the mosquitoes aren't draining your lifeblood, he will say he knows it's way too soon, and please don't freak out, but he thinks he's falling in love with you. You freak out and protest that you've only just met, and he clutches your wrists (so you can't slap; it's a habit) and breathes, "God, don't you think I know that? It's crazy . . . but there's something about you. I've got chills, Rachel. I'm losing control. You have this power. . . it's electrifying."

You start to lean into him, then pull back and say, "Wait a minute. That's from *Grease*."

He is unfazed at being caught and responds, "I know, I know. But Zuko sings what I *feel*."

Because you, too, struggle to form original thoughts in a derivative world, you believe him, and suddenly you are deeply concerned because (1) you haven't polled your friends yet, and (2) his heart is in your hands—his tender, scarred, pulsating Bad Seed heart. You should crush it, of course. You should hurl it to the ground and stomp it into lasagna and *laugh, laugh, laugh* until a panel truck comes for you. Instead, you stroke his palms and say, "I don't want to hurt you." You plumb his earnest, hopeful, Bad Seed gaze and say, "I think you're an amazing person. But I have violation issues, too, and

229

some psoriasis I'm trying to deal with. What I'm saying is, *I need more time.*"

The Bad Seed turns away to battle emotion. "Of course you do," he says thickly. "You'd think I'd know better than to blurt it out like that. You'd think I could get something right for once in my life. I fucking hate myself!"

He bolts and streaks away, past the curly slide and the bouncing ducks. After a startled moment, you realize his demons are chasing him, and because this is the most cinematic thing that's ever happened to you, you follow them.

You are more a skipper than a runner. More a hopper than a skipper. More an ankle twister than any of these. When you finally reach him, you feel you have traveled years into the future instead of fifty yards dragging your left leg. You find you have a flair for drama, and you clutch the Bad Seed, claw at him to communicate something primal, and make an embarrassing statement that involves the phrase "the cold eye of the cosmos."

Then you go home and sleep with him.

IN VERY MANY SPECIES OF PLANTS THE SEEDS, WHEN SHED FROM THE
PARENT, WILL NOT GERMINATE. . . . THESE SEEDS ARE SAID TO
REQUIRE A PERIOD OF AFTER-RIPENING.
—*The Germination of Seeds*

Transcript of a phone call:
You: "Hi, Mom. It's Rachel."

Your mother: "I hope you're not taking those metabolic grapefruit pills. I feel sorry for the women in the commercials. They lose weight, but there's no adjustment period. The fat girl is still there inside them. You can see it in their eyes—the hunger."

You: "Actually, I'm calling because I'm extremely happy. I've met someone, and he makes me extremely happy."

Your mother: "You said that."

You: "What?"

Your mother: " 'Extremely happy.' You said it twice. You sound like you're trying to convince yourself."

You: "I'm not trying to convince myself. I am myself. I mean, I *am* extremely happy."

Your mother: "Your father is picking the raisins out of the raisin bread. Stop it, Linus. You know I hate it when you do that. He knows I hate it when he does that."

You: "You said that."

Your mother: "Of course I did. Rachel, what's wrong, dear? Is your young man giving you trouble?"

You: "Mother, please. I'm trying to tell you something wondrous about my life. I'm in love with Brett."

Your mother: "Isn't that the name of a hair spray?"

You: "No, that's Breck. But I'm not sure they make it anymore."

Your mother: "Well, he sounds like a snake in the grass to me."

After you hang up, you wander around the house touching your possessions to make sure they aren't concealing blades. "You are mine," you tell your candlesticks firmly. To your lamps and curtains you say, "Mine." In the kitchen, you slide open a drawer and palm your bottle of grapefruit pills. You stare at it; it stares at you. "My decision," you say. You throttle the bottle and enjoy its loose-teeth sound. You declare, "I am your master!" Then you twist the cap and pour the pills down the sink and sit on the floor and cry—because your mother is always right. Even when she's not.

Unfavorable germination conditions often
throw seeds into dormancy so they will not germinate
when shifted to a favorable condition.
—*Physiology of Seeds*

But your mother is wrong about the Bad Seed. You know a snake in the grass when you see one, and the Bad Seed is far from snaky (he blinks, for one thing). To prove this, you dedicate yourself to making him giddy with joy at having you in his life. You know relationships don't come easy (because that's the theme of many popular songs), but this one will work because you will crush any threats to your ecstasy.

In front of a mirror, you practice making your expression of blissful transport look less like a death rictus. You employ this expression in private and in public, even at the risk of being mistaken for Julie Andrews. You build up a repertoire of stock moods and responses and alternate them. There is Rowdy You: "I am having such a rockin' time"; Rhapsodic You: "Wow. I mean, wow, wow, *wow!*"; Reverent You: "It's like we're in church. My soul is as quiet as a sleeping child."

231

For a while you imagine that the relationship is a perfect match instead of a tenuous connection between two people who like carob, that it is full of quixotic emotion instead of a strain on your acting ability. You expect your life will become a whirlwind, that you'll get outdoors more, pack picnics, play Frisbee, catch some fish (if you can bring yourself to kill the crickets). You are sure you'll need new clothes to wear to unexpected events, so you buy some, forgetting you aren't a contessa and don't need that much tulle. Actually, the two of you spend a lot of time watching TV at your place (which you did before). You order take-out (ditto). You read your cookie fortune to the Bad Seed instead of the cat and marvel aloud that your fortunes always seem guarded and noncommittal. ("Hard work makes strong back." "You will climb many mountains." "Luck smiles on the few, not the many.")

"Weird, huh?" you say.

And he says, "Weird," but not enthusiastically—so you worry that he is bored with the relationship, and to spice things up you model your new gowns for him, floating diaphanous and barefoot (free spirits fear not tetanus) across the room. You smile a closed-lip, mysterious smile and say, liltingly, "It feels like I have *nothing* on. Not a *stitch*." But he's watching a *Baretta* rerun, and you keep floating in front of the screen, so instead of leaping up and whirling you from wall to wall like a tulle tornado, the Bad Seed gets cranky and barks, "Can't you see he's talking to the bird!"

Your smile wobbles. Your hair (which you have worked into a spun-sugar cloud) feels sticky on your back. Your feet are cold. "I just wanted to be magical, that's all," you quaver, and stump away to throw yourself on the bed.

A little later he comes in to tell you he's a jerk. You say nothing and concentrate on breathing through your snot. He says, "I swear I amaze myself. Here I am with this incredible girl . . . this gorgeous creature from beyond . . . and I screw it up. I wouldn't blame you if you dropped me like a sack of wet garbage. I mean it. Go, Rachel. Fly." Here, he pins your ankle to the mattress. "But know this: You're my Every Woman."

You are aware that (1) he waited until the commercial to come in and console you; (2) these are probably song lyrics. Moreover, the Bad Seed has failed you in a number of respects (no fish, no Frisbee, etc.). But by now you have invested a lot of time you could have spent speculating about supermodels (will Shalom go short for spring?), reorganizing your pantry, watching your married friends jam chapped red nipples into the chapped red mouths of screaming infants (God, it's so beautiful. How you envy them!). Also, he has seen you naked and hasn't criticized anything.

Then the Bad Seed pulls out the stops: "Please say you don't hate me."

LITTLE . . . IS KNOWN ABOUT PHYSICAL AND
CHEMICAL CHANGES OCCURRING IN CERTAIN SEEDS.
—*Physiology of Seeds*

You love him. You do. But as the months pass, certain aspects of the Bad Seed begin to bother you: his dead incisor (is it getting grayer?); how he drinks in stereo (*agunk, agunk, agunk*); his nail-polish fetish ("Shouldn't you fix that chip before we eat? I can wait"); how he always wants you on all fours and pretends it isn't significant ("Can I help it if you're really sexy back there?"). You tell yourself these things make the Bad Seed unique. That you are always too critical. That you have flaws yourself and he overlooks them. Still, thoughts come at you like trucks, carrying the Names of Boyfriends Past with the labels you affixed to them. Larry the Limpet. New Age Nonny (who moved smooth black stones around in a little tabletop sandbox with a tiny rake). You-Gonna-Eat-That?-Matt. Travis Trivia ("Did you know armadillos can be house trained? Quick! List the biblical plagues. EEERP. Time's up!"). The trucks hurtle toward you at unsafe speeds. There are many, many trucks. It's a convoy, Rubber Duck. And here comes another one—appropriately bringing up the rear. What's your handle, good buddy? Brett from Behind.

You resist these thoughts. All thoughts. You decide to live each moment as pure sensory experience, with acceptance and appreciation and a generous, loving spirit. This would work if each moment weren't full of unbearable irritants. Instead of saying, "My stomach hurts," he says, "I have a rumbly in my tumbly." As quickly as you can buy ChapStick, he steals it; then, when your lips crack and bleed, he offers to let you use his tube. His nose whistles like a mad piper, yet he can't hear it. Then you begin to hear it when he's not around—at the office, out shopping, until you are discovered in a Dillard's dressing room clawing your cheeks and rambling, "He's here, he's here, he's here, I know he's here!"

You decide you need space, but resolve to be mature about it, gentle, because he is fragile and you don't want his blood on your hands. A week passes while you wait for the right moment to break the news. Another week. (You are a physiological wonder: completely gutless, yet you can still digest foods.) Another week. Finally, as you are driving to the movies one night, he keeps punching the car lighter, though he doesn't smoke. He just pulls the knob when it pops and stares at the glowing coils, then holds it up so you can see. "These things are great," he says with fresh discovery in his voice.

"Yes," you say slowly, as to a child. "Fire." Then, because you feel your brain swelling like a blowfish, you blurt, "I think we should see other people."

Your statement is greeted with silence, and you hit the automatic door locks (in case he's a leaper) and wedge your elbow against the window (for leverage should he insanely grab the wheel).

But all he says is, "Oops"—and for an instant you think he has dropped the lighter and the car will be engulfed in flames and he'll hold you tenderly as your skin chars and your liver melts, saying, "If this is goodbye, let us burn together, Rachel." But you realize almost immediately that it's not that sort of an "oops." It's a snake-in-the-grass "oops."

So you demand, "Whadda ya mean, 'Oops'?"

And the Bad Seed shrugs sheepishly and confesses, "I didn't know we were supposed to be exclusive. You never said anything."

You are sure you did not hear correctly, hence your reply: "Come again, Zuko?"

And he says, "I didn't mean to lead you on, if that's what you're implying. It just never came up."

Though you feel a nightmare approaching, you inquire, "*Who* never came up?"

The Bad Seed is pained. "Well . . . if you must know, Gina."

"Gina? *My* Gina? My *best friend* Gina?"

He confirms: "She called a while back, when you were in the shower, and we had a really good talk."

You respond through great cotton wads of stupefaction: "You talked to my best friend? You're not allowed to talk to my best friend. That's a rule. It's a very big rule. It's *giganto*." (You have always hated romantic comedies, and now you know it's because they flout the giganto rules intolerably!) You make a new rule: "You will never talk to my best friend again."

The Bad Seed reproaches, "That's a little selfish, don't you think?

234

Gina's going through a transitional phase, and she needs a lot of support."

You have just turned into the theater parking lot, but instead of slowing down and steering so as to miss immovable objects, you press the accelerator and aim for a dumpster at the end of the row of cars. "See that? That's a transitional dumpster," you remark with eerie calm. "When we hit it, we will change." (You are now courting death; this may signal a loss of perspective on your part.)

"Hey, whoa!" the Bad Seed exclaims. "I didn't know you felt so strongly about it. We're exclusive, okay?"

You ease your foot off the gas pedal and coast to a stop, your bumper giving the dumpster a brushing kiss. "Damn right," you say.

Then you begin to tremble because you have no idea who you are.

THE QUESTION UNDER CONSIDERATION AT THIS POINT
IS WHETHER THIS RESTRICTION OF OXYGEN SUPPLY HAS
ANY RELATION TO DORMANCY IN THE SEED.
    —*Physiology of Seeds*

You quickly learn to despise who you have become. Outwardly, you are cheerful and affectionate (so as not to give him an excuse)—but within, you are a cricket cage, acrawl with suspicions and needling chitinous legs that rub together to make sounds, phrases, mean little commentaries on your (appalling) life. You bury your heart again to punish it for misleading you, but the heart has been working out and paddles up through your tulips using its little aortic stubs. It scales your beech tree and howls like a bone-snapping gale. The neighbors are frightened and because they threaten to involve the police, you are forced to take the heart back, though it knows you are bitter and revenges itself by mass-producing unreasoning psycho-bitch rage.

You throw yourself into sex, performing many astonishing acts with your mind's eye blindfolded. You whinny without being asked. When it's over, you press, "Did *she* do that for you? Huh? Did she?"

The Bad Seed, basking in man-melt, replies lazily, "Who? Oh. I could never love Gina. She has inverted nipples."

This does not mollify you (you are beyond the satisfaction of minor disfigurements, *far* beyond), and when you determine he is deep in dreamland ("Breck?" you whisper to the darkness near his ear. "Breck?"), you go downstairs and pick up the phone and have a pizza delivered to Gina's house—pepperoni, so she'll know you know about the nipples.

You insist he spend all his time with you, and though he seems happy to do this, you notice certain tricks of evasion (for instance, the men's room). At the movies, he leaves his seat during the tank chase, and when you search him out a half-hour later, he is craning over the candy counter, chatting it up with the girl who earlier dispensed your Snow Caps (you swear it) icily. The Bad Seed waves when he sees you. "Hey," he says. "I want you to meet Brittany. She's having a hell of a time with geometry."

"Poor thing," you say, linking your arm with the Bad Seed's and pulling him away. "Good luck with it," you cry gaily over your shoulder. To him, you hiss, "What is she? Fifteen?"

His eyebrows gang up on you, two disapproving parabolas: "I didn't know you were such an ageist."

In the car, you smack your palm on your forehead. "Well, heck darn doo. I forgot something. Be back in a sec, lover." In a twinkling you are at the counter, clutching at the glass, darkening the Milk Duds like a poisonous atmosphere. Brittany is alone, mopping orange pools of popcorn butter. Her nose is cutely awrinkle. Her ponytail, pert. She is your enemy and always has been, and you are about to make the sort of menacing claim that results in restraining orders, when she turns to you with a look of urgency on her flushed little freckledy face. "Listen, you don't know me from Dorcas," she says, "but totally trust me when I tell you your date is a complete creepoid. Like slime central."

Instantly you crumble. Even the Junior Mints (so refreshing!) cannot console you. "Oh, Brittany," you wail. "What should I do?"

She ponders a moment, her brow adorably furrowed. "I think," she says, "you should get away from him."

THERE ARE MANY SEEDS. . .WHICH DETERIORATE
RAPIDLY WHEN EXPOSED TO OPEN AIR.
—*Physiology of Seeds*

You try. You let days drag out of fetal dawn and form restless, questing limbs and finally stoop, broken, into the folding dark—all without touching the phone. You do not wonder what he's doing. You do not wonder what he's doing. You do not wonder what he's doing.

You make a gourmet dinner for one, wearing nothing but an apron, and comment to the cat, "I feel so free and joyous right now. I celebrate my independence and individuality. I affirm myself." Then you catch the reflection of your rear in the oven window glass, and you see you are not affirm at all but rather afflaccid. You reverse the apron, but the view does not improve.

After dinner you catch up on the things you always said you'd do but never really meant to. Like reading operation manuals on appliances you've had for years (this involves some ugly realizations about filters), checking under the house for missing children, changing all the light bulbs because you fear they'll go out at once. At midnight you decide you must have a gentler, more nourishing shampoo immediately, so you get in the car and drive straight to his apartment and stare at his empty parking place for the time it takes you to realize how pathetic you are (about an hour). Then you drive home. At 2:00 a.m. you remember you forgot the shampoo, and you are back at his apartment. This time his car is there, so you stare at his darkened windows and smoke a cigarette shakily and do not wonder if he is alone.

By 3:00 you are at an after-hours bar throwing back shots of ouzo, talking to a guy wearing a clip tie (he demonstrates) who thinks your name is Beth. You say, "My name is Rachel."

He responds, "Oh, right, Beth. Like I believe that. You must think I'm some kind of yutz. Okay, I'm a yutz." He winks and says with poke-in-the-ribs levity, "Hello, *Rachel.*" (Run fast, run far, dear Rachel. Flee with your dignity whilst you can.)

You respond with your own poke-in-the-ribs levity, "Hello, *Brian.*" His face crumples like the squeezed half of a grapefruit.

"Beth," he sobs, his fingers scrabbling at his sternum. "It's me, Stewart. Don't you recognize me?"

The ouzo is making the bar seem like an environment, and you are cozy there with the pitiful people. You are all single cells making up a pitiful animal, one that crawls on its belly as a means of locomotion. Stewart is crawling onto your bar stool. "You *know* me, you *know* me," he is saying.

You nod (slowly, because you're not sure he can detect movement) and speak with the wisdom of the ages: "What you say is true . . . but vast."

Then you take Stewart home and sleep with him.

FOR SOME SEEDS EXPOSURE TO FLUCTUATING CONDITIONS . . . IS
AN OBLIGATORY REQUIREMENT FOR GERMINATION.
—*Seed Dormancy and Germination*

You are now the most degraded you have ever been. Your soap shudders when you reach for it. The shower spits in your face. Even your collars reject you, straining away from your clavicles no matter how you beat them. You realize there is no one but yourself to blame—so you blame the Bad Seed. This works well. By using your hate as a stepping-stone, you emerge from the slough of self-mortification covered with scum, but with no ghoulish tattoos or uncomfortable piercings. When the Bad Seed calls, finally, to see "how things are going," your defiance leaps to the fore, so you do not say, "Like a train wreck with mangled bodies marring the countryside," or, "Okay if you discount the herpes scare," but rather, "Great! This is a very exciting time for me," and to show him you're being both productive and whimsical in his absence, you add, "I'm learning to hula hoop."

He says, "Wow, that's really something," and you say, "Yep." And he laughs a little (a trial balloon), but you don't laugh back, so he tries another tack, saying meltingly, "My life is a weeping sore without you. Rachel, you're my sexy salve."

You feel the heart staging a coup (it's now in league with your lungs, bullying your breath to catch), and you know you must be merciless or forever dwell in the land of song-lyric abominations, so you ask, "Do you know Stewart?"

A pause follows while the Bad Seed reassesses. "I don't think so," he ventures, guarded now. "Should I break his legs?"

For reasons you can't fathom, you are filled with absurd disappointment. "I guess not," you say.

And he says suddenly, "Holy smoke, I just remembered I left something in the oven." And though it's nothing like you imagined it, you grasp immediately that *this is the end*, and to let him know you grasp it, you exclaim with dismay, "And here my sock drawer just exploded. Now I'll never get them matched!"

After he hangs up, you sit quietly to await the heart's rib-kicking conniption, but the heart surprises you by ushering blood cells from room to room like a proper tour guide. You take this to mean grace is possible. Of course, there are rough days ahead. You will wallow and snuffle and chew the buds from your tongue. You will deny yourself cookie dough, and this will backfire monstrously. You will pack your sheets in a box and mail them to the Bad Seed, remembering his comment on your "sleep smell," then smash some darling collectibles when he doesn't acknowledge their receipt.

But some days will not be fresh hells. Some days will be ordinary, and you will accomplish things (like breathing, walking unaided, etc.). You will be a bit kinder to yourself. Maybe you will start a support group, write a pamphlet, stand on street corners shouting, "You, too, can like you! It's a guilt-free gift! No agony attached!" And one morning in the not-so-distant future, you will awaken with the idea that you can be happy. The sky will be a study of softness—blue on blue on blue. There will be sunlight you fail to cringe from. You will turn on the shower full force, and when you step into its mist, you'll practically be bursting your skin.

Nominated by David Kirby, David Madden

BEETLES

by STEVE KOWIT

from *The Dumbbell Nebula* (Heyday Books)

> *The famous British biologist J.B.S. Haldane, when asked by a churchman . . . to*
> *state his conception of God, said: "He is inordinately fond of beetles."*
>
> Primo Levi

Spotted blister beetles. Sacred scarabs.
Water beetles whirling on the surface of still ponds.
Little polkadotted ladybugs
favored by the Virgin Mary & beloved of children.
Those angelic fireflies sparkling in the summer evenings.
Carrion beetles sniffing out the dead.
June bugs banging into screens.
Click beetles. Tumblebugs. Opossum beetles. Whirligigs
& long-horned rhino beetles,
Cowpea weevils snuggling into beans.
The diving beetle wintering in mud.
Macrodactylus subspinosus: the rose chafer
feasting upon rose petals, dear to the poet Guido Gozzano.
The reddish-brown *Calathus gregarius*.
Iridescent golden brown-haired beetles.
Beetles living in sea wrack, dry wood, loose gravel.
Clown beetles. Pill beetles.
Infinitesimal beetles nesting in the spore tubes of fungi.
There is no climate in which the beetle does not exist,
no ecological niche the beetle does not inhabit,

no organic matter, living, dead, or decomposed
that has not its enthusiast among the beetles,
of whom, it has been estimated, one and one-half
million species currently exist,
which is to say one mortal creature
out of five's a beetle—little armored tank
who has been rolling through the fields her ball of dung
these past three hundred million years: clumsy
but industrious, powerful yet meek,
the lowly, dutiful, & unassuming beetle—
she of whom, among all earth-born creatures, God is fondest.

Nominated by Charles Harper Webb, Jack Marshall, Jane Hirshfield, Thomas E. Kennedy

KHWAJA KHADIR

essay by DAVID JAMES DUNCAN

from ORION

> *Worship God as though you see Him.*
> Muhammad The Prophet

In the late 1990s, the editor of a renowned fishing magazine sent a letter asking me to pen a portrait of my favorite fly fishing guide. This portrait was to take its place among "a celebrity compendium of great Western fly fishing guides." A color photo of my guide was also requested.

I'm no celebrity and plan to keep it that way. But I do have a favorite guide—an exceedingly quiet fellow of mixed Middle Eastern extraction, named Khwaja Khadir. I wrote a glowing profile, then found a color photograph of a stretch of empty Montana trout water where Khadir has several times given me superb advice. Empty water was the best I could do, portrait-wise, since Khadir happens to be an Islamic immortal being precisely as photogenic as the Holy Ghost.

I mailed this package off to the magazine. A week or so later the editor phoned. His first words—delivered in the for-some-reason ubiquitous drawl of fishing magazine editors—were, "Ah lahked your gahd po'truht veruh much."

I replied, "That's okay. I didn't expect you to print it." Since the editor had given no hint of rejection yet rejection was indeed impending, he was flabbergasted by my "clairvoyance." But it was really just conditioned response. Years of interaction with magazine editors have taught me that the phrase "liked it very much" is as close

242

as they'll come to saying, "I wouldn't print this cockamamie bullshit if it was the last skein of sentences on earth." In fact even the phrases "I loved it!" or "I've GOT to publish this!" don't mean your story will be published. But I digress.

What the editor said next was, "Ah loved your strange po'trayal of fly fishin'. But Ah was troubled by your gahd concept, raht from the openin' lahn. How can Ah include, in mah profawls of great fishin' gahds, a profawl that in effect tells us not to hahr gahds at all?"

"I didn't recommend hiring no guide," I argued. "I recommended hiring an invisible guide. Big difference."

"Not in your photo of Mr. Khadir," the editor countered. "But now listen. Ah do love the fishin' part o' this. That's whaw Ah cawled. Ah'd like you to cut the refer'nces to invisible Arab fellas, bandage up the cuts, run the result by its lonesome. Ah'd pay twice what Ah could for you gahd po'trait."

"But I wasn't fishing alone," I said. "That's why the fishing was so good. What kind of thanks am I showing the best guide I ever met if I brag up my catch but don't mention he was guiding?"

The editor sighed once more. Even it had a drawl. "Ah'm runnin' a fishin' magazine here, son. Evinrudes 'n Eagle Claws. Hawgs 'n crank-baits. Meet me half way is all Ah'm sayin'. Turn the woowoo down a notch, you got yourself a paycheck."

"And a betrayed invisible fishing guide," I said. "Just toss my story, please. Don't feel bad."

"Big mistake, son," said the editor.

"Not my first," I replied.

"Ah won't forgive you," he warned, "till you send me a fishin' yarn as fahn as this one, woowoo-free."

I said, "Compared to hawgs 'n crank-baits, my whole life is woowoo. 'Cept for maybe my mornin' dump."

The editor laughed. He signed off. He returned my "Great Western Guide Portrait," invisible guide intact.

Here it is:

For the past two and a half decades I have rarely gone fishing without my favorite guide, Khwaja Khadir, whose chief virtues are that, being silent and invisible, he is the closest thing on the river to no guide at all. I first learned of my guide not in a fly shop, or a fishing magazine, or by word of mouth, but in a collection of essays on ecstatic utterances of Sufi saints. Midway through this book, way back in the early '70s, I stumbled onto the Arabic word, *al-Khizr*. I don't speak a speck of Arabic. I'd never seen this word before. When, at the sight of it, an unfounded thrill of recognition shot up my spine, I paid attention.

Investigating further, I learned from a scholarly friend that al-Khizr is a bodiless divine servant so close to Allah that to be accompanied by the former is to stand in the hidden presence of the Latter. I discovered that Khizr is both the guardian and purveyor of "the Waters of Eternity"—the caretaker/bartender, so to speak, of the elixir of secret knowledge and everlasting life. I learned that al-Khizr is also known as *Khidr*, the Green Prophet, Khwaja Khadir, and other aliases, and that he is a famed in the Islamic world as is the Holy Spirit in the Christian world for his omnipresence, perfect wisdom, and perfect invisibility.

In this age of global tyranny by short-term economic thought, Americans have developed a tendency to equate what is desirable with what is profitable, and what is invisible with what doesn't exist. My lifelong flyrod-in-the-office, wisdom-literature-in-the-fishing-vest habits have made me pretty un-American with regard to this tendency. I figure love is invisible. Intuition as well. Before I was born I too was invisible, at least to the fellow I am now. When I die I expect to become the same. To be repelled by invisibility is, then, to be repelled by love, intuition, and my former and future selves. I have, on the contrary, spent my life endeavoring to befriend that foursome. This effort naturally includes my fishing life. Upon learning a bit about the invisible al-Khizr, therefore, I did not think, "*Weird!*" and go turn on "The Dave Show." Instead my thoughts ran more along these lines:

"*Invisibility . . . Omnipresence . . . Perfect Wisdom . . . Guardian of Eternity's waters . . .* Holy shitwaw! What incredible qualifications for a fishing guide!"

I then began trying to figure how to get this being on a river with me.

I didn't expect results. I didn't expect anything. I'm ignorant as mud in these matters. But I didn't rule out the possibility of contact, either. Fly fishing, successfully undertaken, builds enormous faith in the human ability to make contact with unseen beings. When you have repeatedly accomplished tasks as unlikely as slinging a size 22 dry-fly on a 6× tippet toward a hidden aquatic being rising eighty feet away, only to hook, battle, and drag that being into your hands, you grow reluctant to say what is or isn't possible in terms of contacting things invisible—including even invisible fly fishing guides.

I won't fib. The first time I hit a high desert river after learning of al-Khizr, I fished my predatory ass off for a day and a half, forgetting all about him. After deceiving, catching and releasing a fair number of trout, though, my predatory ass was pretty near gone. I love this gradual transition from raging fish-lust to inner quiet. Brings to mind the Tai Chi sequence *"Embrace tiger. Return to mountain."* Nothing strained or "spiritual" about it, really. Deploying ordinary perceptions and movement, normal whoops, curses, and obsession, you stalk and embrace tigerish fish and battle current, glare, brush, wind, and mystery, till your predatory energy begins to gutter out. Of course we fanatics resist this guttering. But sooner or later even the fiercest fly fishers find their eyes staring without focussing, their mouths literally hanging open, and their brains gone silent, having printed out so much fishing data that their cartridges have temporarily run out of ink. I suddenly had no interest in making another cast. The fishing had gone dead anyway. Far better to bask my tired back in July sunlight, let the current lap my legs, listen to the call of the canyon wren.

A magpie wandered idly across the river. A blissful, no-reason chill wandered idly up my spine. I thought of the Rumi line: *Love has taken away my practices. . . .* I thought of the John Coltrane line: *God breathes through us so gently, so completely, we hardly feel it. . . .* And suddenly, I was gasping with gratitude for every last thing I could feel, smell, intuit, or see. High desert all around. Fragrance of sage, fragrance of juniper, fragrance of water. Still, nothing out of the ordinary here. During the "return to mountain" phase, no-reason detonations of this sort greet the devotees of every nonmotorized outdoor sport there is. Typically, though, we greet such visitations with our Throw-Away Consumer reflexes: *"Wow! What a feeling! But now it's fading. Oh well. Goodbye. . . ."*

When this particular chill struck, however, I did not say goodbye. Instead, unaccountably, I whispered: *"Khizr?"*

And just that fast: a bolt of yearning pierced me.

"Is this really you?" I asked the air.

And something about the light over the rimrock, heatwaves over the road, emptiness of canyon, smell of the desert river, left me feeling the answer was, most emphatically, *Yes*.

I don't know what got into me then, but I began speaking to the empty canyon, the yearning, the air, as if to a friend. What's more, I imagined this friend to be the mysterious Arabic being of whom I'd read, and referred to it as such, by name.

I don't recall my exact words, but I remember their basic trajectory. I told Khwaja that since he is all-wise, he already knew I loved rivers and fly fishing: loved them like a sickness: loved them the way some scruffy Druid might once have loved his god. I then surmised—aloud, to keep it physical and official—that as the eternal guardian of waters, Khadir might be as fascinated by fly fishing as I am, yet might also be unable to try it, despite his great powers, for simple lack of a physical body, a fly rod, physical flies. I then informed the immortal Green Prophet that, if he liked, he was welcome to borrow *my* crummy body, rod, and flies, and go fishing with that.

Boy did my mind kick up a fuss at this proposal! *"You imbecile! Al-Khizr is an Islamic divine mystery! An intimate of Prophets and ecstatic sages. Whereas* you *are a dopey American fly flinger. Why would the Green One ever want to borrow* you*!?"*

I understood my mind's position. Even in those days, though, I'd read too much wisdom literature to take that kind of shit from the hired help. "If I'm just a dopey American fly flinger," I fired back, "then *you're* just that dopey fly flinger's *mind*! So shut up. I'm talking to al-Khizr here. . . .

"Khwaja, ignore that jerk. I know I'm in many ways unworthy. But I also know that Prophets and ecstatic sages—the ones I've read about anyway—don't fly fish a lick. Whereas I do. So if you're curious to try it, my offer stands. . . ."

I stood quietly for a while then, out in mid-river, waiting to be "borrowed" or some such thing. But nothing happened. And my mind of course assured me that Whoever or Whatever I'd spoken to hadn't been there in the first place.

A few minutes after issuing my invitation, though, I felt a purposeless urge to leave the glide I'd been fishing and hike, despite the heat, to a fierce, boulder-strewn rapid a mile or so downstream. And upon reaching that rapid I felt a second urge—as strong, clear, and utterly absurd as any in my previous fishing existence—to grease up an extremely large Dave's Hopper with floatant, cast it into the whitewater, hold my rod straight up over my head as high as I could reach, and skitter the hopper back upriver against the ripping current, as if in imitation of a depraved six-legged water-skier. This strategy duplicated no insect behaviour or fishing trick I'd ever heard of or seen. And I immediately hooked, and much much later landed, one of the most beautiful twenty-inch rainbow trout I've ever met. What's more, I felt a joy in the take, the blazing runs, the enveloping sunlight and spray round the leaps, fragrance of sage, roar of water— greater than any I'd felt over the day and a half previous. Which led to a second spontaneous outburst:

"*Jeez*, Khwaja!" I exclaimed as the green-backed trout left my hands and shot back into green depths. "*Nice!*"

That was the first encounter. And scoffers and doubters, please, do scoff and doubt: I'm not selling anything. I just feel compelled—in response to a request to portray my favorite fishing guide—to say that the being I have just so bumblingly described is mine.

I issued that first invitation to al-Khizr some twenty-five years ago. I've continued to issue invitations ever since. I have yet to receive an audible reply. If things do get audible, I'll make an immediate appointment with the best available shrink. What I *have* received in "reply," though—beginning that first day—is an occasional post-invitation urge as palpable yet indescribable as river speech, usually involving some very specific, hitherto-unthought-of fly fishing strategy. These strategems are often so bizarre that my mind gets highly exercised about their inanity, and even my body feels idiotic if I obey them within sight of other fly fishers. But I *do* obey them. Paying careful heed to all such impulses year in and year out, I have ended up fishing in some exceedingly odd places, using some exceedingly odd techniques—and in so doing have caught way more than my share of exceedingly unlikely and magnificent fish. So go figure.

A number of people who've glimpsed these bizarre impulses and their often ludicrously good results have declared me a "fly fishing genius." But to accept that compliment feels dishonest to me. The genius, in my experience, is Khwaja.

Khadir's address, ecstatic poets and Sufi scholars agree, is "the cusp between the Unseen and the Seen." Since there is no way to phone, write, or e-mail this cusp, the sole method of contacting my guide is via direct belief. While Muslim mystics, for centuries, have had little trouble with this, American anglers often find it a stumbling block. If you're the type who needs references, you might like to know that Khadir was an intimate of Muhammad, that he also served (according to Sufi tradition) as guide to Moses, and that he has been written of glowingly by some of the greatest poets on earth—Rumi, Hafiz, Ibn al-Arabi, Ruzbihan Baqli, and al-Bistami, to name a few.

If and when you meet the Green One, you'll notice he is way more invisible than green, and that he speaks a language comprehensible to you almost solely in solitude, and that this language will be inaudible to you even then. His skills, however, more than make up for his marked resemblance to thin air. Confining myself to four:

1. Khizr has been on the job for all eternity—which is longer, if you think about it, than all mortal fly fishing guides put together. That's *experience*!

2. Because he's invisible, he has never spooked a fish: *ever*!

3. If you think through his omnipresence, intimacy with Allah, and knowledge of waters, Khadir knows where *every single fish on Earth* dwells, knows in advance whether you're going to catch it, knows (karmically speaking) whether you *should* catch it, knows who you and the fish were before you were born, who you'll become after you die, who creates and sustains you, the meaning and purpose of life, how it all comes out in the wash. And so on. Despite the subtlety of Khwaja's presence and guiding style, this kind of know-how makes for reassuring company. And,

4. if, like Muhammad the Prophet, "poverty is your pride," you just can't beat Khadir's invisible rates.

I took a trip with the Green One, just the other day, which nicely illustrated some of his basic techniques.

The joint adventure began with me in my Montana study, feeling too restless and word-jaded, at the end of a three-week work binge, to cloister myself on another beautiful July morn. Knocking on the door between the Unseen and Seen, I remarked to Khadir that I'd heard a seven-syllable rumor concerning a creek not terribly far from my study, and wondered whether this rumor was worth pursuing. I then dangled the syllables before him:

"Big Cutthroats in Small Water..."

My guide responded with the usual silence—and he is not just poker-faced, he is no-faced: his position proved, as always, very tough to gauge.

I mentioned that if we left at once I had the time, and would be willing to pay the physical price, to check the seven-syllable rumor out. Khadir showed no interest in this "physical price." Lacking a body, what is physical effort or suffering to him? I feel, though, that if we mortals are to relate to Khizr's undying bodilessness, he in return should relate to our doomed physicality. So I described my impending ordeal: "Ninety-degree heat. Seven miles in, seven miles out. Two thousand feet up, two thousand down. Only today to do the hike and the fishing. By sundown you can watch me really hurt, if that turns you on at all. And—thanks to your silence—no guarantee that the rumor is even true. Sound like fun?"

He remained inaudible and imperceptible. Beyond imagination and conception, too. But in all the years I've known him Khwaja has not, to my knowledge, refused an invitation to go fishing yet.

We were in my old Toyota in minutes, my companion withholding comment on the Richard Thompson tapes I blared all the way to the trailhead. We then hiked the seven miles in and two thousand feet up, me sweating, panting and working like a pig, dog, and mule, respectively; Khwaja as invisible, sweatless, and tireless as ever.

Deep in wilderness, we reached the creek of rumor. Completely new water to me, running cold and clear as air. Completely familiar water to Khwaja, he being who he is. I began trying to read the situation. It was a small stream, eight to ten feet wide and only a foot deep, most places. A lot of velocity but no depth. Far from my idea of good trout water. "Khwaja?" I whispered, beginning to doubt the seven-syllable rumor. "A little help here?"

But straightforward Q & A is just not the way he works. Khwaja guides when he wants to, not when I ask him to. That's one of the things I've grudgingly grown to respect about him. William Blake called the intuition "Christ," and worshiped it as such. Khadir's guiding style leaves one little choice, while fishing, but to grow increasingly well acquainted with Blake's Christ.

By a tiny, sunlit pool on a side-channel of the creek, I rested from the hike, rigged my rod, traded hiking boots for wading sandals, and meanwhile studied the insect life over the pool. By the time I'd geared up I'd seen golden stoneflies, three hues of mayfly, two kinds of caddis, and a random smattering of midges and duns. But no species dominated. And Khwaja kept his own counsel. I decided not to choose a fly till I found fishable water.

We began hiking upstream, Khadir flying or emanating or whatever the heck he does, me splashing right up the creek to avoid impenetrable thickets on both banks. The stream veered up a majestic, granite-sided valley choked with wildflowers, streamside willows, and stands of stately tamarack. The initial shallow run turned out to be characteristic, and I definitely felt disappointment over that. When al-Khizr's with me, though, I get almost as stubborn as the forces that create creeks and depth and shallowness, and keep seeking the kind of water I long for, scarcely caring whether I find it or not.

Tiny sandbars formed in the creek each time it changed direction. I noticed elk tracks, beaver tracks, black bear and deer tracks on each of these bars. "No griz or moose tracks," I remarked loudly, to reassure myself—though either could have lurked round any bend. Khadir, being fleshless, could have cared less.

A solitary sandpiper began flitting from sandbar to sandbar just upstream of me, singing a song that sounded as if he hated to complain, but, well, these mountain-creek-sandbars sure were tiny, and it was embarrassing to admit this but, dangit, it was true, he *had* managed to lose track of the entire Pacific Ocean and was beginning to really pine for its far more satisfactory sandbars. So would I mind directing him?

Over the rush of the water I hollered, "West!" pointing with my flyrod. Beeping twice in thanks, the sandpiper shot away.

At last we reached promising water: a long run, four feet or more deep, with overhanging willows and broken boulders for cover. The creek's clarity was amazing. The stones submerged by four feet of water were swirlier-looking, but no less perfectly visible, than the stones lying on dry land. The run appeared fishless, but no trout is better camouflaged than West Slope cutthroats, so I treated the water with respect.

Kneeling in the downstream tail-out, I again tried to get analytical about choice of fly, but now the only visible insects in air or water seemed to be a jillion of those tiny, sunlit, mote-sized buglets which, if you focus your eyes one way, are all flying from left to right over the stream's surface, and if you focus another way are flying right to left.

To my surprise, Khadir suddenly gave me to know—via a wave of goose-bumps and a sudden urge to laugh—that he cherished these little guys. His first communiqué of the day: as unpredictable in content as ever.

"Bug-love?" I teased. "From the Primordial Keeper of Eternity's Fountain? How long do these wee buggers live? Half an hour?"

Look at them, I felt Khwaja urge. So I did—and at second glance began to get the picture: if the ethereal al-Khizr were ever to sire anything so earthly and tangible as children, these deft, silent, near-invisible zippers might be just what they'd look like. For all I knew they *were* his kids, and all live as long as he.

The only other animate life-form was a magnificent six-point whitetail, maybe eighty yards upstream, drinking from the center of the creek. Big bucks are usually the wariest of the deer, but this fellow, after one brief glance, decided my fly rod and I were no threat and bent back to the water. "You can tell it's Montana," I remarked to Khadir. "Even the deer are serious drinkers."

No response. My guide does not, I fear, have a sense of humor about drink. Could be the bartending job at the Fountain. Could be an Islamic thing.

Having failed to spot a dominant insect, I tied on a prospecting favorite: a dry fly called a Stimulator. I then crouched down and tiptoed to the base of the run, made a long cast, dropped the fly in the belly of the best water, and waited.

Nothing. And still no advice from my all-knowing guide. I made four more casts. More nothing. Sitting on a rock to reassess, I noticed the buck, after all this time, was *still* drinking, realized he must not be drinking at all, noticed the tasty-looking cresses growing atop every rock including the one beneath me, and saw that the buck was in fact after these.

I changed fishing strategies, dead-drifting a Hare's Ear nymph through the depths of the run. Four times, eight times. Hooked the same nothing. Tried a black Wooly Bugger. More nothing. Added leechlike twitches. Zilch. Tying on another prospecting pattern—a mayflyish invention called a Crippled Emerger this time—I said, "That's it for this spot. Let's head upstream."

Khwaja didn't say boo to this plan. But the browsing buck was so beautiful up there in mid-creek that I wanted to delay the moment I scared him away. So I fetched the water bottle from my pack and took a long drink. The buck watched me, then drank too. I browsed on fig bars. The buck browsed cresses. I took a leak in the creek. So did the buck. Figuring male-bonding had reached its zenith, I said, "Here I come, big fella," then started upstream.

False-casting as I strolled, I planned to throw my fly into the up-permost tip of the run I'd just fished. But this riffle-tip, I saw as I neared it, was so shallow and sunlit that I could make out every drowned twig and pebble on the bottom. Obviously fishless. I reeled in my line, intending to splash on past, when something stopped me cold . . .

This was the quintessential Khadir moment, so I'll get as technical as I can: first, it was actually *nothing* that stopped me. But when fishing with Khwaja one learns to trust certain nothings—certain no-reason starts or stops. What froze me in my tracks this time was an urge to show the barren tip-riffle the same fly fisherly respect I'd just shown the promising run. Why? There *was* no why. It was naked impulse. Apart from the no-reason chills, naked impulse is the most reliable sign I know that Khadir is transmitting.

The next task, I've learned from long experience, is unquestioning obedience to the urge, even in defiance of reason. My eyes clearly saw the tip-riffle to be as troutless as a city sidewalk. Khadir, it seemed, saw otherwise. *Don't be ridiculous!* huffed my mind. But as Khwaja and I both know, my mind is not my identity, *noumenon*, spirit, *atma, dharma,* soul, *buddhi, anam, nous* or fishing guide. So fuck it. I proceeded to behave as if the "sidewalk" held the fish of my dreams.

Dropping to my knees to lower my silhouette, I inched silently into casting position, stripped enough line from my reel to preclude the need for fish-spooking false-casts, took another glance at the cress-eating buck, then tried to mimic his calm as I made—with a single stroke of the rod—the lightest possible cast up into the riffle-tip. My fly alit on clear-as-air water not ten inches deep. It had floated a yard or so back toward me when one of the big, canteloupe-colored stones so plainly visible on the bottom turned its entire up-stream edge into an enormous white mouth. This mouth gaped clear out of the water, engulfing my fly and a fair fraction of stream with it. I lifted my rod in reply. An animal so huge and strong that I could not believe in its existence began to shake its head, equally unable to believe in me. But the rod throbbed hard. The hook burrowed. Conversion was simultaneous for us both.

The trout shot straight toward me, forcing me to stand, run back-wards, and strip line madly, to keep things taut. It then writhed round the far side of a midstream boulder, forcing me to pay out line, dash out into the creek, un-lasso the rock. The rest of our combat was comparatively uneventful, if ten or so minutes of pure wonder can be considered an unevent. The huge, glowing, green-gold trout ripped tirelessly up and down the identically green-gold and glowing pool. The cress-eating buck watched us both. As the trout finally drew close, its thrashing body was so big it created wakes. When these wakes hit my legs, no-reason chills rose at the feel of the lapping. Desperate for cover, the big fish finally sought it in my shadow, hovering long, by choice, between my knees. The buck watched. Khwaja's tiny insects moved left to right and right to left in sunlight. Fragrance of pine. Fragrance of wilderness. So many intimacies. For a time, I couldn't move. Then the seven-syllable rumor—*Big Cut-throat in Small Water*—entered my hands: the largest West Slope I've ever seen: a female as beautifully plotted, thick through and long in the making as a thousand-page novel.

I knew, as I held her, that I'd encountered her solely because of an irrational impulse to fish empty sidewalk. But when such urges lead you year after year to fish after fish, how rational is it to keep calling them irrational? I'm just a fisherman. As such, I prefer, to any form of fishermanly reasoning, the catching of even the most unreasonable of fish. I therefore expressed, upon releasing this one, my sincere gratitude to the unreasonable cause of its capture: "*Geez,* Khwaja!" I gasped. "*Thanks!*"

The Green One, once he finally starts transmitting, is often surprisingly slow to stop: the way that beautifully plotted West Slope, upon release, did not so much swim as dissolve back into the elements that created her; the way her dissolution then made every sunlit, seemingly barren inch of clear-as-air creek feel rife with invisible life; the way this rifeness then filled the clear-as-creek July sky with intimations of life unseen and the no-reason chills smacked me in a wave and my identity swamped and capsized, leaving just enough residue to work a flyrod and forget how to work a pronoun as not-I and I wandered the cusp between inner and outer creeks and granite ridges, inner and outer aspen groves and sun-flares, paintbrush and bear-sign, tamarack, trout-rise, and pine, overwhelmed and grateful for the whole fragrant, lit-from-within confusion—all of this, I believe, came of the guidance of the one I call Khwaja.

And not-He and He and not-I and I landed four more West Slopes. All of them preposterously large for that tiny creek. All invisible in the beginning; green, gold and glorious in the end. All somehow hidden in the same sort of "barren" tip-riffles, so that for the duration of the day our eyes were fed the sight of stones suddenly possessed of fish-mouths, of seens possessed of unseens, of paradigmatic beauties possessed of invisibility, then strength, then form and colors too lovely to do anything but touch, thank, and let go.

The seven miles out sure as shit hurt.

My guide sure as shit didn't give an Arabic hoot.

But after five fish like those, even that braying donkey, my body, had grown soulful enough that a feared inferno never became more than brief purgatory.

We reached my old truck. I paid up with the usual syllables:

"Geez, Khwaja! Beats church! *Thanks!*"

That was it—the whole guide/client transaction.

"Lovers," said *Jalal al-Din Rumi,* "don't finally meet somewhere. They're in each other all along." Maybe that's why the best guide I know isn't visible: he's not external.

The mind still says: *Did anything really happen? Is anyone but me really there?*

The mind will say this forever. But I mostly fish rivers these days. In so doing, movement becomes stasis, flux is the constant, and *everything* flows around, through and beyond me, escaping ungrasped, unnamed and unscathed. The river's clean escape does not prevent belief in its reality. On the contrary, there is nothing I love more than the feel of a wholeness sliding toward, around, and past me while I stand like an idiot savant in its midst, focussing on tiny idiot-savantic bits of what is so beautiful to me, and so close, yet so wondrously ungraspable.

Nominated by Orion

IT IS HARD
NOT TO LOVE
THE WORLD

by JIM MOORE

from WATER-STONE

but possible. When I am like this,
even the swallows are not God.
Even the yellow school bus.
Even the children inside,
wanting out, are not God.

Nominated by Michael Dennis Browne

THE MOURNING DOOR

fiction by ELIZABETH GRAVER

from PLOUGHSHARES

THE FIRST THING SHE FINDS is a hand. In the beginning, she thinks it's a tangle of sheet or a wadded sock caught between the mattress cover and the mattress, a bump the size of a walnut but softer, more yielding. She feels it as she's lying, lazing, in bed. Often, lately, her body keeps her beached, though today the sun beckons, the dogwoods blooming white, the peonies' glossy buds specked black with ants. Tom has gone to work already, backing out of the driveway in his pickup truck. She has taken her temperature on the pink thermometer, noted it down on the graph—98.2, day eighteen, their thirteenth month of trying. She takes it again, to be sure, then settles back in, drifting, though she knows she should get up. The carpenters will be here soon; the air will ring with hammers. The men will find more expensive, unnerving problems with the house. She'll have to creep in her robe to the bathroom, so small and steady, like one of the pests they keep uncovering in this ancient, tilting farmhouse—powder post beetles, termites, carpenter ants.

She feels the bump in the bed the way she might encounter a new mole on her skin, or a scab that had somehow gone unnoticed, her hand traveling vaguely along her body until it stumbles, oh, what's this? With her shin, she feels it first, as she turns over, beginning to get up. She sends an arm under the covers, palpitates the bump. A pair of bunched panties, maybe, shed during sex and caught beneath the new sheet when she remade the bed? Tom's sock? A wad of tissue? Some unknown object (needle threader, sock darner, butter maker, chaff-separator?) left here by the generations of people who came before? The carpenters keep finding things in the walls and

256

under the floor: the sole of an old shoe, a rusted nail, a bent horse-shoe. A Depression-era glass bowl, unbroken, the green of Key lime pie. Each time they announce another rotted sill, cracked joist, additional repair, they hand an object over, her consolation prize. The house looked so charming from the outside, so fine and perfectly itself. The inspector said go ahead, buy it. But you never know what's lurking underneath.

She gets out of the bed, stretches, yawns. Her gaze drops to her naked body, so familiar, the thin freckled limbs and flattish stomach. She has known it forever, lived with it forever. Mostly it has served her well, but lately it seems a foreign, uncooperative thing, at once insolent and lethargic, a taunt. Sometimes, though, she still finds in herself an energy that surprises her, reminding her of when she was a child and used to run—legs churning, pulse throbbing—down the long river path that led to her cousin's house.

Now, in a motion so concentrated it's fierce, she peels off the sheet and flips back the mattress pad. What she sees doesn't surprise her; she's been waiting so hard, these days, looking so hard. A hand, it is, a small, pink dimpled fist, the skin slightly mottled, the nails the smallest slivers, cut them or they'll scratch. Five fingers. Five nails. She picks it up; it flexes slightly, then curls back into a warm fist. Five fine fingers, none missing. She counts them again to be sure. *You have to begin somewhere,* the books say. *You have to relinquish control and let nature take its course.*

She hears the door open downstairs, the clomp of workboots, words, a barking laugh. Looking around, she spots, on the bedroom floor, the burlap sack that held the dwarf liberty apple tree Tom planted over the weekend. She drops the hand into the bag, stuffs the bag under the bed. Still the air smells like burlap, thick and dusty. She pulls on some sweatpants, then thinks better of it and puts on a more flattering pair of jeans, and a T-shirt that shows off her breasts. She read somewhere that men are drawn to women with small waists and flaring hips. Evolution, the article said. A body built for birth. Her own hips are small and boyish; her waist does not cinch in. Her pubic hair grows thin and blond, grass in a drought. She doesn't want these workmen, exactly, but she would like them, for the briefest moment, to want her. As she goes barefoot down the stairs to make a cup of tea and smile at the men, she stops for a moment, struck by a memory of the perfect little hand; even the thought of it makes her gasp. The men won't find it. They're only working in the basement and the attic, structural repairs to keep the house from falling down.

In her kitchen, the three men: Rick and Tony and Joaquin. Their eyes flicker over her. She touches her hair, feels heavy with her secret, and looks down. More bad news, I'm afraid, Rick tells her. We found it yesterday, after you left—a whole section of the attic. What, she asks. *Charred*, he says dramatically. There must have been a fire; some major support beams are only three-quarter their original size. She shakes her head. Really? But the inspector never— I have my doubts, Rick says, about this so-called inspector of yours. Can you fix it, she asks. He looks at her glumly through heavy-lidded eyes. We can try, he answers. I'll draw up an estimate but we'll need to finish the basement before we get to this. Yes, she says vaguely, already bored. Fine, thanks.

Had she received such news the day before, it would have made her dizzy. A charred, unstable attic, a house whittled down by flames. She would have called Tom at work—You're not going to believe this—and checked how much money they had left in their savings account, and thought about suing the inspector and installing more smoke alarms, one in every room, blinking eyes. Today, though, she can't quite concentrate; her thoughts keep returning, as if of their own accord, to what she discovered in her bed. One walnut-sized hand, after thirteen months, after peeing into cups, tracking her temperature, making Tom lie still as a statue after he comes, no saliva, no new positions, her rump tilted high into the air afterwards, an absurd position but she doesn't care.

After thirteen months of watching for the LH surge on the ovulation predictor kit—the deep indigo line of a good egg, the watery turquoise of a bad, and inside her own body, waves cresting and breaking, for she has become an ocean, or it is an oceanographer? *Study us hard enough*, the waves call out to her, *watch us closely enough and we shall do your will*. She has noted the discharge on her underpants—sticky, tacky, scant. Egg white, like she's a chef making meringues or a chicken trying to lay. *Get to know your body*, chant the books, the Web sites, her baby-bearing friends, and oh she has, she does, though it's beginning to feel like a cheap car she has leased for a while and is getting ready to return.

She still likes making love with Tom, the tremble of it, the slow, blue wash, the way they lie cupped together in their new, old house as it sits in the greening fields, on the turning earth. It's afterwards that she hates. She can never fall asleep without picturing the spastic, thrashing tails, the egg's hard shell, the long, thin tubes stretched like IVs toward a pulsing womb. A speck, she imagines sometimes, the head of a pin, the dot of a period. The End—or maybe, if they're lucky, dot dot dot.

But the hand is so much bigger than that, substantial, real. Her own hands shake with relief as she puts on the tea water. Something is starting—a secret, a discovery, begun not in the narrow recesses of her body, but in the mysterious body of her house. The house has a door called the Mourning Door—the realtor pointed it out the first time they walked through. It's a door off the front parlor, and though it leads outside, it has no stoop or stairs, just a place for the cart to back up so the coffin can be carried away. Of course babies were born here, too, added the realtor, her voice too bright. Probably right in this room! After she and Tom moved in, they decided only to use the door off the kitchen. Friendlier, she said, and after all, they're concentrating, these days, on making life.

When she goes back upstairs, she takes the burlap sack and a flash-light to the warm, musty attic, where Tom almost never goes. With the flashlight's beam, she finds, in one dark corner, the section where the fire left its mark. She touches the wood, and a smudge of ash comes off on her finger. She tastes it: dry powder, ancient fruit, people passing buckets, lives lost, found, lost. She leaves the sack in the other corner of the attic inside a box marked "Kitchen Stuff." Then she heads downstairs to wash her hands.

Three days later she is doing laundry when she comes across a shoulder, round and smooth. She knows it should be disconcerting to find such a thing separated from its owner, a shoulder disembodied, lying in a nest of dryer lint, tucked close to the wall. But why get up-set? After all, the world is full of parts apart from wholes. A few months ago, she and Tom went to the salvage place—old radiator covers, round church windows, faucets and doorknobs, a spiral stair-case leading nowhere. Then, they bought two doors and a useless unit of brass mailboxes, numbers fifteen through twenty-five. Now she wipes her hands on her jeans and picks the shoulder up. It is late afternoon, the contractors gone, Tom still at work. She brings the shoulder up to the attic and puts it in the sack with the hand. Then she goes to the bedroom, swallows a vitamin the size of a horse pill, climbs into bed, and falls asleep.

Whereas before she had been agitated, unable to turn her

thoughts away, now she is peaceful, assembling something, proud. But tired, too—this is not unexpected; every day by four or five o'clock she has to sink into bed for a nap, let in dreams full of floaty shapes, closed fists, and open mouths. Still, most days, she gets a little something done. She lines a trunk with old wallpaper, goes for a walk in the woods with a friend, starts to plan a lesson sequence on how leaves change color in the fall. Her children are all away for the summer, shipped off to lakes and rivers and seas. Sometimes she gets a "Dear Teacher" postcard: *I found some mica. We went on a boat. I lost my ring in the lake.* The water in the postcards is always a vivid, chlorinated blue. She gets her hair cut, sees a matinee movie with her friend Hannah, starts to knit again. One night Tom remarks— perhaps with relief, perhaps with the slightest tinge of fear—that she seems back to her old self.

In the basement, the men put in lally columns, thick and red, to keep the first floor from falling in. They construct a vapor barrier, rewire the electricity. They sister the joists and patch the foundation. In her bedroom, she stuffs cotton in her ears to block the noise. She wears sweatpants or loose shorts now, and Tom's shirts. Each time she catches a glimpse of herself in the mirror, she is struck by how pretty she looks, her eyes so bright, almost feverish, her fingernails a flushed, excited pink.

She finds a second foot with five perfect toes, and a second shoulder. She finds a leg, an arm. No eyes yet, no face. Everything in time, she tells herself, and at the Center for Reproductive Medicine they inject her womb with blue, and she sees her tubes, thin as violin strings, curled and ghostly on the screen. They have her drink water and lie on her back. They swab gel on her belly, and she neglects to tell them that her actual belly is at home, smelling like dust and apple wood, snoozing under the eaves. They say come in on day three, on day ten. They swab her with more gel and give her a rattle, loose pills in an amber jar. Tom goes to the clinic, and they shut him in a room with girlie magazines and take his fish. At home, while he is at the doctor's, she finds a tiny penis, sweet and curled. Tom comes home discouraged—rare for him. He lies down on the floor and sighs. She says don't worry, babe, and leans to kiss him on the arm. She would like to tell him about everything she has found, but she knows she must protect her secret. Things are so fragile, really. The earth settles, the house shifts. You put up a wall in the wrong place and so never find the hidden object in the eaves. You speak too soon and cause—with your hard, your hopeful words—a clot, a cramp. Things are so fragile, but then also not. Look at the ants, she tells herself. How they always find a place to make a nest. Look at the people of the earth, each one with a mother. At the supermarket, she stares at them—their hands, their faces, how neatly it all goes together, a completed puzzle.

She knows her own way is out of the ordinary, but then what is ordinary these days? She is living in a time of freezers and test tubes, of petri dishes and turkey basters, of trade and barter, test and track, mix and match. Women carry the eggs of other women, or have their own eggs injected back into them pumped with potential, four or six at a time. Sperm are washed and coddled, separated and sifted, like gold. Ovaries are inflated until they spill with treasures. The names sound like code words: GIFT, IUI, ZIFT. Though it upsets her to admit it, the other women at the Center disgust her a little. They seem so desperate, they look so swollen, but in all the wrong places—their eyes, their chins, their hearts. Not me, she thinks as the nurse calls her name and she rises with a friendly smile.

One day, she moves the burlap bag from the attic to the back of her bedroom closet. It's such a big house, and the attic is sweltering now, and soon the men will be working up there on the charred wood. Before, she and Tom lived in a tiny, rented bungalow and looked into each other's eyes a lot. She loves Tom; she really does, though lately he seems quite far away. Outside, here, is a swing set made of old, splintered cedar, not safe enough for use. But that same day, she finds an ear in it, tucked like a chestnut under a climbing pole. The tomatoes are ripe now. The sunflowers she planted in May are taller than she is, balancing their heads on swaying stalks. In the herb garden, the chives bear fat purple balls. The ear, oddly, is downed with dark hair, like the ear of a young primate. She holds it to her own ear as if she might hear something inside it—the sea, perhaps, a heartbeat or a yawn. It looks so tender that she wraps it in tissue paper before placing it in the bag.

One night on the evening news, she and Tom see a story about a girl who was in a car accident and went into a coma, and now the girl performs miracles and people think she's a saint. The news shows her lying in Worcester in her parents' garage, hitched to life support while pilgrims come from near and far: people on crutches, children

261

with cancer, barren women, men dying of AIDS. Jesus, says Tom, shuddering. People will believe anything—how sick. But she doesn't think it's so sick, the way the vinyl-sided ranch house is transformed into a wall of flowers, the way people bring gifts—Barbie dolls, barrettes, Hawaiian Punch (the girl's favorite)—and a blind man sees again, and a baby blooms from a tired woman's torso, and the rest of the people, well, the rest sit briefly in the full lap of hope, then get in their cars and go home. The girl is pretty, even though she's almost dead. Her braid is black and shiny, her brow peaceful. Her mother, the reporter says, sponge-bathes her each morning and again at night. Her father is petitioning the Vatican for the girl to be made an official saint.

Days now, while the men work in the attic, she roams. She wanders the house looking for treasures, and on the days when she does not find them, she gets in her car and drives to town, or out along the country roads. Sometimes she finds barn sales and gets things for the house—a chair for Tom's desk, an old egg candler filled with holes. One day at a yard sale, she buys a sewing machine, though she's never used one. I'll give you the instruction book, the woman says. It's easy—you'll see. Also at this yard sale is a playpen, a high chair, a pile of infant clothes. The woman sees her staring at them. I thought you might be expecting, she says, smiling. But I didn't want to presume. As a bonus, she throws in a plump pincushion stabbed with silver pins and needles, and a blue and white sailor suit. It was my son's, she says, and from behind the house come—as if in proof—the shrieks of kids at play.

That night, with Tom in New York for an overnight meeting, she sets up the sewing machine and sits with the instruction manual in her lap. She slides out the trap door under the needle, examining the bobbin. Slowly, following the instructions, she winds the bobbin full of beige thread, then threads the needle. She gets the bag from the closet. She's not sure she's ready (the books say you're never sure), but at the same time her body is guiding, pushing, *urging* her. Breathe, she commands herself, and draws a deep breath. She has never done this before, never threaded the needle or assembled the pattern or put together the parts, but it doesn't seem to matter; she has a sense of how to approach it—first this, then this, then this. She takes a hand out of the bag and tries to stitch it to an arm, but the machine jams so she unwinds a length of thread from the bobbin, pulls a needle from the pincushion, and begins again, by hand.

Slowly, awkwardly, she stitches arm to shoulder, stops to catch her breath and wipe the sweat from her brow. She remembers back stitch, cross stitch; someone (her mother?) must have taught her long ago. She finds the other hand, the other arm. Does she have everything? It's been a long summer, and she's found so much; she might be losing track. If there aren't enough pieces, don't panic, she tells herself. He doesn't need to be perfect; she's not asking for that. He can be missing a part or two, he can need extra care. Her own body, after all, has its flaws, its stubborn limits. What, anyway, is perfect in this world? She'll take what she is given, what she has been able, bit by bit, to make.

She stitches feet to legs, carefully doing the seams on the inside so they won't show. She attaches leg to torso, sews on the little penis. The boy-child begins to stir, to struggle; perhaps he has to pee. Not yet, my love. Hold on. She works long and hard and late into the night, her body tight with effort, the room filled with animal noises that spring from her mouth as if she were someone else. She wishes, with a deep, aching pain, that Tom were here to guide her hands, to help her breathe and watch her work. Finally—it must be near dawn—she reaches into the bag and finds nothing. How tired she is, bone tired, skin tired. She must be finished, for she has used up all the parts.

Slowly, then, as if in sleep, she rises with the child in her arms. She has been working in the dark and so can't quite see him, though she feels his downy head, his foot and hand. He curls toward her for an instant as if to nurse, so she unbuttons her blouse and draws him near. He nuzzles toward her but does not drink, and she passes a hand over his face and realizes that he has no mouth. Carefully, in the dark, she inspects him with both her hands and mind: he has a nose but no mouth, wrists but no elbows. She spreads her palm over his torso, and her fingers tell her that he has kidneys and a liver but only six small ribs and half a heart. Oh, she tells him. Oh, I'm sorry. I tried so hard. I found and saved and stitched and tried so hard and yet—

She feels it first, before he goes: a spasm in her belly, a clot in her brain, a sorrow so thick and familiar that she knows she's felt it before, but not like this, so unyielding, so tangible. Six small ribs and only half a heart. While she holds him, he twitches twice and then is still.

Carrying him, she makes her way downstairs. It's lighter now, the

263

purple-blue of dawn. She walks to the front parlor, past the TV, past the old honey extractor they found in the barn. She walks to the Mourning Door and tries to open it. It doesn't budge, wedged shut, and for a moment she panics—she has to get out now; the weight in her arms keeps getting heavier, a sack of stones. She needs to pass it through this door and set it down, or she will break. Trying to stay calm, she goes to the laundry room and finds a screwdriver, returns to the door, and wedges the tool in along the lock placket, balancing the baby on one arm. Finally the door gives, and she walks through it, forgetting that no steps meet it outside. Falling forward over the high ledge, she lands, stumbles, catches her balance (somehow, she hasn't dropped him) to stand stunned and breathless in the still morning air, her knees weak from landing hard.

Across the road, the sheep in the field have begun their bleating. A truck drives by, catching her briefly in its lights. She lowers her nose to the baby's head and breathes in the smell of him. He's lighter now, easier now. *Depart*, she thinks, the word an old prayer following her through the door. *Depart in peace*. With her hands, she memorizes the slope of his nose, the open architecture of his skull. She fingers the spirals of one ear. Then she turns and starts walking, out behind the house to the barn where a shovel hangs beside the hoe and rake. It's lighter now. A mosquito hovers close to her face. The day will be hot. Later, Tom will return. She buries the baby under a hawthorn tree on the back-stretch of their land and leaves his grave unmarked. My boy, she says as she turns to go. Thank you, she says— to him or to the air—when she is halfway home. She sleeps all morning and gardens through the afternoon.

That night (day sixteen, except she's stopped charting), she and Tom make love, and afterwards she thinks of nothing—no wagging fish, no hovering egg, no pathway, her thoughts as flat and clean as sheets. Tom smells like himself—it is a smell she loves and had nearly forgotten—and after their sex, they talk about his trip, and he runs a hand idly down her back. She is ready for something now—a child inside her or a child outside, come from another bed, another place. Or she is ready, perhaps, for no child at all, a trip with Tom to a different altitude or hemisphere, a rocky, twisting hike. They make love again, and after she comes, she cries, and he asks what, what is it, but it's nothing she can describe, it's where she's been, so far away and without him—in the charred attic, the tipped basement, where

264

red columns try to shore up a house that will stand for as long as it wants to and fall when it wants to fall. Nothing, she says, and inside her something joins, or tries to join, forms or does not, and her dream, when she sleeps, is of the far horizon, a smooth, receding curve.

Nominated by Debra Spark, Ploughshares

IN TRANSIT

by JOHN HOLLANDER

from RARITAN

> All symbols are fluxional; all language is vehicular and transitive, and is good, as
> ferries and horses are, for conveyance, not as farms and houses are, for home-
> stead.
>
> —Emerson

Well, then, if that's the case let's start packing and get
    going—not "packing it all in," of course,
But "-all up"—and with some brawny friends and brainy
    lovers let's get all our stuff loaded on
Some truck and get it on its way, whatever way
    that may indeed be toward whatever place.
Metaphoron in modern Greek conveys the sense
    of "moving van" (if you speak modern Greek)
A vehicle crammed with the mischmasch of tenors
    that should not be allowed to rot at home.
(Too much of the untransferred literal all too
    soon rots in the due course.) On with it then,
And off we go, the cityside, the chartered views
    high from the cabled bridges, the long haul
Through the enclosing tunnel, the wide traverse of
    nonurban sprawl and then the countryside,
Its various selves, all rushing by to fill
    spaces we vacate, one by fleeting one.

Are we talking about the springtime here, early
    forsythia moving the very air
Forward into another place-like state of things
    (the scheduled time for moving)? But even
The dullest February dawn gives up its first
    catatonic sulk and soon starts loading
Up with the innermost of motions assuring
    that each new morning will be moving day.
Semper eadem, constant?—true enough for some
    things (such as Latin mottoes like itself),
But with all the stuff of our lives we have to keep
    going, going, or we will all be gone.

Rumble of diesel, crush of huge tires over
    protesting gravel, shouts, whining and boom
Of boom-box indeterminately modulate
    through the long roar of the road as all is
Transported over the widest but most unseen
    of interstates to where we hear only
Summer's drone at the end of the rhododendrons
    if only the soundless drone of the dark
Shiny green in which its leaves are so dustily
    absorbed as if remembering their time
Of blossoming back in that other place from which
    they had been moved in the vast eight-wheeler
That, getting on with things, has brought them and us to
    the place that yet was right here all along.

Nominated by Raritan

O LOST

fiction by THOMAS WOLFE

from THE PARIS REVIEW

Thomas Wolfe's first novel, titled O Lost, *as submitted to the legendary editor Maxwell Perkins of Charles Scribner's Sons in 1928, contained 294,000 words. Perkins—the genius-spotter who already had F. Scott Fitzgerald and Ernest Hemingway in his stable—was willing to gamble on its publication, but required Wolfe to make cuts, mainly for reasons of economy, but also to remove sideshows and bawdry.* O Lost *was not considered a selling title by Scribners, and Wolfe submitted* Look Homeward, Angel, *which was published in 1929.*

With Wolfe unable to make the required excisions on his own, Perkins identified what he thought were the expendable passages; the final cuts were made by Wolfe, who then wrote the necessary bridging passages—which were sometimes longer than the deleted mate-rial. The published text of Look Homeward, Angel *has 223,000 words—a reduction of 71,000 words (twenty-four percent).*

The first casualties of the editorial operation were the opening of O Lost *describing the Battle of Gettysburg as seen through the eyes of two Pennsylvania Dutch farmboys (one of whom, Oliver Gant, would father Eugene Gant) and a long account of Oliver's pre-Altamont years. That opening was summarized in the fifth and sixth paragraphs of* Look Homeward, Angel.

The Perkins-Wolfe editorial connection became one of the most painful and tempestuous in American letters. After Wolfe's death, Perkins rationalized his editorial practices on the novel:

We then began to work upon the book, and the first thing we did, to give it unity, was to cut out that wonderful scene it began with and the ninety-odd pages that followed, because it seemed to me, and he agreed, that the whole tale should be unfolded through the memories and senses of the boy, Eugene, who was born in Asheville [Altamont]. We both thought that the story was compassed by that child's realization; that it was life and the world as he came to realize them. When he had tried to go back into the life of his father before he arrived in Asheville, without the inherent memory of events, the reality and poignance were diminished—but for years it was on my conscience that I had persuaded Tom to cut out that first scene of the two little boys on the roadside with Gettysburg impending. And then what happened? In Of Time and the River *he brought the scene back to greater effect when old Gant was dying on the gallery of the hospital in Baltimore and in memory recalled his "olden days."* (Harvard Library Bulletin, Autumn, 1947).

The amputated Gettysburg material is summarized—not salvaged—in less than 1,000 words in Of Time and the River *(Book One, Section VI). Whether it is used there "to greater effect" is doubtful. The original material about the Battle of Gettysburg from* O Lost *is printed here. The full text of* O LOST *was published by the University of South Carolina Press in 2000.*

—Matthew J. Bruccoli

Anabasis

. . . a stone, a leaf, an unfound door; of a stone, a leaf, a door. And of all the forgotten faces.

Naked and alone we came into exile. In her dark womb we did not know our mother's face: from the prison of her flesh have we come into the unspeakable and incommunicable prison of this earth.

Which of us has known his brother? Which of us has looked into his father's heart? Which of us has not remained forever prison-pent? Which of us is not forever a stranger and alone?

O waste of loss, in the hot mazes, lost, among bright stars on this most weary unbright cinder, lost! Remembering speechlessly we seek the great forgotten language, the lost lane-end into heaven, a stone, a leaf, an unfound door. Where? When?

O lost, and by the wind grieved, ghost, come back again.

•

One morning at the beginning of July, sixty-five years ago, two boys were standing by a Pennsylvania roadside on the outskirts of the little farming village of York Springs, watching a detachment of the Confederate army, as it tramped past on its way to the town of Gettysburg, about twelve miles away to the south.

The older of the two boys was fifteen, the younger was thirteen: they lived nearby on a tidy little farm, which they helped their mother, a widow, to run. The widow was a rugged woman of forty-three years: she was of Dutch stock, a little under six feet tall, spare, brown, with big high bones—she was as big and strong as a man. She had been born in that region: her people had come over more than a century before in the great migration.

The widow had lost her husband six years before. He was an Englishman: his name was Gilbert Gaunt, which he had later changed to Gant—a concession possibly to Yankee phonetics.

Gaunt, or Gant, had come to America in the autumn of 1837 in a cotton ship bound from Bristol to Baltimore: he had lived in Baltimore for more than two years, buying at first a partnership in a small public house, which he soon lost after his profits began to roll down an improvident gullet, and descending thereafter to the office of bartender and finally to no office at all.

Still bearing upon his tarnished finery the elegant stamp of a London tailor, he drifted westward into Pennsylvania, always ready, when able, to lay a bet on a horse or a dog, or to spur the feet of a fighting cock: he eked out a dangerous living matching these fowls against the crested champions of country barnyards.

Sometimes he escaped leaving his champion dead on the battlefield, sometimes he escaped with the bruise of a farmer's big knuckles upon his reckless face, sometimes he escaped, without the clink of a coin in his pocket, after a night in a village jail. But he escaped, and coming at length among the Dutch during the harvest season, he found so fat a pasture for his easy talents that he dropped anchor for a prolonged visit.

Gilbert Gaunt was a tall thin man, and he looked fondly at the meaty plenty of that rich land. The houses were small and cozy, and were tucked warmly away in the shadows of great barns. The Dutch were a clean and thrifty people who loved abundance: they worked hard, scrubbed their houses bright and ate heartily. All of this Gilbert Gaunt noted with pleasure. He liked people who fed well. He liked to see clean and cozy houses. He liked to look at people who worked hard. He could frequently look at them all day without showing a sign of fatigue.

And the Dutch liked Gilbert Gaunt. He was tall and thin and handsome: he had large black eyes, sunken deep in his head, hollow thirsty-looking cheeks and a fine sweeping flourish of black hair. He wore bright fancy waistcoats and a watch fob with several big seals. And he had a rich sonorous voice of great range and power.

It was a grand sight to see him do Hamlet in the manner of the great Edmund Kean—long legs wide apart, hands clasped behind him, thirsty brooding face bowed down into his collar, voice low and deliberate as he began "O that this too too solid flesh would melt," and rising strongly thereafter, while his long body straightened impressively, coming out loudly with a lifted face on "O God! O God!" falling to weary disgust at "Fie on't! O fie!" rising, rising to a crazy yell at "Heaven and earth! Must I remember—" and sinking to sad finality at "Frailty, thy name is woman!"

I remember an old Dutch farmer past eighty who told about one of these recitals when I was ten years old. He said that he had heard Gil Gant do Shakespeare once and that, although he was only a boy of sixteen at the time, he had never forgotten it. The old man said that Gil Gant was "a born actor" and could have gone far if he had chosen to be one.

"He had the greatest flow of language of any feller I ever knew," the old man said.

The old fellow grinned reminiscently all over his brown Dutch face: his broad craggy features split up into weathered seams, his little eyes closed, and he showed big yellow nubbins of horse-teeth.

"He was a great feller," he said, "a great talker. He could tell one story right after another without a stop, and all with a choice of words it would do you good to hear. He was never cut out for farming—he should have been an actor."

After a moment, the old man added with cryptic significance:

271

"Well, we all have our faults, I guess. But Gil was a good feller. We all liked him."

They had liked him so well, in fact, that for several months after his arrival he had been an assiduous diner out. Many a fat hog was slaughtered in honor of the fascinating stranger. Many a keg of cider was broached to oil his hypnotic tongue. And he found shelter for the night under the low eaves of many a farmhouse. And meanwhile this easy gentleman spoke vaguely of grand affairs. He spoke with affection of Nature and hinted that he might buy a farm and "settle down."

"For, damn it, gentlemen," he would say, with a fine gesture of his hand among his hair, "I begin to weary of the Ways of Men. I am tired of the Falseness and Corruption of Mankind—the frown of the Tyrant, the fawning of the Slave, the sneer of the Courtier, the trickery of the Knave and the gullibility of the Fool. By heaven, sir," he exclaimed as he took another long draught of his host's cider, "I had rather my life had run its course here among simple men where honesty's the only warrant to friendship, than in the Marts of Gold, where a man's worth is measured by the guinea stamp." This was really how he talked.

But after several months even the lavish hospitality of the Dutch began to wear a little thin. Their smile was still broad, but a little detached. Men did not stay so long to hear him talk. And the Dutch, in low asides at first, began thriftily to ask when Gil Gant was going to get to work. Then, just when his welcome was wearing threadbare, Gil married a rugged young Dutch woman of twenty-four who had been left the year before by the death of her husband, a farmer, the owner of a cozy little farm.

Gilbert came back into his own. He was a landed gentleman now, a man of substance. And although his Dutch wife bore the brunt of running the farm, and gained for herself a grudging sympathy, her harsh and honest tongue won few supporters. It was said that she led him a dog's life—but she also did most of the work. Meanwhile, Gil's facile tongue kept wagging, he enchanted the farmers with unending stories of the golden world, he continued to dine out. And whatever his deficiencies as a farmer may have been, many a canny Dutchman discovered to his grief that the Englishman's ignorance did not extend to horseflesh.

The unhastened years prowled in on leopard feet. The thin Englishman was still hollow in the cheeks, but he now carried a com-

272

fortable paunch. The thick black shock of hair was salted with coarse gray; the thirsty eyes grew dull and bogged; he walked with a gouty limp.

One morning when she went to his room to nag him out of sleep, his wife found him dead of an apoplexy. His thin dark face, with its bladelike nose, was thrust sharply upward as if trying to escape strangulation. And his strange bright eyes stayed open, holding in them the secret her harsh tongue had never fathomed, a passionate and obscure hunger for voyages.

So this Englishman, whose cold brain held from its race the twilight intuitions of the ashen stave, the forged byrnies and the red rush of the Spear-Danes, and from itself the memory of Bow Bells and Paternoster Row, and the ripe green fields of England, with the hedges, the squire and the low gray skies, all close and small, came to his death in the ample Dutch country, in a little farmhouse under the shadow of great barns. A destiny that leads the English to the Dutch is strange enough; but one that leads from Epsom into Pennsylvania over the proud coral cry of the cock is touched by that dark miracle of chance that makes new magic in a dusty world.

The Englishman left a mortgage and five children. The oldest, a girl, he named Augusta. The other four were boys: Gilbert, Oliver, Emerson and John. And it was the two oldest of these boys, Gilbert and Oliver, who stood one summer morning six years after his death, by a roadside well, watching the Confederates on their way into Gettysburg.

Young Gilbert, who was fifteen and the older of the two boys, was shorter and stockier than his brother. He had a tough brown body, lean and long, heavy shoulders and a big barrel chest. Both of the boys had powerful knobby bones, and strong big hands, brown and long. Both had thin angular faces of sallow coloring, but Gilbert's face had more grim Dutch stolidity than his brother's.

Oliver, who was only thirteen, was more than six feet tall. He had very little meat on his great skeleton save long stringy muscles. His hands, roughened by the hard labor of the farm, were extraordinary: they hung from his bony wrists like big brown rocks. They were twice too big and too strong for his skinny arms. They were broad sinewy hands, without an ounce of fat, and with huge knuckles, but the thing one noticed immediately was the great length and power of the fingers. They dangled apishly almost to his knees, with a strong brown curve of the paw. But, in spite of their great power, the hands held curious suggestions of delicacy and skill: they were made to lift great weights of stone, and to work cunningly. They were such hands as a sculptor might have had.

And Oliver's thin face, too, had this curious mixture of roughness and delicacy: his nose was a huge angular blade, hooked sharply, very thin and waxen—his nostrils were merely slits. His mouth was thin, and marked at one corner with a small round deeply incised scar, which he had received from a fall on the ice. It gave to his face a marking of grim obstinacy, but the mouth was somewhat petulant and hangdog. His eyes were small, cold gray and shallow—they glanced about restlessly, furtively, but at moments they darkened with some obscure and passionate hunger. He had thick brows that grew across the base of his skull, a bony sloping forehead, abundant dark brown hair and big masculine ears with tufts of hair in them.

But as they stood there by the roadside, while the dusty rebels tramped past them, Oliver seemed to turn timidly, shyly towards the stubborn unflinching column of his brother's body. Both boys wore overalls: their big brown feet splayed out solidly in the dust. Gilbert stood planted on spread legs, paying the enemy back stare for stare with hard unafraid defiance.

But that scarecrow army was in cheerful humor. It was going to fight; it was going to fight barefooted. In a way, it was going to fight because of those bare feet, and it did not care. For, during the morning, some of the men of Heth's brigade had come in from Lee's base at Cashtown to look for shoes in the town of Gettysburg. On the outskirts of that little town the shoeless rebels had come upon a detachment of Union cavalry—the fight had begun then and there. Along the dozen roads that led to Gettysburg the armies of both sides were pouring in and the town no one had wanted to fight in had become the greatest battlefield of the war.

And now this marauding host, which had swung northeastward across the Rappahannock in a gesture of loot and capture, tramped along the road past the two boys in rags and tatters: it came with naked toes, wearing the stovepipe hat it had looted exultantly from a country store; it came, coatless and shirtless, magnificently shod in greased and stolen boots; it came shoeless, switching ironically the unctuous tails of a black frock coat. It streamed past without rhythm, without step, in noisy hilarity, apparently a dusty rabble, but really an army of seasoned fighting men, lean as snakes, nut brown, casual and alert, and able to do its twenty miles a day on a handful of parched corn. And as it passed, tumultuously, with loud good-natured jeers, it saluted the two boys.

"Hi, Yank! Ye'd better hit out fer the woods. Jeb Stuart's lookin' fer ye."

"He'll be looking for you this time tomorrow," Gil shouted angrily. The men roared with laughter. Frightened. Oll drew in a little closer to his brother. Gilbert spat briefly into the dust and stared.

A lean young captain rode in towards the boy on a roan mare and reined up with a strong brown smell of sweat and leather. Oliver shrank back, frightened at this close odor of Mars, but Gilbert stood his ground.

"Give me a drink, Yank," said the officer, with a grin of white teeth between his dusty gray lips.

"Get it yourself, Reb," said Gil. He stared bitterly at the officer for a moment, then, with a sudden blaze of anger, he said: "I wouldn't spit down your throat if your guts were on fire."

The men passing jeered their officer happily: he grinned again and turned to Oliver. "You look like a smart boy," he said.

In a moment Oliver stepped timidly up to the wellhead and drew a cup of water out of the slopping bucket. The man drank with a hot gulp of thirst and gave the cup back to the boy. Then, resting his hands upon the pommel, he stared down at them for a moment.

"You boys got any cattle?" he asked.

Oliver's sallow face went gray. The boys had driven the widow's cows from the farm during the morning and had hidden them in a copse of wood that flanked the meadow behind them. But Gil looked at the officer with hard unwavering defiance.

"What's it to you?" he said.

"Where are you hiding them, Yank? These fellows could use a little meat," said the officer nodding towards the dusty troops.

"Dead men don't have to eat," said Gil.

The young captain laughed. "I'll tell Jeb Stuart about you, Yank. That's what I'll do. He has a little Yank served up for breakfast every morning." Then slapping his dusty gray hat against his boot he rode away.

In a moment, a group of dusty men on horseback rode up to the well. Most of them were grave tired-looking men, past middle age, by their abundant whiskerage, officers of high rank.

"Give us a drink of water, son," their leader said. Oliver filled and refilled the dripping cup until all had drunk.

"How far are we from Gettysburg?" the leader asked.

"It's about twelve miles, sir," Oliver said.

"It's a damn sight further comin' than goin'," said Gil savagely. "You'll find that out soon enough."

The officers laughed.

"This is a fightin' little Yankee," said one. "Let's give him to Jeb Stuart."

"Ah!" said Gil contemptuously. "I've heard that before. To hell with Jeb Stuart."

They roared with whiskered laughter, and one of them shouted: "Damn if he ain't a good one!" Then they rode on.

Then a ragged soldier came up and drank—a young man with lank hair, a little silk goatee and the thin reckless face of a Southerner.

"Know who that feller was?" he drawled.

"What fellow?" said Oliver.

"The one you gave the drink to first."

Oliver shook his head.

"That's General Fitzhugh Lee," said the soldier. "He's old Bob's nephew."

They were silent a moment, awed by the thunder of great names. Then Gil said: "That won't do him no good where he's goin'."

Then they stood as before watching the ragged rebels as they tramped past. The hot sun made a blue glister on the gun barrels. There was a halt. The men leaned dustily at the roadside on their rifles. And there was one, among the drawling and terrible mountaineers, who sang hymns while he marched and preached while he waited. He was a young man of twenty-six, red-faced, bearded, with a broad meaty nose, deep flat cheeks, sensual lips and a smile mixed of pleased complacency and idiot benignity. He was dressed in shapeless rags; his large odorous feet were bandaged with wound sacking; he gave off from his thick hairy body a powerful decayed stench. In moments of piety, his comrades called him Stinking Jesus, but his real name was Bacchus Pentland.

"Hit's a-comin'! As sure as you're livin', hit's a-comin'," he shouted cheerfully. And, seeing the two boys, he shouted his strange message happily to them, smiling kindly with pleased idiocy.

"Hit's a-comin', boys. Tell yore folks. Armageddon's here."

"You don't need to tell 'em Stinkin' Jesus is here," a mountaineer shouted. "They can smell him already."

Bacchus Pentland answered their roar of laughter with a good-humored smile. Then, when he could be heard again he said: "Hit's a-comin'! The kingdom of Christ upon the earth approacheth. He'll be here a-judgin' an' dividin' by eight o'clock tomorrow morning. I've got it all figgered out accordin' to 'Zekiel."

He drew a roll of paper from the hairy bush of his chest, and opened up a soiled chart with elaborate biblical notations.

"Hell, Back," drawled a mountaineer, "you had it all figgered out accordin' to Ebenezer at Chancellorsville, an' all I got out of it was a slug of canister in my tail."

"That was the beginnin' of it," said Bacchus with a smart undaunted wink. He tapped his chart. "Hit all comes out right accordin' to this. Hit's a-comin' as sure as you live. Christ's kingdom is at hand."

"I hope He gits here before the Yanks begin to shoot," said another, spitting drolly.

And another, as he stoppered up his dripping canteen at the well, said: "What air you goin' to be, Back, Brigadier or Vice President? I wish you'd git me a job on yore staff."

And other men came to the well, and drank, jeering at their strange fellow. He bore their mockery patiently, with his benign smile, touched with its tranquil idiocy, with something inner and unearthly like the strange grin of a primitive Apollo. And he held the chart invitingly in his hands, turning from one to another, eager to debate, to persuade, to explain, when their laughter should dwindle away.

Then they were ordered to resume their march and they moved on into battle, jesting at God and sudden death. But before he had passed from their hearing, Bacchus Pentland turned and shouted at the staring boys once more his triumphant prophecy of eternal life.

"Hit's a-comin', boys. Tell yore folks hit's a-comin'."

The boy Oliver stared down the road, the hard Dutch order of his life touched by the scarecrow gallantry of the ragged men, with a gray darkening of his small cold eyes as there arose in him the obscure and passionate hunger for voyages that had led from Fenchurch Street to Philadelphia. And as his gaze followed the burly figure of the prophet, he was touched by something strange and fleeting, far more remote than Armageddon. He had been touched by the dark finger of Chance, but he did not know it.

•

This Bacchus Pentland was of Southern mountain stock that derived some of its vitality, it was said, from the loins of David Crockett. Bacchus had carried a gun and a chart from the outbreak of the war: he had enlisted in order to be present at Armageddon, and he had announced the coming of that final day at Manassas, Fredericksburg and The Wilderness. Each of his failures as a prophet only increased his belief in his infallibility, and enforced, after a little reflection, his conviction that the ending was only beginning. His comrades bore with him because he amused them, his power of invention was enormous, and his heart kind and simple. And his officers bore with him very cheerfully because they were able to find little fault with a marksman who could pick the fingers off a Yankee's hand at ninety yards, and send his enemies into eternity with a Christian sense of having awarded them the honors of Paradise. For there is no commission which so increases a soldier's effectiveness as one which he believes he has received from God.

Wherever he went Bacchus Pentland carried his Bible and his chart. He had been captured at Antietam by a detachment of Joe Hooker's men, and before his escape three weeks later—an escape which his captors did little to prevent—he had shouted his news of Armageddon along the length of McClellan's line. During the two weeks of his three-hundred-mile detour into Virginia, he fed sparingly on parched corn and the roadside carcass of an army mule, which the Divine Providence had bountifully left in his way. And wherever he went he carried his idiotic smile, his chart and his strange message of the end of earth and the beginning of life.

Perhaps, as that ragged horde tramped up the way that led bloodily from Virginia into Maryland, and across the Potomac into Pennsylvania, this prophecy of a day of wrath and judgment, of red tramplings in the vineyard, and an end to pain and labor, touched wearily in them some deep and obscure joy.

So they marched on into the slaughter of July, bearing with them the cracked prophet who had shown the Dutch farmboy the first of that strange clan with which his life was to be mixed.

•

When all the troops had gone by, the boys stood listening to the sudden noise of silence, the sleepy buzz of summer. There was a freshening of warm wind among the blades of corn, the drone of a bee as it reeled home drunk with pollen, the fading creak of a gun-carriage down the road.

Then from a little white farmhouse set up on an elevation under some trees at a considerable distance from the road, they heard the bronze clangor of a bell, broken by the wind. They walked rapidly away towards the house, each lost and silent in the blazing pageantry of his thought.

A woman stood in the front doorway sheltered from the sun by a little stoop. She held the bell in one hand, and shaded her eyes with the other, with the powerful gesture of a man. When they were still some distance away, she called out to them in a harsh, rasping, and impatient voice.

"You boys hurry up! You've idled the whole morning away watching those good-for-nothing rebels. You don't care if your mother, a pore old widow woman, works herself to death as long as you fill yore bellies. Now, I give you fair warning. I'm not going to put up with it any longer: you're both of you big strapping men, and you've got to earn yore keep."

They accepted this tirade casually, without perturbation. When they came up to the door, she said more quietly, "Did you get the cattle put away?"

"Yes," said Gil. "It's all right. They're in the wood."

"Did any of them ask you where they were?"

"Yes," said Gil.

"What did you tell them?"

"I told them," said Gil, "to go to hell."

"Well," said the widow matter-of-factly, "you boys go and wash up. You're not coming in this house with those filthy hands. Hurry, now! You've kept dinner waiting half an hour."

She turned and went back into the house. Gilbert and Oliver went around to the back door. They filled a battered tin pan with water, pumping for each other, and lathering their big hands with gritty soap.

Then they went into the kitchen for dinner. The kitchen was a big room with a low ceiling. There were rows of pots and pans upon the walls, scrubbed to a silver and copper glitter. There was a great oaken cupboard, a flour bin and shelves loaded with preserves. In the pantry there was a barrel of apples, a flitch of bacon and four or five fat smoked hams, which hung by hooks.

The two boys sat down at a table covered by a clean blue linen cloth patterned with stripes and squares of black. The hired man, a bronzed Dutchman of middle age, sat across the table from them, horsily gulping his food. He looked up from his scoured plate after a moment, and said ironically: "You boys are kinda late, ain't you? Did you enjoy your vacation?"

"I'm not going to have any more of it," said the widow Gant, opening the oven door. "You've all got to earn your keep or get out."

"I earn my keep," said Gil calmly. "And more, too."

The hired man rose, wiping his mouth dry of cider.

"Did you see the rebs, Gil?" he asked.

"Yes," said Gil sourly, "and smelled them too."

"There'll be hell a-poppin'," said the hired man. "A Gettysburg man came over this morning. He said the troops are camped all over the country. The rebs have been at Cashtown since yesterday."

"Well," said Gil, "I wish they'd shoot a few on our place. We need the fertilizer."

The grinning Dutchman went out to his work.

Oliver and Gilbert sat together on one side of the long table and waited for their food. Their younger brother, Emerson, a boy of eleven, sat opposite them. Emerson had their mean features: his nose, his small gray eyes and his tight stingy mouth all came slyly to a focal point.

The youngest child, John, a sensitive and delicate-looking boy of eight years with a shock of brown hair, sat next to Emerson, at the head of the table near his mother. Augusta, the only girl, and the oldest, helped her mother put food on the table. She was twenty-three years old, big brown and bony like her mother, with a broad high-boned face, a big nose, a wide straight mouth, and coarse black hair parted in the center and drawn tightly down. But, in spite of her rugged Dutch likeness to the widow, there was a strange tenderness and docility in Augusta.

She had great brown eyes, as big and gentle as a cow's: they gave to her gaunt face an expression of brooding tenderness and fidelity. Her movements were clumsy and deliberate: she had none of her mother's harshness of voice or gesture. She spoke little: she had been formed for obedience.

The widow, opening the oven door again, thrust in her aproned hand and drew out a roasting pan with a smoking quarter of beef, tenderly crisped in its fat, and oozing succulently a rich gravy. Augusta cut up smoking squares of brown cracklin' bread and put it on the table.

"God knows," said the widow, as she ladled the pan gravy over the roast, "what's going to become of us this winter. They're predictin' it will be bitter cold, and there's no one on the place who'll do any work. I'm an old widow woman, and there's nothing left for me but the porehouse. They'll sell the roof over my head for taxes."

"Now, mother," said Gilbert, pouring out a glass of cider from a pitcher on the table, "don't start on that. I'm tired of hearing it. I do my work and so does Oll."

"We'll starve before the winter's out," she said gloomily, putting the roast on the table. Then she went to the cupboard and returned with a great platter of cold jellied smearcase. Augusta meanwhile piled a bowl with meaty smoking ears of yellow corn, and filled other dishes with hot string beans, spinach, sliced tomatoes, and mashed potatoes, whipped to a creamy froth. She put these on the table and returned a moment later with a covered boat of thick gravy. The two women then sat down at opposite ends of the table and began to eat.

Gilbert grasped a carving knife and a steel in his great hands, and after setting up a briefly appetizing clangor, speared the roast to its heart with the long tines of a meatfork, and carved off rich savory slabs of the rare beef. Then he served the women, John, Oliver and himself, pausing finally to stare grimly at Emerson's mean greedy eyes.

"You ain't helped yet," Emerson whined nasally.

He stretched his skinny hand forth for the meatfork. Gilbert rapped him smartly across his knuckles with the steel. He yelped in angry pain.

"Those who don't work," said Gilbert, "don't eat."

"You leave that child alone, Gil," said the widow. She speared a slice of beef and put it on the boy's plate.

"Your brother's right about you," she said harshly. "You're not worth your salt."

"What've I done?" whined Emerson.

"Nothing," said Gilbert. "That's what you've done—nothing. You haven't done any of your chores, and if I had my way you wouldn't eat."

There was the silence of confession for a moment. Then Gil concluded with emphasis: "I do my work. I eat. Oll does his work. He eats. You don't do your work. You don't eat."

281

"Now that's enough, Gil," said the widow. "Don't tease the child any more."

"Mother," said Oliver nervously and eagerly, "I talked to the rebels. I gave General Fitzhugh Lee a drink of water."

"You were a fool to do it," growled Gilbert. "I'd have seen them in hell first."

"Pore fellows," said the widow, "I suppose they're worn out. God knows, there's enough trouble in the world without tramping all the way from Virginia looking for more."

As he heard the strange name of Virginia, Oliver's cold furtive eyes darkened again with their obscure hunger.

"They were a seedy-looking lot," said Gil. "They looked as if they hadn't eaten for the last month."

"I hope they leave us alone," the widow said. "I've trouble enough making ends meet as it is, and if the rebels roost upon me we'll be eaten out of house and home."

"Mother," said Oliver, with the same eager nervousness, "one of the rebels had his feet wrapped up in old rags, and he kept shouting to us that the end of the world is here. He said that Armageddon is coming tomorrow and to tell everyone to get ready."

"He was crazy," said Gil definitely, "and you're a fool for listening to such talk. I don't pay no attention to it."

"He may not be far wrong," said the widow Gant. "It will be the end of the world sure enough for many a pore soldier, and maybe for some of the rest of us if the fighting comes this way."

But, as they sat there listening to the sleepy drone of July jarred only faintly by the guns, it was hard to believe that the ends of the earth had met in so quiet a land. Gilbert took a long draught of cider and put his glass down reflectively.

"Mother," he said at length, "I've decided to go away. I'm going to Baltimore to learn a trade."

Oliver turned quickly to him with stopped breath. Augusta stared quietly with her great faithful eyes. The widow made no answer for a moment.

She leaned thoughtfully forward on her bony elbows.

"Well, Gil," she said quietly at last, "if you want to go I won't try to stop you. You're getting big enough to support yourself. We're pore folks and I've never been able to do much for you. But you're a good boy, and a hard worker, and I know you'll get along."

"Mother," said Oliver huskily. "Mother. Let me go with Gil."

She started violently, and turned upon him.

"No!" she cried fiercely, in strong fear. "No!"

Her bony fingers trembled. In a moment she spoke more calmly, with a kind of prayer in her voice. "Why, Ollie," she said, "my little Ollie. You don't want to go and leave me yet, do you? You don't want to leave your pore old mother all alone, do you?"

"Please, Mother!" said Oliver dryly, desperately. "I want to go with Gil."

She looked, with pain, with an old familiar terror, into his eyes, darkening now with her old enemy—a strange Norse hunger for voyages that she could not understand, darkening with the ghost of the Stranger that she had lost, and that stood specter-wise here now in his son, that she could not bear to lose.

"Why, Ollie," she coaxed desperately, "Ollie. You're only a child, son. You mustn't leave me yet."

She seized his big hands in her bony grip, and dry-lipped, gray-faced, he answered her desperate stare.

"No. You stay here with Mother for a while, Oll," said Gilbert decisively. "You're not old enough to leave home yet. I'll send for you when the time comes."

His downright bluntness released their tension. Oliver slumped dejectedly in his chair. The women rose and began to clear the table.

Then, over the drowsy heat of the day, there came to them faint broken sounds from the road—of men who sang old songs as their bodies swung wearily in saddles, of hoofbeats dumb with dust, a faint creak of leather, a clink of bit and sabre, but all so drowsed in the sleepy day that they seemed to come from a remote and elfin world.

The widow went to the door and looked out with shaded eyes. Gilbert looked up inquiringly.

"What is it?" he asked.

"Cavalry going by—pore fellows," she said.

Oliver got up suddenly and went to the door.

"I can see the light upon their bridles," he said. "But it all sounds so far away."

He turned to Gilbert with a strange calm excitement, brooding and suppressed.

"Gil! Gil! How long will they go by?"

"How should I know?" said Gilbert surlily. "Do you expect them to parade every day for your benefit?" he asked ironically. "They can't go by forever, you know."

Oliver turned toward the road again, with the old hunger darkening in his eyes.

If they only could! (he thought). If they only could!

•

The next day they heard the blasting thunder of great guns. During the night Lee had come through on his white horse, with the rest of his 70,000 ragged men.

Save for the tremor of the guns nothing disturbed the hot blue peace of the countryside. The boys brought the cows back to the fields, studded with the hot dry legions of the daisies. And they went stubbornly about their manful work, rising in the dark before dawn to go do the milking, doing half a day's hard labor before the armies began to fight.

The rumors of blood and battle rolled back to them: Gil spat grimly when he heard of the first day's work and the retreat of Meade's army to Cemetery Hill. Then, after a quiet night and forenoon, while the troops dug in, the terrible fighting of the second day began.

Bacchus Pentland toiled up the grim slope of Little Round Top, shooting his enemies dead among the savage rocks of the place and crying his news of Armageddon as he came in among them clubbing with a brainred gunstock. He was shot through the groin and ripped up the leg with a bayonet, but he managed to get back to the Wheat Field, where he fought, painting the grain with blood until his blistered hands stuck to the gun barrel. Then night came, and delirium, and he was carried back beyond the road to a field hospital, oblivious alike of the coming of the Lord and the cursing mercy of the surgeons who had no time for wounds that did not need the terrible execution of the meatsaw and the cleaver.

Then morning came and the end of rebellion, as the ragged men charged straight across the fields against that hill of death and union. They melted, formed again, toiled to the cannon's barrel, and were erased. The drawling mountaineer, the tenant farmer had fought to the end for the slaves they had never owned—had left one more myth of chivalry and knighthood for the exploitation of those three assiduous and innumerable quacks: the Major, the Senator and the Lady.

It was over. Lee drew his broken army together and on the night of the Fourth, with superb manipulations, fell back through the hills towards Maryland while, in torrential rain, stabbed with flashes of lightning, Jeb Stuart's battered horsemen fought to hold the pass at Monterey, and gave bloodily to the retreating army its hour of precious escape.

No more. No more.

On Sunday, which was the Fifth, Gil hitched up the rig and drove the family over the mired roads to the little village that had gained its eternity in three days. The farmers stood ruefully in among the ruined grain that was soaked in the blood of an army that had come to devour it.

The victorious army breathed wearily, collecting itself slowly, and, unable to follow its beaten enemy, sent out a brigade of cavalry to harry it. Over the fields the stretcher bearers moved with the wounded, taking them from the sopping canvas of field hospitals to dryer quarters.

And from the humid earth there rose the green carrion stench of rotting limbs, which the surgeons had piled up in heaps, and the corrupt smell of the dead men, weltering into the mud with putrid deliquescence. The unburied rebels still lay upon the field: they sprawled thick and gray in the casual postures of violent death among the rocks of Little Round Top and Culp's Hill, they lay upon the Wheat Field and in the Peach Orchard, and across that open shot-mown land where Pickett's men had charged they lay, rotting into the earth. Wheeling low above the field with flapping screech, the rednecked vultures plunged downward to their feast.

Gilbert stared at the friendless bodies with satisfaction. But Oliver strode across the fields peering into the corrupt blur of the faces, searching for one that he had seen listening to the language of the lost world, the forgotten faces. He did not find it.

Over the field of Armageddon lay the trampled corn, the broken wall, the yellow pollution of death.

There were new lands. Where? When?

Nominated by The Paris Review

THE TURNING

by JEANNETTE BARNES

from THE NEBRASKA REVIEW

One aged dun pony, late last spring, vanished—
stolen or perished, we didn't know. Not wolves,
but the season turning. Packing salt, we trotted
out to feed in April's big wet snow.

I dallied a bale from my gray
Spanish mare, the fierce brave one,
dragged it for miles to the leanto
below the tall cottonwood grove.

Beauty, we called that lost pony, a homely range-bred,
cow-savvy, squat, square-jawed grulla dun only kids rode.

However it was, Beauty did not jog home.
Colic, the cold, it could be. Boot deep,
soaked past our knees, we searched high
as we could go, spurning what shelter you'll find
down arroyos. Whistled and yelled. No echo.

Wind shrieked in fence wire; even my bold
dappled Spanish mare slipped, floundered,
hooves balling ice, flailing
drifts that cramped her, belly high. Our gloves froze

on the reins. Snow thickened, fell faster;
wet leather squeaking, the shift of snow.

Numb, streaming, shivering, bent to the quirt-cut wind,
our eyes frosted almost closed; the thud
of the horses' hearts shook us. No answer.
We turned, loped home.

Now in the ease and dust of summer,
I've turned wet cows to graze new ground, rallying
my gray mare. It's her when I crave
joy or buck or lunge against the bull's
tilt of white rim-
reddened eye. This day,

I cantered my gray beyond stones and shadows.
(She snorts and pretends to be wary of those.)

Off this leap, the great birds, dark and golden,
plummet and rise, defying crows. Green

is the sweet sea of brome grass, the land's mane blowing.
Rivers wind the mesa's smoke-stained bones,
down to the chert tools left here: Scrapers, arrows
rest under tough sage where the deep creek flows.

Like a prayer, the water: *We are born and broken,
broken, born*. In this cliff's ten thousand year shade,
her ribs rise, sharp, to gleam like snow.

No undone Beauty, old or dark,
forgets, or turning, lets us go.

Nominated by The Nebraska Review

REFLECTIONS OF AN UNCERTAIN JEW

essay by ANDRÉ ACIMAN

from THE THREEPENNY REVIEW

The MAN in this 1921 photograph is sixty-five years old, bald, with what looks like a white trimmed beard, his left hand poised not so much on his left waist as on his lower left hip, displacing the side of his jacket, his bearing confident, a bit menacing perhaps, and yet, despite the purposeful and intentionally secure posture, always a touch apprehensive. As with all of the older men in my father's family album, in his hand, which is slightly uplifted, he is holding something that looks like a cigarillo, though it is somewhat thicker than a cigarillo, but not quite as big as a cigar; at its tip there seem to be ashes. One might say (if only to mimic a famous reconstructive analysis of how Michelangelo's Moses holds his tablets) that it is almost as though the photographer had not warned his subject in time, and therefore the subject, thinking this was a pause in between takes, went for a quick puff and didn't manage to remove the guilty cigarillo in time, so that the cigarillo, from being an item to be kept out of the picture, once caught, ends up occupying center stage.

Something tells me, however, it might just as easily be a small pen instead. Still, one doesn't hold a pen between one's middle and index fingers, especially with the hand turned outward in so relaxed a manner. No, not a pen. Besides, why would a pen appear when the subject is standing up and when there clearly is no desk anywhere in the background? It must be a cigar.

On closer inspection, it seems that there is something quite studied in his relaxed posture: one hand akimbo, the other almost placing the cigarette on exhibit, not as an afterthought, not diffidently, but declaratively. The ashes themselves say quite a bit: they are not about to spill, as may have seemed at first; they are in fact honed to a point, as with a pencil sharpener, which is why I thought of a pen, a ball-point pen, all the while knowing that ball-point pens did not exist at the time this picture was taken. Stranger yet, there is no smoke emanating from the cigarillo, which suggests either that the smoke was touched up and blotted out in the photo lab, or that the cigarillo was never even lit.

Which means that the cigarillo in the photo has a totally intentional presence.

What is this gentleman—and there is no doubt, since the posture proves he is a gentleman—doing exhibiting his cigarillo that way? Could it be that this is just a cigarillo, or is it much more than a cigarillo, much more than a pen even, the ur-symbol of all symbols, not just of defiance, of menace, of security, or of wrath even, but simply of power? This man knows who he is; despite his age, he is strong, and he can prove it, witness his cigarillo—it doesn't spill its ashes.

Another, younger picture of the same subject, taken around 1905, suggests more or less the same thing. The hair is neatly combed—there is much more of it—the beard, though grayish, is bushier. Behind the seated subject is a reproduction of Michelangelo's statue of a dying slave, standing in naked and contorted agony. The man in this photograph stares at the camera with something like a very mild stoop, his shoulders less confident, uneasy, almost cramped. He looks tired, overworked, worn out; in his left hand he is holding a cigar that seems to have been smoked all the way down; he is holding its puny remains at one or two centimeters above the spot where his thighs meet, almost—and I stress the almost—echoing the flaunted nudity of the dying slave behind him.

I may have made too much of the symbolism here. I would, let me hasten to say, respectfully withdraw every word, were it not for the fact that the subject of these two pictures, ostensibly fraught with Freudian symbolism, is none other than Freud himself. How can anyone look at Freud's cigarillo and not think Freudian thoughts?

However, there is another symbol at work here. Indeed, looking back at the pictures, it occurs to me that something had clearly happened between the older man standing up in 1922 and the somewhat younger man sitting down in 1905. What happened, of course, is success.

The man in the later picture is an established man. A man of property, of substance. His is the pose that all men adopted when being photographed: it conveyed composure, worldliness, confidence, plenitude, security, a touch arch and arrogant perhaps, but without a doubt, this was a man of the world, a much-traveled, sought-after individual who had seen and lived much. In fact he was more than just established, he had made it, he had, as the French say, arrived. An *arriviste* is someone who strives to arrive; a *parvenu*, however, is someone who has arrived. You posed with a cigarette, or a cigar, or a cigarillo, not just because the cigar suggested security—as though those with, as opposed to without, cigars were worthier men—but also because the cigarillo was an instrument, an implement, a prosthesis for grounding oneself in the picture and, by extension, in the world. Smoking doesn't suggest success, it screams success. It locks it in. A successful Jew who smokes is proof that he has attained a degree of prominence.

Let me resort to another word, which is much used nowadays and which conveys a neo-Jewish nightmare: this man had assimilated. *Assimilate* is a strange verb, used without a direct or indirect object to mean being swallowed up, absorbed, and incorporated into mainstream Gentile society. But the verb has another meaning, closely linked to its etymology: to assimilate means to become similar to, to simulate.

The irony is that this was how one posed to simulate success. You were photographed with a smoking implement to appear you weren't posing, to appear as though you had achieved enough stature not to have to pose at all. You posed with a cigar to suggest you weren't posing with a cigar. You belonged and, therefore, no longer had to worry about belonging. The Italians may have called this posturing *sprezzatura*; add a pipe and the complications reach Magrittian proportions. A Jew poses with a cigar to symbolize two things: that he has achieved social and professional success, but also that he has successfully assimilated.

There were many other Jews with cigars.

There is a picture of a plump, extremely groomed, self-satisfied young gentleman wearing clothes that were clearly cut by the best tailor. He is seated with one arm resting on a thigh, and another holding out a cigarillo more or less in the manner of Freud; his face looks up smugly, with a rakish glint on his smile. His name is Artur Schnabel.

Another is caught walking along the street holding his pipe in his hand. He is wearing an unbecoming wide-rimmed hat. He could not look more gawkish or more self-conscious. He is feigning a debonair amble about town, but he is holding a pipe no less gingerly than if he were walking a urine sample to a laboratory. His name is Albert Einstein.

Another is not even looking at the camera, his hand supporting his chin while grasping a cigarette. He looks like the most established intellectual, and yet if there is a man who has come to symbolize the most unestablished intellectual of this century it was precisely Walter Benjamin, who died on the run.

There is, also a picture of a young woman, perhaps one of the boldest intellectuals of her times, looking totally intimidated and fainthearted, having enlisted the help of this implement for the picture, and yet holding her cigarette at bay, almost pushing it out of the picture (the way some New York cabbies do when they hold their cigarette out of the window), all the while desperately clinging to it, hoping it might give her that certain air without which she'd be a simple undergraduate. Her name is Hannah Arendt.

Finally, there is the picture of the greatest Italian novelist of this century, the man who first introduced Freud to Italy and who indeed translated Freud, and who took on a name that is itself quite interesting: Italo Svevo, also known as the man who made compulsive smoking a subject worthy of modern literature. He is sitting with legs crossed, holding a cigar over one thigh in a gesture that could be called Freudian.

Freud, Schnabel, Einstein, Benjamin, Arendt, Svevo—*didn't they know?*

Didn't they know that smoking, besides giving you cancer, confers no power, no composure, no confidence whatsoever?

But this is not the question I meant to ask. This was just my way of dissembling the real question, as though I too had something to dissemble and needed to mislead the reader somewhat before coming out with it, as though by raising the smokescreen of Freudian symbolism I could sneak in another, more disquieting question, which reflects my own very personal worries and anxieties, not Freud's or Einstein's.

Didn't they know they were Jewish?

Or, to turn it around: didn't they know that, even if all of Europe posed this way, it would never wash, that they could never pass, that part of what made them so odious to anti-semites was the very fact

291

that they presumed they could pass? Didn't they know that, while others posed with a cigar to suggest they weren't posing with a cigar, such a pose, when it came to Jews, was a double pose and as such came close to a form of imposture that brought out the killer in every anti-semite?

What was so threatening to a German, to an Austrian, to a Frenchman or an Englishman in this cigar posture was not just that Jews had made it into mainstream German, Austrian, French, or British society. What was really threatening about such Jews was that they were also the very first to have accessed pan-European culture. In fact, they didn't just tap into such a culture; they built it.

They were enamored of cosmopolitan European civilization not only because, unlike national venues, it flung open far wider doors to them, but also because, all the while not being properly speaking theirs, it was more theirs than any other nation's. Their romance with the Christian or pagan culture was irresistible precisely because it allowed them to draw much closer than they had ever been to those cultures which only a few generations before had been barred to them. Moreover, it allowed them to realize that being Jewish did not mean they couldn't get to the center of the Christian universe and understand it, perhaps, even better than did Christians. Benjamin's unfinished doctoral dissertation was on the theater of the post-Reformation; he was one of the very few modern thinkers to appreciate the genius of Paolo Sarpi, the sixteenth and seventeenth-century Venetian friar who remains today the most lucid historian of the Council of Trent. Hannah Arendt wrote her dissertation on Saint Augustine under Karl Jaspers, the existential Christian philosopher. Freud, a font of encyclopedic knowledge, was fascinated by classical antiquity. And Ettore Schmitz, who changed his name to Italo Svevo to reflect both his Italian and Schwabian roots, had intentionally or inadvertently forgotten to make up a third name to reflect his Jewish origins.

The list goes on and on. For cosmopolitan Jews, traditional Judaism and the traditional rewards of Judaism could not compete with the advantages and rewards of this profound and vertiginously rich European culture—could not compete, that is, with Berlin, Vienna, Paris, Rome, Milan, Trieste, London.

The city where my great-uncles posed with cigars or cigarettes between their fingers was a long way from those European cultural capitals. And yet if the world of Alexandria had one wish—and that wish lasted for seventy-five years—it was precisely to be like Berlin, Vienna, Paris, Rome, Milan, and London, to be Berlin, Vienna, Paris, Rome, Milan, and London all in one. I won't repeat the clichés; everyone knows them: Alexandria was a city where all the religions and nationalities of the world were represented, and where each religion lived side by side with the others in perfect harmony. Perfect harmony may be an exaggeration of course, but I mean it no less facetiously than when it is said of married couples living side by side in perfect harmony. Such cosmopolitanism can exist in two ways: as it does in New York and as it did in Alexandria, i.e., in a democracy or in an empire.

In New York, there is a system of social values and beliefs that prescribes mutual toleration and equal opportunities. Prescribed does not mean practiced, but it is there on the books at least, and most people try hard enough to believe it works that they would fight for it if it were taken away from them.

In Alexandria, there were no shared values or shared beliefs. Alexandria was the product of two or even three empires: the Ottoman, the French, and the British. Empires generate their own kinds of capital cities: nerve centers where all of their far-flung populations send emissaries and migrants. You go to exploit multiplicity, not to lose your identity or to respect the other more than is necessary to conduct business. You embrace multiplicity because it ratifies your identity. You learn everyone's language; and if you never lose yours to a dominant language, you do adopt a lingua franca that eventually confers an identity all its own.

Many of the people I grew up with were children of immigrant and low-end colonialist communities: Italian, Syrian, Lebanese, and French immigrants. Many of these continued to maintain contact with their country or community of origin much in the way ancient Greek colonies did: the colony of the colony of a colony frequently continued to claim ties to the mother community, say, of Athens, Thebes, or Corinth.

But then you also had a different kind of population, of which I can recall three: the Armenians, some of whom had settled after the first Armenian massacre; the Greeks from Asia Minor, who had come before but who certainly thronged to Alexandria following their exodus from Turkey and the burning of Smyrna; and then the Jews, many of whom had been in Egypt for a thousand years, while others

293

arrived from elsewhere—in my family's case, from Turkey—in an attempt to found a new home. Armenians, Greeks, and Jews did better than the French or the Italians not only because they were more numerous but because they were more desperate: for them there was really no country to return to.

In this interim oasis they created their own peculiar dynamic, acquiring paper citizenships that were to real nationalities what paper profits are to real money. They thrived in this ideal panopolis, though, as with immigrants elsewhere in the world, no one really expected to stay there permanently. No one identified with Alexandria, and everyone was too busy identifying with the entire culture of Europe to understand what having a single culture really meant.

The more westernized the Jews of Alexandria grew, the more they developed the sensibility of their German, French, and Italian Jewish counterparts: they too allowed their Jewish identity to be displaced, not by a national identity—which was almost entirely imaginary—but by a pan-European, equally imaginary one. We imagined every other city in the world in order not to see the one city we were very much a part of, the way we imagined every other culture in order to avoid seeing we were basically and just Jewish. Some of us could afford to go through all these antic moves because we knew—and feared—that, all things considered, the one thing that would never be taken away from us was precisely our Jewishness. And yet, was Jewishness something at the core, securely lodged, or was it something that had been dislodged and was now spinning forever out of orbit?

Although most Jews did practice Judaism in Egypt and were proud of being Jewish, I was always torn. I was proud of being Jewish, but I could just as easily have been mortified by being Jewish. I wanted to be Christian. But I didn't want to be anything but Jewish. I am a provisional, uncertain Jew. I am a Jew who loves Judaism provided it's on the opposite shore, provided others practice it and leave me to pursue my romance of assimilation, which I woo with the assiduity of a suitor who is determined to remain a bachelor. I am a Jew who longs to be in a world where everyone is Jewish, where I can finally let down my guard; but I am a Jew who has spent so much time defining himself in relation to non-Jews that I wouldn't know how to live, much less who to be, in a world where everyone was Jewish.

I still don't know whether the pan-Europe I dreamt up truly existed or whether it was after all a Jewish invention, a Jewish fantasy.

But it may explain my single-minded devotion to European Christian and pagan literature. These books were the first literature I read during my youth, and it was to these books that I finally turned when I sought to locate the imaginary Europe I had totally lost on landing in Europe after Egypt.

For if anything seemed parochial and provincial and closed-minded when I landed in Europe, it was precisely Europe itself. And more provincial still was America. Yet it was in America that I finally realized that the most provincial place in the world was Alexandria, and that perhaps the ability to spot provincialism in people and places was itself the surest sign of a provincial person: i.e., someone who longs for the great and tiny tokens of cosmopolitanism for fear of being sucked back into the dark alleys of dark small towns in the dark old country which every Jew carries inside of him. We needed our books, our many languages, our broad-mindedness, our ability to disclaim who we were in the interest of adaptability, our fast cars and our tiny cigars, even our willingness to show we could easily live with the most disquieting paradoxes—we needed them because they were a cover for something we no longer knew how to be: Jewish.

As I write of all of these paradoxes, it occurs to me that I am being cosmopolitan in a very Alexandrian way, in the way the Book of Ecclesiastes is a very Alexandrian book, because, in the beginning as in the end, to be a cosmopolitan in Alexandria was to live with every conceivable contradiction. But when it comes to the deeper, thinking self, it takes no great effort to see that without paradox I am out of place, I am a stranger, and that this very paradox, for a cosmopolitan Jew living in Alexandria, is home.

But let us not overromanticize either. What paradox does when it becomes a way of life is to alienate one, to make one a stranger from one's people, one's homeland, one's second and third homeland, and ultimately from who one is.

You become nothing, *nobody*, like Ulysses.

And Ulysses posing with a cigar is like a lotus eater who thinks he's found a new home.

So let me return to Freud's cigar and suggest—and I do so with all the hesitation in the world, because I do hate this sort of thing—that the cigar I've been toying with throughout is a phallic symbol.

But as Nietzsche said, I am giving you the moral before giving you the tale.

So let me give you two tales.

The first is taken from my own experience as the only Jewish boy in a ninety-seven-percent Muslim school in Egypt (the other three or so percent being Christians). We are about to take swimming lessons and I complain to the teacher that I am feeling sick—and for all I know at that moment, I must be sick, because fear will do this to you. The reason is not hard to imagine. I don't want to undress before the other boys because if I did so I'd reveal to the Catholics who thought I was Catholic, to the Greek Orthodox who always suspected I was one of theirs, or to the Muslims who assumed I was soon to convert to their religion, since I was the only European boy who attended Islam Class every week, that I was—to them—a sham. You may not feel Jewish, but Judaism is—pardon the metaphor—cut into you, as though to make sure that, however you quibble over your Jewish identity, you are branded with it for life. You—and others—would never have a doubt. But as every Elizabethan and Jacobean playwright knew, that's precisely the tragedy of impostors. Even when they are totally alone they no longer know where their truth lies. And their awareness of this paradox resolves nothing at all.

When I explained to some of my relatives why I hated swimming class—I who loved the sea and who loved the beach enough to wish to spend my entire life in the water, because if I am ambivalent about all things, I am certainly the most amphibian man alive—they responded with a totally different tale. During the Armenian massacre, when a Jew was mistaken for an Armenian by the Turks, all he had to do was pull down his trousers and he was given his life back.

So let me be totally blunt now and ask questions whose purpose is really not so much to arrive at answers but to give you a sense of how confused I, the writer from cosmopolitan Alexandria, am on this question of the Jewish identity in a cosmopolitan world. To this end, let us assume for a split second that Freud is in fact holding a phallic symbol in his hand.

What is he saying about that phallus? Is he holding out a Jewish member and saying, "Look, ladies and gentlemen, I may be a totally cosmopolitan man, but I can never—nor do I ever wish to—forget I am Jewish"?

Or is he saying the exact opposite? "Look, stare and observe: here is proof I am not and have never been Jewish."

Or, "Would I even allow you to raise the question if I thought you'd come up with this?"

Or is he saying something totally different? That is: "This is just a cigar. And only a Jew from Alexandria who has never understood Freud or confronted his own anxieties about being Jewish would think otherwise. This, sir, says more about you than it ever will about me."

And without hesitating a second I'd say that he was right, that it is all about me and my own reluctant Judaism, which desperately wishes to find similarly reluctant Jews around the world, if only to nurse the illusion that there are other Jews like me, that Jews like me are not alone, that perhaps all Jews are like me, in the sense that all Jews are other, lonely Jews, that no Jew can ever be authentically Jewish once he steps out of the ghetto, that all Jews have the diaspora branded on them so profoundly that feigning they are not Jewish is perhaps the surest way to discover they are nothing but Jewish.

But as Galileo did when forced to recant his theory, I'd still mutter under my breath, as any confused Alexandrian would always end up muttering: *Ceci n'est pas un cigare.*

Nominated by The Threepenny Review

THE POET'S VOICE

by MICHAEL S. HARPER

from THE AMERICAN SCHOLAR

> *love, light, loss, liberty, lunacy and laceration*
> —Gwendolyn Brooks

Too much made of birth in Topeka
too little made of Chicago *Defender*

contributor at sixteen, the odd job
solo moments of community gloss

in each kitchenette clipping
microscopic *tintypes* of losses and gains

without the slightest naivete
of the street, backyard, parlor grid

her masterpiece of the 'singing tree'
"We Real Cool" in 1959

anticipates the rest of the century:
after Fisk in 1967

known by detractors and sycophants
alike as "Mother Afrika"

but she remains a *citizen* in daily
interiors of unassailable synapse

contralto arpeggios released
in bemused attributes of light

at the end of her *lincoln west* tunnel
wordsmith of the 'real thing'

exhortingly brave in every territory
for those unsung-in-service-evermore

(for Gwendolyn Brooks on her 82nd birthday: 6.7.99)

Nominated by Toi Derricotte

MELBA KUPERCHMID RETURNS

fiction by PETER M. ORNER

from THE SOUTHERN REVIEW

MELBA KUPERCHMID WAS A BEAUTIFUL ONE, and everybody knows what happens to the beautiful ones. Scooped up and gone before she turned twenty. He was a traveler; nobody even knew his name or what he did for a living, only that he had daring and never lived in one place for long. But Melba's old friend Sarah Kaplan used to get postcards from places that didn't seem very romantic from the photographs. Windsor, Canada, for one. St. Louis, Missouri, for another. Then, twenty-three years after she left, as everybody claimed they knew in their heart of hearts would happen sooner or later, Melba Kuperchmid came home. Discarded like the beautiful ones always are, one way or another. But when she came back to Fall River, she wasn't fat like everybody expected. She was still gorgeous. Still had all that hair and those enormous black eyes men fell into and flailed. Still Melba, not destroyed, even a little giggly like she always was. Not lamenting being deserted, not even discussing it.

For a few months she went to cocktail parties and talked (politely) to the husbands, letting everybody know from the way she refused to laugh at the men's bad jokes that she wanted no part of them. This of course made the wives suspicious. What else could a returned (spurned, vanquished) divorcée possibly want if not their potbellied husbands? The other curious thing was that not long after she came home (she had no family left, and she'd had no children), Melba— now in her mid-forties—opened a seamstress shop on Corky Row, apparently with her alimony money. She'd always been good at sewing; a lot of the girls remembered that. But Melba Kuperchmid? A seamstress?

Sarah'd always loved her. As girls they often left school in late morning and spent afternoons trudging the mud along Watupa Pond. Slogging and hackling about people. They used to talk about what they'd do when they got to Paris. Twirl in the streets, first of all. Then search for dark Mediterranean men with unpronounceable names and wispy, tuggable mustaches. For Sarah, Melba's return was a strange jolt. She'd been marching forward. She'd raised Rhoda into a girl people talked about (Rhoda'd been elected *Most Garrulous* and *Best Dancer* by her class at Durfee). Sarah'd served as volunteer chair of the hospital charity luncheon eleven years in a row, and was a respected member (and treasurer) of the Hebrew Ladies Helping Hand Society. The new house on Delcar wasn't so new anymore, but the mortgage was far from dead and buried. There was Walt and his cars. He talked about his old junked cars like they were children who'd grown up and gone away. Now he was in love with Volvos, which made him, according to him, avant-garde. Rhoda was already in her fifth term at Simmons the year Melba came home, 1961.

Was it really possible that she wanted nothing more than to open a shop and live quietly, modestly, in a rented apartment mid-hill? Sarah tried to distance herself from the gossip of the girls. There were all kinds of explanations. Dotty Packer said that some cousin of Leddy Levine (of the Harry Levines) told her that Melba's ex-husband was a gambler who fled because he was wanted by J. Edgar Hoover *and* the Sugar House Gang for extortion and unpaid debts. Somebody else—Ruth Gerard—said Melba's husband was a kind of junior-issue sheik who got summoned back to Arabia to marry a sultan's firstborn daughter. That was a good one. Ruth Gerard always came up with good ones, and Sarah chose not to mention that she had in her possession an old photograph (Melba sent it from the Midwest somewhere) of the man she married, and he was white as white could be, shirtless, leaning against a tree, wearing a bowler and a crimped smile that made him look like he was being pinched, but oh, was he handsome, very. The only thing Sarah would offer the gossip-eaters was a lie she claimed she heard from Tenelle Donatello (who was considered close to the new Melba because it was from her husband Felix that Melba rented shop space) that Melba left him, not the other way around. This of course prompted Bea Halprin to huff, "Well in that case, where's her other man? And why come back here if life was so wonderful she could ditch him in the first place?"

The fact was that nobody knew because nobody asked. Even the most fearless Nosey Parker, Edi Dondis, didn't have the courage to broach the subject directly. Because there still floated about Melba a halo of untouchableness, an aura that went beyond her physical beauty into realms no one could describe in conversation. She'd had it since she was a child, and everybody recognized that it still shrouded her with as much force as ever. (For example, they all started wearing hats indoors again.) Yet since Melba was a shop-keeper now, it became a question of class. This didn't bother Sarah, of all people, but it did, after a while, make it awkward to invite her to cocktail parties, and eventually the girls stopped asking her to most things, except the occasional low-profile non-charity luncheon. And when this didn't appear to ruffle Melba's feathers, some of the girls started saying maybe there's something wrong upstairs. Didn't something like this happen to Erma Zagwell's brother Jerome, that one morning he just refused to get out of bed ever again? There was a lot of dispute on this point, because even those who stopped send-ing over invitations still took their dresses to Melba to be fitted or let out. First, out of pity, they took things they no longer wore. Later they relied on her because she was so good they couldn't live without her. Finally the consensus was that anybody that excellent with the needle (particularly after all these years) couldn't possibly be crazy. But that didn't make the socializing problem easier for anybody.

About eight months into Melba's return, Sarah parked the big Lin-coln Town Car on the street in front of the house on Delcar. (Walt al-ways insisted she drive his past loves; this one was so huge it didn't fit in the garage.) But she didn't get out of the car. Instead, she paused and reflected that she'd spent a good chunk of her time in the mar-ket worrying over the mystery of Melba Kuperchmid: her lack of bit-terness, her lack of interest in reclaiming any former glory. They had all been so jealous of what she had—the envy of a thousand girls—that it must have been real. Now her coming home and not caring a lick put everything into question. The way she used to walk the halls, as if stepping on puddles of air nobody else could see, the boys quiv-ering and gnawing their collars. Sarah left the groceries in the car and went inside to look for something that needed mending. Not finding anything, she went into Walt's closet forest of white shirts and ripped a tear in the sleeve of one. Got back in the car, melting strawberry ice cream and all (this was in August), and headed down the hill to Corky Row. She found Melba behind the counter, alone, working the Singer, the clicking monotonous, feverish, loud enough that she did not hear Sarah open the chimeless door.

And Sarah stands mesmerized by the back of Melba's head. Her hair is pulled back tight in a plait; its end rests on her shoulder. Sarah looks at the exquisite columns that form that familiar neck. If she could freeze a moment in time, she'd freeze this one. The one before Melba finally turns around and sees her, because it isn't the new Melba she wants, it's the old one, the one who left here looking for something better. To ask what it's like to be so loved that rolling your tongue around your teeth's enough to make men swoon and need cold water. *And that still not be enough for you.* Melba with your simple black hair and big eyes, still no breasts to boast to the Queen of Sheba about, and yet you're Melba, aren't you? Aren't you? You were two years older than me. And you used to whisper that you'd stolen a pack of Mr. Jalbert's cigarettes. *Come on, Sar. We're as good as gone!* And that was all it ever took.

In the shop, pressing her handbag and the shirt to her chest, listening to the manic click of the machine, watching Melba's head. Maybe Sarah will tell her again (she wrote her about it after, in a flurry, and sent the letter to one of the many addresses she had for Melba then) about her own escape from Fall River. She's sure Melba's forgotten, if the letter even made it to her. And of course it was only for a weekend, but there was Sarah Gottlieb's famous eloping to Rhode Island. People still talk about how Rhoda was born big and healthy barely seven scandalous months later, and how Sarah's mother's rage lasted till the day she died. Didn't Sarah take her risk, too? She never thought it'd matter again (she was just like so many other people now), but now her once running means more.

She clears her throat. "Melba, dear, I thought I'd drop by and bring you—"

Melba swivels her stool. Some wrinkles below her eyes like the veins of a leaf the only change. It could be 1936. They could be on the shore of the Watupa talking about Howie or Hughie, the one from Boston who chased Melba for months, one of the many she didn't choose, the one who kept circling her block in his convertible,

303

hundreds of times. They called them Howie's laps, and they became as much a part of the neighborhood as Mrs. Gilda Rubover's garden of rabbit skeletons.

Yes, the same as ever, but tired now too. Maybe it's the sallow light of the store, but there's exhaustion in that still beautiful face. Melba's eyes linger before she welcomes Sarah with her old closed-mouthed smirk. It's in the way the sweat's pooled on the nape of her neck—a glimpse of what's disappeared in that trickle of moment before Melba calls, sprightly, over the machine's noise. "Ah, Sarah. You brought me some mending."

And Sarah looks at her and thinks, *We're becoming older women, on the verge of being like those fat-ankled waddlers at the club, the ones Walt says keep disappearing into their shoes. Even you.*

Melba waves her closer. "Sit! Sit!" The shop is cluttered and stuffy. Fabric's in piles on the floor. Skirts clipped on hangers draped over ironing boards. There are books on a shelf alongside a stack of sewing magazines. There's a bowl of chocolate and a ripped calendar. *Even you, Melba. You can't hide behind not caring.*

Melba tosses a pincushion away, wipes off a wooden school chair with a rag. "Sit! Sit! For God's sake, sit down, Sarah." She sighs. "So good to see you. Too too long. I haven't laid eyes on you in weeks, ages, honey."

She sits on the edge of the chair to make clear she can't stay long, that she's only pausing for a quick chat. She tells Melba about the shirt, what a klutz Walt is, how he insists on wearing his good clothes around the house to fix things that don't need fixing. But even as she rambles on, she becomes aware of something in the way Melba said "weeks, ages." As if they aren't different. And then she knows, all at once, what should have been the obvious truth all along: that the marriage was short-lived, that the husband probably didn't last a year or two after that shirtless picture by the tree, that it was Melba who did all the moving around, that she'd been alone, that she'd been a seamstress for the last twenty-odd years, a damn good one, and that she came home for the same reason everybody comes home, but that in her case it wasn't to chase her past; she merely wanted to live near it. That proximity itself was comfort.

That she'd been alone, probably many years alone, maybe even because she wanted to be. Sarah thinks of Walt, how during the day she often forgets about him, but how he arrives every afternoon, breathing heavily at the back stoop, arms full of more junk they'd

304

never need; but he arrives, always, some afternoons knocking on the door with his head because he's got no free hand. And yes she feels pity, but Sarah's first instinct is to rub Melba's unchanged face in everything she doesn't have, to unbuckle her handbag and wave pictures of Rhoda. Rhoda's report cards, her hundred boyfriends, her honor society pins, her still-life drawings of fruit and vegetables. . . .

They make small talk about the shop and some things Melba's working on. She's doing Nina Shetzer's daughter's wedding party. (*An absolutely horrid plum! The bridesmaids are going to look like the walking wounded.*) But after a couple of awkward, too-long silences, Sarah can't keep herself from blurting: "I hate myself for saying this, Melba, but the girls all talk about your life like it's a train wreck."

Melba laughs and swoops her arm in an arc to dismiss them all, every last one of them. And what's incredible is that even her voice is the same, thick and direct like a man's, like the rocks she used to throw into the Watupa. "Tell them I was never a whore. Tell those yappies that."

Sarah doesn't nod, only stares and seeks forgiveness from Melba's eyes for being no better than everybody else, for reveling in such a miraculous and perfect failure. She thinks of the early postcards, the black-and-white photographs, Melba's zigzagged scrawl. *Darling Sarah, We've moved to a place called Wabash in Indiana. We live in a house on a small hill overlooking a dirty rushing river. Reminds me a bit of home, but the rivers are so much smaller here. Please write! I don't know two souls here. Your M*

"Not one of them ever once called you that. Not one."

But Melba's still laughing at the thought and doesn't care if they did or they didn't. She scoots her stool closer, leans, and squeezes Sarah's wrists. Her palms are hot and wet from work.

Nominated by Pat Strachan, James Reiss

MEMORY

by ANTHONY HECHT

from SOUTHWEST REVIEW

Sepia oval portraits of the family,
Black-framed, adorned the small brown-papered hall,
But the parlor was kept unused, never disturbed.
Under a glass bell, the dried hydrangeas
Had bleached to the hue of ancient newspaper,
Though once, someone affirmed, they had been pink.
Pink still were the shiny curling orifices
Of matching seashells stationed on the mantle
With mated, spiked, wrought-iron candlesticks.
The room contained a tufted ottoman,
A large elephant-foot umbrella stand
With two malacca canes, and two peacock
Tail-feathers sprouting from a small-necked vase.
On a teak side-table lay, side by side,
A Bible and a magnifying glass.
Green velvet drapes kept the room dark and airless
Until on sunny days toward midsummer
The brass andirons caught a shaft of light
For twenty minutes in late afternoon
In a radiance dimly akin to happiness—
The dusty gleam of temporary wealth.

Nominated by Maura Stanton

ALCYONE

by TALVIKKI ANSEL

from THE INDIANA REVIEW

Alcyone walking the dirt road at dusk's
even flush sees bats above the harbor,
an owl in a dark tree, smudgy fire of sticks
in a weedy lot, two lambs nurse, monstrous
big, for a moment like two grown sheep
nursing from a third. Her skin
smells of smoke. Ceyx is gone to Claros
to the oracle, to learn of his brother.
Family, family. Things we know we must not do—
stone the finch when it comes so close
irresistible, to pick seed for its mate,
look at the eclipse when the shadows grow
larger and the cicadas intensify, more loud
than brightness, the sun's black disc
is lipped in flames—how can that be stronger
than the sun itself full exposed? She shouldn't
look, shouldn't think of her husband, weather.

•

To get lost in all this—terraces leading
to terraces in the low evening light,
a gray donkey, man in faded clothes,
sage, sweat, dust and heat lessening.
But premonitions—
a sheep's blind eye turned her way, spume
blown off the jagged wave. She cannot sleep,

the worst nights spin away from her
like a white rock, smoothed, rattles down
the endless cold gorge of stone, falling
below the Taurus Mountains. Wind draws
the curtains in and out, she distrusts
the winds, how they teased, capricious.
As a girl at her father's house she knew them,
hanging about, they charmed Aeolus,
half in his power, three-quarters not.
Why does he let them free to trouble us?
They cannot hurt me, will not hurt me I
will stay calm. She wills the stone of herself
back into her mind, her body into sleep,
dolphins' glass bodies sew through waves,
waves become fish. As a girl she'd envied
Thetis, body turning to the muscled flanks
of the spotted leopard, lifting open arms
up into the angle of a hawk. To rise above
Aeolus's playthings, who will toy with Ceyx,
she wishes to have gone on the passage.
To Claros, there is only the stone dovecote here,
thought, the jetty shouldering the waves' three.

•

From this journey you will come back
changed, as slowly, surprisingly
the puffer fish cast down on the dry shore
expands into air when breathed on.
As leaning forward to hear one's story
you are filled with another, and listening
one thinks—no, this person contains more
than I thought before. This person.
On deck, the night's air condenses,
forms dew, dampens the sleeper's hair and skin.
Boats slip out of the harbor, spot
of a deck lamp lit, though morning is coming,
the mountains pink on the far shore.
Rattle of anchor chains, a dying
star's burning embers, *and my mouth*
calling your name had only salt to drink

but it was only a dream. Calm morning,
prequel to the afternoon's shifting winds,
no rumor, no doubtful message this,
let him return, let him love no other.
Maybe his boat rounding the island's point,
but it is too soon for Claros, and back.

•

If only she could separate these fears, put each
in its own peaked-roofed sarcophagus
on the hill, silhouetted against the sky.
Before a hurricane one sinks in shallow water
the boats, below the surface curl and crash,
to rock on the bottom, unbroken, waiting
until the seas are calm as an August day,
when from the water, flat and hot as beaten
metal the flying fish startle up, skitter
the surface, wings spread like stunted
hands, racing through air.
Two goats on the cliffs bleat to each other,
tiny, teaching perspective—how large
the cliffs loom over the fishing boat.
Inland, winds turn the pear leaves to gray.
That he would come back, in whatever form.
The theater's filled with sand, dead snails
bleached white as cotton dot the bushes.
She wants to walk, walk to the foothills
below the mountains. That snow-capped, hard,
impervious from a distance, so distant
from her would yield this—endless cold water
falling on dust, dry stones, her face,
surprises her still, the freshness.

•

In the cove where the common sandpiper
teeters on the bleached shore and the *serin*
buzz calls from the dry sage, their kingfisher
bodies dive and rise from the cool water.
They shake drops from wing coverts, turquoise
blue barbs. What they so admired—arms, calves,

309

legs for walking—is now changed. Their young
peck free of eggs, will not resemble their younger
selves. The shapes of their kingfisher lives—
flash of fish in the shallows, muddy nest cavity,
rock for perching. Sheltered here they rest
on the bank, below the olive trees ringing the cove,
where there is no wind and the spring pools
unsalty. You can open your eyes underwater
and see walls, stairs of a ruined village
descending, rocks and shore, the direction
that you swim, and your eyes will not sting.

Nominated by Maura Stanton, David Wojahn

THE FIREMAN

fiction by RICK BASS

from THE KENYON REVIEW

THEY BOTH STAND on the other side of the miracle. Their marriage was bad, perhaps even rotting, but then it got better. He—the fireman, Kirby, knows what the reason is—that every time they have an argument, the dispatcher's call sounds, and he must run and disappear into the flames—he is the captain—and while he is gone, his wife, Mary Ann, reorders her priorities, thinks of the children, and worries for him. Her blood cools, as does his. It seems that the dispatcher's call is always saving them. Their marriage settles in and strengthens, afterward, like some healthy, living, supple thing.

She meets him at the door when he returns, kisses him. He is grimy—black, salt-stained and smoky-smelling. They can't even remember what the argument was about. It's almost like a joke—the fact that they were upset about such a small thing—any small thing. He sheds his bunker gear in the utility room and goes straight to the shower. Later, they sit in the den by the fireplace and he drinks a few beers and tells her about the fire. Sometimes he'll talk about it till dawn. He knows he is lucky—he knows they are both lucky. As long as the city keeps burning, they can avoid becoming weary and numb. Always, he leaves, is drawn away, and then returns, to a second chance.

The children—a girl, four, and a boy, two—sleep soundly. It is not so much a city that they live in, but a town—the suburbs on the perimeter of the city—and it could be nameless, so similar is it to so many other places: a city in the center of the southern half of the country—a place where it is warm more often than it is cold, so that the residents are not overly familiar with fires—the way a fire spreads from room to room, the way it takes only one small errant thing in a house to invalidate and erase the whole structure—to bring it all down to ashes and send the building's former occupants— the homeowners, or renters, or leasers—out wandering lost and adrift into the night, poorly dressed and without direction. They talk until dawn. She is his second wife; he is her first husband. Because they are in the suburbs, unincorporated, his is a volunteer department. Kirby's crew has a station with new equipment—all they could ask for—but there are no salaries, and he likes it that way; it keeps things purer. He has a day job as a computer programmer for an engineering firm that designs steel girders and columns used in industrial construction: warehouses, mills, and factories. The job means nothing to him: he slips along through the long hours of it with neither excitement nor despair, his pulse never rising; and when it is over each day he says good-bye to his coworkers and leaves the office without even the faintest echo of his work lingering in his blood. He leaves it all the way behind, or lets it pass through him like some harmless silver laxative.

But after a fire—holding a can of cold beer, and sitting there next to the hearth, scrubbed clean, talking to Mary Ann—telling her what it had been like—what the cause had been, and who among his men had performed well, and who had not—his eyes water with pleasure at his knowing how lucky he is to be getting a second chance, with every fire.

He would never say anything bad about his first wife, Rhonda— and indeed, perhaps there is nothing bad to say—no fault or failing in which they were not both complicit. It almost doesn't matter; it's almost water under the bridge.

The two children asleep in their rooms; the swing set and jungle gym out in the backyard. The security of love and constancy—the *safety*. Mary Ann teaches the children's choir in church, and is as respected for her work with the children as Kirby is for his work with the fires.

It would seem like a fairy-tale story; a happy marriage, one which turned its deadly familiar course around early into the marriage, that day he signed up to be a volunteer for the fire department, six years ago. One of those rare marriages, as rare as a jewel or a forest, that was saved by a combination of inner strength as well as the grace and luck of fortuitous external circumstances—*the world afire*. Who, given the chance, would not choose to leap across that chasm be-

312

tween a marriage that is heading toward numbness and tiredness, and one that is instead strengthened, made more secure daily for its journey into the future?

And yet—even on the other side of the miracle, even on the other side of luck, a thing has been left behind. It's almost a perfect, happy story; it's just this side of it. The one thing behind them—the only thing—is his oldest daughter, his only child from his first marriage, Jenna. She's ten, almost eleven.

✿   ✿   ✿

There is always excitement and mystery on a fire call. It's as if these things are held in solution, just beneath the skin of the earth, and are then released by the flames as if the surface of the world, and the way things are, is some errant, artificial crust—almost like a scab—and that there are rivers of blood below, and rivers of fire, rivers of the way things used to be and might some day be again—true but mysterious, and full of power, rather than stale and crusty.

It does funny things to people—a fire, and that burning away of the thin crust. Kirby tells Mary Ann about two young men in their thirties—lovers, he thinks—who, bewildered and bereft as their house burned, went out into the front yard and began cooking hamburgers for the firefighters as the building burned down.

He tells her about the man with a house full of antiques in a house that could not be salvaged. The attack crew was fighting the fire hard, deep in the building's interior—the building "fully involved," as they say to one another when the wood becomes flame, air becomes flame, world becomes flame. It is the thing the younger firemen live for—not a smoke alarm, lost kitten, or piddly grass fire, but the real thing, a fully involved structure fire—and even the older firemen's hearts are lifted by the sight of one. Even those who have been thinking of retiring (at thirty-seven, Kirby is far and away the oldest man on the force) are made new again by the sight of it, and by the radiant heat, which curls and browns and sometimes even ignites the oak leaves of trees across the street from the fire. The paint of cars that are parked too close to the fire sometimes begins to blaze spontaneously, making it look as if the cars are traveling very fast. . . .

Bats, which have been out hunting, begin to return in swarms, dancing above the flames, and begin flying in dark agitated funnels back down into the chimney of the house that's on fire, if it is not a winter fire—if the chimney has been dormant—trying to rescue their

313

flightless young, which are roosting in the chimney, or sometimes the attic, or beneath the eaves. The bats all return to the house as it burns down, but no one ever sees any of them come back out. People stand around on the street—their faces orange in the firelight, and marvel, hypnotized at the sight of it, not understanding what is going on with the bats, or any of it; and drawn, too, like somnambulists, to the scent of those blood-rivers, those vapors of new birth that are beginning already to leak back into the world as that skin, that crust, is burned away.

The fires almost always happen at night.

This fire that Kirby is telling Mary Ann about—the one in which the house full of antiques was being lost—was one of the great fires of the year. The men work in teams, as partners—always within sight, or one arm's length contact of one another, so that one can help the other if trouble is encountered—if the foundation gives way, or a burning beam crashes across the back of one of the two partners, who are not always men; more and more women are volunteering, though none have yet joined Kirby's crew. He welcomes them, as from what he's seen from the multiple-alarm fires he's fought with other crews in which there are women firefighters, the women tend to try to outthink, rather than out-muscle the fire, which is almost always the best approach.

Kirby's partner now is a young man, Grady, just out of college. Kirby likes to use his intelligence when he fights a fire, rather than just hurling himself at it and risking getting sucked too quickly into its loom-again maw and becoming trapped—not just perishing, in that manner, but possibly causing harm or death to those members of his crew who might then try to save him—and for this reason Kirby likes to pair himself with the youngest, rawest, most adrenaline-rich trainees entrusted to his care—to act as an anchor of caution upon them; to counsel prudence and moderation, even as the world burns down around them.

The fire in the house of antiques—Kirby and Grady had just come out to rest, and to change oxygen tanks. The homeowner had at first been beside himself, shouting and trying to get back into his house, so that the fire marshal had had to restrain him—he had the homeowner bound to a tree with a canvas strap—but now the homeowner was watching the flames almost as if hypnotized. Kirby and Grady were so touched by his change in demeanor—by his coming to his

314

senses—the man wasn't struggling any longer, was instead only leaning out slightly away from the tree, like the masthead on a ship's prow, and sagging slightly—that they cut him loose so that he could watch the spectacle of it in freedom, unencumbered.

He made no more moves to rejoin his burning house, only stood there with watery eyes—whether tears of anguish, or irritation from the smoke, they could not tell—and taking pity, Kirby and Grady put on new oxygen tanks, gulped down some water, and though they were supposed to rest, they went back into the burning building and began carrying out those pieces of furniture that had not yet ignited, and sometimes even those which had—burning breakfronts, flaming rolltop desks—and dropped them into the man's backyard swimming pool for safekeeping, as the tall trees in the backyard crackled and flamed like giant candles, and floating embers drifted down, scorching whatever they touched; and the neighbors all around them climbed up onto their cedar-shingled roofs in their pajamas and with garden hoses began wetting down their own roofs, trying to keep the conflagration, the spectacle—the phenomenon—from spreading. . . .

The business of it has made Kirby neat and precise. He and Grady crouched and lowered the dining room set carefully into the deep end (even as some of the pieces of furniture were still flickering with flame), releasing them to sink slowly, carefully to the bottom, settling in roughly the same manner and arrangement in which they had been positioned, back in the burning house.

There is no longer any space or room for excess, unpredictability, or recklessness; these extravagances can no longer be borne, and Kirby wants Grady to see and understand this, and the sooner the better. The fire hoses must always be coiled in the same pattern, so that when unrolled, they can be counted upon; the male nozzle must always be nearest the truck, and the female, farthest. The backup generators must always have fresh oil and gas in them and be kept in working order; the spanner wrenches must always hang in the same place.

The days go by in long stretches, twenty-three-and-a-half hours at a time, but in that last half hour, in the moment of fire, when all the old rules melt down and the new world becomes flame, the importance of a moment, of a second, is magnified ten thousandfold—is magnified to almost an eternity, and there is no room for even a single mistake. Time inflates to a density greater than iron. You've got to

315

be able to go through the last half hour, that wall of flame, on instinct alone, or by force of habit, by rote, by feel.

An interesting phenomenon happens when time catches on fire like this. It happens to even the veteran firefighters. A form of tunnel vision develops—the heart pounding two hundred times a minute, and the pupils contracting so tightly that vision almost vanishes. The field of view becomes reduced to an area about the size of another man's helmet, or face: his partner, either in front of or behind him. If the men ever become separated by sight or sound, they are supposed to freeze instantly, and then begin swinging their pike-staff, or a free arm, in all directions; and if their partner does the same, and is within one or even two arms' lengths, their arms will bump one another, and they can continue—they can rejoin the fight, as the walls flame vertical, and the ceiling and floors melt and fall away. The fire-fighters carry motion sensors on their hips, which send out piercing electronic shrieks if the men stop moving for more than thirty seconds. If one of those goes off, it means that a firefighter is down—that he has fallen and injured himself, or has passed out from smoke inhalation—and all the firefighters stop what they are doing and turn and converge on the sound, if possible, centering back to it like the bats pouring back down into the chimney.

A person's breathing accelerates inside a burning house—the pulse leaps to over two hundred beats a minute—and the blood heats, as if in a purge. The mind fills with a strange music. Sense of feel, and the memory of how things *ought* to be, becomes everything; it seems that even through the ponderous, fire-resistant gloves, the firefighters could read Braille if they had to. As if the essence of all objects exudes a certain clarity, just before igniting.

Everything in its place; the threads, the grain of the canvas weave of the fire hoses, is canted such that it tapers back toward the male nipples; if lost in a house fire, you can crouch on the floor and with your bare hand—or perhaps even through the thickness of your glove, in that hypertactile state—follow the hose back to its source, back outside, to the beginning.

The ears—the lobes of the ear, specifically—are the most temperature-sensitive part of the body. Many times the heat is so intense that the firefighters' suits begin smoking and their helmets begin melting, while deep within, the firefighters are still insulated and protected, but they are taught that if the lobes of their ears begin to feel hot, they are to get out of the building immediately: that they themselves may be about to ignite.

It's intoxicating; it's addictive as hell.

✿　✿　✿

The fire does strange things to people. Kirby tells Mary Ann that it's usually the men who melt down first—who seem to lose their reason sooner than the women. That particular fire in which they sank all the man's prize antiques in the swimming pool in order to save them—that man becalmed himself, after he was released from the tree (the top of which was flaming, dropping ember-leaves into the yard, and even onto his shoulders, like fiery moths), and he walked around into the backyard and stood next to his pool, with his back turned toward the burning house, and began busying himself with his long-handled dip net, laboriously skimming—or endeavoring to skim—the ashes from the pool's surface.

Another time—a fire in broad daylight—a man walked out of his burning house and went straight out to his greenhouse, which he kept filled with flowering plants and where he held captive twenty or more hummingbirds of various species. He was afraid that the fire would spread to the greenhouse and burn up the birds, so he closed himself in there and began spraying the little birds down with the hose, as they flitted and whirled from him, and he kept spraying them, trying to keep their brightly-colored wings wet so they would not catch fire.

✿　✿　✿

Kirby tells Mary Ann all of these stories—a new one each time he returns—and they lie together on the couch until dawn. The youngest baby, the boy, has just given up nursing; Kirby and Mary Ann are just beginning to earn back moments of time together—little five- and ten-minute wedges of time—and Mary Ann naps with her head on his fresh-showered shoulder, though in close like that, at the skin level, she can still smell the charcoal, can taste it. Kirby has scars across his neck and back, pockmarks where embers have landed and burned through his suit, and she, like the children, likes to touch these; the small, slick feel of them is like smooth stones from a river. Kirby earns several each year, and he says that before it is over, he will look like a Dalmatian. She does not ask him what he

317

means by "when it is all over," and she holds back, reins back like a wild horse to keep from asking the question, "When will you stop?" Everyone has fire stories. Mary Ann's is that when she was a child at her grandmother's house, she went into the bathroom and took off her robe, laid it over the plug-in portable electric heater, and sat on the commode; but as she did so, the robe quickly leapt into flame. The peeling old wall-paper caught on fire, too—so much flame that she could not get past—and she remembers even now, twenty-five years later, how her father had had to come in and lift her up and carry her back out—and how that fire was quickly, easily extinguished.

But that was a long time ago and she has her own life, needs no one to carry her in or out of anywhere. All that has gone away, and vanished; her views of fire are not a child's, but an adult's. Mary Ann's fire story is tame, it seems, compared to the rest of the world's.

She counts the slick, small oval scars on his back: twenty-two of them, like a pox. She knows he is needed. He seems to thrive on it. She remembers both the terror and the euphoria, after her father whisked her out of the bathroom: as she looked back at it—at the dancing flames she had birthed. Is there greater power in lighting a fire, or in putting one out?

He sleeps contentedly, there on the couch. She will not ask him—not yet. She will hold it in for as long as she can, and watch—some part of her desirous of his stopping, but another part not.

She feels as she imagines the street-side spectators must, or even the victims of the fires themselves, the homeowners and renters: a little hypnotized, a little transfixed; and there is a confusion, as if she could not tell you, nor her children—could not be sure—whether she was watching him burn down to the ground, or was watching him being born and built up, standing among the flames, like iron being cast from the earth.

She sleeps, her fingers light across his back. She dreams the twenty-two scars are a constellation in the night. She dreams that the more fires he fights, the safer and stronger their lives become.

She wants him to stop. She wants him to go on.

They awaken on the couch at dawn to the baby's murmurings from the other room, and soft, sleep-breathings of their daughter's, the four-year-old. The sun, orange already, rising above the city. Kirby gets up and dresses for work. He could do it in his sleep. It means nothing to him. It is its own form of sleep, and these moments on the

318

couch, and in the shells of the flaming buildings, are their own form of wakefulness.

✿ ✿ ✿

Some nights he goes over to Jenna's house—to the house of his ex-wife. No one knows he does this: not Mary Ann, and not his ex-wife, Rhonda, and certainly not Jenna—not unless she knows it in her sleep and in her dreams, which he hopes she does.

He wants to breathe her air; he wants her to breathe his. It is a biological need. He climbs up on the roof and leans over the chimney, and listens—*silence*—and inhales, and exhales.

✿ ✿ ✿

The fires usually come about once a week. The time spent between them is peaceful at first, but then increasingly restless, until finally the dispatcher's radio sounds in the night, and Kirby is released. He leaps out of bed—he lives four blocks from the station—kisses Mary Ann, kisses his daughter and son sleeping in their beds, and then is out into the night, hurrying but not running across the lawn. He will be the first one there, or among the first—other than the young firemen who may already be hanging out at the station, watching movies and playing cards, just waiting.

Kirby gets in his car—the chief's car—and cruises the neighborhood slowly, savoring his approach. There's no need to rush and get to the station five or ten seconds sooner, when he'll have to wait another minute or two anyway for the other firemen to arrive.

It takes him only five seconds to slip on his bunker gear; ten seconds to start the truck and get it out of the driveway. There used to be such anxiety, getting to a fire: the tunnel vision beginning to constrict from the very moment he heard the dispatcher's voice. But now he knows how to save it, how to hold it at bay—that powerhousing of the heart, which now does not kick into life, does not come into being, until the moment Kirby comes around the corner and first sees the flames.

In her bed—in their bed—Mary Ann hears and feels the rumble of the big trucks leaving the station; hears and feels in her bones the belch of the air horns, and then the going-away sirens. She listens to the dispatcher's radio—hopefully it will remain silent after the first call—will not crackle again, calling more and more stations to the blaze. Hopefully it will be a small one, and containable.

She lies there, warm and in love with her life—with the blessing of her two children asleep there in her own house, in the other room, safe and asleep—and she tries to imagine the future: tries to picture being sixty years old, seventy, and then eighty. How long—and of that space or distance ahead, what lies within it?

❖   ❖   ❖

Kirby gets her—Jenna—on Wednesday nights, and on every other weekend. On the weekends, if the weather is good, he sometimes takes her camping, and lets the assistant chief cover for him. Kirby and Jenna cook over an open fire; they roast marshmallows. They sleep in sleeping bags in a meadow beneath stars. When he was a child Kirby used to camp in this meadow with his father and grand-father, and there would be lightning bugs at night, but those are gone now.

On Wednesday nights—Kirby has to have her back at Rhonda's by ten—they cook hamburgers, Jenna's favorite food, on the grill in the backyard. This one constancy—this one thing, small, even tiny, like a sacrament. The diminishment of their lives shames him—especially for her, she for whom the whole world should be widening and open-ing, rather than constricting already.

She plays with the other children, the little children, afterward, all of them keeping one eye on the clock. She is quiet, inordinately so—thrilled just to be in the presence of her father, beneath his huge shadow; she smiles shyly whenever she notices that he is watching her. And how can she not be wondering why it is, when it's time to leave, that the other two children get to stay?

He drives her home cheerfully, steadfastly; refusing to let her see or even sense his despair. He walks her up the sidewalk to Rhonda's like a guest. He does not go inside.

By Saturday—if it is the off-weekend in which he does not have her—he is up on the roof again, trying to catch the scent of her from the chimney; and sometimes he falls asleep up there, in a brief cat-nap, as if watching over her and standing guard.

A million times he plays it over in his mind. Could I have saved the marriage? Did I give it absolutely every last ounce of effort? Could I have saved it?

No. Maybe. *No*.

❖   ❖   ❖

It takes a long time to get used to the fires; it takes the young firemen, the beginners, a long time to understand what is required: that they must suit up and walk right on into a burning house.

They make mistakes. They panic, breathe too fast, and use up their oxygen. It takes a long time. It takes a long time before they calm down and meet the fires on their own terms, and the fire's.

In the beginning, they all want to be heroes. Even before they enter their first fire, they will have secretly placed their helmets in the ovens at home to soften them up a bit—to dull and char and melt them, slightly, so anxious are they for combat and its validations: its contract with their spirit. Kirby remembers the first house fire he entered—his initial reaction was, "You mean I'm going in *that*?"—but enter it he did, fighting it from the inside out with huge volumes of water—the water sometimes doing as much damage as the fire—his new shiny suit yellow and clean amongst the work-darkened suits of the veterans. . . .

Kirby tells Mary Ann that after that fire he drove out into the country and set a little grass fire, a little piss-ant one that was in no danger of spreading, then put on his bunker gear and spent all afternoon walking around in it, dirtying his suit to just the right color of anonymity.

You always make mistakes, in the beginning. You can only hope that they are small or insignificant enough to carry little if any price; that they harm no one. Kirby tells Mary Ann that on one of his earliest house fires, he was riding in one of the backseats of the fire engine, so that he was facing backwards. He was already packed up—bunker gear, air mask, and scuba tank—so that he couldn't hear or see well, and was nervous as hell; and when they got to the house that was on fire—a fully involved, "working" fire—the truck screeched to a stop across the street from it. The captain leapt out and yelled to Kirby that the house across the street was on fire.

Kirby could see the flames coming out of the first house, but he took the captain's orders to mean that it was the house across the street from the house on fire that he wanted Kirby to attack—that it too must be burning—and so while the main crew thrust itself into the first burning house, laying out attack lines and hoses and running up the hook-and-ladder, Kirby fastened his own hose to the other side of the truck and went storming across the yard and into the house across the street.

He assumed there was no one in it, but as he turned the knob on the front door and shoved his weight against it, the two women who lived inside opened it so that he fell inside, knocking one of them over and landing on her.

Kirby tells Mary Ann that it was the worst he ever got the tunnel vision; that it was like running along a tightrope—that it was almost like being blind. They are on the couch again, in the hours before dawn; she's laughing. Kirby couldn't see flames anywhere, he tells her—his vision reduced to a space about the size of a pinhead—so he assumed the fire was up in the attic. He was confused as to why his partner was not yet there to help him haul his hose up the stairs. Kirby says that the women were protesting, asking why he was bringing the hose in their house. He did not want to have to take the time to explain to them that the most efficient way to fight a fire is from the inside out. He told them to just be quiet and help him pull. This made them so angry that they pulled extra hard—so hard that Kirby, straining at the top of the stairs now, was bowled over again.

When he opened the attic door, he saw that there were no flames. There was a dusty window in the attic, and out it he could see the flames of the house across the street, really rocking now, going under. Kirby says that he stared at it a moment and then asked the ladies if there was a fire anywhere in their house. They replied angrily that there was not.

He had to roll the hose back up—he left sooty hose and footprints all over the carpet—and by this time the house across the street was so engulfed, and in so great a hurry was Kirby to reach it, that he began to hyperventilate, and blacked out, there in the living room of the non-burning house.

He got better, of course—learned his craft, his calling, better—learned it well, in time. No one was hurt. But there is still a clumsiness in his heart, in all of their hearts—the echo and memory of it—that is not that distant. They're all just fuckups, like anyone else, even in their uniforms: even in their fire-resistant gear. You can bet that any of them who come to rescue you or your home have problems that are at least as large as yours. You can count on that. There are no real rescuers.

*   *   *

Kirby tells her about what he thinks was his best moment of grace—his moment of utter, breathtaking, thanks-giving luck. It happened when he was still a lieutenant, leading his men into an apartment fire. Apartments were the worst, because of the confusion;

322

there was always a greater risk of losing an occupant in an apartment fire, simply because there were so many of them. The awe and mystery of making a rescue—the holiness of it, like a birth—is in no way balanced by the despair of finding an occupant who's already died, a smoke or burn victim—and if that victim is a child, the firefighter is never the same and almost always has to retire after that; his or her marriage goes bad, and life is never the same, never has deep joy and wonder to it again. . . . The men and women spend all their time and energy fighting the enemy, *fire*—fighting the way it consumes structures, consumes air, consumes darkness—but then when it takes a life, it is as if some threshold had been crossed—it is for the firemen who discover that victim a feeling like falling down an elevator shaft, and there is sometimes guilt, too, that the thing they were so passionate about, fighting fire—a thing that could be said to bring them relief, if not pleasure—should have this as one of its costs. . . .

They curse stupidity, curse mankind, when they find a victim, and are almost forever after brittle, rather than supple. . . .

This fire, the apartment fire, had no loss of occupants, no casualties. It was fully involved by the time Kirby got his men into the structure, Christmas Eve, and they were doing room-to-room searches. No one ever knows how many people live in an apartment complex: how many men, women, and children, coming and going. It can never be accounted for. They had to check every room.

Smoke detectors—thank God!—were squawling everywhere, though that only confused the men further—the sound slightly less piercing, but similar, to the motion sensors on their hip belts, so that they were constantly looking around in the smoke and heat to be sure that they were all still together, partner-with-partner.

Part of the crew fought the blazes, while the others made searches: horrible searches, for many of the rooms were burning so intensely that if they did still house an occupant, no rescue could be made, and indeed, the casualties would already have occurred. . . .

You can jab a hole in the fire hose at your feet, if you get trapped by the flames. You can activate your ceased-motion sensor. The water will spew up from the hose, spraying out of the knife hole like an umbrella of steam and moisture—a water shield, which will buy you ten or fifteen more seconds. You crouch low, sucking on your scuba gear, and wait, if you can't get out. They'll come get you if they can.

This fire—the one with no casualties, the one with grace—had all the men stumbling with tunnel vision. There was something different about this fire—they would talk about it afterwards—that they could sense as no one else could: that it was almost as if the fire wanted them, had laid a trap for them.

They were all stumbling and clumsy—but still they checked the rooms. Loose electrical wires dangled from the burning walls and from crumbling, flaming ceilings. The power had been shut off, but it was every firefighter's fear that some passerby, well-meaning, would see the breakers thrown and would flip them back on, unthinking.

The hanging, sagging wires trailed over the backs of the men like tentacles as they passed beneath them. The men blew out walls with their pickaxes, ventilated the ceilings with savage maulings from their lances. Trying to sense, to *feel*, amidst the confusion, where someone might be—a survivor—if anyone was left.

Kirby and his partner went into the downstairs apartment of a trophy big-game hunter. It was a large apartment—a suite—and on the walls were the stuffed heads of various animals from all over the world. Some of the heads were already ablaze—flaming rhinos, burning gazelles—and as Kirby and his partner entered, boxes of ammunition began to go off: shotgun shells and rifle bullets, whole caseloads of them. Shots were flying in all directions, and Kirby made the decision right then to pull his men from the fire.

In thirty seconds he had them out—still the fusillade continued—and thirty seconds after that, the whole second floor collapsed: an inch-and-a-half thick flooring of solid concrete dropped like a fallen cake down to the first floor, crushing the space where the men had been half a minute earlier; and the building folded in on itself after that and was swallowed by itself, by its fire.

There was a grand piano in the lobby and somehow it was not entirely obliterated when the ceiling fell, so that a few crooked, clanging tunes issued forth as the rubble shifted, settled and burned: and still the shots kept firing.

No casualties. They all went home to their families that night.

✿　✿　✿

Grace. One year Rhonda tells Kirby that she is going to Paris with her new fiancé for two weeks, and asks if Kirby can keep Jenna for that time. His eyes sting with happiness—with the unexpected grace and blessing of it. Two weeks of clean air, a gift from out of nowhere. A thing that was his and taken away, now brought back. This must be what it feels like to be rescued, he thinks.

324

Mary Ann thinks often of how hard it is for him—she thinks of it almost every time she sees him with Jenna, reading to her, or helping her with something—and they discuss it often, but even at that—even in Mary Ann's great lovingness—she underestimates it. She thinks she wants to know the full weight of it, but she has no true idea. It transcends words—spills over into his actions—and still she, Mary Ann, cannot know the bottom of it.

Kirby dreams ahead to when Jenna is eighteen; he dreams of reuniting. He continues to take catnaps on the roof by her chimney. The separation from her betrays and belies his training; it is greater than an arm's-length distance.

The counselors tell him never to let Jenna see this franticness—this gutted, hollow, gasping feeling. To treat it as casual.

As if wearing blinders—unsure of whether the counselors are right or not—he does as they suggest. He thinks that they are probably right. He knows the horrible dangers of panic.

And in the meantime, the new marriage strengthens, becomes more supple and resilient than ever. Arguments cease to be even arguments anymore, merely pulsings of blood, lung-breaths, differences of opinion, like the sun moving in its arc across the sky, or the stars wheeling into place—the earth spinning, rather, and allowing these things to be scribed into place. It becomes a marriage as strong as a galloping horse: reinforced by the innumerable fires and by the weave of his comings and goings, and by the passion of it. His frantic attempts to keep drawing clean air are good for the body of the marriage.

Kirby and Mary Ann are both sometimes amazed by how fast time is going by. She worries about the fifteen or twenty years she's heard get cut off the back end of all firefighters' lives: all those years of sucking in chemicals—burning rags, burning asbestos, burning formaldehyde—but still she does not ask him to stop.

The cinders continue to fall across his back like meteors: twenty-four scars, twenty-five, twenty-six. She knows she could lose him. But she knows he will be lost for sure, without the fires.

She prays in church for his safety. Sometimes she forgets to listen to the service and instead gets lost in her prayers. Her eyes blur upon the votive candles. It's as if she's being led out of a burning building herself: as if she's remaining calm and gentle, as someone—her rescuer, perhaps—has instructed her to do.

She forgets to listen to the service. She finds herself instead holding in her heart the secrets he has told her: the things she knows about fires that no one else around her knows.

The way light bulbs melt and lean or point toward a fire's origin—the gases in incandescent bulbs seeking, sensing that heat, so that you can often use them to tell where a fire started: the direction in which the light bulbs first began to lean.

A baby is getting baptized up at the altar, but Mary Ann is still in some other zone—she's still praying for Kirby's safety, his survival. The water being sprinkled on the baby's head reminds her of the men's water shields: of the umbrella-mist of spray that buys them extra time, time on earth.

As he travels through town to and from his day job, he begins to define the space around him by the fires that have visited it, and which he has engaged and battled. The individual buildings—some charred husks, others intact—begin to link together in his mind. *I rescued that one, there, and that one*, he thinks. *That one.* The city becomes a tapestry, a weave of that which he has saved and that which he has not—with the rest of the city becoming simply all that which is between points, waiting to burn.

He glides through his work at the office. If he were hollow inside, the work would take a thing from him—would suck something out of him—but he is not hollow, is only asleep, like some cast-iron statue from the century before. Whole days pass without his being able to account for them. Sometimes at night, lying there with Mary Ann—both of them listening for the dispatcher—he cannot recall whether he even went into the office that day or not.

He wonders what she is doing: what she is dreaming of. He rises and goes in to check on his other children—to simply look at them.

❊   ❊   ❊

When you rescue people from a burning building, the strength of their terror and panic is unimaginable: enough to bend iron bars. The smallest, weakest persons can strangle and overwhelm the most burly. They will always defeat you. There is a drill that the firemen go through, on their hook-and-ladder trucks—mock-rescuing someone from a window ledge, or the top of a burning building. Kirby picks the strongest fireman to go up on the ladder, and then demonstrates how easily he can make the fireman—vulnerable, up on that ladder—lose his balance. It's always staged, of course—the fireman is roped to the ladder for safety—but it makes a somber impression on

326

the young recruits watching from below: the big man being pushed backward by one foot, or one hand, and falling backwards and dangling: the rescuer suddenly in need of rescuing.

You can see it in their eyes, Kirby tells them—speaking of those who panic. You can see them getting all walleyed. The victims-to-be look almost normal, but then their eyes start to cross, just a little. It's as if they're generating such strength within—such *torque*—that it's causing their eyes to act weird. So much torque that it seems they'll snap in half—or snap you in half, if you get too close to them.

Kirby counsels distance to the younger firemen. Let the victims climb onto the ladder by themselves when they're like that. Don't let them touch you. They'll break you in half. You can see the torque in their eyes.

Mary Ann knows all this. She knows it will always be this way for him—but she does not draw back. Twenty-seven scars, twenty-eight. He does not snap; he becomes stronger. She'll never know what it's like, and for that, she's glad.

Many nights he runs a fever, for no apparent reason. Some nights, it is his radiant heat that awakens her. She wonders what it will be like when he is too old to go out on the fires. She wonders if she and he can survive that: the not-going.

✿ ✿ ✿

There are days when he does not work at his computer. He turns the screen on but then goes over to the window for hours at a time and turns his back on the computer. He's up on the twentieth floor. He watches the flat horizon for smoke. The wind gives a slight sway, a slight tremor to the building.

Sometimes—if he has not been to a fire recently enough—Kirby imagines that the soles of his feet are getting hot. He allows himself to consider this sensation—he does not tune it out.

He stands motionless—still watching the horizon, looking and hoping for smoke—and feels himself igniting, but makes no movement to still or stop the flames. He simply burns, and keeps breathing in, detached, as if it is some structure other than his own that is aflame and vanishing; as if he can keep the two separate—his good life, and the one he left behind.

Nominated by Joyce Carol Oates, Wally Lamb, Jessica Roeder

BIKE RIDE WITH OLDER BOYS

by LAURA KASISCHKE

from THE IOWA REVIEW

The one I didn't go on.

I was thirteen,
and they were older.
I'd met them at the public pool. I must

have given them my number. I'm sure

I'd given them my number,
knowing the girl I was . . .

It was summer. My afternoons
were made of time and vinyl.
My mother worked,
but I had a bike. They wanted

to go for a ride.
Just me and them. I said
okay fine, I'd
meet them at the Stop-n-Go
at four o'clock.
And then I didn't show.

I have been given a little gift—
something sweet

and inexpensive, something
I never worked or asked or said
thank you for, most
days not aware
of what I have been given, or what I missed—

because it's that, too, isn't it?
I never saw those boys again.
I'm not as dumb
as they think I am

but neither am I wise. Perhaps

it is the best
afternoon of my life. Two
cute and older boys
pedaling beside me—respectful, awed. When we

turn down my street, the other girls see me . . .

Everything as I imagined it would be.

Or, I am in a vacant field. When I
stand up again, there are bits of glass and gravel
ground into my knees.
I will never love myself again.
Who knew then
that someday I would be

thirty-seven, wiping
crumbs off the kitchen table with a sponge, remembering
them, thinking
of this—

those boys still waiting
outside the Stop-n-Go, smoking
cigarettes, growing older.

Nominated by James Harms, Pinckney Benedict, The Iowa Review

SELF AND ATTRIBUTES

by SUSAN WHEELER

from THE EVANSVILLE REVIEW

When the wind shifts, the dirt—uh, earth—kicks
up. It skirts the pages of the catalogues

that line the steel link, it scarifies the retina, it
scumbles up the new gas line in Mr. Rodriguez's

U.V.I see you levitate before you risk the
plunge. Swinging into the western blast, the screen

door sings although the brothers oiled it—gone
to flaxseed, gone to hay—afore the late moon dis-

appeared. The crux is alive at the fork of me, in
a particulate breeze that rakes. *Ai-ay-ai-ee*

the prairie hums, *ai-ay-ai-ee* — as if this filtering,
dandled, upswung thing could hear it sing,

as if the particles of the earth were populate,
as if each trailed a self in the whining wind,

——*what*? the self that is you interjects. *Let's
get the roadside back in view*. It's just Lester's

daft mutt Seagram's grave the winds kicked
up. He'd had him spayed cockeyed is how it's

told, and ever doting dug him there. We reassert
the selves but the Seagrams of the earth they

sift us with silt no mind our gear in a wind that takes
going off to heart, or what heart a silt self has

in the greater earth it constitutes. *Go get the truck*
you say and then the band picks up.

Nominated by Molly Bendall, Laurie Sheck

THE THIEF OF TAY NINH

fiction by KEVIN BOWEN

from MĀNOA

I LOOK AT THE PICTURE in the newspaper; a man stands on a bunker by a ridge, carrying the flag of the North Vietnamese. The caption says QUANG TRI, 1972. I look at the picture, can almost feel the wind blowing in from the mountains. I know this place well. The man has come to the place four years after we left. His presence here on the page sets me on a journey to another photograph, one found in a book in a small library: a photo of a room full of women standing before a raised altar—one woman bending, dressed in bright, flowing robes. She wears a turban on her head, money sticking out of the folds. She is lost in a spell, the caption says. The two women beside her fan her face. Lilies spike up from the altar behind the swirl of incense smoke. In the front row, a small boy looks quizzically into the camera.

Where do I begin? Like so many, I remain confused about those days. When I look back, I wonder how much of it was real, how much imagined; perhaps I should start with him, the thief, for so much of it, so many memories of that place, remain tied to him.

What struck us all from the start was the craziness of it—a thief in the middle of a war—and the way he appeared so suddenly, only after the move south. It was as if he had been some ghost, waiting for us. Life was to be much better for us there in the south. Much better than up north. Only mountains and rain up there. And cold, the cold that had surprised us all. Nothing to do up there, all day sitting around the bunkers, passing radio traffic, listening to the North Vietnamese trying to jam us. At night, guard duty or maybe sitting up on the berm to watch LZ Jane or Betty down the road get hit, listening to the far sound of the guns, seeing the red flares parachute down in the smoke, wondering if it would be our turn next. Maybe once or twice a week pulling road security, sweeping for mines—the rest of the time digging new bunkers, fighting off the rats. Even the rats we got used to.

But the thief, no. It was as if he had been there waiting for us even as the first planes flew in, waiting there among all the abandoned buildings and bunkers of the base, the scattered old buildings, the wood stripped from their sides, tin roofs caved in, sandbags bleeding back into the earth, the base camp like a great bleached skeleton spread out over a half square mile in the midst of acres of deep-green paddy—the rotting structures sitting like that, maybe since the days of the French.

The thief made his appearance soon after we'd arrived. We were still living above ground then. We were playing cards—Blackburn, Rodriguez, Willy, and myself—sitting in Willy's area in the hootch. Blackburn was winning, Rodriguez was telling the story of LZ Julie again. The rains were falling. Outside, the duck boards swam a few inches above the mud, weaving a maze through the compound. Once or twice we could hear a footstep pass along on them, a door slam shut in another hootch—someone getting back from radio watch. It was when Blackburn got up to go outside that it came to us, the distinctive panicked sound of men running. I can still hear Blackburn's rough voice calling to us through all the years that followed.

"Hey, you. Hey you, hey you, stop—" He yells, his voice choked, half in panic. "Hey, someone, stop him!"

Rodriguez, Willy, and I leap fast, but by the time we are outside the hootch, all we see is a hunched-over figure running off in the darkness. Rodriguez, half in shock, stands, shaking his head, waiting for us back in the hootch. His is the first of the six cots that line the walls of the ten-by-twenty-foot wooden building where we live— each sleeping area walled off by sandbags and short plywood walls scavenged from the base's abandoned buildings. Rodriguez stands, mumbling, talking half to himself, half to whomever is there to listen.

"Jesus, Jesus. I don't believe it. What sorry bastard would want to go and do something like this." He shakes his head again and again. "Man, no one's even got real money here. Look at this shit—he even took my wallet." We stand confused, trying to decipher exactly what has happened, watching Rodriguez's dismay turn to anger and then back to amazement again. We watch as he sits down on the floor, just plops himself down by the cot and drops his head, then turns back to us with that strange, disembodied smile.

It was only a few days later that the thief struck again. That was when they started, the stories. They were always the same: the thief struck only at the most dangerous times, times when people were all around, someone always managed to catch a glimpse of him, he always just missed getting caught. A ghost, some said. Or someone made plain crazy by the war. A death wish for sure.

Maybe it was the strangeness of it that made him seem superhuman, that set against the overwhelming boredom of our work. Every day the same. There are many kinds of work men may do in war. Some carry the weight of heavy packs and weapons through the jungle, every day a slog through sun and mud and rain. Some drop bombs from planes. Some are lifeguards at pools on the white beaches of the coast. Our lot was somewhere in between: all day working the radios, sometimes the small ones down at the landing pad, guiding the Chinooks in and out, sometimes the big VSC-2s, passing traffic back to Battalion and Brigade. Casualty reports, daily stock reports, situation reports. But every day ended the same: the spider flight lifting off from the pad beside us, the Chinook loaded down with the weight of the dead. We looked up as it circled over our heads, kicking up dust, swinging out over the last strands of razor wire. We turned back to our hootches then to drink or walk up the road to stand formation for guard. Life could have been better; life could have been worse. We had learned to be philosophical that way.

Still the seven of us then. Rodriguez, my brother from basic, Rodriguez with his love for the *cao dai*, the strange monks in their white robes, Rodriguez who loved to take the jeep and head straight off through the gate for the temple. It made him feel good to get beyond the wire, he said, to listen to the sounds of the chanting rising from the aisles, to see the lines of believers retreating on their knees from the altar. And Harry, who thought there was a girl. And Willy who agreed. And Kelley and Caspar. And Blackburn, farm boy from Oklahoma who never saw a city until he got drafted, a man whose wife back home was carrying his child, who could never get himself to look at Rodriguez's pictures, the ones he'd brought back after the attack on LZ Julie, the ones with all the bodies in them. The odd angles they took, as if in repose, torsos torn in half. He would look neither at the pictures or the letters: the letters with the pages that had what looked like poems and flowers drawn on them, the ones Ro-

334

driguez said he'd taken from a man he'd killed, along with what must have been pictures of the man's family back in Hanoi. Rodriguez said he was going to write to them someday.

Seven of us digging in for the dry season, the whole firebase digging in, everyone digging bunkers as deep as they could, scouring the base for timbers, sandbags, metal sheets of PSP. This the first year after Tet Mau Than, the great offensive of the Year of the Monkey that the whole world had watched at home on television sets. A year later, how many were watching? Soon they began: the small probes along the perimeter; the mortar rounds that fell more and more frequently—before long, coming even in daylight; each morning, reveille a cluster of delay fuse rockets slamming into the compound. Replacements arrived. The dead and the wounded were carried off. By the end of January, we were all living underground. And even in the middle of all this, the thief still continued to strike.

So much uncertain, even today, even after studying the history, the maps, even after going back, walking the road to the temple. But I am getting ahead of myself. I did not have the book then, the one with the photograph. Then, there was only the war—and the thief. I did not know then about the mysteries, the legends of the king and queen of the forest, of the princes and princesses who lived in a world just beyond ours—a world happier, sweeter, and more harmonious than ours. I did not know then of the princesses, young girls who carry the names of flowers, Cong-chua Que and Cong-chua Quynh, of their dresses made of deep-red roses, of how, when not in human form, they lived in the Palace of Heavenly Spirits in a region east of Con Lon Mountain or on the moon in a vast and cold forest.

It was a month later that Blackburn and I got our passes to Saigon—a reward for survival. Rodriguez, too, but he chose to stay behind. In the jeep he drove us across the compound to the landing strip, waved as the Caribou took off, lifted us high over the pitted brown landscape, and flew us to company headquarters at Bien Hoa. We slept our first night in the safety of the compound, then at dawn made our way out to the gate, where we climbed up on the back of a tank to catch a ride to the city. To the west, the fields took us by surprise: farmers still working the paddy so close to the heart of the war. Boys in the fields stretched their thin bodies across the brownish gray backs of water buffalo as the paddy turned that shade of blue only paddy water can when the sun is just right, the water reflects the sky, and the rice stalks burn bright green and yellow. No other place to find those colors. Two buffalo boys in the field waved to us; a crane stood up on the back of an old buffalo lumbering along the dike. We passed through the ARVN roadblocks, the MPS checking papers to catch Viet Cong and draft dodgers. I knew I had never before heard noises like the ones we heard along that road or smelled air like that: thick with ash and dung and dust, the heavy smell of petroleum and penoprene. It was as if we were driving into the belly of some dying god. Inside the city, at the intersections and in alleys, garbage burned in open piles. On motor bikes young men in sunglasses zipped in and out of the traffic, beautiful girls in *ao dai* sitting sidesaddle behind them. At every crossing, MPS stood like they were waiting for someone important to drive through.

It was true that it was sex and not love we were seeking back then. I think Blackburn and I had already even lost some of our hunger by the time we arrived at the small stucco house by the airfield the cabdriver took us to. Two girls waited in the courtyard to greet us when we walked in. Blackburn quickly fixed on the prettier one and in a moment disappeared with her to the room above the courtyard. I remained, looking at the girl before me. She seemed so young, not more than seventeen. Quy was her name. I was all of twenty. She asked if I was hungry, then pulled me to the room.

The room was spare, just a bed and a small bureau. It opened onto a dirt alley maybe five feet wide. Across the alley, a family—it must have been hers—sat watching television, the figures on the screen dressed in ancient costumes, looking like Chinese kings and queens. They were singing to each other. The people in the room seemed to ignore me as I fumbled with the weapons, an M-16 and Chicom 44. The girl tried to take them from me and place them in a corner of the room, but I was afraid to have them anywhere but beside me.

"Be calm," she told me. "Be calm." She was not beautiful. She did not have the movie-star looks so many of the women seemed to. Sometimes I think someone made them grow such women just for us. But she had another kind of beauty.

"*Em, co met khong?*" she asked. I looked blankly at her. "You are tired."

"Yes, I am tired," I told her, "very tired." I wished then I could tell her how tired I was, how much I wanted to peel off all the layers of the war from my body, all the clinging fatigue, the nights of not sleeping.

Her eyes rested on my shirt. I was surprised at how gentle she was, how true her actions seemed. Her hands still had the roughness of the fields creased in their lines. Later she brought a bowl of water and a damp towel to the bed. She washed me. Perhaps she was far away then, imagining I was somebody else. But still she made me feel human there in that room, made me feel even more deeply what it was I was doing to her, to her family across the alley, sitting quietly and watching TV, to her country, half on fire.

Again? she asked. I nodded no, wanting to reassure her she was not at fault. She then took me by the hand through the courtyard, up the stairs to where Blackburn and his girl sat, drinking on a small veranda. For a few moments we felt it, felt what was soon to become that savage nostalgia of the war. For a few moments we watched the flares go up around the city and on the other side of the river, the gunships, our guardian protectors, swirling in the distance.

When we returned, we went straight to the Filipino compound at the far edge of the base. Why, I am not exactly sure. The Filipino soldiers were all gathered around the grills, cooking steaks, drinking San Miguel. None of us knew what they were doing there in Viet Nam, in their tight, starched fatigues. Some of them might have even been left over from the Kennedy years, or their time with Lansdale. Some might have even gone out with him into the jungle and kidnapped villagers, drawing their blood in an effort to convince other villagers that we Americans were vampires. We were there because of the Red Cross library—Rodriguez hungry for books on the *cao dai*. It was in this small, strange library that I found the book, the one with large print and expensive binding, lush color prints and photographs, *Les Techniques et Chants des Mediums Vietnamiens*—a strange book that opened to a photograph of a room full of women standing before a raised altar, one of them in a turbaned headdress, moving as if in a spell. In the background, a young boy standing before a mirror, a strange expression on his face. With high-school French as my guide, I began to read the book.

That first night back, the thief was at work again. I woke, unsure at first of what I was hearing. "Get him. Get him!" someone was calling. The call seemed to come from a great distance. Rodriguez stirred slowly beside me, then suddenly bolted upright. I could hear what sounded like the heavy thud of footsteps, someone running.

"Get him, get him!" I heard the words again, and the slap of the footsteps, headed straight in my direction.

It all happened with great speed now, Rodriguez turning, pushing the poncho liner off and reaching for the rifle. The night was clear. I could see the compound three hundred degrees around. I knew where he would come from. He would be coming down the path between the red hats' hootch, he would reach the small clearing and then be running right at us. Rodriguez had turned his body to face him. But the thief must have known that the voices had alerted the compound ahead. At the corner of the red hats' hootch, he made a sharp right. Rodriguez registered the change and drew his weapon up, followed the silhouette along the line of hootches for twenty yards before it suddenly turned right again, then back into the cluster of the burned-out buildings of the artillery compound.

But Rodriguez didn't fire. Neither did I. Something held us back. I still don't know what. Maybe the thought that there were men sleeping and moving all about us. And why should we want to shoot him? Was that the proper punishment for a thief? What had he really done? And what had we really seen? A silhouette, a shadow? A ghost? Later that night, we woke once more—this time to the long, wailing cry of a feral cat. Rodriguez threw a rock. We watched the cat's outline slink down from an old bunker. We tried to fall back to sleep, hollow and shaken.

I was like a bird who seeks shelter beneath a broken bridge from rains. The words keep coming back to me. I don't know how she remembered me or knew how to find me. *Con gai.* Those were the first words that told me she existed. A daughter, the letter said. For days, I slowly let the words sink in. A daughter. My daughter. Our daughter. In the letter, she said she knew it the day I left, felt something change inside her the night I went back to Tay Ninh. She had given birth to the girl in Hue, where she had gone for refuge. A Buddhist, she went home to the city of her mother.

So many years later, this need to find me, to tell me. This need, perhaps the same need I had then. "I knew you would understand," she wrote. "Those difficult days." Her life of sewing names on silk jackets for soldiers. How many hundreds, thousands of jackets until the baby came. An aunt had taken her in. But the fighting grew worse. She knew I would understand. He was a businessman, Chinese. He wanted to marry her, move back to Saigon. But what would she do with the child? She knew I would understand. "I was like a bird who seeks shelter beneath a broken bridge from rains," she wrote. She left the girl with friends. But then came the great battles: Dung Ha falling, Quang Tri. She tried to get back to the girl in the last days, but when she got there, she found the family had packed up and left.

She asked me to come help. What could I say? My life had not taken a straight course. I had wandered from job to job, place to place—always something missing, a hollow place the war had left behind, or maybe filled. And those were the days when men were first going back to Viet Nam. Stories of these kinds of reunions ran in the papers.

I recognized her face right away—the same lonely eyes, the hair frayed and slightly graying—pressed against the glass in the transit area at the airport. Eighteen years gone by, and still I recognized her. Two days later, we watched the mountains rise up in the west as the plane tipped for its descent into Phu Bai. Only grass and rotting tarmac where the airfield had once been. We stood outside the control tower where I had once waited for a chopper to take me to my first home in that place—the firebase north, along route nine—where I had once watched truckloads of prisoners pass, seen the c123s, planes with great mouths swallowing and disgorging arriving and departing soldiers. But now all I could hear was the wind ripping down from the mountains across the empty fields.

Her face seemed not to have changed since that night so many years before. We took a small bus along the bumpy route up Highway One, and there we began our pilgrimage, walking day and night, from house to house, along both banks of the river, asking for her, asking for her aunt, asking for word of what had happened to them. But the stories were always the same. So many families went south, to America, Australia, Canada. Over the weeks, we slowly made our way through the foothills, stopping in the pagodas to light incense.

The book says that in this life we play a brief comedy before a closed curtain, always with the sense that there is something behind the curtain. Some of us go back and forth freely; others always remain on this side, walk past that curtain without ever trying to look through. The book says this is the difference between East and West. On that journey north, I came to believe more and more that I could see through the curtain. At the temples, I saw the young nuns at the pagodas, listened to the stories of the women who, after the war, made their way to distant monasteries. The young nuns, dressed in brown, aged seventeen and eighteen, walked with such ease and

339

grace through the courtyards, their heads shaved, their eyes clear, their faces unlowered in the sun. They would be her age, my daughter's age. Perhaps she had become one of them.

For weeks, we walked or travelled by bus along the mountain roads. Once, we crossed the border over into Laos. By chance we came upon an old village and a familiar-looking temple. Its rooms were empty. Only an old white horse sat, rotting under a back window beside a half-broken, dull glazed mirror. I recognized it then: it was the temple in the photograph in the book, I stood there, staring hard through the mirror, and for a second, I swear, I saw him: the young boy. He seemed to be looking out at me. Maybe she was there with him, she and all the others. I don't know. I only know that in that moment in the temple, I realized how much I had come to hate the war and all the men who had made it.

So we went on, village to village. But after a time, I started to doubt Quy's story, to note the small tic that sometimes ran across her face. Perhaps there was no child at all and she had sought me out as another soul with whom to perform this strange penance. But then I realized it was the war that had done this to her. At the airport, I kissed her one last time.

So much reduced to memory. Those days together searching, hoping. Sometimes when I think of them, they seem so real, the only real things in the world. Then at other times, like the war itself, they seem to be a dream that I am not sure I ever had. And the thief—he too dissolves into that same dream, even though his end is known. A month after our return from Saigon, Blackburn was just getting back from leave—from seeing his wife and new daughter—waiting at Bien Hoa for the chopper to take him back out to us. I can still hear his voice drawling through the static that travelled to where I stood at the base of the mountain. As if from another world, I told him slowly over the radio about that night: how the mortars and rockets had come; how the sappers had risen up from the tunnels; how Rodriguez had been right beside me, the first to see the figure coming up from the tunnel, he drawing a bead on the figure as I turned to look; and then the flash, the rocket hitting the bunker, throwing me in one direction; Rodriguez in another. Blinded at first, then crawling over to search for him in the darkness, only to feel his mangled body passing through my fingers, his arm and legs shredded. I tried to stop the bleeding, but in the end just cradled his head to my chest like a baby until the others came to take him to die in triage.

But Rodriguez was not the only one to die that night. Toward dawn the medics pulled another body out from a bunker near the green line. By midmorning the news had travelled through the compound. Soon lines of men circled the spot. He was no more than eighteen, a homesick mail clerk from Battalion. I stood there with the others, waiting my turn to see where the rocket had opened a small tunnel leading to a deeper, older bunker, perhaps one left by the French. There they had found his hiding place, the footlocker crammed with wallets, the small box stuffed with money. When my turn came, I crawled down like the others. I stood and stared at those four walls covered with the pictures he must have taken from the wallets: pictures of lovers, fathers and mothers, sons and daughters back home. I tried not to look too closely for I knew if I did, somewhere I would see Rodriguez's pictures. And the pictures of the man he killed and his family. I never learned what they did in the end with all those pictures or the money. Maybe they returned them to the men and their families, or maybe they sent them on with the thief's effects. Something in me believes, though, that they just placed them in a barrel, dragged them out to the green line, and then burned them there at sunset—their smoke rising up like incense to the mountain, to that blue, unforgettable light.

Nominated by H. E. Francis, Mānoa

LIMEN

by NATASHA TRETHEWEY

from DOMESTIC WORK (Graywolf Press)

All day I've listened to the industry
of a single woodpecker, worrying the catalpa tree
just outside my window. Hard at his task,

his body is a hinge, a door knocker
to the cluttered house of memory in which
I can almost see my mother's face.

She is there, again, beyond the tree,
its slender pods and heart-shaped leaves,
hanging wet sheets on the line—each one

a thin white screen between us. So insistent
is this woodpecker, I'm sure he must be
looking for something else—not simply

the beetles and grubs inside, but some other gift
the tree might hold. All day he's been at work,
tireless, making the green hearts flutter.

Nominated by Graywolf Press, Philip Levine, Rita Dove

LABOR

fiction by MADISON SMARTT BELL

from NEW ENGLAND REVIEW

Saint Domingue, 1797

THAT FIRST MORNING when she woke in the inn at Dondon, Isabelle was seized with nausea the moment she sat up. Her throat bubbled up, and she hunched over, spilling vomit onto a square of cloth she had just time to snatch underneath her chin. She spat, swallowed, and regained partial composure, though her eyes watered still and her gullet burned.

Nanon was asleep, or feigning to be, and without any servant at all, Isabelle hardly knew what to do next. She felt ashamed. But she rolled up the cloth into a damp, foul-smelling package, and, holding it away from herself in her left hand, she tiptoed outdoors, barefoot and wearing only her shift.

It was still very early and quite cool. The town was unusually quiet, since almost all the soldiers had poured out of it the day before. A few chickens scratched in the dust of the main square and at the well, several women were filling clay vessels and swinging them to graceful balance atop their heads. Isabelle was ashamed to approach them, though water was what she wanted. In the other direction she could hear the sound of a stream and so she turned and walked toward that.

A few black women sitting on their doorsteps looked at her curiously. The cloths that shut their doorways had been cinched in the middle, like a woman's waist, for light and ventilation indoors. After two blocks of low houses like these, a ravine bordered the edge of the town. Isabelle peered over the edge and decided she could manage to get down there, skipping from boulder to boulder and holding onto the hanging vines. The effort focused her, and by the time she reached the level spit of gravel by the water, the last traces of her nausea had receded. She knelt at the stream bed and let the current wash clean her soiled cloth. The stain came out easily enough when she rubbed it over the stones. She washed her face in the cold water, and took a cautious sip—only enough to moisten her throat. She wanted next to nothing in her stomach, still.

With the damp cloth wrapped around her wrist, she walked downstream, looking for an easier way to climb back to the town. As she followed the stream around a bend she came face to face with another woman, younger than herself and bare to the waist as she labored over her own washing. Startled, the other woman broke into a bright white smile. Isabelle curtsied, blushing at the absurdity of her gesture, which still somehow felt right. The black woman straightened, her hands on her hips, her full breasts trembling as she threw back her head to laugh.

Behind her, two small children played on a strip of fine sand. The infant boy was bare-naked, his polished skin a rich iridescent black. Whenever he crawled for the water's edge, the older child retrieved him. It was a sweet moment, and the sun was warming on her back, but when she heard a bell begin to ring in the town, Isabelle knew she had better return.

"*Koté m kab monté?*" she asked, and the other woman smiled again, and turned to point further down the stream, where Isabelle could see the foot of a much more feasible trail than the one she'd descended. She made her thanks and walked by. Halfway up the trail, she stopped and looked down through the hanging lianas, and waved the free end of the cloth turned round her wrist at the woman and her children, but they were all unaware of her now. Nevertheless her feeling of exhilaration sustained itself. At this instant she had nothing, was constrained by nothing but her body and the cloth that covered it, and there was no connection to her history here, except Nanon, who was herself such a mystery.

The feeling could not last forever, and already she began to feel oppressed as she walked back toward the tavern in the mounting heat. The others were eating a morning meal which she declined to

344

share (though Madame Fortier cautioned her she'd see no more till nightfall): bananas and warm runny eggs and pork dried on the *boucan*. Her stomach writhed at the odor. Monsieur Fortier seemed to be looking with disapproval at her bare dusty feet. She went to the room she'd shared with Nanon and put on more confining clothing, along with her shoes and a bonnet which hid her hair and most of her face.

Madame Fortier sat on the wagon box beside her husband, while Nanon and Isabelle used the bed, which was three-quarters full with provisions purchased or bartered for in the town. There were various clay vessels packed in straw, and barrels of dried fish and dried peas and salt meat, and several rolls of calico against which they could recline, so they were not so terribly uncomfortable, though nothing could completely blunt the jouncing of the wagon over the worst parts of the road.

By midday, Isabelle's stomach had begun to turn, for all the pains she'd taken to leave it empty. The hollowness cramped upon itself, and the heat made everything worse. She found herself hanging over the edge of the wagon, coughing and retching up clots of burning foam. A line of Fortier retainers who were following the wagon with baskets balanced on their heads carefully sidestepped around the wet spots in the dust. Nanon rose to her knees and laid a gentle hand on Isabelle's shoulder, but this had no real effect for better or worse.

Then the wagon lurched to a halt, so that Isabelle bruised her breastbone against the siderail. Presently she felt a hard grip on the back of her neck, thumb gouging, probing between the tendons at the base of her head. She was lifted, and the same grip dug harshly into the underside of her wrists. It was painful, but the nausea receded. Madame Fortier was holding her by the chin and peering at her face in the shade of the bonnet.

"How long has it been?"

"What do you mean?" Isabelle began weakly, but the evasion seemed pointless under Madame Fortier's firm hand and keen eye. She pulled back and covered her face with her forearm. "Between two months and three—I can't be certain."

She felt the tang of vinegar on her lips; Madame Fortier had shifted her arm aside and was cleaning her face. The sharp smell of the vinegar brightened her.

"Eat this," the older woman said, pressing a wedge of cassava in her hand. "Or only hold it in your mouth—it will do you good." She folded the fingers of Isabelle's other hand over the soaked rag. "And use the vinegar." She pointed to one of the stoppered clay jars.

"Yes," said Isabelle. "I'll do as you say. And thank you."

The firm hands squeezed her shoulders, then withdrew. Cautiously, Isabelle nibbled a corner of the cassava. Her stomach clenched, and she simply held the bread in her mouth, letting its faint sweetness dissolve. Monsieur Fortier muttered something to his mules, and the wagon wheels began to turn. Isabelle lay back, propped against one of the long bolts of cloth. They had stopped just short of a peak in the zig-zag trail, and now as they passed into the descent, the wagon began to roll faster, with M. Fortier grunting from time to time as he pulled back on the long bar of the brake. The barefoot women behind the wagon swung into a rhythmic trot to match the quicker pace, singing as they jogged along, words which Isabelle could not completely understand. If the nausea rose, a sniff of the vinegar rag seemed to quell it, and it was true that the cassava bread had put a more stable foundation beneath her stomach; without realizing it, she seemed to have eaten it all.

She became aware that Nanon was watching her with her usual air of self-enclosed composure, a moment before the other woman spoke.

"Is it always so with you," she said, "when you are expecting a new child?"

"Not always," said Isabelle. "With the first, but not the second."

"Ah," said Nanon. "Robert." Her molasses tongue softened the name so wonderfully: *Wobè* . . . "I remember him well from the time when I first came to your house. And the second, Héloise, was only a baby then."

"Let us not speak of it." Isabelle's eyes were pricking; she turned her face away and looked out blurrily over the precipitous fall of jungled escarpments, down into the basin of Grande Rivière. She could still hear the strange singing of the women who trotted behind the wagon. Some language of Africa; it was not ordinary Creole. She felt a terrible loneliness that seemed to come from her own hollow core. The moment she'd shared with the black woman and her children by the river returned to her. It seemed to her now that never in her whole life had she been so free as that woman was, unless in her earliest childhood. Perhaps even then her sense of liberty had been illusion. All the twists and turns of her life so far had been a struggle

346

against constraints she could not see or feel. All her maneuvers had been forced, and futile, insufficient in the end to keep her children with her. This thought especially oppressed her, weighing down with the chant of the alien voices and the bitter brightness of the sun.

Then a shadow blocked the light, and she felt Nanon's warm weight settle against her side. The soft, rather heavy arm about her shoulders drew her in.

"When Paul was lost from me," Nanon murmured, "I was sad two times each day. In the morning when I woke, and at night, before sleeping."

"How terrible it is, sometimes." Isabelle heard her own whisper as if from a long echoing distance, returned to her from the vertiginous valley below.

"At night was worse," Nanon said. "But the morning was bad too."

Isabelle stirred against her, drowsily. She felt herself beginning to drift. Long ago, a lifetime it seemed, she had had an intense romantic friendship with a colored girl of her father's household in Haut de Trou. They had been permitted great intimacy, and had adventured considerably into one another's bodies, before either of them had ever known a man. Isabelle did not know what had become of her, afterward.

This was not that. But it was pleasant. A kind of mother comfort— how long since she'd known that? She let herself be cuddled, like a little cat, feeling Nanon's fingers loosening her bonnet strings and walking the taut tendons of her neck. She let her head slip down to Nanon's shoulder. Before she knew it, she was sleeping, so soundly that she did not wake until that evening as the wagon began to climb the rim of Haut de Trou.

Madame Fortier claimed the front bedchamber, which Nanon had formerly occupied with Choufleur, for herself and her husband to share. Nanon had no objection, while Isabelle was in no position to object. Nanon sensed this, though she had no certain knowledge. The charade of Isabelle supervising *her* pregnancy had seemed rather thin from the beginning, and since Isabelle's own condition had been discovered, Nanon supposed there must be something irregular about it, though she did not give her notion any further thought.

On the evening of their arrival, Madame Fortier inspected the front bedchamber with her lips pursed and her nostrils flaring. She ordered all the bedding to be aired, and the mattress to be thoroughly beaten. With an air of distaste she fingered the collar of scars which Nanon's chain had left on the heavy mahogany bedpost, during that time when she'd been left to circle the room like a dog tied to a tree and abandoned.

Next morning, Nanon found Salomon working round and round the bedpost with a file made of sharkskin wrapped round a lathe. His eyes flashed white when he noticed her, and then he bent more closely over his work, giving her his shoulder. By the end of that day he'd ground down both posts at the bed's foot to the same degree, so that they remained symmetrical, and oiled them so carefully that scarcely any trace of the alteration could be seen.

But Nanon had spied Madame Fortier, sitting on the gallery with a couple of mildewed ledgers under her hand; as she had no refreshment by her, Nanon went at once to the kitchen herself. The women were preparing coffee, but Nanon took the task out of their hands. She prepared a tray with two cups, a pot, a bowl of brown sugar, some wedges of cassava bread, and a sprig of bougainvillea in a vase.

Madame Fortier looked up abstractedly as Nanon placed the cup before her and poured. "My son, your particular friend, was not a great hand with his accounting," she said. "All this is the work of his father." She turned the pages fretfully. The paper was wormholed through and through, but still mostly legible; scrambling over the lace-like sheets Nanon recognized the pale insectine script of the Sieur Maltrot.

"Jean-Michel never opened this book, I don't imagine," Madame Fortier said. "It's been years since any note was made at all." Peevishly she slammed the ledger shut and looked up. "Well?"

"*C'est pour Monsieur,*" Nanon said, glancing at the second cup.

"Oh," said Madame Fortier. "He has gone to the terraces, long ago. The second coffee is yours, my dear. Sit down and drink it."

Nanon obeyed. After she had taken her first sip, Madame Fortier covered her hand with her own. "You are not to play the servant, child," she said. "You are at home, as much as anyone here."

Nanon felt a warmth spread across her face. She lowered her head and looked at the dark swirl of her coffee. Madame Fortier applied a light pressure to the back of her hand. Then they both turned toward the interior of the house, their hands slipping apart, as they heard the distantly disagreeable sound of Isabelle retching.

In the next weeks, Monsieur Fortier labored mightily in the coffee terraces, which had fallen into desuetude once again, since Choufleur had vanished from the region. For her part Madame Fortier took inventory of the *main d'oeuvre*, comparing the slave lists of the Sieur Maltrot (which were detailed and thorough) with the present population of free blacks on the plantation. The discrepancy was less, she told Nanon and Isabelle, than she might have expected. Toussaint's orders were generally respected in this region, and most of the former field hands remained on the property, though many of them, perhaps more than half, seemed much more inclined to work their own gardens for their own benefit, rather than trouble themselves with the coffee. Also there had been more births, and more surviving children.

There was at first some difficulty in returning a sufficient work force to the coffee groves, but after certain messages had been sent down the mountain, a troop of Moyse's regiment appeared from Ouanaminthe, and stayed for long enough to remind the field hands that work was the price of freedom. By the time Isabelle had passed through her phase of morning sickness, the coffee trees had been carefully freed of parasitic vines and weeded round their trunks and returned to a state of productivity.

Nanon's own pregnancy went more smoothly; she had no nausea to contend with, and though she was further along than Isabelle, she carried the child more easily. Of course, she was the larger woman, if not so clearly the stronger. Isabelle was more resilient, far less fragile than she looked; Nanon knew her toughness well. But this pregnancy looked as if it would try her strength severely. Even Madame Fortier whispered, privately to Nanon, that it had been inadvisable for the *blanche* to have come horseback as far as Dondon.

For a month, six weeks, it did go badly with Isabelle. She could scarcely eat, so she lost her strength and grew spectrally thin, with the bones standing out on her face, as if the flesh were no more than a veil for her skull. She began to avoid the mirrors of the house for that reason—it was no aspect for a pregnant woman, though maybe not so inappropriate for her case. Maybe the child would starve in the womb, come rattling out like a dry, shriveled pea. But she could not quite bring herself to wish for that. Even the bitter remark she'd made from the saddle to Captain Maillart had only been half-intended. She could feel the child's life fully wrapped around her own, and she still clung to life herself, in spite of everything.

Then the period of illness passed, and she could eat again, and she did eat—like a tiger, to the frank amazement of Nanon and Madame

Fortier. Even Monsieur Fortier, usually so inexpressive, would study her with interest at the table, stroking his beard with his long graceful hand and humming to himself, as Isabelle demolished entire platters of food.

Her color came back, and so did her strength. Useless, for she had no future. The outcome of her situation was something which her thought refused. Fortunately, this middle phase of pregnancy always made her stupid. She could feel, but could not think, and she embraced her feeling.

Nanon began to take her around the countryside. They might do whatever they liked all day, as the Fortiers required nothing of them at all, but indulged them like two spoiled children. For some few blissful weeks, Isabelle felt herself carried back to her own childhood, a time when no one could gainsay her—her mother had died soon after her birth and her father had no will to oppose her. She had been the princess of Habitation Reynaud, admired and obeyed by all her father's six hundred slaves. The slaves had mostly been fond of her, for though capricious, she had not been cruel. Now, as she went rambling with Nanon, she remembered with a strange emotion certain kindnesses they'd shown her, which she had not recalled for many years.

She and Nanon got the use of two little donkeys, and rode them all around the country in the style of two market women—side saddle but without stirrups, the forward knee hooked up over the animal's shoulder. Nanon showed her the tombs of the *caciques*, and the places where one could gather wild orchids, or better yet, wild mushrooms. She took Isabelle to a cavern full of Indian relics, now inhabited only by bats—which were reputed to smoke pipes of tobaccos, like ghosts of the old *caciques*. The two women giggled like girls over this tale, but afterwards were perhaps a little frightened by it.

Then one bright morning Nanon brought Isabelle to a new place. Isabelle had felt, from the moment they set out, that her friend had some particular plan. Nanon had packed an elaborate lunch in one of her donkey's panniers, and had put two blankets in the other. They rode an unfamiliar path, and presently Isabelle began to hear the sound of rushing water, then they came out into a green glade in the center of which was a deep foaming pool, fed by a twenty-foot waterfall.

"Oh," Isabelle said. "Oh . . ." She could say nothing more at all, the place was so very special, like a gift.

Nanon was tying up the donkeys, on long tethers so that they had space to graze. She spread one of the blankets over the grass, and set the basket of food and the other folded blanket on top of it. Then she took Isabelle by the hand.

"Come," she said, and Isabelle let herself be led. They climbed alongside the waterfall to about half its height, with the help of hand-and-footholds worn in the stone by long years of use. Ten feet up, they balanced on a ledge, and Nanon thrust her free arm to the elbow into the curtain of falling water.

"Come," she said, and she drew Isabelle forward into the current, before she could think of resisting. The cold drenched her, shocked her to the bone. Then she was through. She and Nanon stood in a little grotto behind the fall, hugging each other for warmth and laughing from excitement.

The sun, filtered through the falling water, covered them with a strange liquid light. Nanon pulled her dress over her head and balled it up and hurled it through the barrier. She turned to Isabelle and kissed her on the corner of the mouth.

"Don't be afraid," she said. Then she stepped through the veil, as if she were herself translated into water, and disappeared into the tumbling light.

Isabelle stood poised a moment, with her finger laid on her open mouth where she had been touched. The waterfall made a weird window, where everything appeared magnified, distorted, rearranged by the ropes of crystal fluid. She could not really see what lay beyond it.

She took off her own dress and jumped through the waterfall, holding the garment stretched out at arm's length like a flag. As she launched into the bright air she shouted out a mixture of joy and fear and surprise at the chill water washing over her again. The water of the pool was warmer than she had expected when she went under, though it was very deep. She came up spluttering. Nanon reached out her hand to pull her up over the bank into the glow of the sunshine.

For a moment they stood side by side, studying each other's bodies, each pearshaped from pregnancy. Nanon set her arm against Isabelle's; they were now almost the same honey shade, for in these last weeks Isabelle had abandoned all her usual precautions against the sun. Only her breasts and belly were still pallid, of course, and the parts of her limbs which were usually covered, and soon they

351

were both giggling at the effect of this. Then they turned and stood side by side, looking into the pool, where their dresses floated like two great crumpled water lilies.

"The water is not so cold as I thought," Isabelle said. "And it seems to get warmer the deeper you go."

"A warm spring feeds it from below," Nanon said. She wrinkled her nose, and Isabelle thought she caught a hint of sulphur in the air.

"But come," Nanon said, "you will burn." She brought Isabelle to the spread blanket and covered her with the folded one. They stretched out on their backs, side by side, with their fingers lightly laced and the sun red against their eyelids.

Later when they roused from their doze, they were both very hungry. Isabelle busied herself laying out the cold chicken, bread, and fruit, while Nanon hooked their dresses from the pool with a long stick and spread them on the grass to dry. Then she climbed again to the grotto behind the waterfall. When she came out this time, she was brandishing a bottle of white wine.

"*Miracle*," Isabelle said, when she had tasted it. "But this is very good, it is certainly French. How is it possible?"

Nanon gave her only a sly smile. For a time they went on eating and drinking in silence.

"But it must be witchcraft," Isabelle said finally, as she drained her glass.

"No," said Nanon, a little sadly, it seemed. "No witchcraft. Choufleur kept his wine here, so it would not sour in the heat. Now I am the only one that knows." She smiled distantly. "There are still a great many bottles hidden there. I think I shall not tell the Fortiers."

"All this place must be your secret, then."

"It was one of the first secrets I shared with him. Later, after he had changed, it was all spoiled for me." Nanon turned to Isabelle, her heavy red lips curving. "But now I can love it again, because of you."

"Why, you touch my heart," Isabelle said. As she spoke, she felt a shadow pass over her. She leaned back on her elbows. A hawk was circling the crown of the sky, but the hawk could not have cast such a shadow.

"No," said Nanon, as if to answer the unspoken question. "I would rather remember him as he was then."

"You speak of him as if he were dead."

"Yes," Nanon said slowly. "I suppose I do." She stood up and walked over to her dress, which had dried by then, and slowly stooped to lift it, like a burden she was reluctant to resume.

When Nanon's child was born, Isabelle assisted her as she had first promised. The birth was uncomplicated, and Madame Fortier, though older and more experienced in midwifery, stepped back at the last moment, so it was Isabelle who received the bloody infant into her own hands. A boy. She slapped his back to start him crying, as she'd seen others do, then cleaned and dried him all over and swaddled him carefully in soft white cloth. Nanon was insensible; Isabelle passed the baby to Madame Fortier for a moment while she dried her own hands. When she looked again, the older woman seemed to be in the grip of some interior struggle, her hands trembling, her face tightly drawn, so that Isabelle took the infant back at once, and so quickly that she almost snatched him.

During the next three days, the newborn began to take on the face he would wear through life. His features were very much those of his father, and it was plain enough to Isabelle that this father must be Choufleur, rather than Antoine Hébert, though no one spoke openly of the matter. Madame Fortier had none of the affection one might have expected for a grandson. She handled the baby seldom, and whenever she did pick him up, Isabelle had the disturbing impression that Madame Fortier could barely restrain herself from dashing his brains out on the floor.

At the end of three days, Nanon was on her feet again, and Madame Fortier announced her own departure. She and her husband must go, she said, to see to their holdings near Dondon. Here at Vallière, all was now in satisfactorily good order. Salomon had the field workers well in hand and—Madame Fortier implied—the two younger women would know well enough how to manage him.

At this announcement, Nanon merely lowered her head with her usual self-obscuring modesty, but Isabelle found a moment alone with Madame Fortier, just before they left.

"It is only a child," she said carefully, having chosen her words in advance. "Only a baby—and given to us to make the best we can of him."

"Is it so?" said Madame Fortier, drawing herself up to such a sharpness that Isabelle quailed, believing for an instant that the other woman had penetrated her own secret.

"A mother may fully give her love," Madame Fortier said, in a terrible voice. "But there is blood too, and nothing—nothing!—will wash blood away."

Then she softened ever so slightly. "But perhaps you are right," she said more quietly. "In any case, I admire your sentiment, though what this child will do for a father, I do not know. I do not say I am leaving forever, though it's best that I leave now, for a time."

She took up, and with her usual stately grace went down from the gallery into the garden. Beyond the open gateway, Fortier was already waiting on the wagon seat. But Madame Fortier paused at the foot of the stairs, and beckoned Isabelle to come down within earshot of her whisper.

"For your sake too, it may be better that I leave now, young woman."

Inwardly, Isabelle wilted again, though she thought she kept her expression calm.

"You may find that Nanon has small enough experience in certain practical matters," Madame Fortier said, with a dubious smile. "If you are in trouble, when your time comes, you must send for a woman called Man Jouba."

"But where?" said Isabelle, who'd grasped her meaning well enough.

"Only say her name. They will bring her, out of the mountains." Without saying anything more, Madame Fortier glided across the garden, her back faultlessly erect, like a soldier's, as she stepped up into the wagon.

The management of the plantation now fell into the hands of the two women, which meant that it fell into Isabelle's. Madame Fortier had judged Nanon correctly, at least to this extent. But Isabelle took up the ledgers where Madame Fortier had laid them down. In the older woman's hand she found a meticulous record of all events on the plantation: the weather, positions of the stars and phases of the moon, progress of work in the coffee groves and drying sheds, a thorough record of illness, death, and birth (not only among the people but for the animals too). Of the new child in the *grand'case* she had written this: "To the *quarteronée*, woman, Nanon, was born, 6 January 1800, a male child, *quarteroné*, to be called François."

There were no more excursions, no larks in the countryside. Not only because of the burden of management, but because Isabelle felt the weight of her pregnancy much more heavily now. In fact she was ill, and full of foreboding. That halcyon day by the waterfall seemed aeons from her now.

One morning at the breakfast table, she felt herself give way, but not till she saw Nanon's startled face did she look down and see her skirts all stained with blood.

"Now let me die," she said.

"Oh, what can you mean?" said Nanon, shocked. But she bypassed her own question and called a housemaid to help Isabelle to her bed.

The contractions, convulsions rather, came quickly, then subsided, then came again in viciously stabbing sets. So it went all through the morning, afternoon, into the night and the next day. The child was not descending properly. Isabelle felt that her own body would crush it to a lifeless pulp, and take her with it too. She held the name of the midwife to her like a secret weapon she would not draw. At last she passed from consciousness into fevered dream. It was night again when she awoke, enough to be aware of Nanon dabbing her temples and her lips with a cool cloth. In the light of a candle behind her head, Nanon whispered to her to hold on.

"No," said Isabelle. "It is better I should die, and the child too."

"You can't mean that," Nanon said to her.

"Oh yes," said Isabelle. "If you knew the father."

"No father could merit such a wish. No matter who."

"It is Joseph Flaville."

She felt Nanon draw back. For a moment she knew herself abandoned, utterly alone, and she wished she had not spoken. Then Nanon took one of her hands in both of hers, and pressed and rubbed it till Isabelle began to feel a thread of energy returning to her through this contact.

"Even so," Nanon said. "Even so, we shall find some way."

"There is no way," said Isabelle. "From the day it happened I was ruined."

"There is. You will live for your children already born, Robert and Héloïse."

Isabelle felt the wetness of her tears against the pillow. "If I live," she said, "I will ruin them too."

"Do not say that!" Nanon hissed. "Listen to me. I will not let you go this way. When I was alone, and with child, and helpless, when the whites were killing women of my kind all through the streets of Le Cap, you took me in and saved my life and you saved Paul."

"But . . ." Isabelle was thinking that she had not taken Nanon in

355

with her whole heart, but had done it at the doctor's insistence, and that at the time she had partly resented it. But there was no way for her to say such a thing, not now. So she did not, but let Nanon go on massaging her hand, until she began to feel that maybe Nanon was right about everything.

"Man Jouba," she muttered at last.

"What?" Nanon's breath was warm and sweet against her ear.

"Send for Man Jouba," Isabelle said. Then she slipped backward, toppling into the delirium of her pain, and for a long time she knew nothing more.

When she came to herself again, it was night and she was alone. All the house was very quiet. She did not know if it was the same night, but thought it must be at least the next. Nothing in her memory was clear. There had been dreadful pain, which had now abated. The memory of pain was never perfect.

Outdoors, the wind shivered the leaves and branches, and a cool current swirled through her room. Somewhere in the house nearby an infant voice began to wail, but was as quickly muffled by a breast.

She rose, but was stopped for a moment by a thrust of the pain she had forgotten. She bowed over, pressing both hands against the spot, gathering her flattened, slackened belly. It passed, and she straightened and reached for her robe. Fastening it around her, she crossed the hall to the opposite bedchamber. In the orb of light of a single candle, Nanon lay abed, suckling a tiny jet-black infant.

"You see," she said, as if she'd been expecting Isabelle's appearance at that moment. "He is already strong. Oh, he is like a little bull."

"*Li foncé anpil*," Isabelle remarked.

"*C'est ça*," Nanon agreed. "He is very dark." She looked up. "He has already needed his strength," she said. "The cord was wrapped two times around his neck. Without Man Jouba, you would both be dead."

"Yes," said Isabelle. "I shall certainly send her a present." She paused. "I must do it quickly, before my husband learns of this event, and I am murdered."

"This child will be mine," Nanon said calmly. "Brother to my François, but you shall name him."

"Gabriel," said Isabelle. "Let us call him Gabriel." She studied the black baby, who pummeled the breast with one hand as he sucked.

"But it is all impossible, this scheme," Isabelle said. "The servants know, and Madame Fortier . . ."

"Madame Fortier has taken good care to know nothing for certain," Nanon said. "What she may know, or suppose, she will not tell. I think no one at all understood your condition, before we had reached Dondon—but if need be we will say that your child was born dead." Nanon shook her glossy black hair back over her pillow. "That much is near enough to the truth, besides."

"But Man Jouba," Isabelle said. "The servants."

"Man Jouba has gone back to the mountains, where no one will find her if she does not want to be found. The servants will not speak of it, not to anyone who might harm you."

"Nanon," Isabelle said quietly. "What of yourself, and your own situation?"

If a shade crossed Nanon's face, it did not linger.

"Now that is a thought for another day," she said. "Tonight I am thinking only of you, and of these two children."

As if she had signaled him, François began to cry. When Nanon shifted to reach for him, the black infant lost his hold on the breast, slipped down and began to wail.

Isabelle lifted the crying baby and held him to her. He was not comforted by the movement, but howled louder than before. He felt much heavier than the other infant, denser, as if he were entirely carved from the cliff rock of the mountains. Tears were running down her face, and her own milk had started, bleeding out through her robe.

"No," Nanon said. "You must give him up. Give him to me."

Isabelle obeyed her. She settled Gabriel at Nanon's other breast, so that he and François could nurse together.

"*Marassa yo*," Nanon said with a crooked smile. "You see? They are my twins."

Isabelle saw. She knew she must not reach for what she saw. She must be grateful for her life and whatever it gave her, for the two children fastened to her friend's breasts, and the dark hand groping blindly toward the light one.

Nominated by Stuart Dybek, Gibbons Ruark

SPLINTER

by JEFF DOLVEN

from THE PARIS REVIEW

I am singing now of the splinter of wood
you got in your knee as a child and never
got out. Of the splinter that sank out of sight
in your flesh and was gone.

I am singing of something that cannot be lost,
that cannot be changed like your clothes or your voice
(your voice that sinks over time to a low
and incredulous moan

as you know); I am singing of something that cannot
be found, as the querying steel first confessed
in her gentle now outlasted ministering hand
who sought it in vain;

I am singing of something loose in your blood
where it roves without homecoming, never turns back,
traveling even when you are at rest:
that wears you away

like the diamond tip of a phonograph needle
tracking the seams of your bones, scoring
the delicate tissues, and singing *I
am the splinter of wood*

I am singing the truth that your skin tries to hide:
that within you are only the wound that you got
as a child on your knees on the splintering floor,
or sometime before.

Nominated by Lloyd Schwartz

BIT-O-HONEY

fiction by BERNARD COOPER

from THE THREEPENNY REVIEW

ALL DAY, while Ross's customers made small talk, snippers of hair raining down around them, he couldn't stop thinking about his father. Even that evening as he swept the floor, turned the sign in the window to Closed, and bundled up the barber drapes he took home to wash, Ross kept coming back to his dad.

He'd meant to drive straight home after work, but the car made a sharp, last-minute turn and wound through narrow foothill roads. Tonight was Halloween, and a fittingly eerie sliver of moon had risen over Hollywood. Ross turned up Ridgecrest Avenue, a street where the houses stood far from the curb and walkways led to large front doors. Amber porch lights glowed through the trees. Pumpkins leered from front steps. Children who'd waited impatiently all day were spilling onto the sidewalks in costume, clutching paper bags at their sides and scavenging for candy.

Ross parked his car in front of Mrs. Hartounian's, his old next-door neighbor. He considered getting out and walking past his father's house; maybe he'd discover some clue to what had happened between them—a silhouette in a window, a stranger's car parked in the driveway, some sign of illness or dereliction. But he hated to think that his father might see him alone in the dark, a son who had nothing better to do than lurk in the street like a spy.

In the past year, Ross had called and hung up on his father at least a dozen times. Despite how childish he considered the act, the need to phone his father was as urgent as hunger, and when it struck, his body obeyed. As soon as he heard the familiar voice, Ross would cover the mouthpiece with his hand to mask the sound of his quickening breath. The silence that followed was a contest of wills. "Whoever this is," Mr. Gold finally blurted, "you better stop pestering me!" Ross would wince, depress the lever, and listen to the hum of the dial tone.

Occasionally, he'd reach the answering machine. *Hello. This is the telephone machine. I am not at home at this present time.* He was saddened by his father's halting voice. More and more isolated since his retirement from the insurance firm, Mr. Gold had lost contact with other agents from the office, and had few friends as far as Ross knew. Still, the message's jolly, incongruous coda—*Have a nice day!*—filled Ross with fury. How dare he wish happiness to any stranger who happened to call, when he wouldn't even speak to his only son.

A boy and girl dressed in the pantaloons and eye-patches of marauding pirates walked up the flagstone path to his old house. He leaned toward the dashboard and tried to see what happened when they rang the bell, but Mrs. Hartounian's hibiscus bush obscured his view of the front door. The same kids walked away moments later, rowdy with satisfaction as they rooted through their bags. Ross watched as they vanished into the night, taking with them booty from his father.

There were times as a child when some petty deprivation—a toy or a favor he'd been denied—had made Ross red-faced, contorted with tears, and he felt a phantom of that wanting now, stark and inconsolable. He swallowed hard, gripped the wheel.

And then a plan lit him from inside.

Ross reached around and grabbed one of the barber drapes he'd tossed into the back seat. He spread the fabric across his lap, guessed at its center, and jabbed two ragged holes with his car key. After cloaking himself beneath the disguise, he examined it in the rearview mirror. If he didn't move his head too much, the eyeholes worked, and his view of the world was unobstructed.

As he stepped onto the sidewalk, the drape fanned behind him like ectoplasm. Breath warmed the cotton that covered his face. Because he wore running shoes, his footsteps were muffled against the pavement, air moving beneath his feet. He felt like himself, but ethereal, freed from the laws of propriety and physics, as if he were dreaming himself toward home.

A warm Santa Ana gusted through the city, shook the trees and electrified the air. Every now and then he had to grip the drape from inside and brace it against the gusts of wind. He took a moment to compose himself beside Mrs. Hartounian's hibiscus bush. Mitsy, the arthritic, white-faced cocker spaniel that Mrs. Hartounian never bothered to lock in her yard or keep on a leash, lay on the grass like a dusty throw rug. She opened her eyes when she sensed Ross's presence, then grunted once before she closed them.

A mother dressed as Vampira walked past, dragging a tiny hobo behind her. Thanks to wrinkled clothes and a face smudged with charcoal, the child gave an excellent impression of indigence and filth. Ross chirped a "Hi" to assure them he was harmless, that he had some reason for loitering. Vampira smiled and led the hobo up his father's walk, long black hair swaying behind her. Peering around the bush, Ross could see the colonial house he'd once lived in, as immense and stately as an ocean liner. The hedges were trimmed, the shutters freshly painted. Apparently, dispossessing a son hadn't put a dent in his father's life, or at least in his home. Ross realized then that he'd hoped to see some evidence of his father's regret, some blow to pride of ownership: the paint peeling, the shutters unhinged. Instead, framed within the wide bay window, the living room, which had never seemed particularly inviting to Ross when he was a child, glowed now with lamplight, an inaccessible sanctuary, every pillow within it plumped, the mahogany furniture sturdy and burnished.

Mr. Gold opened the door, wearing a polyester safari suit that those less familiar with his wardrobe might have mistaken for a costume. Only the rifle and pith helmet were missing. He took a moment to beam at the boy and pat his head, finally pouring chocolate bars from a crystal bowl. The hobo held up a gaping paper sack and gazed into his benefactor's face. Ross eyed the waterfall of chocolate and, once the boy and his mother had left, wafted toward his father's house.

At the lip of his father's walkway, he met a trio of unsupervised boys who were dressed as Bat-, Spider-, and Superman. After scrutinizing him from behind their masks, they accepted him into their midst; Ross was just another stranger begging for sweets. When the four of them reached the porch, Ross took it upon himself to ring the doorbell, something he'd never done in the past when he'd felt entitled to use his key. The doorbell chimed three mellow notes, prelude to countless welcomings he used to hear from inside the house. The pack of trick-or-treaters waited, shifted their weight on the flagstone porch.

Although it had been a year since he'd actually seen his father, Ross thought he saw him everywhere. Almost once a week, if the cast of light and the distance conspired, any balding, bespectacled old man might trip the alarm of recognition. Ross would catch his mistake before he called out and waved to the stranger, but the sound of *Dad?* would stick in his throat.

What baffled Ross most was how their fight had started. They'd been sitting in his father's sunny kitchen, discussing one of Mr. Gold's recent parking tickets; he parked his Regal wherever he pleased. His father's refusal to pay the fine wasn't surprising—he'd always been a stubborn man, slow to admit he'd been in the wrong—but as he talked to Ross about the ticket his age-spotted hands began to tremble and his brown eyes, magnified by horn-rimmed glasses, clouded with rage. It was as if every injustice, every tribulation of his seventy years had been written down on a pink slip of paper and slapped on his windshield for all the world to see. Ross sat back, thinking it best to let his father fume. "Bet you wouldn't pay it," his father snapped, "if you were me. You probably couldn't afford to on that income of yours."

"Just a minute," Ross insisted, so stunned by his father's remark that he wasn't aware his voice had risen. "I make a decent living cutting hair." Day after day, men marveled at a flawless part, or the symmetry of bristling sideburns. He refused to let his father's insult slide. But the second Ross protested, Mr. Gold had grabbed his son's shirt, his face clenched and alien with effort. "Don't you ever raise your voice at me," he'd yelled. "Don't forget that I'm your father. Now get the hell out and don't come back."

Taller and stronger than his father, Ross could have easily fought back or wrenched himself free, but he let himself be shoved toward the door. Once outside, he turned on the landing. He expected to see his father purged of anger, hands in his pockets, embarrassed by his flaring temper and ready to make amends. Instead his father was slamming the door. Ross reached out and stopped it from closing, but Mr. Gold heaved against it with his shoulder.

"This is crazy," said Ross, pushing back from the other side.

"I'm not as crazy as you think."

"Not you. This. Over parking tickets." The door began to creak with pressure, the brittle sound of wood giving way.

"I'm old," said his father, breathing hard. "I'm an old man and I can do whatever the hell I want. I don't have to answer to anyone. Not anymore I don't. And that includes you."

His father's voice, enraged and frail, caused the fight to drain from Ross's body. The whole house rattled when the door hit the jamb, the lock clicking, definitive.

Standing among a bunch of kids, Ross faced the door through which he'd been ejected; it was painted green with a small brass knocker, like the entrance to hundreds of other homes. And just as that door began to swing open, an updraft ballooned within the drape and threatened to send it flying away. Ross caught it and pulled it taut. He tugged on the cotton and angled his head, but one crooked eyehole wouldn't straighten out and a circle of Ross's cheek was exposed. He gazed at his father with the other eye. Gaunt and unsteady on his feet, Mr. Gold nevertheless managed to gawk at his visitors with great theatricality, arching his unruly white eyebrows, his mouth an "O" of surprise. As if on cue, the kids crooned a chorus of "Trick or treat!" Ross piped in a little too late. He'd intended to keep quiet, but that Halloween cry was a deep-seated reflex. He hoped his father hadn't recognized his voice, deeper and yet more eager than the others. When Mr. Gold turned to face him, Ross noticed, as though for the first time, the freckled scalp, the tired eyes, and patches of stubble the razor had missed—a glimpse of his future face in his father's.

"My, my," said Mr. Gold. "You're a big one."

Before Ross could think of a response, the superheros thrust out their bags, reminding Mr. Gold of his obligation. While his father went to retrieve the crystal bowl from a table in the foyer, Ross adjusted his eyeholes and sidled closer to the door. The grandfather clock ticked in a corner. The checkered floor of the foyer was spotless, and Ross figured his father still employed the maid who'd worked at the house since his mother's death. His father's solitude was muted by money; Ross gazed at the comforts from which he'd been banished. Had his comparative poverty embarrassed his father? Maybe so, but wasn't Ross a person who paid his bills, kept his appointments, washed his Chevy Nova once a month? *I'm a responsible adult*, he assured himself, tugging the costume taut.

The hobo must have absconded with all the chocolate, because the crystal bowl now brimmed with Bit-O-Honey, a candy Ross might never have recalled had he not seen it again this evening. His father dumped fistfuls of the stuff into bag after bag—those delectable rectangles pelting the paper!—until he came to Ross. The sight of his father reaching toward him caused Ross's arms to levitate. The drape slid down to the crook of his elbows and he found himself forming a cup with his palms. He hoped his hairy forearms and broad hands wouldn't give him away. "Where's your bag?" his father asked, the Bit-O-Honeys poised in midair.

Ross continued to stand there, a pillar of cotton rippling in the wind. The kids stared up at the two adults and waited for something to happen. "Hey, look!" Superman shouted when Mitsy hobbled through his legs and into Mr. Gold's house. She stopped to sneeze in the middle of the foyer, the tags on her collar tinkling like a wind-chime, then limped into the living room. Mr. Gold turned in pursuit, his hearing aid squealing from the sudden motion. The door blew shut, groaning on its hinges, but Ross reached out and stopped it from closing.

He spun around and faced the kids. "You can go now."

"Who died and made you king?" said Batman.

"Yeah," said Spiderman.

"This is my house," said Ross.

"Oh, sure," said Superman.

Ross pointed into the night. "Get off my property." How nostalgic to invoke that threat, just like he had as a boy.

"Asshole," one of them mumbled.

Ross lunged. Superheroes leapt off the porch and scattered across the front lawn, epithets trailing in their wake.

After the kids had disappeared, Ross scanned the street in both directions. Leaves rattled in the warm, insistent wind and a few trick-or-treaters laughed in the distance. He slipped through the door as smoothly as vapor. He could hardly believe what he was doing, but now that he haunted his father's house, he had to be stealthy and insubstantial; one clumsy move and he might get arrested, or scare his father half to death. He padded past the archway that led to the living room and saw his father bending over Mitsy. Feedback still shrieked from the hearing aid. Frightened by the noise, Mitsy cowered against the sofa. When Mr. Gold reached out to touch her, she raised her face and bayed, her howl milder and more forlorn than any Ross had ever heard. Mr. Gold finally quieted the hearing aid, but he continued to stroke the spaniel's ears and tried to calm her by talking nonsense. *Crazy pooch, sneaky little goof.* Ross could hear the faint, absurd endearments as he glided up the stairs of the house where he was born. He recalled precisely which steps creaked—how intimate he was with this house, would always be—and skipped them with ease.

Once he reached the second-story landing, he held onto the banister and stared into the room below, trying to stay as calm and inconspicuous as possible. Mr. Gold carried Mitsy into the foyer and set her down. "Shoo," he said, holding open the door. As soon as the dog hobbled off, Mr. Gold locked the front door and switched off the porch light, giving up on Halloween early. Hovering above his father, Ross remembered hearing how the dead, before they transcend to another plane, peer down from the heights of the life they once lived and view it with a new detachment. Mr. Gold gathered up packages of candy, sighing deeply now and then, his pate shining beneath the chandelier. Ross had wanted to believe his father was a monster, mean to everyone he met, but Mr. Gold had spent the night tending to children and a neighbor's ancient dog.

Only after his father carried the leftover candy into the kitchen did Ross become aware of a woman's voice emanating from the master bedroom down the hall. Although he couldn't make out what the woman was saying, she seemed to be making promises. *So this has been his secret,* thought Ross: a lover sprawled on the king-size bed, rehearsing invitations to kiss and caress her. Perhaps his father had been afraid all along that Ross would find out he kept a woman—by the sound of her, young and practiced in seduction. Maybe his girlfriend, clearing a path to Mr. Gold's money, had encouraged him to cut off contact with Ross. Or maybe she'd convinced his father to turn his back because Ross was gay, appalled that Mr. Gold had taken his sexuality in stride. These possibilities, only a few among the dozens he'd ruminated over for the past year—*maybe if I hadn't raised my voice, had visited him more often, had been another kind of son*—suddenly seemed plausible. He drifted toward the master bedroom, a migration of pure curiosity, certain he was close to an answer at last.

His eyes adjusted to the dark hallway. Leather-bound classics lined a shelf. The print of a mallard gleamed under glass. When he heard a sudden creaking from the stairwell—could it be his father climbing the stairs?—Ross dashed into his old room. It surprised him to find the door wide open; he would have guessed that his father kept it closed. He pressed against the bedroom wall, his muscles tense, his

366

breathing ragged. When the creaking subsided—the house must have been settling—so did his panic. Ross fluffed his costume and walked around the room. His desk and bureau, a high school pennant tacked to the wall—*Go Rovers!*—had remained unchanged for nearly fifteen years. The smell of wood polish and moth balls was stronger than he remembered. Cold, preserving moonlight fell through the windows and made his room seem like a diorama, each artifact in its place. Ross touched the lampshade, the bedspread, the chair, as separate from his boyhood as he was from his father.

The woman's distant, sultry voice roused him from his reverie. Once he was certain there was no one in the hall, he tiptoed out of his room, determined to finish his mission. He crept beside the door to the master bedroom and tried to figure out how he could peek inside without being seen. The drape might help him blend into the walls of the hallway. Or else his father's girlfriend, in the middle of her monologue, would glimpse a ghost in the doorway and scream. Either way, he needed to see this woman through his own two eyeholes, and the fact that he might made his mouth go dry. "I've got what you've been waiting for," she murmured. "Here it comes, ready or not." Then came the chords of "We've Only Just Begun." The instant Ross understood his mistake, an electric piano glissandoed. He stepped into the moonlit room and there was the radio on his father's nightstand. "Hey, out there," said the DJ. "This is Lila O'Day bringing you *Sounds In The Night.*"

Ross had grown hot beneath his costume. He yanked off the drape—the drag of fabric caused his short brown hair to crackle with static—and bunched it under his arm. Here was the room where his father came to brood. Without farewell or explanation, Mr. Gold would rise from the dinner table before he'd finished a meal, or from the couch before *Six O'Clock News* had ended. Once he began his ascent up the stairs, no entreaty could bring him back. Sometimes he disappeared when company was visiting, the guests too shy or polite to ask Mrs. Gold if anything was wrong. Ross and his mother knew to let him go, knew that he'd return an hour or two later; purged by silence and isolation. Since Ross could never fathom the reasons behind these flights into privacy, he'd wondered instead if his father paced the floor, or stared through the window, or slumped on the edge of the bed. Only as a small child was Ross granted the privilege of entering the master bedroom unannounced; when frightened by

367

the leafy people who appeared in the trees outside his bedroom window, he'd barged into his parents' room, finding rest in the valley between their bodies.

Even in the gloom, Ross saw the pink of several parking tickets piled atop the desk in the corner. Drawn closer, he sat in the desk chair, its claw feet gripping the floor. His father kept the tickets weighted down by the Lucite picture cube his mother had bought shortly before her death. Cancer had stripped Mrs. Gold of her flesh, but gave new life to her sentiment; she'd intended to fill each side of the cube with snapshots of friends and relatives, though she'd quickly grown too sick. His father hadn't bothered to replace the photographs of models that came in the cube: frisky kids, loving couples, and spry old folks. Bland and random examples of family.

Ross couldn't resist thumbing through the unpaid tickets. He squinted at the range of violations—from double parking to an expired meter. His father had accumulated over a dozen fines. How long before they clamped a Denver Boot onto his car? Ross carefully began replacing the tickets just as he'd found them, as if he'd never set foot inside the house. Tonight his erasure was within his own power, not his father's.

Hunched over the desk, his back to the door, Ross suddenly stopped what he was doing, alert to a shift in the atmosphere. He spun around and faced his father. Wearing a bathrobe and a pair of fleecy slippers, Mr. Gold was framed in the doorway. His knee-joints cracked as he walked toward his son. His legs, the hair grown sparse with age, were white as bone. Ross held his breath and drew back toward the desk, gripping the picture cube until its edges dug into his palm. Mr. Gold hadn't switched on the bedroom light; his face was in shadow and it was impossible to tell whether he was approaching with astonishment or rage or tenderness. Ross searched the farthest reaches of his imagination for a legitimate excuse to be sitting in his father's bedroom, uninvited, in the middle of the night. There was no excuse, only the obdurate need to see him. *I'm sorry*, he was about to say aloud, but he'd said it in a letter to no avail, and there seemed no point in saying it again. When his father walked through a stripe of moonlight, Ross saw that his face held neither wonderment nor animosity nor love. Except for the effort of moving forward, he bore no expression whatsoever. Mr. Gold stared through his son. He carried his bifocals and hearing aid in one hand, and a glass of effervescing liquid in the other. The closer he came, the louder the sound of hissing bubbles. It seemed an act of divine intervention when Mr. Gold turned before he reached the desk a few yards away from his gaping boy. He moved to his side of the bed and laid his belongings on the nightstand. Ross watched him pluck out his dentures and drop them into the glass. Teeth touched bottom with a subaquatic clink. They left behind a mouthful of emptiness, like something unsaid, when Mr. Gold yawned.

Having shed his senses, Mr. Gold was unable to see or hear the intruder huddled in the far corner of the room. He removed his bathrobe, nude underneath. Flesh sagged from his shoulders and hips. A shock of pale hair covered his groin. Mr. Gold laid the robe at the foot of the bed and pulled back the blanket. Oblivious to the news issuing from the radio—a report on the usual Halloween pranks and hooliganism—Ross's father climbed into bed and closed his eyes, a remote, dismantled man.

Once the immediate danger of being caught had passed, Ross realized he was trembling. Blood banged in his temples. It took him a while to feel his hands and feet, to wrench himself out of the chair. Hugging the bundled drape to his stomach, he moved through the bedroom in slow motion, the floorboards creaking with every step. All the while he kept an eye on his father to make sure he didn't stir. Mr. Gold began to snore, drifting deeper and deeper into enviable forgetfulness.

Ross had reached the bedroom door when his father asked a question. The words were airy and unintelligible, more like the wind than the voice of a man. His eyes fluttered but didn't open. His arms twitched briefly then stilled at his sides. The old man looked so slack in the bed, he spoke in such a plaintive tone, that Ross couldn't help but answer back. "Yes," he said, though he wasn't sure to what he'd assented. Mr. Gold suddenly heaved himself up and rolled onto his stomach.

Ross flew down the staircase and through the foyer, nearly slipping on the polished tile. The front door was a riddle of brass latches and stubborn deadbolts. When the door finally opened, brittle leaves blew over the threshold and scratched across the checkered floor. Ross didn't stop to close the door behind him. Not until he raced down the flagstone path and leapt into his Chevy, not until he'd stepped on the gas and lurched from the curb did he dare to look back. In the rearview mirror, his old house hurtled into the night at twenty, twenty-five miles per hour, the roof and windows and clap-board walls vanishing like an apparition.

The outlandishness of what he had done began to fade on the drive back to his apartment. Breaking and entering seemed almost ordi-nary compared to the trees festooned with toilet paper streamers, a fish pond frothing over with soap suds, or a headless man filling his tank at a Standard Station.

It wasn't until he arrived home that he found the Lucite cube. It lay in the folds of his crumpled costume. He must have run off with it gripped in his fist. The missing picture cube, the unlocked door, the leaves strewn across the foyer—he worried that his father might report the break-in to the police. But who could make sense of such a crime? It was a mystery Mr. Gold would have to live with.

The next day, Ross told a few friends that he'd finally seen his fa-ther in the flesh, though he downplayed the fantastic circumstances surrounding their reunion. When pressed for details, Ross told them he was "all talked out" about his father, weary of guesses and specu-lation.

The picture cube found a prominent place on his counter at the shop, next to a tin of talcum powder and a bottle of styling gel. Some-times a client asked who the people were. Ross would turn off his electric clippers and brush stray hairs from the nape of the man's neck. He'd pick up the cube—it weighed next to nothing—and turn it in his hand. A stranger gazed from every side.

Nominated by The Threepenny Review

THE STORY OF THE DOOR

fiction by DAVID HUDDLE

from THE IDAHO REVIEW

In THE BEGINNING, of course, it had been a window. Which was probably what gave the student the idea in the first place. During one of the instructor's dreary monologues, this student had glanced over at the little staircase—three steps—that led up to its threshold, and she'd thought to herself *What goes up*, etc. But in fact there wasn't a *down* on the other side of that door. There was merely an *out*, a step out onto the fire escape. You could go out there and gaze over at the mountain range in the distance. That was pleasant enough. She'd done it a few times. But something about the asymmetry of the arrangement irked her: Three steps up—there should be three steps down, or the architectural equivalent of three steps down. Psychospiritually the lack of that *down* began to piss her off: step step step? step step step. What the hell?

This student had done her best to fit into the class and into the school. She was forty-five years old and a little plain, but strong and fit as a new Corvette. And she had the clothes, the manners, the tone of voice, the vocabulary, and the generally polite opinions that allowed her to be considered one of them. She'd grown her hair out to an acceptable length, and in the dormitory, she took care not to let anyone see the tattooed predators' wings across her shoulders and talons down either side of her spine. She'd borne the pain of lying about who and what she was. When asked, she had cast her eyes down and said she was a reference librarian from Echo City, South Dakota. Nobody ever asked her for more information. She'd earned her place among these students. She'd earned the right to live normally among normal people.

She was in fact a retired Master Sergeant, a former Airborne Ranger and one of the first women officially to be sent into combat in a combat role, albeit on a somewhat experimental basis. And the Department of Defense wasn't eager to let the public know the details of what she'd done in Operation Desert Storm. Suffice it to say that she had demonstrated something disturbing: Some women were better suited to be warriors than men. Some women could make most men look like candy asses. Suffice it to say that Iraqi Intelligence—which term she could never voice without guffawing—had a name for her which translated more or less as "hell-demon" or "the remorseless one." Her last posting had been at the U.S. Army Swamp School outside of Bobwhite, Louisiana.

So here she was in a classroom full of exceptionally nice people who had devoted their lives to educating the youth of America, a classroom that exuded more decency than the Louisiana swamp generated methane gas, and she was still feeling little tremors of bloodlust and the old desire to step out onto the dance floor to have a little waltz with the King of Bones. step step step? step step step, by god, or else somebody better watch out. She really did have to do something, or else her whole plan for retirement was going to collapse, and they'd find her crawling through the woods up there on the mountain with a bayonet in her teeth and wearing a necklace of bear molars.

She used the Internet to locate the nearest rigging shop, which turned out to be in Starksboro, for god's sake, Vermont, and the guy who ran it turned out to be an old Navy Seal, who took one look into her eyes and was ready to do whatever she asked. He had the latest equipment, which he was delighted to demonstrate for her up on the Falcon Cliffs above Bristol. That was not a bad time she had with him up there in the medium-altitude thermals, and she thought about letting that be that, not going any further. Maybe just driving over here occasionally and having a little climb-and-plummet with the old Seal would do it for her. But even as she thought it, she knew it couldn't be so. When they got back to his shop, he helped her stash the twelve sets of rigging into the back of her Cherokee.

That night—or rather, deep in the early hours of the morning—she carried out the delicate mission of torching through the bars of the fire escape to make an exit opening. She even went to the trouble of blacking her face, putting socks over her boots to muffle her steps, and strapping the tanks and the torch on her back. It made her homesick for combat.

Something happened to the class when she explained it to them—a combination of parachuting and hang-gliding, easier than riding a bike and so technically advanced that there was no way you could make a mistake. "Trust me on this," she told them. "I've done all the research. It will work." As she spoke, she looked each of them in the eyes, one by one. At first they got quiet, and she didn't blame them for being scared. Not everybody liked cozying up into death's armpit the way she did, and she was ready for the two or three of them that she was certain would opt out. But as she put on the rigging, explaining it each step of the way, and then as she moved up to the door—step step step?—she could feel excitement hit the bunch of them like a match to gasoline-soaked sticks of kindling. She stood out there on the fire escape and spoke to the class very softly through the door, back into the classroom where they crowded into a pack around the steps. Then, turning and taking the position at the edge, feeling their eyes on her back, she stepped off into the air.

Immediately she caught an updraft that might have sailed her all the way up over Lincoln Ridge if she hadn't tilted the left foil enough to release air faster than it could fill. Even so, she had enough of a ride to take her out to the edge of the woods beyond the volleyball court. She thought she could even hear them applauding when she came down to land soft as a thrush's feather on the meadow. She felt just fine as she gathered up her rigging and started the jog back to the classroom building. And when they streamed out of the building to meet her in the parking lot, yammering like chimps at the banana store, she felt too exhilarated to speak. She knew she'd done the right thing. Even the instructor came out and shook her hand and told her that in thirty years of teaching he'd never seen anything as inspiring as the sight of her aloft and rising toward the clouds. "What a lady you are!" he said. She started to say, "Well, sir, what a pussy you are!" but she got a hold of herself just in time. Better that he go on thinking of her as a librarian.

So they strapped themselves up in the classroom while she walked among them, checking them out, patting their equipment up and down, tugging their buckles and straps to be sure they were tight, and then slapping their butts to signal they were okay. When they were all ready, she went over the basic stuff with them one last time—check your feet to see that your toes are over the edge, look at the horizon, take a deep breath, step forward at exactly the same moment you yank your chest handle, take hold of your foil cords, try a couple of turns, maybe try to catch a thermal, then ease back and enjoy the ride. She let the class members and the instructor line up in front of the door in whatever order they wanted. When the line was formed, they quieted right down.

The fact was, she thought that one of them might die—and if there had to be a casualty, then she hoped that it would be the instructor, whom she considered pretty useless. And of course she would be held responsible, which would damn sure gum up her plans for retirement. But she also knew that this event was mandatory. She was deep into it now. Her life—if she was going to have a life—depended on going forward, and maybe theirs did, too. Maybe they needed this little ride just as much as she needed to give it to them. At any rate, she wasn't about to feel bad. They were waiting.

step step step? She took her place beside the exit platform and sent them off at fifteen-second intervals, just enough of a pause to stop the line if one of them got it wrong and stepped out without yanking the chest handle. She knew what the splat would look like down there in the gravel, she even knew what it would sound like, because she'd had more than one experience like that in her past. But the whole class got it right, every single one of them.

Not only did they get it right, but the updraft over the building was so steady and gentle that they each got a lift that sent them up over the meadow, rising slow and even, their billowing sails above them white as angel wings. And while they were up there, they started calling to each other, laughing in the air, the instructor even crying with the silly joy of feeling himself suspended in mid-air. She had to admit he was right. She herself felt like weeping right then, but she was also in the throes of knowing something that shocked her. She wasn't going to need to step out into the air even this one last time. step step step. She started loosening the straps and buckles to release herself. She could stay right here beside the door to wait for her teacher and her classmates. If they wanted to go again, she'd help them. But she was through with all of it forever. She was finally going to be able to tell the Bone King to go fuck himself. But oh my Christ! Weren't they beautiful up there soaring in the mountain's clear light!?

Nominated by The Idaho Review

BY A SWIMMING POOL OUTSIDE SYRACUSA

by BILLY COLLINS

from THE GETTYSBURG REVIEW

All afternoon I have been struggling
to communicate in Italian
with Roberto and Giuseppe, who have begun
to resemble the two male characters
in my *Italian for Beginners*,
the ones who are always shopping
or inquiring about the times of trains,
and now I can hardly speak or write English.

I have made important pronouncements
in this remote limestone valley
with its trickle of a river,
stating that it seems hotter
today even than it was yesterday
and that swimming is very good for you,
very beneficial, you might say.
I also posed burning questions
about the hours of the archaeological museum
and the location of the local necropolis.

But now I am alone in the evening light
which has softened the white cliffs,
and I have had a little gin in a glass with ice

which has softened my mood or—
how would you say in English—
has allowed my thoughts to traverse my brain
with greater gentleness, shall we say,

or, to put it less literally,
this drink has extended permission
to my mind to feel—what's the word?—
a friendship with the vast sky
which is very—give me a minute—very blue
but with much great paleness
at this special time of day, or as we say in America, now.

Nominated by Robert Wrigley, Henry Carlile, David Kirby

DEATH AS A
FICTITIOUS EVENT

essay by BERT O. STATES

from THE HUDSON REVIEW

> Strictly speaking, the duration of the life of a living being is exceedingly brief,
> lasting only while a thought lasts.
>
> —Borges, "A New Refutation of Time"

> . . . one day we were born, one day we shall die, the same day, the same second,
> is that not enough for you?
>
> —Pozzo in Waiting for Godot

OUR TALENT for creating imaginary worlds comes to a sly perfection in our thinking, or not thinking, about death. The truth is, we will have none of it and so we have devised delicate stratagems for whistling our way past the graveyard, or at least around the topic. I am speaking, of course, of people in the bloom of life, people who have good health, lots to do and better things to think about. These are the whistlers, of whom I normally count myself one.

Quite simply, death is a fictitious event because, as Gertrude Stein might say, there is no *here* there. Better still, there is no there *here*, only a weak *when*, meaning *when*, in the vague future-bound sense, as when we say "When you are old enough," or "When the cows come home," the *when*, in other words, that we toss off as being so far down the road that there is no point thinking about it now. Prometheus' greatest gift to humankind is to have erased from each mortal's consciousness the knowledge of the hour of death. Imagine it otherwise. Imagine how day and night, love and work and play, and time and anything done or thought about therein, would be altered if you knew for certain that on, say, August 8, 2004 at 3:17 P.M., EST—exactly—you would cease to be among those who are *here*. But Prometheus took away this knowledge, planted in us by wicked gods, and he gave us fire, or progress, which has preoccupied us ever since. So instead of anticipating, we have learned to whistle, and death comes to have the status of a fiction, something that may well be true but isn't real, something toward which we can willingly suspend our belief, if not our disbelief. And as a result, there is a careless ambiguity in our thinking about death, as if certain exceptions might be made, or as if we might one day pick up the newspaper and learn, through a new study done at MIT, that death can be significantly postponed in 75% of the cases if Dyosilide-2B, a derivative of dandelion, soon available to all (following approval by the FDA), is added to the diet.

Chief among our strategies we wrap death in the social shroud of the "they," "the others," and "all of us," as if by generalizing we might third-person Death to death. Everywhere, except in the homes of those (as they say in the Middle East) at whose door the black camel has already knelt, this "other-ness" pervades our language. Even our proverbs bear it out: "Charon waits for us all"; "Nothing so certain as death"; "Death combs us all with the same comb"; "A piece of churchyard fits everybody"; and so on, by the carload. One could crochet such bland sayings on sofa cushions and wall hangings for all the shudder they arouse. Where we and they are congregated the "I" is mercifully lost in the crowd.

There is a certain contradiction in using the word death at all for almost any purpose beyond the daily idiomatic, idioms being semantically invisible, like the hinges on which doors open and close. In fact, most of our uses of the word death are euphemistic. If the word were truly considered in its fundamental meaning and inevitability—its preposterous *unfairness*—death would be the one word that is never uttered or written, as the word for God is not spoken (and certainly not written) in certain religions because it reduces God to the category of understandable and tangible things, like rivers, buildings, persons, and places. "If you understand," Augustine says somewhere, "it is not God." So too with death, for which there is no true category, except the weak verbal one which reduces it to a figure of speech.

For example, "I'll be in my grave by then," or "That child will be the death of me," or "Sarah's lasagna is to die for."

Perhaps the most perfect specimen of this attitude is the little joke told by Freud of one lover saying to the other, "If one of us should die I will move to Paris." Here the whole apparatus of repression of one's own personal death slips into casual conversation without the slightest ripple of awareness. The truth of the joke is that even the unity of love is haunted by a primal certitude of self-endurance; and though the lover might (in a moment of madness) die for the beloved—take the bullet meant for her (or him)—even this is no proof to the contrary of our universal repression of death as a forth-coming *personal* event.

In one sense, this all has to do with our having no tool of thought or voice to name what death is, or to come into its presence. Even if you can somehow face the fact of your death, or wanted to talk frankly about it, you remain tongue-tied, and all of the great death speeches of literature and history are concerned with the anticipa-tion ("I die, Horatio—"), the terror ("Aye, to die and go we know not where—"), or the release ("I am fire and air; my other elements I give to baser life"), rarely with the brutal contradiction involved in your own inevitable absence. For all descriptions of death are auto-matically false in taking a point of view on what it is, a point of view being, after all, something that proves you are alive and well. Even the sentence, "One day I too will die," reeks of life, being less a pre-diction than a self-assertion. It is not the worst, the line runs in *King Lear*, so long as we can say, "this is the worst." Precisely. There is something like a Zeno paradox at work in all death-thought and speech: death itself disappears in thought about it as nothingness dis-appears when one walks, like Achilles, to the extreme edge where the void begins and throws a spear into it, thus refuting it with sub-stance.

So we are hobbled, coming and going, by the very notion and thought of death. It escapes us like a tomato seed under the finger of definition. Finally we throw up our hands and get on with life, as should be. And that is the other side of the matter. Outwardly, most people face death bravely. Death is taken as an eventuality about which we can do nothing; therefore we accommodate ourselves to the fact and live as best we can, hoping ("when the time comes") for a quick release, a "good" death, or lacking that a creditable manner of meeting it, in whatever form it comes ("To the end, she never complained, though the pain must have been unbearable"). There is, in short, a decorum of dying—or at least to the point where the rattle sets in, and the bedside is all confusion and disbelief. In any case, it is part of the business of being alive that the death you have coming be faced with the same stalwart courage that you weather a financial crisis, a troublesome child, or a failed marriage—as if these things were somehow the equivalents of Death. Or, if not courage, gallows humor, as in the braggadocio of the old man saying in mock-cheeriness, "I'll be eighty-five next week," that ironical pride in negative achievement that we have perfected over the decades in dealings with government offices.

We assume "lower" animals are spared a good deal of this fine-tuned sensibility and die quite "naturally," though I doubt that our instruments for defining human sensibilities can accurately assess those of animals. Animals die *too*, and they know it. For instance, I recall a nature film about the death of an infant elephant. Somehow, the baby had been ill-born, was unable to stand on its own feet, and was becoming increasingly feeble. The other elephants in the group—five or six perhaps—made every attempt to keep it standing, trying to assist it by every possible elephant skill. There was a kind of panic in the group; it simply could not—what? accept the fact? But how do I know? But it was clear that there was a primary concern in every elephant's mind for the plight of this young defective issue from its mother's loins. Finally, the young elephant collapsed and ceased to move and the pain radiated visibly from the group. It was dreadful to watch, and tears ran down my face.

Of course baby elephants are cute, unlike baby scorpions and sow bugs. They are properly grotesque, having the right disproportions in naturally comic parts of the body (nose, ears, feet). They are like us. So perhaps the idea here is that I cried because the elephant was really a human child, and that I read my own idea about death and loss into the minds of the adult elephants. Still, what was this incomprehension on their faces? What was behind this strange attention? What was the bellowing about? For it was abundantly clear that the very sinews of elephant life were somehow at stake.

The truth is, in order to live life, to enjoy its favors, you must put death in your hip pocket and keep it here until it makes its move; then of course it infects everything and you move gradually through Kubler-Ross's four stages, ending in acceptance. Or so we are told. Example: you have six months to live and you elect to take a last vacation to an exotic place. Why not? Why waste the time sunk in despair? And you actually have fun.

But not the same kind of fun others are having there.

Perhaps we should make at least some distinction between those who accept death with God's blessing and promise and those who do it, or can't do it, on their own. Unfortunately, it is my belief that "believing" in God must inevitably spring from the same convincing sources that cause me to believe in pain, beauty, bigotry, and human imperfection. On the other hand, there are other sorts of gods who promise nothing, offer nothing, and exist by virtue of a philosophy anchored in selflessness and the continuity of nature which make death one event amongst many in a lifetime. This, it seems to me, is a much more acceptable idea of divinity than the one that dominates religion in the United States which somehow strikes me as a metaphysical form of capitalism based on the profit/loss principle.

In any case, it is the "secular" class of whistlers who interest me, those who have no spiritual antidote for mortality. My concern is primarily in sneaking into the graveyard and looking at some of the things you don't find on the epitaphs. Is it possible to discuss death as what it is, or seems to me to be: that is, the termination of an exquisite phenomenon called consciousness that has the unique capacity to experience both the world and itself, its own continuation in the world, its past and its possible future, not to mention a palette of emotions as delicate as the colors of a Monet lily pond? To me, there is no fact that proves more definitively that nature is helmless and pointless than the way death snatches consciousness back into the void without regard for its value and its appreciation (or overappreciation) of its own existence. The most stunning question of all is: what happens to it, to this *awareness*, when I am gone?

It is faintly embarrassing, if not vulgar, to talk about such private matters. But it is the only way to illustrate how the psychology of avoidance innocently betrays itself at the cell level of everyday thought and language. As it turns out, the thing that causes all this is not death itself—which is, literally, *nothing*—but the fiction we spin about Time. Consider, for example, the lifelong implications of our language having three basic tenses, past, present and future. One goes through life using them much as one performs the little economies of survival, putting on shoes, setting the table, making phone calls. Thus our temporal world is as three-dimensional as the spatial world, and we come to count on the future as effortlessly as we drive to the pharmacy to buy remedies for this and that. Not only that, time soon becomes confused with space and we find ourselves not only thinking of the past in terms of particular places but imagining that to return there might be to re-live—and perhaps even re-do or un-do—what happened there (as if the Time were still there!). One knows it would be futile to go back, but the awful part is that the only external signs of one's life are the now alien places in which it has been lived. Thus time, in absentia, finds its surrogate in space.

This brings us to the passages from Borges and Beckett, both very poor whistlers. What exactly do these strange sentiments mean? Are they only metaphors? If not, how is it that life can be a "thought" or a "second" long, that we are born "astride of a grave" when we know very well that most of us lead decently long lives—not long enough, but longer than that.

There are a dozen philosophical routes by which we might approach the question, as Borges does in "The New Refutation of Time," in which the quotation appears. For simplicity I would turn first to one of Beckett's favorite philosophers, St. Augustine, and specifically to the passage in the *Confessions* where Augustine asks God (very politely) about the mystery of time. What is time? Where, O Lord, are the past and the future? The present, Augustine felt (at first), was easy enough to understand; it was simply what one could see—hence its emblem *sight*—and feel around one; but where are the other two "parts" of time? God's answer, of course, was not forthcoming; indeed, one sees Him, like an embarrassed priest in a confession stall, taking the divine Fifth. So Augustine concluded on his own that the past and future are here only in the present, not as "the things themselves" but as memory and expectation—the "present of things past" and "the present of things future." And if this is the case the present itself—all of life—is "a distraction." For we are unavoidably "divided amid times" that are either not here yet or have only been here before. This is our lot: never—apart from a few keen moments: the stab of pain, the first sip of the martini, the moment of orgasm (these are not Augustine's examples)—to be precisely here, in the present, but always ahead of it or behind it, never *in* it, endlessly living life on the specious knife edge where memory and expectation commingle to create the illusion of time *actually passing*.

As a devout man bent on the life to come, Augustine did not bother about this much. But his modern student Beckett was bothered, devoting a considerable part of his thought to what he called the Time cancer. The conclusion we draw is that the present in which we dwell is nothing more or less than the mind's never-changing window on the world, not a thing or a form of time in itself but, to move to Borges (citing Schopenhauer), "the condition of all that is knowable." The time that constitutes a "second" or a "thought," therefore, is nothing more (or less) than the time that constitutes all so-called (and mis-named) time. Time itself is an "extensionless present," a rolling "second," according to a Buddhist text of the fifth century, where the chariot wheel meets the earth. Time, in short, is a deceit of the mind, and what passes as time, as Beckett expressed it, is simply "the place where we finish vanishing," the space that exists outside the mind in which all things slide effortlessly along an invisible path in which there are no events, no thoughts, no befores, no afters, no important or unimportant things taking place (including The Big Bang), only a constant metamorphosis of *whatever happens to be there*.

Alas, even the physicists have it all wrong in their little "time games," as Borges would call them. Space-time is simply a "useful" concept devised so that physicists can do physics. Oh, we can grant them their so-called imaginary time, their mathematics, and their neat little fictions like Planck's Constant, the Uncertainty Principle, light traveling at 186,000 miles per second, and so forth; but electrons aren't uncertain of anything, light doesn't give a damn how fast it's traveling. It has no awareness of time because it hasn't got one of these consciousnesses that insist on measuring everything in sight. All of these things are metaphors, pure metaphors. Oh perhaps in a trivial sense, you might insist that light *still* travels at 186,000 mps whether or not there is someone around to clock it. But right there you've sneaked physics back into the picture and physics, like art or religion or anything else we do, is just another Cartesian euphemism for consciousness: I think; therefore time exists (because, trivially, it takes time to think).

In this regard, consider the fascination of the photograph. As Roland Barthes saw so well, the photo is steeped in death. But—you may argue—is it not also clear proof of Time's existence, a true instant of time plucked out of the stream of change? For—behold—time has been caught like a thief in the act of stealing away. Yes, but look what has happened to it. It is not time that was caught. Though "taken" at a time—say, 2:12 P.M.—the photo is itself timeless. Or, if you prefer (it's the same thing), it is filled with *all* time; for as in

Muybridge's still photos of the running horse anyone can plainly see that a past and a future inhere in the subject's unnatural posture of being trapped *in medias res*. But whatever we mean by running, or time passing, is now a mile down the road. But again, this is the time of the mind—the lie told by space. The paradox of the photograph is that though we view it as an image of life we know, in the viscera, that it is *precisely* the negative of life, that it is Death that we hold between two fingers: the replica of a memory; something present, as Beckett says of Proust, at its own absence. Thus we say, "This is a good picture of you," in vague surprise that you have been preserved in a likeness reminiscent of your animation. Or, of a poor picture we say, "This is not you at all," meaning that the eye of the camera may have objectively recorded (though at a "bad" angle) what was standing in front of it but not the "you" we have over the years come to know, love and (above all) anticipate. Or, at a funeral "viewing," we hear, "She looks so like herself" (thanks to the mortician's body-photography), well-intended nostalgia but a grotesque revelation that the body at "final rest" should, of all things, resemble itself—that likeness should survive alacrity.

Or, take a painter who understands the fictitious nature of time. Of all the artists in our era, including Cézanne, it was Edward Hopper who painted the Now in all its sumptuous vacancy. In the world's estimation Hopper is probably no match for Cézanne as a painter, but he caught something about the being of things that is the very essence of deathliness. In Hopper time does not pass, as it does on those lazy afternoons in Impressionist painting; the very illusion of time has been extracted from Hopper's world, as if some metaphysical pump had sucked the past and future from everything and left only the husk of a Now as it reflects the light rays of the world. Cézanne said that he wanted most to paint "the world's instant"; what Hopper painted was not so much its instant (as in the photo) as its intrepid constancy—the *real* extensionless Now. No accident that Hopper could not paint *motion*, or when he tried, as in his equestrian and nautical paintings, everything seems awkwardly suspended, the ships too dense to float, the horses escapees from a merry-go-round. But the time-dead Now was his true province: the midnight cafe, the cadaverous "girlie shows," *Early Sunday Morning* in the city, the pale woman in *Room in New York* who idly depresses a single piano key with her index finger, the man in a chalk-white shirt sunk in his newspaper, are not "doing" things. They have a story, no doubt, and the surface of the painting hints at it—she lonely, he distracted, over something we are not told—but that is not what Hopper paints; rather, he paints their silent tolerance of a world infected to the core by an atrocious torpor. Indeed, Hopper's people are no different from his lighthouses, country gasoline pumps or the turrets of those great Victorian seaside homes he loved so much to paint because they were like harps for light to play on. It is all one, for they are all made of the same congealed paste. Hopper is our greatest painter of still life, that is, of the death sentence that is carried out constantly in everything under the radiant light of the sun.

What is literature itself but a beautiful charade on this whole subject? Its precise mission is to convert life and death into a timely experience that one would otherwise never have, a kind of Apocalypse—an action with a beginning, middle and end (Aristotle)—inserted into our ongoing continuity. All fiction offers the false solace of one's exemption from death. For example, my favorite death scene: Hamlet lying, mortally wounded, on the floor of the palace, in the arms of Horatio, saying "O I die, Horatio, the potent poison quite o'ercrows my spirit!" (What lucidity!), Horatio desperately trying to wrest the goblet from his friend's hand ("Here's yet some liquor left!"), and join him in the other world; but Hamlet, the saner of the two, prevailing, "And in this harsh world, draw thy breath in pain to tell my story." An unparalleled death to behold (unless it is Lear's): the eye's fruitful river overrunning the cheek, the breath forced, the visage wan and dejected, the stifled cry from the soul, the loss of an intimacy unknown in a lifetime of real friendships; it's all there, the works. And yet, what is this quintessence of death but a negation of death since, once again, *I survive it*? ("When Hamlet dies, I shall go home.") Words like "o'ercrow" and phrases like "harsh world" are stunningly beautiful but deeply untrue, if only because they carry the cool equanimity of poetry's immunity to death, the phrase "harsh world" having already outlasted its maker—long since "food for worms"—by some four centuries. *Ars longa, vita brevis*! And so too beautiful words like infarction, edema, pneumonia and carcinoma. These so-called technical words, this poetry of the hospital, like "o'ercrow my spirit"—what a soothing definition of death—are pure anesthesia, pure euphemism compared to *the thing itself* ("Your father, I'm afraid, has suffered an embolism"), necessary to proper diagnosis, but then diagnosis itself is but a weak description dwarfed by the event, spoken by a white-coated doctor who will return to family within the hour, with nothing more to do with "how it is" (Beckett's phrase) than the fiction that light travels at 186,000 mps.

Anyway, this would be my exegesis of these two dark passages. Of course, I speak only for myself. If Beckett (who mistrusted all interpretation) were able to respond, I imagine him saying, "Pozzo's beliefs are not necessarily my own." But I doubt it. Borges, on his part, would certainly say that my reading was a contradictory verification of his claim, at once coherent and absurd, original and plagiarized, like everything else. Finally, I could hardly fault the reader for finding this whole meditation the indulgence of a lugubrious mind. But having made the case for my own refutation of time (and death?), I must add that my thoughts are not necessarily my beliefs either. I still whistle Dixie, if only because my life is composed of memory and expectation, and I like it that way. I am used to it. The truth is, I live by the clock. Like everyone else, I Spring ahead and I Fall back. Whenever possible, I am never late to a meeting or an event, I consider promptness a substantial virtue, I hold to a fairly structured routine and am put out when it is disrupted. Moreover, I have left instructions that my ashes not be scattered in a bucolic meadow or mountain stream, and certainly not put into an airless box in a concrete columbarium facing the sea. Rather I want my wife, or someone (if she has moved to Paris), to run them through the blender until the chunks are downsized to uniformly even grains, put a cup or so of the mix into a small hourglass, place it on the mantle, and now and then turn it over to allow me the posthumous pleasure of measuring the thing that killed me. With the proper family commitment (abetted perhaps by a small revolving stipend), that should keep me going well into the nineties of the next century, surely enough life for anyone.

Nominated by The Hudson Review, Emily Fox Gordon, Richard Burgin

GOING

by DANIEL HOFFMAN

from THE GETTYSBURG REVIEW

Your time has come, the yellowed
light of the weary sun
wavers in the foliage.
It's no use, no use to linger.
So, goodbye, day. See,
the shadows join each other
as the air turns shadow
and the light fails. You
are gone, gone into the ghostly
light of all my days, of all
my hungers only partially assuaged,
of all desires
which in the rush of hours
I reached and stooped to grasp.
They're gone, receding like the light,
like the shadows, receding
into subsidence, to come
again as the day comes,
as the night
comes, bringing its own
going in its coming
again, and again.

Nominated by Grace Schulman

PART OF THE STORY

fiction by STEPHEN DOBYNS

from DOUBLETAKE

THERE WERE DAYS when Lily Hendricks would look from the picture window of her mobile home for an hour or more, watching the clouds making round, hopeful shapes in the air. What was hopeful for Lily was anything ongoing: clouds moving west to east, birds keeping busy, progress being made. But mostly the western Michigan sky was overcast and life didn't care squat. Mostly life tried to pen you up within its chain link fence. Lily had a little dog named Joyce that would bring her the box of Kleenex whenever Lily cried and the tears spilled onto her lap. The dog, half cocker, half beagle, would yip and wag her tail. Joyce was always upbeat. Lily had also tried teaching Joyce to fetch the bottle of Old Crow, but Joyce could only manage a pint bottle, and Lily liked to buy her bourbon by the gallon.

Lily was sixty-three. She had had five children and she had given all five up for adoption. But that was long ago. In those days, whenever she was with a new man and she asked herself should she or shouldn't she, the wildness always won. Maybe two of the children had had the same father, but Lily wouldn't put money on it. She hadn't played the field; she'd played the county. But that was history. Now she had Burt on Saturdays and Herbert on Wednesdays and weeks would go by when neither of them could get it up. They were older men who liked their quiet, and they did what they were told.

In the past year Lily had thought more about her five children than in the previous twenty-five. This was not a result of awakened conscience: they had tracked her down. Robbie had been first. He was forty-five and taught high school in Monroe, outside of Detroit. Lily felt proud that one of her children was a schoolteacher. He had phoned, and she was a little cool until she realized that he didn't want money and he wasn't going to complain. Robbie's father was one of three possible men. All dead now. Maybe it had been that time she had done it in the hayfield, or maybe that time in the back seat of a Plymouth. She had asked Robbie: "What color's your hair?"

"Brown."

"Curly?"

"Straight."

"And your eyes?"

"Brown."

She had asked more questions. Maybe Robbie's father had been Jerry Lombardi, who died in Jackson, where he had been serving a term for armed robbery. Somebody had stuck a knife in his back. When Lily had heard the news, she thought he deserved it. He had always been a mean man, someone who'd cross the street just to kick a stray dog. She wanted to ask Robbie if he had a mean streak, but she didn't feel it was something she could discuss over the phone.

In that first conversation she had told Robbie about his four half brothers and half sisters. It was just chitchat as far as she was concerned. She would have told anybody. Now, however, she felt he had wormed the information out of her: he had asked questions, and she'd been too truthful to lie. She gave him the dates of their births, more or less. She had used the same Catholic agency, in Lansing, with each adoption. She'd call up Sister Mary Agnes to tell her she had another little parcel on the way. Sometime later Sister Mary Agnes would give her a new name to remember in her prayers. Not that Lily did much praying, but it was more convenient to have a name other than "Baby X" to think about. If Robbie was the oldest at forty-five, then Marjorie was the youngest at twenty-five. Five babies in twenty years. And lucky she was to have had only five. After the last, Lily had had her tubes tied.

Robbie had contacted his brothers and sisters, and one by one they had called. They had hushed voices, as if talking to somebody important. They didn't want anything, seemingly, except to hear her voice and let her know they were okay. But she knew that was only part of the story, and for months she had been expecting the next installment. "I'm waiting for the other shoe to drop," she told Burt and Herbert. "It's going to be the big one."

The next installment had come in spring, in the middle of April. Robbie had called on a Sunday—one of those gray, bourbon-drinking Sundays. He said he'd been talking to his brothers and sisters, and they had decided to take a big step. They wanted to make her acquaintance. When would be a good time to visit?

"All of you?" asked Lily.

"That's right, all five. We want to meet our mom."

"Won't that be too much trouble for you?" Lily said.

"Nope, we've been talking about it. I've met Gwen and Frank, but this would be a good time for all of us to get to know one another."

Lily wanted to ask why, but she kept silent. She didn't see why they wanted to meet her, and she didn't see why they wanted to meet each other. She wished them well; she hoped they had happy lives; but she didn't want to get to know them. They were mistakes, bloopers. The rubber had broken, or the man hadn't used a rubber, or she had stopped taking her pills, or they had been in too much of a hurry. She had opened the door a crack and one by one her children had sneaked into the world. They were like ghosts, but they were living. She was glad they were living. She even liked it when they called. But she didn't want to meet them.

"I got a pretty tight schedule during the next few months," she said. The lie sounded so obvious that she felt bad about it. Twenty hours a week she worked at Rex's Diner and that was about it. Sometimes she played cards with a couple of the girls. Then on Saturdays and Wednesdays she had Burt and Herbert. She considered saying that she was off to Disneyland or Indianapolis, but the prospect of a whole string of lies exhausted her. It was not that she felt any allegiance to the truth. God knows she had cheated on too many men for the truth to be more than a stumbling block. But sometimes falsehood took more strength than she could summon up.

"What do you have to do?" asked Robbie patiently.

"Oh, it's nothing I can't get out of," said Lily. "You come whenever you want and I'll make the time. But there's no room in the trailer. You'll have to stay at the motel." And Lily felt it was only right that they should stay where at least one of them had been conceived.

Robbie handled the arrangements. He was practical and efficient, and it made Lily think that he probably wasn't Jerry Lombardi's kid after all. Jerry was a fuck-up. In the afternoons Lily sat staring at the clouds through her picture window and she knew that Robbie was pushing his plans forward. It frightened her. It was like what she had heard about soil erosion or the ice caps melting. Bit by bit it was going on, even while you slept or brushed your teeth. There was nothing hopeful about such activity, nothing upbeat. The negatives were rushing to get a leg up on the positives, and some day soon she would be knocked for a loop. Little Joyce lay her furry head in Lily's lap and stared up into her eyes. Even the dog knew trouble was coming.

A week later Robbie called back. "We want to come in May," he said.

"Just don't make it on Mother's Day," said Lily. "I don't think I could stand it."

They settled on the Saturday after Mother's Day. Many phone calls were made. Robbie took care of the reservations at the motel. Lily thought of these five adults and their expectations. In her imaginings they had question marks instead of faces. Soon those question marks would be exchanged for specific features. Would they all have her brown eyes? Her straight nose? She felt anxious and hopeful. She would give them pancakes for breakfast. She was afraid they wouldn't like her, that they would feel disappointment.

•   •   •

Most likely, the weekend would have been pleasant, even slightly dull, if events hadn't conspired to make it otherwise. Lily had known something would go wrong. She had even ticked off the possible disasters on her fingertips, but she hadn't thought of this one. She had never thought that Burt would cash in his chips right in her own bed. Kicked the bucket, bought the farm—whatever Lily called it, the whole business took about ten seconds from beginning to end. Maybe it was a stroke, maybe a heart attack. In days to come, Lily would think of Burt's death and want to blame him for the trouble he had caused, as if his death had been an act of petulance.

Burt was a retired hardware salesman, and he was soft. That was the problem. No exercise. Too many sweet things over a lifetime on the road. Jams and jellies. Thick butter. He felt hurt that he had to miss his Saturday with Lily just because Lily's children were coming to visit. He grew sullen and made remarks about how things should stay where you put them and not come back to plague you. So at last Lily said, "Then come Friday night, but you have to be gone by eight o'clock Saturday morning." Which, in a manner of speaking, he was.

Later, when Lily blamed Burt for dying, what she mostly blamed was his appetite, that on this particular occasion he had wanted to have sex more than once. "Burt had a greedy streak," Lily would tell the girls over cards, without bothering to explain herself. Often Burt didn't want to have sex at all, and they played gin rummy instead. But because Lily's children were coming, Burt must have felt a need to assert himself. He got himself all inspired again around seven-thirty that morning, and fifteen minutes later he was dead, lying naked on the sheet with his mouth open and his teeth still on the dresser. Lily had scrambled away and watched as Burt had seemed unable to catch his breath. He had choked and gasped, and his face had reddened. Then he was gone.

"For crying out loud!" Lily had stared at him, waiting for him to do something. He lay on his back with his arms flung out. After a minute she leaned forward and gently slapped his face. "Burt, Burt." She was so used to his doing exactly what she said that she felt some exasperation when he failed to respond.

Once she realized he was dead, she hurried to the phone in the kitchen. She could call the rescue squad or she could call the police. She glanced at her watch. It was eight o'clock. At eight-thirty her five children were due to arrive to have breakfast with their mom. She stood with the receiver in her hand. She thought of her children, the accidents of their births. Late nights in parked cars. Twice in the diner on the kitchen counter after closing. And here was Burt, the last of the men, or at least the most recent, sprawled naked on her bed. The rescue squad would have to come from town. Most likely they would arrive at the same time as her children. She imagined Robbie and Frank and Gwen and Merton and Marjorie standing by the door watching Burt being removed from their mom's bedroom. What she saw on their faces was disappointment. Their mom was up to her old tricks again. Sixty-three years old and still having fun. Lily hung up the phone. Burt was in no hurry. He could wait. Lily returned to the bedroom to get dressed and make herself look pretty. Then she'd get started on the pancakes.

●   ●   ●

Robbie arrived at eight-thirty on the dot and brought Gwen with him. Robbie was a tall man wearing a blue plaid sport coat, and Lily could see something of her face in his, like looking at herself through several inches of water. Gwen, who was forty-one, didn't favor her at all: a stout black-haired woman who would look like she was crying even when she was laughing. She wore a dark-green suit with some lace at the collar, and glasses with thick black frames. Little Joyce barked and barked. Lily kept nudging the dog with her foot and telling her to shush. She would have shut her in the bedroom if she hadn't been afraid that Joyce would take a bite out of Burt's nose. Lily had dressed Burt, even putting on his shoes and socks. There was an easy chair in the bedroom, and she had dragged him over to it. She had stuck a *Reader's Digest* in his lap, put in his teeth, and shut his mouth. She brushed his hair and set his reading glasses on his nose. Now he looked as if he had just happened to die in the bedroom. Maybe he had reached an exciting part of the story and popped his ticker. His death didn't look sex-related; it looked reading-related.

Gwen stood just inside the door with her arms folded, looking around the trailer. "This is really very nice," she said.

Robbie was trying to keep the dog from jumping up on his trousers. "Active little fellow," he said.

"It's a girl," said Lily, with a smile that hurt her cheeks. "Her name's Joyce. But come in. Have some coffee. It's almost ready." She had put on dark slacks and a beige turtleneck sweater. On a chain around her neck was a good-luck medallion showing a rainbow in four colors and a little pot of gold.

"Do you have any decaf?" asked Robbie.

"I'll check," said Lily, knowing that she didn't.

"It must be nice living in a mobile home," said Gwen. "Everything's always within reach."

Lily set her two children down at the kitchen table. It was a red vinyl booth, just like the booths at Rex's Diner. Lily had even taken one of the diner's chrome napkin dispensers and a glass sugar shaker with a chrome screw top. "What about tea?" she asked her son. Both her children were glancing around while trying not to appear nosy. They kept making sideways looks.

"That would be fine," said Robbie. When he spoke, he leaned forward and opened his mouth more than was necessary. His teeth reminded Lily of a wolf in a story. The front ones were as big as postage stamps. They didn't look like her teeth, nor did they look like Jerry Lombardi's. She couldn't stop staring at her children. Her fascination with their faces almost frightened her.

Lily poured coffee for Gwen. Her daughter's mouth was puckered as if a drawstring had been pulled tight. She wore no makeup, and her eyebrows were dark and shaggy. Lily herself plucked her eyebrows, and she liked to wear the brightest lipstick she could find. That morning she was wearing one called Passionate Appeal.

Joyce kept jumping up on Robbie's knees. "You can just whop her if you want," said Lily. "She's used to it." Then she thought of poor dead Burt and hoped he wouldn't topple onto the floor. She hadn't even had time to grieve yet. She put the kettle on the stove. "So you're from Toledo?" she asked Gwen.

"That's where my adoptive parents lived," said Gwen, "and that's where I was raised."

Lily wondered if she heard a note of complaint in her voice. Gwen was an accountant. Numbers were her life, she said. It amazed Lily that all her children did things. She took down the flour and baking powder and began to prepare the pancake batter as Gwen talked about Toledo. There was more to it than met the eye, she said.

A few minutes later Lily heard the rumble of motors and she glanced from the kitchen window. A Ford pickup had pulled up behind Robbie's Chevrolet, and a little green Toyota was right behind it. Two men and a woman got out. The woman was to be Marjorie, her youngest. She had been riding in the Toyota with one of the men. She was pretty, with strawberry-blond hair, but nervous-looking. Lily noticed that she fidgeted with her hands. The two men were Frank and Merton, but Lily didn't know who was who. For a second Lily felt she lacked the strength to open the door.

Frank was the taller one; he was thirty-six. Merton was pudgy and soft; he was thirty-two. Soon all five were crowded around the kitchen table. Lily was struck by how different they were from one another. If she had shoved a pencil blindly into the phone book she couldn't have found five people more different. They were as different from one another as she was different from a Chinaman. Lily couldn't recall having had sex with a Chinaman, though she might have had sex with one had she known one.

"I can't tell you how long I've hoped for this happy event," said Frank. He was a lay Baptist preacher in Marshall. He wore a dark-brown suit and had elaborate sideburns that curved forward and ended in points. His face was long. It didn't seem thin so much as squished, as if something had squeezed his head at the ears. He wore black shoes and white socks.

"I've been waking up early every morning just from excitement," said Merton. He was a druggist in Flint and still unmarried. He kept fooling with red spots on his face. His hands seemed swollen and soft. He wore a baby-blue corduroy sport coat, a red plaid shirt, and no tie. His jeans were white.

"Sometimes I start to weep," said Marjorie, "and I don't know why. I've been dreaming of this moment all my life." She was a dental hygienist in Saginaw. There were tears in her eyes. She kept pushing her hands through her blond hair, which would rise up and float back down like a cloud. When she spoke, she never looked at the person she was speaking to until the very end of her sentence. She wore a light-green summer dress with a full skirt that rustled when she shifted in the booth.

The five of them had gotten acquainted over dinner the previous evening, but Lily could tell they were still strange to one another. They kept looking at one another as if seeking resemblances. Lily stirred her pancake batter; it seemed the one safe thing. Gwen poured coffee and made tea for Robbie. Then she began hunting for dishes. She was short but efficient. Like her mother, she seemed to take comfort in activity.

Later Lily decided there was never really a specific moment when she felt it wasn't going to work. Rather, she had experienced an increasing dread. Her children's collective grievances were like a sixth person in the room. Lily could almost see his face: a real troublemaker. She thought of Burt sitting in her bedroom getting stiffer and stiffer. She almost envied him.

"I can't tell you what a special occasion this is for me," Lily said. It seemed her only hope lay in falsehood. "Seeing you together is like having all my eggs in one nest." She cracked two eggs into the bowl and stirred vigorously.

Gwen gave a tight smile. Marjorie's eyes welled up. Robbie gave the dog a push. Frank lowered his head and nodded. Merton scratched his face and stared at the breadbox. Their neediness oppressed her.

"The pancakes will be ready in a jiffy," she said. The bacon was already sizzling on the grill. Once they started eating, they would be occupied. But what would they do after that?

Frank said grace, and they bowed their heads. Her children's mouths filled with food seemed a reasonable alternative to silence. Chewing, after all, was akin to talking. They all sat crowded at the table and bumped one another with their elbows. Lily had real maple syrup. She kept sneaking furtive looks at her children, and she sensed them taking quick looks at her as well. It was barely nine o'clock. The day stretched ahead like an alp.

She was struck by how they chewed in similar ways: slowly and methodically. Frank ate with the tines of his fork pointing up; Robbie ate with the tines of his fork pointing down. Lily asked them about sports, and Merton talked about dart games. Marjorie said she played bingo at her church. Lily considered the passion that had sparked their lives into being and wondered where it was now. Robbie, Frank, and Gwen were all married with children, which made Lily a grandmother. Even this surprised her. She imagined generations proceeding into the future just because Jerry Lombardi had gotten her drunk in the back seat of his old Plymouth. She found herself suddenly yearning for actions without consequences, for simple routines like taking food orders or wiping off tables with a clean white rag. She remembered all those nights when some faceless man had had his way with her. She had thought of those actions as having clear beginnings, middles, and ends, but she had been mistaken. There weren't any ends. Never were, never would be. There was only a dull ongoingness, as if she had taken it into her head to walk all the way from Grand Rapids to Detroit. But even that journey would end, while this one didn't seem to. It was just one foot plopped in front of the other for the duration. She had had these children, and they had had children, and those children would have more children. Again she thought of Burt propped up with his *Reader's Digest*—the lucky devil.

Her children went on to talk about things they had recently read in the newspaper: troubles in Russia, troubles at home. Frank told about a circus elephant that had rampaged through a shopping center in Cleveland and had to be shot. Marjorie spoke of how Boy Scout leaders seemed to be getting in trouble almost everywhere. Lily felt touched by how they were trying to be conversational and civilized. They stumbled between one subject and the next while the subjects closest to their hearts remained lurking to the side. Lily wondered how long it would take them to speak their minds. If things got too far out of control, she thought, she could always walk into her bedroom and scream. Then they would find Burt and that'd be that. In the midst of Burt's death, her children wouldn't have the courage to ask their mother embarrassing questions about her life.

396

After breakfast, when the dishes were washed and put away, they moved into the small living room. Her three sons sat in a row on the sofa. They were crowded and leaned forward with their elbows on their knees. Whenever they did anything in the same way—scratched their noses or wrinkled their foreheads—Lily wondered if it was genetic. Marjorie sat in the easy chair, and Gwen sat on the arm. It seemed affectionate, but they weren't touching. Lily stood in the entrance to the kitchen.

Robbie glanced around at the others and cleared his throat. "We were wondering," he said, "if you could tell us anything about our fathers."

Even as the question was articulated, Lily had an image of their fathers. Oh, she didn't know who they were exactly, but she visualized a row of men who might have been their fathers: a rogue's gallery of male longing. The dim-witted and lustful. The meanspirited and carnal. Lily doubted there was a high school graduate in the bunch. And their accumulated jail time approached triple digits. Think of the beer and whiskey these men had consumed. The cars crashed, the women beaten or bullied, the jobs lost. In her imagination the men peered at her, leering and moronic. They had wanted her and she had been unable to say no.

"Your fathers were all grand men," said Lily at last.

"Were they all different?" asked Frank. "I mean, are any of us full brothers or sisters?"

"Five fathers for five children," said Lily. "They were all different, yet they were men you'd be proud of."

"Can you tell us their names?" asked Merton.

Lily had been afraid of this. In her bedroom stood a tall bookshelf packed with paperback romances: intimate tales to soothe her solitary hours. Now she called on them for inspiration.

"You have to ask yourself why we never married," she began. "Love was experienced and exchanged. Deep truths were shared. These were men with families, with positions in the community. In their youth they made mistakes. They had married the wrong women. As the years passed they came to realize the error of their ways. It was then we met."

"And this happened five different times?" asked Merton.

"More than that, but only on five occasions was a child conceived.

In fact, three times I had miscarriages. Somewhere your little heavenly half siblings are circling the globe. But if you could have known your fathers, then how proud you'd be."

"You mean they're dead?" asked Gwen in a whisper.

"Every single one." Lily covered her eyes with her hand. She was thinking hard. In her mind's eye she saw the dark-haired, bare-chested men on the book jackets, the women whose torn gowns were kept in place only by the magnitude of their bosoms.

"What was my father like?" asked Robbie.

"The colonel," said Lily. "He disappeared during Tet. Missing in action. He had sent me a note from Saigon saying he was going underground. Without doubt, he was one of the bravest men I've ever met. They never found his body. Could be he's still in some dank jungle cell, chained to a post."

"And my father," asked Frank, "what about him?"

"He raced cars. He was no stranger to Indianapolis. He was at home on a thousand tracks. Your father was one of the great ones. How ironic that he should be burned to death at a small county fair in Tennessee. He swerved to avoid a child who had strayed out onto the track. His wife was a strict Catholic and dead set against divorce."

"And mine?" asked Merton.

"The priest," said Lily. "The only one who wasn't married. He looked just like Gary Cooper."

The others pressed forward with their questions.

"Your father," Lily told Gwen, "was a state senator. One of the grand old men of Michigan politics. When we were together he was over seventy, still vigorous and full of life. Had he been a younger man we'd have married. He was eighty-five when he passed away. He knew you lived in Toledo. He kept his eye on you."

"I got a scholarship to the Brothers School," said Gwen.

"That was the senator's doing," said Lily.

"And your father," Lily told Marjorie, "was a Navy stunt pilot. You remember that crash over the fairgrounds in Detroit twenty years ago? No matter. He was about to tell his wife he wanted a divorce. I've carried his picture in my heart. Compared to him, other men were flotsam in the wind."

Now her children were perking up. Their faces were developing lively expressions. Lily brought out the bottle of Old Crow, and Gwen got ice and glasses. Marjorie no longer wept, and Frank no

398

longer looked dour. Robbie sat a little straighter. Even Gwen began to smile. Merton stopped picking at the red spots on his face.

"But how did you happen to be with my father, the colonel?" asked Robbie.

"It was shortly after the Miss Michigan contest," said Lily. "He had seen me on television."

"You were Miss Michigan?" Robbie asked, respectfully.

"No, no. Only a runner-up. The colonel called me at my parents' farm in Okemos. We agreed to meet at the state fair. One thing led to another and we ran away together. I've always been a sucker for a uniform. Then the colonel was sent overseas. After that, life was very hard. Of course I never inherited a penny."

"You must have met the senator shortly after that," suggested Gwen, pouring her mother a little Old Crow.

"He saved me. I was sitting on the lawn outside the capitol, weeping, and he found me. Without him, it would have been the white slavers, or worse. He had a shock of pure white hair that nearly reached his collar. And a white mustache as well. Can you blame me for going with him? He had a stretch limousine with a smoked-glass partition. Even the chauffeur couldn't see us."

"You did it in the limousine?" asked Gwen.

"Not only was the senator impetuous," said Lily, "he was forceful. He wanted to take my mind off my troubles. He swept me away." Lily was beginning to enjoy herself, but then she thought of Burt, how he was becoming stiffer in death than he had ever been in life.

"My father must have come next," said Frank.

"The dentist," said Lily.

"You said he raced cars," said Frank.

"Yes, a dentist who raced cars. I was hitchhiking out of Lansing, and he picked me up in his Jaguar. He drove like the wind—and he fixed my teeth as well."

Her children's eagerness propelled her forward. To Merton she told the story of the priest who had given her confession and how she had become his housekeeper. The first domesticity she had ever experienced. She had cooked him sweet things, but in the end his temptation had been too great and he had thrown his clerical collar to the floor. To Marjorie she described the amorous excesses of the stunt pilot and how they had once had sex parachuting over Sleeping

Bear dune. "When we hit the sand, we were still coupled," said Lily. "His organ was black and blue for weeks."

Their willingness to believe drove her to further excesses. But as she spoke she remembered how it really had been, with high school dropouts pulling her down between parked cars. She visualized how the sleeves of their jean jackets had been cut off at the shoulders, and how they wore little silver chains across the instep of their motorcycle boots. They kept packs of Luckies in the rolled-up sleeves of their T-shirts. They had flat bellies, and freckles, and they chewed toothpicks. Although they had seemed tough and virile, they were lousy lovers. Had they stayed around, they would have been lousy fathers: slapping their children just as they had slapped her. With them in the house, none of her children would have found a profession. Robbie wouldn't have been a teacher; Gwen wouldn't have become an accountant.

Lily had had a hunger that overswept her, and she had squandered it on riffraff. It was only as an older woman that she had begun to exert some control over her male companions. There had been Burt and Herbert and others. If they weren't all kind, they were at least obedient.

But hadn't Burt been kind? He had bought her a new TV and had her refrigerator fixed. He talked to her about her life and told her she was a good woman even when he got nothing out of it. Again and again she had kicked him out, calling him a sorry brute and a worthless dead sausage. He had sold farm equipment in Illinois, a childless man, and had wandered into western Michigan and taken a part-time job with the hardware store. "My biggest regret," he often told her, "was I never had kids." Now he was dead in the bedroom armchair with a *Reader's Digest* propped in his lap. And at that thought Lily, who had been laughing and joking with her children, burst into tears.

Her little dog Joyce was sitting beside her. When Lily began to cry, Joyce trotted out of the room. Lily didn't stop to think that Joyce was off to fetch the Kleenex and the Kleenex was in the bedroom.

"I've been a bad mother," Lily said, sobbing.

"No, no," said Marjorie.

"I have. I've been with men it was wrong to be with, and I've been irresponsible with my body."

"You were following your inner needs," said Merton.

"I've cheated and I've done what I shouldn't."

"But we're glad to be alive," said Frank. "We're grateful for that."

Her five children stood in a semicircle around her. Their foreheads all wrinkled in the same way.

It was then that Joyce began her ferocious yapping. By the time Lily got her thinking in order and called to Joyce to stop, it was too late. Gwen had gone to see what the trouble was and screamed. Then she came running back to the living room. Little Joyce trotted after her with the box of Kleenex.

"There's a dead man in the bedroom!" Gwen said. "And he's reading the *Reader's Digest*!"

"How can you tell he's dead?" asked Merton.

Frank and Robbie went to look. The others stared at Lily.

She covered her eyes with her hand. Truth and falsehood stretched ahead like two roads. But truth was a dark and muddy track compared to which falsehood was all fresh macadam. "I've been a terrible liar," she said.

"But who is it?" asked Gwen.

Lily buried her face in a wad of Kleenex. "That man's your father," she said.

"You mean Gwen's father?" asked Merton.

"No," said Lily, with her face still in the Kleenex. "That's Burt. He's the father of all five of you."

There was silence. Lily looked over her wad of Kleenex and saw she was alone. From the bedroom she heard the hushed voices of her children. Little Joyce jumped on Lily's lap to have her neck scratched. Lily wondered if she could escape while her children were occupied. But where could she go? She had to see her story through to the end.

Robbie was the first to return. The others trailed after him. Their faces showed surprise, grief, and confusion. It gave them a family resemblance.

"But how?" said Robbie. "Are you sure he's our father? Who is he?"

"That's Burt," said Lily. "Burt Frost. He drove out to meet you. He lives just this side of Grand Rapids. The excitement was too much for him. All night he talked about you, talked about seeing your dear faces. He got wound up tighter and tighter. He died just before you arrived."

"He's the father of all five of us?" asked Marjorie. They all began to sit down again.

"That's right. You're full brothers and sisters. Burt and I were

401

lovers for over forty-five years. His wife wouldn't give him a divorce. He was a salesman and she was a rich woman. She didn't want children and he yearned for them. I wanted you to think you had grand and important fathers. Burt never did a mean thing in his life. He was gentle as a kitten. When his wife died, he didn't get a penny. He moved here from Illinois to be near me."

"But why didn't you get married?" asked Merton.

"By that time it seemed too much like locking the barn door after the horse was gone," said Lily. "We were companionable, but we didn't want to tie the knot."

Lily then recounted the history of her sexual escapades, and it wasn't far from the truth. She described how and where each of her children had been conceived. But instead of Jerry Lombardi or Bobo Shaw or Leftie Meatyard, she inserted Burt. She had loved only one man, and she had been faithful. Now they were still together in their twilight years, but the fire of sexual passion had cooled. They were companions over poker and pinochle. They discussed their children's careers with pride.

"But he sounds like a wonderful man," said Marjorie.

"He was," said Lily. She was struck by the eagerness of their belief. They had a mother, but they wanted a father, too. And wouldn't Burt do? Lily's story was leaky but it would float. Outside, it began to rain.

All during their talk, one or another of her children would go into the bedroom to take a look at their new dad.

"I was going to wait till you'd gone," said Lily, "then take him back to his place. He's got a little house. It would embarrass him to be found here. If Burt had a fault, it was his love of privacy."

"I'm like that myself," said Robbie.

"You favor him in more ways than one," said Lily.

"People are going to wonder why you kept him here so long," said Frank. "You could get in trouble with the authorities."

"I figured I could take him home, then call the rescue squad," said Lily, "but I just don't feel I could do it now."

"Maybe we could take him," said Robbie. "Is it far?"

"Not far at all," said Lily.

And so it was settled. There were loose ends but Lily snipped them off. There were doubts but Lily slowly rubbed them away. She drew a map to Burt's house. She made sandwiches for everybody. They drank more whiskey. Frank said Baptist prayers over Burt, and they had a little service with all six of them crowded into the bed-

402

room. They stared at Burt fondly. Lily felt how glad Burt would have been had he known. She found herself happy.

Around dusk they put Burt into the back of Frank's Ford pickup, chair and all. They couldn't bend him; it was best to keep him seated. The rain had stopped and there was a red glow in the sky.

"We'll buy you a new chair, Ma," said Merton.

Robbie, Gwen, and Marjorie sat in the back of the pickup to keep Burt from toppling over. Merton followed in his Toyota. They were only going about ten miles. In the dim light Burt didn't look dead. He looked fatherly and alert. His new children sat at his feet as if he were telling them a story. And perhaps, in a way, he *was* telling them a story, because weren't they learning the story of their lives? What did it matter that it wasn't a true story? They would commit it to memory. They would embroider it and pass it along to their children and grandchildren. It would be a bright color in a dim world. And wasn't that more useful than a sentimental allegiance to a series of events called truth?

Lily stood by the window and watched. She held little Joyce in her arms so that she could watch too. Lifting the dog's right paw, Lily moved it up and down. From outside it would seem that the little dog was waving good-bye.

Nominated by Nancy Richard, Stuart Dischell, DoubleTake

PAIN THINKS OF THE BEAUTIFUL TABLE

by LAURIE LAMON

from ARTS & LETTERS

the way water looks up Pain thinks of the beautiful table
surrounded by light Pain thinks of glass & cup iridescence
& afterwards paper & mouth the wall Pain is used to craving
the hand lifting the usual thing Pain thinks of the body's
meekness the fork without hunger without interruption Pain
thinks of going for days without the beautiful table without
food or expression so that flowers & cold are drawn in

Nominated by Arts & Letters

THE PRICE OF EGGS
IN CHINA

fiction by DON LEE

from THE GETTYSBURG REVIEW

It was noon when Dean Kaneshiro arrived at Oriental Hair Poet Number Two's house, and as she opened the door, she said, blinking, "Hello. Come in. I'm sorry. I'm not quite awake."

He carried his measuring rig through the living room, noting the red birch floor, the authentic Stickley, the Nakashima table, the Maloof credenza—good craftsmanship, carefully selected. This poet, Marcella Ahn, was a woman who knew wood.

"When you called," she said in her study, "I'd almost forgotten. It's been over two years! I hope I wasn't too difficult to track down."

Immediately Dean was annoyed. When she had ordered the chair, he had been clear about his backlog, and today was the exact date he'd given her for the fitting. And she *had* been difficult to track down, despite his request, two years ago, that she notify him of any changes of address. Her telephone number in San Francisco had been disconnected, and he had had to find her book in the library, then call her publisher in New York, then her agent, only to learn that Marcella Ahn had moved an hour south of the city to the very town, Rosarita Bay, where he himself lived. Never mind that he should have figured this out, having overheard rumors of yet another Asian poet in town with spectacular long hair, which had prompted the references to her and Caroline Yip, his girlfriend of eight months, as the Oriental Hair Poets.

He adjusted his rig. Marcella Ahn was thin and tall, but most of

405

her height was in her torso, not her legs—typical of Koreans. She wore tight midnight-blue velvet pants, black lace-up boots, and a flouncy white Victorian blouse, her tiny waist cinched by a thick leather belt.

"Sit, please," he said. She settled into the measuring rig. He walked around her twice, then said, "Stand up, please." After she got up, he fine-tuned the back supports and armrests and shortened the legs. "Again, please."

She sat down. "Oh, that's much better, infinitely better," she said. "You can do that just by looking?"

Now came the part that Dean always hated. He could use the rig to custom-fit his chairs for every part of the body except for one. "Could you turn around, please?"

"Sorry?"

"Could you turn around? For the saddling of the seat?"

Marcella Ahn's eyes lighted, and the whitewash of her foundation and powder was suddenly broken by the mischievous curl of her lips, which were painted a deep claret. "You mean you want to examine . . . my *buttocks*?"

He could feel sweat popping on his forehead. "Please."

Still smirking, she raised her arms, the ruffled cuffs of her blouse dropping away, followed by the jangling release of two dozen silver bracelets on each wrist. There were silver rings on nearly every digit, too, and with her exquisitely lacquered fingers, she slowly gathered her hair—straight and lambent and hanging to mid-thigh—and raked it over one shoulder so it lay over her breast. Then she pivoted on her toe, turned around, and daintily lifted the tail of her blouse to expose her butt.

He squatted behind her and stared at it for a full ten seconds. It was a good butt, a firm StairMastered butt, a shapely, surprisingly protuberant butt.

She peeked over her shoulder. "Do you need me to bend over a little?" she asked.

He bounced up and moved across the room and pretended to jot down some notes. Then, pointing to her desk, he said, "You'll be using the chair here?"

"Yes."

"To do your writing?"

"Uh-huh."

"I'll watch you, then. For twenty minutes, please."

406

"What? Right now?"

"It'll help me to see you work, how you sit, maybe slouch."

"It's not that simple," she said.

"No?"

"Of course not. Poets can't write on demand. You know nothing about poetry, do you?"

"No, I don't," Dean said. All he ever read, in fact, were mystery novels. He went through three or four of them a week—anything with a crime, an investigation. He was now so familiar with forensic techniques, he could predict almost any plot twist, but his head still swam in delight at the first hint of a frame-up or a double cross. He looked around the room. More classic modern furniture, very expensive. And the place was neat, obsessive-compulsive neat.

Marcella Ahn had her hands on her hips. "And I don't slouch," she said.

Eventually he did convince her to sit in her present desk chair, an ugly vinyl contraption with pneumatic levers and bulky ergonomic pads. She opened a bound notebook and uncapped a fountain pen, and hovered over the blank page for what seemed like a long time. Then she abruptly set everything aside and booted up her laptop computer. "What do you do with clients who aren't within driving distance?"

"I ask for a videotape, and I talk to their tailor. Try to work, please. Then I'll be out of your way."

"I feel so silly."

"Just pretend I'm not here," he said.

Marcella Ahn continued to stare at the computer screen. She shifted, crossed her legs, and tucked them underneath her. Finally, she set her fingers on the keys and tapped out three words. She exhaled heavily. "When will the chair be ready?"

"I'll start on it next month, on April 20th, then three weeks, so May 11th," he told her, though he required only half that time. He liked to plan for contingencies, and he knew his customers wanted to believe—especially with the prices they were paying—that it took him longer.

"Can I visit your studio?" she asked.

"No, you cannot."

"Ah, you see, you can dish it—"

"It would be very inconvenient."

"For twenty minutes."

407

"Please don't," he said.

"Seriously. I can't swing by for a couple of minutes?"

"No."

Marcella Ahn let out a dismissive puff. "Artists," she said.

Oriental Hair Poet Number One was a slob. Caroline Yip lived in a studio apartment above a hardware store, one small room with a Pullman kitchen, a cramped bathroom, and no closets. Her only furnishings were a futon, a boom box, and a coffee table, and the floor was littered with clothes, CDs, shoes, books, newspapers, bills, and magazines. There was a thick layer of grease on the stove top, dust and hair and curdled food on every other surface, and the bathroom was clogged with sixty-two bottles of shampoo and conditioner, some half-filled, most of them empty.

Dean had stayed in the apartment only once—the first time they slept together. Surveying his erection, Caroline had said, "Your penis looks like a fire hydrant. Everything about you is short, squat, and thick." It was true. Dean was an avid weightlifter, not an ounce of fat on him, but his musculature was broad and tumescent, absent of definition. His forearms were pickle jars, almost as big as his thighs, and his crew-cutted head sat on his shoulders without the relief of a neck. "What am I doing with you?" Caroline said. "This is what it's come down to, this is how far I've sunk. I'm about to fuck a Nipponese fire hydrant with the verbal capacity of tap water."

There were other peculiarities. She didn't sleep well, although she had done almost everything possible to alleviate her insomnia and insistent stress—acupuncture, herbs, yoga, homeopathy, tai chi (interestingly, she didn't believe in psychotherapy). She ran five miles a day, and she meditated for twenty minutes each morning and evening, beginning her sessions by trying to relax her face, stretching and contorting it, mouth yowling open, eyes bulging—it was a horrific sight.

Even when she did sleep, it was fitful. Because she ground her teeth, she wore a plastic mouthpiece to bed, and she bit down so hard on it during the night, she left black spots where her fillings were positioned. She had nightmares, a recurring nightmare, of headless baby chickens chasing after her, hundreds of decapitated little chicks tittering in rabid pursuit.

The nightmares, however, didn't stop her from eating chicken, or anything else, for that matter. She was a waif, five two, barely a hundred pounds. Her hair—luxuriant, butt-length, and naturally kinky, a rarity among Asians—seemed to weigh more than she did. Yet she had a ravenous appetite. She was constantly asking for seconds, picking off Dean's plate. "Where does it all go?" he asked over dinner one night, a month into their courtship.

"What?"

"The food."

"I have a very fast metabolism. You're not going to finish that?"

He scraped the rest of his portion into her bowl, and he watched her eat. He had surprised himself by how fond he'd become of her. He was a disciplined man, with solitary and fastidious habits, yet Caroline's idiosyncrasies were endearing to him. Maybe this was the true measure of love, he thought—when you willingly tolerate behavior that, in anyone else, would be annoying, even abhorrent to you. Without thinking, he blurted, "I love you."

"Yikes," Caroline said. She put her chopsticks down and wiped her mouth. "You are the sweetest man I've ever met, Dean. But I worry about you. You're so innocent. Didn't anyone let you out of the house when you were young? Don't you know you're not supposed to say things like that so soon?"

"Do you love me?"

She sighed. "I don't now," she said. Then she laid her hands on top of his head and shook it. "But I think I will. Okay, you big boob?"

It took her two months. "Despite everything, I guess I'm still a romantic," she said. "I will never learn."

They were both reclusive by nature and most of the time were content to sequester themselves in Dean's house, watching videos, reading, cooking Japanese dishes: *tonkatsu, oyako donburi, tempura, unagi.* It was a quiet life, free of catastrophe, and it had lulled Dean into believing that Caroline was no longer particularly neurotic, that there would be no harm in telling her about his encounter with Oriental Hair Poet Number Two.

"That cunt!" she said. "That conniving Korean cunt! She's moved here on purpose!"

It was all she could talk about for three days. Caroline Yip and Marcella Ahn, it turned out, had a history. They had both lived in Cambridge, Massachusetts, in their twenties, and for several years, they had been the best of friends—inseparable, really. But then their first books had come out at the same time, Marcella's from a major New York publisher, Caroline's from a small, albeit respected press.

409

Both had very similar jacket photos, the two women looking solemn and precious, hair flowing in full regalia. An unfortunate coincidence. Critics couldn't resist reviewing them together, mocking the pair, even then, as "The Oriental Hair Poets," "The Braids of the East," and "The New Asian Poe-tresses."

But Marcella escaped these barbs relatively unscathed. Her book, *Speak to Desire*, was taken seriously, compared to Marianne Moore and Emily Dickinson. Her poetry was highly erudite, usually beginning with mundane observations about birds or plant life, then slipping into long, abstract meditations on entropy and inertia, the Bible, evolution, and death, punctuated by the briefest mention of personal deprivations—anorexia, depression, abandonment. Or so the critics said. Dean still had the the book from the library, and he couldn't make heads or tails of it.

In contrast, Caroline's book, *Chicks of Chinese Descent*, had been skewered. She wrote in a slangy, contemporary voice, full of topical, pop-culture allusions. She wrote about masturbation and Marilyn Monroe, about tampons and moo goo gai pan, about alien babies and her strange, loopy obsession with poultry. She was roundly dispatched as a mediocre talent.

Worse, Caroline said, was what happened afterwards. Marcella began to thwart her at every turn. Teaching jobs, coveted magazine publications, awards, residencies, fellowships—everything Caroline applied for, Marcella got. It didn't hurt that Marcella was a shameless schmoozer, flirting and networking with anyone who might be of use, all the while ridiculing them behind their backs. The fact was, Marcella was rich. Her father was a shipping tycoon, and she had a trust fund in the millions. She didn't need any of these pitifully small sinecures which would have meant a livelihood to Caroline, and it became obvious that the only reason Marcella was pursuing them at all was to taunt her.

"She's a vulture, a vampire," Caroline told Dean. "You know she won't go out in the light of day? She stays up until four, five in the morning and doesn't wake up until past noon."

And then there was the matter of Evan Paviromo, the English-Italian editor of a literary journal whom Caroline had dated for seven years, waiting patiently for them to get married and have children. He broke it off one day without explanation. She dogged him. Why? Why was he ending it? She refused to let him go without some sort of answer. Finally he complied. "It's something Marcella said," he admitted.

At first Caroline feared they were having an affair, but the truth was more vicious. "Marcella told me she admired me," Evan said, "that I was far more generous than she could ever be. She said she just wouldn't be able to stay with someone whose work she didn't really respect. I thought about that, and I decided I'm not that generous after all. It's something that would eat away at me, that's bothered me all along. It's something I can't abide."

Caroline fled to California, eventually landing in the little nondescript town of Rosarita Bay. She completely disengaged herself from the poetry world. She was still writing every day, excruciating as it was for her, but she had not attempted to publish anything in six years. She was thirty-seven now, and a waitress—the breakfast shift at a diner, the dinner shift at a barbecue joint. Her feet had grown a full size from standing so much, and she was broke. But she had started to feel like her old self again, healthier, more relaxed, sleeping better. Dean had a lot to do with it, she said. She was happy—or as happy as it was possible for a poet to be. Until now. Until Marcella Ahn suddenly arrived.

"She's come to torment me," Caroline said. "Why else would she move to Rosarita Bay?"

"It's not such a bad place to live."

"Oh, please."

"A coincidence," Dean said. "How could she have even known you were here? You said you're not in touch with any of those people anymore."

"She probably hired a detective."

"Come on."

"You don't understand. I suppose you think if anyone's looking for revenge, it'd be me, that I can't be a threat to her because I'm such a failure."

"I wish you'd stop putting yourself down all the time. You're not a failure."

"Yes I am. You're just too polite to say so. You're so fucking Japanese."

Early on, she had given him her book to read, and he had told her he liked it. But she had pressed him with questions, and finally he'd had to confide that he had not really understood the poems. He was

411

not an educated man, he had said. He only read detective stories; the only movies he liked were whodunits.

"You pass yourself off as this simple chairmaker," Caroline said. "You were practically monosyllabic when we began seeing each other. But I know you're not the gallunk you make yourself out to be."

"I think you're talented. I think you're very talented." How could he explain it to her? Something had happened as he'd read her book. The poems, confusing as they were, had made his skin prickle, his throat thicken, random images and words—*kiwi, quiver, belly, maw*—wiggling into his head and taking residence.

"Are you attracted to her?" Caroline asked.

"What?"

"You're not going to make the chair for her, are you?"

"I have to."

"You don't have a contract."

"No, but—"

"You still think it's all a coincidence."

"She ordered the chair *sixteen months* before I met you."

"You see how devious she is?"

Dean couldn't help himself. He laughed.

"She has some sick bond to me," Caroline said. "In all this time, she hasn't published another book, either. She *needs* me. She *needs* my misery. You think I'm being hysterical, but you wait."

It began with candy and flowers, left anonymously outside the hardware store, on the stairs that led up to Caroline's apartment. Dean had not sent them.

"It's her," Caroline said.

The gifts continued, every week or so, then every few days. Chocolates, carnations, stuffed animals, scarves, hairbrushes, barrettes, lingerie. Caroline, increasingly anxious, moved in with Dean and quickly came down with a horrendous cold.

Hourly he would check on her, administering juice, echinacea, or anti-histamines, then go back to the refuge of his workshop. It was where he was most comfortable—alone with his tools and wood, making chairs that would last hundreds of years. He made only armchairs now, one chair, over and over, the Kaneshiro Chair. Each one was fashioned out of a single board of *keyaki*, Japanese zelkova, and was completely handmade. From the logging to the tung oil finish, the wood never touched a power tool. All of Dean's saws and chisels and planes were hand-forged in Japan, and he shunned vises and clamps of any kind, sometimes holding pieces between his feet to work on them. On first sight, the chair's design wasn't that special— blocky right angles, thick Mission Style slats; its beauty lay in the craftsmanship. Dean used no nails or screws, no dowels or even glue. Everything was put together by joints, forty-four delicate, intricate joints, modeled after a traditional method of Japanese joinery, dating from the seventeenth century, called *sashimono*. Once coupled, the joints were tenaciously, permanently locked. They would never budge; they would never so much as squeak.

What's more, every surface was finished with a hand plane. Dean would not deign to have sandpaper in his shop. He had apprenticed for four years with a master carpenter in the city of Matsumoto, in Nagano Prefecture, spending the first six months just learning how to sharpen his tools. When he returned to California, he could pull a block plane over a board and produce a continuous twelve-foot-long shaving, without a single skip or dig, that was less than a tenth of a millimeter thick—so thin you could read a newspaper through it.

Dean aimed for perfection with each chair. With the first kerf of his *dozuki* saw, with the initial chip of a chisel, he was committed to the truth of the cut. Tradition dictated that any errors could not be repaired and had to stay on the piece to remind the woodworker of his humble nature. More and more, Dean liked to challenge himself. He no longer used a level, square, or marking gauge, relying only on his eye, and soon he planned to dispense with rulers altogether, maybe even pencils and chalk. He wanted to get to the point where he could make a Kaneshiro Chair blindfolded.

But he had a problem. Japanese zelkova, the one- to two-thousand-year-old variety he needed, was rare and very expensive— amounting to over one hundred and fifty dollars a pound. There were only three traditional wood-cutters left in Japan, and Dean's sawyer, Hayashi Kota, was sixty-nine. So much of the work was in reading the trees and determining where to begin sawing to reveal the best figuring and grain—like cutting diamonds. Hayashi san's intuition was irreplaceable. Afraid the sawyer might die soon, Dean had begun stockpiling wood five years before. In his lumber shed, which was climate-controlled to keep the wood at a steady thirty-seven-percent humidity, was about two hundred thousand dollars' worth of zelkova. Hayashi-san cut the logs through and through and air-dried them in Japan for a year, and after two weeks of kiln heat, the boards were shipped to Dean, who stacked them on end in *boule* order. When he went into the shed to select a new board, he was always overcome by the beauty of the wood, the smell of it. He'd run his hand over the boards—hardly a check or crack on them—and want to weep.

Given the expense of the wood and the precision his chairs required, anyone seeing Dean in his shop would have been shocked by the rapidity with which he worked. He never hesitated. He *attacked* the wood, chips flying, shavings whirling into the air, sawdust piling at his feet. He could sustain this ferocity for hours, never letting his concentration flag. No wonder, then, that it took him a few moments to hear the knocking on the door late that afternoon. It took him even longer to comprehend why anyone would be disturbing him in his workshop, his sanctum sanctorum.

Caroline swung open the door and stepped inside, looking none too happy. "You have a visitor," she said.

Marcella Ahn sidled past her. "Hello!"

Dean almost dropped his *ryoba* saw.

"Is that my chair?" she asked, pointing to the stack of two-by-twos on his bench. "I know, I know, you told me not to come, but I had to. You won't hold it against me, will you?"

Without warning, Caroline let out a violent sneeze, her hair whiplashing forward.

"Bless you," Dean and Marcella said at the same time.

Caroline snorted up a long string of snot, glaring at Oriental Hair Poet Number Two. They were a study in contrasts, Marcella once again decked out as an Edwardian whore: a corset and bodice, miniskirt and high heels, full makeup, hair glistening. Caroline was wearing her usual threadbare cardigan and flannel shirt, pajama bottoms, and flip-flops. She hadn't bathed in two days, sick in bed the entire time.

"When you get over this cold," Marcella said to her, "we'll have to get together and catch up. I just can't get over seeing you here."

"It is incredible, isn't it?" Caroline said. "It must defy all the laws of probability." She walked to the wall and lifted a mortise chisel from the rack. "The chances of your moving here, when you could live anywhere in the world, it's probably more likely for me to shit an egg for breakfast. Why *did* you move here?"

"Pure chance," Marcella told her cheerily. "I happened to stop for

414

coffee on my way to Aptos, and I saw one of those real estate circulars for this house. It looked like an unbelievable bargain. Beautiful woodwork. I thought, What the hell, I might as well see it while I'm here. I was tired of living in cities."

"What have you been doing since you got to town? Going shopping? Buying lots of gifts?"

Dean watched her slapping the face of the chisel blade against her palm. He wished she would put it down. It was very sharp.

Marcella appeared confused. "Gifts? No. Well, unless you count Mr. Kaneshiro's chair as a gift. To myself. You don't have a finished one here? I've actually never seen one except in the Museum of Modern Art."

"Sorry," he told her, nervous now, hoping it would slip by Caroline.

But it did not. "The Museum of Modern Art?" she asked. "In New York?"

Marcella nodded. She absently flicked her hair back with her hand, and one of her bracelets flew off her wrist, pinging against the window and landing on some wood chips.

Caroline speared it up with the chisel and dangled it in front of Marcella, who slid it off somewhat apprehensively. Caroline turned to Dean. "Your chairs are in the Museum of Modern Art in New York?"

He shrugged. "Just one."

"You didn't know?" Marcella asked Caroline, plainly pleased she didn't. "Your boyfriend's quite famous."

"How famous?"

"I would like to get back to work now," Dean said.

"He's in Cooper-Hewitt's permanent collection, the MFA in Boston, the American Craft Museum."

"I need to work, please."

"Don't you have a piece in the White House?"

"Time is late, please."

"Can I ask some questions about your process?"

"No." He grabbed the chisel out of Caroline's hand before she could react and ushered Marcella Ahn out the door. "Okay, thank you. Goodbye."

"Caroline, when do you want to get together? Maybe for tea?"

"She'll call you," Dean said, blocking her way back inside.

"You'll give her my number?"

"Yes, yes, thank you," he said and shut the door.

Caroline was sitting on his planing bench, looking gaunt and exhausted. Through the window behind her, Dean saw it was nearing dusk, the wind calming down, the trees quieting. Marcella Ahn was out of view, but he could hear her starting her car, then driving away. He sat down next to Caroline and rubbed her back. "You should go back to bed. Are you hungry? I could make you something."

"Is there anything else about you I should know? Maybe you've taught at Yale or been on the Pulitzer committee? Maybe you've won a few genius grants?"

He wagged his head. "Just one."

"What?"

He told her everything. Earlier in his career, he had done mostly conceptual woodwork, more sculpture than furniture. His father was indeed a fifth-generation Japanese carpenter, as he'd told her, but Dean had broken with tradition, leaving his family's cabinetmaking business in San Luis Obispo to study studio furniture at the Rhode Island School of Design. After graduating, he had moved to New York, where he was quickly declared a phenomenon, a development that baffled him. People talked about his work using terms like "verticality" and "negation of ego" and "primal tension"; they might as well have been speaking Farsi. He rode it for all it was worth, selling pieces at a record clip. But eventually, he became bored. He didn't experience any of the fractious, internecine rivalries that Caroline had, nor was he too bothered by the monumental egos, pretension, and fatuity that abounded in the art world. He didn't see these art people. He didn't go to parties, and he avoided openings. He just didn't believe in what he was doing anymore, particularly after his father died of a sudden stroke. Dean wanted to return to the pure craftsmanship and functionality of woodworking, building something people could actually *use*. So he dropped everything to apprentice in Japan. Afterwards, he distilled all his knowledge into the Kaneshiro Chair, which was considered as significant a landmark as Frank Lloyd Wright's Willits Chair. Ironically, his work was celebrated anew. He received a five-year genius grant that paid him an annual fifty thousand dollars, all of which he had put into hoarding the zelkova in his shed.

"How much do you get a chair?" Caroline asked.

"Ten thousand."

"God, you're only thirty-eight."

416

"It's an inflated market."

"And you never thought to tell me any of this in the eight months we've been going out? I thought you were barely getting by. You live in this crappy little house with cheap furniture, your pickup is ten years old, you never take vacations. I thought it was because you weren't very savvy about your business, making one chair at a time, no advertising or catalog or anything, no store lines. I thought you were as anti-intellectual as they came. I thought you were *clueless*."

"It's not important."

"Not important? Are you insane? Not important? It changes everything."

"Why?"

"You know why, or you wouldn't have kept this secret from me."

"It was an accident. I didn't set out to be famous. It just happened. I'm ashamed of it."

"You should be. You're either pathologically modest, or you were afraid I'd be repelled by how successful you are, compared to me. But you should have told me."

"I just make chairs now," Dean said. "I'm just like you with your poetry. I work hard like you. I don't do it for the money or the fame or to be popular with the critics."

"It's just incidental that you've gotten all of those things without even trying."

"Let's go in the house. I'll make you dinner."

"No. I have to go home. I can't be with you anymore."

"Caroline, please."

"You're not like me at all. You're like Marcella. Everything's come so easily to you, and you don't even appreciate how lucky you've been. You look at people like me, and you sneer. You must think I'm pathetic, you must pity me. You represent everything I despise."

They had had fights before, puzzling affairs where she would walk out in a huff, incensed by an innocuous remark he'd made, a mysterious gaffe he'd committed. A day or two would go by, then she would talk to him, peevishly at first, ultimately relenting after she had dressed him down with a pointed lecture on his need to be more sensitive, more supportive, more complimentary, more assertive, more emotive, more sympathetic, and, above all, more *communicative*. Dean would listen without protest, and, newly educated and humbled, he would always be taken back. But not this time. This time was different. On the telephone the next day, Caroline was cool and resolute—no whining or nagging, no histrionics or ultimatums or room for negotiation. "It's over, Dean," she said.

The following afternoon, he went to her apartment with a gallon of miso soup. "For your cold," he said.

She looked down at the tub in his hands. "I'm fine now. I don't need the soup. The cold's gone."

They were standing outside on the stairway landing. "You're not going to let me in?" he asked.

"Dean, didn't you hear what I said yesterday?"

"Just tell me how I should change. I'll change."

"It's not like that."

"What's it like, then? Tell me what you want me to do."

"Nothing," she said. "You can't fix this. Don't come by again, don't call, okay? It'll be easier if we just break it off clean."

He tried to leave her alone, but none of it made any sense to him. Why was she ending it? What had he done wrong? It had to be one of her mood swings, a little hormonal blip, a temporary synaptic disruption, all of which he'd witnessed and weathered before. It had to be more about Marcella Ahn than about him. She couldn't really be serious. The best course of action seemed to be to wait it out, while at the same time being solicitous and attentive. So he called—not *too* frequently, maybe once a day or so—and since she wouldn't pick up her phone, he left messages: "I just wanted to see how you're doing. I miss you." He drove to her apartment and knocked on her door, and since she wouldn't answer it, he left care packages: macadamia nuts, coffee, cream, filters, toilet paper, sodas, granola bars, spring water, toothpaste—the everyday staples she always forgot to buy at the store.

Five days passed, and she didn't appear to be weakening. A little desperate, he decided to go to Rae's Diner. When Caroline came out of the kitchen and saw him sitting in her station, she didn't seem surprised, but she was angry. She wouldn't acknowledge him, wouldn't come to his table. After twenty minutes, he flagged down Rae, the owner. "Could you tell Caroline to take my order?" he asked.

Rae, a lanky, middle-aged brunette with a fierce sunlamp tan, studied him, then Caroline. "If you two are having a fight, I'm not going to be in the middle of it. You want to stay, you'll have to pay."

"That's what I'm trying to do. She won't take my order."

"Why don't you just move to another station?"

"There aren't any other tables."

"The counter, then."

"I'm a paying customer, I should be able to sit where I want."

Rae shook her head. "Any screaming, one little commotion, and you're out of here. And no dawdling over a cup of coffee, either. The minute your table's cleared, you go."

She had a brief conference with Caroline, who began arguing with her, but in the end Rae won out, and Caroline marched over to Dean's table. She didn't look well—pale and baggy-eyed. She wasn't sleeping or eating much, it was clear. He tried to make pleasantries. "How have you been?" he asked her. She would not say a word, much less look at him. She waited for his order, ballpoint poised over her pad. A few minutes later, when his food was ready, she clattered the plate down in front of him and walked away. When he raised his coffee cup for a refill, she slopped the pot, spilling coffee over the brim, almost scorching his crotch. He left her a generous tip.

He came to a similar arrangement with the manager of Da Bones, the barbecue restaurant where Caroline worked nights—as long as he paid, he could stay. He ate meals at every one of Caroline's shifts for a week, at the end of which he had gained eight pounds and was popping antacids as if they were gumballs. His typical breakfast now consisted of six eggs over easy, sausage, hash browns, blueberry flapjacks, coffee, orange juice, biscuits, and milk gravy. Dinner was the hungry man combo—beef brisket, half a rack of baby backs, kielbasa, blackened chicken, rice, beans, slaw, and cornbread—accompanied by a side of mashed and two plates of conch fritters. But it was worth it. Caroline's resolve, he could tell, was beginning to crack (although the same could be said about her health; she looked awful). One night, as he asked for his fifth glass of water, she actually said something. She said, "You are getting to be a real pain in the ass," and she almost smiled. He was getting to her.

But two days later, he received a strange summons. A sergeant from the sheriff's office, Gene Becklund, requested he come down for a talk concerning Caroline. Mystified, Dean drove over to the sheriff's and was escorted into an interrogation room. Gene Becklund was a tall, soft-spoken man with prematurely gray hair. He opened the conversation by saying, "You've been going over to your

419

ex-girlfriend's apartment a lot, dropping off little presents? Even though she told you not to call or visit?"

Unsettled, Dean nodded yes.

"You've also been bothering her at her workplace nearly every day?"

" 'Bothering'?"

"And you've been leaving a lot of messages on her machine, haven't you?"

"We haven't really broken up," Dean said. "We're just having a fight."

"Uh-huh."

"I'm not harassing her or anything."

"Okay."

"Did she say I was harassing her?"

"Why don't we listen to something," Becklund said and turned on a cassette player. On the tape was a garbled, robotic, unidentifiable voice, reciting the vile, evil things that would be done to Caroline—anal penetration, disembowelment. "You think you can treat people the way you've treated me, Miss Mighty High?" the voice said. "Think again. I'm going to enjoy watching you die."

"Jesus," Dean said.

Becklund clicked off the tape. "That's just a sample. There have been other calls—very ugly. The voice is disguised. It's hard to even know whether it's a man or a woman."

"The caller used a voice changer."

"You're familiar with them?"

"I read a lot of crime novels."

"I was surprised how cheap they are. You can get them off the Internet," Becklund said. "The calls were made from various pay phones, mostly between two and four in the morning. Ms. Yip asked the phone company to begin tracing incoming calls a couple of weeks ago, but we can't trace these." Almost as an afterthought, he asked, "You didn't make them, did you?"

"No. Is that what Caroline thinks?"

"Here's what I never understand. She *should* think that, everything in my experience says so, but she doesn't. She thinks it's this woman, Marcella Ahn. I've talked to her, too, but she claims she's only left a couple of messages to invite Ms. Yip to tea, and to see if she would do a poetry reading with her at the bookstore."

Dean had never really believed it was Marcella Ahn who was leaving the gifts. Maybe a neighbor, or the pimply clerk in the hardware store, or an enamored restaurant customer, but not Marcella. Now he reconsidered. "Maybe it's not all a coincidence," he said. "Maybe it is her." Suddenly, it almost made sense. "I think it might really be her."

"Maybe," Becklund said. "But my money's on you. Unfortunately, I can't get a restraining order issued without Ms. Yip's cooperation. But I can do this. I can tell you that all the things you did before—the presents, the calls, the workplace visits—weren't prosecutable under the anti-stalking laws until you made a physical threat. You crossed a line with the physical threat. Then all those things can be viewed as a crime. Then I can arrest you." He tapped the tabletop with his fingertip. "I suggest you stay away from her."

Dean ignored Becklund. He was frightened for Caroline, and he would do all he could to protect her. The next morning, he waited across the street from the diner for Caroline's shift to finish. When she came outside, he didn't recognize her at first. She had cut off all her hair.

She was walking briskly, carrying a Styrofoam food container, and he had to sprint to catch up to her. "Caroline, please talk to me," he said. "Will you talk to me? Sergeant Becklund told me about the messages."

She stopped but did not turn around. As he stepped in front of her, he saw she was crying. Her hair was shorn to no more than an inch, matted in clumps and tufts, exposing scalp in some places. Evidently she had chopped it off herself in a fit of self-immolation. "Oh, baby," he said, "what have you done?"

She dropped the container, splattering egg salad onto the sidewalk, and collapsed into him. "Do you believe me now?" she asked. "Do you believe it's her?"

"Yes. I do."

"What makes one person want to destroy another?" she asked. "For what? The pettiness, the backstabbing, the meanness—what's the point? Is it fun? She has everything. What more does she want? Why is she doing this to me?"

Dean held her. "I don't know."

"It's such a terrible world, Dean. You can't trust anyone. No matter where you go, there's always someone who wishes you ill will. You think they're your friends, and then they're smearing you, trying to ruin you. I can't take this anymore. Why can't she just go away? Can't you make her go away?"

It was all Dean needed to hear. He took her to his house, put her to bed, and got to work.

It didn't take long to learn her routine. Caroline had been right: Marcella Ahn never left her house until near sunset, when she would go to the Y to attend a cardioboxing class, topped off with half an hour on the StairMaster. She usually didn't shower at the Y but would go straight home in her workout clothes. Around nine or so, she might emerge and drive to the bookstore in town for a magazine and a cappuccino. Once, she went to a movie. Another time, the supermarket at 2 A.M. She had one guest—a male, dressed in a suit, a doctor, according to the hospital parking sticker on his BMW. He spent the night. She didn't go anywhere near Caroline's apartment or make any clandestine calls from pay phones.

Dean didn't try to conceal his stakeouts from Caroline, but he misled her into thinking he wanted to catch Marcella in the act. He had no such expectations. By this time, she had to know that she was—however unlikely—a suspect, that she might be watched. Dean had an entirely different agenda.

One afternoon, he interrupted his surveillance to go to a spy hobbyist shop in San Francisco. He had found it through the Internet on the library computer—Sergeant Becklund had given him the idea. At the store, he bought a lock pick set, $34.95, and a portable voice changer, $29.95. (The clerk also tried to sell him a 200,000-volt stun gun, on sale for $119.95.) Dean paid cash—no credit card records or bank statements to implicate him later.

In the dead of night, he made a call from a pay phone to his own answering machine, imitating the taunts he'd heard in the sheriff's office with the voice changer. "Hey, Jap boyfriend, you're back together with her, are you? Well, fear not, I know where you live." Before leaving the house, he had switched off his telephone's ringer and turned down the volume on the answering machine. He didn't want to scare Caroline, even though she was likely asleep, knocked out by the sleeping pills prescribed by a doctor he'd taken her to see. Still, in the morning, he had no choice but to play the message for her. Otherwise, she wouldn't have called Becklund in a panic, imploring him to arrest Marcella Ahn. "She's insane," Caroline told him. "She's

422

trying to drive me crazy. She's going to try to kill me. You have to do something."

Becklund came to Dean's house, listened to the tape, and appeared to have a change of heart. Dean and Caroline had reconciled. There was no reason to suspect him anymore. Becklund had to look elsewhere. "Keep your doors and windows locked," he told Dean.

After that, the only question was when. It couldn't be too soon, but each day of waiting became more torturous. Finally, the following Wednesday, he could stand it no more. He dropped Caroline off at Da Bones, then nestled in the woods outside Marcella's house. On schedule, she left for the Y at 6 P.M. After a few minutes, he strolled to the door as casually as possible. She lived on a dead end, and she didn't have a neighbor within a quarter mile, but he worried about the unforeseen—the doctor lover, a UPS delivery, Becklund deciding belatedly to serve a restraining order. Wearing latex surgical gloves, Dean inserted a lock pick and tension bar into the keyhole on the front door. The deadbolt opened within twenty seconds. Thankfully she had not installed an alarm system yet. He took off his shoes and walked through the kitchen into the garage. This was the biggest variable in his plan. If he didn't find what he needed there, none of it would work. But to his relief, Marcella Ahn had several cans of motor oil on the shelf, as well as some barbecue lighter fluid—it wasn't gasoline, but it would do. In the recycle bin, there were four empty pinot grigio bottles. In the kitchen, a funnel and a dishrag. He poured one part motor oil and one part lighter fluid into a bottle, a Molotov cocktail recipe provided by the Internet. In the bedroom, he pulled several strands of hair from her brush, pocketed one of her bracelets, and grabbed a pair of platform-heeled boots from her closet. Then he was out, and he sped to his house. All he had to do was press some bootprints in the dirt in front of the lumber shed, but he was running out of time. He drove back to Marcella's, hurriedly washed the soles of the boots in the kitchen sink, careful to leave a little mud, replaced the boots in the closet, checked through the house, and locked up. Then he went to Santa Cruz and tossed the lock pick set and voice changer into a dumpster.

He did nothing more until 3 A.M. By then Caroline was unconscious from the sleeping pills. Dean drove to Marcella Ahn's again. He had to make sure she was home, and alone. He walked around her house, peeking into the windows. She was in her study, sitting at her desk in front of her laptop computer. She had her head in her hands, and she seemed to be quietly weeping. Dean was overcome with misgivings for a moment. He had to remind himself that she was at fault here, that she deserved what was coming to her.

He returned to his own property. Barefoot and wearing only the gloves and his underwear, he snagged the hairs along the doorframe of the lumber shed. He threw the bracelet toward the driveway. He twisted the dishrag into the mouth of the wine bottle, then tilted it from side to side to mix the fluids and soak the rag. He started to flick his lighter, but then hesitated, once more stalled by doubt. Were those mystery novels he read really that accurate? Would the Hair & Fiber and Latent Prints teams be deceived at all? Was he being a fool—a complete amateur who would be ferreted out with ease? He didn't know. All he knew was that he loved Caroline, and he had to take this risk for her. If something wasn't done, he was certain he would lose her. He lit the rag and smashed the bottle against the first stack of zelkova inside the shed. The fire exploded up the boards. He shut the door and ran back into the house and climbed into bed beside Caroline. In a matter of seconds, the smoke detectors went off. The shed was wired to the house, and the alarm in the hallway rang loud enough to wake Caroline. "What's going on?" she asked.

Dean peered out the window. "I think there's a fire," he said. He pulled on his pants and shoes and ran to the shed. When he kicked open the door, the heat blew him back. Flames had already engulfed three *boules* of wood, the smoke was thick and black, the fire was spreading. Something had gone wrong. The sprinkler system— his expensive, state-of-the-art, dry-pipe sprinkler system—had not activated. He had not planned to sacrifice this much wood, one or two stacks at most, and now he was in danger of losing the entire shed.

There was no investigation, per se. Two deputies took photographs and checked for fingerprints, but that was about all. Dean asked Becklund, "Aren't you going to call the crime lab unit?" and Becklund said, "This is it. We're a small town."

It was simple enough for the fire department to determine that it was arson, but not who set it. The insurance claims adjuster was equally lackadaisical. Within a few days, he signed off for Dean to receive a seventy-five-thousand-dollar check. Dean and Caroline had kept the blaze contained with extinguishers and garden hoses for the seventeen minutes it took for the fire trucks to arrive, but nearly half of Dean's wood supply had been consumed, the rest damaged by smoke and water.

No charges were filed against Marcella Ahn. After talking to Becklund and a county assistant district attorney, though, she agreed—on the advice of counsel—to move out of Rosarita Bay, which was hardly a great inconvenience for her, since she owned nine other houses and condos. Caroline never heard from her again, and, as far as they knew, she never published another book—a one-hit wonder.

Caroline, on the other hand, finally submitted her second book to a publisher. Dean was relentless about making her do it. The book was accepted right away, and when it came out, it caused a brief sensation. Great reviews. Awards and fellowships. Dozens of requests for readings and appearances. Caroline couldn't be bothered. By then, she and Dean had had their first baby—a girl, Anna—and Caroline wanted more children, a baker's dozen if possible. She was transformed. No more nightmares, and she could nap standing up (housekeeping remained elusive). In relation to motherhood, to the larger joys and tragedies that befell people, the poetry world suddenly seemed silly, insignificant. She would continue to write, but only, she said, when she had the time and will. Of course, she ended up producing more than ever.

Marcella Ahn's chair was the last Dean made from the pristine zelkova. He would dry and clean up the boards that were salvageable, and when he exhausted that supply, he would switch to English walnut, a nice wood—pretty, durable, available.

He delivered the chair to Marcella just before she left town, on May 11th, as promised. Most of her belongings had already been packed in boxes. He set the chair down in the living room, and she sat in it. "My God," she said, "I didn't know it would be this comfortable. I could sit here all day."

"I'd like to ask you for a favor," Dean said. He held an envelope in his hand.

"A favor?"

"Yes. I'd like you to read Caroline's new poems and tell me if they're good."

"You must be joking. After everything she's done?"

"I don't know poetry. You're the only one who can tell me. I need to know."

"Do you realize I could have been sent to state prison for two years? For a crime I didn't commit?"

"It would've never gone to trial. You would've gotten a plea bargain—a suspended sentence and probation."

"How do you know?" Marcella asked. "Your girlfriend is seriously deranged. I only wanted to be her friend, and she devised this insidious plot to frame me and run me out of town. She's diabolical."

"You stalked her."

"I did no such thing. Don't you get it? She faked it. She set me up. *She* was the stalker. Hasn't that occurred to you? Hasn't that gotten through that thick, dimwitted skull of yours? She burned your *wood.*"

"You're lying. You're very clever, but I don't believe you," Dean said. And he didn't, although she made him think for a second. He pulled out the book manuscript from the envelope. "Are you going to read the poems or not?"

"No."

"Aren't you curious what she's been doing for the past six years?" Dean asked. "Isn't this what you came here to find out?"

She did not respond.

"Haven't you always been afraid that Caroline's the one with the real talent?"

Marcella slowly hooked her hair behind her ears. "Give it to me."

For the next hour, she sat in his chair in the living room, reading the seventy-one pages, and Dean watched her. Her expression was unyielding and contemptuous at first, then it went utterly slack, then taut again. She breathed quickly through her nose, her jaw clamped, her eyes blinked.

"Are they good?" Dean asked when she finished.

She handed the manuscript back to him. "They're pedestrian. They're clunky. There's no music to the language."

"They're good," Dean told her.

"I didn't say that."

"You don't have to. I saw it in your face." He walked to the door and let himself out.

"I didn't say they were good!" Marcella Ahn screamed after him. "Do you hear me? I didn't say that! I didn't say they were good!"

Dean never did ask Caroline about the stalking, although he was tempted at times. One summer afternoon they were outside on his deck—Caroline leaning back in the rocker he'd made for her, her eyes closed to the sun, Anna asleep in her lap. It had rained heavily that spring, and the eucalyptus and pine surrounding the house were

426

now in full leaf. They sat silently and listened to the wind bending through the trees. He had rarely seen her so relaxed.

Anna, still asleep, lolled her head, her lips pecking the air in steady rhythm, dreaming an infant soliloquy.

"Caroline," he said.

"Hm?"

"What do you think she's saying?"

Caroline looked down at Anna. "Your guess is as good as mine," she said. "Maybe she has a secret. Can babies have secrets?" She ran her hand through her hair, which she had kept short, and she smiled at him.

Was it possible that Caroline had fabricated everything about Marcella Ahn? He did not want to know. In turn, she would never question him about the fire. The truth wouldn't have mattered. They had each done what was necessary to be with the other. Such was the price of love among artists; such was the price of devotion.

Nominated by Fred Leebron, Elizabeth Gaffney, E.S. Bumas

MEMOIR

by LOUISE GLÜCK

from THE THREEPENNY REVIEW

I was born cautious, under the sign of Taurus.
My family lived on an island, prosperous,
in the second half of the twentieth century;
the shadow of the Holocaust
hardly touched us.

I had a philosophy of love, a philosophy
of religion, both based on
early experience within a family.

And if when I wrote I used only a few words
it was because time always seemed to me short
as though it could be stripped away
at any moment.

And my story, in any case, wasn't unique
though, like everyone else, I had a story,
a point of view.

A few words were all I needed:
nourish, sustain, attack.

Nominated by The Threepenny Review

SEVEN TYPES OF AMBIGUITY

fiction by DAN CHAON

from TRIQUARTERLY

Age 49:
This is a braid of human hair. The braid is about two feet long, and almost two inches wide at the base. It seems heavy, like old rope, but is not brittle or rough. Someone has secured each end with a rubber band, so the braid itself is still tight—the simplest braid, which any child can do, three individual strands twined together, A over B, C over B and A, etc. It smells of powder. There is a certain violety scent which over the years has begun to reek more and more of dust. The color of the hair is like dry corn husks. At first, Colleen thought it was gray.

But it must have been blonde, she now thinks. There was a newspaper clipping among the effects in her father's strongbox, concerning the death of a girl who would have been Colleen's aunt: her father's older sister, though he'd never mentioned her, that she could remember. The clipping, which is dated October 9, 1918, is a little less than an eighth of a column. "Death came to the home of Julius Carroll and wife Sunday evening and claimed their daughter, Sadie, aged eleven years, who had been ill with typhoid fever for two weeks. All that loving and willing hands could do did not save the child." The article goes on to describe the funeral, and to offer condolences. Perhaps erroneously, Colleen has come to believe that the braid belonged to that long-ago girl. There is no one to ask, no one alive who can confirm anything. She found it curled in the bottom of a trunk along with some of Colleen's grandfather's papers. The braid wasn't labeled. It seems to have been removed rather abruptly, or at least uncarefully. The edges at the thickest end of the braid are ragged and uneven, as if it has been sawed off by a dull blade.

It reminds her of a conversation she'd had with her father years ago. She'd been very interested in genealogy at the time, and had sent him a number of charts, which he'd dutifully filled out to the best of his ability, but he'd really wanted no part of it. When she'd asked to interview him about his memories of their family, he'd balked. "I don't remember anything," he'd said. "Why do you want to know about this garbage, anyway? Let the dead rot in peace," he said. "They can't help you." She'd made some comment then, quoting something she'd read: Genetics is destiny, she told him. Don't you ever wonder where the cells of your body came from? she asked.

"Genetics!" her father said. "What's the point of it? All that DNA stuff is just chemicals! It doesn't have anything to do with what's real about a person." Anyway, he said, a cell is nothing. Cells trickle off our body all the time, and every seven years we've grown a new skin altogether. The whole thing, he said, was overrated.

Nevertheless, for years now she has carried the braid with her. She keeps it in an airtight plastic bag, in a zippered compartment of her suitcase. No one else knows that she carries it with her, and most of the time she herself forgets that it is there. She cannot recall when, exactly, the braid began to travel with her, but it has become a kind of talisman, not necessarily good luck, but comforting. Occasionally, she will take it out of its bag and run it through her hands, like a rosary. The braid has traveled all over the world, from Washington D.C. to the great capitals of Europe, from Mali to Peru. She supposes that this is ironic.

For the last ten years, she has worked for an international charitable organization which gives grants to individuals who, in the words of the foundation's mission statement, "have devoted themselves selflessly to the betterment of the human race." For years, she has anonymously observed candidates for the grants, and written reports on them. Her reports are passed on to a committee which divides its endowed moneys among the deserving. It is a great job, but it leaves her lonely. She is divorced, and she rarely speaks to her grown son. Most of the relatives that she remembers from her youth died a long time ago. There are a number of regrets.

430

*

Age 42:

She is in a motel room in Mexico City when her son, Luke, calls. "Mommy?" he says, in a voice that is drunk or drugged. He is twenty years old, telephoning from San Diego, where he had been a student before he dropped out. The last that Colleen had heard, he was working as a gardener for a lady gynecologist from Israel and living in a converted greenhouse out behind the woman's house.

"She's really weird," her son says now, trying to carry on a normal conversation through his haze. "Like, when I'm clipping the hedges or something, sometimes she lies out on a lawn chair, totally naked. I mean, I'm no prude, but you'd think she could wait until I was done. It's not a pretty sight, either. I mean, my God, Mom, she's older than you. I'm starting to wonder if she's trying to come on to me."

He is drunk, Colleen thinks. What sober person would talk about this kind of thing with his mother? But the comment about her age sinks in, and she hears her voice grow stiff: "It must be really grotesque, if she's older than me," Colleen says.

"Oh, Mom!" Luke says. Yes: there is the petulant slur in his voice, a wetness, as if his mouth is pressed too close to the phone. "You know what I mean." And then, as is Luke's habit when he is intoxicated, his voice strains with sentiment. "Momma, when I was little, I thought you were the most beautiful woman in the world. I just idolized you. You remember that blue dress you had? With the gold threads woven in? And those blue high heels? I thought that you looked like a movie star." Any minute now, Colleen thinks, he will start bawling, and it disturbs her that she can't muster much compassion. He has used it up, expended it on the histrionics of his teenage years, on the many, many ways he has found to need "help" since going off to college. He has already been treated once for chemical dependency.

"Oh Mommy," Luke says. "I'm so screwed up. I'm so lost." He takes in a wet breath. "I really am."

"No you're not, Honey," Colleen says. She clears her throat. He is still a kid, she thinks, a child yearning for his mother, who has been cold. But what else can she say? They have had these conversations before, and Colleen has learned that it is best to simply pacify him. "You'll find your way," Colleen says, soothingly. "You've got to just keep plugging away at it. Don't give in." Of course, Colleen thinks, the truth is that Luke is clearly wasting his life. But he'd never listened to any advice when he was sober, and to say anything when he was drunk would only lead to an argument. She considers asking Luke if he is on anything. But she knows that he will deny it—deny it until he is desperate. What could Colleen do for him at such a distance, anyway? "Are you all right, baby?" Colleen whispers. "Is everything okay?"

Luke is silent for a long time, trying to regain his composure. "Oh," he says. And his voice quavers. "Yes—I'm fine, I'm fine. I'm not doing drugs, if that's what you're thinking."

"I'm not thinking anything. You just sound—"

"What?"

"Sad."

"Oh." He thinks about this. Then, as if to contradict Colleen, his voice brightens. "Well," he says, "How are things going for you? Anything exciting happening?"

"No," Colleen says. "The usual." He is her son, and she has failed him.

"How's grandpa?" Luke says. "Is he still holding up?"

"He's okay," Colleen says. She pulls the shade, shutting out the lights of Mexico City. There is nothing special about this place, nothing particularly outstanding about the candidate she is observing, a man who runs a free AIDS clinic for street people, but who is not nearly selfless enough to be awarded money by her firm. Does Luke realize how endless the world's supply of sorrow and hard luck stories is? Does he ever think that even if he were a saint, he might not be worthy of notice among a planet of billions? She is so tired. She can't believe how far away she is, how distant from the people that she should love.

Age 35:

"Why does everyone have to be so smart-alecky," her father says, and throws his tennis shoe at her TV screen. "That was a steaming pile of crap."

He has been drinking a lot since he came to her house, sitting alone in her guest room—the only place he is allowed to smoke— sipping at a never-empty tumbler of Jack Daniels. She has seen him drunk before, but he has never been this belligerent, this temper-prone.

"That didn't even make any sense," he says. He is referring to the video they just watched together, which she'd loved, and which she'd thought he would like too. "Why can't they just tell a good story any-more," he says sullenly. She can't believe that he actually threw his shoe at her television.

"Dad," she says. "You can't just throw things! This is my home!"

"Jesus H. Christ," he says, and stalks out of the room.

He has been staying with her for almost a month. She hadn't known he was coming: he just pulled into the driveway one morning. He'd been trying to get ahold of her for over a week, he said, and Colleen had frowned. "How did you try to get ahold of me," she wondered. "Smoke signals? Telepathy?"

"Well," her father said. "Your damn phone's always busy. How many boyfriends do you have, babygirl?" He tried to smile, tried to ease things a bit by evoking this old pet name from her child-hood. But he knew that things were not as simple as that. The last time he'd stayed with her, they'd fought constantly; he'd left one night after an argument and hadn't called her for almost two months.

The argument had been about her son, Luke. Her father thought she was spoiling him; she said that she didn't dare to leave Luke alone with him because he drank so much. Each had hurt the other's feelings, which was how it often was. Neither one could bear the other's disapproval.

After a time, she goes to his room. He is sitting on the bed, smoking, and he looks at her balefully as he lifts his tumbler to his mouth. He has taken off his toupee and it lies beside him on the bed, like a fur cap. She could have never imagined him wearing a hairpiece; he has always been embarrassed and scornful of male vanity, but she sees that he is right to wear it. He is completely bald, except for a few fine tufts wisping here and there over his pinkish scalp, like the head of a four-month-old baby. Without the toupee, he looks awful—frighten-ing, even.

He is going to live a while longer. The cancer, much to the doctor's surprise, is gone. It is not merely in remission; as far as they can tell, it has completely left his body. Sometimes, he seems aware that something miraculous, or at least vaguely supernatural, has hap-pened to him. But not often—more frequently, he seems frazzled, even haunted by his good fortune, and he turns even more fiercely toward his old habits.

"I brought your shoe," she says. He looks at her, then down.

"I'm sorry I didn't like your program," he says. "I guess I didn't understand it."

"Well," she says. "You've never been one for ambiguity."

He frowns. He knows these "two-dollar words," as he calls them—he has done crossword puzzles all his life—but he disapproves of people actually using them. He thinks it's showing off.

"*Ambiguity*," he says. "Is that what you call it?"

"Dad," she says, quietly. "What's wrong with you? You never used to . . . go off on little things like that. It's not good."

He shrugs. "I guess I'm just getting old. Old and cranky." His hands shake as he puts the nub of a Raleigh cigarette to his lips, and she thinks of how badly she needs him to be normal and happy, to be an ordinary father. *Don't be this*, she thinks urgently. She is a divorced woman with a thirteen-year-old son, and she works forty hours a week as an administrator at a charity organization, where all she thinks about is helping people, helping, helping, helping. She does not want him to need her, not right now. But she can see that he does. His eyes rest on her, gauging, hopeful.

"I don't have anywhere to go, Colleen," he says. "I don't know what to do with myself. I'm sixty-two years old, and I'm damn tired of working construction."

"Well," she said. "You know that you can stay here . . ." But she hesitates, because she knows it's not true. He can't stay here if he's going to drink and smoke like this. He knows this, and his eyes deepen as he looks at her. She doesn't love him as much as he'd hoped—she sees this in his eyes, sees him think it, struggling for a moment. Then he lifts his tumbler and tastes his drink again.

"That's all right," he says.

Age 28:

From time to time, she loses her temper. Like this one time, he pushes her, for no reason, teeth gritted: "Leave me alone!" he says, and that gets to her. Oh, I'll leave you alone, she thinks. See what it's like, see how you like to be alone.

She knows it is wrong, even as she presses her back to the bark of the tree that conceals her. It is a bad thing, but her anger buoys her, makes her breathing tight and slow. She isn't hurting him, she thinks. She is teaching him a lesson.

It takes him a while to realize that she is gone. It is a warm day in early summer, a little breezy. From her hiding place, she can see the wobbly reflection of the sun and clouds floating in Luke's inflatable swimming pool. Luke plays without noticing for some time. Then, as if he's heard a sound, he stands straight and alert. "Mom," he says. He scopes the yard and the roads and the pasture beyond. They live a few miles outside of the small college town where she is studying for her Master's degree; the nearest neighbor is a mile away. "Mom?" He says again, but she doesn't move. An army man drops from his hand into the grass, near where the hose makes a sinewy, snake-like curve through the lawn. "Mommy?" he says, more anxiously. Her heart beats, quick and light, as she presses herself into the shadows. She has the distinct, constricting pleasure of having disappeared—a pleasure that, since her divorce, has occupied her fantasies with odd frequency: to leave this life! To vanish and be free!

And, more than that, as he begins to panic—there is a kind of tingly relief. For what if he hadn't noticed that she was gone? What then?

She lets it go on too long, she knows. He is almost hysterical, and it takes a long time to get him calmed down—rocking him, his face hot against her shoulder, whispering: "What's wrong? It's okay. Don't cry!" A kind of warm glow spreads through her. "I thought you wanted Mommy to go away," she whispers—Horrible! Horrible!— she can sense that it is wrong but she keeps on, running her hand through his hair, long-nailed, thin fingers: vampire fingers. "I thought you wanted Mommy to go away," she murmurs. "Isn't that what you said?" And then she begins to weep herself, with shame and fear.

Age 21:
She is just out of college, staying at her father's house for a week or so, when the tornado hits. It is the most extraordinary thing that has ever happened to her. Parts of the roof are whisked away. The windows implode, scattering shards of glass across the carpets, the beds, into the bathtub. Apparently, there had been a beehive in the upper rafters, because dark lines of honey have run down the kitchen walls.

Colleen and her father have been hidden in the cellar, among rows and rows of dusty jars: beets and green beans and apple sauce that Colleen's mother had canned, or that her grandmother had canned, when her father was a boy. Some of the jars go as far back as 1940, their labels written in a faded, arthritic cursive. Her father has been planning to get rid of this stuff for as long as Colleen has been alive. She had been warned, as a child, never to open anything from the cellar. Her mother had heard of poisonous gas coming out of ancient, sealed containers.

She recalls this, sitting on the cool earthen floor that reminds her of childhood. As the storm roars overhead, she and her father huddle close together.

When they come up to see the world, after the howling has stopped, it is raining. There are no trees standing as far as they can see, only the flat prairie and branches and stumps everywhere, as if each tree had burst apart—as if, Colleen thinks poetically, there were some terrible force inside them that they finally could not contain.

"Jesus H. Christ," her father keeps saying. He goes to the door of the house, and Colleen follows after him. The rain is falling into the kitchen, dripping off scraps of insulation that hang down like kudzu. Her father touches the kitchen wall and puts his finger to his mouth. "Honey!" he says, and laughs. The room is full of the smell of honey, and the sound of water. She doesn't know what to say. It is the house that both she and her father grew up in, and it is destroyed.

Her father finds his bottle of Jack Daniels under the kitchen sink; he finds ice, still hard, in the refrigerator's freezer; and he pours them each a drink.

"At least the liquor's okay," Colleen's father says. "There's one blessing we can count."

Colleen smiles nervously, but accepts the drink that's offered to her. She had thought that this would be a rest period in her life—that it would be the last time she really lived at home, and that there would be a number of conversations with her father that would bring closure to this stage of her life. She had been a psychology major, and is very fond of closure. She likes to think of her life in segments, each one organized, analyzed, labeled, stowed away for later reflection: Another stage along her personal journey. Nevertheless, a tornado seems a melodramatic way to end things. She would have preferred some small, epiphanic moment.

Her father settles into the kitchen chair beside her, leaning back. The sky is beginning to clear; cicadas buzz from the dark boughs strewn about the lawn. Through the hole in the roof, they can see a piece of the evening sky. The constellations are beginning to fade into view.

"Well," her father says. He puts his palm on top of her hand, then removes it. He sighs.

"Now what?"

Age 14:
"Here's babygirl, with her nose in a book!" Colleen's father crows. "As usual!"

She is stretched out on her bed and looks up sternly, closing the book quickly over her index finger, hoping maybe that he will let her alone. But it is not likely. He is standing in the doorway, in a clown-ish, eager mood. He does a weird little dance, hoping to amuse her, and she is terribly embarrassed of him. Still, kindly, she smiles.

"What good is sitting alone in your room," he sings, and capers around. She leans her cheek against her hand, watching him.

"Dad," she says. "Settle down." She takes a tone with him as if he is a little boy, which has become their mode, the roles they act out for one another. Her mother has been dead for a little over a year, and this is how things go. They have accepted that she is smarter than he, more capable. They have accepted that things must some-how continue on, and that she will leave him soon. He says that she is destined for great things. She will go on to college, and become educated; she will travel all over the world, as he himself wanted to; she will follow her dreams. They don't talk about it, but she can see it—in the morning, as he sits hunched over his crossword puzzle, sip-ping coffee; after dinner, as he sits, watching the news, rubbing salve onto his feet, which are pale and delicate, the toes beginning to curve into the shape of his work boot. She can feel the weight of it as he stands in her doorway, looking in, trying to get her attention. He dances for a moment, and then he stands there, arms loose at his sides, waiting.

"Do you want to go out to Dairy Queen and get a sundae," he says, and she looks regretfully down at her book, where the hobbit Frodo is perhaps dead, in the tower of Cirith Ungol.

"Okay," she says.

She is a pretty girl. Older boys have asked her out on dates, Juniors and Seniors, though she is just a Freshman, and she is flattered, she takes note, though she always turns them down. Her hair is long, the color of wheat, and her father likes to touch it, to run the tips of his fingers over it, very lightly. These days, he only touches her hair very rarely, such as when she's sitting beside him in the pick-up and he stretches his arm across the length of the seat. His hand brushes the back of her head, as if casually. He believes that she is too old to have her father touch her hair. He will only kiss her on her cheek.

Their little house is just beyond the outskirts of town, and as they drive through the dark toward Dairy Queen, she wonders if she will ever not be lonely. Perhaps, she thinks, being lonely is a part of her, like the color of her eyes and skin, something in her genes.

Her father begins humming as he drives. The dashboard light makes his face eerie and craggy with shadows, and his humming seems to come from nowhere: some old, terribly sad song—Hank Williams, Jim Reeves, something that almost scares her.

Age 7:
On Saturday after supper, Colleen's father asks her if she'd like to go on over and see his place of employment. He tilts his head back, draining his beer. He smiles as he does this, and it makes him look sly and proud. "It's a nice night," he says. "What do you say, babygirl?" He seems not to notice as Colleen's mother reaches between his forearms to take his plate. He is not inviting *her*.

Colleen is not sure what is going on between them. It is an old story, though, extending back in time to things that happened before Colleen was born—things Colleen's mother should have gotten, things she is still owed. Every once in a while, it begins to build up. Colleen can feel the heat in her mother's silences.

But her father doesn't appear to notice. He gives Colleen's hair a playful tug, and makes a face at her. "I'm only taking you, babygirl, because you're my favorite daughter."

Colleen, who is sensitive about being teased, says: "I'm your only daughter."

"You're right," her father says. "But you know what? Even if I had a hundred daughters, you'd still be my favorite."

Colleen's mother looks at him grimly. "Don't keep her up too late," she says.

Colleen's father works for the Department of Roads, and he drives her out to a place where a new highway is being built. The road is lined with stacks of materials, some of them almost as tall as houses; and with heavy machinery, which looks sinister and hulking in the dusk. Her father stops his pick-up near one of these machines, a steamroller, which she has seen before only in cartoons. He wants to show her something, he says.

Just at the edge of the place where the road stops, they are building a bridge. The bridge will span a creek, a tiny trickle of water where she and her father occasionally come to fish. Every few years or so, the creek has been known to flood, and so it has been decided that the bridge will be built high above it. The bridge, her father says, will be sixty feet off the ground.

The skeleton of the bridge is already in place. She can see it as they walk toward the slope that leads down to the creek. Girders and support beams of steel and cement stretch over the valley that her father tells her was made by the creek—over hundreds of years, the flowing water had worn this big groove into the earth. They have cleared earth where buffalo and Indians used to roam, he says, and then he sings: "Home, Home on the Range."

She is only vaguely interested in this until they come to the edge of the bridge. It *is* high in the air, and she balks when her father begins to walk across one of the girders. He stretches his arms out for balance, putting his one foot carefully in front of the other, heel to toe, like a tightrope walker. He turns to look over his shoulder at her, grinning. He points down. "There's a net!" he calls. "Just like at the circus!"

And then, without warning, he spreads his arms wide and falls. She does not scream, but something like air, only harder, rises in her throat for a moment. Her father's body tilts through the air, pitching heavily, though his arms are spread out like wings. When he hits the net, he bounces, like someone on a trampoline. "Boing!" he cries, and then he sits up.

"Damn!" he calls up to her. "I've always wanted to do that! That was fun!" She watches as he crawls, spider-like, across the thick ropes of net, up toward where she is standing, waiting for him. The moon is bright enough that she can see.

"Do you want to try it?" her father says, and she hangs back, until he puts his hand to her cheek. He strokes her hair, and their eyes meet. "Don't be afraid, babygirl," he says. "I won't let anything bad happen to you. You know that. Nothing bad will ever happen to babygirl."

"I know," she says. And after a moment, she follows him out onto the beam above the net, cautiously at first, then more firmly. For she does want to try it. She wants to fly like that, her long hair floating in

439

the air like a mermaid's. She wants to hit the net and bounce up, her stomach full of butterflies.

"You're not afraid, are you?" her father says. "Because if you're afraid, you don't have to do it."

"No," she says. "I want to."

Her father smiles at her. She does not understand the look in his eyes, when he clasps her hand. She doesn't think she will ever understand it, though for years and years she will dream of it, though it might be the last thing she sees before she dies.

"This is something you're never going to forget, babygirl," he says. And then they plunge backward into the air.

Nominated by Martha Collins, Joyce Carol Oates, TriQuarterly

I AM MRS. LORCA

by RAFAEL CAMPO

from PARTISAN REVIEW

—for Kim Vaeth and John Vincent

Dark love is all I've ever known; the dance
is nearly over, but I think the world
will not allow another end. The lights

burn bright, and I am married to romance,
his eyes betraying secrets that his words
conceal. He never speaks to me at night,

our bed as arid as the flat interior
of Spain. I love him just the same, the way
he combs his hair straight back, his hands

so womanly in shape. I'd be his whore,
but I am not as young as this new day,
this century we dance around;

I'd be his son, but I am not as sad
as dying is, as any son of his
inherits only death's queer finery;

right now, instead, I'm only going mad,
the dance and any meaning that it has
dissolving to the perfect thing he sees.

Nominated by Marilyn Hacker, Partisan Review

BEETHOVEN, MONET, TECHNOLOGY AND US

essay by BURTON RAFFEL

from PALO ALTO REVIEW

CONSTRUCTING A WORK OF GENIUS, like any other building proj-
ect, necessarily involves issues of depth, width, and height. Good
friends gave me a small desk calendar last Christmas. Printed in Ger-
many, with captions in three languages, it has a tear-away page for
each of the year's three hundred and sixty-five days, every single
sheet festooned with a gorgeously rendered reproduction of a Monet
canvas. These reproductions are no more than three and a half by
two and a half inches—distinctly miniature, yet incredibly sharp and
true. The paintings of lilies and ponds are all there, of course. But
there is also an enormous, overwhelming display of dazzlingly in-
tense work totally unfamiliar—paintings not so much obscure as sim-
ply never before seen. And as one turns the pages, day after day, it
becomes startlingly obvious that Monet's range of treatment and con-
cept, of subject and visual attack, is immensely greater than, on the
basis of what we are able to know, anything that could ever have
been dreamed. Even the very early work, though stylistically not fully
formed, shows a fascinating depth of emotion and understanding.

I am looking, as I write, at a likeness of *Eglise de Varengeville, temps
gris*, painted in 1882, an "oil on canvas, 65 x 81 cm." This is an
epochally stunning exploration of mist-transformed daylight, sur-
rounding a mountain, the church in the distance, at the top left, and
two small trees, bottom right. I would dearly love to see it, as it were,

443

in the flesh. But it can be viewed only at the J.B. Speed Art Museum, Louisville, Kentucky. I have been many places, in my long life. Alas, Louisville, Kentucky is not one of them—but, for the sake of this canvas, Louisville may have to become the site of a future visit.

And from the slow, steady parade of experiment and achievement, as one after another the glorious paintings emerge, the genius ("height") of Monet cannot help but rise triumphantly. Far from the flower-drunk colorist he may sometimes seem, on the relatively slender evidence most of us have been offered, Monet is revealed as a hunter after virtually every variety of visual experience he can find. Nor does he wait until experience somehow manages to locate him. Plainly, he scoured the face of the civilized earth as he knew it— France, England, Italy, Holland, Belgium, Denmark—passionately haunting cathedrals, train stations, rivers, mountains, cities, fields, houses and forests, the omnipotent sun and changing sky, confronting and wrestling with the images so freely presented to him by his (and our) world. His is the never-ending urgency of a driven sensibility and alert intelligence which description might readily serve as a definition of the compulsions that underlie genius.

Years after, reflecting bitterly on the whirling, cataclysmic study he had made in 1879 of his wife, Camille, on her deathbed, Monet clearly frames his art as a sort of bondage, labeling it perverse and unnatural that, instead of mourning, he was forced to paint. This is no Frederic Chopin, brilliant but narrowly engaged "poet of the piano." This is Ludwig van Beethoven, stamping and roaring as he struggles, almost maniacally, to beat the *Missa Solemnis* into functional submission. The Viennese poet and playwright, Franz Grillparzer described the process in an oration at Beethoven's funeral, 29 March 1827:

> As Beethoven rushes, tempestuous, over the oceans, so he flew over the frontiers of his art. From the cooing of doves to the rolling of thunder, from the most subtle interweaving of the self-determined media of his art to the awe-inspiring point where the consciously formed merges in the lawless violence of the striving forces of Nature, all these he exhausted, all these he took in his stride.

Such vast new exposure to art has been made available through the not-quite-natural means of mechanical reproduction. That is, these

444

are not Monet's paintings, either in actual fact or, certainly, in size. I can see my small calendar's parade of Monet strictly on the printed page, not in their true, unique splendor, triumphantly displayed as we are accustomed to viewing great canvases, for the most part hanging on the walls of museums. Each Monet painting, and especially those I have never seen before, in real life or in reproduction, comes to me only in tiny rectangles. But even thus compressed, these superbly manufactured simulacra are profoundly accurate in their color registration: I have seen enough of Monet, in more usual forms, to recognize scrupulously faithful reproductions.

In a sense, then, one does not need the "true" experience of Monet to kindle new levels of admiration and understanding. And mechanical reproduction can become the vehicle for new and miraculously extended appreciation virtually straight across the spectrum of art, a new appreciation that is often, in sometimes profound ways, quite unlike the traditional variety.

Mechanical reproduction allows us to hear Beethoven, for example, as we see Monet, in new dimensions of genius—and once again these dimensions are not necessarily available when the music is experienced in traditional performance. Nor are these new possibilities limited to large-ensemble pieces, requiring dozens of musicians, sometimes vocalists, sometimes a chorus, and in our time both a well-trained *chef d'orchestre* (or *regisseur*, German *Dirigent*, Italian *direttore*) and significant amounts of pre-performance rehearsal time. Small ensembles, such as violin and piano duos, piano soloists, are in fact almost equally subject to the same limitations: musicians of more or less professional caliber cannot be summoned by a magic wand, even when not congregated in full-sized orchestras of much less than a hundred strong. How often do we have the opportunity to hear, say, the magnificent string quartets of Beethoven, or any one of his string quartets, performed seriatim by two, or three, or four different ensembles? But any reasonably determined home listener can do exactly that, simply by plucking the music in recorded form, right off the shelves.

And the experience, though neither natural nor, before the twentieth century ever available to human ears, can indeed be incredibly rewarding. We tend to think of the six quartets of Beethoven's Opus 18, numbered 1 through 6 (though probably not composed in exactly that order), as essentially apprentice work. It is the three

Rasamovskys of Opus 59 which have come to mark the great Beethoven for us, and the late quartets which magnificently cap that achievement. These judgments have their reasons and their merits. I have been saying exactly such things for years, myself, and it is only now, after suddenly deciding to listen to the Quartet in F Major, Opus 18 #1, as recorded by four premier ensembles—the Budapest, Guarneri, Fine Arts, and Hungarian quartets, mine being entirely an LP library—that I have had my eyes opened. Or, strictly speaking, my ears.

The experience has been much like a very particular listening transformation I experienced more than fifty years ago, at the intermission of a Beethoven cycle given by the Budapest Quartet. The site was New York City's Town Hall, a small, relatively intimate hall of warm acoustical timbre. A well-dressed man of forty or so suddenly appeared in the back rows of the balcony, where I was sitting, along with other young men and women, most of them, like me, university students. "Anybody want to sit in the front row downstairs, for the second half of the concert?" he asked cheerfully. I think we were all stunned—but I not only put up my hand, about as fast as I could, I also nodded and said, loudly, "Yes!" Smiling, he handed me his ticket stub, and I gave him mine. "I just want to see what it sounds like, from up here," he explained, dropping into what had been my seat. All I can recall saying in return is "Thanks," because I wanted to know how it sounded down there.

Sitting in the front row, dead center, was a brand new and a strange sensation, as I had thought it might be. Instead of my not-very-elaborately-dressed friends, there were older and visibly more prosperous concert-goers, every one of them a stranger to me. But once the musicians came back on stage and began to play, the people around me no longer mattered, for the quality of sound, the immediacy and soul-drenching intensity of the music, was incredible. "It felt," I explained to my balcony-confined friends, afterwards, "almost as if I was sitting at Mischa Schneider [the Budapest's cellist]'s feet." No recital, no recording, nothing had ever so washed me in such rich, swirling layer upon layer of music-making.

I apprenticed myself to this music and vividly remember having borrowed and then played over and over a Budapest recording of Beethoven's *15th Quartet*. It came, in those days, as five fragile

78 rpm records of the 12-inch size, which I carefully lifted on and off my turntable, tracking through the quartet something like seventy times or more, bit by bit struggling to at least partially disentangle Beethoven's profoundly radical, monumentally drawn-out intricacies, especially those of the long, somber central movement, the quartet having five in all. That movement, which I had recognized as the fulcrum around which the entire quartet was levered, had for a long while completely defeated me; I could not follow where, surely, Beethoven was trying to lead. Slowly, very slowly, I developed at least a modicum of the necessary capacity.

To this day, I do not think I am capable, or ever will be capable, of fully grasping what Beethoven is up to, in the *15th Quartet*'s third movement. And that same *15th Quartet*, with that same tremendous, *molto adagio* central meditation, that same wrenching, stupendous dialogue with the Almighty, was—God be praised!—what the Budapest were playing, that night, as the second half of their concert. I sat just beneath them, in the front row of Town Hall, close enough to have reached out and touched them, had I dared, as the true believer I was. The experience was rhapsodic, heavenly, utterly exalting. It seemed to go on for hours and hours, a long quartet—but no music on earth is truly as never-ending as the 15th seemed to me, that night.

And so back to the much earlier and nowhere near so highly regarded *F Major Quartet #1*, in multiple recorded incarnations. The first performance I played was a Budapest recording—"the classic 1951 recording," proclaims the album cover. It is predictably vibrant, the sound rich and complexly clear (despite what may seem, these days, like a quasi-medieval recording date), the instruments not only warm and live but at suitable times wonderfully lush. And as should be almost immediately apparent, listening to this music on its own terms, the quartet fully deserves so dedicated a rendering.

Beethoven was roughly twenty-nine when, in 1799, he composed the *F Major Quartet*. He was emphatically not a tyro, groping and stumbling after his unknown way. Without even mentioning all the earlier work he did not publish in his lifetime, much of it of extraordinary quality, Beethoven had already completed the first two sonatas for cello and piano, the first three sonatas for violin and piano, the sonata for French horn and piano, a string quintet, a trio for clarinet, cello, and piano, three trios for violin, cello, and piano, one or perhaps two piano concerti, and the first ten piano sonatas. The piano concerti have complex orchestral scoring, the first symphony, finished and first played in 1800 as op. 21, was quite directly on the horizon.

What the Budapest performance brings out, indeed, is that, while Beethoven knows exactly what all of the instruments can and should be doing, there is an unprecedentedly intricate, almost orchestral voicing to these four string parts. On every level, from scoring to harmony, from rhythm to chromatic modulations, Beethoven's technical mastery is complete. Even though what he expresses is not in many ways what he puts into his music later on, he phrases every note richly, with passion, wit, and charm. Were this pop music, one might well say that it swings. But not only is this serious music, it is also fundamentally new, and inherently path-breaking. In an essay on "Music, Poetry, and Translation," thirty-five years ago, I commented on "a thoroughly third-rate piano concerto by John Ireland, a British composer":

> Parts of the slow, middle movement could have been written by Shostakovitch; whole sections of the allegro third movement were obviously derived from Darius Milhaud (the bright strings and deft woodwinds) and, alternately, from Prokofiev (the bouncy abruptness of the solo piano part). There were incidental quotations from Jean Francaix and from Hindemith and Honegger; Ravel had a hand in shaping the composer's approach, and I suspect Debussy did too (*The Forked Tongue*, pp. 154–55).

No one could say things of this sort about Beethoven's Opus 18—but, on the other hand, it is starkly obvious how much other composers, over the next half century and more, learned from precisely this as well as the later Beethoven.

What the multiple performances of the *F Major Quartet* show perhaps most abundantly is how, by this relatively early point in his career, Beethoven was already busily enlarging, and deeply influencing, music itself. *Everyone* studied at Beethoven's knees; in the Budapest performance we cannot help but hear what other musicians heard, and from which they proceeded to borrow, and borrow, and borrow. There probably is no such thing as a perfect rendering of any musical score, but if that is a possibility, the Budapest has I think achieved it. Remember, please, that my approach to quartets generally, and Beethoven quartets in particular, was over many years shaped primarily by this same ensemble, both in concert and on recordings.

But if, to my mind at least, the Budapest's playing of the quartet exhibits Beethoven's massive influence in virtually universal terms (again, no one could and no one did escape), the other recorded performances to which I listened are more focused, as it were, to the left and to the right of Beethoven. The Guarneri—a younger and more Americanized ensemble—performs with a lighter, perhaps more whimsical touch. As played by the Guarneri, there are upper-register fillips in the violin, for example, which are plainly the egg, or some large part of it, out of which the fantastic cadences of Hector Berlioz were born. And the often more playful sides of Franz Schubert are audible, too, as are some of the dashing surges of Chopin's melodies. The Guarneri articulates Beethoven's music beautifully, glowingly, always respectfully, but a touch more freely (in the faintly pejorative sense the word sometimes has) than does the Budapest. One could do a lot worse than have this as the only version of op. 18 in one's collection.

The Hungarian Quartet offers a more problematic version. The group is composed of performers even older and certainly more Europe-centered than the Russian-Jewish emigrants who became, though they did not found, the Budapest. Here is the Beethoven Brahms revered. But not only Brahms: Rheinberger and Raff, Reinicke and Farrenc, Volkmann and Draeseke, Hiller and Rietz and many, many more, all of whom have perished, drowned by time, having tried to walk in the tracks left by Beethoven's gigantic footsteps. This is Respectable Beethoven, Correct Beethoven, Punctilious Beethoven—not academic and lifeless, not unworthy, even magnificent in its way, but not capable of sustaining and inspiring, not offering a welling of inspiration, pure and undefiled. I enjoy Reinicke's proper Victorian melancholy; I appreciate the sonorous proprieties of Rheinberger. But I listen to them only at intervals, and only when I want the smallish flavors they are able to add to the larger brew. Deep draughts are simply not available from vessels like these. But Johannes Brahms, though palpably intimidated by Beethoven, had enough inner strength to learn from his Master and then to move on. Imitation which remains no more than imitation has become not flattery, but slavery.

449

In all fairness, the Hungarian Quartet's approach is not stolid so much as faintly predictable, touched perhaps with too much obeisance, and even with an unhealthy dash of self-importance. From this view of Beethoven, which is neither untenable nor uncommon, one comes not only to Wagner (who in all of musical history was ever more self-important?), but also to Schönberg, and to Bartok, and in turn to their progeny.

The Fine Arts Quartet, the youngest and most American of the four to which I listened, is only subtly unlike its model, which seems to me plainly the Budapest—and no wonder, for in its prime the Budapest towered above all string ensembles on the American musical scene. The Fine Arts is good, very good. They have thought and felt their way to a first-rate synthesis, entirely true to Beethoven. But at crucial moments, they are not the executants the Budapest were. I am never bored (as, truthfully, I can become, listening to the Hungarian), the music flows. But it does not always excite, it does not continuously captivate. And from this very good but, alas, not great performance we learn, if we did not already know, that only genius can authentically replicate genius. Only that which is inexhaustibly new can forever endure. Whoever brings us a Beethoven in any way worn, to any degree threadbare, has brought us a false Beethoven, for the true Beethoven can never be emptied into any container.

Yet what of those most universal of all mechanical reproductions of art, namely, the printed and bound products we call books? There can be no doubt either that they are or can be genuine treasures, that we have cherished them longer and far more variously, as well as far more deeply, than the relatively new phenomena I have been discussing. Even in the days of the classic Greeks and Romans, almost three millennia ago, long before the invention of movable typefaces and of the printing press, humans relished and drew deep strength and pleasure and comfort from books. Still, the wealthiest of Greeks, and even the wealthiest of the far wealthier Romans, could not have possessed and housed, as I myself do, something like fifteen thousand volumes. I keep roughly five thousand of these in a room known as The Library; the rest are shelved, all arranged in my own ordering, in literally every room of my home. Nor in all of recorded history did humans enjoy either the range or the variety of books in which we can revel.

We think less exclusively than we did, not too many years back, of knowledge, learning, and entertainment as essentially book-derived. But to the films, the videos, the tapes and discs and all the rest has now been added perhaps the most potent threat ever to be mounted against the hegemony of the book, namely, all the devices and capabilities linked in one way or another to the computer—which include telephones, fax and copy machines, scanners, CD-ROM players, and more. The facts are that the book has not always been with us, any more than writing itself has, and that new technologies always have and always will constantly change our sources of verbal information, instruction, and entertainment.

"Who in all the world reads an American book?" that infamous British taunt, will predictably become, at some point we cannot yet accurately date, "Who in all the world reads a book?"—and then, at last, "Who in all the world remembers those strange, primitive creations people once called 'books'?" In many of the future worlds imagined by C. J. Cherryh, a writer too little known outside the genre of science fiction, there in fact are no books, not even for accounting purposes. She has humans employing a direct-to-the-brain transfer system which permanently implants knowledge, or at lesser levels of usage provides entertainment, at rates and with a thoroughness and effectiveness beyond anything we now know. And why not?

New systems of mechanical reproduction in the arts do not damage, but extend and deepen artistic understanding and appreciation. Studies in oral tradition have flourished, in the past several decades, in part because rather than in spite of the fact that new technologies have at the same time increased the function of orality in contemporary art and life. Speech came before writing, as writing came before printing and fingers before forks. Let us savor rather than cavil at human ingenuity, as we ride it (and it rides us) into the twenty-first century and beyond.

—*Lafayette, Louisiana*

Nominated by Palo Alto Review

YELLOW FEVER

by BARBARA HAMBY

from VERSE

Aureole of golden hair, my darling, my shimmering
buttercup, my dandelion, Tweety Bird, dipsomaniacal

canary, too chickenhearted to say chicken shit,
dear bee sting, yellow jacket, sunshine of my life,

elegant, graceful arc of light, Nordic, Swedish,
flaxen, braided, cruel, barbarous, shining inner domes of

gilded cathedrals, gold rush, golden delicious, apple of my eye,
he can do no wrong, no right, no one, nobody

is in a position to revile me as I lie here,
jaundiced, flipping through the yellow pages of my own personal

Kama Sutra of sulfurous yearning, acid, sour,
lemon ice, face like fresh cream, girl with the flaxen hair

meets boy with the sandy crew cut, true love screams
neon sighs—no, signs—sighs come later with the startling

opalescence of birth, bright wail of life turning
picaresque as ego tries on its splendid primrose jacket, no

quelque chose there, and later when rusty with age,
remembering sitting over steaming bowls of gummy

saffron risotto alla Milanese on a honeymoon, harvest moon,
topaz sliver of reflected glory, a slight memory of being

under someone, over someone, someone yourself, where is that
vain creature, that one, who calls Mirror, mirror, on the

wall, plague upon your house, car, yacht, palazzo,
xanthic acropolis of regret called heartbreak, two amber

yolks, rich, heart-clogging ache, muddled gold
zeppelin of heat, distorted luster of my disordered heart.

Nominated by David Kirby, Ed Falco, Verse

GRAFTING

fiction by MARIKO NAGAI

from NEW LETTERS

Harvest. another failure. Third year in a row. Now. The posted sign in the village center: *All people unable to work must leave within two weeks. Children exempted.*

The summer had been too long. The short rain season followed by overwhelming heat, sucking every drop of moisture, cracking the earth. The ground opened in the field like mouths waiting for water that never came. We waited for rain. It never came. The green wilted before our eyes. We were helpless. And gods did not hear our prayers this summer; the heat had settled too near the earth, sucking our prayers as soon as they came out.

The village was quiet this summer. Everyone hid, afraid to breathe deeply. Cattle died, their limbs fleshless, taut skin over bones, skeletal, even ghost-like while alive. We were no better than them. Our flesh hung loosely around us; bellies grumbling loudly like a nearing storm. Hands shook; sometimes, we became too lightheaded that we forgot where we were, for an instant, but not long enough to forget that we were hungry. The communal rice bins became lower and lower until we could see the bottom—this summer, no children dared to go to the stream because they knew they would find only a shallow, muddy puddle at the bottom of a deep crevice. Where the stream once was. A wound of the earth, we call it around here. A deep scar. Third crop failure in the row.

Now the sign. Now, old people must leave.

I tried to tear off the sign before anyone read it. Before anyone woke up. But it was too late. When I got there, women were wailing in each others' arms; men stood with downcast eyes. They had all read the post. And they understood. Their backs said more than words; their backs hung in resignation, in acceptance. We knew. We had known all along. We had known that something like this would happen. Somehow, something or someone must be sacrificed in order for the rest to live. If they stayed, if our old people stayed, we would all be hungry. More than hungry.

We were hungry the first year. We were cold, but somehow we managed. Last year was even worse; we were hungrier than a year before, and we were colder, but somehow, we managed again. But with a heavy price. One by one, the girls left the village. Strange men came from afar with heavy wallets in their hands, as if they knew— bad news travels quicker than the good ones—and the girls went with them, one by one. Hanging their necks, their necks bobbing with sobs. Not one disobeyed their parents: not one tried to escape. They were not yet women. Some of them haven't even had their first bleeding. Most of them would never live to be my age; most of them would never go past twenty-five. Their breasts would be forced into growth under the constant sucking; their breasts would grow under the touches of strangers. And after all these men, what would become of these girls? They all bore it like women, and they didn't even know what it meant. I know which one has a mole between her shoulder blades. I know which one has a scar on her neck. I know all the marks each brought to this world. I saw them come to this world, this cruel and exacting world.

And I miss them. No one talked about them after they left. Some of the parents erased the names from their doors, erasing them from their daily lives. They were banished even from our memory. But money from selling a daughter can go only so far. It never lasts. When spring came, we sighed in relief. We finally breathed. We ate roots and grasses, pretending them to be feasts fitted for the nobleman. It's easy to lie, really; the mind and and body are easily fooled. We prayed earnestly. We all did. But gods were busy, or indifferent; I do not know. And we were hungry. More than we wanted to admit.

So now, this again.

The only way to eliminate hunger is by cutting down the number of mouths. Old people. They cannot stand up straight. They cannot raise anything heavy over their shoulders; they cannot even raise their own arms. Some cannot see farther than their fingers; some cannot hear our loudest whispers. There are some, like my mother, who don't remember their lives.

My mother doesn't remember my name. My mother doesn't remember much of her life. She lives in the different time than I do— sometimes before I was born, perhaps even before she herself was born. But somehow, wherever she is, whenever she is, she seems content. Contained in her world. Or, perhaps, worlds. Perhaps she lives in many worlds, all of it better than where we are, where I am.

She bridged the other world and this one, a midwife. Every man in this village had come through the mother's canal and fell into my mother's hands. Sometimes, she coaxed the baby because they did not want to leave the other world. They were stubborn in their refusal, but she lured them out, somehow, with promises of sweet things this world offers. Cold water against the bare skin, the feeling of wet grass under bare feet, how laughter could never be explained with words. She helped with everyone's birth here until her hands hardened like hands on the woodcarvings, and she could no longer feel women's insides. She said that fingers must be delicate, must be flexible because women's insides are delicate and fragile. Then her memory began to leave her one by one, as if the doors of cages of canaries opened, birds taking flight timidly, then boldly one by one. First, what medicine she is mixing in the bowl. Then, the names of the pregnant mothers. Then her own name. The birds each took something of her past. Now, she is left with nothing. The birds keep flying away, one by one, each minute. Only time she speaks now is when she, somewhere deep inside of her, somewhere most primordial, speaks out for necessity like a baby wailing when in hunger, or wet, and even those come out weakly, as if she is not even sure of what she needs, herself.

Time leaves her, as quickly as it passes through her. She's living the past as she sits in front of me, asking me questions. Future hasn't happened to her yet, though I know what happens. She lives in a time when the past and present become one. Sometimes, she waves her spotty wooden hands gracefully in the arch, as if she's tracing a train of thought that no one can see. She doesn't say anything; she seems content. She looks like she doesn't need anything else in the world when she's like that. Coaxing her to go for a walk is hard, is simple—I never know when she wants to be led, or to lead, or to stay. When tugging becomes too much, when I pull her too hard, she stubbornly stands where she is, time leaving her quickly, and she can stand there for an hour, for two hours, forever if I let her. Times like that, she looks young for a second, like she's the girl she must have been more than a half a century ago, her eyes sparkling like a pair of shiny stones on the bottom of the stream. She seems to enjoy her own stubbornness. It's beautiful to see her when she's like that. She is a child, mine, as I was hers, and I love her because she doesn't remember anything. Because she cannot see how she is now.

She, too, must leave.

The villagers come to me one by one, late at night. They ask what they should do, what we should do. We have no more daughters to sell; we have nothing to eat. And this is only the beginning. We survived eating roots in spring. . . Must we all die? Must we all die? I cannot tell them anything. They have sold their daughters; their daughters will live for ten years at most, domesticated beasts, really. Their insides will rot with each year they are penned in the bedrooms and back rooms of inns and bars that sell women more than alcohol. But these villagers have sold their daughters so that they can live just for a season. I sent them away with a quiet blessing, a packet of herbal tea or a carved branch, anything just to quiet them. Tell them that these charms will give them the answer. They do not want an answer; they just want someone to agree with them. Anything I tell them, they will turn deaf ears. They will not have enough courage to kill their parents; they will take their parents up to the mountain and leave them. So they will die somewhere away from them, somewhere they cannot see. As they did with their daughters.

My mother will have to leave. I will have to carry her on my back, go up the mountain to the waterfall and leave her with the others. So they will not starve, so they will not go thirsty, so they will not die alone; they will live, so the villagers say, they will live longer than we will, the villagers say. And they say many things more. Many many more. And there are only twelve nights left before I, too, leave her.

She sleeps. In one of her many worlds. Her mouth open slightly, she looks like a child in her deep prayer. A look of deep concentration. She moves slightly. I turn away from her sleeping body. The villagers may not have mercy, but I, too, have no mercy. I will rather take my mother somewhere I cannot see her, have her fight for short life than to strangle her in her sleep. Or smother her. It's easy. It must be easy. A pillow over her head, it will not take too long. It must be easy to kill a child without a common memory. I have seen so many mothers do it to their children, infants, umbilical cords still warm and thick. A child without an arm, some that looked too much like cats, their lips split right beneath the nose. We have angered the fox god, so the child looks like a fox. What kind of future would she have? One child, I remember, did not have legs or arms, its head grotesquely open like the crushed pomegranate. The mother cried; she had cried and cried as she put a pillow over its misshapen head. It did not struggle. It just accepted, tiny chest rising and rising, and slowly, slower and slower until it stopped moving. It left without memory, perhaps only the memory of its mother's cry that did not end. The mother died a few days later. We found her body in the village well, her belly bloated as if she were once again pregnant. The villagers had kicked her body around, kicked until her belly burst. They left her carcass for the crows to pick on. That bitch fouled our water supply, they cursed; now we have to walk so far to get the water from the stream. I took her body back to her family before anything got to her. They did not take the body; they just told me to let it rot. I buried her in my yard. My mother had looked at the ground and smiled. She even placed a wild chrysanthemum on the grave. All the babies came and went, lived for a minute, two minutes, then disappeared. From one world to another.

Will it be that easy? It will be easier than knowing that she will live without me, looking for me. It will be short. Her cry under the pillow will be muffled. It will be short. It will have to be short, two minutes at most. She is so weak she will not be able to fight me.

I take my pillow from my bed and stand over her.

She opens her eyes. It is clear: it is like the way I remember her eyes as before her past flew away. She whispers, "I heard what they said. Take me to the mountain," then she smiles, closes her eyes.

The next day, day after, I look at my mother. That night must have been a dream, a waking dream, I tell myself. One by one, the old people disappear from the village. The children have grown sullen and quiet. They know. Their eyes are unusually calm with redness.

A scream from one house, a scream so mournful, so much like a pig about to get slaughtered. An old man runs as fast as he can from the yard. He is half-blind, but rocks and the uneven road mean nothing to him now. He runs past me. His son catches up with him. The old man yells, Help me, please. I don't want to leave my home. How can you do this to me? How can you banish me, just like that? I won't eat; I promise I won't eat; just let me die here. Just let me die where I was born. His son cries. His grandchildren stand by the gate, looking at the play with startlingly calm eyes. Then the son hits the bald wrinkled head with an axe, the blunt side lightly on the side of the old head. Not hard enough to kill, but hard enough to quiet. The old man crumbles. The son cries. He cries like the child he once was. The son has no mercy. He cannot even kill his father with his own hands. He'd rather let the father die alone, so far away from home.

I avert my eyes. I make my way home. My mother lies in her bed, staring at the ceiling as if there is a universe right there, right in front of her face. Her mouth gaped open, lips caved in without the teeth. Cheeks sunken in. She is somewhere else today.

I tell her that we're going on a trip, somewhere far, and that I am bathing her for the journey ahead. My mother lies on her back, still lingering in the ceiling, but something flickers in her eyes, something, and she closes her mouth for a second as if she is licking her lips to say something. But nothing comes out.

I get the bath water ready. Keeping one eye on my mother, I stir the bath water, evening the hot and cold; my reflection on the water swirling, swirling until it is only a blended colored blur.

Stand up, mama, stand up, I say, nudging my mother with my hand. She looks blankly at the ceiling. I lift the blanket from her; I get her on her legs slowly. She wobbles like a young animal learning to walk for the first time, a newborn doe taking its first step.

That's right, mama, that's right, slowly, slowly, we're going to take a nice bath today, you like bath, don't you, yes, we're taking the bath, I say. I talk to her as if she is a baby, though she is far from being a child, a beautiful child, my baby. My mother stands with her legs apart, bent knees, her back slumped. The robe has become undone, already half-naked as she stands. One of her breasts exposed, her breast that hangs low around her wrinkled stomach. Her flesh hangs loosely around her, colorless, flesh hanging loosely. The cloth around her hip is already soiled from a half day of lying down, heavy in my hand. Leading her slowly to the bathroom, one step at a time—she is obedient today, an obedient child.

Yes, mama, one step at a time, one step, I coo, and she seems happy to oblige. I lift her up; I lift her into the bathroom, the body shaven into less than half, less than one-third of what it used to be, shaven down to the bare essential, a grafted tree. Even privacy—what sets us apart from beasts—is taken from her; her shame is for all to see, her shame no longer her shame, but mine. My mother lies on her back, lies on her back as she did on her bed, floating in water, her body weighing nothing on my hand in water. She does not resist the water like a young body; nor is it let go like the dead body. Her eyes keep looking at the ceiling; she does not see me, she does not see anything except what she can only see, somewhere inside of her.

I pack the essentials. This robe, that thick jacket for cold nights, each cloth bringing me closer to the common memory my mother and I share. Forget long enough, but not long enough. Outside on the street, I see a villager with an old woman on his back, a ragged sack, really. The old woman sits on the broad back. She looks around and, as if she is shying from remembering, of too much remembrance, she glances around lightly, just enough to remember the outlines of the village, but not the details. Our eyes meet. She nods at me. She is wearing her best robe. They walk toward north, where the mountain waits. Where other old people wait, where others will join, even my mother.

I take my mother's hand; I tell her that it is time to go. She grasps it, hard. My knuckles turn white.

I strap her on my back, binding us hard with a belt. Binding us together.

The path becomes thinner and thinner. Thin line, wide enough for the sole. The past travelers seem indecisive; the path is crooked, veering left for no reason, then tight curve right. I carry her on my back, and soon, she falls asleep, trusting all her weight on me. Her face nestles on my neck, her breath rising and falling on my hair that has become undone. How far must I carry her before I must abandon her?

The night closes in, and the path starts to fade into darkness. She wakes up and says that she is hungry. Stopping where we are, I spread her bed next to mine; we make a small fire and cook little rice in the pan. She opens her mouth while I am cooking, waiting for me to feed her. She opens her mouth, not closing it while I feed her little by little.

Then I tell her that we must rest. Sleep, I tell her, sleep.

And she does.

The next day is like the day before. I carry her on my back. She is making a soft sound, a mewling sound, gently opening her hands, then closing them.

I let her be. She is happy where she is.

The mountain is close enough, in front of us.

We enter the thickets of trees the next day. She is becoming heavier and heavier. All the past she carries with her weighs me down. My feet do not go as fast as they did when we set out. The belt binding us together must be rebound every hour, becomes loose from my mother falling off of my back slowly and slowly, an inch every minute. The mountain is in front of us.

Each tree we pass, she bends the branch, breaks it enough that the branch still hangs with the rest. I ask her what she is doing.

"For you to get back without getting lost."

She continues to do so, even after I tell her that I know my way back, I know our way back. She reaches over to the branch her height, no more than height of my own shoulder, splinters each branch as landmark. I will be the only one to see it. She does not care. I cannot see the villagers before me or behind me; they have not come this way. I don't know where they have taken the old people. Maybe we have lost our way already. I have never gone through this path. She does not care. She continues to bend the branch, lets it hang there.

The path slopes upward. It is no longer a path, but a trail of beasts. But beasts never walk in uniformity the way we do. They roam where they want; they are not creatures of habits. Habits will kill them. They follow a certain rhythm, but no more. Habits will mark them into weakness; they will be caught by predators or hunger if they followed the same path each day of their lives.

461

The back of my mother is bruised. There are Xed blue marks on my chest from the rope. The blisters on my feet have burst. I have discarded my sandals.

My mother has refused to be on my back today. As I tried to put her on my back, she stood there, twenty minutes, thirty minutes.

Mama, please, get on my back, Mama. Mama, please, please, I coo.

No one answers me.

She tugs my shoulder.

My mother comes no higher than my shoulders, but she is stronger. She leads me by my hand, her hand tugging strongly. Her feet so light I think about squirrels.

We rest.

She is restless. She continues to break the branches. Our supply is getting low.

We start. I have lost the count of how many days we have been traveling like this, this aimless travel, this journey that must end eventually, like her life.

We must be somewhere near the clearing. We see more light. The leaves, green-yellow green-red, seem brighter. I know that we are near the end. I now lead, all the tiredness gone. All the worries gone.

We reach the clearing. It is beautiful. Somewhere close by, there must a stream running by. There's a little concave hollow there, a huge boulder jutting out to provide a shelter. I know this is where my mother will live.

I tell her that this is where we will rest for a while, and I begin to gather twigs to build a fire. Taking out the pot, and boiling the last supply of rice I brought with us, she helps me as much as she can, though her gnarled hands cannot hold anything properly. Her hands just wave around as if she is cooking herself, but she is nowhere near me. That is enough—that she wants to help. She seems a bit distant. She has left me again.

I feed her in silence.

As I lay out her clothing near her, she leans against the rock, looking far ahead.

Mama, let's play hide-and-seek, O.K.? You be the it, and I'll hide, is that O.K.? Mama, are you listening? You be the it, start counting, one . . . two . . . three . . . O.K.? I tell her.

She looks at me blankly, then something in her flickers in recognition.

Yes, Mama, like this, one . . . two . . . three . . . you say it Mama, I say.

One . . . two . . . my mother opens her mouth as much as she can as if she is actually saying the number.

I want to touch her before I hide. I reach over, then stop. Six . . . Seven . . . I begin to run across the clearing, toward the thicket we had exited from. Ten . . . Eleven . . . I count in my head. I cannot see where I am going, except that I must follow the broken twigs on the tree. Seventeen . . . Eighteen . . . I run as fast as I can.

Twenty . . . I run down the path. The path to the village will take more than fifty counts. The village. They must be near deserted. I can go back, not reminded of my mother because there will be no old people to remind me of her. She will be erased, as the other old people have been erased, disappeared from history as the houses disappear in darkness. But what of the morning? When the light brings about the disappeared houses? Will we be reminded? Can we ever erase our past? The daughters may be gone, somewhere far in the big cities, selling their nights to strange men, but I remember. The mother could not forget the limbless child; she killed herself. And everyone else wanted to forget her, even her family; everyone wanted to forget the shame she had brought when she killed herself, when she gave birth to the monster. But I still remember her. She will not go away.

I stop. I strain my ears to hear the count.

Thirty-nine . . . forty.

I close my eyes. I am no different from the villagers. I can say that I am different, that I am not like them. The villagers who can sell their daughters to survive for a season, a mere season; the villagers who can abandon their old parents. How different am I? My story is like theirs. Our stories are the same. I am no different. I am here, where they are. Or, have been. In the mountain. With my mother. I am no different.

Forty-three . . . forty-four . . . I begin to walk. Where I came from. Where my mother is. Forty-seven . . . forty-eight . . . I begin to walk faster. Forty-nine . . . Fifty . . . The leaves turn brighter and brighter. I stand by the tree closest to the clearing.

My mother stands in the middle of the clearing. Her arms in front

463

of her as if she is searching for something in the dark. This darkness, this darkness that has invaded our lives for a long time. Not caring that her robes have become loose in motion.

I stand, quiet.

The bird whistles by. The wind rustles the trees. And my mother stands still with her back bent, her arms in front of her. Her robes flap around her, wings of a bird about to take a flight if it could.

Nominated by New Letters, Jewel Morgan

RECITATION

by SCOTT CAIRNS

from WESTERN HUMANITIES REVIEW

He did not fall then, blind upon a road,
nor did his lifelong palsy disappear.
He heard no voice, save the familiar,

ceaseless, self-interrogation
of the sore perplexed. The kettle steamed
and whistled. A heavy truck downshifted

near the square. He heard a child calling,
and heard a mourning dove intone its one
dull call. For all of that, his wits remained

quite dim. He breathed and spoke the words he read.
If what had been long dead then came alive,
that resurrection was by all appearances

metaphorical. The miracle arrived
without display. He held a book, and as he read
he found the very thing he'd sought. Just that.

A life with little hope but one, the lucky gift
of a raveled book, a kettle slow to heat,
and time enough therefore to lift the book

and find in one slight passage the very wish
he dared not ask aloud, until, that is,
he spoke the words he read.

Nominated by Western Humanities Review, Kathy Fagan, Jim Barnes

A LITTLE LEARNING

fiction by SHARON DILWORTH

from THIRD COAST

FATHER-IN-LAW WORSHIPS KNOWLEDGE. *Pessimmism of the intellect, optimism of the will*, reads a T-shirt he wears nearly every day.

The printer at Fast-n-Ezee Tee's is to blame for the misspelling. Father-in-law would never have made such a mistake. "Look at the store sign," Father-in-law says. "I should have known they don't own a dictionary."

"Never trust a man who can think of only one way to spell a word," Janet says. She recognizes Antonio Gramsci, but quotes Bernard Shaw, not one of Father-in-law's favorite's, but appropriate, given the situation.

Father-in-law believes stupidity, not ignorance, is the central issue of the times. He thinks most people waste their days in the pursuit of shallow and useless endeavors. "Mastery of a stationary bicycle is not a cultural achievement."

He laments the fact that Moses did not include an 11th Commandment—Thou Shall Not Be Dim.

"It's not just the dumbing down of the average American," he complains. "The Void includes everybody. Society is bereft of public intellectuals. Look at our heroes," he says and then points to his feet. Janet knows he's talking about professional athletes. He doesn't understand how people wearing high-top tennis shoes could earn the respect and admiration of the masses.

"Grown men throwing balls?" he asks, then puts his hands on either side of his face like Munch's *The Scream*.

Janet, a.k.a. daughter-in-law/business partner, would like to go to France. She doesn't care how stupid the world is—doing nothing but

467

criticizing everyone else is not profitable. She wants to make money and thinks she's found a way to do it in Pittsburgh.

She's read about a bookstore town in France that has brought business and tourists flocking to a depressed region. There, in the southwest part of the country, is a whole village devoted to the buying and selling of books. People come from all over the globe to shop. Janet would like to build a similar tourist attraction in southwestern Pennsylvania. The steel is gone—it's not coming back—why not try something new?

Father-in-law cannot contemplate leaving the country—he's too busy complaining about the state of the Union.

"People are no longer searching for knowledge, they're looking for a short cut that will take them to the pot of gold at the end of the rainbow," Father-in-law says, when Janet shows him the low airfares to Paris listed in the *Pittsburgh Post-Gazette*.

Father-in-law uses television—the talk shows, the cop shows, the news shows to support his tirades. The O.J. trial sent him into a tizzy—everyone and anyone with letters after their name getting air time. "Listen to them, professing their opinions as if they mean something. They have no sense of history. No sense of irony. They buy expensive suits, put gel in their hair, and somehow that gives them the right to enlighten the public about the human spirit."

What Janet likes about his anger is that it is constant. He is in continual mourning for the way the world is moving. "To the dogs," he says. "Not even worth saving."

"Which is why we should go to France now," Janet says. The E-saver fares on US Air will not last forever. "Two-twenty-nine. Round-trip," she emphasizes.

"When is the earth going to be eaten up by the sun?" he asks.

"Two billion years," Janet says.

"Not soon enough if you ask me," Father-in-law tells her.

Janet is tired of Pittsburgh. She would like to get things moving, but she needs Father-in-law's financial support.

She is impatient and talks constantly about France, hoping enough discussion will prompt Father-in-law to take some action.

But nothing pleases Father-in-law. He is "pessimmistic" about everything.

With one exception.

His son; her Spouse.

Their marriage is over. Soon he will be her ex-spouse, so why bother with names?

Father-in-law is not just optimistic when he considers his son, he's delusional; he believes his son to be a genius.

Spouse is obedient, pleasant, caring, funny, all qualities you would expect or at least desire in a newborn puppy. Spouse is potty trained. He can eat with a spoon. He has a certain charm, he's not bad to look at, but he is definitely not a genius.

Spouse is not even smart.

Janet has never met a more needy, more careless, more utterly dependent person than Spouse, and Father-in-law's adoration of his son's "fine mind" annoys her to no end.

Spouse can order, but cannot scramble, eggs. He has a bank card, and money in his account, but doesn't always remember his PIN number. Ambition is a word that Janet is not sure he could define. He definitely couldn't spell it.

When people ask what he does, Spouse tells them he's an inventor.

That's how he sees himself—a twentieth-century Ben Franklin, an up-and-coming Thomas Alva Edison. Of course, he has yet to invent anything. He's not ready for invention. Right now he's processing— simply thinking about things. Spouse doesn't work. With all these thoughts, he doesn't have time for a job. Unfortunately, he doesn't have to work. His uncle, Father-in-law's only brother, died, leaving all his money to the family. The inheritance embarrasses Father-in-law and makes Spouse a lazy adult.

During the thirteen months of their marriage, Spouse thought about a brake for in-line skaters. Certain that roller bladers needed to stop, he thought they should carry a long stick with a sharp point on the end.

"Like a ski pole?" Janet asked.

"A roller blade brake," he insisted.

After talking about it for more than a year, he finally sketched it out for her.

"It looks like a ski pole," Janet said.

"It's just what these in-line skaters need to keep them from getting hurt," he said, full of bravado.

Janet wasn't sure the sleek, quick-moving skaters she saw zooming around the neighborhood would want to carry a stick that looked like a ski pole, and if they did, why wouldn't they just buy a ski pole?

When she told Spouse this, he gave up.

"In-line skating is just a fad anyway," he told his father, who agreed wholeheartedly.

"Make something that will carry this generation into the future," Father-in-law advised.

A few days later, Spouse began thinking about a garbage chute. It was to work on the same principles as a laundry chute—a hole-in-the-wall theory.

"What an idea, huh?" Spouse asked. He was clearly pleased with himself. "No more trash bags. No more garbage trucks. No more unsightly dumpsters."

There were glitches, of course—things he had to think through. "Give me some time," Spouse said. "A few months and I'll get this thing off the ground."

"Time is not money," Janet said. She was already thinking about the cost of a divorce.

Spouse reminds Janet of a fly. He's harmless, not buzzing around annoying anyone like a mosquito might, but as he isn't doing anything useful, why not just shoo him out the window?

Janet and Father-in-law are in business together. They own a bookstore. OUT WITH THE NEW, a shop that specializes in rare and used books. Second-hand goods are turned into treasures. That's the party line, though there's not much truth to it. They have new books—paperbacks that come from a North Carolina wholesaler. Most of the other books are from the Goodwill Store in Wilkinsburg. The stock is cheap, mark-up is high, and Janet is good at finding valuable first editions that professors from the Universities will buy.

The way Janet sees it, OUT WITH THE NEW is just a start.

She's not talking illusions of grandeur here. It's not like Spouse's inventions—she's actually going to do something. Janet thinks a whole street of bookstores is a fantastic idea. She will call it an empire. An empire of bookstores. She can imagine shoppers moving from store to store carrying their overstuffed paper bags full of books. The shops will be warm, welcoming. People will come to spend a day or two. Bed and breakfasts will pop up and restaurants will move to the street to support the traffic. She will make the Fortune 500 list by the end of the century.

Why can't bookstores make money?

Father-in-law has no head for business and he watches with worry as the street goes to the chain stores—The Gap, Banana Republic, Victoria's Secret.

"There's no end to this madness," he laments.

People tell him he should put in a coffee machine—something to attract the customers, but Father-in-law refuses. "If I want to eat I'll go to a cafeteria. Bookstores are sacred. They're like temples, places of worship. General meeting places. A safe enclosure in which to share ideas."

Father-in-law looks at the chain stores on the street and shakes his head.

"Every place the same. No variety. No individuality. The street used to have character. Now it looks like every other place in America."

"They make money," Janet says. "Tons and tons of money." She wonders how much down payment one needs to open a Starbucks franchise.

"It's a wonderful legacy we're leaving our children, isn't it?" Father-in-law asks. "They'll think we intended for them to do nothing but consume."

It is ugly, but it is profitable.

Occasionally someone comes into the bookstore. They want to use the bathroom.

"You can't go back," Father-in-law says. "Once beauty is gone, it's gone. Not just faded but destroyed."

Janet had been a regular customer at OUT WITH THE NEW before becoming the only employee. The dark wood room with its large bay window was comfortable, the best place in Pittsburgh to spend an afternoon. Father-in-law, ignoring the safety codes, would build a fire when it got cold. He tended to the wood with more care than he paid the customers.

Father-in-law was a terrible salesperson. Janet was there when the woman came in to buy a carton of hardback books. She wanted fifty or sixty; titles were not important. Nothing too moldy or too dusty; she didn't want them smelling up her living room. They were to be decorative, antique looking so they would match the things she had bought at the Dargate Auction House.

Father-in-law exploded.

The store was very quiet after she left. Father-in-law looked over to where Janet was sitting.

"What?" he said.

"You can't care why people want to buy books," Janet scolded.

He was dispirited, obviously conflicted, but she still thought he shouldn't have quoted Foucault.

"She was a cultural watershed," he said.

"Money is money," Janet said. "I should know. I don't have any."

"Talk like that causes pain," he said, clutching his chest as if suffering from heartburn.

He was also rude to the pretty woman in the bike shorts and neon pink nylon jacket who came in looking for *The Anarchist Cookbook.* Father-in-law, not familiar with the text, heard only what he wanted.

"Cookbook?" he asked and rolled his eyes as if she was a brainless twit. Then he suggested she might be happier at the Barnes & Noble, permanently.

"She's a professor," Janet told him after the woman had stormed off, vowing never to buy another book from OUT WITH THE NEW. Janet recognized her from the University. "A Ph.D. from Berkeley."

"She certainly doesn't dress like a person with an advanced degree."

"Would tweed have been better?" Janet asked. "What happened to not judging a book by its cover?"

Father-in-law doesn't want to sell books. He wants people to read. He expects the shoppers to be curious, to be anxious to learn. He wants them to know more than they do.

"Aim for the ideal, but appreciate the real," Janet warned, paraphrasing Jean-Jacques Jaures.

"The universal promise of earthly well-being includes a curious mind," he came back without a moment's pause. "What gets me is their pride. Stupidity is something they should be ashamed of."

"That woman was not stupid," Janet said.

"She looked like a case of arrested development."

"Your business is to sell books," Janet said.

"If you know so much, why don't you do it?"

Janet became an employee of OUT WITH THE NEW that afternoon. She asked Father-in-law to pay her in cash, which was fine with him. When business was slow, he paid her in shares of the store.

Plans for the empire came later.

Father-in-law is awkward with Janet when Mother-in-law explains that Spouse and Janet plan to divorce.

"Very very sorry," Father-in-law says. He moves around her, clumsily raising his arms, then lowering them as if he means to give her a hug.

"I guess it was inevitable," Janet says. She is not comfortable discussing Spouse with Father-in-law. She has not been totally honest in her dealings with Spouse. At one time, marriage had seemed like a good idea. Spouse was single, she was single. He was there. She was there. It had been easy, convenient—more like a business deal than a marriage.

"You were in love," Father-in-law tells her.

"Okay," Janet says. She does not argue.

She thought she could change Spouse. She wanted him to take his ideas and do something with them. Instead, Spouse spent all his days thinking.

He didn't care about being rich; he wanted to be famous.

Janet could not tolerate so much thought.

"Vision is cloudy when the heart beats boldly," Father-in-law says. "People don't think clearly when they're in love."

Janet does not think Father-in-law is talking from experience.

Mother-in-law is a huge fan of daytime soaps. She tapes the NBC ones and watches these at night after three hours of ABC. When not watching television, Mother-in-law cleans. On good days, she does both. The house is spotless, but even when the place shines she doesn't like to go anywhere. "I'm happy here," she says. "Very happy right here."

Mother-in-law has never been out of the city of Pittsburgh. Not even as a kid. She's seen photographs, but has never been to Niagara Falls. She talks about New York City as if it is some kind of exotic fairyland rather than an eight-hour car ride.

Father-in-law and Janet do not talk about Mother-in-law's cloistered ways. Genetic laziness seems to prevail in that household, but Father-in-law is protective, he insists it's something medical. As they are so far apart on Spouse, Janet doesn't verbalize her opinion of

473

Mother-in-law. Father-in-law has never said anything about being unhappy, but once when he'd had too much wine, he said something about how different his life would be if he had married a woman with a thought in her head.

It is January. The other merchants on the street have warned her that things get bad after Christmas. What they don't tell her is that business comes to a complete halt in the winter months. She is not sure how long they can operate without customers.

The only person who ever comes in is Spouse.

He arrives every day at noon, and stays until closing.

"Find something else to do," Janet tells him. "You are no longer my responsibility."

"It's my father's store," he says. "I have every right to be here."

The days are boring enough with just Janet and Father-in-law, but with Spouse spending every minute of the day there, it is intolerable.

Spouse is processing a new invention. The idea came from a book he read, something which pleases Father-in-law.

Janet knows the source. It is a biography of Frank Sinatra, filled mostly with black and white photographs. There is almost no text.

Spouse is fascinated by the story of how women in New York City would trail after the singer, collecting the footprints he left on the snow-covered sidewalks. Spouse thinks it would be great to actually have a machine that would trap the footprints of famous people.

Father-in-law likes the idea, but wants to improve it.

"It's not their feet we care about, but their minds," he lectures Spouse. "Can't you think of a machine that would save their minds?"

Spouse is too enthusiastic to listen to criticism.

"Think about it. Women could have Elvis' footprints hanging on their wall. All kinds of movie and television stars. Mom would love to have had Ed Sullivan's. Think of the money I could have made had I saved Princess Diana's footprints."

Janet is sick of Spouse.

"Saving stars' footprints only adds to the commodification of their uselessness," she says. "Adults dressing up in other people's clothes, memorizing lines someone else wrote. We lavish them with praise and call them artists? Talk about stupidity."

Father-in-law excuses himself and disappears to the rest room in the basement.

"When a true genius appears in the world, you may know him by this sign, the dunces are all in confederacy against him," Spouse says.

"You've never even read Jonathan Swift," Janet yells across the store. "A little learning is a dangerous thing. Drink deep or taste not the Pierian Spring. Pope."

"I know what I'm capable of achieving."

"Fool someone else," Janet says. "I recognize a fake when I'm married to one."

They close the shop early that night. Three dollars and fifty cents is no reason to stay open past four o'clock.

"It's time for us to do something," Janet announces.

She is worried. This is her one chance to get a business going. She must do something now or she will lose all opportunity for a prosperous future.

Father-in-law is tired and asks if they can talk in the morning.

"Our expansion depends on our knowledge of what to do," Janet says.

"Knowledge?" Father-in-law asks. He raises his eyebrows. This is his kind of conversation.

"Of course," Janet says. "We have to learn how to run a successful book town."

"Learning without thought is labor lost; thought without learning is perilous," Father-in-law says.

"Confucius would have approved," Janet says and shows him the map of France.

"You mean leave?" he asks. "Now?" He is nervous, but curious.

"We're not doing anything here," Janet says. "It's not like we're losing business." She opens her palm and shows him the day's sales.

"I could always have my son watch the store."

"A sign in the window, saying we've gone to replenish stock, will suffice," Janet says.

It is not an easy trip.

Paris is crowded. It seems that everyone in the world has chosen this particular week to profit from the low fares to France.

"I came to Europe to see history, to see culture, to witness things I have never seen before. Instead there are only lines and crowds of people trying to get through doorways. This, I can see this at any Steelers game." Father-in-law is not happy.

He complains about the global economy. "It's only an illusion of choice," he says, pointing to the Ikea, the Pier One, the fast-food restaurants lining the highways outside Paris. "What is the difference between this and Pittsburgh?"

Janet does not have an answer, nor can she convince him that there are things to admire in the chaos of the overcrowded city.

But this is not why they have come to France. She is there to learn how to make money on books. She keeps her head clear and focuses on her goal.

Things are better when they get to Montolieu, the bookstore town in the south. Eight hundred residents, fourteen bookstores, a thirteenth-century cathedral in the town square. Charm prevails.

The hotel/cafe where they are staying is run by three Australians who are the most cheerful people Janet has ever met. They drink red wine until their lips and teeth are stained blue. They are enthusiastic about the small village, though they don't seem to know much about it. Janet questions them endlessly about the history of the town, how it came to be a book town, how many visitors come every year, how many books are sold.

They prefer to talk about their own country.

"Tourism is very big down-under. At any given time, a quarter of the population of Australia is out of the country. Being away is our national pastime," they tell Janet and ask for her telephone number back in Pittsburgh. "You never know when we'll be in your neighborhood."

At night, the Cafe fills with the bookstore owners from the town who drink wine and talk until well after midnight. Father-in-law's French is limited, and though he cannot keep up with their conversations, he sits and listens to their arguments, certain that they are talking of lofty things.

"There is not a television in the place," he says and rubs his hands gleefully. "This is heaven."

The trip has suddenly turned wonderful.

"What a glorious idea you had," Father-in-law tells Janet. "We should have done this months ago."

The trip is not successful. The bookstore owners are friendly, they certainly like to talk, but they cannot help her with the construction of her empire. The town, while charming, is financially dismal. The tourists are few and far between. Not at all like the *New York Times* article bragged about. The tourist buses go to Angorra, where there is no tax. Not on anything. Sales in the bookstore town are infrequent. Money does not change hands often.

No one is getting rich.

"I've never been happier," Father-in-law tells her.

Saturday, they are sitting outside the Cafe, waiting for Nigel to make their lunch—lamb shanks, for the third day in a row. Janet sips at her wine and reads from her true crime book. Father-in-law insists she wrap them in brown paper packaging so no one will see what she is reading.

"This is the zenith of my life," Father-in-law says. "This village is a miracle. All kinds of wonderful things can happen here."

Janet prefers his maudlin rants to this bubble-gum personality.

Father-in-law's energy and cheerfulness are not infectious.

Janet is bored. The village of Montolieu is incredibly small. One hundred of the town's eight hundred residents are retired nuns who live at the convent on the river. The nightlife is nil.

Janet is on her fifth true crime book.

Nigel brings their lunch. He's already been sipping the cooking wine. He gives them a big blue smile. "Enjoy," he says.

"I wish he'd speak to us in French," Father-in-law says.

"What's the point in that?" Janet says. She opens her book, but sets it down when Father-in-law makes a strange noise in his throat. Janet wonders if he's going to choke.

"Look," he says and points towards the cathedral.

Janet turns to see Spouse, walking across the town square.

Janet could not be more surprised.

He is not doing well. The trip over the ocean, changing planes at Gatwick, the car rental in Toulouse, this is the most Spouse has accomplished in his entire life. He looks ill.

"What are you doing here?" Janet asks.

Spouse ignores her questions. He speaks to Father-in-law. "You left a note for mother on the kitchen counter."

"She's very fond of cleaning the counters in the kitchen," Father-in-law says without humor. "I thought she'd see it there."

Spouse turns to Janet. "You."

"Me?" Janet asks.

Spouse punches her arm.

It is a treat to see him angry. His range of emotions has always been so limited.

"My mother is furious," Spouse says. "She'll never speak to you again. Never."

Janet asks, "What have I done?"

"I suppose you don't care that my mother is dying of shame," Spouse says. A bright red spot appears on his cheek, and when Janet looks more closely, she sees that it is a rash and that it continues down his neck.

"Why should she be dying of shame?" Janet asks. "Why should she be dying of anything?"

Janet is confused. Utterly and completely in the dark.

Father-in-law excuses himself. He pushes his chair away from the table, and wanders over towards the cathedral.

"Explain," Janet demands of Spouse.

"My father says you've changed his life."

"I've never changed anything of his," she tells Spouse.

It is the first she's heard about Father-in-law's plans to travel the world. Like the Australians he is never going home again. It seems that he called Mother-in-law a few days ago and told her she was on her own. He is following his dreams which have nothing to do with a wife or a house, or a son in Pittsburgh. He is a wanderer, moving to higher grounds, gaining knowledge and experience with each footstep into a new culture and country.

Janet did not know that he sent her a telegram. GONE FOR GOOD. NOT TO WORRY. I'M FOLLOWING MY HEART, NOT MY REASON. XXXOOO, TED.

Of course Mother-in-law, trained in the intricacies of soap opera plots, thinks Janet is to blame.

"She called you a hussy," Spouse tells Janet.

"This is great," Janet says.

"How do you think I feel?" Spouse asks. "He's my father. You're still married to me."

"Believe me. There is nothing going on between your father and me."

She wishes she had a machine that would make the whole family disappear. Now that would be an invention worth talking about.

Father-in-law is in the cathedral, near the front, staring at the stained-glass windows surrounding the altar.

"Why are you lying to your wife?" Janet talks in a loud voice so there will be no mistake that she is angry.

"It's true," he says. "I'm not going home."

"Don't be stupid." Janet sits beside him. The cathedral is ancient. It smells of mold and mice droppings. "Of course we're going home."

Father-in-law folds his arms under his chest. "You, maybe. Me? Never."

"What about your wife?"

"I no longer care about her. She seems distant, a part of my life I no longer want to be involved in."

"You can't just walk away from her. Or the bookstore. Think what will happen if you're not there to run it?"

"Here," he says. He has a napkin from the Cafe. He puts it on his knee and scribbles something. He pushes it into her hand.

It is difficult to read the scrawl in the darkness of the thirteenth-century cathedral, but Janet understands that Father-in-law has signed over his shares of the bookstore to her.

"Do you think this will stand up in court?" Janet asks hopefully.

"I won't fight you. The bookstore is yours," Father-in-law promises. "You can go back to it or you can travel with me. I don't mind you coming along. Except for those trashy books, your mind is good. You're not afraid to say what you think."

"I think you're being an idiot." She asks him to sign the napkin in ink.

"I can't spend my life caring what others think of me."

"You've never cared what others think of you," Janet reminds him.

"Empires rise and fall, but man's desire to wander the earth burns through eternity like the brightest star in the night sky."

"You're not quoting anyone important. For all I know, it's poetry," Janet says. The rear doors open. A nun enters. She drags a large broom behind her and begins to sweep in between the pews.

"It's the poetry of my heart," Father-in-law says as Janet walks away.

"I wouldn't try to publish it," Janet calls over her shoulder. She is anxious to get back to the States.

Mother-in-law wants to fight it, but Father-in-law does nothing.

He is home three days after Janet. He went to Spain. He took the train which was crowded and uncomfortable. "Madrid looked just like New York. McDonald's. Wendy's. Burger Kings. Pizza Huts.

479

Why leave home? Why go anywhere anymore? Let the world blow up. Tomorrow is not soon enough, if you ask me."

There is no mention of his travels around the world. There is no more talk of him following his heart.

"I was stupid," he says about signing over the bookstore to Janet.

"That's right," Janet nods. "You were."

She disagrees with Mother-in-law. There is nothing low-class about taking advantage of someone's weakness

Father-in-law likes definitions, so she defines what was his. Nothing.

"Art is long, life short: judgment difficult, opportunity transient," Janet reminds Father-in-law.

"Goethe would not have recognized any of this as art," he argues.

"It's a start," Janet tells Father-in-law. "The strongest empires were built one brick at a time."

"More like one brick-head at a time," Father-in-law says. He doesn't approve of any of the changes at the store.

Janet no longer needs his approval or his financial support. She lets him rant and rave, and does not interrupt—they have history—reason enough to be polite.

The lottery machine brings in an enormous amount of revenue.

"We're doomed," Father-in-law complains.

He comes in every day and sits in the chair by the fireplace. He no longer talks about the greatness of her mind. He no longer tells her she's brilliant.

"Optimism of the will," Janet chants like a mantra. The customers repeat it after her. "Optimism of the will." They do not know or care who Gramsci is, but they're enthusiastic; they want to win big time.

Father-in-law grunts at her determination.

"Action," she says when she sees the sour expression on his face.

"Contemplation," he insists.

"You've got to take the bull by the horns and go for it," Janet says. "You've got to fight to get what you want. The eye of the tiger."

"Clichés," Father-in-law shudders. "Mindless banter. Semiotic nonsense. Babble."

"Money made," Janet says. She has netted a profit three months running. Expansion is on the horizon, though not with books. The new Barnes & Noble Superstore convinced her to move in another direction.

She will sell what the public wants to buy. There's no sense shoving things they don't want down their throat. The new espresso machine attracts a young, hip crowd. Videos are cheap. Magazines, even easier to stock. Everyone loves a cold Coke. People will pay for flavored water.

Spouse is still overseas.

The book town in France agrees with him. The Australians hired him to work at the Cafe. They're not a particularly motivated group, and Spouse is a welcome addition. They think his footprint saver is a great invention. They don't care about the particulars. They sit around and discuss how famous they could have been had they had the footprint saver when Genghis Khan was alive.

Spouse is thinking about a new invention. He is not saying what it is, but he writes and tells his father that he finds the Australians most supportive of his ideas. "Not like some people I know." Of course, nothing has come to fruition. Spouse isn't ready for the invention stage. He's just thinking, a pastime Father-in-law has no problem supporting.

"At least my son dreams," Father-in-law tells Janet. "Which is more than I can say . . ."

"Who's got time for dreaming?" Janet interrupts. "I'm too busy making money."

The line at the counter grows longer—only a half hour until the Daily Seven Drawing.

"Pessimism of the intellect," she chants, making another $15 sale. "Spell it any way you like."

The cash register sings.

Nominated by Jane McCafferty, Third Coast

ARCHAEOLOGY

by MARGARET GIBSON

from THE IOWA REVIEW

You who come here, if you come, cannot know how it tasted,
        this hook of dried root—
whether its flesh were ocher, gold, color of wild mustard in a field.
You'll have seen photographs of harvest, if archives last longer
        than houses.
You'll think, whoever lived here had a taste for the holy—here is
        a monk with no hands to fold in prayer,
none to protest the imperial episodes, their wars.
And this—was it a flower? Did the woman (Was there a woman?)
        wear it in her hair,
this blue whorl of a tidal wave and night-blind wind?
You say it may have sprung out of a fetid wetland log—
and in the twisted root of dream, if you still dream, *parasite*
        turns to *paraclete*,
a word pebble as whole as the blue stone earring tumbled in with
        the midden of mussel shells and chips of china.
Who lived here? Ask the corn husk masks. They watched the man
        and woman, like a mist,
drift over the threshold of a door frame that stood, despite everything,
sentinel a while. They let the screen door fall gently to,
they knew where they were going, just down the road, past the bog
        and its stench of mutant frogs,
a rotted sump of skins and carcasses. They knew what it was to lose
        everything. They gave away
their bodies, as the monk his hands. When they prayed—if they prayed,
        and only for the bland

safety of the dead bolt, the comforts of ownership—it was not
                to the wild throb of fire
God is, but to its humbled image. Icon and evidence. These you can store.
There was the skull of a beast hung on the wall, and a tree grew out of
            it, once.

Nominated by Ted Deppe, Eamon Grennan

BLOOD SPORT

fiction by THOMAS LYNCH

from WITNESS

Most times the remembrance was triggered by color—that primary red of valentines or Coca Cola ads—the color of her toenails, girlish and perfectly polished. He remembered her body, tiny and lifeless and sickeningly still as she lay opened and autopsied on the prep-room table. He could still bring to mind, these many years since, the curl of the knot in the viscera bag the pathologist had tied, with all of her organs examined inside, and the raw edge of the exit wound in her right leg and the horrible precision of the hole in her breast where the man who murdered her put the muzzle of the gun.

And he remembered the dull inventory of detail, the hollow in her mother's voice the morning she called him at the funeral home.

"Elena's been shot, Martin. Up in Baldwin. She's at the Lake County Morgue. Go and get her, Martin. Bring her home."

Elena had been only fifteen when her father died—the darkly beautiful daughter of a darkly beautiful mother and a man who'd had cancer. He was laid out in an eighteen-gauge metal casket. The funeral was huge. Martin could remember standing between them, Elena and her widowed mother, when they'd come to see the dead man's body. He figured he was ten years older than the daughter, ten years younger than the mother. He had asked, as he'd been trained to ask, if everything was "satisfactory." It was the failure of words that always amazed him.

"He got so thin."

"Yes."

"At least he's not suffering anymore."

"No."

"Thank you, Martin."

"Yes."

And he remembered how Elena, after trying to be brave for her mother, after standing and staring at the lid of the casket as if she could tough it out, as if she could look but not see, had let her gaze fall on the face of her dead father and cried, in one great expiration of pain, "Oh Daddy! Please, no," and nearly doubled over at the middle holding her tummy and how her knees buckled and how he grabbed her before she fell to the floor. And how she had pressed her sobs into his shirt and how he'd hugged her close and felt her holding on and could smell her hair and feel the form and perfect sadness in her shaking body and how he'd said that everything would be all right because he really didn't know what to say. It made him feel necessary and needed and he wanted to hold her and protect her and make everything better, because she was beautiful and sad and though he could not fix it he would not let her go until she could stand on her own two feet again. And he thought that being the only embalmer in town was no bad thing when you stood among the widowed and orphaned and they would thank you for the unhappy work you'd done on their people.

Five years after that and it was Elena, killed by her husband with a gun.

Martin could not get his mind off how mannish the violence was, how hunter-gatherly, how very do-it-yourself, for the son-of-a-bitch to stand on the front deck of their double-wide out in the woods while she loaded the last of her belongings in the car—her boom box and a last armful of hanging things—how he must have carefully leveled the rifle, his eyes narrowing to sight her in. He put the first bullet through her thigh. An easy shot from fifteen yards.

He must have wanted to keep her from running.

"The way you would with any wild thing," the fat pathologist, smelling of stale beer, had told Martin in the morgue, taking the cigar out of his mouth to hold forth like an expert. "You hobble it first, then you don't have to chase a blood trail through the woods all night." He warmed to his subject. "Bow hunters go for the heart or lungs most times. They don't mind chasing through swamps and marshes after a wounded buck. It's part of the sport to them. But shooters go for the head shot or the legs."

And as she lay in the thick leaf-fall beside the car, bleeding from the severed femoral artery, he'd walked over, put the barrel to her left breast and squeezed off another round.

"She'd have bled to death either way," the pathologist said. The sight of that fat hand with the cigar touching the spot on Elena's thigh where the bullet tore its exit out sickened Martin. And when the same hand pulled the sheet back to show the terrible carnage to her torso—the post-mortem incisions very loosely stitched up and the black and blue and red little wound where her killer must have reckoned her heart would be, Martin quickly moved his stretcher beside the morgue tray, covered her body and took charge before the pathologist carried his hapless lecture any further. He signed the log book beside Elena's name and case number, got the death certificate marked "gunshot wounds to leg and chest" in the section that asked for the cause of death and "homicide" where it asked for manner and had her name and date of death, all of it scrawled in the sloppy hand of the pathologist, and got her out of there.

All the way home he tried to imagine how it must have happened—if anyone could have heard it, the small caliber outrage of it, as if she'd been a doe feeding among the acorns or come to the salt lick, her large brown eyes full of panic and stillness. He wondered if she knew he was dangerous. He wondered if she realized, after the first shot, that he was going to kill her. He wondered if she died with fear or resolve. He wondered if bleeding from the first wound, she might have passed out, and never saw the face of her killer or the barrel of the gun or felt it on her body or saw his eyes as he pulled the trigger.

Taken as a thing itself, undistracted by his professional duties, considered as a bit of humanity, the aberration was incomprehensible. How could someone kill someone so coldly, someone with whom you had made plans, had sex, watched television, promised love? It left him with a functional ambiguity. Martin tried to assemble a reasonable sentence in which the last line went like *and then he shot her, twice, because . . .* but he was always unsuccessful.

He looked in the rearview mirror at the length of the stretcher in the back of the hearse with its tidy blue cover under which Elena's body was buckled in, her head on the pillow, a small bag with her bloodied clothes, her jewelry and personal effects beside her. He tried to connect this horror with his remembrance of a sad, beautiful girl sobbing at the graveside of her dead father a few years before, waiting for the priest to finish with his prayers.

The morning was blue and sunlit, the buds of maples just busting loose, the men who'd been pallbearers lined up on one side of the grave, Elena and her mother and grandmother on the other. And all around, a couple hundred who'd come to pay their respects—women who worked with Elena's mother at the real estate office, men who worked with her father at the shop, parishioners from Our Lady of Mercy and kids from the freshman class of the high school. And after the priest had finished, Martin had nodded to the pallbearers to remove their gloves and solemnly place them on the casket—a little gesture of letting go. And then, from the pile of dirt next to the grave, under the green grass matting, he'd given a small handful of dirt, first to the dead man's mother, then to the dead man's wife and then to Elena; and at his direction, each stepped up to the casket and traced a cross on the top with the dirt that Martin had given them. He put a hand on their elbows as they stepped on the boards in a gesture of readiness and ever vigilant assistance. And after that, Martin made the announcement he had practiced saying out loud the night before.

"This concludes the services for Mr. Delano."

He reminded himself to speak slowly, to enunciate, to articulate, to project.

"The family wishes to thank each of you for your many kindnesses—for the floral tributes and Mass cards and most especially for your presence with them this morning."

He took a breath, tried to remember what part came next.

"You are all invited to return now to Our Lady of Mercy Parish Hall where a luncheon has been prepared in Mr. Delano's memory. You may step now directly to your cars."

At this direction, people began to move away, relieved at the end of the solemnities, talking freely, trading news and sympathies. Martin had been pleased with the performance. Everything had gone off just as he'd planned—a fitting tribute, a good funeral. The pallbearers walked away as a group, looking official. Someone assisted the grandmother from the grave. Elena's mother, her eyes tired and red, took Martin's arm as they walked to the limousine, holding the rose Martin had given her, the crowd of people parting as they made their way. And Martin was thinking this is no bad thing for people to see

487

what a dependable man their new funeral director was—a reliably upright, lean-on-me kind of man—less than a year out of mortuary school, mortgaged to the eyes for the business he'd bought from the widow of the man who'd been here before, but clearly a responsible, dependable citizen, someone to be called on, night or day, if there was trouble.

At the door to the car Mrs. Delano stopped, turned toward Martin with a brave smile, tilted her head slightly, opened her arms and Martin, sensing that she wanted him to, without hesitation bent to embrace her. She was saying, "Thank you, Martin," and "I could never have made it through this without you," loud enough for bystanders to hear and he was patting her back professionally, all caring and kindness as you would with any hurt or wounded fellow human, saying to her, "You did good, he'd be proud of you," and she was patting his shoulders and then, once the hug was over, holding the hankie to her eyes, she quickly disappeared into the back seat of the car in a rush of grief and relief and gratitude, and Martin straightened up and held the door.

Elena, who'd been following Martin and her mother to the limousine, holding two roses she'd picked from her father's casket spray, paused at the car door and, perhaps because she was following her mother's lead, perhaps thinking it was the proper thing to do, looked Martin in the eyes and said, "Thank you, thank you for everything," and reached up to lock her hands around Martin's neck and just as Martin was starting to say, in a voice all caring and kindness, "You're very welcome, Elena," she rose on her tiptoes, pressed her body firmly against his and kissed him squarely on the mouth. Martin could feel her chest on his chest, her small hands holding the sides of his face, and her soft mouth opening and the wet tip of her tongue on his lips. He let go of the door handle and held her at the waist, first pulling her towards him, then opening his eyes, gently pushing her away and when she stopped kissing him, he could feel his face reddening and he was wondering if the priest and the pallbearers and the townspeople could see his blush and the flash of desire he could feel in himself and the wish beginning to form in his mind that everyone would disappear so that he could hold her and touch her and comfort her and have her and then, before he could pat her on the back professionally, before he could say, "There, there, everything is going to be all right," before he had a chance to restore the air of solemnity and order, Elena proffered, with a brave smile, one of the roses she was holding. He took it from her, and as her mother had, Elena disappeared head first into the back of the long black Cadillac, which then drove away.

There was a safety in dealing with only the parts—the arteries and chemistries, the closure of eyes and lip-lines, the refitting of cranium and sternum, the treatment of cavities and viscera, the placement of hands, the suturing of wounds and incisions, the rouge and lipstick and nail polish, the dressing and hairdo and casketing. Duty had a way of separating Martin from what it was he was doing. Stuffing the opened cranium with cotton, fitting the skull cap back in place and easing the scalp back over the skull (thereby restoring the facial contours), and minding the tiny stitches from behind one ear to behind another were only part of the process of embalming and embalming was only part of the process of laying out the dead which was only part of the process of the funeral and the funeral was only a part of the larger concept of a death in the family and a death in the family was a more manageable prospect, more generic somehow, than the horror—round and witless and recognizable and well beyond his professional abilities—of a lovely girl, grown lovelier as a woman, who leaned on him and counted on him and had kissed him once as if she meant it and who moved away and then got shot like an animal in the woods by a man about whom Martin knew next to nothing.

For months after her father's funeral, Martin kept an eye out for Elena. Her mother came to pay the bill, and pick up more holy cards and thank-you notes. And then she came to order a stone. "Beloved Husband and Father" is what it said. Martin had advised her against a double marker. She was young and would surely remarry he thought.

And Martin would always ask, "How is Elena doing?" in his most professional, caring voice.

"She's having some trouble with her schoolwork. She doesn't sleep well. I'm a little worried."

Martin gave Elena's mother a list of grief support groups, run by the local hospice and area churches. He reminded her that there used to be "a year of mourning" and said that Elena's feelings were probably "very normal" and that "time heals all wounds."

"Yes," said Elena's mother. "It's just so hard."

She thanked Martin again for everything and said she hoped

he'd understand if she said she hoped she wouldn't be seeing him again.

Martin smiled and nodded and said he understood completely.

The next June, Martin read in the local paper how Elena had been captain of the debate team that went to the regional finals in Ann Arbor, and the year after that she had gone to Italy on a Rotary Exchange Scholarship, and in her senior year she was pictured on the front page smiling in her prom dress beside the son of the man who owned the Lincoln-Mercury dealership in town, over a caption that read "A Night to Remember" and Martin remembered how very happy she looked, how very pretty. After that he pretty much lost track of her.

"After her father died," Elena's mother told Martin when she came in to pick out a casket and arrange the funeral, "she seemed a little lost."

Martin listened and nodded as Elena's mother, looking so much older now, outlined the details of her dead daughter's life. She'd finished school, applied to college, spent the summer after graduation waitressing in a bar-restaurant in western Michigan, to get out on her own and earn a little money.

"She met him there. At the Northwoods Inn."

He worked for the county road commission and came in weeknights after work and weekends after fishing or hunting. He was handsome and chatty. He had a trailer in the woods. He gave her compliments and brought her flowers and bought her beer and cheeseburgers. And when it came time to go to the university, to get the education her father had saved for, she called her mother and told her that she was moving in with this man.

"I didn't approve but what could I do, Martin? Her father would never have allowed it. But what could I do?"

Martin shook his head and nodded.

"I told her she was throwing her life away on a summer fling, but she said she loved him. She loved him and he killed her, shot her like a damn dog, Martin."

Elena's mother's sobs grew heavy. Martin poured her a glass of water, moved the box of Kleenex nearer to her.

"Thank you, Martin," she said. "I'm sorry."

"Not at all," he said. "It's OK."

"In no time she was pregnant and he said he wanted to 'do right' by her. I told her he would always feel trapped, or always feel like he had done her a big favor, always feel like he was such a big man and she was just nothing without him, but she said she loved him and maybe it was all meant to happen like this and what could I do, Martin? What could I do? Her father would have gone up there and brought her home, but I had no one, no one."

They were married in the county offices in a civil ceremony, Elena wearing her prom dress and her new husband wearing a cowboy hat and a blue jean jacket and a string tie.

Elena's mother took the wedding snapshot out of her purse and told Martin, "Cut him off of there and use that picture for the paper and the holy cards. She was so happy then."

Elena miscarried in her third month and took a job working dispatch for the sheriff's office. By the following midsummer things were getting bad. Her husband's appetite for Budweiser and blood sport hadn't abated.

"She'd call home crying, Martin. He still went to the bar weeknights and came home boozy and, well, unpredictable. And he spent the weekends tramping through the woods shooting small game which he'd bring home for her to clean and cook.

"He'd go out at night and snag spawning salmon and bring them back to freeze and smoke and put up in jars.

"Her letters home got so sad, Martin. 'He doesn't bathe enough,' she wrote me once, 'he seems so angry.'"

She had taken from her purse a packet of pink envelopes and was holding them and rocking a little in the chair across the desk from Martin.

"She had such beautiful handwriting."

Martin nodded, smiled, understood.

"She called me crying horribly once and I asked her if he'd hit her but she said no, no. He had killed a fawn, right outside their trailer. It had come with its mother to feed at the pile of carrots he baited them with. They were in bed. Sunday morning. He sat up, walked to the window, went to the door where he kept his rifle. It was months before the legal season. He shot it right from the door. The fawn, Martin. The little fawn."

She was shaking now again, sobbing and rocking in the chair.

"Do you know what he told her, when she yelled at him for shooting the fawn?"

491

Martin shook his head.

"He told her it couldn't live without its mother anyway."

Now she was sobbing and shaking fitfully and Martin reached across the desk to take hold of her hands in which she held the packet of her daughter's letters.

"We don't have to do this now," Martin told her.

But she wanted to go on, to get it out, to get this part behind her.

After he killed the baby deer, Elena applied to the state university in Mt. Pleasant, using as return address the sheriff's office. When the letter came from the admissions department, beginning Dear Ms. Delano: Congratulations! she made a copy and mailed it home with a note asking her mother if there was still money left for her education.

"Of course is what I told her," Elena's mother told Martin. "I wanted her to get her education before she settled down. After she lost the baby, she had no reason to stay with him. And he was drinking and depressed. He worked and drank and grew more distant. She could see she had made a big mistake. I could tell she wasn't happy."

Elena told her mother how she gave her husband back his leather coat and the tiny diamond ring and said she would always care about him but that she had been too young and she felt she owed it to her father to return to school and get her life on track and she would always treasure their time together but she really had to go. She thought it would be the best thing for them both. She was sure he wasn't happy either.

The night before she had planned to leave, she did her hair and polished her nails and cooked him pheasant and they ate by candle-light—"for old time's sake" she had told her mother when she called to say she'd be home tomorrow. She really wanted no hard feelings. It had been her mistake and she was sorry to have involved him in it. Surely, they would always be friends.

"He's OK with it. He doesn't like it but he's OK with it," is what she told her mother when her mother asked her how he was taking it.

And, near as the coroner and the sheriff could piece it together, it was after everything she owned had been loaded in the car, the trunk full of books and photo albums, the back seat packed with her stereo and a rack of hanging clothes and the front passenger seat with the one suitcase full of toiletries and socks and underwear; maybe she was turning to wave good-bye before going, or maybe he'd been drinking Budweiser all night, or maybe he'd helped her and then went berserk but whatever happened, whether it was passion or calculation, before she sat into the driver's seat, he got the rifle from wherever he kept it. Near as they could figure by the angle of the wound, he stood on the front porch, aimed and fired, then walked over to where she lay in the leaf-fall beside the car and shot her again, in the breast.

This was the part that Martin could never imagine—the calculation of shooting her in the leg, then slowly, deliberately walking over and pressing the barrel against her left breast and pulling the trigger. Wouldn't such madness in a man give signs before? Wouldn't the first gun shot wake him from the dream?

Elena's mother was rocking in the chair across from Martin, sobbing quietly, clutching the letters, staring at the snapshot of her daughter on the desk standing next to the man who had just killed her.

"You pick out the casket, Martin. I can't do it. Something like her father's. Please, Martin. You do it."

He used the cherry casket with the moss pink velvet interior and though it was considerably more costly than what Elena's father was buried in, he charged the same and thought it was the least he could do.

And now, twenty years since, nearing fifty, he could still not shake the sense of shame, that the men in her life had let her down badly. The father who died too young, the husband who murdered her, even the embalmer who could only treat her viscera with cavity fluid, inject her arms and legs and head, stitch the horrible incisions of the post-mortem—from left shoulder to breastbone, breastbone to right shoulder, then breastbone to pubic bone—the little bulge in her tummy where the bag full of organs made her look almost expectant, then cover the stitches with cotton and adhesive. And then put a little blush on her cheeks, brush her lipstick on, curl and comb her hair. He had dressed her in the sweater and jeans her mother brought in and lifted her into the casket, put her First Communion rosary in her hand, a crucifix in the head of the casket and put an arm around her mother when she came to look.

"Oh no, no, no," she sobbed, her shoulders rising and falling, her

493

head shaking, her body buckling at the sight of her daughter's dead body. Martin held her at the elbows, whispering, "Let it go, I'm so sorry," because he never could think of the right thing to say.

Over time Martin learned to live with the helplessness and the sadness and the shame. He quit trying to figure the right thing to say. He listened. He stayed.

Still, all these years since, whenever the right shade of red turned up, he could see the fat old pathologist and his cigar and stupid tutorial manner there in the morgue with its cold smell of disaster and formalin, and the hearse that he drove up to get her that October. And the way they lay in coolers in the corner of the room, the two bodies in trays beside one another—Elena and the son-of-a-bitch that shot her.

He had shot himself, after killing her. He walked back in the house, sat on the edge of the bed and taking the muzzle of the rifle in his teeth pulled the trigger with his thumb, dividing his face at the septum in the process.

"Isn't that always the way?" the old pathologist had said, yanking the tray out with Elena's body on it. "It's love sickness. A man kills his wife then kills himself. A woman kills her man then does her nails."

Martin hated those sentences and couldn't forget them. That they rang true sometimes and false at others had never been a comfort.

Eventually, after the wake and Mass, her body was buried beside her father's, leaving another grave on the other side for her mother. It was all Martin could do—to get her where she was supposed to be. Her mother had a stone cut that read "Beloved Daughter" with a rose between her dates and another with her own name on it and her year of birth and a dash and had it placed over the empty plot beside her husband. She moved away some few years after that. Martin never heard from her again.

Nominated by Witness, Michael Heffernan, Joan Murray, Gibbons Ruark

IN PRAISE OF COLDNESS

by JANE HIRSHFIELD

from TIN HOUSE

"If you wish to move your reader,"
Chekhov wrote, "you must write more coldly."

Herakleitos recommended, "A dry soul is best."

And so at the center of many great works
is found a preserving dispassion,
like the vanishing point of quattrocento perspective,
or the tiny packets of desiccant enclosed
in a box of new shoes or seeds.

But still the vanishing point
is not the painting,
the silica is not the blossoming plant.

Chekhov, dying, read the timetables of trains.
To what more earthly thing could he have been faithful?—
Scent of rocking distances,
smoke of blue trees out the window,
hampers of bread, pickled cabbage, boiled meat.

Scent of the knowable journey.

Neither a person entirely broken
nor one entirely whole can speak.

In sorrow, pretend to be fearless. In happiness, tremble.

Nominated by Bob Hicok, Kay Ryan, Tin House, David Means

THINGS NOT SEEN
IN A REAR-VIEW MIRROR

essay by DEBRA MARQUART

from NEW LETTERS

On the morning of my father's funeral, there was a house on the road that blocked, for a time, all flow of traffic on Hwy 3, the two-lane blacktop that stretches south of I-94 to my hometown. I spotted the house first as a sliver of roof and eaves in the distance, weaving like an apparition above the horizon.

"Is that a house?" I asked my husband, Peter, who knows best to drive and remain quiet the closer we get to ground zero. We had driven 600 miles the day before and collapsed into bed late, 75 miles away at a hotel in Jamestown, the nearest city, in order to avoid the crowded bedrooms and cold morning showers that a wedding or a funeral or any kind of major family reunion can create in one household.

I kept expecting the next curve or rise to correct my vision, for the growing roof to slither to the right or left and become simply one more farmhouse on the side of the road. I know the topography of this drive from every conceivable angle, could read it with my fingers like braille. If you installed my memory like a slotted reel on a player piano, the ghostly keys would play out this tune: there is the gravel turnoff to Grandma and Grandpa Geist's old place; there's the farm where the Doll triplets lived, and the field that fills with water in the spring and empties in the summer; there's the ruin of the old country store where the little boy was run over by a milk truck. This is the place of dust where I spent my childhood; the place that my childhood cost.

Although writing about early Kansas, Willa Cather most accurately captures the enduring feeling of these plains when she describes them as "flatland, rich and somber and always silent; the miles of fresh-plowed soil, heavy and black, full of strength and harshness; the growing wheat, the growing weeds; the toiling horses, the tired men; the long empty roads," and "the eternal, unresponsive sky." And "against all this," Cather writes, "Youth, flaming like the wild roses."

I know the plains as that flaming impatient youth, a seventeen-year-old girl scanning the horizon for all possible methods of escape, and I know it from the next twenty years, gazing through the air-tight windows of cars, arming myself like an astronaut entering a rarefied environment every time I pass through for a short visit. For a long time, it seemed to me, North Dakota looked best only when glanced at briefly while adjusting the rear-view mirror.

As we came over the next rise, I saw we had three miles to go. This is Logan County. While it may be just another patch of flat horizon to someone driving through, to the people of my family it's the navel of the earth—the place from which all things flow, and to which all things return in time. In front of us now stretched the low-lying bowl of land that once belonged to my great-grandfather, Joseph Marquart. Although I did not know my great-grandfather—he was born in south Russia in 1856, exactly 100 years before me, and he died a wealthy man in central North Dakota in 1937—the headline of his obituary describes him as the "Logan County Wheat King for a Quarter Century."

This is big: to be king of wheat in a part of the country where wheat is king. In my own day, I was Dairy Princess of Logan County, a short-lived title I was stripped of when I refused to attend the state competition and pit my creamy milkmaid thighs and flashing farmer's daughter eyes against those of beauties from across the state.

How many times did I ask my father to recount for me the number of sections great-grandpa had owned. And he'd sit and think, ticking them off on his fingers—the north fields, the south fields, the ones that bordered the lake, the gravel pit, the ones by the wild woods—nine full sections of land, 5,760 acres, not counting the lots he owned in town, and the land in western North Dakota he inherited from his brother-in-law, and the land in Canada he bought during his salad days.

What must it have been like for him, an immigrant refugee from Russia, to come over this small ridge in the second half of his life and know that everything in sight belonged to him, had been shaped by his hand and the hands of children of his blood.

Before he died at the age of 80, my great-grandfather distributed his wealth by "set[ting] off in severalty a parcel to each of his children," the obituary says, "in appreciation of their cooperation." Even this description, which was written by Jay A. Bryant, the longtime editor of the Napoleon *Homestead*, makes him sound kind of baronial—dispatching his land in parcels, like there was an ermine cape, rolls of parchment, bowing servants, and hot-wax seals involved.

My own grandfather, as the eldest son, also named Joseph, took over the heart of the farm, the land with the orchard and the original farmstead and these low-lying fields surrounding it. And in his own time, my father Felix, who did not have the temperament to be a farmer—who had no aptitude with machinery, no affinity for livestock, who was impatient with nature, and believed he could will it to deliver sun or rain if he just got angry enough or stared out the window at it long enough—took over this farm and the life of frustration that went with it just so the land would not go out of the family.

In the end, my father fulfilled his generation's part of the agreement. A mile ahead and to the right was the nest of white buildings on a gentle hill at the center of what was now my brother's farm. The land spread out flat for miles. It was early June; the fields lay in rich black furrows, the seeds buried deep under the topsoil were just cracking their husks and letting go of tender green shoots; the grass in the pastures was lush. We were close to home now. If not for the small rise on the northern edge of town, I would have been able to see the three elevators jutting into the sky and the thin spire of the church belltower, which would be ringing, in moments, for my father.

The funeral was at 10:00, but the rosary vigil began at 9:00. It was now 9:15. I imagined my distraught mother at the funeral chapel, clutching a ragged Kleenex, her nose red from crying. She sits in the front pew as mourners pass by to view my father stretched out flat in his coffin. My brother and his wife, all my sisters and their husbands, and all the grandchildren will have arrived by now. But where am I,

499

she will be wondering. Have we been killed in a car accident? My mother is a woman who believes in multi-part tragedies, in life unraveling in complex and ironic ways, and as her youngest daughter, I have given her more grist for her worry-mill than all of her other children put together.

If we had come upon this magnificent house on the road on any other stretch of Hwy 3, we could have just pulled off the lane, hung in the ditch at a fierce angle, and stared in wonder for a few moments as it passed by. But on this day, we meet up with the house precisely on the spot where county workers have decided, this anonymous morning, to repair a forty-foot stretch of the road. Men in orange vests are shoveling and packing down the soft tar. The right lane is cordoned off with a line of orange reflector cones stretched across the highway.

Peter pulls our van onto the gravel shoulder, and we join a growing column of cars all waiting to see what will happen. Down the road, on the south side of the tarred lane, we see the house hulking and bouncing on its springy flatbed like an over-anxious bull.

This is not one of those sad double-wides with their backsides marked "wide load," and their vivisected halves roaring by you on the freeway. When I'm passed by these trailer houses, their cross-sectioned walls battened down by tarps, I stretch to look inside the blowing corner always hoping to see an entire mobile-home-life going on: a man in a sleeveless T-shirt sprawled on a couch and watching a grainy TV, a woman making cupcakes in the small island kitchen, and a collection of Holly Hobby collectors plates resting on wire pedestals in the space above the cupboards that nobody knows what to do with. But all the tarp reveals is a hollow cavern of wind-blown emptiness.

Not so, this house on the road. Here is a sturdy brick, two-story complete with a wraparound three-season porch and an attic full of spooky gables. A house worth tearing off its 100-year-old foundation and rolling with logs and pulleys onto a monstrous flatbed. And on this day it makes its thirty mile journey north to the town of Dawson where it will become, I learn later, a lodge house for weekend hunters. For now it is solemn and dignified, moving at a queenly pace, as if rolling through a parade in its honor.

The flatbed is flanked on all sides by the flashing red lights of police escorts and the nervous moving crew. Also shadowing the house, moving as it moves, are several orange trucks from the power com-

500

pany, their hydraulic baskets hoisting men in hardhats in the air. Wearing long rubber gloves, the men stretch the electrical wires over the complicated matrix of eaves and chimneys with long, slatted poles. This is delicate work, dangerous. A small slip and more than one person could die right before our eyes this morning.

I look at my watch. It is now 9:20. Peter doesn't say anything, just gets out of the car and approaches one of the roadworkers. I watch them talk for a while on the side of the road as only men can talk. The county worker spits a prodigious wad onto the blacktop; Peter lifts his shoulders and sinks his hands deep in his pockets.

My husband doesn't look like he belongs in this part of the country. Even in the more populated and slightly more diverse eastern part of the state where his family lives, people will approach him in stores and say, "You're not from around here, are you?" He's Greek-American, has a thick head of dark wavy hair, and soft coffee-brown eyes. He has deep, slanted cheekbones and an arching Roman nose.

If I were to have gotten out of the car and approached the county worker, the man would have said, "Oh, you're one of the Marquart girls." So identifiable to the region are my family features—a narrowness of chin and angularity of eyes—that I'm sometimes called Little Felix by perfect strangers. But this is how small my hometown is. Even when Peter approaches him, the county worker still says, "Oh, you're on your way to the funeral in town." How does he know this? Who else would be on this road at this time of day except someone going to the funeral. I look at my watch. It's now 9:25.

Peter turns in the wind and walks back to the van. I can tell by the look on his face the news is not good. "Twenty minutes," he says, getting in and slamming the car door. "They've got to move the house before we can pass."

I look around at the standing water in the ditches. There's almost enough dry room to pull the van off the blacktop, down the grassy incline, and make a quick getaway into town. But with all the cops around, I'm not about to transform into Cousin Daisy from the Dukes of Hazzard and invite the pursuit of the drunken sheriff. This is how catastrophes happen, I know from experience—one bad decision follows another.

Had I done this on purpose? Gotten up a little later than I should have at the hotel in Jamestown, taken a little too long to get dressed before we checked out, so that I could arrive here at this moment. Three miles down the road my father lies in the funeral chapel, the spooky building we kids passed by on our way from school, past the bowling alley, to the rec center downtown, hurrying by that corner because we were so repulsed by the faded green funeral parlor sign stuck in the lawn.

There was a game we played when we passed that corner. First, you made a palm sandwich by cupping one of your hands against someone else's hand. Then you'd run your thumb up and down the side of your hand, and your first finger along the side of the other person's hand. Yuck, we'd scream and pull our hands away. You can feel the backside of your own hand with your thumb, but the other side, the part that is someone else's hand, is numb against the stroke of your finger.

This is what death feels like, we'd whisper creepily to each other. It was as if the other half of your hand was nothing more than a numb shape in this world—busy, we theorized, doing advance work in the other world, being a hand for you across that unknown threshold to which your now half-a-feeling hand would eventually be pulled.

I thought of my father in that building that morning, wearing his blue suit inside a steel-blue coffin lined with satin. I didn't want to see his hands held together in eternal prayer, a black rosary wound around his fingers as if to help him keep track of his Our Fathers and Hail Marys during his long journey. I didn't want to shake the hand of the sympathetic undertaker, or admire the sheaf of ripe wheat bound with a blue ribbon and placed inside my father's coffin as a parcel of seed for the fields he would plant in the afterlife. I didn't want to hear family friends tell me "how good he looks," and I didn't want my mother to force me to get up close and stroke his lapel one final time.

I wanted to remember those hands shuffling a deck of cards, dealing ten to me, ten to him, picking up spares and slapping down discards as he looked to complete his run of queens or diamonds or hearts. And when I snapped my fan of cards down on the table and gave him my rummy smile, I wanted him to rise again and scream in playfulness, "You had my gin card!" and chase me around the house with a shoe until my mother makes us stop.

I wanted to remember him scruffing the top of my head, tickling me, bending my ears, messing my hair, saying, "Ah, you're just a rotten kid." Wah, I wanted to protest back, I am not. I wanted to remember him on the couch with the remote in his hand, or in the hospital after his last heart attack with the plunger in his hand calling for more medication or for the nurse.

I remember one spring when I was about thirteen, my mother asked me to drive the pickup to the north field to take my father his lunch. He had been seeding the land for weeks, and this section was the last to be done. The water levels were high that year, and this particular field had a slope and a small spring in the center that even under normal conditions never dried to more than a slough halfway through the summer.

My father adored straight, even rows, and he couldn't bear wasted acreage. Each year, he circled the wet spot like a jealous husband, seeding as close in as possible. How many times as a child had I seen him walking home from the field after he had gotten the tractor stuck in that field. From the second story of our farmhouse, one could observe him coming along the section line, his short legs jutting sharply in front of him as he stamped toward the house to get another tractor to pull himself out.

When he got closer, you could see, he'd be swinging his seed cap madly by his side. And with his cap off, you could make out the leathery sunburnt darkness of his face, smudged and dirty from planting, set against the pallor of his bone-white forehead—the one place that lived a pristine, sunless life under the constant protection of his seed cap. And when he'd get close enough to be addressed, my mother would dare to ask, "What happened," and he'd just storm by saying, "goddamit."

That day when I was thirteen and got to drive lunch to Dad in the north field, I remember sitting on the gravel road in the pickup with the cooler beside me on the seat. I watched my dad go around in circles seeding the circumference of the wet spot. It was common to have to wait like this. Farming was serious business, and you were just a kid. You could afford to listen to the radio and wait until the next row was finished.

I remember my dad circling and circling with the tractor, then getting a little too close to the spring, cutting too deep with one of the big back tires, its deep grooves spinning in place—clogged and slick with dark mud. And I remember him trying to back his way out of the mess, jackknifing with the seeder attached behind the tractor, and then his other back wheel sliding down the incline and getting sucked into the mud.

The angry groan of the tractor's engine roared against the quiet backdrop of the morning. The grinding gears gnashed and rocked the tractor back and forth as the wheels dug down looking for pay-dirt, anything solid for the deep rubber grooves to catch on, but they only spun and kicked up more mud.

Just when he was about to give up, just about to cut the engine, pull the brake and hop down, the front end of the tractor began to lift off the ground—first, touching lightly into the air, then elevating slowly higher and higher, rising into the sky. It happened so slowly that there was time to contemplate the outcome. Would the balance shift and the tractor flip backward over him? This is the most common story of the plains; each year some farmer must die on his machinery, sacrifice his blood to this dry land.

My father held firm in his seat. High in the air now, he grasped the steering wheel and leaned his small body forward to counteract the light front end. I watched from the pickup, unable to move or help. It was a moment of sheer weights and balances—the physical world ticking off its equations, none of which included me. That is when my father looked in my direction, to see if I was registering all this, and our eyes met. I could see that he wasn't afraid at all, that he was just his usual self—small and fierce and impatient to know what would happen next.

That's the way I want to imagine him that last day in the hospital. Except for the beeping equipment and the health workers trying to save his life, he was alone. But I want to be there floating above him. And when that part of him that is now gone begins to lift up, I want to meet his eyes one last time, so that I am the last thing he sees, so that he will remember me—the daughter who watches silently by the side of the road, the one who is getting this all down.

Nominated by New Letters

THE PALACE AT 4:00 A.M.

by DEBORA GREGER

from THE KENYON REVIEW

> *Who's sleeping next to you?*
> *It's not loneliness—it's your wife.*
> —Nazim Hikmet

And then one morning the courtship is over.
No longer does the male hold forth at 4:00 A.M.

to impress the female enough to mate.
Now only the note of alarm is given voice

by the blackbird or its cheeky, petrified young:
a *chink* in the air—as if stone were being dressed,

the way you mend a wall in an old cathedral town,
the local clunch too soft to last. Almost fifty,

you wake almost alone, in a foreign country.
That's not a husband next to you, that's loneliness.

You can hear the electric whine of the milk float,
muezzin of the neighborhood, a few doors down,

near the mosque, once Methodist chapel—
but who worships it now? The *chink* of bottle against stone

drowns under the dead weight of casks being rolled
down to the cellar of the Live and Let Live pub.

The wind is wrong, but the hour's quartered
and tolled by Our Lady of the English Martyrs.

O Fisher, Campion, and More, admit to your circle
Hikmet, Communist, poet exiled to Russia and there

kept company by a woman younger and blonder
than his wife. For this small warmth let us give thanks.

Nominated by The Kenyon Review, Henry Carlile

MILES

fiction by RICHARD BURGIN

from CHELSEA

"You're the rookie, I'm the veteran—you should listen to me," the veteran said, turning toward her in the front seat. She didn't acknowledge him, just kept driving her route, staring ahead poker-faced, maddeningly placid from the veteran's point of view, Miles thought. "See, it's not about what's comfortable and convenient for you, it's about time-is-money; you hear me, rookie?" She still said nothing. Kept her poker face, although Miles thought it was a pretty poker face and he'd been trying, so far without luck, to make eye contact with it from the backseat via the mirror in the front seat where the rookie and veteran sat. In that regard he sympathized with the veteran. Miles' hope was that if she would look back at him he'd show some sympathy for her, try to talk to her and maybe find a way to get her phone number later. But, realistically, he thought this could never happen. She was simply driving the shuttle to his home—there was no basis for contact. Besides there were several other factors going against him. She was probably black, she hadn't said more than three words to him and was under a great deal of pressure from her mentoring fellow driver who might or might not be involved with her, and who was certainly more than a little mean.

It was starting to get dark out. Five minutes ago, the last people besides Miles left the shuttle and the veteran began to get even angrier. He pointed out with more than a little contempt that the elderly couple they'd just dropped off lived in one of the wealthiest communities in Delaware County, then said how he hadn't appreciated their oversized guard dog that'd charged him. The veteran

507

described the dog's charge in some detail and then its relentless barking, although nothing happened to him bite-wise.

"I wish that dog did bite me so I could sue their ass," he said and Miles made a little supportive sound—something like a part laugh, part uh-huh.

Speaking of money made the veteran think again about the longer cost-ineffective route the rookie was taking and he lit into her once more. Now Miles started to worry. It was like becoming aware there was a bee flying near him, not exactly on his nose but perhaps two or three feet away.

He thought it was hard to know if it was worse being a rookie or a veteran, then checked again and saw that the rookie being criticized was definitely black. He tried one last time for eye contact with an expression that he hoped combined both lust and sympathy, but she still didn't respond. Once more he wouldn't get his way.

He remembered sitting in the backyard of his building complex a week ago, shortly before he started packing for his company's latest trip. He'd moved his white plastic chair off the five feet of concrete in front of his sliding doors onto the backyard itself, then started picking some blades of grass and rubbing them against his face. A fat bumblebee was flying around in an irregular pattern as if it were drunk. Miles had been thinking: there are as many people in the world as blades of grass in this yard but it's only the few blades you can pick and rub against your face that you feel. It was the same with people. The ones you picked weren't any more different from each other than the blades of grass were. They wanted light and water and growth and maybe to be picked by the right hands. They wanted their way—it was built into them, just as it was built into the grass. But how long could you accept your will being denied?

It was a tricky question, especially with women. He remembered when he started with them in his late teens and early twenties he thought the pleasure lay in getting as much of your way as you could. He would look for and eventually find ones who would let him mostly do what he wanted but they always thwarted him one way or another. Either they said too many words, or not the right ones afterwards or none at all or else they would simply lie to him or ultimately leave him, or if one ever did do what he wanted he found out that wasn't what he really wanted either.

The veteran was talking warmly to the rookie now, even laughing, and Miles wondered what was behind this good cop/bad cop behavior. Was the veteran simply becoming worried about the way he acted in front of a customer or was he merely trying another approach to get some response from her? Then the rookie asked Miles in a toneless voice if his home was off Route 113. Miles answered and the veteran started speaking sarcastically to the rookie again, but by then Miles had turned back to his own thoughts.

He was thinking about his sister now—sibling rivalry would be too weak a word to describe the intense, complicated power struggles between them that took place over the years on the playground, in their yard and, of course, inside their home in the form of endless games and competitions. Much more often than not, however, when he would win in Chinese checkers or badminton (and especially when she'd cry afterwards), instead of feeling happy he'd feel a sadness verging on despair. It was almost the same thing, years later, when he got divorced. The fact that his ex-wife didn't find anyone for years, and he did, didn't make him feel happy or vindicated—though she'd left him, and falsely accused him of so much. Instead her loneliness caused him more pain than if she'd married again right away and he was left like a dog chasing its tail or like that drunken, useless bee.

"O.K., you gonna stop this bullshit right now," the rookie said. She still wasn't looking at the veteran when she spoke, but then she'd just left a red light and couldn't afford to.

"You saying something to me?"

"You heard me."

"You talk that way to me, you're looking for trouble."

"You're the one done all the talkin'. You're the one in trouble talking like that to me in front of a customer."

"I'll talk any goddamn way I want to. I'm the supervisor in this car."

"I'll talk to the supervisor, alright. You can be sure of that."

There was another red light; then catlike, she got out of her seat belt and slammed the door.

The veteran swore out the window at her but she was running and soon turned a corner (perhaps into the woods) and disappeared. Meanwhile, cars were honking behind him and the veteran had to switch to the driver's seat and start driving.

"Jesus Christ, do you believe that?" he said.

Miles couldn't think of anything to say in response and made one of his semi-supportive sounds again.

"That woman's crazy. I'm trying to help her do her job, I'm *supposed* to ride with her and help her do her job and she refuses to take the route I tell her to take. It's like she wanted trouble right from the start."

"Do you think she'll be all right?" Miles blurted.

"Oh, she'll be all right. That bitch is tough as nails. I'm the one's gonna come out getting screwed by all this. She's got a cell phone that she's probably using right now to file a complaint on me."

"I thought I saw her run into the woods. How will she get home?"

"She'll get home okay. She'll get them to pick her up and when they come she'll say I abused her, maybe even tried to rape her. I wouldn't put it past her. Matter of fact, you're my only chance here 'cause you're the only goddamn witness knows what really happened."

"I really wasn't paying attention."

"That right? Funny, I thought I saw you looking at her a couple of times, like you were interested . . . anyway, you know I didn't lay a goddamn finger on her. If I lose this job, it's all over for me. Your telling the truth—that's my only chance. What's your name . . . sir?" he said, adding the sir as a kind of afterthought.

"Miles."

The veteran pulled the car onto the soft shoulder and stopped. "Miles, I'm gonna have to get your name and address, okay?"

The veteran produced a notebook and pen and turned on the light in the shuttle. Miles thought briefly of lying, but what would be the point since the veteran would see where he lived when he dropped him off? Besides he'd already given the company his last name and phone number when he called the shuttle service from the Philadelphia airport.

The veteran wrote rapidly (though his hand was shaking) asking Miles to repeat everything twice. He had a mustache and dark, intense eyes. Then he started the car up and drove in silence for a while. When they were ten to fifteen minutes from Miles' housing complex, the veteran finally spoke.

"Hey Miles, I hope I didn't offend you with what I said earlier about you looking at the driver."

"No, forget it. Besides, I guess I was looking a little."

"Hey, I don't blame you. We all look, right?"

"Sure."

"Be worse than hell if we couldn't even look."

"That's for sure . . . these days."

"Hey Miles, you mind if I ask if you're married?"

"No, I'm not married. I was once, but I'm not now."

"Anyone special in your life?"

"No, not now. I couldn't say there was."

"So it must have ruined the ride for you when she left the car, huh?"

"The whole thing was just upsetting."

"But if me and her didn't argue, she might not have left and then you could have kept looking and maybe talked with her and who knows what might have happened? So I guess I ruined that and I owe you one, right?"

It was a strange, though not inaccurate line of argument—like a panicked kind of logic—and Miles didn't know what to say.

"Yeah, I can see what I ruined for you—especially since I'm gonna need you to be on my side and say that I never touched or threatened her, never did nothing like that to make her leave the car and desert her job."

"You don't owe me," Miles said, although he was thinking the veteran did owe him for this nightmare of a ride and should give him the ride for free.

"No, no, I think I do, and I think I know a way I can pay you back and square things between us, but first I need to know if you'd like a little action tonight; I mean a woman, Miles. Could you use one?"

He thought of his perfectly empty apartment. The traveling life of his new job in a new place made it almost impossible to meet anyone, and the only women who'd been in his place in the year that he'd been there were the building manager once—for two minutes—and an equally brief visit from a middle-aged tenant with a petition. It was as if his will to find anybody at this point had been worn away. At 29, he knew he shouldn't be feeling that way.

"Yeah, I could use one, I guess."

"It just so happens I know one who lives pretty near you. I can make a little detour and get her for you right now. If you want me to."

"What's this gonna cost me?"

"No, no, you don't get it. She's for you, on me, to show my appreciation for your testimony for me in the future, okay?"

"Yuh, okay," Miles said, feeling uneasy.

"Good, so long as we understand each other. 'Cause I didn't hear

511

you volunteering to speak for me, and I have to be completely clear about what you're gonna say, you hear me? I can't take no chances with you."

"Yes, yes, I hear you."

" 'Cause if I lose this job it's all over for me. I'd rather be a corpse in the ground than be out of a job, and I'll never get work in this business again if that bitch starts flapping her lips. See I've got no defense, you get the picture, Miles. You sure you get it?"

"Yes, I understand . . ."

"So that's why I'm rewarding you like this."

"Okay. So how's it going to work with this girl you're gonna get me?"

"I'll pick her up, we'll drive to your place or you can do it at hers. You do it at hers, I'll wait in the shuttle and drive you home after. You do it at yours, I'll wait in the shuttle and drive *her* home. Would an hour be enough time? Maybe you could have a little more."

"Yeah, sure."

He was trying to figure where it would be better. He didn't like the idea of a stranger in his house with the veteran right outside. On the other hand it would be easier to do it in his own apartment and safer, too, since he knew where everything was.

"You just say the word, buddy, and I'll call her on my cell phone right now so she'll be ready."

"Yes, okay. I guess my house would be better."

"You got it, chief."

The veteran began to dial and Miles leaned forward slightly like a jockey. He was trying to figure if he was getting his way or if the veteran was. Or was this one of those rare times when both could benefit? The veteran was talking in a low voice and it was difficult to hear much of what he was saying. Miles thought he said, "You *have* to do it," then, "Be ready . . . ten minutes, no more."

The veteran cursed softly, but with great bitterness, after he hung up. Neither of them said anything for a while.

"What's her name?" Miles suddenly said, surprised by his question.

"Who? The one I'm getting for you?"

"Yes."

"Her name's Silver."

"Sylvia?"

"No, Silver, like the horse, and you can be the Lone Ranger. Me,

I'll be Tonto waiting off-screen. There a place I can get a drink near you?"

"Yuh, there's a couple."

"Good. You tell me where they are when we get there so I'll have something to do. I could use one."

"Okay," Miles said. He was wondering just how big a pimp the veteran was, how many girls he had in his stable. It couldn't be too many otherwise he wouldn't be so worried about losing his driving job.

They reached Paoli (15 minutes or so from his home), the veteran still muttering about the rookie. Then he took a couple of side streets and a moment later pulled the car over and said, "Wait here, I'm gonna get her."

Was it his home? Hers? A few seconds after the veteran left the car, Miles looked out the window to get a sense of the neighborhood. It looked dim and gray, even under the stars, more shabby than sinister. The few people he saw walking were not well-dressed but appeared to be ordinary citizens.

He heard them walking, or thought he did, a split second before he saw them, and saw them too late to tell which building they came from. He felt oddly frightened and exhilarated at the same time—like a child at a horror movie. Then they were at the car door—Silver making a move to get in front.

"You get in the back seat," the veteran said authoritatively. "Come on, don't start getting shy on me now, I'm in no mood."

Miles moved over to give her room, then tried to figure out how old she was. It was hard to tell because she didn't look at him directly and, at any rate, seemed to have an unnatural expression on her face. As for her body, again Miles couldn't be sure. She was wearing jeans and a long black shirt. No skin was showing, but he thought she was maybe a little overweight.

As if he were reading Miles' mind, the veteran said, "I told her to get in a dress but she wouldn't. I guess this is the night no one listens to me."

Miles looked at Silver reflexively, wondering if she'd start fighting with the veteran like the rookie did, but she said nothing. This time he noticed that her eyebrows were dark and quite pronounced (which made him think she was hairy in other parts of her body too—something he had mixed feelings about). Her eyes were also dark, though smaller than he would have hoped, as if they were on the verge of closing to protect her from something.

513

They rode in silence, no one talking except the veteran occasionally cursing the rookie or else life in general.

"I like your name, Silver," Miles finally said, to say something.

"Oh yeah? Thanks. What did you say yours was?"

"Miles."

"Right . . . 'And Miles to go before I sleep.' That was the name of a poem I learned in school. You know it?"

He did know what she was talking about but didn't want to correct her and so said, "No, I don't know."

"Where'd you say that bar was?" the veteran said.

"On 113 about a half mile from where you'll drop me."

"Gonna get wasted tonight. 'Cause it's a cruel bitch world, right Silver?" the veteran said.

She said something under her breath, then settled back in her seat, rigid like a mummy. "Hey Miles-to-go, you got anything to drink at your place?" Silver said

"Yeah, I got something," Miles said.

"Good."

Miles made his little supportive laugh, trying to make eye contact with her. Instead he saw the veteran glaring at him in the mirror. Silver still hadn't looked him straight in the eye, and Miles began feeling that this all wasn't going to go well. It had been exciting at first, the thought of a girl in his apartment, and it all happening so unexpectedly. It was as if, to return to his earlier thoughts, he was not only getting his way but in a guilt-free manner and with the full cooperation (enthusiastic in the case of the veteran) of the other people involved. Of course it was unclear how much he would have to say later about the rookie. That was troubling since the veteran had scared her and he didn't blame the rookie for leaving the car. As a result, he had to remind himself that the rookie had never really spoken to him. There'd been one plaintive look that had encouraged him, falsely he now saw, so really what was she to him? Still, it was troubling. Was it really, then, his conscience bothering him about her that could account for his mood, or simply how sullen Silver was acting?

Once again, the veteran seemed to read his mind. "Hey, Silver. I don't hear you talking to Miles. You supposed to be friendly, I told you that. Miles is going to do something very important for me, and he's supposed to be happy, you got that?"

514

She said a single "yeah" in reply. He didn't like the way the veteran was bullying her.

At his home, Silver got out of the car and walked ahead of him through the parking lot, still not looking at him, stopping only so he could open the door. He turned on the light immediately and walked to the refrigerator where there was a bottle of gin.

"You want a gin and tonic, or maybe a beer?"

"Gin's good. I'll fix them."

He stood a few feet away now, thinking that there was something oddly sweet in the way she looked, that she was really pretty and that perhaps this would work out after all.

"Hey Miles, what're you thinkin' about?" Silver said, handing him his drink. He saw that she'd finished half of hers. "You look a million miles away."

He quickly took a large swallow of his drink. He liked that she was speaking lightly to him. She asked him about his job and he told her, without telling her how much he hated it. They joked for a few minutes more until he said, "I'm thinking you have a pretty face," and touched it with his free hand. Then he drank some more. He was pleased that she let him touch her there, since he thought prostitutes usually didn't like to be kissed or even touched on their faces. She looked at him closely and he saw a softness in what he'd thought were her hard little eyes.

"I like looking at it," he said, continuing to touch it and then her hair. She seemed to be under his spell for a minute, but then broke away.

"It's not my face you want to spend time with."

"What do you mean?"

"That's not the part of me you're interested in, right?"

Miles made a semi-shrug, uncertain what to say. The alcohol seemed to have made her much bolder. She was walking ahead of him toward his room, holding the little bottle of gin and her glass, which she set down on his bureau. He was embarrassed that his room was so small and uninteresting. It lacked distinction or even any secrets. He thought it would be fun to share secrets with a woman under his spell but they were all in his mind and there seemed no way to get them out. He thought he would drink some more then, like Silver.

"What are you looking at? You keep looking outside," she said.

515

"My blinds are open and I can see him in the car."

"Yeah, that don't surprise me."

"Feels kind of weird, like he's spying on us."

She finished her drink and started another. She was standing a few feet away from him by the far side of the bed.

"Why don't you shut them then?"

"Think it would make him mad? I notice he's got quite a temper."

"It's your house. Besides, he told me he was doing you a favor. He's worried about making you feel good, not about me."

Miles shut the blinds, then walked towards her. He thought of kissing her but began trying to unbutton her shirt.

"I'll handle the clothes," she said, turning away from him. "Why don't you shut off the light? You'll like me better in the dark."

"I like you now," he said, but shut off the lamp anyway. He was starting to trust her more now or at least her judgment since he did feel both more excited and confident in the dark. The only thing that bothered him was that she was still drinking in bed, apparently straight from the bottle.

"Put the bottle away, will you?"

"One second," she said.

The only thing that bothered her once they started having sex was his attempts to satisfy her. "Quit doing that, will you. What are you trying to do?" Then later, "Go faster, okay? No point in anything else." She said the latter remark so ardently that he finally obeyed, uncertain again if he'd gotten his way or she'd gotten hers, but reasonably content for a few seconds with the outcome. Then she started talking in a rush. It was like a fast and complicated passage in a piece of music that took him by surprise and seemed to be already well under way by the time he tuned in.

"I was always like that," she was saying, "wanting to know the reasons for things, even as a kid. But after a while you got to wonder what's the point of learning about dresses and makeup or even brushing your teeth if you end up like this," she said, starting to cry softly.

"What's the matter?"

"Nothing. Don't worry about it."

"Come on, tell me. What is it?" he said, embracing her and letting her cry against his chest. It was a refined kind of crying too, that almost made him want to cry himself.

"I shouldn't have drunk so much. It makes me weepy afterwards."

"Haven't you done this a lot? I mean. . ."

"No, not a lot. A few times when he made me."

"What do you mean? What are you saying?"

"What do I mean? What am I saying?" she repeated.

"You mean you never get paid?"

"I'm no whore. It's him, he gets paid from it one way or another."

"So why do you do it? I don't understand."

"You're asking a lot of questions, aren't you? Especially since you wouldn't like none of the answers."

"I like you, I . . ."

"Oh really."

"Yeah, that's why I want to know."

"It's an evil story, Miles."

"He's your boyfriend, right?"

She laughed ironically, but said nothing.

"That's it, right? And he gets off making you do this for him whenever he wants to use you."

"No, that's not it."

"What else could it be? He's not your pimp, you don't get paid. Why don't you just tell me?"

"It's not that way."

"Come on, why bother to lie about it?"

"I'm not lying. He's my brother, okay? You satisfied now?"

"Your brother?"

"You couldn't understand. We've been together a long time. You couldn't understand. My father crossed the line on both of us. My brother helped us get away. We've been together a long time. He seems mean, but he's kind too."

"So, you're lovers, right?"

"What? Why are you asking me that?"

" 'Cause I'm thinking that you are unless you want to lie and tell me otherwise. Look, I have a sister. I've had dreams about her. It's not like I don't understand."

"It was only once or twice; we did it years ago when we were first away from my father, but then he stopped 'cause he said he wanted to live right."

"Then why does he make you sleep with people?"

"You couldn't get it. He has to do that 'cause he's like me. He has to ruin things. See, you were a nice man, you touched my hair and face and said nice things and I had to ruin it by telling you this. All my secrets."

517

He picked up the bottle from the floor and took a drink. Silver was perceptive enough, he decided, she *had* ruined things. He thought he wanted her to talk but as had been the case before, he regretted it when she did. If only people would occasionally say things you wanted to hear. The way it was, it was nothing but a recipe for confusion. You pleaded for communication and you got over-communication that ended in pain. No wonder you couldn't win.

He sat down on the bed feeling angry and sorry for himself, but not wanting her to leave either.

"My problem is I'm never able to get my way in anything," Miles said, "no matter how hard I try. It's like you can ruin things just by wanting them. Sometimes it looks like I'll get my way but then something always ruins it in the end."

"Well, I'm sure I kept your streak going."

"No, I didn't mean you," he said, thinking that of course he did mean her. "I'd like to get to know you."

"You'd be disappointed." She had stopped crying now and said the last line coldly. It made him miss her crying. He felt he had to do something lest he lose her completely, but first got up from the bed and peered through a slat of his blinds.

"He's still out there."

"I'm not surprised. I hate it when he waits outside like that."

"Why's he doing it?"

She shrugged. "Like I said, he's a ruiner."

"You think he's getting madder by the minute?"

"Probably."

"Why?"

"Just the way he is."

"What if you wanted to stay longer? Could you?"

"How would I get back? I have a regular job, you know. I work behind a counter."

"I could call a cab. I just want to know if that's something we could do, or would he blow his stack?"

"Probably."

"What?"

"Probably blow his stack."

"What would he do?"

"Try to make you pay one way or another."

"But it was *his* idea."

"The sex part was his idea, not anything else. He'd probably feel

518

you were cheating him—he's a great one for feeling cheated. Not that he cares much about me. I don't flatter myself that way."

"I don't get why he'd feel cheated."

"He'd feel you were trying to get more out of the deal than you agreed on. He'd end up turning you against him too. That's one of the ways he ruins things for himself."

"Maybe we could see each other another time. You could give me your phone number."

"My phone number is his phone number."

"You could call me. I could give you my number. I really want to see you," he said, squeezing her hand before getting out of bed to check on the veteran's whereabouts.

"This night would torture you once you started to remember it. I ruined it by telling you too much."

There was a sudden loud knocking at the door.

"Jesus!" Miles said, trying frantically to at least step into his underpants before walking to the door.

Should he open it? It was the veteran, of course, and the knock sounded angry. But if he didn't answer it, the veteran would only get angrier. Besides, hadn't the veteran made good on his deal? He had no grounds not to answer the door. He certainly couldn't bring up about what Silver told him without getting her in trouble, so after hesitating and listening to it again, he opened the door, then immediately stepped back as if he'd just let in a cold blast of air.

The veteran stared hard at him. He was actually an inch or two shorter than Miles, not heavy at all, and probably at least five years older. Yet there was something menacing not only in the face, but in his whole lean, tight body.

"Hey Miles."

"Hey," Miles said, feeling childlike by merely echoing him.

"You enjoy being the Lone Ranger? It looks by the way you're dressed that you did."

Miles looked at him silently.

"Now I need to have you write a statement about the incident tonight with my co-driver. You know, like we agreed."

Had he agreed? He wasn't sure but he said he'd write the statement (thinking what will it mean, if it isn't notarized? He's really not so smart after all).

"Just write a few lines on your stationery saying I didn't abuse her in any way and that she left the car completely on her own . . . impulse. Then sign your name."

Miles nodded. "Will do," he said. "Did you ever go to that bar?" Miles asked as he wrote out the requisite lines on his TV table a few feet away.

"No, but I see that you been doin' some drinkin'. Where's Silver anyway? Silver!" he called, raising his voice a little.

She walked into the room, shirt hanging out, head averted from both of them.

"You been drinking, Silver?"

"What?"

"You been drinking this man's liquor?"

"Just a little. Why's that so bad?"

" 'Cause we all know how easy it is for you to keep your mouth shut when you drink."

She looked away and Miles looked down at the floor.

"You been flapping your lips again? You flap your fucking lips worse than Donald Duck, don't you?" The veteran turned toward Miles. "She been telling you her life story?"

"No," Miles said.

"You been telling him all about us, haven't you?" he said to Silver. She shook her head unconvincingly. It was almost as if she couldn't lie to him, Miles thought jealously.

"Christ, what difference does it make, anyway. My life's over. I ain't gonna keep my job no matter what he writes, they're gonna believe that bitch over me, we all know that. My life's over. You could flush it down the toilet in less than a second—that's how little of it's left, so why the fuck should I care what you two talked about? You always were a stupid snitch, anyway. So how 'bout letting me have a drink too?"

"You sure?" said Miles.

"What do you mean 'am I sure'? You ask a man with a dagger hanging out of his heart if he's feeling any pain? Jesus Christ, what do I have to do to get a drink in this world?"

Silver left the room then.

"Where you going?" the veteran said, taking a step forward, but Silver returned with the gin before he walked any farther, handing the bottle to her brother.

She didn't even ask me if it was all right, Miles thought, as the veteran hoisted the bottle and drank it straight.

"Jesus Christ, this stuff stinks!" he said after the first long swallow.

Then, "Damn it to hell," and, simply, "Christ," after the second and third. He seemed to get high immediately—perhaps he'd been drinking from a bottle of something in his car all along.

Silver's eyes never left the veteran's face, Miles noted, like an actress waiting for her cue. Miles was also watching the veteran, anxious and dumbfounded.

"Jesus Christ, I'm a real spectacle, drinking and crying in front of you two."

"You aren't crying," Silver said.

"Whoring out my goddamn sister to . . ."

"Don't," Silver said.

". . . a stranger. A stranger, for Christ's sake."

"Don't say any more."

"Depending on a goddamn stranger to save my life. You can't get any lower than that, for Christ's sake, can you? . . . So, you enjoy her?" he said, turning toward Miles, with a strange smile on his lips.

"Why don't you sit down?" Miles said.

"If I sit down I will sit down in hell, that's why. I will fall into hell and never get up. You learn to stand, after a while. I sit all day and night in my job . . . So you sorry you did her now? . . . Now we're like family and you got to listen to me."

"I said I was on your side."

"I don't even care about the fucking job. What kind of job is it anyway? You think it's so wonderful driving strangers back and forth from the airport all hours of the day and night for peanuts. For peanuts! You drop them off and get attacked by their dogs in the dark. You get lost, your fellow driver deserts you, you have to pimp for a stranger so he'll testify *if* they even give you a hearing? What am I fighting for? For twelve hours a day of that? It's over, it was over a long time ago."

"Why don't you sit down?"

"I told you why already. Are you completely unaware of hell?" he said, raising his voice and glaring at Miles. "Nothing can save you when you're in hell. You can't rest in hell. You got to stand at attention, that's all. You're trying to get me to sit in hell so you can squash me like you squashed my sister."

"Stop it," Silver said.

"I've been squashed by better than you my whole life," the veteran said, his face wrinkled with grief and rage. He pointed directly at Miles and Miles felt a rage of his own surge up in him.

521

"Give me that," he said, snatching the piece of paper which Miles had been holding for several minutes now.

"This is what I think of your fucking statement," he said, tearing it into several pieces and throwing them on the floor.

We are going to fight now, Miles thought. It will be my first fight.

"Come on," the veteran said to Silver, "let's go. Let's leave this squashing factory."

"He didn't do nothing," Silver said.

"He took *ADVANTAGE!*" the veteran said, screaming the last word before he stormed out the door. Silver followed, but walked slower, turning toward Miles at the open door.

"Goodbye, Miles-to-go," she said, somewhat sadly. He wanted to say something to keep her but she followed the veteran into the car. A moment later the tires screeched and they were gone, Miles staring after them from behind his blinds.

At first he felt as if he were spinning like a top as he walked around and around his apartment, checking for something they might have stolen. Except for his TV and stereo, there was nothing worth taking, from an objective point of view—he had no jewelry (they'd left his car) nor any money hidden, yet he kept checking anyway.

Finally he stopped. It was totally silent in his apartment except for the crickets outside. The next thing he knew, he opened the sliding door onto his five-foot patio, then kept walking through the grass in his bare feet. It was dark out despite the stars. He could feel himself tempted to go back to his apartment, as if to recapture some traces of Silver, who he already was missing but resisted and kept walking, concentrating on the countless blades of grass. He wondered if he could avoid a bee in the dark that could well be outside about to sting him, but he decided to sit down on the grass anyway. He thought about the grass, then looked up at the stars, trying to keep from thinking about Silver. If the world goes on forever, it doesn't matter what anyone does anyway, he thought. That was the world— nothing but endless miles. . . . Then he started worrying about the bee as if it were hovering a few feet from him, poised to attack, and he headed back quickly, locking himself inside his silent home.

Nominated by Emily Fox Gordon, Josip Novakovich, Jana Harris, Lee Upton, Susan Hahn

INHERITANCE

by KWAME DAWES

from THE CARIBBEAN WRITER

for Derek Walcott

I

In the shade of the sea grape trees the air is tart
with the sweet sour of stewed fruit rotting
about his sandalled feet. His skin,
still Boston pale and preserved with Brahmanical
devotion by the hawkish woman
who smells cancer in each tropical wind,
is caged in shadows. I know those worn eyes
their feline gleam, mischief riddled;
his upper lip lined with a thin stripe
of tangerine, the curled up nervousness
of a freshly shaved mustache. He is old
and cared for. He accepts mashed food
though he still has teeth—she insists and love
is about atoning for the guilt
of those goatish years in New England.
A prophet's kind of old. Old like casket-
aged genius. Above, a gull surveys
the island, stitches loops through the sea and sky—
an even horizon, the bias on which

teeters a landscape, this dark loam of tradition
in which seeds split into tender leaves.

II

I can see the smudge of light colors
spreading and drying quickly in the sun.
The pulpy paper takes the water color,
and the cliché of sea and a fresh beach
seems too easy for a poem. He has written
them all, imagined the glitter and clatter
of silver cuirasses, accents of crude
Genoese sailors poisoning the air,
the sand feeling for the first the shadow
of flag and plumed helmet—this old story
of arrival that stirred him as a boy,
looking out over the field of green,
as he peopled the simple island
with the intrigue of blood and heroes,
his gray eyes searching out an ancestry
beyond the broad laughter and breadfruit-
common grunts of the fishermen, pickled
with rum and the *picong* of *kaiso*,
their histories as shallow as the trace
of soil at the beach's edge where crippled
corn bushes have sprouted. That was years ago;
he has exhausted the language of a broken civilization.
These days he just chips at his epitaph,
a conceit of twilight turning into
a bare and bleak night. He paints, whistling
Sparrow songs while blistering in the sun.

III

The note pad, though, is not blank. The words start,
thirteen syllables across the page, then seven
before the idea hesitates—these days
he does not need to count, there is in his head
a counter dinging an alarm like the bell
of his old Smith Corona—his line breaks

are tidy dramas of his entrances
and exits, he will howl before the darkness.
This ellipsis is the tease of a thought,
the flirtatious lift of a yellow skirt
showing a brown taut thigh—a song he knows
how to sing but can't line-up the lyrics again—
an airy metaphor of one taken up
by a flippant sea breeze going some place
inland, carrying the image, snagged
by the olive dull entanglement
of a bramble patch. At eight he lays
the contents of his canvas book bag
on the sand, organizing the still life
in honed stanzas. He scoops the orange pulp
of papaya relishing the taste of fruit, this bounty
harvested from the ant-infested fragile
tree behind the cottage, a tree that bleeds
each time its fruit is plucked away. The flesh
is sunny. He knows the fishermen warn
that it will cut a man's nature; dry up
his sap, that women feed their men pureed
papaya in tall glasses of rum-punch
to tie them down, beached, benign pirogues
heading nowhere. He dares the toxins
to shrivel him, to punish him
for the chronic genius of crafting poems
from the music of a woman's laugh
while he chews slowly. A poem comes to him
as they sometimes do in the chorus
of a song. It dances about in his head.
He does not move to write it down—it will wait
if it must, and if not, it is probably
an old sliver of long discarded verse.

IV

The old men in the rum shop are comforted
as they watch him limp along the gravel
road, wincing at the sharp prod of stones
in his tender feet, the knees grinding

at each sudden jar—just another ancient
recluse with his easel folded under
his arm, a straw hat, the gull-like eyes
seeing the sea before he clears the hill.
They know him, proud of the boy—bright as hell
and from good people. There is no shared language
between them, just the babel of rum talk
and cricket sometimes. Under his waters
he talks of Paris, Florence, barquentines,
Baudelaire, rolling the words around
like a cube of ice—they like to hear
the music he makes with tongue; the way
he tears embracing this green island,
this damned treasure, this shit hole of a treasure.
Sometimes when you don't mind sharp, you would think
he white too, except for the way he hold
the rum, carry his body into the sun
with the cool, cool calm of a drinker.
He say *home* like it in a book;
hard to recognize when he say *home*.
Yes, they like it anyway, the way
they like to hear "Waltzing Matilda" sung
with that broad Baptist harmony to a *cuatro*
plucked, to hear it fill an old time night.

V

If he is my father (there is something
of that fraying dignity, and the way
genius is worn casual and urbane—aging
with grace) he has lost much over the years.
The cigarette still stings his eyes and the scent
of Old Spice distilled in Gordon's Dry Gin
is familiar here by the sea where a jaunty
shanty, the cry of gulls and the squeak
of the rigging of boats are a right backdrop—
but I have abandoned the thought, the search
for my father in this picture. He's not here,
though I still come to the ritual death watch
like a vulture around a crippled beast,

the flies already bold around its liquid
eyes, too resigned to blink. I have come
for the books, the cured language, the names
of this earth that he has invented,
the stories of a city, and the way
he finds women's slippery parts in the smell
and shape of this island, the making
and unmaking of a city through
the epic cataclysm of fire,
eating the brittle old wood, myths dancing
in the thick smoke like the gray ashen debris
of sacrifice. It is all here with him—
this specimen living out his twilight days,
prodigious as John's horror—the green
uncertain in the half light. When we meet
he is distant, he knows I want to draw
him out, peer in for clues—he will not be drawn
out, he is too weary now. He points
to the rum shop, to an old man, Afolabe,
sitting on the edge of a canoe, black
as consuming night. I can tell
that he carries a new legend in his terrible
soul each morning, a high tower over the sea.

VI

I could claim him easily, make of him
a tale of nurture and benign neglect;
he is alive, still speaks, his brain clicks
with the routine of revelations
that can spawn in me the progeny
of his monumental craft. These colonial
old men, fed on cricket and the tortured
indulgences of white school masters
patrolling the mimic island streets
like gods growing gray and sage-like in the heat
and stench of the Third World; they return
to the reactionary nostalgia
during their last days—it is the manner
of aging, they say, but so sad, so sad.

I could adopt him, dream of blood and assume
the legacy of a divided self.
But it would ring false quickly; after all
my father saw the Niger eating out
a continent's beginnings; its rapid
descent to the Atlantic; he tasted
the sweet *kelewele* of an Akan
welcome, and cried at the uncompromising
flame of *akpetechi*. The blood of his sons
was spilled like libation into the soil,
and in nineteen twenty six, an old midwife
buried his bloodied navel string, the afterbirth
of his arrival at the foot of an ancient
cotton tree there on the delta islands
of Nigeria. My blood defines the character
of my verse. Still, I pilfer (a much better word),
rummage through the poet's things to find the useful,
how he makes a parrot flame a line
or a cicada scream in wind; the names
he gives the bright berries of an island
in the vernacular of Adam and the tribe.

VII

I carry the weight of your shadow always,
while I pick through your things for the concordance
of your invented icons for this archipelago.
Any announcement of your passing
is premature. So to find my own strength,
I seek out your splendid weaknesses.
Your last poems are free of the bombast
of gaudy garments, I can see the knobs
of your knees scarred by the surgeon's incisions
to siphon water and blood from bone;
I stare at your naked torso—the teats
hairy, the hint of a barreled beauty
beneath the folding skin. I turn away
as from a mirror. I am sipping your blood,
tapping the aged sap of your days while you grow
pale. You are painting on the beach, this is how

the poem began—I am watching you watching
the painting take shape. I have stared long enough
that I can predict your next stroke—your dip
into the palette, your grunts, your contemplative
moments, a poised crane waiting for the right
instance to plunge and make crimson ribbons
on a slow moving river. These islands
give delight, sweet water with berries,
the impossible theologies
of reggae, its metaphysics so right
for the inconstant seasons of sun and muscular
storm—you can hear the shape of a landscape
in the groan of the wind against the breadfruit
fronds. I was jealous when at twenty, I found
a slim volume of poems you had written
before you reached sixteen. It has stitched in me
a strange sense of a lie, as if all this
will be revealed to be dust—as if I learned
to pretend one day, and have yet to be found out.

Nominated by The Caribbean Writer

THE NAMES

fiction by CAROLE MASO

from CONJUNCTIONS

I NAMED MY CHILD Mercy, Lamb.

Seraphina, the burning one.

I named my child the One Who Predicts the Future, though I never wanted that.

I named my child Pillar, Staff.

Henry, from the Old High German Haganrih, which means ruler of the enclosure, how awful.

I named my baby Plum, Pear Blossom, Shining Path.

I named my child Rose Chloe—that's blooming horse. I almost named her Rose Seraphina, that would have been a horse on fire.

Kami, which is tortoise. The name denotes long life.

Kemeko—tortoise child.

Kameyo—tortoise generation.

So she might live forever.

And Tori—turtledove.

I named my child Sorrow, inadvertently, I did not mean to. In the darkness I named her Rebecca—that is noose, to tie or bind. In the gloom I named my baby Mary—which means bitter, but I am happier than before and name my baby Day and Star and Elm Limb.

I named my child Viola, so that she might be musical. And Cecilia, patron saint of music, so she might play the violin.

Vigilant was the named of my child. Daughter of the Oath. Defiance. I named my child Sylvie so that she will not be frightened of the sunless forest.

I named my child War, my mistake. That would be Marcella or Martine. I named my child Ulrich—Wolf Power. Oh my son! After a

530

while, though, I wised up and passed on Brunhilde, Helmut, Hermann, Walter. And Egon—the point of the sword. I did not value power in battle and so skipped over Maude.

Instead I named my child Sibeta—the one who finds a fish under a rock. Sacred Bells, and Ray of Light. And Durga—unattainable. Olwynn—white footprint. Monica—solitary one. I named my child Babette, that is stranger. I named her Claudia: lame—without realizing it.

How are you feeling Ava Klein?

Perdita.

I named her Thirst. And Miriam—Sea of Sorrow. Bitterness. And Cendrine—that's ashes. But I am feeling better now, thank you. I named my child God is With Thee, though I do not feel Him.

I named her Isolde—Ruler of Ice. Giselle—Pledge and Hostage. Harita, a lovely name derived from the Sanskrit denotes a color of yellow or green or brown, a monkey, the sun, the wind and several other things.

I named her Clothed in Red, because I never stopped bleeding.

I named my son Yitzchak—that's He Will Laugh. And Isaiah, Salvation.

I named him Salvation. And Rescue. Five Minutes to Midnight.

I named my daughter Esme, the past participle of the verb esmer, to love. I named her She Has Peace, and Shining Beautiful Valley. I named my baby Farewell to Spring, just in case.

I named my child Ocean for that vast, mysterious shifting expanse. I named her Marissa, that's of the sea—because naming is what we do I guess. There is a silliness to us.

I named my child Cusp and Cutting Edge and Renegade, to protect her from critics.

I named my child Millennia, because the future is now—whether we like it or not.

It is a distinct pleasure to be here on this earth naming with you.

They lift a glass:

New Year's Eve and the revelers. Dizzy, a little more than tipsy. At the edge of what unbeknownst to them has already happened, is already happening. It gives them a sepia tone. In their paper hats and goblets and blowers and confetti. *Happy*—that old sweet and hopeful *New*—there is not one day that I have not thought of you my child—*Year*. And time passes. As if we had a choice.

A strange photographed feeling. The black hood over the box on

531

its legs. That wobbly feeling come from champagne and last things. As the new century moves into us—1900.

Time immemorial—so they say.

What is to come unimaginable.

I named my baby Many Achievements, Five Ravens, Red Bird. I named her Goes Forth Bravely. Beautiful Lake. Shaking Snow, Red Echo, Walking by the River.

And we relish the saying. While we still can. And in the saying, inhabit our own vanishing, in the shadow language, its after-image, a blue ghost in the bones, the passage of time, intimacy of the late evening—seated by a fire—embers.

Pipe smoke when you were a child come from under the crack in the door, letting you know that Uncle Louis was near. The distant sound from your nursery of the revelers—they come in to peer at you in your crib in the eerie masks of Victoriana on the dying year's last eve. Louisa and Herman move toward the lamplight. Oohs and aahs and then quiet. All disperse: a proper German gentleman, an American with a handlebar moustache, a chorus girl, a rabbit-faced widow, a bursar or stationmaster, a man in a turban, a geisha—a chic Orientalism. A sultry gypsy girl. They meander through the Ramble, weaving a little, with the odd premonition that they are all playing their parts—on this elaborate stage, the world hurtling forward, the year on the verge of turning. Snow begins to fall. The lights twinkling. They lift a glass.

New Year's Eve and we dream—of a music, a book never seen before, at the edge of its obsolescence—the light pale opal. On the shards of story and sound. What is left now.

On the last day of the last year of the last one thousand.

And the dead stream by with their names. And all the ways they tried to say—

Clint Youle, 83, Early Weatherman on TV

H.S. Richardson, Heir to Vicks Cold Remedies

Hazel Bishop, an Innovator Who Made Lipstick Kissproof

Linda Alma, Dancer in Greek Movies

Walter O. Wells, a Pioneer in Mobile Homes

The future already with us. Its advance implacable and the revelers, having rested up that afternoon, begin their foray. To play out the passing of time—thrilled, a little frightened, tinged with melancholy, struck as they leave now by the intense desire to stay.

"To earn one's death," writes *Mary Cantwell, 69, Author*, "I think of it as a kind of parlour game. How, I shall ask my friends, would you like to earn your deaths? And how would I like to earn mine?"

And we are charmed. I named my baby The Origin of Song—and then The Origin of Tears. Angel Eyes and Angel Heart. And Sweetie Pie and Darling One.

We've relished the naming—eased by it. And all the other games we made up, and all the things we thought to do. New Year's Eve and the revelers.

At the end of the century a whisper. The Berlin Philharmonic plays seven finales in a row.

And the year 2000 is issued in, scraps of story and sound. That beautiful end of the century debris.

We were working on an erotic song cycle. It was called: *The Problem Now of the Finale*.

Today, where the sense of key is weaker or absent altogether, there is no goal to be reached as in earlier finales, as a closing gesture, what, what now?—a joke, a dissolve, a fast or slow tearing, intimations of a kind of timelessness, the chiming of bells, a wing and a prayer—perhaps, a solemn procession toward—what then?

New Year's Eve and the revelers.

Another sort of progress.

I named my child Farewell to Spring.

How strange the dwindling—pronounced as it is on this night where we deliberately mark its passage. Happy New Year. Lost in the naming, in the marking of time as it slips—distracted from the strangeness for a minute.

It's been a privilege. And how quickly all of a sudden . . . Pipe smoke when you were a child.

Or the alarming forced jollity of a Shostakovich finale—

Where are you going?

Where have you gone?

I named her Century. I named her Bethany—House of Figs. I named her Lucia to protect her from the dark. And Xing—which is Star. Dolphin, Lion, Lover of Horses.

I named her Arabella—Beautiful Altar, and Andromeda—Rescued.

My child was made almost entirely of blood in the end. She slipped through my hands. They say ordinarily such a child is not named.

A flock of birds. Bells that descend. A rose on the open sea.

The pages of the baby name book ragged. Nevertheless—I could not pass up

Mercy.

Tenderness.

Lamb.

I wish I could decipher the Silence. Understand its Whims. The century a Chalice of Heartbreak. We put our lips to it and whisper.

What now?

What then?

And Bela—derived from a word that means wave—or a word that means time—or a word that means limit. It is also indicative of a type of flower or a violin.

Nominated by Conjunctions, Lance Olsen

HER GARDEN

by DONALD HALL

from TIN HOUSE

I let her garden go.
let it go, let it go
How can I watch the hummingbird
Hover to sip
With its beak's tip
The purple bee balm—whirring as we heard
It years ago?

The weeds rise rank and thick
let it go, let it go
Where annuals grew and burdock grows,
Where standing she
At once could see
The peony, the lily, and the rose
Rise over brick

She'd laid in patterns. Moss
let it go, let it go
Turns the bricks green, softening them
By the gray rocks
Where hollyhocks
That lofted while she lived, stem by tall stem,
Dwindle in loss.

Nominated by Tin House

535

FUNKTIONSLUST

fiction by MELISSA PRITCHARD

from THE PARIS REVIEW

Copulation is the lyric of the mob.
—Baudelaire

Happy gorillas are said to sing.
—Jeffrey Moussaieff Masson,
When Elephants Weep

Up AND DOWN THE DULL COASTLINE of her desk, Amerylys ticked her fingernails, Minnie Mouse airbrushed onto each bismuth pink shield. She was back from Ladies where she'd flattened out *Newsweek* from its bug-swatter twist to read about the chief of the Cloud People, his vow to leap off a high cliff if a certain foreign petroleum company purchased his tribe's ancestral land from the Colombian government. Who would want that sort of thing on their conscience? There was a stamp-sized photograph of the chief, pudding faced, with black, beveled hair and the sexy, charismatic gaze of the not-quite-holy man. His story sat to the left of another article (both were recipe-card sized), about world forest fires and greenhouse temperatures, beside a pink graph nobody would leap off of anything for. Flags—not math—inspired sacrifice, thought Amerylys. With her Disney nails, she sliced out the Cloud Chief's small story, not wanting to lose his heroic possibilities. This was the second bit of news sparking the dry foolscap of her afternoon. The first was the gorilla, recently delivered to her garage by a young eco-terrorist, Moser, now airborne, leaving Phoenix for a week's walking tour through Cluj, a medieval city in Romania—at the sudden behest of his newest lover, an aspiring historian named Boris.

At the tether end of her forties, Amerylys Stanch lived alone. A former Miss Gilbert, she had worked nine years in this auto-collision inspection station, an exotic bloom turning brown around the edges, potted into her gray cubicle. Her one window allowed a mean view of a spinach-colored hedge and, beyond, the diminished rear ends of a McDonald's and an urban dairy. Nine years dragging her pink nails over clients' paperwork, outlining where and when to take their cars for repair, handing over fat checks based on Rorty's estimates. Unnerved by their collisions, clients grabbed at their checks until Amerylys reminded them it was for repair, for vehicular damage, then offered a consoling peppermint along with a customer satisfaction card. She had won the Employee Recognition Award six years running, tallying the highest number of positive remarks, never mind they were mostly about her smile, her legs, her hair or, like the retired fireman wrote, how she was a dead ringer for Reba McIntyre, as if that would make her drop like a stunned fly into his bed (which it nearly did). Amerylys hammered all six of her awards onto the spongy gray wall in a circle, like a clock, around her Miss Gilbert photograph. That contest had been years before, and recently she felt it, that she was coasting, picking up speed, going downhill. The sex-kitten rigamarole, the glam-o-rama, the I-enjoy-being-a-girl mindset, the sequins and folderol, where had it gotten her? Where, for instance, was Mr. Right? Moser's answer was biologically terse. It's secretions, he would rant, secretions and scent. Take any woman who smiles and ovulates at the same time—no question—she'll mow the men down. *Baloney*, Amerylys shot back. Now she wasn't so sure, plus she was finished ovulating, so where did that leave her? Flailing about in a crisis she couldn't identify. Dragging open the file-cabinet drawer, she raked up a tangle of fried calamari with her nails, ate it, formed a squadron of green Tic Tacs, then flicked them into her mouth with her tongue. She did this to keep from screaming, to keep from jumping off the squat gray cliff of her desk.

In the waiting room, a tall, long-bellied man paced with his cell phone, shouting in German. Behind him was a jacked-up white van with Rorty, the inspector, standing underneath the dented portion holding his clipboard. Amerylys once asked Rorty, at an office party, if he ever worried he'd be crushed. Biting down on a bacon-wrapped chicken liver, he'd winked—*only by my wife, sweet thang*. That's who

537

she worked with, had to jack her own life up above and keep it there, in the clouds. For the first two or three years, Amerylys tried livening things up around the holidays, wearing leprechaun hats to work, Santa suits, Easter bunny ears, green makeup and a witch's pointed hat. One year she gave everyone—even Rorty—a personalized Easter egg. For close to six months, she'd written and posted a Daily Inspiration on the announcement board, and nobody said a word. When she ran dry of inspiration, everyone complained. Lately, her thoughts kept contracting into one shrill, pinpoint ambition: find a husband. She'd never had one; now she kept her list of Eligibles under the inflatable Mr. Potato Head anchored to the far corner of her desk. She'd won Mr. P. at a party for her friend Rhoda, whose current husband drove a Frito-Lay truck. They had all gotten drunk and played potato games, peel the potato, find the potato, roll the potato, etcetera. Mr. Potato Head, a door prize, had detachable Velcro trimmings, an orange beard, felt glasses, a red turnip-shaped nose, lips, ears. Everyone except Amerylys had wanted the other door prize, a Mr. Potato Head vibrator.

He was not her only inflatable. In her bedroom closet, stashed behind a tiered rack of athletic shoes (until it disappeared in a gas explosion, pelting the strip mall with a clunking blizzard of white athletic shoes, she'd worked two evenings a week at the Strapless Jock), Amerylys kept a blow-up security guard, a gift from a Turkish journalist who became concerned, even panicky, about her living alone without a gun, an alarm or Mace, not even a dog—undefended!—a woman with her hair, smile, legs, etcetera. He'd ordered the security guard shipped to her from an airplane shopper catalog on his way back to Ankara. Amerylys had never bothered to inflate the man, who resembled Burt Reynolds right down to the five o'clock shadow; he was still doubled and tripled over in his clear, soft plastic bag. She sometimes thought it might be nice to have a complete assortment of past lovers, puddled into plastic bags like so much dry cleaning, ready to be inflated, strapped into the passenger seat of her car, seated in the wing chair by the picture window or made to stand by the stove—deterrents, tall male balloons planted like mines. On her fiftieth birthday, she could inflate them all— hooray!—her bloated village of nostalgia, starting with angst-ridden, myopic Victor Leipzig when she was seventeen, to now. Now was different, though. Amerylys was considering "closing up the lab" as Rhoda called it. Until she met Moser, who'd seen three of his ex-lovers cremated and was only twenty-six, the whole thing hadn't seemed real.

Hilton, a juvenile gorilla, had been slated for AIDS research in a local university laboratory. He was scheduled to be injected with the virus, given experimental treatments and combinations of drugs, to live out his short, tortured life in a small, gray cage (familiar enough, thought Amerylys). Moser intended to release Hilton into the jungle he had been captured from, but now, because of love's abrupt seizure, he had flown to Romania in the middle of his rescue project.

The world, it seemed to Amerylys, had shrunk to the size of a cocktail napkin. Claustrophobic, excessively connected . . . Moser's was a green, ecological awareness intended perhaps to morally refresh, but Amerylys felt suffocated, like being part of somebody's big, nosy family. Okay. She picked up Rorty's call. *Five minutes till my guesstimate, sweet thang*, he said, adding that the cell-phone German with the weirdo skinny braid was on his way in to see her.

After he bought the Harley, Moser couldn't sleep. He kept running down from his fourth-floor apartment to make sure the black and salmon bike wasn't stolen. When he told Amerylys he was thinking of sleeping on the gravel next to it, holding a pistol, she told him that was silly and gave him her spare garage-door opener. She'd never ridden with him on the bike, but one night, wearing only her Disney World T-shirt, she'd sat on the Harley, playing with the black beaded fringe on its handles like a kid on a ride outside Wal-Mart. That night, when she pulled into the garage, Moser's bike was in its usual spot, but when she opened the door, she caught what had to be the gorilla's rank, blunt smell. Then she saw the metal cage wedged between her suitcase and a neat stack of Pine Logs. (To gain sympathy, Moser'd told her countless animal horror stories, like the one about the chimpanzee rescued from a birdcage that had hung ten years in a dark garage.) A purple box of dog biscuits sat on top of her suitcase, a yellow note taped to its side. Were the biscuits his? What if he escaped when she opened the door to feed him? Should she tell the German man when he showed up to take her to dinner that Hilton had been spirited out of a laboratory the night before, that she was an accomplice—not to mention a sitting duck—now that the actual thief was in Romania, in Cluj, and what kind of name was that for a city—it sounded like luggage. What was the reason Moser couldn't wait until after Cluj to steal Hilton? Leaving her—fool!—

holding the bag? She couldn't remember. Amerylys crouched down in front of the cage.

"Hilton? I'm here. Amerylys. Your hero, Moser, went away for a few days. I don't want you to worry. See?" She pointed to the yellow note. "Instructions."

The gorilla regarded her gloomily—almost cynically it seemed to her, before shifting to turn his back. The fuschia metal tag punched into his left earlobe gave him a disconcertingly punk look. For some reason, Amerylys thought of the Patty Hearst kidnapping, how the Symbionese Liberation Army had kept Patty in a closet, only letting her out to rob banks.

Sitting naked and tailor fashion on her floral chenille bedspread, Dieter (like *tweeter*) Heinrichs unbraided his hair. Two Apache women had dyed it for him. He sounded as if he was bragging as he gave the blackened hair a vain, girlish toss. "And *Funktionslust*? Ah." He sucked air through his gapped teeth, a wet, sensual sound. "It means taking huge pleasure in what one does best, enjoying one's abilities."

"What a word." Still fully dressed, Amerylys emerged from her closet, where she had rushed to hide her Affirmations board. On this board was a list of qualities she sought in a husband: dark, virile, cultured, emotionally sensitive, loves opera, oral sex and pink bubblegum ice cream . . . she'd been drunk when she'd made the list. "So what are you good at?"

"Oh, that's easy. I find all of [*suck*] life so beautiful. I find you [*suck*] most incredible of all."

For pity's sake. Wow. He was certainly corny, but so pleased with himself, with his funny hair and long soft tummy, she decided, sure, make love with this man who told her he was an adopted Lakota and knew a lot of Indians, knew them really well. Dieter Heinrichs, physical therapist turned cultural entrepreneur, regularly flew Indians to Germany to conduct sweat lodges and feather circles. Maybe he would take her, too? Was he an Eligible? she wondered. Not after he'd complained that monogamy was a negative "thought frame," interfering with his *Funktionslust*. Nature is my model, he'd proclaimed, and she is too clever for monogamy's straitjacket.

What was it about Amerylys lately that turned normal conversation into a monologue, with the other person doing all the talking? When he ended his philosophic chat with himself, Dieter Heinrichs took so

540

long singing the praise of every curve of her as he uncovered it (much like the time Amerylys thought to prolong Christmas by taking an eternity to unwrap each of her presents until her parents both shouted at her), he was forced to wake her up by the time he'd gotten her completely nude. Napoleonic and noisy, Dieter *funktionslusted*, exuberant and gamboling, carnal as a child. Then he fell asleep, a pink snoring starfish, a probable monster who, eyes closed and mouth open, looked incapable of harm. On her hands and knees, Amerylys crept around him, felt a faint, fickle sense of endearment as she studied the pale, relaxed umbrella handle of his penis. She wasn't tired anymore. Her house felt charged up with two males in it, one here on her bed, one caged in the garage.

Not wanting to wake him by flushing the toilet, Amerylys went into her backyard to pee behind the blossoming, poisonous oleanders. Back in the kitchen, she stared at his shoes, at his fringed, butter-colored leather jacket with the red and black beadwork, at the cell phone on the table beside the jacket (throughout the evening he had made a series of rambling phone calls in German). She stared at his shoes so long and so suspiciously, she began loathing them and by extension loathing him, the raw-looking starfish in her bedroom. All at once Amerylys knew a man could be laid bare by his shoes. These were light brown skidders, sliders, slippery, sloppy rundown roadsters, big and nasty looking. The nasty-looking shoes spoke, saying she'd better be a sharp cookie and look through his wallet, which lay under the cell phone. The trifold wallet fell open to a snapshot of his wife and three children tricked out like Indians—odd, as if she tried to be German by wearing lederhosen—like the year she was six and wore her Annie Oakley costume, cap guns included, every single day. Then she heard him cough, a phlegmy smoker's cough and, quick as a wink, shoved the wallet back under the phone. His teeth were bad too, crooked, stained, gapped. Shoes and teeth. Lord. The evening was losing its dignity. Time to check on Hilton.

He was wilted on his side, asleep. What's my *Funktionslust*, Amerylys wondered. What's his? Retreating to the kitchen, she swallowed two times the recommended dosage of Celestial Seasonings sleeping pills before flopping down on the living room sofa to mentally review her Eligibles. Discounting Dieter (married, dyed hair, bad teeth, telltale shoes) and disqualifying Moser (homosexual, twenty-eight, the closest she had to family, a sort of nephew/son combination) left her with:

1. Gub Mix, the Christian plumber who'd answered her ten P.M. emergency call and stayed until two A.M. When he started talking religion from under her kitchen sink, his legs splayed like blue cornstalks across her linoleum, she admitted to having had a vision of the Virgin Mary where Mary foretold she would one day give up all she owned and travel south. This pushed Gub's one button. Sliding out from under the sweating pipes, he'd asked permission to pray over her, then cupping his grimy hands over her head, prayed long and loud while she stared at the black rubber bell of the plunger. Gub had heavenly blue eyes and a squashed-in head. His head made her think of a square gift box bashed in on one corner, but she refused to ask questions. When he was ready, he would explain. Last week he dropped off a pot of miniature yellow roses and a double CD of Christian rock music.

2. George Dorsey, the Mormon who'd showed up to empty last year's water out of her swimming pool. She'd sat by the side of the slowly draining pool, swinging her bare feet while he brushed clean the plaster sides of the pool and told her increasingly off-color stories about people he'd met on his mission in New York City, like the man who had sex every Saturday night with his wife's dog, a blond Afghan. George spoke humorlessly about "pumping iron," and his muscled skin was so tan, Amerylys imagined chomping affectionately into his thigh would be a lot like sinking her teeth into a hollow chocolate rabbit. What worried her, though, was his vehicular rage. Driving her home from a lunch of Chinese dim sum, he'd become agitated, hurling grapefruits out his window at offending cars. And reaching down for her purse, she'd encountered an aluminum baseball bat under the front seat. So when he kept calling, asking her to one of his church dances, she stalled, telling herself that for a Mormon man as handsome as he was to still be unmarried, something must be drastically wrong.

3. Duke Ruff taught Tae Bo part-time at a community college, part-time at the Ak-chin Casino. He lived out in the desert in a trailer the color of dead daffodils, stuck up on cinderblocks. He had no shower curtain, and, like a fool, she bought him one, installed it herself, then made her prized osso buco before discovering the pile-up of unreturned casserole dishes in his broom closet and realizing how many other women had tried to win this man with desperately competing casseroles. In bed, he said the same thing

542

over and over—*it feels like you and me've done this 150,000 times before*—and she never knew what to say to him except maybe he'd worked too long at the casino.

4. Doc Sparkles, an eighty-nine year old millionaire, married five times. He played squash on Tuesdays / Thursdays and wanted her to fly to Puerto Vallarta with him, then go on a Russian cruise. She'd met Doc at the El Charro Lounge one night, where he'd rambled on and on, his talk vortexing like a tiny tornado up into his stained cowboy hat. For now she kept that flirtation barely going, the faintest of embers.

What did Gub, George, Duke and Doc all have in common? Loneliness? She should get up from the couch right now and call Mose in Romania. Use the German's cell phone, let him foot the bill. Wearing nothing but her flourescent Tweety Bird slippers, she changed her mind and stood cooling in front of the open refrigerator, munching on a handful of Hilton's salad mix. She swallowed three more pills and thought of women she'd read about in certain societies (she couldn't remember which ones) who, when their hair turned gray, were allowed to touch all men, women and children with impunity. She remembered a friend of hers, a film developer, describing medical photographs of a sixteen-year-old girl's ovaries as a series of botanically succulent O'Keefe paintings, then saying how a single photograph of a sixty-year-old woman's ovaries looked like a sentimental illustration of death.

She peeked in on them—on Hilton and the German—then, woozy from all the skullcap, passion flower and valerian root, clamped her headphones on and lay naked on the floor beside the CD player, falling asleep to *Cosi fan tutte,* Mozart's cheery, inane libretto.

The very next night, with Dieter gone to his powwow in Sedona, Amerylys woke from a hugely perplexing, erotic dream. Before bed, she had changed the sheets, lit her pumpkin candle and lavender incense (Moser claimed studies showed men consistently aroused by the smells of lavender and pumpkin) and fallen asleep with her headphones on, blaring a tape about intuitive awareness. As she lay in the dark, the fan paddling above her, she dreamed that a small, dark ape climbed on top of her and began to fuck her, his penis small, glistening and quick. Waking up in a state of lubricious excitement, she yanked her now silent headphones off and sniffed. Overwhelming the mix of lavender and pumpkin was a thick stripe of smell, rank, almost scorched. Attaching her reader's light to her forehead like a miner's lamp, Amerylys followed the smell, tiptoeing out to the garage. There he was, in the crown of white light cast by her lamp, asleep, his salad hilled in the corner of the cage, bleached and dingy looking.

Why not let him out? Surely he was intelligent and sensitive, more so than Dieter, who had called three times already, leaving breathy New-Age messages, powwow drums thumping in the background.

Pensive, Amerylys shook out a fresh panful of salad for Hilton while listening to the Three Tenors—Pavarotti, Domingo, who was the third?—when the phone rang. Answering, she heard a distinctly alto hum from the garage.

"Amerylys?"

"Mose?"

"Hey. I'm stuck here for awhile."

"What?"

"Yeah, I'm sorry."

"But—"

Stealthily, the portable phone to her ear, she opened the door to the garage. Hilton was thrumming his fingers along the cage mesh, eyes upturned, his guttural hum charged with a sorrowful yearning; she actually lost track of what Moser was saying from his end in Romania.

". . . what can I say, I'm in love—with Boris obviously, but with Cluj, the Romanians, the air, the trees, the sinks, toilets, toothbrushes, trust me, dog shit smells divine here . . . "

The CD ended, the house a tomb.

"Enough, Moser. It's biology, right?" Her voice startled her so she lowered it. "Look, I'm happy for you, and I can handle it."

"Ever-awesome Amerylys. I suddenly want to marry you. How's our man?"

"Ah . . . good. Really good. I'm not sure he's eating enough though. Listen." (Here she shut the door to the garage and whispered.) "The truth. Can he undo his cage thingy?"

"The latch? Absolutely. I trained him as part of a contingency plan. Then again, I've never seen him do it without heavy coaching. Why? Did he get out?"

"No. I don't know. I'm not sure." Amerylys whipped open the

544

garage door to see what he was doing. Nothing. Plinking through his lettuce. "Does he like music?"

"Oh yeah, Hilton adores opera. It makes him kind of sing. Why? It sounds like you two are hitting it off."

Though his back was to her, Hilton was listening, she knew it. "Would it be okay to let him out? I think he's getting bored."

"I don't know. Look, I . . . "

The operator cut in demanding money.

Quickly, Moser told her where to find maps, instructions, forged paperwork—in the saddlebags on his Harley, along with his apartment key. *Piece of cake* was the last thing she heard before the call cut off. It dawned on her that because of love or the crime he had committed, or both, Moser might never come back.

Amerylys showered, dressed, went to work, stayed late. That night she crawled into bed with her headphones, reading light, pumpkin candle, herbal eye pillow and sleeping pills, the exotic distractions of the lonely. Really, the bedside table looked like a sexual convalescent's.

Then she was asleep and the ape was on her again, this time lollopping down past her stomach with his warm, black, slick-honeyed tongue. Against her navel, she thought she heard an operatic vibration, a low hum. Stunned, she raised up on her elbows, looked around the empty room. She refused to get up and look in the garage, see if the latch was undone, if Hilton was where he was supposed to be. She had her suspicions and did not want the truth either way. Didn't happiness have the right to go unquestioned? And adult happiness, Amerylys knew, lasted longest when confined to tender arenas of ambiguity.

At the end of that night, Amerylys Stanch changed the course of her life. She left an upbeat message on her manager's voice mail saying she quit, no hard feelings, she was now self-employed as a living Barbie at little girls' birthday parties. And truthfully, before the inspection station, before the Strapless Jock, Amerylys had done exactly that, thus her deceit was technical, her fib chronological. After investing in a slew of glittering costumes, she'd advertised that as Living Barbie she promoted a positive role model, teaching little girls that in modern day America you could be both glamorous and successful. At the parties, the little girls were cold to her concept, whining and begging to try on her jewelry, bickering and tugging on her platinum wig with sticky, greedy fingers. Amerylys wound up putting an ad in the local alternative-lifestyles newspaper and practically giving away her slinky wardrobe to a Presbyterian cross-dresser. She finished the message by asking that somebody make certain Rorty got her Mr. Potato Head.

Hilton's cage was jammed sideways in the back seat, the deep hem of a blue thermal blanket overhanging it like a limp awning. He was looking at her amorously, sucking water out of a pink jogger's bottle. The security guard floated in the passenger seat, stuffed into a sort of Brinks outfit and wearing reflective sunglasses. "Well boys." Amerylys rechecked Moser's maps, forged papers and instructions before switching on the ignition. "I don't know where the hell we're going, but here the hell we go." With that, she sped south out of Phoenix, down into Mexico and beyond. All doors and portals swung open, few questions were asked, hardly anyone stopped them. It was as if they possessed triune powers of invisibility or, more likely, the kind of visual absurdity that inspired long and cautious distance. Amerylys bit off her cartoon nails, gave away her spike heels and educational tapes. Glamour fell like confetti all along the way until she was barefoot, wearing a broomstick skirt and a *Save the Rainforest* T-shirt, her hair a little gray, though mostly still a flaming, hibiscus-cooler red.

She was spotted in Mexico City, Panama City, Managua and Bogotá, always with her clipping about the Cloud Chief, always asking directions. Before she vanished altogether, she was seen working in an orphanage, a soup kitchen, a General Motors plant, an AIDS clinic, a leper colony, behind the wheel of a lime-green taxi. Like a rogue saint, Amerylys Stanch was sighted here and there, most often by the innocent, by the child working in a soybean field who said the lady gave him a message he couldn't remember, or the mute who signed he'd seen her in a diamond mine, a reading lamp blazing from her forehead. On occasion, she was seen in the company of a little ape. In bars and brothels, in certain classrooms and lunchrooms, there were heated debates and even fistfights over the whereabouts and purpose of the ape. The security guard? He went to the first listless knot of children she came across in Nogales. Living like cockroaches in dank, poisonous sewers, they sold the toy for food, a slowly deflating joke to help them laugh.

Her image appeared on *retablos* made of tin or of wood, crude icons painted onto Coke bottles and votive candles. Red-haired, big-rumped piñatas swayed on poles in marketplace booths. She was a giantess on urban wall murals, cloud-skinned with snaking red hair, a banana-leaf hat, long feet. When rumor took hold that La Gringa had been abducted and murdered, bits of her flesh strung like superstition, like milagros around the necks of government soldiers, a second rumor sprang up to contradict the impossibility of the first—that she had found the Cloud People, and that their Chief, obedient to the riddle governing this lower world of dust and ash and insects, found strength to take La Gringa for his bride. Those of a melancholic temperament clung to the first rumor, while those with faith in the brutality of love defected, with fever, to the second.

Nominated by Elizabeth Gaffney

TO THE TUNE OF A SMALL, REPEATABLE, AND PASSING KINDNESS

by CARL PHILLIPS

from MID-AMERICAN REVIEW

In the cove of hours-like-a-dream this
is, it isn't so much
that we don't enjoy watching

a view alter rather little, and each time
in the same shift-of-a-cloud
fashion. It's the

swiftness with which we
find it easier, as our cast
lines catch more and more at nothing,

to lose heart—
                    All afternoon, it's
been with the fish as with

lovers we'd come to think of as
mostly forgotten, how
anymore they less often themselves

surface than sometimes
will the thought of them—less
often, even, than that, their names . . . .

But now the fish bring to mind
—of those lovers—
the ones in particular

who were knowable
only in the way a letter written
in code that resists

being broken fully can be
properly called a letter we
understand: *If*

you   a minute   could you   when
said I might   however
what if   haven't I loved

—who?
            As I remember it, I'd lie
in general alone, after, neither in

want nor—at first—sorry inside
the almost-dark I'd
wake to. The only stirring

the one of last light getting
scattered, as if for
my consideration. All over the room.

Nominated by Mid-American Review, Robert Pinsky, Rita Dove, Michael Waters, Cyrus Cassells, David Baker, Alan Michael Parker, Martha Collins

THE MOOR

fiction by RUSSELL BANKS

from CONJUNCTIONS

I‍T'S ABOUT TEN P.M., and I'm one of three, face it, middle-aged
guys crossing South Main Street in light snow, headed for a quick
drink at the Greek's. We've just finished a thirty-second degree in-
duction ceremony at the Masonic Hall in the old Capitol Theater
building and need a blow. I'm the tall figure in the middle, Warren
Low, and I guess it's my story I'm telling, although you would say it
was Gail Fortunata's story, since meeting her that night after half a
lifetime is what got me started.

I'm wearing remnants of makeup from the ceremony, in which I
portrayed an Arab prince—red lips, streaks of black on my face here
and there, not quite washed off because of no cold cream at the Hall.
The guys tease me about what a terrific nigger I make, that's the way
they talk, and I try to deflect their teasing by ignoring it, because I'm
not as prejudiced as they are, even though I'm pleased nonetheless.
It's an acting job, the thirty-second degree, and not many guys are
good at it. We are friends and businessmen, colleagues—I sell
plumbing and heating supplies, my friend Sammy Gibson is in real
estate and the other, Rich Buckingham, is a Chevy dealer.

We enter the Greek's, a small restaurant and fern bar, pass through
the dining room into the bar in back like regulars, because we are
regulars and like making a point of it, greeting the Greek and his
help. Small comforts. Sammy and Rick hit uselessly on one of the
waitresses, the pretty little blond kid, and make a crack or two about
the new gay waiter who's in the far corner by the kitchen door and
can't hear them. Wise guys. Basically harmless, though.

The Greek says to me, "What's with the greasepaint?" Theater

550

group, I tell him. He's not a Mason, I think he's Orthodox Catholic or something, but he knows what we do. As we pass one table in particular, this elderly lady in the group looks me straight in the eyes, which gets my attention in the first place, because otherwise she's just some old lady. Then for a split-second I think I know her, but decide not and keep going. She's a large, baggy, bright-eyed woman in her late seventies, possibly early eighties. Old.

Sammy, Rick and I belly up to the bar, order drinks, the usuals, comment on the snow outside and feel safe and contented in each other's company. We reflect on our wives and ex-wives and our grown kids, all elsewhere. We're out late and guilt-free.

I peek around the divider at her—thin, silver-blue hair, dewlaps at her throat, liver spots on her long flat cheeks. What the hell, an old lady. She's with family, some kind of celebration—two sons, they look like, in their forties, with their wives and a bored teenaged girl, all five of them overweight, dull, dutiful, in contrast to the old woman, who despite her age looks smart, aware, all dressed up in a maroon knit wool suit. Clearly an attractive woman once.

I drift from Sammy and Rick, ask the Greek, "Who's the old lady, what's the occasion?"

The Greek knows her son's name, Italian—Fortunata, he thinks. "Doesn't register," I say. "No comprendo."

"The old lady's eightieth," says the Greek. "We should live so long, right? You know her?"

"No, I guess not." The waitresses and the gay waiter sing Happy Birthday, making a scene, but the place is almost empty anyhow, from the snow, and everybody seems to like it, and the old lady smiles serenely.

I say to Sammy and Rick, "I think I know the old gal from some-place, but can't remember where."

"Customer," says Sammy, munching peanuts.

Rick says the same, "Customer," and they go on as before.

"Probably an old girlfriend," Sammy adds.

"Ha-ha," I say back.

A Celtics-Knicks game on TV has their attention, double-overtime. Finally the Knicks win, and it's time to go home, guys. Snow's piling up. We pull on our coats, pay the bartender and, as we leave, the old lady's party is also getting ready to go, and when I pass their table, she catches my sleeve, says my name. Says it with a question mark. "Warren? Warren Low?"

I say, "Yeah, hi," and smile, but still I don't remember her.

Then she says, "I'm Gail Fortunata. Warren, I knew you years ago," she says, and she smiles fondly. And then everything comes back, or almost everything. "Do you remember me?" she asks.

"Sure, sure I do, of course I do. Gail. How've you been? Jeez, it's sure been a while."

She nods, still smiling. "What's that on your face? Makeup?"

"Yeah. Been doing a little theater. Didn't have any cold cream to get it all off," I say lamely.

She says, "I'm glad you're still acting." And then she introduces me to her family, like that, "This is my family."

"Howdy," I say, and start to introduce my friends Sammy and Rick, but they're already at the door.

Sammy says, "S'long Warren, don't do anything I wouldn't do," and Rick gives a wave, and they're out.

"So, it's your birthday, Gail. Happy birthday."

She says, "Why, thank you." The others are all standing now, pulling on their coats, except for Gail, who hasn't let go of my sleeve, which she tugs and says to me, "Sit down a minute, Warren. I haven't seen you in what, thirty years. Imagine."

"Ma," the son says. "It's late. The snow."

I draw up a chair next to Gail and, letting go of the dumb pretenses, I suddenly find myself struggling to see in her eyes the woman I knew for a few months when I was a kid, barely twenty-one, and she was almost fifty and married and these two fat guys were her skinny teenaged sons. But I can't see through the old lady's face to the woman she was then. If that woman is gone, then so is the boy, this boy.

She looks up at one of her sons and says, "Dickie, you go without me. Warren will give me a ride, won't you, Warren?" she says, turning to me. "I'm staying at Dickie's house up on the Heights. That's not out of your way, is it?"

"Nope. I'm up on the Heights, too. Alton Woods. Just moved into a condo there."

Dickie says, "Fine," a little worried, due to the weather. He looks like he's used to losing arguments with his mother. They all give her a kiss on the cheek, wish her a happy birthday again, and file out into the snow. A plow scrapes past on the street. Otherwise, no traffic.

The Greek and his crew start cleaning up, while Gail and I talk a few minutes more. Although her eyes are wet and red-rimmed, she's not teary, she's smiling. It's as if there are translucent shells over her bright blue eyes. Even so, now when I look hard I can glimpse her the way she was, slipping around back there in the shadows. She had heavy, dark red hair, clear white skin smooth as porcelain, broad shoulders, and she was tall for a woman, almost as tall as I was, I remember exactly, from when she and her husband once took me along with them to a VFW party, and she and I danced while he played cards.

"You have turned into a handsome man, Warren," she says. Then she gives a little laugh. "Still a handsome man, I mean."

"Naw. Gone to seed. You're only young once, I guess."

"When we knew each other, Warren, I was the age you are now."

"Yeah. I guess that's so. Strange to think about, isn't it?"

"Are you divorced? You look like it."

"Shows, eh? Yeah, divorced. Couple of years now. Kids, three girls, all grown up. I'm even a grandpa. It was not one of your happy marriages. Not by a long shot."

"I don't think I want to hear about all that."

"Okay. What do you want to hear about?"

"Let's have one drink and one short talk. For old times' sake. Then you may drive me to my son's home."

I say fine and ask the Greek, who's at the register tapping out, if it's too late for a nightcap. He shrugs why not, and Gail asks for a sherry and I order the usual, Scotch and water. The Greek scoots back to the bar, pours the drinks himself because the bartender is wiping down the cooler and returns and sets them down before us. "On the house," he says, and goes back to counting the night's take.

"It's odd, isn't it, that we never ran into each other before this," she says. "All these years. You came up here to Concord, and I stayed there in Portsmouth, even after the boys left. Frank's job was there."

"Yeah, well, I guess fifty miles is a long ways sometimes. How is Frank?" I ask, realizing as soon as I say it that he was at least ten years older than she and is probably dead by now.

"He died. Frank died in 1982."

"Oh, jeez. I'm sorry to hear that."

"I want to ask you something, Warren. I hope you won't mind if I speak personally with you."

"No. Shoot." I take a belt from my drink.

553

"I never dared to ask you then. It would have embarrassed you then, I thought, because you were so scared of what we were doing together, so unsure of yourself."

"Yeah, no kidding. I was what, twenty-one? And you were, well, not scary, but let's say impressive. Married with kids, a sophisticated woman of the world, you seemed to me. And I was this apprentice plumber working on my first job away from home, a kid."

"You were more than that, Warren. That's why I took to you so easily. You were very sensitive. I thought someday you'd become a famous actor. I wanted to encourage you."

"You did." I laugh nervously because I don't know where this conversation is going and take another pull from my drink and say, "I've done lots of acting over the years, you know, all local stuff, some of it pretty serious. No big deal. But I kept it up. I don't do much nowadays, of course. But you did encourage me, Gail, you did, and I'm truly grateful for that."

She sips her sherry with pursed lips, like a bird. "Good," she says. "Warren, were you a virgin then, when you met me?"

"Oh, jeez. Well, that's quite a question, isn't it?" I laugh. "Is that what you've been wondering all these years? Were you the first woman I ever made love with? Wow. That's . . . Hey, Gail, I don't think anybody's ever asked me that before. And here we are, thirty years later." I'm smiling at her, but the air is rushing out of me.

"I just want to know, dear. You never said it one way or the other. We shared a big secret, but we never really talked about our own secrets. We talked about the theater, and we had our little love affair, and then you went on, and I stayed with Frank and grew old. Older."

"You weren't old."

"As old as you are now, Warren."

"Yes. But I'm not old."

"Well, were you?"

"What? A virgin?"

"You don't have to answer, if it embarrasses you."

I hold off a few seconds. The waitress and the new kid and the bartender have all left, and only the Greek is here, perched on a stool in the bar watching *Nightline*. I could tell her the truth, or I could lie, or I could beg off the question altogether. It's hard to know what's right. Finally, I say, "Yes, I was. I was a virgin when I met you. It was the first time for me," I tell her, and she sits back in her chair and looks me full in the face and smiles as if I've just given her the perfect birthday gift, the one no one else thought she wanted, the gift she never dared to ask for. It's a beautiful smile, grateful and proud and seems to go all the way back to the day we first met.

She reaches over and places her small crackled hand on mine. She says, "I never knew for sure. But whenever I thought back on those days and remembered how we used to meet in your room, I always pretended that for you it was the first time. I even pretended it back then, when it was happening. It meant something to me."

For a few moments neither of us speaks. Then I break the spell. "What do you say we shove off? They need to close this place up, and the snow's coming down hard." She agrees, and I help her slide into her coat. My car is parked only halfway down the block, but it's a slow walk to it, because the sidewalk is a little slippery and she's very careful.

When we're in the car and moving north on Main Street, we remain silent for a while, and finally I say to her, "You know, Gail, there's something I've wondered all these years myself."

"Is there?"

"Yeah. But you don't have to tell me, if it embarrasses you."

"Warren, dear, you reach a certain age, nothing embarrasses you."

"Yeah, well. I guess that's true."

"What is it?"

"Okay, I wondered if, except for me, you stayed faithful to Frank. And before me."

No hesitation. She says, "Yes. I was faithful to Frank, before you and after. You were a virgin, dear, and except for my husband, you were the only man I loved."

I don't believe her, but I know why she has lied to me. This time it's my turn to smile and reach over and place my hand on hers.

The rest of the way we don't talk, except for her giving me directions to her son's house, which is a plain brick ranch on a curving side street up by the old armory. The porch light is on, but the rest of the house is dark. "It's late," I say to her.

"So it is."

I get out and come around and help her from the car and then walk her up the path to the door. She gets her key from her purse and unlocks the door and turns around and looks up at me. She's not as tall as she used to be.

"I'm very happy that we saw each other tonight," she says. "We probably won't see each other again."

"Well, we can. If you want to."

"You're still a very sweet man, Warren. I'm glad of that. I wasn't wrong about you."

I don't know what to say. I want to kiss her, though, and I do, I lean down and put my arms around her and kiss her on the lips, very gently, then a little more, and she kisses me back, with just enough pressure against me to let me know that she is remembering everything, too. We hold each other like that for a long time.

Then I step away, and she turns, opens the door and takes one last look back at me. She smiles. "You've still got makeup on," she says. "What's the play? I forgot to ask."

"Oh," I say, thinking fast, because I'm remembering that she's Catholic and probably doesn't think much of the Masons. "Othello," I say.

"That's nice, and you're the Moor?"

"Yes."

Still smiling, she gives me a slow pushing wave with her hand, as if dismissing me, and goes inside. When the door has closed behind her, I want to stand there alone on the steps all night with the snow falling around my head in clouds and watch it fill our tracks on the path. But it actually is late, and I have to work tomorrow, so I leave.

Driving home, it's all I can do to keep from crying. Time's come, time's gone, time's never returning, I say to myself. What's here in front of me is all I've got, I decide, and as I drive my car through the blowing snow it doesn't seem like much, except for the kindness that I've just exchanged with an old lady, so I concentrate on that.

Nominated by Conjunctions

THE CHILDREN OF THIS LAND

by WOLE SOYINKA

from MICHIGAN QUARTERLY REVIEW

The children of this land are old.
Their eyes are fixed on maps in place of land.
Their feet must learn to follow
Distant contours traced by alien minds.
Their present sense has faded into past.

The children of this land are proud
But only seeming so. They tread on air but—
Note—the land it was that first withdrew
From touch of love their bare feet offered. Once,
It was the earth of their belonging.
Their pointed chins are aimed,
Proud seeming, at horizons filled with crows.
The clouds are swarms of locusts.

The children of this land grow the largest eyes
Within head sockets. Their heads are crowns
On neat fish spines, whose meat has passed
Through swing doors to the chill of conversation
And chilled wine. But the eyes stare dead.
They pierce beyond the present through dim passages
Across the world of living.

These are the offspring of the dispossessed,
The hope and land deprived. Contempt replaces
Filial bonds. The children of this land
Are castaways in holed crafts, all tortoise skin
And scales—the callus of their afterbirth.
Their hands are clawed for rooting, their tongues
Propagate new social codes, and laws.
A new race will supersede the present—

Where love is banished stranger, lonely
Wanderer in forests prowled by lust
On feral pads of power,
Where love is a hidden, ancient ruin, crushed
By memory, in this present
Robbed of presence.

But the children of this land embrace the void
As lovers. The spores of their conjunction move
To people once human spaces, stepping nimbly
Over ghosts of parenthood. The children of this land
Are robed as judges, their gaze rejects
All measures of the past. A gleam
Invades their dead eyes briefly, lacerates the air
But with one sole demand:
Who sold our youth?

Nominated by Michigan Quarterly Review

FUGUE

by ELIZABETH ALEXANDER

from SHENANDOAH

1. WALKING (1963)

after the painting by Charles Alston

You tell me, knees are important, you kiss
your elders' knees in utmost reverence.
The knees in this painting are what send the people forward,

Once progress felt real and inevitable,
as sure as the taste of licorice or lemons.
The painting was made after marching
in Birmingham, walking

into a light both brilliant and unseen.

2. 1964

In a beige silk sari
my mother danced the frug
to the Peter Duchin Band.

Earlier that day
at Maison Le Pelch
the French ladies twisted

her magnificent hair
into a fat chignon
while *mademoiselle* watched,

drank sugared, milky tea,
and counted bobby-pins
disappearing in the thick-

ness as the ladies worked
in silence, adornment
so grave, the solemn *toilette*,

and later, the bath,
and later, red lipstick,
and later, L'Air du Temps.

My mother without glasses.
My mother in beige silk.
My mother with a chignon.
My mother in her youth.

3. 1968

The city burns. We have to stay at home,
TV always interrupted with fire or helicopters.
Men who have tweedled my cheeks once or twice
join the serial dead.

Yesterday I went downtown with Mom.
What a pretty little girl, said the tourists, who were white.
My shoes were patent leather, all shiny, and black.
My father is away saving the world for Negroes,
I wanted to say.

Mostly I go to school or watch television
with my mother and brother, my father often gone.
He makes the world a better place for Negroes.
The year is nineteen-sixty-eight.

4. 1971

"Hey Blood," my father said then
to other brothers in the street.
"Hey, Youngblood, how you doin'?"

"Peace and power," he says,
and, "Keep on keepin' on,"
just like Gladys Knight and the Pips.

My stomach jumps: a thrill.
Sometimes poems remember small things, like
"Hey, Blood." My father

still says that sometimes.

5. THE SUN KING (1974)

James Hampton, the Sun King
of Washington, DC,
erects a tin-foil throne.
"Where there is no vision, the people perish."
Altar, pulpit, light-bulbs.

My 14th and "U," my 34 bus, my weekday winos,
my white-robed black Israelites
on their redstone stoops,
my graffiti: "Anna the Leo as 'Ice,' "
my neon James Brown poster
coming to the DC Coliseum
where all I will see is the circus,
my one visit to RKO Keith's Theater
to see "Car Wash"
and a bird flew in, and mania,
frantic black shadow on the screen,
I was out of the house in a theater full of black folks,
black people, black movie, black bird,
I was out, I was free, I was at RKO Keith's Theater
at 14th and "U"

and it was not "Car Wash" it was the first
Richard Pryor concert movie
and a bird flew in the screen
and memory is romance
and race is romance,
and the Sun King lives
in Washington, DC.

Nominated by Cathy Song, Maureen Seaton

SPECIAL MENTION

(The editors also wish to mention the following important works published by small presses last year. Listing is in no particular order.)

POETRY

Vacation Sex—Dorianne Laux (Shenandoah)
Mercy—Tim Seibles (New Letters)
Potatoes and Point—R.T. Smith (Georgia Review)
She Goes to Confession—Meg Kearney (Washington Square)
Plutonium—Sascha Feinstein (Crab Orchard Review)
High Desert Snow—Dabney Stuart (Gettysburg Review)
A Mission—Ha Jin (Kenyon Review)
Priest—Kurt Brown (The Ledge)
The Dune House—William Logan (Southwest Review)
My Soul At Nude Beach—Terri Witek (Southern Review)
Hallway—Sam Sanvel Rubin (The Laurel Review)
Second Skin—Theodore Deppe (The Recorder)
My Last June In Chelsea—Alfred Corn (James White Review)
The Art of Distance, V—Ellen Bryant Voigt (TriQuarterly)
The Loon—Mary Oliver (Image)
My Daughters in New York—James Reiss (*Ten Thousand Good Mornings*, Carnegie-Mellon University Press)
Pennywort, After The Storm—Pete Makuck (Poetry)
Giacometti Portrait in Four Parts—Carol Anne Davis (Doubletake)
donor—Lucille Clifton (*Blessing the Boats*, BOA)
Beads—Lia Purpura (*Stone Sky Lifting*, Ohio State U. Press)
Southern Man Like Elvis—Fleda Brown (Beloit Poetry Journal)
Fragment (found inside my mother)—Nick Flynn (Paris Review)
Sailing At Sunset—Patricia Corbus (Green Mountains Review)

When The Great Chinese Papermakers Came to Cuba, The Great Poets Followed—Virgil Suarez (Beloit Poetry Journal)

Common Property—Bruce Bennett (Laurel Review)

A Small Song for Luke—Gerald McCarthy (Rattle)

Three Twelve O'Clocks in a Day—Victoria Redel (Alaska Quarterly Review)

Sea Below Rocks—JoEllen Kwiatek (American Poetry Review)

Typing and Typing in the Wandering Countryside—Charles North (Barrow Street)

NONFICTION

The Insult—Howard Norman (TriQuarterly)

Wrongful Death—Melanie Hulse (Threepenny Review)

Traps—Lee Martin (Creative Nonfiction)

Notes From the Catwalk—Elissa Wald (Creative Nonfiction)

Berenger At Bard—Norman Manea (Partisan Review)

Sweeney Revisited—Thomas Lynch (Southern Review)

Plan Of A Story That Could Have Been Written If Only I Had Known It Was Happening—Gail Hosking Gilberg (Post Road)

Promises, Promises—Adam Phillips (Noon)

Could It Be Read to Flaubert?—Nora Sayre (Yale Review)

Mail Romance—Tom House (Chicago Review)

Candy Jernigan—Alec Wilkinson (Doubletake)

The Watery Labyrinth—Floyd Skloot (Boulevard)

How To Pray—Ben Birnbaum (Image)

Cliffs of Despair—Tom Hunt (Gettysburg Review)

Fargo—Steve Heller (Fourth Genre)

Richard Bautigan: A Millennium Paper Airplane—Eric Lorberer (Rain Taxi)

The Bible Tells Me So—Jeffrey Hammond (Shenandoah)

Glenn Gould, the Virtuoso As Intellectual—Edwards W. Said (Raritan)

A Leg, A Hand, A Foot, A Finger—Peggy Shinner (Another Chicago Magazine)

The Countess's Tutor—Philip Lopate (Doubletake)

Lovey-Dovey Dove—Jeanne Dixon (Northern Lights)

Good Poems, Good Funerals—Thomas Lynch (Island)

Aborigine In the Citadel—Marilyn Nelson (Hudson Review)

True Believer—Erin McGraw (Gettysburg Review)
Why I Played the Blues—Richard Terrill (Fourth Genre)

FICTION

That Winter—Fred G. Leebron (TriQuarterly)
Things That Make Your Heart Beat Faster—Jennifer Anderson (The Missouri Review)
Des Moines, Iowa—Thea A. Goodman (New England Review)
Kami—Mary Yukari Waters (Black Warrior Review)
But, Microsoft: What Byte Through Yonder Windows Breaks?—Melvin Jules Bukiet (Agni)
The Rubbed-Away Girl—Mary Gaitskill (Gulf Coast)
Mister Henry's Trousers—William McCauley (Missouri Review)
Shards—Adria Bernardi (*In The Gathering Woods*, University of Pittsburgh Press)
The Gauntlet—Ernest Hebert (*The Old American*, University Press of New England)
A Cheerful Death—Thomas E. Kennedy (Gulf Coast)
Heat—Lynne Sharon Schwartz (Ontario Review)
The Mappist—Barry Lopez (Georgia Review)
The Carnival Tradition—Rick Moody (Paris Review)
California—Angela Pneuman (Iowa Review)
Virga—Mary Hood (Georgia Review)
You Are Not A Stranger Here—Adam Haslett (Bomb)
Neighbors—Josip Novakovich (TriQuarterly)
At Copper View—Ron Carlson (Five Points)
All Hallow's Leaves—Trudy Lewis (New England Review)
Public Relations—George Singleton (Georgia Review)
Female Trouble—Antonya Nelson (Epoch)
Tarzan Among the Agents—Paul Maliszewski (Boulevard)
Jolie-Gray—Ingrid Hill (The Southern Review)
Words—Joyce Carol Oates (Yale Review)
Wool Tea—Coleman Dowell (*The Houses of Children*, Dalkey Archive Press)
The Rest of Your Life—John Barth (TriQuarterly)
Notes—Molly Johnson (Mississippi Review)
Flake White—Jennifer Lapidus (Happy)
I Was Evel Knievel—Keith Regan (Alaska Quarterly Review)

The Catherine Wheel—Patricia Page (Epoch)
Fortitude—Lily Tuck (Epoch)
Commandments—Rose Moss (Massachusetts Review)
Gunnison Beach—Rita Welty Bourke (Witness)
The Man Who Would Be Kafka—Steve Stern (Salmagundi)
Solicitation—RJ Curtis (McSweeney's)
L'Art Ecosse 2000—Rob McClure Smith (Chelsea)
What It's Worth—Elizabeth Searle (Chelsea)
Love Him, Petaluma—Rebecca Barry (Ploughshares)
The Resolution of Nothing—Daniel Coshnear (Other Voices)
Something Horrible Is About To Happen—Mathew Blackburn (Fiction International)
Pipers At the Gates of Dawn—Lynn Stegner (*Pipers At the Gates of Dawn*, University Press of New England)
Transmitting and Receiving Information—Paul Diamond (Mississippi Review)
Where We Last Saw Time—Peter LaSalle (New England Review)
Before The Wedding—Mark Brazaitis (Shenandoah)
Thaw—Max Ludington (Tin House)
Hunting Country—Stephen Coyne (Southern Review)
Sabbath Night In The Church of the Piranha—Edward Falco (Missouri Review)
Overtime—Dwight Allen (Shenandoah)
A Family of Kruks—Askold Melnyczuk (StoryQuarterly)
Melvin In The Sixth Grade—Dana Johnson (Missouri Review)
Requiem—Ken Silber (StoryQuarterly)
Betty Hutton—Roy Parvin (Five Points)
Try Not To Lose Her—Tod Goldberg (West Wind)
Delivrez-nous—Karen Hollenbeck (Literal Latte)
A Bride For My Son—Dorothea Freund (Missouri Review)
Cooks, Camouflage, and Number 10 Cans—Paul Bellerive (Worcester Review)
In The Snow Forest—Roy Parvin (Glimmer Train)
Pinch-Hitter—Kristen Desmond (High Plains Literary Review)
Mother—David Evanier (Southwest Review)
Planet Big Zero—Jonathan Lethem (Lit)
Fog—Bill Roorbach (Another Chicago Magazine)
American Primitive—Lisa Norris (Helicon Nine Editions)
The Empiricists—Abby Frucht (Ontario Review)
Shooting—Lidia Yuknavitch (Fiction International)

566

PRESSES FEATURED IN THE PUSHCART PRIZE EDITIONS SINCE 1976

Acts
Agni Review
Ahsahta Press
Ailanthus Press
Alaska Quarterly Review
Alcheringa/Ethnopoetics
Alice James Books
Ambergris
Amelia
American Letters and Commentary
American Literature
American PEN
American Poetry Review
American Scholar
American Short Fiction
The American Voice
Amicus Journal
Amnesty International
Anaesthesia Review
Another Chicago Magazine
Antaeus
Antietam Review
Antioch Review
Apalachee Quarterly
Aphra
Aralia Press

The Ark
Art and Understanding
Arts and Letters
Artword Quarterly
Ascensius Press
Ascent
Aspen Leaves
Aspen Poetry Anthology
Assembling
Atlanta Review
Autonomedia
Avocet Press
The Baffler
Bakunin
Bamboo Ridge
Barlenmir House
Barnwood Press
The Bellingham Review
Bellowing Ark
Beloit Poetry Journal
Bennington Review
Bilingual Review
Black American Literature Forum
Black Rooster
Black Scholar
Black Sparrow

Black Warrior Review
Blackwells Press
Bloomsbury Review
Blue Cloud Quarterly
Blue Unicorn
Blue Wind Press
Bluefish
BOA Editions
Bomb
Bookslinger Editions
Boston Review
Boulevard
Boxspring
Bridges
Brown Journal of Arts
Burning Deck Press
Caliban
California Quarterly
Callaloo
Calliope
Calliopea Press
Calyx
Canto
Capra Press
Caribbean Writer
Carolina Quarterly
Cedar Rock
Center
Chariton Review
Charnel House
Chattahoochee Review
Chelsea
Chicago Review
Chouteau Review
Chowder Review
Cimarron Review
Cincinnati Poetry Review
City Lights Books
Cleveland State University Poetry Center
Clown War
CoEvolution Quarterly
Cold Mountain Press
Colorado Review

Columbia: A Magazine of Poetry and
    Prose
Confluence Press
Confrontation
Conjunctions
Connecticut Review
Copper Canyon Press
Cosmic Information Agency
Countermeasures
Counterpoint
Crawl Out Your Window
Crazyhorse
Crescent Review
Cross Cultural Communications
Cross Currents
Crosstown Books
Cumberland Poetry Review
Curbstone Press
Cutbank
Dacotah Territory
Daedalus
Dalkey Archive Press
Decatur House
December
Denver Quarterly
Domestic Crude
Doubletake
Dragon Gate Inc.
Dreamworks
Dryad Press
Duck Down Press
Durak
East River Anthology
Eastern Washington University Press
Ellis Press
Empty Bowl
Epoch
Ergo!
Evansville Review
Exquisite Corpse
Faultline
Fiction
Fiction Collective

Fiction International
Field
Fine Madness
Firebrand Books
Firelands Art Review
First Intensity
Five Fingers Review
Five Points Press
Five Trees Press
The Formalist
Fourth Genre
Frontiers: A Journal of Women Studies
Gallimaufry
Genre
The Georgia Review
Gettysburg Review
Ghost Dance
Gibbs-Smith
Glimmer Train
Goddard Journal
David Godine, Publisher
Graham House Press
Grand Street
Granta
Graywolf Press
Green Mountains Review
Greenfield Review
Greensboro Review
Guardian Press
Gulf Coast
Hanging Loose
Hard Pressed
Harvard Review
Hayden's Ferry Review
Hermitage Press
Heyday
Hills
Holmgangers Press
Holy Cow!
Home Planet News
Hudson Review
Hungry Mind Review
Icarus

Icon
Idaho Review
Iguana Press
Image
Indiana Review
Indiana Writes
Intermedia
Intro
Invisible City
Inwood Press
Iowa Review
Ironwood
Jam To-day
The Journal
The Kanchenjuga Press
Kansas Quarterly
Kayak
Kelsey Street Press
Kenyon Review
Kestrel
Latitudes Press
Laughing Waters Press
Laurel Review
L'Epervier Press
Liberation
Linquis
Literal Latté
The Literary Review
The Little Magazine
Living Hand Press
Living Poets Press
Logbridge-Rhodes
Louisville Review
Lowlands Review
Lucille
Lynx House Press
The MacGuffin
Magic Circle Press
Malahat Review
Mānoa
Manroot
Many Mountains Moving
Marlboro Review

Massachusetts Review
McSweeney's
Meridian
Mho & Mho Works
Micah Publications
Michigan Quarterly
Mid-American Review
Milkweed Editions
Milkweed Quarterly
The Minnesota Review
Mississippi Review
Mississippi Valley Review
Missouri Review
Montana Gothic
Montana Review
Montemora
Moon Pony Press
Mount Voices
Mr. Cogito Press
MSS
Mudfish
Mulch Press
Nada Press
Nebraska Review
New America
New American Review
New American Writing
The New Criterion
New Delta Review
New Directions
New England Review
New England Review and Bread Loaf
    Quarterly
New Letters
New Virginia Review
New York Quarterly
New York University Press
News from The Republic of Letters
Nimrod
9 × 9 Industries
North American Review
North Atlantic Books
North Dakota Quarterly

North Point Press
Northern Lights
Northwest Review
Notre Dame Review
O. ARS
O. Blēk
Obsidian
Obsidian II
Oconee Review
October
Ohio Review
Old Crow Review
Ontario Review
Open City
Open Places
Orca Press
Orchises Press
Orion
Other Voices
Oxford American
Oxford Press
Oyez Press
Oyster Boy Review
Painted Bride Quarterly
Painted Hills Review
Palo Alto Review
Paris Press
Paris Review
Parnassus: Poetry in Review
Partisan Review
Passages North
Penca Books
Pentagram
Penumbra Press
Pequod
Persea: An International Review
Pipedream Press
Pitcairn Press
Pitt Magazine
Pleiades
Ploughshares
Poet and Critic
Poet Lore

Poetry
Poetry East
Poetry Ireland Review
Poetry Northwest
Poetry Now
Prairie Schooner
Prescott Street Press
Press
Promise of Learnings
Provincetown Arts
Puerto Del Sol
Quarry West
The Quarterly
Quarterly West
Raccoon
Rainbow Press
Raritan: A Quarterly Review
Red Cedar Review
Red Clay Books
Red Dust Press
Red Earth Press
Red Hen Press
Release Press
Review of Contemporary Fiction
Revista Chicano-Riquena
Rhetoric Review
River Styx
Rowan Tree Press
Russian *Samizdat*
Salmagundi
San Marcos Press
Sarabande Books
Sea Pen Press and Paper Mill
Seal Press
Seamark Press
Seattle Review
Second Coming Press
Semiotext(e)
Seneca Review
Seven Days
The Seventies Press
Sewanee Review
Shankpainter

Shantih
Sheep Meadow Press
Shenandoah
A Shout In the Street
Sibyl-Child Press
Side Show
Small Moon
The Smith
Solo
Solo 2
Some
The Sonora Review
Southern Poetry Review
Southern Review
Southwest Review
Spectrum
The Spirit That Moves Us
St. Andrews Press
Story
Story Quarterly
Streetfare Journal
Stuart Wright, Publisher
Sulfur
The Sun
Sun & Moon Press
Sun Press
Sunstone
Sycamore Review
Tamagwa
Tar River Poetry
Teal Press
Telephone Books
Telescope
Temblor
The Temple
Tendril
Texas Slough
Third Coast
13th Moon
THIS
Thorp Springs Press
Three Rivers Press
Threepenny Review

571

Thunder City Press
Thunder's Mouth Press
Tia Chucha Press
Tikkun
Tin House
Tombouctou Books
Toothpaste Press
Transatlantic Review
TriQuarterly
Truck Press
Undine
Unicorn Press
University of Georgia Press
University of Illinois Press
University of Iowa Press
University of Massachusetts Press
University of North Texas Press
University of Pittsburgh Press
University of Wisconsin Press
University Press of New England
Unmuzzled Ox
Unspeakable Visions of the Individual
Vagabond
Verse
Vignette

Virginia Quarterly
Volt
Wampeter Press
Washington Writers Workshop
Water-Stone
Water Table
Western Humanities Review
Westigan Review
White Pine Press
Wickwire Press
Willow Springs
Wilmore City
Witness
Word Beat Press
Word-Smith
Wormwood Review
Writers Forum
Xanadu
Yale Review
Yardbird Reader
Yarrow
Y'Bird
Zeitgeist Press
Zoetrope: All-Story
ZYZZYVA

CONTRIBUTING SMALL PRESSES FOR PUSHCART PRIZE XXVI

A

Adept Press, P.O. Box 391, Long Valley, NJ
Advocado Press, P.O. Box 145, Louisville, KY 40201
After Hours, 538 N. Kenilworth, Oak Park, IL 60302
Agni, 236 Bay State Rd., Boston, MA 02215
Alaska Quarterly Review, 3211 Providence Dr., Anchorage, AK 99508
Algonquin Roundtable Review, 135 Woodroffe Ave., Rm. B336, Nepean, Ont. K2G 1V8 CANADA
Alligator Juniper, Prescott College, 301 Grove Ave., Prescott, AZ 86301
Always in Season, P.O. Box 380403, Brooklyn, NY 11238
American Letters & Commentary, 850 Park Ave., New York, NY 10021
American Literary Review, P.O. Box 311307, Univ. of North Texas, Denton, TX 76203
American Scholar, 1811 Q St. NW Washington, DC 20009
Amherst Writers & Artists Press, Inc., P.O. Box 1076, Amherst, MA 01004
Ancient Paths, PMB #223, 2000 Benson Rd. S, #115, Renton, WA 98055
Angel Heart Productions, Inc., P.O. Box 5224, Glendale, CA 91221
Antietam Review, 41 S. Potomac St., Hagerstown, MD 21740
The Antioch Review, P.O. Box 148, Yellow Springs, OH 45387
Apogee Press, P.O. Box 8177, Berkeley, CA 94707
Arbiter Press, P.O. Box 621082, Orlando, FL 32862
Arctos Press, P.O. Box 401, Sausalito, CA 94966
Argonne Hotel Press, 1620 Argonne Pl., NW., Washington, DC 20009
Arkansas Review, Arkansas State Univ., P.O. Box 1890, State University, AR 72467
Art Word Quarterly, P.O. Box 14760, Minneapolis, MN 58414
Artful Dodge, English Dept., College of Wooster, Wooster, OH 44691
Artifact Press, 1701 Stanley Rd., Cazenovia, NY 13035
Arts & Letters, Georgia College State Univ., Milledgeville, GA 31061
Ascent, English Dept., Concordia College, Moorhead, MN 56562
Asterius Press, P.O. Box 5122, Seabrook, NJ 08302
Atelos, 2639 Russell St., Berkeley, CA 94705
The Aurorean, P.O. Box 219, Sagamore Beach, MA 02562
Axe Factory Review, P.O. Box 40691, Philadelphia, PA 19107

B

Ballast Quarterly Review, 2022 X Ave., Dysart, IA 52224
The Baltimore Review, P.O. Box 410, Riderwood, MD 21139
Bamboo Ridge Press, P.O. Box 61781, Honolulu, HI 96839
bananafish, 35 Pequosette St., Watertown, MA 02472
The Barcelona Review, C/Correu Vell 12–2°, 08002, Barcelona, *SPAIN*
Barrow Street, P.O. Box 2017, Old Chelsea Sta., New York, NY 10113
Bathtub Gin, see Pathwise Press
Baybury Review, 40 High St., Highwood, IL 60040
Bellingham Review, MS-9053, WWU, Bellingham, WA 98225
Bellowing Ark Press, P.O. Box 55564, Shoreline, WA 98155
Beloit Fiction Journal, P.O. Box 11, Beloit College, Beloit, WI 53511
Beloit Poetry Journal, 24 Berry Cove Rd., La Moine, ME 04605
Berkeley Fiction Review, 201 Heller Lounge, UC, Berkeley, CA 94720
Bilingual Review/Press, P.O. Box 872702, Tempe, AZ 85287
Bitter Oleander Press, 4983 Tall Oaks Dr., Fayetteville, NY 13066
BkMk Press, Univ. of Missouri, 5101 Rockhill Rd., Kansas City, MO 64110
Black Dress Press, P.O. Box 126515, San Diego, CA 92112
Black Hat Press, 508 2nd Ave., Goodhue, MN 55027
Blue Collar Review, P.O. Box 11417, Norfolk, VA 23517
BOA Editions, Ltd., 260 East Ave., Rochester, NY 14604
bomb magazine, 594 Broadway, Ste. 905, New York, NY 10012
BoneWorld Publishing, 3700 County Rte. 24, Russell, NY 13684
Boulevard, 18 S. Kingshighway, Apt. 10JK, St. Louis, MO 63108
Brain, Child, P.O. Box 1161, Harrisonburg, VA 22803
Briar Cliff Review, Briar Cliff College, P.O. Box 2100, Sioux City, IA 5110
Bridge, 1957 N. Ashland Ave., #3A, Chicago, IL 60622
Brilliant Corners, Lycoming College, Williamsport, PA 17701
Browder Springs Books, 6238 Glennox La., Dallas, TX 75214
Burning Bush Publications, P.O. Box 9636, Oakland, CA 94613
Buttonwood Press, Box 206, Champaign, IL 61824
Byline, P.O. Box 130596, Edmond, OK 73013

C

The Cafe Review, 20 Danforth St., Portland, ME 04101
The Caribbean Writer, Univ. of Virgin Islands, RR2-10000 Kingshill, St. Croix, U.S. Virgin Islands, 00850
Carolina Quarterly, Univ. of North Carolina, Chapel Hill, NC 27599
Carve Magazine, Univ. of Washington, P.O. Box 352238, Seattle, WA 98195
Chapiteau Press, 24 Blue Moon Rd., South Stafford, VT 05070
The Chariton Review, Truman State Univ., Kirksville, MO 63501
Chattahoochee Review, 2101 Womack Rd., Dunwoody, GA 30338
Chelsea, Box 773, Cooper Sta., New York, NY 10276
Chicago Review, 5801 S. Kenwood Ave., Chicago, IL 60637
Chico Puntos Press, 2709 Louisville Ave., El Paso, TX 79930
Clackamas Literary Review, 19600 S. Molalla Ave., Oregon City, OR 97045
Cleveland State University Poetry Center, 1983 E. 24th St, Cleveland, OH 44115
Coal City Review, English Dept., Univ. of Kansas, Lawrence, KS 66045
Colorado Review, English Dept., Colorado State Univ., Ft. Collins, CO 80523
The Comstock Review, 4958 St. John Dr., Syracuse, NY 13215
Confrontation, Eng. Dept., C.W. Post of L.I. Univ., Brookville, NY 11548
Conjunctions, Bard College, Annandale-on-Hudson, NY 12504

Connecticut Review, Eng. Dept., So. Connecticut State Univ., New Haven, CT 06515
Controlled Burn, 10775 N. St. Helen Rd., Roscommon, MI 48653
Copper Canyon Press, P.O. Box 271, Port Townsend, WA 98368
Crab Orchard Review, Southern Illinois Univ., Carbondale, IL 62901
Critique, 254 Dogwood Dr., Hershey, PA 17033
Crone's Nest, 94 Sandy Point Farm Rd., Portsmouth, RI 02871
CrossConnect, Inc., P.O. Box 2317, Philadelphia, PA 19103
Crucible, Barton College, Wilson, NC 27893
C-ville, 222 South St., Charlottesville, VA 22947

D

Dalkey Archive Press, 6271 E. 535 North Rd., McLean, IL 61754
John Daniel & Co., P.O. Box 21922, Santa Barbara, CA 93121
Defined Providence Press, 34-A Wawayanda Rd., Warwick, NY 10990
Designer/Builder, 2405 Maclovia La., Santa Fe, NM 87505
Dial-A-Poem, 576 Horseshoe Tr., SE, Albuquerque, NM 87123
Disquieting Muses, P.O. Box 640746, San Jose, CA 95164
The Distillery, Motlow College, P.O. Box 8500, Lynchburg, TN 37352
D-N Publishing, 6238 Old Monroe Rd., Indian Trail, NC 28079
DoubleTake, 55 Davis Sq., Somerville, MA 02144

E

Eastern Washington University Press, 705 W. 1st, Spokane, WA 99201
The Eighth Mountain Press, 624 SE 29th Ave., Portland, OR 97214
Ekphrasis, P.O. Box 161236, Sacramento, CA 95816
Emrys Journal, P.O. Box 8813, Greenville, SC 29604
Epoch, Cornell Univ., 251 Goldwin Smith, Ithaca, NY 14853
Eureka Literary Magazine, Eureka College, Eureka, IL 61530
Evansville Review, 1800 Lincoln Ave., Evansville, IN 47714
Event, Douglas College, P.O. Box 2503, New Westminster, BC *CANADA* V3L 5B2
Exquisite Corpse, P.O. Box 25051, Baton Rouge, LA 70894

F

Faultline, Eng. Dept., Univ. of California, Irvine, CA 92697
Fence, 14 Fifth Ave., Apt. 1A, New York, NY 10011
Fiction International, San Diego State Univ., San Diego, CA 92182
First Intensity, P.O. Box 665, Lawrence, KS 66044
5 AM, P.O. Box 205, Spring Church, PA 15686
580 Split, P.O. Box 9982, Oakland, CA 94613
Five Points, Georgia State Univ., Univ. Plaza, Atlanta, GA 30303
The Florida Review, Univ. of Central Florida, Orlando, FL 32816
Flyway, 203 Ross Hall, Iowa State Univ., Ames, IA 50011
The Folio, Box 3490, San Diego, CA 92163
Folly Cove Chapbooks, 3 Essex St., Beverly, MA 01915
The Formalist, 320 Hunter Dr., Evansville, IN 47711
Fourth Genre, Michigan State Univ., Dept. of ATL, East Lansing, MI 48824

Free Lunch, P.O. Box 7647, Laguna Niguel, CA 92607
Frith Press, P.O. Box 161236, Sacramento, CA 95816
Fugue, Eng. Dept., Univ. of Idaho, Moscow, ID 83844
Futures Magazine, 3039 38th Ave. S, Minneapolis, MN 55406

G

A Gathering of the Tribes, P.O. Box 20693, Tompkins Sq. Sta., New York, NY 10009
George & Mertie's Place, P.O. Box 10335, Spokane, WA 99209
The Georgia Review, Univ. of Georgia, Athens, GA 30602
The Gettysburg Review, Gettysburg College, Gettysburg, PA 17325
Glimmer Train Press, 710 SW Madison St., Ste. 504, Portland, OR 97205
Global City Review, 105 West 13th St., Ste. 4C, New York, NY 10011
Goss Press, 6604 Walnutwood Circle, Baltimore, MD 21212
Grain, Box 1154, Regina, SK, S4P 3B4 *CANADA*
Gravity Presses, 27030 Havelock, Dearborn Heights, MI 48127
Graywolf Press, 2402 University Ave., Ste. 203, St. Paul, MN 55114
Green Bean Press, P.O. Box 237, New York, NY 10013
Green Hills Literary Lantern, P.O. Box 375, Trenton, MO 64683
Green Mountains Review, Johnson State College, Johnson, VT 05656
The Greensboro Review, P.O. Box 26170, Greensboro, NC 27402
Guidelight Productions, P.O. Box 233, San Luis Rey, CA 92068
Gulf Coast, Eng. Dept., Univ. of Houston, Houston, TX 77204

H

Hanover Press, Ltd., P.O. Box 596, Newtown, CT 06470
Happy, 240 East 35th St., 11A, New York, NY 10016
Harvard Review, Lamont Library, Harvard Univ., Cambridge, MA 02138
Hawaii Pacific Review, 1060 Bishop St., Honolulu, HI 96813
Hayden's Ferry Review, Arizona State Univ., Tempe, AZ 85281
heart, P.O. Box 81038, Pittsburgh, PA 15217
Helicon Nine, P.O. Box 22412, Kansas City, MO 64113
Heyday Books, P.O. Box 9145, Berkeley, CA 94709
The Higginsville Reader, P.O. Box 141, Three Bridges, NJ 08887
High Plains Literary Review, 180 Adams St., Ste. 250, Denver, CO 80206
Hip Pocket Press, 228 Commercial St., #13B, Nevada City, CA 95959
Hubbub, 5344 SE 38th Ave., Portland, OR 97202
The Hudson Review, 684 Park Ave., New York, NY 10021
Hutton Publications, P.O. Box 2907, Decatur, IL 62524

I

The Iconoclast, 1675 Amazon Rd, Mohegan Lake, NY 10547
The Idaho Review, 1910 University Dr., Boise, ID 83725
Illumination Arts, P.O. Box 1865, Bellevue, WA 98009
Illya's Honey, P.O. Box 225435, Dallas, TX 75222
IMAGE, 3307 Third Ave., W, Seattle, WA 98119
Indiana Review, Indiana University, 1020 E. Kirkwood, Bloomington, IN 47405

Indigenous Fiction, P.O. Box 2078, Redmond, WA 98073
In Posse Review/Web Del Sol, 239 Duncan St., San Francisco, CA 94131
Iowa Review, 308 EPB, University of Iowa, Iowa City, IA 52242
Italian Americana, 80 Washington St., Providence, RI 02903

J

Jewish Currents, 22 East 17th St., #601, New York, NY 10003
The Journal, Eng. Dept., Ohio State Univ., Columbus, OH 43210
Journal of New Jersey Poets, Co. College of Morris, 214 Center Grove Rd., Randolph, NJ 07869

K

Kalliope. Florida Community College, 3939 Roosevelt Blvd., Jacksonville, FL 32205
Karawane, 402 S. Cedar Lake Rd., Minneapolis, MN 55405
Kelsey Review, Mercer Co. Community College, P.O. Box B, Trenton, NJ 08690
The Kenyon Review, Kenyon College, Gambier, OH 43022
Kerouac Connection, P.O. Box 7250, Menlo Park, CA 94026
Krater Q, P.O. Box 1371, Lincoln Park, MI 48146

L

La Petite Zinc, 134 Lincoln Place, #5, Brooklyn, NY 11217
The Larcom Press, P.O. Box 161, Prides Crossing, MA 01965
The Laurel Review, Northwest Missouri State Univ., Maryville, MO 64468
The Ledge Magazine, 78–44 80th St., Glendale, NY 11385
Licking River Review, Nunn Dr., Highland Heights, KY 41099
Linnaean Street, 7 Linnaean St., Cambridge, MA 02138
lips, P.O. Box 1345, Montclair, NJ 07042
Literal Latte, 61 East 8th St., Ste. 240, New York, NY 10003
The Literary Review, 285 Madison Ave., Madison, NJ 07940
Louisiana Literature, S.E. Louisiana Univ., Hammond, LA 70402
Lummox, P.O. Box 5301, San Pedro, CA 90733
Lynx Eye, 1880 Hill Dr., Los Angeles, CA 90041

M

The MacGuffin, Schoolcraft College, 18600 Haggerty Rd., Livonia, MI 48152
Magazine of Speculative Poetry, P.O. Box 564, Beloit, WI 53512
The Manhattan Review, 440 Riverside Dr., #38, New York, NY 10027
Manoa Journal, Eng. Dept., Univ. of Hawaii, Honolulu, HI 96822
Many Beaches Press, 1527 N. 36th St., Sheboygan, WI 53081
Margin, 9407 Capstan Dr., NE, Bainbridge Island, WA 98110
The Marlboro Review, P.O. Box 243, Marlboro, VT 05344
Maryland State Poetry & Literary Society, Drawer H, Baltimore, MD 21228
Meridian, Univ. of Virginia, P.O. Box 400121, Charlottesville, VA 22904

Michigan Quarterly Review, Univ. of Michigan, Ann Arbor, MI 48109
Mid-American Review, Bowling Green State Univ., Bowling Green, OH 43403
Mid-List Press, 4324 12th Ave., S. Minneapolis, MN 55407
Milkweed Editions, 1011 Washington Ave. S, Ste. 300, Minneapolis, MN 55415
Mississippi Review, Univ. of Southern Mississippi, Hattiesburg, MS 39406
The Missouri Review, Univ. of Missouri, Columbia, MO 65211
Montag Publishing, P.O. Box 368, Waite Park, MN 56387
The Montserrat Review, 6307 RFD, Long Grove, IL 60047
Mudfish, 184 Franklin St., New York, NY 10013

N

Natural Bridge, English Dept., Univ. of Missouri, St. Louis, MO 63121
The Nebraska Review, FA212, Univ. of Nebraska, Omaha, NE 68182
New England Review, Middlebury College, Middlebury, VT 05753
New England Writers/Vermont Poets Assoc., P.O. Box 483, Windsor, VT 05089
New Letters, Univ. of Missouri, 5100 Rockhill Rd., Kansas City, MO 64110
New Orleans Review, Box 195, Loyola Univ., New Orleans, LA 70118
New Orphic Review & Publishers, 706 Mill St., Nelson, B.C., *CANADA* VIL 4S5
the new renaissance, 26 Heath Rd., #11, Arlington, MA 02474
New Rivers Press, 420 N. 5th St., Ste. 1180, Minneapolis, MN 55401
New York Stories, La Guardia Community College/CUNY, E-103, Long Island City, NY 11101
NFSPS Press, 3128 Walton Blvd., PMB 186. Rochester Hills, Mi 48309
night rally, P.O. Box 1707, Philadelphia, PA 19105
Nimrod International Journal, Univ. of Tulsa, 600 S. College, Tulsa, OK 74104
96 Inc., P.O. Box 15559, Boston, MA 02215
NOON, 1369 Madison Ave., PMB 298, New York, NY 10128
North American Review, Univ. of Northern Iowa, Cedar Falls, IA 50614
Northern Lights, P.O. Box 8084, Missoula, MT 59807
Northwest Review, Univ. of Oregon, 369 PLC, Eugene, OR 97403
Notre Dame Review, Eng. Dept., Univ. of Notre Dame, Notre Dame, IN 46556

O

The Ohio Review, Ohio Univ., Athens, OH 45701
Ohio State University Press, 1070 Carmack Rd., Columbus, OH 43210
Ontario Review, 9 Honey Brook Dr., Princeton, NJ 08540
Open City, 225 Lafayette St., Ste. 1114, New York, NY 10012
Orchises Press, P.O. Box 20602, Alexandria, VA 22320
Orion Society, 195 Main St., Great Barrington, MA 01230
Osiris, P.O. Box 297, Deerfield, MA 01342
Other Voices, Univ. of Illinois, 601 S. Morgan St., Chicago, IL 60607
Oxford America, P.O. Box 1156, Oxford, MS 38655
Oxford Magazine, Miami Univ., Oxford, OH 45056
Oyster Boy Review, P.O. Box 77842, San Francisco, CA 94107

P

Painted Bride Quarterly, 230 Vine St., Philadelphia, PA 19106
Palo Alto Review, Palo Alto College, 1400 W. Villaret Rd., San Antonio, TX 78224

Pangolin Papers, P.O. Box 241, Nordland, WA 98358
Papyrus Publishing, P.O. Box 7144, Upper Ferntree Gully, Vic., 3156 *AUSTRALIA*
The Paris Review, 541 East 72nd St., New York, NY 10021
Partisan Review, 236 Bay State Rd., Boston, MA 02215
Paterson Literary Review, Passaic Co. Community College, Paterson, NJ 07505
Pathwise Press, P.O. Box 2392, Bloomington, IN 47402
The Paumanok Review, 254 Dogwood Dr., Hershey, PA 17033
Pendragon Publications, P.O. Box 719, Radio City Sta., Hell's Kitchen, NY 10101
Penny Dreadful, see Pendragon Publications
Penumbra, 801 W. Monte Vista, Turlock, CA 95382
The Permanent Press, 4170 Noyac Rd., Sag Harbor, NY 11963
Perugia Press, P.O. Box 108, Shutesbury, MA 01072
Phoebe, George Mason Univ., 4400 Univ. Dr., Fairfax, VA 22030
Picadilly Press, 10965 W. Reed Valley Rd., Fayetteville, AR 72704
Pleasure Boat Studio, 8630 NE Wardwell Rd., Bainbridge Isl., WA 98110
Pleiades, Eng. Dept., Central Missouri State Univ., Warrensburg, MO 64093
Ploughshares, Emerson College, 100 Beacon St., Boston, MA 02116
Poems & Plays, Middle Tennessee State Univ., P.O. Box 70, Murfreesboro, TN 37132
Poet Lore, The Writer's Center, 4508 Walsh St., Bethesda, MA 20815
Poetry, 60 West Walton St., Chicago, IL 60610
The Poetry Porch, 158 Hollett St., Scituate, MA 02066
Polyphony Press, PMB 317, 207 E. Ohio St., Chicago, IL 60611
Porcupine, P.O. Box 259, Cedarburg, WI 53012
The Portland Review, P.O. Box 347, Portland, OR 97207
Post Road, 853 Broadway, Ste. 1516, New York, NY 10003
Potomac Review, P.O. Box 354, Port Tobacco, MD 20677
Potpourri Publications Co., P.O. Box 8278, Prairie Village, KS 66208
Prairie Schooner, P.O. Box 880334, Lincoln, NE 68588
Primavera, Box 37-7547, Chicago, IL 60637
Provincetown Arts Press, P.O. Box 35, 650 Commercial St., Provincetown, MA 02657
Puerto del Sol, New Mexico State Univ., Las Cruces, NM 88003
PWJ Publishing, P.O. Box 238, Tehama, CA 96090
Pyrczak Publishing, P.O. Box 39731, Los Angeles, CA 90039

Q

QECE, 406 Main St., #3C, Collegeville, PA 19426
Quarter After Eight, Ellis Hall, Univ. of Ohio, Athens, OH 45701
Quarterly West, Univ. of Utah, Salt Lake City, UT 84112

R

Rain Taxi, P.O. Box 3840, Minneapolis, MN 55403
Raritan, 31 Mine St., New Brunswick, NJ 08903
Rattapallax, 532 LaGuardia Pl., Ste. 353, New York, NY 10012
Rattle, 13440 Ventura Blvd., #200, Sherman Oaks, CA 91423
RE:AL, Stephen F. Austin State Univ., P.O. Box 13007, SFA Sta., Nacogdoches, TX 75962
Red Hen Press, P.O. Box 902582, Palmdale, CA
Red Moon Press, P.O. Box 2461, Winchester, VA 22604
Red River Review, 1729 Alpine Dr., Carrollton, TX 75007
Red Rock Review, Community College of So. Nevada, N. Las Vegas, NV 84030
Red Wheelbarrow, 21250 Stevens Creek Blvd., Cupertino, CA 95014

River City, Eng. Dept., Univ. of Memphis, Memphis, TN 38152
River King, P.O. Box 122, Freeburg, IL 62243
River Styx, 634 N. Grand Blvd., 12th fl., St. Louis, MO 63103
River Teeth, Eng. Dept., Ashland Univ., Ashland, OH 44805
Rivertalk Poetry Magazine, 3359 Braemar Sr., Santa Barbara, CA 93109
Rosebud, N. 3310 Asje Rd., Cambridge, WI 53523

S

Sacred Beverage Press, P.O. Box 10312, Burbank, CA 91510
Salt Hill, Eng. Dept., Syracuse Univ., Syracuse, NY 13244
Santa Monica Review, Santa Monica College, 1900 Pico Blvd., Santa Monica, CA 90405
Sarabande Books, Inc., 2234 Dundee Rd., Ste. 200, Louisville, KY 40205
Sarasota Review, P.O. Box 35355, Sarasota, FL 34242
School of Visual Arts (SVA), 209 East 23rd St., New York, NY 10010
Seal Press, 3131 Western Ave., #410, Seattle, WA 98121
Seeding the Snow, 2534 N. St. Louis, Chicago, IL 60647
Seneca Review, Hobart & William Smith Colleges, Geneva, NY 14456
Sensations Magazine, 2 Radio Ave., A5, Secaucus, NJ 07094
Shades of December, P.O. Box 244, Selden, NY 11784
Sheila-Na-Gig Magazine, 23106 Kent Ave., Torrance, CA 90505
Shenandoah, Washington & Lee Univ., Lexington, VA 24450
Skylark, 2200 169th St., Hammond, IN 46323
Slipstream, P.O. Box 2071, Niagara Falls, NY 14301
Small Brushes, see Adept Press
Smallmouth Press, P.O. Box 661, New York, NY 10185
The Southern Review, 43 Allen Hall, LSU, Baton Rouge, LA 70803
Southwest Review, Southern Methodist Univ., Dallas, TX 75275
Sou'Wester Magazine, Eng. Dept., So. Illinois Univ., Edwardsville, IL 62026
The Sow's Ear Press, 19535 Pleasant View Dr., Abingdon, VA 24211
Spectacle, PMB 155, 101 Middlesex Trnpke., Ste. 6, Burlington, MA 01803
Spinning Jenny, see Black Dress Press
Story Quarterly, P.O. Box 1416, Northbrook, IL 60065
Stringtown, 2309 West 12th Ave., Spokane, WA 99224
Sulphur River Literary Review, P.O. Box 19228, Austin, TX 78760
The Sun, 107 N. Roberson St., Chapel Hill, NC 27516
Swan Scythe Press, Eng. Dept., Univ. of California, Davis, CA 95616
Sweet Annie Press, 7750 Hwy F-24 W., Baxter, IA 50028
Sycamore Review, English Dept., Purdue University, W. Lafayette, IN 47907
Symbiotic Oatmeal, P.O. Box 14938, Philadelphia, PA 19149

T

Tampa Review, see Univ. of Tampa Press
Tatlin's Tower, 78 North St., Bristol, VT 05443
Tebot Bach, 20592 Minerva La., Huntington Beach, CA 92646
The Temple, see Tsunami, Inc.
Ten Pell Books, 303 P.A.S., #500, New York, NY 10010
Thema, Box 8747, Metairie, LA 70011
Third Coast, Western Michigan University, Kalamazoo, MI 49008
Three Mile Harbor, P.O. Box 1951, East Hampton, NY 11937
Threepenny Review, P.O. Box 9131, Berkeley, CA 94709

Tin House, 120 East End Ave., Ste. 68, New York, NY 10028
Tiny Lights Publications, P.O. Box 928, Petaluma, CA 94953
Towers & Rushing, Ltd., P.O. Box 691745, San Antonio, TX 78269
TriQuarterly, Northwestern Univ., 2020 Ridge Ave., Evanston, IL 60208
Tropical Press, P.O. Box 161174, Miami, FL 33116
Tsunami, Inc., P.O. Box 100, Walla Walla, WA 99362
Turning Wheel, 50 Black Log Rd., Kentfield, CA 94904

U

University of Georgia Press, 330 Research Dr., Athens, GA 30602
University of Massachusetts Press, P.O. Box 429, Amherst, MA 01004
University of Nevada Press, MS 166, Reno, NV 89557
University of Tampa Press, 401 W. Kennedy Blvd., Tampa, FL 33606
University Press of New England, 23 S. Main St., Hanover, NH 03755
U.S. Catholic, 205 W. Monroe St., Chicago, IL 60606

V

Valentine Publishing Group, P.O. Box 902582, Palmdale, CA 93590
Valley Contemporary Poets, P.O. Box 5342, Sherman Oaks, CA 91413
Van West & Co., Publishers, P.O. Box 662, Port Townsend, WA 98368
Verse, Eng. Dept., Univ. of Georgia, Athens, GA 30602
Vestal Review, 2609 Dartmouth Dr., Vestal, NY 13850
The Vincent Brothers Review, 4566 Northern Circle, Riverside, OH 45424

W

Wake Up Heavy, P.O. Box 4668, Fresno, CA 93744
Washington Square, NYU, 19 Univ. Place, Rm. 22, New York, NY 10003
Washington Writers' Publishing House, P.O. Box 15271, Washington, DC 20003
Web Del Sol, 517 Lorimer, Brooklyn, NY 11211
West Anglia Publications, P.O. Box 2683, LaJolla, CA 92038
West Branch, Bucknell Univ., Lewisburg, PA 17837
Western Humanities Review, University of Utah, Salt Lake City, UT 84112
White Pelican Review, P.O. Box 7833, Lakeland, FL 33813
Willow Springs, EWU, 705 West 1st Ave., Spokane, WA 99201
Witness, 27055 Orchard Lake Rd., Farmington Hills, MI 48334
The Worcester Review, 6 Chatham St., Worcester, MA 01608
Word Works, Inc., P.O. Box 42164, Washington, DC 20015
Word Wrights, see Argonne Hotel Press
Wordcraft of Oregon, P.O. Box 3235, La Grande, OR 97850
The Writer's Garret, P.O. Box 140530, Dallas, TX 75214
The Writer's Voice, 5 West 63rd St., New York, NY 10023

Y

Yale Review, Box 208243, New Haven, CT 06520
Ye Olde Font Shoppe, P.O. Box 8328, New Haven, CT 06708

Z

Zoetrope, 1350 Ave. of the Americas, 24th fl., New York, NY 10019
ZYZZYVA, P.O. Box 590069, San Francisco, CA 94159

CONTRIBUTORS' NOTES

ANDRÉ ACIMAN is the author of *Out of Egypt* and *False Papers*. He lives in New York. He won the Whiting Award in 1994.

ELIZABETH ALEXANDER's *Antebellum Dream Book* was published by Graywolf in 2001. She teaches at Yale.

GARY AMDAHL's work has appeared in *The Santa Monica Review*, *Fiction*, *The Nation*, *The Quarterly* and other journals and newspapers. He lives in Redlands, California.

TALVIKKI ANSEL's book of poems *My Shining Archipelago* won the Yale Series of younger Poets Award.

RUSSELL BANKS is the author of *Cloudsplitter*, *Rule of the Bone*, *Sweet Hereafter* and other books. He lives in upstate New York.

JEANNETTE BARNES is winner of *The Nebraska Review Award* in Poetry for 2000. Her work has appeared in *Kalliope*, *Wind*, *Shenandoah*, *Crucible* and *Louisiana Literature*.

KIM BARNES is the author of memoirs from Doubleday and Random House. Her essay appears in *A Year In Place*, just out from the University of Utah Press.

RICK BASS lives in Northwest Montana. He is the author of fifteen books of fiction and nonfiction. *My Colter* is just out from Houghton Mifflin.

ANN BEATTIE is the author of *What Was Mine* and *Picturing Will* (Random House). This is her first appearence in this series.

MADISON SMARTT BELL's most recent book *Masters of the Crossroads*, (Pantheon) includes "Labor." He lives in Baltimore.

MARIANNE BORUCH has published four volumes of poetry plus a collection of essays. She lives in West Lafayette, Indiana.

KEVIN BOWEN is a poet and translator. Curbstone Press publishes his books. This is his first published short story.

RICHARD BURGIN is the author of the novel *Ghost Quartet* (TriQuarterly Books) and two recent story collections from Johns Hopkins University Press. He is the editor of *Boulevard*.

SCOTT CAIRNS' book *Philo°Kalia: Poems New and Selected* will appear in 2002. He lives in Columbia, Missouri.

RICK CAMPBELL is the director of Anhinga Press. His most recent book, *Setting the World In Order*, was published by Texas Tech University Press in 2001.

RAFAEL CAMPO teaches and practices general internal medicine at Harvard Medical School. His next book, *Landscape With Human Figure*, will be published by Duke University Press in 2002.

DAN CHAON's *Among the Missing* is just out from Ballantine. His previous collection was published by TriQuarterly Books. He lives in Cleveland Heights, Ohio.

BILLY COLLINS is Poet Laureate of the United States. He is also the past poetry co-editor of *Pushcart Prize XXV*. His *Sailing Alone Around the Room: New and Selected Poems* is just out from Random House.

BERNARD COOPER's books are *Guess Again* (stories) and *Truth Serum* (memoirs). He is art critic for *Los Angeles Magazine*.

ROBERT CORDING is the author of books from Copper Beach Press and Alice James Books. His latest book, *Against Consolation*, is just out from Cavankerry Press.

KWAME DAWES was born in Ghana and raised in Jamaica. He has published six collections of poetry and teaches at the University of South Carolina.

SHARON DILWORTH lives in Pittsburgh. This is her first appearance in this series.

STEPHEN DOBYNS has published ten books of poems, twenty-one works of fiction and a book of essays on poetry. He lives near Boston.

JEFF DOLVEN teaches at Princeton. His poems have appeared in *Yale Review*, *Southwest Review* and elsewhere.

DAVID JAMES DUNCAN the author of novels, *The River Why* and *The Brothers K*, a collection of stories and a memoir, *River Teeth*, and *My Story as Told by Water*, a collection of nonfiction. He has lectured all over the U.S. on wilderness, the writing life, the nonmonastic contemplative life, the fishing life, and the nonreligious literature of faith.

IAN FRAZIER writes essays and nonfiction. His most recent book is *On the Rez*.

MARGARET GIBSON's seventh book of poetry, *Icon and Evidence*, will soon be published by LSU Press.

DAGOBERTO GILB is the author, most recently, of *Woodcuts of Women*. He lives in Austin, Texas.

LOUISE GLÜCK received the Bollingen Prize. She teaches at Williams College. Ecco/HarperCollins issued her poetry collection, *The Seven Ages*.

ALBERT GOLDBARTH lives in Wichita, Kansas. His work has appeared several times in this series. His most recent books have been published by Ohio State University Press and Graywolf.

ELIZABETH GRAVER is the author of *Have You Seen Me?*, *Unravelling*, and *The Honey Thief*. Her stories have appeared in *Best American Short Stories* and *The O'Henry Awards*.

DEBORA GREGER's new book, *God*, is just out. She teaches at the University of Florida.

EAMON GRENNAN is from Dublin and teaches at Vassar. His *Relations: New and Selected Poems* was published by Graywolf in 1998.

ALYSON HAGY is the author of three collections of short stories. She lives and teaches in Laramie, Wyoming.

DONALD HALL has published thirteen books of poetry, most recently *Without*, a book of poems about the illness and death of his wife Jane Kenyon.

BARBARA HAMBY's second book of poems, *The Alphabet of Desire*, won the New York University Prize for poetry in 1998 and was published by NYU Press. Her work has appeared in *The Paris Review*, *The Southern Review*, *TriQuarterly* and elsewhere.

MICHAEL HARPER's *Songlines In Michaeltree* was published by the University of Illinois Press in 2000. He is co-editor of *The Vintage Book of African American Poetry*.

ANTHONY HECHT has received the Pulitzer Prize, the Robert Frost Medal, the Bollingen Prize, and the Wallace Stevens Award.

JANE HIRSHFIELD's *Given Sugar, Given Salt* appeared in 2001 (Harper-Collins). She has received fellowships from the Guggenheim and Rockefeller Foundations.

DANIEL HOFFMAN was poetry consultant at the Library of Congress 1973–74. Today the office is called Poet Laureate of the United States. His tenth book of poetry is due from LSU Press in 2002.

JOHN HOLLANDER is Sterling Professor of English at Yale. His book *Figurehead* is available from Knopf, and *Reflections on Espionage* has been reissued by Yale University Press.

DAVID HUDDLE's novel, *The Story of A Million Years* (Houghton Mifflin) was a *Los Angeles Times* Best Book of the Year in 1999. A second novel is just out from Houghton.

HA JIN first appeared in *Pushcart Prize XVII*. He is the author of several books of poetry and fiction. His latest poetry collection is *Wreckage*.

DENIS JOHNSON lives in Bonners Ferry, Idaho. He previously appeared in PPXI. His essay was first commissioned by The National Millennium Survey of the College of Santa Fe.

LAURA KASISCHKE's newest collection, *Dance and Disappear*, won the 2001 Juniper Prize. In 1999 Hyperion published her second novel, *White Bird In Blizzard*.

STEVE KOWIT edited *The Maverick Poets* anthology. He also founded the first animal rights organization in San Diego and is the author of several poetry collections.

LAURIE LAMON has poems forthcoming in *Ploughshares* and *Colorado Review*. She teaches at Whitworth College, Spokane.

DON LEE edits *Ploughshares*. He is the author of the story collection *Yellow* (W.W. Norton, 2000).

RACHEL LODEN's *Hotel Imperium* was published by the University of Georgia Press recently. She lives in Palo Alto.

THOMAS LYNCH is the author of *Bodies in Motion & At Rest, Still Life in Milford*, and *The Undertaking*, all from W.W. Norton Co. He lives in Milford, Michigan.

DEBRA MARQUART teaches at Iowa State University and is the poetry editor of *Flyway Literary Review*. A short fiction collection is just out from New Rivers and a poetry collection is forthcoming from Pearl Editions.

JIM MOORE has just completed a book of new and selected poems entitled *For You*. His awards include The Minnesota Book Award for Poetry.

CAROLE MASO teaches at Brown. She is the author of nine books including *Defiance* (a novel), *Break Every Rule* (essays) and *The Room Lit by Roses* (journal of pregnancy and birth).

NICOLA MASON lives in Baton Rouge. This is her first appearence in this series.

MARIKO NAGAI teaches at Keio University, Toyko, Japan. This is her first fiction publication. She has published poetry in several literary journals.

PETER ORNER's first book, *Esther Stories*, is just out from Houghton Mifflin. His stories have appeared in *Epoch, North American Review*, and *Michigan Quarterly Review*.

PAMELA PAINTER has two story collections published recently. She is a founding editor of *StoryQuarterly*, and she teaches at Emerson College, Boston.

CARL PHILLIPS is the author of five books of poetry. He teaches at Washington University in St. Louis.

DAVID PLANTE appeared here last in *Pushcart Prize V*. He teaches at Columbia University.

CAROL POTTER teaches at Holyoke Community College. Her third book of poems, *Short History of Pets*, was the winner of the Cleveland State University Poetry Center competition in 1999.

MELISSA PRITCHARD teaches at Arizona State University. She is author, most recently, of *Selene of the Spirits* (Ontario Review Press).

KEVIN PRUFER'S second book, *The Finger Bone*, will be issued by Carnegie-Mellon in 2002. He is editor of *Pleiades* and *The New Young American Poets* (Southern Illinois University Press, 2000).

BURTON RAFFEL was once a Wall Street lawyer and he now teaches at the University of Louisiana. He has published "sixty or so" books.

STACEY RICHTER is author of the story collection *My Date With Satan*. She won the National Magazine Award and lives in Tucson.

JESS ROW teaches at the University of Michigan. His work has appeared in *Green Mountains Review*, *Ploughshares* and elsewhere.

WOLE SOYINKA is the winner of the 1986 Nobel Prize in Literature. He teaches at Emory University, Atlanta.

BERT O. STATES is a retired teacher. He has just finished a book on metaphorical seeing and thinking. He lives in Santa Barbara.

NATASHA TRETHEWEY is the winner of the 1999 Cave Canem Poetry Prize. Her poems have appeared in numerous journals and anthologies. She holds a Bunting Fellowship at Cambridge.

SUSAN WHEELER's poetry collection, *Smokes*, was published by Four Way Books. Her work has been published in *Best American Poetry* several times. She lives in New York.

THOMAS WOLFE lived from 1900 to 1938 and wrote *Look Homeward, Angel* and other novels.

CHARLES WRIGHT is the author of five poetry collections from Farrar Straus and Giroux. He lives in Charlottesville, Virginia.

INDEX

The following is a listing in alphabetical order by author's last name of works reprinted in the *Pushcart Prize* editions.

591

593

597

601

608

611

612

615

616